*The*
# Inn at Eagle Hill

## Books by Suzanne Woods Fisher

*Amish Peace: Simple Wisdom for a Complicated World*
*Amish Proverbs: Words of Wisdom from the Simple Life*
*Amish Values for Your Family: What We Can Learn from the Simple Life*
*The Heart of the Amish: Life Lessons*
*on Peacemaking and the Power of Forgiveness*

---

*A Lancaster County Christmas*
*Christmas at Rose Hill Farm*
*Anna's Crossing*

### LANCASTER COUNTY SECRETS

*The Choice*
*The Waiting*
*The Search*

### STONEY RIDGE SEASONS

*The Keeper*
*The Haven*
*The Lesson*

### THE INN AT EAGLE HILL

*The Letters*
*The Calling*
*The Revealing*

### THE ADVENTURES OF LILY LAPP
### (WITH MARY ANN KINSINGER)

*Life with Lily*
*A New Home for Lily*
*A Big Year for Lily*
*A Surprise for Lily*

### THE BISHOP'S FAMILY

*The Imposter*

# *The* Inn at Eagle Hill

**3-IN-1 COLLECTION**

## THE LETTERS
## THE CALLING
## THE REVEALING

# SUZANNE WOODS FISHER

**Revell**

a division of Baker Publishing Group
Grand Rapids, Michigan

© 2013, 2014 by Suzanne Woods Fisher

Published by Revell
a division of Baker Publishing Group
P.O. Box 6287, Grand Rapids, MI 49516-6287
www.revellbooks.com

Combined edition published 2016
ISBN 978-0-8007-2786-4

Previously published in three separate volumes:
*The Letters* © 2013
*The Calling* © 2014
*The Revealing* © 2014

Printed in the United States of America

Published in association with Joyce Hart of the Hartline Literary Agency, LLC.

16   17   18   19   20   21   22          7   6   5   4   3   2   1

# The Letters

Dedicated to my dear dad,
as well as his brothers and sister,
who were raised on the real Inn at Eagle Hill
in Buzzards Bay, Massachusetts

# 1

The air had the sweet burn of frost. Long out of habit, even in the winter months, Rose Schrock woke before dawn to carve out a little time for herself before the day began. She liked the bitter cold, a cold that seemed to sharpen the stars in the wide Pennsylvania sky. Dawn was her favorite hour, a time when she felt most keenly aware of how fragile life truly was. Between one breath and the next, your whole world could change. Hers had.

On this morning, wrapped in her husband's huge coat, she walked along the creek bordering the farm and climbed the hill. The thin February moon, low in the horizon, lit the sky but not the ground. Her golden retriever, Chase, trotted behind her, saluting trees along the path, baptizing each one as he went. When Rose reached the top of the hill, she sat with her back against a tree. In its awakening hour, the farm below seemed peaceful, lovely, calm. The birdsong symphony had just begun—something that always seemed like a miracle to Rose. How did that saying go? "Faith is the bird that feels the light and sings when the dawn is still dark." And wasn't that the truth?

Rose Schrock had been raised not to complain, so she didn't, but the truth of the matter was, the last seven months had been the hardest stretch of her life: so many things had gone wrong that it was hard to know which trouble to pay attention to at any given time.

Her mother-in-law, Vera, assured her cheerfully that increase in trouble was something she had better get used to. "You can't expect mercy."

"I don't expect it," Rose had told Vera. "I just wish things would go wrong one at a time. That way I could handle them."

Soon, she would need to head back down the hill and wake her boys. Her girls would already be stirring. They were unusually helpful and did whatever chores there were to do without being asked, whereas her two young sons were so sluggish in the morning that it took them half an hour just to get themselves dressed and downstairs. Before Rose left this quiet spot, she had something to do. To say. No, no. She had something to pray.

*Lord, I beg your pardon, but I am in a fix. I'm about wrung out from all this, and it's getting so I can barely tell which way is up. I've got four fatherless children—five, if I knew where that oldest boy had run off to— an addle-minded mother-in-law, and barely thirty-six dollars left in my pocket. I'm fresh out of backbone, Lord. And near out of fight. Near out. Lord, if you'd be so kind, look down here and let me know what to do. I need a Plan B.*

Rose waited quietly, hoping for a word from above, or maybe just an inkling. Reflecting, she decided it was funny how life could change so fast. She used to have so many plans. Now, her plans for the future were foggy at best. Years ago, money had been the last thing on her mind. Now it was all she thought about. Scarcely seven months ago, she had a husband. Now Dean was gone. A few years earlier, she hadn't minded so much being with her mother-in-law. Not so much. Now she couldn't think of anything worse.

*Anything you want to say, Lord? Any advice? A word of wisdom?* Rose heard the gentle hoot of a screech owl, once, then twice. A rooster began to crow. That would be Harold, the loudest rooster in the county. The day would soon begin.

A moving bright light in the sky caught her eye. She watched for a moment, intrigued. Then, fascinated. It was a shooting star, darting over little Stoney Ridge in all its glory and majesty. Her jumbled thoughts gave way to a feeling of peace.

What a thing to see at a time when she needed it so badly!

───── ☙ ◊ ❧ ─────

Whenever Miriam had visited her grandmother's farm, it had seemed like an adventure to adapt to the lifestyle of the Old Order Amish. But living someplace was different than visiting and Mim felt she came from a different world. She was raised in a Mennonite church in a large town in Pennsylvania—where her family had used electricity and drove a car. Here, it was quiet. No electricity, no car, not even normal lights. In the kitchen there was the kerosene lantern hanging from the ceiling, which hissed and gave off a flat white light.

It was all different, all new to her. For a girl who didn't like change, it was too much change, all at once. She wished life could just go back to the way it was. She felt sad at all she'd had and what was no longer.

Her eyes blew open. *Just like my grandmother,* she thought, shocked. *I am sounding just like my grandmother.* Whatever Mammi Vera had, it was catching!

Right then, she decided to start a list of things she liked about moving to Stoney Ridge. She scrambled off her bed and took out a clean sheet of paper from her desk drawer.

Number One: Danny Riehl, the boy who sat next to her at school and wore glasses that were hinged together with a paper clip.

Number Two: School.

Mim had mistakenly assumed it would be as easy here as it was back in their old town. After all, here it was a one-room schoolhouse. But this teacher believed in pushing students. It wasn't all bad to be challenged, she had discovered. She loved math. She loved language. The teacher, Mary Kate Lapp, called Teacher M.K., had noticed Mim. She gave her extra math problems. She loaned her a used Latin textbook and told her to study root words. Each week, she assigned Mim new vocabulary words. Words like *modicum, interim, aplomb, insipid, pseudo.* She was told to use the words in one sentence. She spent hours constructing descriptive sentences.

Mim looked out her bedroom window and thought about how someone might describe her in one sentence. Where to begin? She was thirteen years old, with dark hair like her father and gray eyes like her mother. She was average height, average weight. Entirely average. Entirely unremarkable. In her mind, she erased those boring descriptions and started all over again.

What else? Mim liked her brothers and her sister and her mother and, some of the time, her grandmother. Mostly, she liked school and loved book learning and was fond of the month of March because no one much liked March. Her favorite color was bright red for the same reason: her new church frowned upon the color red. She didn't understand what made red so offensive, but that was an Amish tradition and so that was that.

But what Mim loved more than anything else was to collect facts. She was excellent at collecting facts. Excellent. She liked to find facts in ordinary things. Her grandmother was always spouting proverbs and Mim would find the fact in them. She shortened her name to Mim from Miriam because she had read that one-syllable names were easier to remember. That was a fact.

Still, so far she hadn't come up with a very scintillating way to describe herself. Scratch all that. So far, her sentence was entirely unremarkable. She wiped down the chalkboard that she had imagined in her mind and started again: "Say what you will about thirteen-year-old Mim Schrock, but don't leave out that she was organized. Very organized. Exceedingly organized." She smiled. Everyone knew that fact about her.

"And she is a champion problem solver," she added to her imaginary description.

That was the main reason she loved to read so much. In books, she learned to find answers to questions. Clean and simple. It was a pity that her grandmother was so against book learning. She only allowed a handful of books in the house. Too much book learning, her grandmother insisted, would make your brain go soft. Mim pointed out that there was no research to support that thinking, and her grandmother shut that conversation down with a Penn Dutch proverb: "De meh gelehrt, de meh verkehrt." *The more learning, the less wisdom.*

Happily, Mim's mother disagreed. With a quiet blessing from her mother, Mim kept her library books hidden in the barn. Most of the barn was crammed with useless junk, especially in the hayloft, but she had found a little corner by a dusty window to claim as her own. Ideal for quiet moments to read, hidden from overly nosy brothers, like the one who was peering in around the doorjamb at her right this very moment.

Eight-year-old Sammy came in and sat on her bed, humming, tossing a softball up a foot or two in the air, then catching it in his mitt. Mostly missing it. She looked over at him and smiled as he scrambled to find the ball under the bed. Sammy was small and stocky and compact like a suitcase.

He always told the truth, even when he shouldn't. She would never admit it to anyone, but Sammy was her favorite brother. He was a kind person and enjoyed discussing unusual facts with Mim. And he lent her money from the coffee can he kept beneath his mattress. Her ten-year-old brother Luke had his good points: he was funny and smart and was a bottomless pit of good ideas to do on a Sunday afternoon, but he had a sneaky side to him, like Tobe, the oldest in the family. A person needed to be careful about business transactions with Luke.

Sammy took a very black banana out of his pocket and peeled it.

"That is disgusting," Mim said.

Sammy didn't seem to mind. He finished off that bruised banana in just a few bites. "Did you know that the Great Wall of China can be seen from the moon?"

Now that was a fine fact. Mim scribbled it down in her school notebook, color coded under "Yellow" for Fine Facts. Teacher M.K. would like it. The class would like it. Danny Riehl, he would like it.

Delia Stoltz was running late to her doctor's appointment. Her day had been so busy that she hadn't even stopped for lunch. A boring meeting for the Philadelphia Historic Preservation Society, followed by another tedious fundraising meeting for the Children's Hospital, a mind-numbing Daughters of the American Republic tea, and then a complete waste-of-time board meeting for the local bank, where she listened to a heated debate about whether to provide free coffee for their customers. Delia wasn't sure anyone really wanted her opinion about how to run businesses or charities, but she was in great demand as a benefactress. It was one of the responsibilities of being married to Dr. Charles Stoltz.

Charles Stoltz was the most prominent neurosurgeon on the eastern seaboard. Quite possibly, in the entire country. Delia and Will, their only child—who was now in his last year of vet school at Cornell—wanted for nothing. Charles kept track of all of their investments and financial dealings. She wasn't interested in the actual figures or details of her portfolio, but Charles said she had plenty of money to live well and be a generous benefactor to the community, so she did and she was.

Delia glanced at her watch. She thought about skipping the doctor's appointment altogether, but she was driving right by the office to get home. She would allow fifteen minutes, but if the doctor kept her waiting, she would leave.

She took her Lancome Mulled Wine lipstick from her purse and pulled out a compact mirror. She would be sixty years old next summer. Just this morning, someone had asked her a blunt question: "Delia, have you had a little touch-up surgery? You look *so* good for a woman your age!"

Delia withered that someone with a glance.

She supposed asking such a personal question about whether she ever had cosmetic surgery might seem perfectly normal, but as far as she was concerned, it was perfectly rude.

If that person had a clue about what made Delia Stoltz tick, she would have known that Delia would scoff at the thought of cosmetic surgery. Everyone aged. She never understood why people spent so much time and money trying to avoid it or pretend it wasn't happening. She worked hard at keeping herself up—she had a personal trainer at the gym and swam laps twice a week. When it came to makeup and fashion, she felt simplicity was best. A little mascara, a little blush, a good lipstick. Her closet was filled with classic clothing of excellent quality—well-cut lined wool slacks, silk blouses, an array of cashmere sweaters, and for more formal occasions, an assortment of black cocktail dresses. A good purse was a must. Her preference was Prada. In the purse was a creamy pashmina scarf, at the ready. Add a nice pair of shoes and a few pieces of well-chosen jewelry: pearls, matching earrings, and perhaps, one simply spectacular ring, like the enormous diamond her husband had given to her on their twentieth wedding anniversary.

Now, a woman's hair was a different story. Delia had a standing monthly appointment with Alessandro at the salon for a root touch-up. She accepted most of the signs of aging, but not when it came to hair. Going gray was simply unacceptable.

If that rude someone truly knew Delia, she would know all of that. But while everyone in Philadelphia knew who Delia Stoltz was or knew of her, no one really knew her. She preferred it that way. Utterly private.

When she stepped through the door from the waiting room, Dr. Zimmerman was there to greet her. "Hello, Delia, how are you today?" he said.

"I'm fine. Shouldn't I be?" she said offhandedly, smiling, but she felt the tiniest little pinch in her stomach. A few days ago, she'd had a needle biopsy of a cyst in her left breast. No big deal, even Dr. Zimmerman had said so. It was so routine that she hadn't even bothered to mention it to Charles. He would have gotten overinvolved, would want to speak to Dr. Zimmerman himself, would order extra tests. Not necessary. She had harmless fibroids in her breasts—lumpy breasts, the doctor had told her—and she was vigilant about yearly mammograms. To the day. Delia was precise about everything.

Every few years, she faced some annoying round of post-mammogram testing. After ultrasounds and biopsies, it never amounted to anything more than a nuisance. This year, Dr. Zimmerman called and said he wanted a tissue biopsy, but because her test results had always come back negative before, she was sure it would be the same this time. Busy as she was, as she always was, it hadn't crossed her mind to be worried. Until now.

Something in Dr. Zimmerman's avuncular tone as he asked about her day, something about the weight of his arm across her shoulders as he escorted her into his private office, made a shiver travel up her spine. But it wasn't until she was sitting in his office and Dr. Zimmerman steepled his fingers together on his desk and said, "I'm so sorry, Delia. The biopsy was positive. You have cancer," that she understood what was happening.

Three little words. *You have cancer*. And for a moment, everything stopped. Her heart. Her mind. Her breath. Everything.

Delia couldn't remember how she got home. She must have been driving on autopilot. She pulled into the garage and noticed the trunk was lifted on Charles's BMW. His suitcases were in the back. She hadn't realized he had business travel planned, but he was often called away for consultations on difficult cases. She hoped he could change his plans after she told him her news. She walked into the kitchen and put her purse on the countertop. Charles was waiting for her at the kitchen table. Strange. Charles never waited for her. She was always waiting for him. She looked at him and knew something terrible was about to happen, like the quiet right before a storm was due to hit. But a storm had already hit at the doctor's office. Surely, there couldn't be two storms in one day. In a moment of clarity, she realized she was in the eye of the hurricane, about to face the dirty side of the storm. The worst part.

Her son.

Her heart missed a beat. "Did something happen to Will?"

"Will is fine. Studying, I hope, with midterms coming up." Charles licked his lips. It was a habit when he was nervous. Why was he nervous? Had Dr. Zimmerman called him? Did he already know? His face was so pale. Charles was never pale, always tan. He was in his early sixties, close to six feet tall; his looks reminded Delia of Gregory Peck playing Atticus Finch in *To Kill a Mockingbird*. She had a tendency to do that—liken people to movie stars. It was something her son Will forever teased her about.

Dee saw a trickle of sweat on Charles's forehead. "Delia, there's something I need to tell you." He took a deep breath and exhaled. "I've fallen in love with someone else. I'm sorry, honey. I'm moving out."

She saw his lips move, but she couldn't understand what he was saying. She just stared at him.

He tried to get her to talk, but she felt nothing, said nothing.

Finally, Charles rose to his feet and said that his attorney's office would be contacting her, and not to worry, he would take care of everything. She would never have to worry about money. And one more thing—he would like to wait to tell Will since he would be going through midterm exams soon.

Then he left.

When Delia heard the garage door close, she took the first breath she had taken in what felt like an hour, since she had left the doctor's office. One deep breath and everything had changed. She had reached her breaking point. It was an indescribable feeling of pain, sheer pain.

How was it possible for a few words to have such power? "I'm in love with someone else." "You have cancer."

Delia felt all the strength leave her body. The body she cared for so thoroughly had betrayed her. There was an enemy within her that, left unchecked, would end her life.

The husband whom she adored and who loved her had failed her. Life as she knew it was over.

Alone and lonely, she covered her face with her hands and gave herself up to despair, weeping until she was dry.

Rose Schrock turned the horse and buggy into the Bent N' Dent's parking lot and tied the reins to the hitching post. The late February sky was filling with lead-colored clouds, threatening to snow. Grabbing a basket by the door, she hurried down the aisle with her list in hand. She had run out of ground cinnamon and needed it for a cake for Sunday church, so she stopped by the spices. She felt distracted, preoccupied with the ongoing worry of trying to find a way to support her family. She'd been on the lookout for Plan B for days now, but nothing had happened; not even the tiniest glimmer of an idea or opportunity had appeared on the horizon.

An English lady with Sharpie pen eyebrows, a tuft of woodpecker red hair, and frosty orange lipstick ringing her big white teeth stood planted in front of the spices, oohing and aahing over the low prices. "Look at this, Tony," the lady called out. "Only fifty cents for a half pint of freshly ground pepper."

Rose watched the lady load up her cart with spices and felt a spike of panic. *Please don't take all the cinnamon. Please, please, please . . .*

An English man came down the aisle to join the lady. "I asked the clerk at the counter about places to stay in Stoney Ridge," he told her. "She said there was nothing around here. No inn. No bed-and-breakfast. Said we'd need to head closer to Lancaster." He was every bit as flamboyant looking as his wife, with a white walrus mustache under his substantial nose and pointed cowboy boots on his feet.

"That's a shame," the lady said, standing on her tiptoes to reach the top shelf of spices. "I wouldn't mind spending more time in this town and mosey through the shops. It doesn't feel as tourist-y as the other towns."

Something started ticking in Rose's head, a sound as real as a clock.

The man watched his wife fill up the cart with spices. "Do we really need all those spices? You don't bake."

"I can give them as gifts," the lady answered. She pushed the cart up the aisle and the husband trotted behind.

Rose looked through what spices remained on the shelves: cardamom, cloves, curry. No cinnamon. Cleaned out. She sighed.

The man and the lady stood in line to pay for their groceries. Rose wheeled her cart behind them, debating if she should ask the lady if she would mind giving up one of the containers of cinnamon. Just one. "The weather's turning real sour, Lois," the man said, peering out the storefront window. "We should get on the road. Might take us awhile to find a place to stay and it's getting late."

*Tick, tick, tick.* The sound in Rose's head got louder.

"What are we going to do, Tony?" The lady's voice took an anxious tone. "You know you can't drive at night. And I've got a dreadful headache."

Rose's head jerked up. The ticking sound stopped in her head and a bell went off.

There *was* no place for visitors to stay in Stoney Ridge. Her mind started to spin. What if she started an inn at the farm? The basement of the farmhouse was finished off with drywall and had an exterior entrance. It was filled with her mother-in-law's junk-that-Vera-called-heirlooms but it could be emptied out. And she could cook breakfast for the guests. Rose was a good cook. Even Vera had said so, and she wasn't a woman given to handing out compliments.

But would the bishop let tourists stay at the farm? Maybe there was a rule about this kind of thing. Maybe that's why there weren't any bed-and-breakfasts in Stoney Ridge. But then, she thought, maybe it's better not to ask. It was always easier to apologize later. Besides, Bishop Elmo seemed like a kind man. Surely, he would understand a mother's plight. The church had been good to them, generous and gracious, but she needed to find a way to take care of her family.

Would an inn bring in enough cash to solve her ongoing cash shortfall? She doubted it. But it would certainly help.

She paid for the groceries with the wad of bills wrapped in a rubber band that she kept in her dress pocket. As she picked up the bags, her heart felt lighter than it had in months. The best cure for sadness was doing something. Her eyes searched the skies, finding a small opening where the clouds parted and blue sky showed through. "Thank you," she said, grinning ear to ear. "Thank you for Plan B."

She ran over to the car where the man and the lady were loading groceries and invited them to stay at the farm.

# 2

The kitchen smelled as sweet and spicy as Christmas Day. Bethany Schrock took the cake out of the hot oven and set it on the counter to cool. She saw her younger brothers, Luke and Sammy, cut eyes at each other, sniffing the air like foxes. Those boys could eat any time of the day, any day of the week. They crowed with happiness as she mixed butter and powdered sugar to make icing for the cake. Then they hollered when Bethany told them they had to wait until after supper to sample it. Finally, fed up with them underfoot, she shooed them upstairs to clean their room.

Bethany was still reeling over her stepmother's big news. Rose had met her at the door as she walked in from work. She told her that there were English strangers staying for the night. In Bethany's very room! Rose had a new business idea: to turn the farm's basement into an inn. Bethany knew Rose was under pressure, but now it appeared she had gone raving mad. Yes, clearly too much pressure.

Rose had seemed so excited about this idea that Bethany didn't have the heart to tell her all the reasons it wouldn't work—how awful it would be to have strangers poke around their property, how easily influenced her little brothers could be by English visitors, how impossible English folks were to please. She knew that from personal experience, but that information was best to keep private.

Most importantly, having Rose so excited about this venture would delay the inevitable—they needed to return to York County, where they belonged. Where Bethany belonged. Where her sweetheart, Jake Hertzler, lived.

A sound of pounding footsteps came from far above her. Those brothers were either just coming or just going. It was hard for them to ever settle.

Then Luke came tearing down the stairs like a scalded cat, with Sammy following on his heels, threatening to hang him out of a window. About halfway down, Luke tripped and went nose over like a barrel down the rest of the stairs. He landed at the bottom with a thud and sprawled, unmoving.

Bethany watched in horror and flew to his side. "Luke?" Sammy galloped down the stairs and stood over his brother.

Luke opened one eye. "Sammy wants to throw me out the window."

Sammy stamped his foot. "I knew you were just playing possum! You rat!"

"No name-calling," Bethany said, helping Luke to his feet. She was sure she'd be worried into an early grave for trying to keep these little brothers out of *theirs*. "What's gotten into you two?"

Sammy pointed at Luke. "He said there's a ghost on the third floor. He said he saw a lady with bright red hair and lips. And she called him 'honey.' He said that, Bethany. He's a liar."

This was such a typical scenario. Sammy and Luke were barely two years apart, but Luke was taller, faster, smarter, more clever. He was constantly tricking or baiting Sammy and it drove Sammy crazy. But Bethany wasn't worried about Sammy. He may not be quick or fast, but he had his own talents. "He's no liar, but he's only half right. There is a couple up there, staying in my room. Rose invited some people she met at the Bent N' Dent to stay here."

"Why'd she do that?" Sammy said.

In walked Rose through the kitchen door, carrying a basket of eggs from the henhouse, with Mim trailing behind her. "I met them at the store," Rose said after she hurried to close the door to Mammi Vera's room. "They needed a place to stay and we are people who try to help others in need." She set the basket on the table.

Mim looked shocked. Bethany realized that Rose hadn't told her the news about the inn. Mim's eyebrows knit together in a frown. It was a look Bethany knew well. Mim was the logical, practical one in the family. Rose often said that if an idea could get past Mim, it was probably a pretty good idea.

"Boys, go bring the sheep into the pen for the night," Rose said. "The goat too. And lock those latches! We don't want them wandering over to the neighbor's again. The girls and I are going to get dinner ready." Luke and Sammy went outside, whooping and hollering about how fast they could run. She watched them through the window. "Everything's a contest with those two."

Mim set the table and Bethany mixed up some biscuit dough, while Rose topped the casserole with some cheese and melted it under the broiler. Bethany remained silent, spooning biscuit dough onto an oven tray and putting it in the oven, as Rose explained the inn idea to Mim. Bethany chanced a look at Mim out of the corner of her eyes, watching her absorb the news. Mim's eyes had widened behind her large round glasses, and she was blinking rapidly, a sign that she was listening hard. Bethany had repeatedly told her to stop blinking like that—she looked like a newborn owl. But Mim could be the one to set Rose straight. She could be the leader of the campaign to pop the balloon of this harebrained scheme. Yes, she was the one.

Rose took the casserole out of the oven. "Bethany, would you please take this tray up to Lois and Tony? I invited them to join us for dinner, but Lois has a headache." She began heaping two plates with spoonfuls of casserole.

*They're strangers!* Bethany wanted to say but thought twice before saying it. She felt confident that the idea would fizzle out of its own accord. Still, if Bethany *were* to say something, this was what she would say:

*Rose, you don't know anything about them. Folks are always saying that the Amish are too naïve, too trusting, and you've just proved them right. You met these people at the Bent N' Dent. All we know about them is that the lady uses very strong perfume and she's stinking up my room with it. That's probably the very reason she's not feeling well. Her perfume is making her sick. You just watch and see—I'll be sick too, all because of that heavy perfume poisoning the air in my room.*

Rose topped each plate with a warm biscuit, added two slices of cake on the side, and handed her the tray. Bethany sighed a grievous sigh.

"Bethany, they're very nice people," Rose said, reading her mind. "Go!"

Bethany stole a look at her sister. Mim's glasses had misted over; that was always a sign that she was thinking deeply. *Come on, Mim, say it.*

*Don't hold back,* Bethany thought. *List all the flaws with new ideas the way you usually do.* She could count on Mim. Her little half-sister did not like change.

Mim opened her gray eyes wide and took a deep breath. "I think it might just work."

Bethany squeezed her eyes tight. As usual, she was going to have to be the one who righted the ship for this family. With Tobe gone missing, she was the eldest, and so the worries reached her first.

She looked at her stepmother, so hopeful and eager. She even looked young again. Her sparkle was coming back. It was a sad and sorrowful state of affairs that Bethany had to be the one to do this, to say this. But someone had to. "Rose, have you spoken to Mammi Vera about this? After all, it is her house."

The next morning, Rose could hear her sons' high-pitched voices carry from the barn all the way up to the porch. She hoped Vera couldn't hear them. It had taken some finagling to make sure Vera didn't catch on that there were English people staying in the house last night. It worked out surprisingly well. No lies were told and none were needed—may God forgive her for even thinking such a thing. Last night Lois had a headache and stayed upstairs. Vera had stayed in her room all evening and slept late this morning.

Luke and Sammy were giving Tony and Lois a tour of the farm and were finishing up by the horse pasture. "All I have to do is catch sight of Silver Girl and whistle, and she'll come running," Sammy was telling them. "That's how good a horse she is." The way he said it, the way he looked at the horse with such admiration in his small face, gave Rose a deep, swift rush of love for her youngest. He was growing up so fast.

Silver Girl was a maiden mare, soon to deliver. Rose had bought her for a song from Galen King, her closest neighbor, a younger fellow who was known for his horse smarts. Two for the price of one, Galen had said. He was being kind. Flash, Vera's buggy horse, was getting along in years, and he told Rose he would train the foal to take Flash's place in a few years.

At first, just the name *Flash* raised a red flag to Rose. Her buggy skills were rusty. She needed a horse that wouldn't break out and bolt. Galen told her the flash was for the streak of white down his forehead. Rose's confidence in Flash and her driving skills was improving, but she still didn't drive at night, though Galen assured her that Flash could drive the buggy himself. She hadn't forgotten that she had once heard Galen tell her boys, "Es is em beschde Gaul net zu draue." *Even the best horse is not to be trusted*.

Tony lifted the suitcases into the trunk of the car as Lois continued the conversation with the boys. Rose wiped her hands on her apron and hurried out to relieve Lois of the ever-increasing complications of any conversation with Luke and Sammy.

"Now, who again is the oldest of you two?" Lois asked the boys.

"I am," Luke answered quickly. "By almost two whole years. Taller, too."

"Nuh-uh," Sammy said, standing on his toes. "Look how them pants are short."

"Those pants," Rose corrected. He was right, though. His skinny ankles showed clear. Something else to add to her to-do list—let down the hem in Sammy's pants.

When Lois and Tony asked Rose how much she charged for a night's lodging and two meals, she gave them a blank look. She hadn't given any thought about what to charge guests. Tony handed her a one-hundred-dollar bill and called her an angel. She was glad to have it, sorry to take it, relieved to know she could pay some bills, and mortified to need it, all at the same time.

Tony said that after news of Rose's fine, buttery blueberry cornbread leaked out, she had better batten down the hatches. "Folks will be beating a path to your door."

Rose doubted that, but it was a nice thought. Lois gave Rose a hug and handed her a container of ground cinnamon. "A pretty little bird named Bethany told me you needed this."

She waved goodbye to Lois and Tony as the car drove out of the driveway. It had turned out well, inviting those two to stay over. Rose had gone to bed feeling more right and quiet on the inside than she had in many, many a night.

She inhaled the scent of cinnamon. A little bird named Bethany? From the look on Bethany's face as she headed upstairs to deliver the tray of food to Tony and Lois—like she was heading to the gallows—Rose would have thought she would be back downstairs in the blink of an eye. Not so. Bethany stayed upstairs talking to them until dinner was on the table.

Rose smiled. Mim was easier for her—what you saw, you got. She was still a little girl. The boys? They were easy to read. But with Bethany, Rose felt as if there were two trains of thinking going on and she wasn't sure which track she was on. She could never predict what Bethany would think or do.

Take last night. Rose wasn't sure why Bethany had objected so strongly to the idea of starting an inn at the farm. She would have thought Mim would list out objections, in her frank way. Mim was the pessimist of the family—so like Vera in that way. Every picnic was going to get rained on, every cup half empty. Vera was only sixty-four, but she'd been dying of old age since she was thirty-five. Mim and Vera should be closely aligned, good friends, because they saw things in the same way, but they weren't. There was often a tension between them. Too much alike, perhaps? Bethany was a polar opposite to Vera—and yet she was the one who had a sweet way with Vera.

Bethany was clever and headstrong. She acted first, thought about things later. Being full of vinegar and spunk wasn't a bad trait, but that combined with being prettier than a girl had any business being . . . mix in her poor judgment and—oh my!—she was a continual worry to Rose.

She was well aware that Bethany kept holding out hope that they would return to their old town, back to Jake Hertzler. He was a good enough fellow, charming and amusing, but Rose was never quite convinced that Jake was as besotted with Bethany as she was with him. She had hoped that Bethany's enthrallment with Jake would fade away, that she wouldn't hold out hope to return to their former town. Besides, they had no home to return to. Vera's farm was their only refuge. Bethany, nineteen now, should have an understanding of their circumstances, but maybe she was expecting too much from her. For all of Bethany's charm and beauty, she gripped tightly to cockeyed optimism. She was like Dean that way.

She remembered when Dean had hired Jake, almost two years ago. Was it that long ago? Jake had an accounting background and was a whiz with numbers. Rose had questioned the wisdom of hiring someone—even an hourly employee—when the business's profit margins were so thin. Schrock Investments had been paying over 6 percent dividends a year until the recession hit. Then, those same investments were barely paying out 1 percent and Dean was scrambling to keep up the same rate of dividends. He assured her that with Jake handling the paperwork details, he and Tobe were freed up to find more investors. "It's the answer to our cash flow problem," he had told her. "An inflow of more investors will keep us afloat. We'll weather this downturn in the economy and be back on our feet." He snapped his fingers, to indicate how quickly things could turn around.

Rose had been curious, bordering on suspicious. It struck her as slightly off—as if they were using money from the new investors to keep the old investors from fleeing. It didn't seem like it was addressing the basic problem—the investments were no longer bringing in high returns. But what did she know? She didn't ask Dean anything more. Now she wished she had.

Harold, their big Barred Rock rooster, strutted along the gable of the henhouse, all puffed up and sassy. Rose led Silver Girl out to the far pasture to graze in the morning sun. She ran a hand along the horse's big belly. As she unclipped the lead off of the horse's harness, she saw her neighbor, Galen King, try to corral their straying goat through an opening between their yards. She hurried to meet him.

"I'm sorry, Galen!" The boys had forgotten to bring the goat in for the night. To their way of thinking, he was never hard to catch, so they didn't bother tying him. The goat wasn't given to wandering far from anything green he could nibble. Usually, that meant Galen's yard.

Galen shooed the goat into the pasture. His manner was slow, befitting a man who worked with animals and knew not to frighten them. He lifted his chin toward the pregnant mare. "How's she doing?"

She turned back to look at Silver Girl. "Just fine. She's not due for another month or so." Nearby, Harold let out a piercing crow.

"Every day, that rooster thinks he's king of the world and has to tell everyone all about it." Galen glanced up at him and cupped his hands around his mouth. "Graeh net zu gschwind, Harold." *Don't crow too soon.*

Rose grinned. Dark and wiry, Galen had a quiet, watchful look about him—until he gave up one of his rare smiles. He had been Vera's neighbor for years, yet up until the last year, Rose hadn't spoken to him of anything more than weather or horses. He wasn't overly blessed with the gift of conversation, but she had found his words always held something good in them—like a satisfying drink of cold lemonade on a hot summer day. Rose shielded her eyes and looked at the crowing rooster, strutting along the roofline of the henhouse. "Sometimes I wonder if we're all a little like Harold. Real life carries on around us while we strut in our own yards, thinking we're the ones in charge of things."

As she spoke, she turned to look at Galen. She saw his eyes lift quickly to the hills behind the farmhouse, as if he didn't want to be caught looking at her.

"Rose, I just bought some new Thoroughbreds off the racetrack. Turning them into buggy horses. They're green, very green, and they're skittish. They'll bolt at anything."

Oh. Rose latched the pasture gate behind her, wanting Galen to see that they did, occasionally, latch gates around here. "We'll take care to make sure the goat doesn't wander off."

Galen gave her a quick nod. That was what he had come over to hear. "Did the goat cause you any trouble?"

Galen lifted a shoulder in a half shrug. "Just the usual. It likes the compost pile."

"I'll send the boys over to clean it up."

He shook his head. "Don't worry yourself. Naomi was raking it up as I brought the goat over." He folded his arms. "Sure you need a goat, Rose?"

No, she didn't need a goat. Or twelve cranky hens. Or five sheep. Certainly not a bossy rooster. But especially, she didn't need a goat. A goat was nothing but a nuisance. She wished she could sell it, or just give it away, but Dean had brought it home for the boys on a whim. Rose didn't have the heart to get rid of it. She couldn't take that away from Luke and Sammy. Too hard to explain all that to Galen, though. "I haven't seen Naomi lately. Is she well?"

Naomi was Galen's seventeen-year-old sister, the baby of the family, the only sibling still at home. She suffered from fierce headaches that forced her to stay in bed for days. Galen was very protective of her. It was a quiet joke around the church that if Naomi sneezed, Galen dropped everything to be at her side with a tissue. "She's had a headache the last few days but seems to be feeling better today."

He started to leave, so she quickly said, "Would you like a cup of coffee? I just brewed a fresh pot for Vera."

"Can't." He was in a hurry, usually was.

Rose knew Galen wouldn't slow down for a cup of coffee. But she needed to talk to him and hurried to catch him before he slipped through the privet. "Galen, could I ask your advice on a matter? A business matter?"

He stopped, turned to face her, didn't say anything, but he was listening.

"I'm thinking of converting the basement into an inn," she went on. "As a business."

Galen was quiet for a moment, thinking. "Why would you want that kind of an undertaking? You've got a lot on your shoulders as it is."

With the Securities and Exchange Commission lawyer hounding her, he meant. With children at home, especially two young boys, who needed constant surveillance. With a mother-in-law who was ailing.

"The thing is . . . it seemed like a way to support my family." She bit her lip, waiting for his reaction.

Tipping his head, he studied her, his lips a speculative twist. "I see." His expression said he didn't see at all.

Rose's heart sunk. She shouldn't have told him. She braced herself, expecting him to point out that she had no real idea what she was doing. And wasn't that the truth?

What if Galen said something to Bishop Elmo? To others? She wasn't ready to discuss this. The last thing she needed was another reason to have folks eyeballing her. She couldn't afford to make mistakes in this new church. Why had she said anything to Galen? They were neighbors, that's all. He'd always been kind to them in his quiet way, especially after what happened to Dean, but she shouldn't expect him to be an advisor to her. Gracious sakes, the man had enough troubles of his own with his frail sister.

"Why?"

Hadn't she just told him? "To make a living."

"No," Galen said firmly, almost impatiently. "No, that must not be all there is to it."

The past seven months had been difficult as she adjusted to widowhood and being a single mother. She knew it was time to pick up the threads of her life and move forward.

"You're here in Stoney Ridge for a reason. Is this the reason?"

Rose spotted her mother-in-law on the front porch steps to the house. The easy answer to Galen's question would be to say they were here for Vera. For the longest time, the older woman just stood there, looking out at the yard and pastures, a slightly confused expression on her face. Rose watched her turn and head back into the house, feeling a spike of concern. Vera was getting more and more forgetful.

Galen cleared his throat. "There must be one hundred easier ways to make a living than operating an inn. Think. Why do you really want to do this?" His voice was urgent. "What was it that gave you the idea in the first place?"

Rose closed her eyes, conjuring the image in her mind. "I've always wanted to have people come to my home, to be restored and refreshed. I love the feeling I get when people are eating at my kitchen table. It makes me feel so good inside, deep down."

An awkward feeling slid over her. She looked down, watching her own fingers make a pleat in her apron. Galen's eyes were on her, waiting for her to continue. She could practically feel them boring in her soul.

"I like the idea of it," she continued. "Of creating a place where folks can catch their breath and feel welcomed. And I do need to find some ways to bring in money. I don't want to have to work in town and have the boys come home to an empty house." Not entirely empty. Vera would be home. Nearly empty.

She chanced a glance at him.

He gave her a soft, slow smile. "Well, let's check out the basement and see what it would take."

For a moment, all she could do was stare at him, stunned. Galen King was *nothing* like she'd thought he'd be. He was a helpful neighbor to Vera but preoccupied with the task of raising his younger siblings. Ten years ago, his father had broken his neck after being thrown from a horse and Galen became the man of the house, overnight, without warning. People tended to think that Galen was surly, recalcitrant, a real grump. He had a tough exterior that made him seem older than he was. It was an image he liked to cultivate, but he was never able to pull it off for long. Underneath his curmudgeon exterior, he had a heart as soft as butter left on a sunny windowsill.

Over the last seven months, Galen had gone out of his way to look after the Schrocks—fixing fences, finding the right horse for Rose, returning straying animals and straying little boys. He made himself quietly useful. Soon, Rose began to see that was what he did, the kind of man he was— and that everyone, including the Schrocks, depended upon him to do it.

Rose took the basement key from her pocket as she walked to the basement door. Even that was a plus—the basement had its own exterior opening. That topped the list of Bethany's many objections—that guests would be interfering with the family. Meals and all. Rose didn't see it that way—as soon as she got the basement fixed up, guests wouldn't need to go to the house. She would deliver breakfast to them. As for dinner, she didn't plan to offer dinner at all. She only did so last night because Lois and Tony were in a fix on a stormy night. She reached into her pocket and felt the one-hundred-dollar bill. Imagine that! God's blessing.

Galen and Rose walked toward the musty, dusty basement. She hadn't been in it since they'd moved to the farmhouse last year. That realization triggered memories of their move. Her mother-in-law was the one who had insisted that Dean and Rose bring the children and live with her after their home was taken over by the bank. Dean had put it up as collateral to the bank for loans, and lost that bet. "I'll have someone in the church help me set up that small room beyond the kitchen for a bedroom for me and we're right as rain," Vera had told them.

"But it's putting you out of your own house—" Rose had said.

"No, it's not. I'm not really able to climb those stairs anyway. Bad knees. This way I have company and a little place to myself. What could be better? I've been waiting for the day when Dean and his children would come back where they belonged."

Vera kept insisting, Dean acquiesced, so Rose knew she had no choice. They moved the family and all their belongings into the large farmhouse in Stoney Ridge—about an hour's drive from Dean's office in York County. Rose had hoped that moving to Stoney Ridge might be a turning point. Instead, it became a point of bracing oneself for the storm.

Rose worked the key in the lock. The door was warped, so Galen had to use his shoulder to push it open. As they stepped inside, something scurried by their feet—a gray mouse. Then another. When Rose's heartbeat returned to normal, she followed Galen the rest of the way inside. She could see just enough to make her cringe. She waited for Galen to say something, the way she waited for her children to talk. People would talk when they got their mind around the subject.

When Galen had looked all through the basement, he folded his arms across his chest. "It's worth a try." It wasn't entirely below ground, another plus. The house was built into a hillside, so the front window of the basement was large and the room was filled with sunlight. It was a big enough space that Galen thought it could be divided into two bedrooms and a sitting area. Maybe a small kitchen could go against one wall—cabinets and a refrigerator and an oven. And a bathroom. Definitely a bathroom. He took the pad and paper from her hands, his fingers brushing hers.

He scribbled down a list of things Rose would need to do to make the basement ready for company. He started a new page with a list of people he thought she should talk to, including his sister in Indiana who had started a bed-and-breakfast. When he was finished, he handed Rose back the paper. There was something fundamentally reassuring about how he took her idea seriously, and she was touched. Rose felt an excitement for the future she hadn't felt in months. Years, maybe.

"You're doing a lot for a neighbor," she said.

He held her gaze. "A friend, you mean." He walked to the door, then turned to her. "Of course, you'll need to run this all past Bishop Elmo."

Rose noticed how smudged and dirty the windows were. She could get the boys working on that this very afternoon.

"Rose? Did you hear me? I think you should talk to Bishop Elmo."

She glanced up at him. "Dean used to say that it was easier to apologize later than to ask for permission first."

Galen's dark eyebrows lifted in surprise. "Wammer eppes oft dutt, waert mer's gewehnt." *Do a thing often and it becomes a habit.*

She gave him a sharp look. Was that Galen's way of commenting on Dean's character? Or lack of. He had known Dean for many years, but

Rose didn't realize that he understood his nature too. One more thing she had underestimated about Galen.

He kept his eyes fixed on her. "I find it hard to believe that Vera would go along with this idea."

"I haven't quite . . . told her yet." Galen opened his mouth to say something, but Rose beat him to the punch. "I know. I know. I will tell her. I just wanted to sort a few things out first."

Galen let out a puff of air. "Good luck with that."

# 3

Bethany rolled up her spare clothes and stuffed them in her cubby, pinned her prayer cap into place, then slipped out the kitchen door of the Stoney Ridge Bar & Grill. She had to hurry. She needed to get to the post office before the mail went out at three. She had received a letter from Jake Hertzler yesterday and wrote one back, immediately.

Jake wrote, regularly at first, then with less frequency. Sometimes, when weeks had gone by with no word from him, Bethany would get angry and tell herself that she was going to end it and move on with her life. After all, they were only about an hour apart and he had never come to visit her, not once, despite her many invitations. But about the time she told herself it was over, a letter from Jake would arrive full of apologies, explanations, and the endearments she longed to hear, and she would forgive him yet again. She let out a sigh. Jake was lucky to have her. Not many girls would be as patient and understanding as she was.

She needed to drop by the farmers' market and pick up a bag of Brussels sprouts from the Salad Stall to take home later today. She paid the young man, Chris Yoder—whom she happened to know was courting her friend, M.K. Lapp—for the Brussels sprouts and retrieved the scooter she hid behind the market dumpster each morning. Her sister, Mim, didn't like any green vegetables, but lately she was willing to try Brussels sprouts, if smothered in fried bacon. Two weeks ago, it was broccoli. Mim's finicky eating habits were beneficial to Bethany. Bringing things home from the farmers' market served as a beneficial decoy.

Rose was under the impression that Bethany worked at the farmers' market five days a week, and Bethany didn't feel any compulsion to correct that impression. She couldn't remember how that impression got started—maybe, when she told Rose that she had *applied* for a job at the farmers' market. But the only job Bethany was *offered* came from the Stoney Ridge Bar & Grill. So she took it. And on a dare one day from another waitress, Ivy, she wore English clothing. Her tips doubled that day. Tripled the next. Since then, Bethany kept spare English clothing in her cubby and changed into them each day. The good thing was that no Amish ever came into the Stoney Ridge Bar & Grill.

Too expensive. Too worldly. In that order.

The bad thing was, she was living a whopper of a lie. But that was a worry for another day. A person shouldn't worry about too much at one time. Women were prone to worry and men didn't like women who worried too much. She had read that very thing in *A Young Woman's Guide to Virtue*, published in 1948, one of the few books allowed in her grandmother's house besides the Holy Bible and the *Ausbund* and the *Martyrs Mirror*. All very serious stuff for a nineteen-year-old girl.

She had retrieved her hidden scooter from behind the dumpster when she heard someone call out her name—a young Amish fellow from her church. She had never noticed him. Maybe once or twice. His name was Jimmy Fisher, he was dangerously good-looking, and anyone could see that he thought he was something special. All the girls at church talked about him as if he could charm the daylight out of the sky.

She had to walk the scooter through the farmers' market to reach the road, but she kept up a quick pace, ignoring Jimmy Fisher.

"Hey! Hey, Bethany! Bethany Schrock!"

Too late.

Bethany didn't slow down but turned her chin slightly, just to acknowledge his existence. Just to be polite. Not so that he would think she had any idea who he was.

Jimmy jogged to catch up to her. "I don't think we've formally been introduced. Aren't you a friend of M.K. Lapp's?"

She slowed to a stop. Just to be polite. "Maybe," she said coolly. So, she was face-to-face with the famous Mr. Irresistible. *A Young Woman's*

*Guide to Virtue* warned of forward and bold young men. They were to be avoided. She started walking on her way.

Jimmy followed behind. "Couldn't you slow down for a moment. Be sociable?"

Bethany turned to face him. It occurred to her that he might just be friendly.

Jimmy took off his hat, held it to his chest, and grinned. "I'm James Fisher, proprietor of Fisher Hatchery. Friends call me Jimmy." He thumped his heart. *Thump, thump, thump.* "My heart leaps to make your acquaintance."

She tried not to roll her eyes. "Well, James, I am in a hurry."

"You're always in a hurry. I see you zooming in and out of here each day. But I can't quite figure out what the big hurry is." Jimmy stroked his chin, deep in thought. "That scooter gets stashed behind the dumpster and you seem to disappear. Makes a fellow wonder where a girl spends her day." His blue eyes sparkled with mischief.

M.K. Lapp had warned her to stay clear of Jimmy Fisher—that he was crazier than a loon. Right now, he didn't strike her as unhinged—more like a fellow who was too clever for his own good. His was a charming scalawag's smile, and she trusted it for about as long as it took to blink.

Jimmy took a step closer to her. "Maybe if you let me take you home in my buggy, we could get to know each other." He took another step toward her. "I can keep secrets."

In such situations, *A Young Woman's Guide to Virtue* recommended that a young woman hold up her head, ignore such ungentlemanly behavior, and quietly remove herself. Remain pious and ladylike at all times, the book said. Unflappable. Imperturbable.

He wiggled his eyebrows in an outrageously flirtatious manner. "What do you say, good-looking?"

*Shootfire!* The arrogance of this fellow really ground Bethany's grits. She narrowed her eyes and planted her fists on her hips. "You, Mr. Irresistible, can just take your buggy and—"

"Bethany! Mom's looking for you!" Luke and Sammy ran up to her, red-faced and panting. "Mammi Vera's having a sinking spell!"

Rose had waited for just the right moment to speak to Vera about turning the basement into an inn. The right moment had yet to come, but she couldn't wait any longer. She had stopped by the phone shanty to pick up her messages and discovered a paying guest wanted to arrive tomorrow. He said his cousin Tony had recommended the place to him after learning he had a business trip in Lancaster County. Rose's first reaction was sheer panic. This was all happening too fast! She wasn't in a position to have people stay at the farm yet—the basement would take time and work to get into shape. That meant a guest would have to stay in the house . . . and this particular guest happened to be a *man*. A stranger. This was a bad idea. A very bad idea.

But on the heels of that thought came another one. Maybe this turn of events was from God. After all, the entire idea came about because she had opened the conversation with God. At Galen's urging, she had gathered her courage one afternoon and driven over to Bishop Elmo's. He met her out by her buggy and listened, without any hint of expression, as she explained about the inn. A thoughtful, kindly man, he stroked his scraggly white beard for a moment, then his face brightened and he clapped his hands together in delight—as if he had only wished he'd thought of it himself. She left with his blessing and a lightness in her heart.

Maybe God was encouraging her to step out in faith and trust that it would all work out. This man wasn't entirely a stranger—he was a cousin of Tony's, who seemed like a good man. She remembered that one-hundred-dollar bill Tony had slipped into her palm. Think how nice it would be to have some steady income right now.

Rose picked up the phone and called Tony's cousin. She tried to sound as if she did this every day of her life—took reservations and gave directions to find the farm. As she hung up the phone, she blew out a puff of air. She had to face Dean's mother about this . . . new venture. She couldn't keep hiding guests in the house.

She rubbed her face. How often must Vera rue the fact that she was the one who encouraged Dean to move his family to Stoney Ridge?

While Rose had been grateful for her mother-in-law's provision of a home, especially after Dean had passed, she knew Vera well enough to know she had an ulterior motive to such a generous offer. Not long after Dean's funeral, Vera spelled out her expectations: return to the Old Order Amish church and all that went with it—school, clothing, no car, no electricity.

"Those are my rules," Vera told Rose firmly. To Vera's way of thinking, this was the chance to bring her grandchildren back to their roots, back to where she felt they belonged.

"Fine," Rose said without any objection, which shocked Vera. Rose had never minded standing up to Vera, but she was prepared for this. She had been raised Old Order but left the church, long ago, before she had been baptized. She sensed that she needed to keep the family intact and united, so she went through the instruction classes, confessed her sins, renounced the world, and joined the church. That vow wasn't made to a group of people, but to God. She felt joined, like a limb to a tree, to the church and to her family and to God.

The children went along with it—switching schools, adjusting their clothing, selling the old minivan. Even Bethany was accommodating, though she said she wasn't ready to attend instruction classes with Rose.

Aside from missing the convenience of her minivan, Rose and the children adapted surprisingly well to the lifestyle change. They had always spoken the Penn Dutch language in their home, and they were familiar with Old Order ways from visits to Vera's home. In so many areas, they were making adjustments and weathering the storm.

But another storm started to brew. Vera had become forgetful. She misplaced objects, forgot dates right after she looked at the calendar, couldn't remember little words like "hat" or "horse," or she would say another word in its place. She had weakness in her right side. The doctor diagnosed it as a series of mini-strokes, brought on by stress. This doctor put her on a blood thinner and gave her daily exercises.

Even if Rose wanted to leave (and to be entirely truthful, she often did), how could she ever justify it? Dean had been Vera's only son.

Rose pulled open the curtains to let the natural light into the room. "It's a beautiful day today. Spring will be here soon."

Vera blinked her eyes. "Where's Bethany? I only want Bethany."

Rose sighed. "Bethany works each day at the farmers' market. She'll be home after three. I have time now to help you with your exercises."

"I'll do them later. With Bethany."

"We need to do these every morning and every afternoon. The doctor explained that to you."

"Women shouldn't be doctors."

And thus began the morning routine with her mother-in-law. Rose slowly coaxed Vera's right hand open, rubbed lotion into each little nook and cranny. "The doctor said that hands often curl up tight when someone suffers apoplexy."

"She was a quack."

"She wasn't a quack. She said your strokes are causing this weakness, but in time you'll regain some of these skills. She said these exercises will help keep your fingers limber."

"That's enough for now."

"Each one needs to be bent and straightened half a dozen times, and your wrist needs to be rotated." A routine of exercises needed to be done twice a day, morning and night, and Rose or Bethany did them faithfully. While Rose patiently started working Vera's fingers in her lifeless right arm, Vera kept a steady stream of rebukes, complaints, and criticism flowing. No amount of soothing calmed her.

Rose knew embarrassment over having to be tended to in such a way was what fueled Vera's sharp tongue. She always forgave her. She knew God was calling her to meet this situation with grace. "Do you see how much stronger you're getting? Dean would have been proud of you."

"Don't think I don't know why Dean did what he did." Vera pushed Rose's arm away. "I know you pushed him to the brink. I heard that argument. Everyone did. The whole county could've stayed home and heard every word."

*Patience. Patience. We are living in her house.* "So you've told me." Rose was accustomed to Vera's vinegar and beans, but those sharp words still stung. The thing was—Vera spoke the truth. She had a hard time forgiving herself for that argument, for what happened the next day. Maybe she did push Dean to the brink.

She took Vera's hand in hers and started bending the elbow, straightening and bending, straightening and bending. Five more, four more, three more. "I have something to tell you. Some good news." Rose tried to keep her voice as calm as a summer day.

Vera looked away.

"I've come up with an idea about how to support my family."

"It's about time. I might be land rich but I'm money poor. And this land is going to Tobe, when he comes home. It's rightfully his. You can't expect me—"

Rose lifted a hand to stop another onslaught. "I've been praying on this and I think I've found a solution. I'll be able to be home for the children and to take care of you." She tried to keep the statement flat, to mask the swells of uncertainty inside her.

Vera peered at her with her one droopy side of the face, curious.

"I'm going to start a bed-and-breakfast. An inn. Here at the farm. Convert the basement. You won't even know guests are here." In the awkward silence that followed, Rose's already-shaky confidence plummeted. "I spoke to Bishop Elmo and he gave me his blessing. Of course, I'd like your blessing on it." She chanced a glance at Vera, who was blinking in surprise, her mouth hung wide open. Rose carefully straightened Vera's blanket. She was taking this news better than she thought she might. What a pleasant surprise.

"Absolutely not!" Vera shouted.

Naturally, Vera Schrock did not brood upon things of the past, the way some people dwelled on such things, but the old ways of her people still came to mind from time to time, often at unexpected moments. Such as this morning.

Her daughter-in-law Rose did not follow the old ways. The old ways would never have approved of turning a home into a . . . stopping station for strangers. The old ways respected that the Plain people were set apart, that they were not to mingle with the English. The old ways . . . She could go on. And what was the point? No one listened to her. She was always the last to know anything, anyway.

Vera tried to lift a coffee mug and couldn't raise it an inch off the table. Her chest tightened with sudden despair. Something terrible was happening to her, something she couldn't fight and simply could not stop. Her right side kept getting weaker and weaker—not stronger like the quack lady doctor promised, after tossing all kinds of pills at her and charging her an arm and a leg. Vera couldn't get words out the way she used to, but she had them in her head. Lately, her thoughts felt like a tangled ball of yarn. They flitted through her mind like a robin hopping from tree to tree, never staying in one place long. The confused state she often found herself in was occurring more and more often, and she didn't like the idea of Bethany and those other children—what were their names? the dark-haired girl and those two wild boys?—well, whatever their names were, she didn't like them seeing her this way.

She was frightened.

Terrified.

At least she was when she remembered.

And then those horrid hiccups would return.

Rose had tried a number of fail-safe cures to stop hiccups that she got from the healer, Sadie something-or-other. She used to be Sadie Lapp, Vera did remember that, but she couldn't remember her married name. Anyway, last week, she had Vera pinching her nose shut with her two thumbs, and plugged up both ears with her fingers, while Rose or Bethany would pour a glass of water down her throat. Vera stomped her foot when she was close to drowning, and then the glass was taken away. It had worked.

Just thinking of that horrid cure made her even more anxious, and sure enough, those awful hiccups started up.

# 4

If it was going to happen, Bethany just wished it would go ahead and happen. The basement had been cleared out, remodeled, freshly painted. She couldn't wait to get the furniture moved in and a shingle hung so that Rose's ridiculous bed-and-breakfast was officially under way. She was sick and tired of giving up her bedroom for strangers. Twice now, she'd had to sleep with Mim in a scrunched-up bed and listen to her whiffling snores all night long. Mim should know that any little thing would wake Bethany. She hardly slept. Too much responsibility weighed on her mind. She was the oldest now, since Tobe had vanished, and she had to take care of everybody.

The man who stayed in Bethany's room had the gall to come downstairs for breakfast and complain about the loud sound of mooing cows! "Well, we *are* close to a dairy farm," Rose said. "And this *is* the countryside."

But the man was not happy. And his "donation" was a mere twenty-five dollars.

To top it off, Mammi Vera heard the man's complaints about the mooing cows and pitched a fit. No wonder her grandmother kept having these mini-strokes. She was constantly pitching fits.

And here was another thing: Bethany was growing weary of getting yanked away from whatever she was doing to settle her grandmother down. It took a fair bit of work to calm Mammi Vera. Being her grandmother's favorite wore her out. She knew the only reason was because she looked so much like a Schrock. The younger ones took after Rose, her father's second wife.

40

Bethany didn't think of Rose as a stepmother but as a real mother. Part of the reason, she supposed, was because Rose didn't believe in labels that fractured a family and divided them up. She insisted that Bethany and Tobe think of Mim and the boys as siblings, not steps or half. Rose referred to herself as Bethany and Tobe's mother. She did all she could to keep the family together. Including Mammi Vera.

But mostly, Bethany thought of Rose as her mother because she was always there for her. She was a rock. She was safe.

Unlike her real mother.

Bethany could hardly remember her real mother. It was sad that there were no pictures of her. If Bethany were a bishop, she would change that rule, first thing. She grinned. Imagine that—a woman becoming a bishop. It would never happen! But she would love to have a picture of her mother. She had deserted their family when Bethany was just a toddler.

A few years later, her father married Rose, and Rose became her stepmother. That was the happiest day of Bethany's childhood. Bethany admired her more than anybody she had ever met. Rose was always thinking of others and she took the brunt of everything, especially her grandmother's sour tongue, yet she wasn't beaten down by it. When Mim complained about the work required to get the basement into shape as an inn, Bethany replied, "But isn't the point to give Rose a chance? Isn't that the whole point?"

As close as Bethany felt to Rose, she couldn't call her "Mom." In her heart, she had a real mother and, one day, she hoped to find her. To ask her why she left.

Luke and Sammy came galloping through the back door. "Bethany, come see! Galen's brought over some furniture for the basement." They galloped back out again.

Hallelujah! If Rose was determined to see this crazy notion through, at least get those strangers out of their house and into the basement.

"You boys quiet down out there!" came a cry from the depths of Mammi Vera's gloomy bedroom.

"They're already back outside, Mammi Vera," Bethany called back. She looked out the window and saw Naomi alongside her brother, Galen, coming up the driveway, in an open wagon filled to the brim with furniture. She wiped her hands on a dishrag and hurried outside.

Naomi waved eagerly when she saw her. It always surprised Bethany that Naomi was so fond of her. There couldn't be two more opposite girls in all the world over. Naomi was frail and thin and often took to her bed. Bethany was strong, curvy, and had never been sick a day in her life. Naomi was pious and pure and reserved, while Bethany was blunt and outspoken, with a hot temper. Why, hadn't she nearly spouted off a curse word or two at Jimmy Fisher just yesterday?

And all the while, Jimmy Fisher just watched her with those mischievous eyes, enjoying her outburst. Not at all offended, he had made good on his offer to give her a ride home in his buggy so she could hurry back to Mammi Vera's side. It was her job to settle Mammi Vera down after pitching one of her fits that ended in relentless hiccups.

Nonetheless, the buggy ride home did not change Bethany's opinion of Jimmy Fisher: he was arrogant and cocky just because he was so handsome and charming and likable.

She wondered if he might drop by sometime. She didn't want him to, but she wondered if he might.

Naomi hopped off the wagon and hurried to Bethany. "My brother emptied out the attic! He brought over extra beds and rugs and tables for the new bed-and-breakfast."

"Not a minute too soon," Bethany said. "I can't handle having strangers in the house. Asking questions and poking around the house. One of them walked right into Mammi Vera's room yesterday and she screamed bloody murder."

"She's always lathered up about one thing or another," Luke piped up.

Bethany pointed a finger at him. "You respect your elders." Then she shooed him away. "Get Sammy and make yourself useful. Go help Galen unload the wagon." She turned back to Naomi. "Come and see how the basement's starting to take shape. You won't believe it."

Naomi followed Bethany to the basement door. It had been divided into two bedrooms, a bathroom, and a living room with a small kitchen. A week ago, after Rose and the boys had emptied everything out and put it in the hayloft, Galen brought a few young fellows from church and they built the interior walls, added drywall, and installed a bathroom and a kitchen, tapping into plumbing that was already there. All in two days. Then Rose and Bethany and Mim painted the entire interior a fresh creamy butter color with white on the woodwork. The place was transformed.

Naomi clapped her hands in delight. "I think this is going to be wonderful, Bethany! And best of all—it means you won't be moving back to your old town."

"Well, I don't know about that," Bethany started. "I'll help Rose get some debts cleared, then I'll be heading back, for sure." No doubt.

"I hope not." Naomi leaned forward to whisper in her ear. "Did I happen to see Jimmy Fisher drop you off in his buggy yesterday?"

"That was purely an accident," Bethany said. She hoped her reputation wasn't sullied because she had been seen with the likes of Jimmy Fisher. "And it won't be happening again, I can guarantee you of that."

"He is awfully good-looking," Naomi said, blushing a deeper shade of red. "But just so you're warned, he goes through girls faster than a bag of potato chips."

*What?* What was Naomi implying? Did she think Bethany was sweet on Jimmy Fisher? She wanted to scotch that suspicion. She was just about to say so when the boys burst through the door, carrying a big rug under their arms.

"I'll go help Galen," Naomi said.

Bethany instructed the boys to lay the rug straight in the big room—the only room it would fit in. The boys ran outside to bring in some more furniture. Bethany looked around the room. She had to hand it to Rose. It was starting to look less like an afterthought and more like a place someone would want to come to stay. Galen deserved a lot of the credit too. Encouraging Rose, organizing the work to get done. Rose kept insisting that she could manage herself, but Galen ignored her objections and kept at it. She wondered why he was being so kind. She looked out the window, watching Galen hand something to Rose and tell her something. Rose laughed in response.

Oh. Of course! He must think of her as an older sister.

Rose tried not to let it show, as she helped unload Galen's wagon full of spare furniture, but her stomach was still churning from this morning's phone call. Allen Turner, a lawyer for the Security Exchange Commission Legal Affairs, called to inform her that Tobe was under suspicion for altering the company books.

She put a box of towels in the bedroom and sorted through them to see which could be used and which should be cut up into rags. As each pile grew, her thoughts drifted to Tobe, to Dean, to that awful time when everything imploded.

Someone had sent a letter to the Security Exchange Commission asking for an inquiry about Schrock Investments. How could they keep up such high returns, the letter had asked, when the rest of the economy was doing so poorly? It didn't add up, the mysterious letter writer accused. That was the first portent—when Dean received a phone call from Allen Turner requesting a meeting after receiving that letter. A tipoff, Allen Turner called it.

Not much later, checks from Schrock Investments started to bounce. Dean made the appalling discovery that there was no money in the bank, though statements said otherwise.

Investors caught wind that Schrock Investments was in trouble and demanded their money. Trapped between a rock and a hard place, Dean declared bankruptcy. Then the claims began from investors, which heightened the concern of the Securities and Exchange Commission. Allen Turner was waiting at the office one morning for Dean to arrive. He had a subpoena for the company books, which Dean handed over. He had nothing to hide, Dean insisted. Allen Turner was stunned to realize that the books were actually physical books, ledgers—no electronic transfer of funds. But Dean didn't use computers. "I'm a Plain man," he explained to Allen Turner, "and I run my company in a Plain way."

"With the added benefit of no paper trail," Allen Turner pointed out, unkindly and with suspicion. He left, shaking his head, those black ledgers tucked under his arm.

It made her sick to think Allen Turner would doubt Dean's integrity. To her knowledge, Dean had never once broken the law. He was a straight-as-an-arrow type. She couldn't even remember that he had ever gotten a parking ticket. But something had happened and no one seemed to understand what. Rose couldn't sleep nights, knowing how many folks had lost so much money. It wasn't like Dean had just spilled punch at a Sunday picnic. For a moment, she closed her eyes as she thought of all the people, scattered across the country, who had invested in Dean's company, Schrock Investments, trusting him with their savings.

That was the day that Tobe ran away. He left a note on his pillow that said,

*Dad and Rose, Don't worry about me. Don't try to find me. I'll be fine.*

Tobe had worked for Dean's company since he turned sixteen. Dean didn't know where Tobe had run off to, or why.

Throughout their marriage, Rose and Dean had had their share of quarrels and misunderstandings like any married couple, but they argued that night in a way they had never argued before. Finally, Dean grew silent, sullen. Then he said to her, "I'm going to fix it. I'm going to fix everything." He went to the door, snagged his hat off the bench, and jammed it onto his head. At the threshold, he turned back and gave her a long look, then shoved the door open and headed down the driveway. She watched him disappear into the darkness. The next morning, his body was found, drowned, in a pond. Even now, months later, she shuddered as she thought of that day. The worst day of her life.

She dropped the towel and rubbed her face with her hands. This entire situation was so complicated and—almost eight months later—only seemed to get more complicated. When would it end? Would Tobe ever show up again? A part of her didn't want him to. What might happen to him if he showed up? She couldn't bear thinking of him, indicted, faced with jail time. If . . . *if* he was guilty.

It seemed Allen Turner thought he was. This morning Allen Turner had told her that Jake Hertzler had been called in for questioning and reluctantly admitted that he suspected Tobe might have been involved in keeping a second set of books. Jake said if that were true, then it was possible Dean had handed over cooked books to the SEC—ones that had been altered to appear as if they complied with accounting regulations.

"Tell me everything you know about Jake Hertzler," was how Allen Turner had started the telephone conversation this morning.

"He's a nice young man. Very polite, very likable. He was new to our church and looking for work. When Dean learned he had some experience with accounting, he hired him on an hourly basis to help with some paperwork."

"What kind of paperwork?"

"Preparing statements to the investors. He never handled money, other than to make bank deposits. Never withdrawals. I know that for a fact."

"But your husband trusted him?"

"Of course. Of course he did. There was never a reason not to."

"Mrs. Schrock, was it possible that your husband had stopped paying attention to details?"

Maybe. *Probably.* "I find it hard to believe that Jake would accuse Tobe of keeping a set of altered books. Jake was a good employee. He worked hard to help Dean and Tobe. Everything changed when he came on board." At least for a while.

"How did everything change?"

"Dean was able to spend more time finding investors. He was very grateful for Jake's help. And don't forget that the problems had started long before Jake had been hired. Dean had been struggling to pay dividends for over a year."

"I see." He paused and Rose knew that he didn't see at all. "But you didn't answer my question. Could your husband have stopped paying attention to details?"

"Is that what Jake said?"

Silence.

"Why would you believe Jake?" she asked.

"He gave us information in a deposition," Allen Turner explained. "He was under oath."

*Well, that's the problem right there. Plain people don't take oaths. They shouldn't need them. Telling the truth isn't optional.* She was afraid it would sound like a deflection, a distraction from what he was after, and that wasn't how she wanted to seem to Allen Turner. She wanted to convey an image of strength, of confidence, that she was sure Dean and Tobe would not have done something illegal—not intentionally.

"When did your husband realize that there was a cash problem?"

"When checks started bouncing and he discovered there was no money in the bank. Soon after that, he filed for bankruptcy. He needed protection from investors and he needed help from the bank to try to figure out what was going on. But he was always planning to make good on the principal investments. He didn't declare bankruptcy to avoid anything. I have no doubt of that." Dean had been adamant that declaring bankruptcy was the only choice—no one could go after them personally, they could only go after the assets of the company—the office, the land it was on, the office equipment. Still, she hated living with those debts over her head. Allen Turner said he was optimistic that up to fifty cents on the dollar could be returned to investors who made claims.

But those claims, only about one fourth of the investors, came from non-Amish, non-Mennonite investors. The rest were all Plain folks who had put their trust in one of their own. What about them? she had asked Allen Turner. "If they aren't willing to pursue the claim in court," he said, "there's nothing that can be done for them, legally."

And *that* was a burden, among others, that weighed on Rose. She was determined to pay every single person back the principle they had invested in Schrock Investments, even if it took her years and years. She felt responsible for these people.

"Mrs. Schrock, it's imperative that we find your stepson. Do you know where he could be? Any idea at all?"

When he asked her that question, her heart started to race. Tobe was in danger, as surely as he was when he was a reckless young boy, doing foolish things like Luke did now—climbing to the tops of trees, teasing the goat. He thought he was invincible. "You've caught me unprepared," she said. "I can't think of anything. But I'll try. I'll . . . make a list."

Allen Turner said he would call again soon to see if she had any idea where he could be. "If you hear from him, you need to let me know."

As if she would need a reminder.

When would it ever end? She threw the last towel into the rag pile and grabbed the empty box, startling Chase, the dog, into action. He sprang from sleeping by her feet and began to bark, then chased his tail. Watching that silly old dog act like a puppy made her lips tug in a smile. *Maybe that is one of the reasons God gave us dogs*, Rose thought, watching Chase spin in a circle. A gentle nudge from above to "hangeth thou in there," even on days when you just feel like you're only chasing your tail.

Bethany lifted a large tray filled with dishes to take out to the dining area to a group of Rotary businessmen. Her friend Ivy had started their orders but needed to leave early today for a dentist appointment, so Bethany agreed to stay and finish up her section. She set up the tray and looked at Ivy's orders to see how the meals should be served around the table: left to right was how they were taught. When she finished serving, she refilled coffee cups and water glasses, made sure everyone had serving utensils. Hopefully, this big table would guarantee generous tips. Not always, but usually.

As she spun around to check the other tables in Ivy's section, she noticed the unmistakable black felt hat of an Amish man who had been seated at a table against the window. Her heart caught for a moment. The man's head was tilted down to look at the menu. It didn't matter—she wouldn't be recognized, not with her English outfit and hair pulled in a ponytail. And lots of makeup too. Ivy had treated her to a makeover a few weeks ago and given Bethany her old mascara, eyeliner, and blush. Lipstick too.

Bethany turned to a fresh page on her pad and went to the table. "Do you know what you'd like to order for lunch?"

When he didn't answer, Bethany looked up from the pad. Her heart dropped. The Amish man was Jimmy Fisher, grinning at her like a cat that cornered a mouse.

"That feisty girl was late bringing me supper again!" Vera said, sitting by the kitchen window.

Rose knew whom she meant: Mim. Whether Vera truly forgot her grand-children's names or she was just being ornery, Rose didn't know.

"I told you that I'd help you with supper, Vera."

"Last time you tried to cut my food, I nearly choked to death."

"Now that's not true, Vera. It was just broth."

"Because you think I'm fat."

Rose swallowed another sigh. Vera constantly raked conversations, looking for slights or insults. She had always been sharp tongued, never been a picnic to be around, but Dean's passing brought out her mean nature on a full-time basis. It caused Rose endless distress. The children deserved a home filled with laughter and love, not sadness and strife.

*I'm not going to think like that. I'm not.*

She went outside to get a fresh breath of air. A breeze soon made the sheets on the clothesline lift and luff. Rose reached out to touch one. Cold but dry. She unclipped the pins and folded the sheet. The sun felt good on her face. *Lord, Sir, I know I keep petitioning you for a string of miracles, but could you please give me patience to endure that woman? Not just patience, but sincere gratitude. She's put a roof over our heads. Help me be truly grateful.*

She saw Bethany come hurrying toward the house with the boys trotting close behind, spilling with news about the bald eagle pair they had been watching for a few days.

Vera knocked on the window and hollered to them to hush up. "Er is en re Saegmiehl gebore." *He was born in a sawmill.* It was what she said to the boys whenever they were too loud, which was often, or didn't close doors, which happened regularly.

"Sorry, Mammi Vera," Bethany called out, but there was fire in her eyes. Something must have happened at work, but Rose didn't know what. There were times when Bethany seemed to get in a frame of mind that was prickly as a stinging nettle. Bethany went right into the kitchen. Rose saw her crouch beside her grandmother to talk to her. It was Vera's only bright spot of the day—when Bethany came home from work.

"Mom, we think them eagles is going to build a nest in the dead tree on the top of the hill. Near the creek," Luke said.

"*Those* eagles are going to build a nest," Rose corrected.

"Exactly," Sammy piped up. "Wouldn't that be something?"

Grammar was forgotten when the boys were excited. Rose couldn't help smiling at the look of wonder on the boys' faces. "It would be something special to watch." Before the boys could start in on more details about the eagles, Rose sent them to the barn to fill the wheelbarrow with hay to feed the goat and sheep. "Don't forget to latch the gates, Luke and Sammy. That goat's been getting out on a regular basis. We want to be good neighbors to Galen."

"We *are* good neighbors," Luke said. "He just doesn't like goats."

No one liked goats, Rose thought, but didn't say. She had already soundly scolded Luke today for trouble at school. Sometimes, she thought that boy learned everything at school but his lessons. Mim said she was mortified to own up to having him for a brother. Today, it appeared Luke drew a very exaggerated picture of Sammy's ears on his arithmetic workbook. Sammy was sensitive about his rather sizable ears. He took it upon himself to correct Luke with a sound punch as soon as they were out to recess and away from the teacher's eyes. Mim said that the boys were rolling together across the playground, each trying to get in a good punch.

Teacher M.K. had little patience with such boy nonsense. They were kept after school and sent home with a note, explaining their crimes. Rose knew she was a fine teacher and needed to keep discipline in the school-house, but she had to smile when she pictured them tumbling around the playground. Rascals to the end.

As she finished folding the last sheet, Rose felt her heart set to right. She was ready to face the evening. *Thank you, Lord, for bringing a little sunshine into a winter day.*

# 5

Lately, Miriam Schrock had set her mind to finding solutions. A few nights ago, she had gone down to the kitchen, late at night, and had seen her mother at the kitchen table, answering letters from investors. She had sneaked a peek at the letters one time and found a similar theme in all of them: "Greetings in the Name of Jesus! I had $2,452.95 (or $3,497.34 or $1,496.75) . . ."—mostly amounts under $5,000. It was impressive to Mim that each letter-writer knew the figure down to the penny—"in Schrock Investments with Dean Schrock and I would like you to know I need that money very badly." The writer would describe his or her current ailment or financial need and conclude with: "I hope and pray you can send me my money back. Thank you kindly."

That night, Mim could see the anxiety in her mother's face as she tucked a $10 or $20 bill in the letters. She knew what her mother was doing. Rose Schrock would pay back every cent, no matter how long it would take her. She was advised by the SEC man to not do anything until the claims had been settled. But her mother didn't pay any attention to the advice of that SEC man. So Mim insisted that her mother keep track of what she was paying people and created a color-coded accounting book for her. It included pages for income from the new inn, pages for outgo, pages to pay bills, and pages to keep track of payments to former investors.

Her mother was pleased and said Mim was a first-rate problem solver. That made Mim feel very happy, because she knew her mother was facing a mountain of problems. Frankly, Mim didn't know how some of the problems created by her father's investment company would ever get solved, but it made her feel good to help where she could.

Bethany's suggestion was to ask the letter writers to forgive the loans. Her mother refused. She said it was a matter of honor. Those people offered the money in good faith, and in good faith, her mother would return it to them.

"Dad was the one who lost those people's money, not you," Bethany would respond. Her sister was angry with their father, for many reasons, mostly because of his puzzling and untimely passing. "Are you going to spend the rest of your life paying for his sins?"

Her mother always had the same answer to give. "Bethany, your father didn't set out to hurt people. He got in way over his head and didn't know how to find a way out of it. He got desperate. That's why he made the decisions he made."

That answer didn't make any sense to Mim. Instead, she refused to think about her father. At least not about his passing. Everything about his death was complicated and illogical, and Mim liked logical and uncomplicated problems.

Besides, she had another pressing problem on her mind.

Mim had fallen in love. She did not fall in love quickly. She had been in love only 1.5 times. One time with an Irish boy named Patrick who had carrot red hair and worked at the library near Mim's old house. She thought that any boy who would work at a library must be a wonderful boy, even though Patrick had never noticed her. The .5 time was when she first laid eyes on Jimmy Fisher, whom Bethany called Mr. Irresistible in a sneering voice. He had made Mim breathless with his winks at church. When she discovered that he winked at all the girls, including the ancient ladies who lived in the Sisters' House, she reversed her feelings. That was the only logical thing to do.

But then she was seated next to Danny Riehl in school last August, and she knew her heart was in trouble. Danny Riehl was the smartest, nicest boy she had ever met. He knew more facts than anyone she had ever met. She watched Danny Riehl's long fingers curl around his book, one leg stretched out, one bent under the chair. She liked to hear him read aloud. He was at that age when a boy's voice was especially squeaky.

Today, Teacher M.K. had asked Mim and Danny to stay late and help her take old pictures off the wall and put up new ones. When they were done, Mim and Danny were in the coatroom, gathering their overcoats, hat and bonnet, and lunch containers. Mim felt she must say something. "My mother saw a shooting star streak across the sky."

Danny looked up in interest. Great interest. To her knowledge, he had never noticed or acknowledged Mim before that moment. "A few weeks ago? When there was a new moon?"

She nodded.

"It was a meteor."

Dumb, she thought with a sinking feeling in her stomach. Of course it was a meteor. She should know that. It was as obvious as saying that he had a black hat on. Or both his legs ended nicely below his trousers. She searched her mind for something better. "Astronauts can see the Great Wall of China from outer space."

He nodded. "It's the only man-made object that can be seen from the moon." Danny put on his jacket, then opened up his lunch cooler. Inside was a small mouse, quiet and friendly looking. "I found it in the schoolhouse. If Teacher M.K. had seen it, she would have whacked it senseless with her broom. I'm going to set it free in a field behind the schoolhouse." He looked at Mim. "Want to come?"

"Yes," Mim said before he could change his mind.

They walked to a farmer's field and Danny carefully set the mouse free near the base of a corn shock. It stayed in one place for a moment, whiskers quivering, before scurrying off. When it disappeared, he turned toward Mim. "What would you be, if you could be anything?"

Mim frowned. Was this a test? She saw an eagle circling over the pond and wondered if it was one of the eagles that had been buzzing around her farm, and if so, if it was the mister or the missus. "I suppose I might like to be an eagle." She shielded her eyes to watch the eagle soar in the sky. "They live for thirty years and like to eat fish best of all and their nests can weigh up to two tons. And they mate for life, which I think is terribly romantic." She cringed. *Oh no!* Why had she added that part about mating for life? Why couldn't she have just stopped at the nest part? It's actually true, she thought, that you could feel your own flush crawl up your neck.

But Danny didn't seem at all embarrassed. He nodded solemnly. "Do Luke and Sammy know those facts?"

"I have told them but I don't know if they listen."

"Sammy, probably."

"Yes. Sammy might be listening. Not Luke."

"Come on," Danny finally said, as if he had been deciding something. "I'll show you what I want to be."

Danny led Mim on a trail up a hill that framed one side of the lake. There was a telescope in a case, wrapped inside a big plastic trash bag, hidden in the branches of a tree. "This is a reflector telescope that my dad bought for me at a yard sale. We had to fix it up, but it's better to use a reflector than a refractor because it uses mirrors to reflect the light, instead of lenses."

Reflectors? Refractors? Mim had no idea what he was talking about.

Carefully, he unwrapped the telescope, set it on the ground, aimed the scope at the sky, and slipped in an eyepiece from a little velvet-lined box. "This is the best spot I've found for studying the planets. Usually I come at night, but lately I've been coming early in the morning. Looking for Saturn. It's just starting to be visible in the east. Since I keep my scope outside but covered, it remains the same temperature as the air. Otherwise the lens can get fuzzy."

He stepped away so she could look through the eyepiece. He had it centered on the thin moon, rising in the east. It was amazing to see it through a telescope—even in the daylight, she could see the faint tracing of the dark side of the moon.

"That's called earthshine," Danny said. "A few days after a new moon, when there's just a very slim crescent, you can sometimes see earthshine on the unilluminated portion of the moon. Earthshine is caused by sunlight reflected off the earth and onto the moon."

Fascinating facts! "I've never noticed earthshine before, but I've never looked through a telescope before, either."

"You can use binoculars. Beginning astronomers don't realize they don't need an expensive telescope. Really, just a dark night and sharp eyes. You don't need much else."

She straightened. "Danny, do you want to be an astronomer?"

He pushed his glasses up the ridge of his nose. He hesitated, as if he was weighing whether he should admit something of such great importance. "No. I want to be an astronaut." He took off his hat. "Almost. I want to be almost-an-astronaut."

The sun had already begun to set by the time Mim parted ways with Danny and walked up the driveway. There had been a spurt of snow the day before, and a little of it lingered in shady places. It crunched under her feet as she approached the house.

Her mind was filled with the moon and school and facts. Mostly she thought about Danny, stargazer and mouse rescuer. Danny with the lovely blue eyes and the glasses that were held together at the hinges with a paper clip.

Mim stood outside her mother's room, watching her fold a mountain of laundry that was on top of her bed. Her sleeves were pushed up past her elbows, her curly brown hair wild around her face. By her mother's feet there were laundry baskets, one piled on top of another, clothes pouring out, one basket filled to the brim with socks.

"Ah! I see you there." Her mother smiled at her.

*Ask me. Ask me about being in love.* "Hello."

"You look as happy as Christmas morning," her mother said, turning her attention back to the laundry basket. "You must have had a good day at school."

Just as Mim opened her mouth to tell her about why it was a good day, about Danny Riehl and his telescope, a ringing bell sound floated up the stairs. Her grandmother needed something.

Her mother's shoulders slumped. "Mim, would you finish folding this laundry while I tend to Mammi Vera?" She tossed a crunchy sun-dried towel to Mim and hurried down the stairs.

Delia Stoltz didn't know which was worse: the discomfort and soreness from yesterday's lumpectomy, waiting to hear from the doctor if the margins were clear, or waking up fresh to the knowledge that her husband was gone and he would never come back. Her life would never be all right again.

Her bed felt huge and empty now, and when she slept, she did so with her arm around a pillow. She dreamed of Charles almost every night, sometimes good dreams of happy and joyful times; mostly, terrible dreams of abandonment, loss, and sorrow.

The phone rang and rang. All Delia Stoltz wanted was to be alone. She was sore from the lumpectomy. The only call she wanted was from Dr. Zimmerman's with the pathology report about the sentinel node biopsy—and don't expect that for a week or ten days, they had said. Why did it have to take so long? She tried to focus on the good news, that the cancer seemed to have been caught in early stages, and that the initial tests in the hospital looked like the lymph node was clear of cancer cells. But she knew enough to wait for results from the extensive testing before she could allow herself to feel relieved.

Each time the phone rang, she jumped. And each time it turned out to be someone other than the doctor, she became more and more irritable. Like now. Caller ID showed it to be Charles's office. She hadn't seen Charles since the day he left. He had called a few times, but she had never picked up her phone. The messages he left infuriated her—patronizing, with avuncular concern.

Slowly, she got up from the wing chair she'd been sitting in. The pain from the incision made her wince a little as she rose to her feet. In the kitchen, she filled the teakettle and put it on to boil. The phone rang again. Maybe Charles was finally feeling remorse and regret over his impulsive behavior. Maybe he wanted to come home. She hurried to the phone and picked it up without looking at Caller I.D. "Hello?"

"Hello, Mrs. Stoltz, I'm calling for Robyn Dixon." Robyn Dixon, Charles's attorney, daughter of Henry Dixon, who handled their living trust. Henry was semi-retired and had passed many of his clients on to Robyn. She was representing Charles in a malpractice suit, the first he had encountered in twenty-five years of neurosurgery. "Ms. Dixon would like you and Dr. Stoltz to meet her at the office tomorrow afternoon to go over some initial paperwork for the—"

"For the what?" *What did Charles want? A divorce?*

"Legal separation," she said. "Two o'clock, tomorrow afternoon. Do you know where the office is? Shall I send a car?"

*To make sure I get there?* "No. I can manage just fine."

Softer now, the assistant added, "Mrs. Stoltz, would you like to have your attorney present? I could call your attorney and set it up."

Delia swallowed. She thought Robyn Dixon *was* her attorney. "Yes. Please call Henry Dixon and tell him I will require his presence at tomorrow's meeting."

She could practically hear the whirl of confusion in the assistant's mind. "I'm not sure that would be appropriate—"

"My teakettle is whistling." Delia put the phone down on its cradle and stared at it for a long while.

The next day, just two days after the lumpectomy, it took Delia most of the morning to get ready for the two o'clock meeting. She wanted to look her best, her absolute best, and she was determined to keep Charles from learning of her surgery. She had warned Dr. Zimmerman's office to keep this private, and even had the surgery done using her maiden name, just to avoid any chance that someone might recognize her name and inform Charles. She had all kinds of feelings about Charles—deep anger, betrayal, even hatred. And love, yes, love. How could you shut that off after twenty-seven years? They had raised a wonderful child together. She didn't know what she wanted from Charles today, but not pity. Never pity.

She allowed herself an hour to get to Robyn Dixon's office and was grateful for the extra time when she noticed the fuel warning light for her gas tank. She sighed. She pulled into the gas station and stared at the pumps for a while, trying to figure out which buttons to push. As busy as Charles was, he had always taken care of these little things for her. He didn't want her to ever pump her own gas.

Suddenly it all seemed too much. Too much to deal with, too much to figure out on her own. She was trying her best to put up a brave front, but it was too hard. Everything was too painful. A tear rolled down her cheek.

Now she knew what she wanted out of this meeting today: she wanted Charles to stop this nonsense and come home. She didn't want a legal separation or a divorce. Tears came faster now, streaming down her cheeks, one after another after another. Her face would look red and puffy for this meeting. And she had worked so hard to look good today.

"Darlin', can I help you with something? Are you having trouble with that pump?" A woman fit the gas nozzle into Delia's car and pushed the right button to start the fuel. Delia stared at her. She had sprigs of bright red hair jutting up from her head like a firecracker in mid-explosion. "My name's Lois."

Embarrassed, Delia swallowed back her tears. "I'm sorry. I've just had too much on my plate lately."

"Oh, I know how that can be. I surely do. About once a month, my Tony and me have to get out of the city and clear the cobwebs. We like to head over to Amish country and breathe some fresh air." She picked up the squeegee and started to wash down Delia's window, then squeegee the excess water off of it. Delia wondered if she might work here and if so, should she tip her? How much would be appropriate?

"Just last month," Lois continued, "we went to a wonderful new place in Stoney Ridge and met this darling Amish family and we just feel so renewed and refreshed. My Tony can't stop talking about that Amish gal's blueberry cornbread. We came home feeling like we'd gone to Hawaii. Good as new." She finished cleaning the window as the gas nozzle clicked. "I'm telling you, sugar. A trip to Lancaster County cures what ails you." She patted Delia's arm and turned to go.

*Oh!* So Lois was a customer. Delia stared at the gas nozzle as Lois's words sunk in.

Cured what ailed you? Renewed? Refreshed? Good as new? "Wait. Wait! Lois! Where did you say that Amish hotel was?"

Lois was getting into her car but popped her head back up, over the roof of the car. "Town is called Stoney Ridge, east of Lancaster. Off Route 30. Head to Main Street, turn right at the Sweet Tooth Bakery, drive a mile or so, and you can't miss it. Big white farmhouse with an even bigger red barn. A goat is in the front pasture and sticks his head over the fence. Tell that little innkeeper—Rose Schrock is her name—that Tony and Lois sent you. She'll treat you right." Lois climbed in the car, then popped her head back up again. "If you get lost, stop at the Sweet Tooth Bakery and ask where Rose lives. Be sure to get a cinnamon roll. Don't miss that!" She waved goodbye and drove out of the gas station.

Delia got back in her car and glanced at the clock. One thirty. She drove to the attorney's office, parked under a shade tree, and took a moment to reapply her lipstick in the rearview mirror. Across the parking lot, she saw

Charles's BMW pull in. She decided to wait until he went inside so she wouldn't appear slow moving as she got out of the car. If she moved too fast, she felt dizzy, or pinched by pain, or both. Delia saw Charles reach over and kiss someone, a passenger in the car, then he jumped out of the car and hurried to the passenger side to open the door for the woman. He was practically skipping, with a lilt in his step that she hadn't seen in years. When had he last opened her car door? She couldn't remember.

Out of the car stepped Robyn Dixon. The other woman.

Delia's heart felt like a jackhammer. She watched the two of them head into the office building, laughing together over something. Delia leaned her forehead against the steering wheel, trying to gather her thoughts, to pull herself together. She couldn't do it. She couldn't go to that meeting. She felt as if she might hyperventilate or have a coronary episode or have a seizure. Or all three. She started the car, drove out of the parking lot, stopped by the bank and withdrew as much cash as the ATM would permit, then headed west on I-76 to Lancaster County.

# 6

For a few days, Rose and the children were all a-flurry, setting things right in the basement, turning it into a cozy place. With everyone helping, the basement began to look like a real home. Sammy and Luke tumbled in and out, underfoot, but every time they got near, Rose gave them a chore.

Rose could hardly believe the transformation. It smelled different, looked different. She went around all the windowsills with a wet rag and then . . . it was ready for the first guest. Whenever, whoever, that might be. No one had stayed with them since the fellow who didn't like the sounds of cows mooing in the morning. Rose felt a spike of worry, that all of this effort to create an inn would be for naught, but then she dismissed those doubts. Already, this venture was bringing the family together. Why, for that matter, the neighborhood too. Galen and Naomi had gone the extra mile for them. Good was coming out of it. God always had a plan, she reminded herself.

After she finished dusting, Rose walked through the rooms. She needed to get sheets on the beds, towels in the bathroom, maybe a few calendars to hang on the walls. She turned in a circle and felt an inside-out excitement. She said a prayer over each room, asking God to fill it with his chosen guests—those who needed rest and refreshment. In his time.

Rose heard the boys shrieking outside, chasing each other. She was just about to tell them to stop acting like wild Indians when they disappeared. She closed the door to the basement, thinking about how she needed a different name than the basement. What was it Galen called it? A flat? Yes, that was it. She liked that idea, because it was flat. A guest flat.

A car pulled into the driveway and came to a stop. Ever so slowly, a woman opened the door and eased out. Rose stood at the window a minute studying her, wondering if she was lost and needed directions. She was tall and elegant, with pale hair pulled back in a bun. She wore dark sunglasses, but Rose could see that her features were fine, delicate. Suddenly the boys were back, whooping and hollering like they were being chased by a swarm of yellow jackets. Rose went out and shooed the boys away before she turned her attention to the driver of the car.

"By any chance are you Rose Schrock?" the woman asked, pulling her sunglasses off her face.

"Yes. Yes, that's me." Rose took a step closer. Something about the abject relief in the woman's face spiked concern in Rose. "Are you all right?"

"I'd like to book a room at your hotel."

Oh. *Oh!* A guest. A guest! "Well, I need to get fresh sheets on the bed, but then you would have the entire base—flat—to yourself. How long did you want to stay?"

The woman looked at the setting sun. "I have absolutely no idea."

As Delia Stoltz got out of the car, she suddenly heard shrieks of laughter, and a little boy flew around the corner of the house, another slightly taller boy in hot pursuit. The boy in the lead ran to one of the sheds between the house and the barn and tried to hide in it, but his brother caught him before he could get inside, and they tusseled and shrieked. The older boy was trying to put something down the younger boy's shirt and finally succeeded, at which point the smaller boy began to hop up and down while the older one ran off, laughing.

The mother, Rose Schrock, appeared out of the basement to the house. She wore a plum-colored dress and a matching apron and had a stack of sheets in her hands. Clearly out of temper, she yelled something in another language at the two boys, who immediately stopped their shrieking, looked at one another, and slowly approached her. Rose addressed herself to the older boy, who made some excuse, and the younger boy, in his own defense, pointed back toward the shed. She listened a minute and began to talk rapidly in a low voice, too low for Delia to hear. She was giving her sons the what for, Delia supposed.

At first Delia hesitated. If the woman were the quick-tempered type, perhaps she should get back in the car and leave. The last thing she needed right now was a woman out of temper. But as Delia watched her, she found she couldn't stop looking at her. Her eyes flashed as she lectured her sons, neither of whom was taking the lecture silently—both were trying to talk back, but Rose Schrock didn't pause to listen. She had abundant brown hair tucked into a bun, covered with a thin organza cap, though the bun had partly come loose in little ringlets around the nape of her neck. Her eyes were gray and warm, fringed by dark lashes and framed by dark eyebrows. She was quite pretty, without a stitch of makeup.

The boys looked around and became aware for the first time that a stranger had come. They instantly stopped fidgeting and stood like statues.

"Pardon the commotion," Rose Schrock said with a smile. "We're a noisy crowd. So you aren't sure how long you'll be staying?"

"If that's all right," Delia said. "I don't want to trouble you."

Rose only laughed. "You don't look like the type to trouble anybody. We grow our own troubles—it would be a novelty to have some we aren't already used to. These are my sons, Luke and Sammy." She reached for Delia's hand. "Why don't you come inside?"

A moment or two later, Delia watched Rose put fresh sheets on the bed and plump the pillows. Delia thought it was strange that she didn't ask for any money or registration information. She showed Delia how to turn the lanterns on and off, and the pilot light on the stove.

When Rose went up to the house and Delia was alone in this sparsely furnished . . . basement! . . . panic rose. She hadn't thought this through. She had a toothbrush in her purse, of course, who didn't? She had a change of clothing in her gym bag, kept in the trunk of the car. But that was all. No nightgown. No face cream. Not even a book to read.

Maybe she should go back to Philadelphia. She could leave some cash on the nightstand and leave. She heard a knock on the door and Rose popped her head in again. "I noticed that you didn't have much luggage, and thought that maybe something had happened to your things. So, I brought a few items for you." In her arms was a nightgown, a *Farmer's Journal* magazine, a spare toothbrush and toothpaste, and a hairbrush. She lowered her voice. "I included some ladies' unmentionables." Color filled her cheeks, and her voice dropped. "Just in case you might have forgotten to pack some."

Mouthwatering aromas wafted down from the house. Delia's stomach rumbled. She hadn't eaten much today.

A big yellow dog came bursting through the door and hurried over to sniff Delia.

"That's Chase," Rose said. "He's a good friend and companion."

Delia looked at the dog. "Is he named Chase because he chases squirrels?"

"No. Because he chases his tail."

The big dog watched Delia. It took a few steps forward, sat on its haunches, and lifted a paw as if it was saying hello to Delia. She tentatively reached out to shake its paw. It was the oddest thing—there was a look in this dog's soulful eyes as if he knew Delia was hurting and felt empathy for her. What an absurd thought!

"Oh, you've passed the test. He likes you. You must have a knack for pets."

Delia had never had a pet. Why did it suddenly seem as if she had missed something? "I'm afraid not." Her son had always wanted a dog but Charles refused. He said that he'd had enough animal rearing in his childhood to last a lifetime. A slight smile tugged at Delia's lips. It was ironic that Will was going to be a vet—not a neurosurgeon like Charles had planned for him to be. She had never told Will, but she had been a little disappointed by his decision too. She had hoped he would follow in Charles's footsteps. After shaking this big dog's paw, she felt a glimmer of understanding of something Will talked about—that when an animal knew you, you felt some kind of special connection to it.

Already, Delia's life was changing. She was changing. Her stomach tightened. She had never liked change, and here she was faced with overwhelming change.

A knock at the door startled Delia.

Rose looked over at the door. "That's my daughter, Mim, bringing some dinner down to you. Just in case you haven't eaten."

Tears pricked Delia's eyes. How long had it been since someone had fussed over her? Maybe she would stay one night. Just one. She put down her purse. "Thank you, Rose. For everything."

After Rose and Mim set dinner up, they left. Delia sank down in a chair at the table. It was after six and she was hungry, exhausted, and sore. She ate like she hadn't eaten in days. Afterward, she took a long hot bath, climbed into bed with the *Farmer's Journal*, and listened to the peculiar sound of buggy horses as they clip-clopped along the asphalt road. It was so quiet here, so strangely quiet. Tomorrow, or maybe the next day, she would decide what she needed to do next. For now, she was right where she needed to be. She had no doubt of that. In the middle of an article about raising feeder pigs, she fell into a dreamless sleep.

Bethany didn't know what to make of the newest guest in the farmhouse basement. The lady drove up in a fancy car and went straight to bed. Three days had passed and she still lay there. Mim said she spoke in the manner of a British queen.

"Am I to presume you are Miriam?" the lady had asked her when they first met, shaking her hand. She said everything about the lady was stylish and expensive.

Rose brought meals to her and tried to keep the boys away from playing near the basement windows. She said that it was obvious the woman needed a good rest and that was the least they could give her.

Well, that lady could sleep all she wanted, but Bethany did suggest to Rose that she ask for room payment up front, just in case the lady expired in her sleep. "It happens, you know," she whispered to Rose. "I heard about it at work. A maid walked into a hotel room to clean it and there was a dead body. Just lying there. Decomposing."

Rose laughed. "Delia Stoltz isn't dying. She's just . . . I don't know what. She's worn out. And she's here for a reason. The Lord brought her to us. He has a plan."

That was just like Rose—always attributing unexplained events to God's sovereignty. Bethany believed in God, how could she not? But there were a lot of things that happened in life that were just . . . bad. She didn't think it was fair to blame God for a person's bad choices, bad decisions. Take her father's final choice, for example. That certainly wasn't God's fault.

Then whose fault was it? Bethany didn't know. Mammi Vera blamed Rose for his death, but that wasn't right and it wasn't fair. Bethany didn't know what would have become of them without her stepmother. Rose was taking care of her father's cranky mother, she was looking after his children, and she was determined to pay back all of her father's debts, one by one.

Bethany was doing all she could to help. It was the least she could do for Rose. Before she and Jake got married.

She heard a horse and buggy come up the drive. Curious, she wiped her hands on a rag and peeked out the window. Why, it was that audacious, flirtatious Jimmy Fisher. Bethany quickly looked in the washstand mirror Rose had left on the kitchen counter. She pinched her cheeks and bit on her lips to give them a little blush, smoothed back her hair, and hurried outside.

Jimmy jumped out of the buggy when he saw her. "Well, well, hello there."

"I don't know why you act so surprised," Bethany said. "You know I live here."

"I haven't seen you at the market in a while and thought I'd stop by. I was passing through."

"Passing from where to where?"

"From there to here." He grinned. "I have a little side job for Amos Lapp, down the road. Snow geese are causing damage to his winter wheat field. If they're left alone, they'll leave a bare spot of wheat several acres in size."

Bethany had heard about them. Thousands of snow geese had been wintering in a wildlife area of Stoney Ridge.

Luke and Sammy appeared out of nowhere, wide-eyed. "You gonna shoot all them birds?"

"Nope," Jimmy said. "There's a limit to the amount a fellow can shoot." He bent down to the boys' height. "I'm gonna set some firecrackers and flush them out."

The boys let out a whoop. "Think it'll work?"

"Will a frog hop?" Jimmy stood and wiggled his eyebrows at Bethany. "I'm known far and wide for my pyrotechnical skills."

How could he say something so ridiculous? Why was she even listening to him?

"Speaking of work," Jimmy said, "I came by to let you know I've heard of a job opening. A good one." He lowered his voice. "One that does not require the art of deception." His eyebrows hopped up and down.

"Where?" she asked.

"The Sisters' House." He took in Bethany's confused look and explained. "Not too far from here. You would know them from church. They're a bunch of elderly sisters, living together. They need a little extra help and I thought of you."

She knew those old sisters at church. Everybody did. They sat in the front row, looking like a chain of cutout dolls in their starched white prayer caps and matching dresses, all of them nodding off during the second sermon.

Still, Bethany hesitated. "What kind of help?"

"Get their house organized. It's a little cluttered up."

Organizing a bunch of little old ladies? She saw herself carrying out chamber pots and hanging wet sheets to dry. And what if they were all cranky like Mammi Vera could be? Older people often got cranky.

He winked. "Gotta strike while the iron's hot, if you know what I mean."

She didn't. This fellow's winking and eyebrow wiggling was scandalous. She had never met anyone as bold and coarse and outrageous as Jimmy Fisher.

Luke pulled on Jimmy's sleeve. "Are you gonna blow up them birds?"

"I'm not blowing up anything. I'm just trying to scare those birds out of Amos Lapp's wheat field. He wouldn't even let me take a single shot at them. Said they're too beautiful to eat. I might disagree, but I always respect my employer's wishes."

"Can we come with you to watch the firecrackers?" Luke asked. Sammy nodded.

Jimmy looked at Bethany. "Sure, if it's okay with your big sister. It's quite a sight to see all those geese take to the sky at one time."

"I suppose they can go." She glared at the two boys. "As long as they promise to stay out of your way."

"Maybe you'd like to come too. It won't take too long. We could talk about your new employment at the Sisters' House." There was more eyebrow wiggling.

Bethany wondered if Jimmy Fisher suffered from facial tics. Or Tourette's syndrome? She had seen someone with Tourette's once, over at the Stoney Ridge Bar & Grill. But that particular fellow swore like a sailor and he didn't wiggle his eyebrows.

She decided she should go along, just to keep the boys in check.

Rose didn't know where the boys had gone, or Bethany either. She was moving the goat and the sheep from the far pasture toward the pen attached to the barn. She waved to Galen, who was exercising a horse in a fenced paddock. A strange sound, like the steady rat-a-tat of a drumbeat, filled the air. The goat and the sheep started to bolt, splitting off into different directions. Galen's horse reacted nervously, rearing and running in the paddock. Chase barked frantically, trying to get the animals into the pen. Then the air was filled with honking geese.

Galen ran over to help Rose gather the goat and sheep. "Are you all right?" He scooped up one of the stray ewes in his arms like it was a bag of potatoes and carried it into the pen.

"Yes," she said, shielding her eyes against the setting sun, watching the geese overhead. "Just surprised. What was that noise?"

"Sounded like gunshots." Galen closed the pen latch and turned to face her. "I'll help you get those sheep to market this spring."

Rose cringed. "I just can't do it. They've become pets for the boys."

Galen looked at her with that slightly amused look he often gave her, as if he wondered if she might be a little dotty.

"I'm thinking about shearing them, though, and selling the wool."

"To whom?"

"I haven't planned that far," Rose said honestly. "Seems like every time I make a plan, something happens to change it."

"Well, life's a twisting stream."

Most wouldn't think to hear such quiet philosophizing out of Galen, but she had come to expect it. Luke and Sammy galloped down the driveway. "You wouldn't believe it, Mom!" Sammy said. "Hundreds and dozens of snow geese flew in the air! A couple fell to the ground. Jimmy Fisher said it was easier than shooting fish in a barrel."

"What type of gun did Jimmy use to shoot the geese?" Galen asked.

"He didn't!" Luke said. "He used firecrackers! He thought the ones that fell to the ground died of sheer fright. My eagles came flying around to see what was going on." Luke spread out his arms and soared around the barnyard.

Galen frowned. "Doesn't that boy realize how dangerous it is to set off firecrackers at this time of day? Livestock is feeding. Why, your mother was practically trampled by the sheep."

Trampled? There were only five sheep. But Rose thought it was kind of Galen to remind the boys to show concern. Those two little boys needed constant reminding.

Galen looked at Sammy. "Where is Jimmy Fisher now?"

"He's on his way home with Bethany," Sammy said.

"With two geese!" Luke added. "Mom, he's bringing them to you to cook for dinner."

Rose's spirits lifted. "A goose delivery? It's too late to start for tonight, but maybe I'll cook it for Sunday supper."

"Jimmy said he'd dress them for you," Sammy said. "And guess what else? We saw the eagles carrying branches in their talons. We think they're building a nest in the big tree up there." He pointed to the very tree, high on the hillside, that Rose liked to sit under some mornings to greet the dawn.

Rose shielded her eyes and looked up. There, in the dead branches of the oak tree, was the start of a big mess of sticks. "Well, I'll be." She turned to Galen. "An aerie. Right here. Wouldn't that be something? To have a bald eagle pair choose this very farm for their home?"

Galen's gaze turned to one of the eagles, bringing in sticks to the tree. "It'd be a pity for us all."

"You may call it a pity, but I'll call it a blessing," Rose said. "Think of all the publicity the inn might get. Why, this could be very good for business."

Galen frowned. "You might be changing your mind when folks set up telescopes to gawk at the eagles after the game commissioner tapes off your property."

"I would still feel blessed that an eagle couple had sensed that this farm would be a good place to raise their young."

Galen lifted his eyebrows, as if he didn't know what to make of that. "Tell Jimmy Fisher I want to talk to him before he heads home," he said before he slipped back through the hole in the privet.

Luke and Sammy exchanged a look. "Jimmy's in trouble," Luke whispered.

For three days, Delia had stayed in her nightgown, mostly in bed. Rose's daughters, with anxious faces, brought meals on a tray down the stairs. Delia tried to appear calm and reassuring to them, but inside she felt that she had lost the will to live.

Last evening Rose asked her if she needed a doctor, because there was a very nice doctor in town who made house calls, but Delia assured her that she just needed some rest. So Rose refilled her mug of tea and promised to do a better job of keeping the boys shouting distance away from the basement.

Rose must be a restful person to live with, Delia thought. The farm was a restful place. She had been lucky to meet red-haired Lois at the gas station and find this place.

It felt so strange, so troubling, that she could not sleep well. She lay down, slept and woke, slept and woke, disturbed each time by foolish dreams. She dozed for a few minutes now and then, because when she opened her eyes, she remembered shreds and pieces of disjointed, implausible dreams. Then she would be wide awake. These senseless dreams came from being over-tired. She had heard on *Oprah* once that dreams are never really senseless, that if you take the disjointed sections apart and rearrange them properly, they will make sense. She decided that was foolish fodder.

This afternoon, Delia stood at the window and watched ordinary people do ordinary things. Rose's eldest daughter had come back from work, a handsome fellow had stopped by in a buggy to pay a call on her, those two little boys with small black hats ran back and forth from barn to house and back to barn. Those two looked like they were always up to something. Every once in a while, Rose would call to the boys from the house, but it seemed to Delia like trying to herd cats.

She watched Amish men and women drive past the lane in buggies or zoom on the road in those odd-looking scooters. These were people with families—men, women, and children who lived normal lives. Their hearts were not heavy with anxiety as hers was. They knew what each new day was going to bring, while she had no idea what was going to happen. She envied them, their sense of security. She didn't think she would ever feel secure again. How could life change so quickly?

One morning, you woke up on a sunny winter day, happy, your mind filled with nothing weightier than the thought of where to have lunch with your friend or what to cook for dinner. And then a conversation began, or the telephone rang, or the lab report arrived, and everything you thought you knew for certain was suddenly called into question.

Tomorrow would be Sunday. Rose had brought her a handwritten list of churches in the area, gently suggesting that Delia might want to consider going. She looked over the list and saw one for the denomination she belonged to in Philadelphia.

After Will was born, Delia and Charles used to go to church each week. Delia had insisted that they provide Will with some kind of spiritual foundation. Charles didn't object, nor did he ever get involved. Over the years, Charles accompanied them less and less. At first, there was always a reason—an emergency at the hospital, an out-of-town conference. Then the excuses stopped and he just admitted he was tired and needed a morning to relax. Delia kept going until Will became a teen and started to object too. He said the youth group kids were weird. Charles insisted that Delia not force Will to attend church if he didn't want to. So she didn't. Naturally, Will slept in on Sunday mornings. And then Delia stopped going too.

She heard the faint buzz of a saw from a neighboring farm and remembered when she and Charles were first married, how the two of them would work together, fixing up their first house. They had loved each other back then, passionately and thoroughly. They enjoyed each other's company. She wondered what had happened to make it end. Life, she supposed. A child, busyness, schedules. And there was Charles's success. She knew she was the envy of her friends, of everyone in town. She wanted for nothing. But success had a price too. Loneliness. Charles was hardly home, and when he was, he was very distracted and distant.

A few months ago, just as they had sat down to Thanksgiving dinner, Charles was called away on an emergency. That wasn't unusual, but Delia felt so let down, more than she typically did. Will had told her not to be disappointed—it was easier without Charles. He was right. She and Will had a wonderful evening together—watching old movies and eating so much until they couldn't move from the couch.

Still, it saddened her that Charles missed so much. Will wasn't home very often and who knew where he would land after he graduated from vet school? His concentration on ornithology was very rare. He had offers from the states of Florida and Alaska. An organization in Europe had showed interest too. Who knew where he might land? All she knew for certain was that their days together as a family were coming to an end.

When Will decided to go to Cornell for vet school after college, Delia's loneliness became more acute. She'd been hoping he'd attend graduate school closer to home, someplace where he could come home for holidays or drop by on weekends. Now she was almost relieved that he lived so far away, too far to get caught in the complications of dismantling a marriage.

She wondered what would happen to her friendships if Charles divorced her. She remembered a woman named Carla whose husband had left her for a younger woman. Everyone dropped Carla like a hot potato, as if she suddenly carried a contagion that threatened to infect their own marriages. Delia, included. How stupid of her. How uncaring.

She also felt betrayed, bereft, heartbroken, abandoned, all those emotions she'd imagined women must feel when their husbands walked out on them. She was so sure she would never, ever be one of those women—but here she was, in Carla's shoes. And just like Carla, she had never seen it coming.

A wave of exhaustion hit Delia. As she eased back onto the bed, she considered calling Charles, but she was afraid if she phoned, he would be angry that she hadn't come to the lawyer's meeting and then she would cry. She refused to cry one more tear over this failed marriage.

Soon, she should call the doctor's office for a follow-up visit, to see if her pathology report was in. But what if it was bad news? What if the cancer had spread? That news could wait. She didn't think she could handle anything more right now.

She told herself she didn't care, anyway.

# 7

Bethany was horrified when Rose invited Jimmy Fisher to come over for a big goose dinner on Sunday. Never mind that he had provided the geese, dressed them too. Yesterday afternoon, after Jimmy had returned from his talk with Galen, he was cheerful as ever and set to work butchering the geese. Bethany couldn't get her head around that—everyone was sure Galen would chew him out for setting off those firecrackers, but Jimmy came back acting like he was having the best day a man could have. When the boys asked what Galen wanted with him, Jimmy only said that Galen preferred to volunteer what he wanted you to know.

As Jimmy butchered the geese, he found the stomachs full of wheat, even their throats, almost to their beaks. The boys couldn't stop talking about it. The whole topic turned Bethany's stomach, which only amused Jimmy Fisher.

She did *not* trust that boy with the blue, blue eyes. She was just waiting for Jimmy to spill the beans that she worked at the Stoney Ridge Bar & Grill and wore English clothes. She knew he was holding it over her head, acting smug, like he'd got the best of her.

Rose had invited Naomi and Galen for the goose dinner. The strange lady in the basement too. Somehow Rose had convinced that lady to try going to church in the morning—which she did—and to come for the goose dinner when she returned. Bethany figured Rose wanted to try to get that lady out of bed.

Around one in the afternoon, the guests arrived at the house, acting quiet and uncomfortable. Except for Jimmy, who didn't have enough sense to know how awkward the situation was; Galen, who didn't speak much and kept to himself; a depressed English lady; a grandmother who got the hiccups if she had a fit; a little sister who spouted off facts; and two brothers who couldn't sit still. At least Bethany had sweet Naomi to talk to.

Rose didn't seem to realize it was an awkward collection of people, either. She welcomed everyone in as if they were family. She gave them jobs to do to help get dinner on the table—Jimmy and Galen brought chairs in from the other room, Delia cut carrots for the salad, Mim set the table, Bethany and Naomi made biscuits while Rose made gravy.

All this bustle made Mammi Vera, seated at the kitchen table, frown with disapproval. She complained that Rose was always telling people what to do, but the truth was, everyone relaxed when they had tasks. Soon, there was cheerful conversation and banter going on. Rose was able to do that—to create that kind of atmosphere. Why couldn't Mammi Vera see that?

When Rose pulled the roasting geese out of the oven, Naomi breathed in the scent and thanked Jimmy Fisher for providing such a good dinner. It hadn't occurred to Bethany to thank him. Sometimes, she wished the Lord would just knock her over with sweetness and goodness, because she didn't seem to be getting the knack of it on her own.

"You wash up good, boys," Rose said to Luke and Sammy as they burst through the door. "I'm going to civilize you if it's the last thing I do."

"Civilize them?" Mammi Vera said. "They need so much more than civilizing."

Rose ignored that remark and steered Delia to a chair at the table. As everyone found their seats, Galen moved to the head of the table.

"That's Dean's place!" Mammi Vera said, her voice as shrill as a penny whistle. Galen froze, midair. He was the last to sit down; there were no other available chairs.

"Galen, you just sit right down and don't give it another thought," Rose said, frowning at Mammi Vera.

"She's getting more and more like a dictator," Mammi Vera muttered to no one in particular.

"Yes, but a benevolent dictator," Rose answered, tying napkins around the boys' necks, for all the good it would do. After the silent prayer ended, a flurry of activity began. Rose began to carve the geese.

Luke sniffed appreciatively. "Do I get a leg?"

"Here you go. But save the wing for your brother." Rose served him and passed the platter of goose meat as Bethany passed the gravy.

"The gravy would be better if it had more substance," Mammi Vera said, peering into the gravy bowl. "Next time, add a little more flour."

"The goose is cooked just right," Jimmy Fisher said cheerfully.

Mammi Vera sniffed. "It's passable."

Bethany's discomfort had taken a new turn. What must Jimmy Fisher think of them? The boys' stomachs were grumbling unpleasantly as they tore into their meal. They were practically inhaling their food; their stomachs were bottomless pits. Their plates began to look like graveyards of bones. Mammi Vera made caustic comments every chance she could, and Mim used a finger to capture the absolute last drop of honey that dripped off her biscuit. She reached out to kick Mim in the shin.

"Ooph!" Galen, sitting next to Mim, grimaced in pain. Bethany had kicked the wrong person. She kept her eyes lowered, suddenly fascinated by what was on her plate.

Mim, oblivious, looked up. "Does everyone know that honey is the world's purest food?"

Her sister was always spouting off odd facts. Bethany had heard enough details on the subject to have already forgotten more than most people ever know about the properties of honey. "Yes, we all know that, Mim," she said, to cut short the talk of honey.

"I didn't," Jimmy Fisher piped up.

"Mammi, you have some food on your chin." Bethany reached over to wipe her grandmother's chin with her napkin.

Luke reached out and grabbed a biscuit, then another.

"Do not bolt your food, Luke," Bethany whispered. "Teeth are quite useful for chewing." He was half wild, was Luke. Boys were.

Luke stuffed a biscuit in his mouth and talked around it. "Sammy and I are starting a business. Renting sheep. To make money."

Galen tried, unsuccessfully, to swallow a grin. "Now, tell me what exactly can a sheep be taught to do?"

"Mow grass, for one," Sammy said. "Warn you about snakes and coyotes and wolves."

"And they can add fertilizer while they're working," Jimmy said. "No extra charge."

Vera let out a cackle of a laugh, like the sound a hen might make if the hen were mad about something.

Luke turned to Galen. "A good sheep can be trained. I could train one to bring your mail up to your house."

"Why not just train the goat?" Galen said. "He spends more time at my place than yours anyhow."

Luke and Sammy looked at each other. "We could rent the goat!" Luke said. He turned to Galen. "Want to be our first customer?"

"I'll give it some thought. I'm pretty busy now, though, with buggy training a green batch of Thoroughbreds. Jimmy is going to start working for me. Starting Monday." Galen glanced at Jimmy. "Early."

Sammy's face lit up. "Jimmy, you'll be able to come by here every day!"

Jimmy Fisher did that crazy up-down eyebrow wiggling at Bethany and she felt a flush creep up her neck.

"Rose, have you thought of giving a handle to your bed-and-breakfast?" Galen said.

"Like what?" Mim said.

"What about Eagle Hill?"

Everyone stilled. It was Delia Stoltz who volunteered that suggestion. She had been so quiet during dinner, they had practically forgotten she was there.

"Why, Eagle Hill is a fine name, Delia," Rose said. "A wonderful choice."

"It is *my* farm," Vera added, her feathers ruffled. "Everyone seems to forget that."

"Every farm needs a name," Rose said.

Vera turned to Rose and narrowed her eyes.

"Now you're taking over my farm. I can't imagine what's next. Maybe you'll be the first woman bishop of Stoney Ridge."

And a silence like cold, still air filled the kitchen.

Bethany could see Rose look at Vera for a moment, holding her peace. Then Rose laughed and the tension was broken. "No, I don't have aspirations to be a bishop, Vera. I'm having enough trouble with this tribe of wild Indians, right here."

Bethany exhaled. Rose had a way of defusing a difficult situation; she never failed.

Vera sat there, sulky.

Bethany knew that look on her grandmother's face. It was time to take action, before something worse happened. "Come, Mammi Vera," Bethany said as she jumped up to help her grandmother rise to her feet. "You've been sitting all day. It's bad for your circulation. You have to get up and walk around." She caught Jimmy looking at her, then quickly away, as if she had caught him at something. She glanced around the table. "We'll be out on the porch if you need us. Mammi needs fresh air."

It was no great surprise to Rose to hear those kinds of remarks come out of her mother-in-law. Rose knew Vera wasn't in favor of creating an inn in the basement, but she also knew Vera wasn't in a position to make decisions about the farm's future. She had no understanding of the dire financial situation they were in. She had always turned a deaf ear and blind eye to any talk or news about Schrock Investments and acted as if it was all too complicated for her.

Rose felt a flash of annoyance, most of it with herself. When Vera insinuated she was taking over the farm, she couldn't disagree. Somebody had to steer this ship before it sank. Sometimes, she felt as if she had turned into another person, as if someone else walked around in her shoes. But the hardness Vera referred to was a result of dealing with the mess Dean had left behind.

As she dried the last dinner dishes and put them away, she hung the wet rag over the faucet and went to the window to see what was going on in the yard. Galen and Jimmy had the boys and Mim engaged in a game of horseshoes. Bethany and Naomi's capped heads were together, talking earnestly. Vera was resting in her room. Delia sat on the porch step in the sunshine, head bent back, watching the sky. What was she looking at? Soon, Rose figured it out. Some kind of noisy drama in a tree. She watched one of the eagles descend like an arrow into the tree, and a flock of birds blasted into the air, filling it with strident, high-pitched squawking.

Eagle Hill was a fine name for the farm. No matter what Galen had said about the game commissioner and people nosing around, she considered it a blessing that an eagle couple had chosen it for their nest. She walked out to join Delia on the porch step. On the western horizon, the sun was a crimson orb, sinking into the treetops.

"The big one is Mrs. Eagle," she said to Delia. "The smaller one is the mister."

Delia had smiled at that and Rose felt pleased. Just as pleased that Delia had agreed to come for dinner, though she didn't say much and she didn't eat much—she just nibbled at her food.

"What kind of eagles are they?"

"See their white heads? That's how you know they're bald eagles. They're a threatened species in Pennsylvania. Thankfully, they're no longer an endangered species. It's a wonderful comeback story. Things can get good again."

Rose smiled and Delia gave her a curious look.

"Someday, I hope to get a porch swing out here," Rose said. "Seems like porch swings are just as good for grown-ups as they are for children."

Rose and Delia watched the eagles dip and dart above the row of pines that lined one edge of the driveway. A whole dancing flock of birds disappeared, dark little dots against the sky.

"I hope you don't mind me saying that your mother-in-law is a ball of fire," Delia said.

Rose burst out laughing. "I don't mind at all. You're right. And she hasn't been well lately. It's made her an even hotter ball of fire."

"Your eldest daughter is very patient with her. Goodness, she reminds me of an Egyptian servant girl, all but fanning your mother-in-law with palm fronds."

Rose smiled. This, to Rose, was Bethany's greatest gift—her patience and kindheartedness to Vera. Bethany was always showing care to Vera in special ways: giving her shampoos, rubbing lotion into her crepe-papery arms and legs, asking her questions about her life as a little girl. No wonder Vera adored her.

Delia brushed off her trousers. "Didn't you go to church today?"

"It was an off Sunday," Rose said. "We have church every two weeks. A good day for a big goose dinner." She looked over at Delia. "I saw your car leave this morning. Did you go to church in town?"

"I did."

That was all she had to say and Rose didn't want to push her.

Delia stood up to leave. "Thank you for including me today."

"I'm glad you came. We can be a noisy crowd."

"Yes, but you're a noisy crowd of love," Delia answered.

To Rose's surprise, she suddenly felt Galen listening to their conversation. Not just watching, but listening. When she turned her head and saw his eyes, she thought she caught a glint of something—amusement? Pity? She couldn't tell.

It had to be admitted that Rose Schrock set a fine table. Naomi had been the one to accept the supper invitation of those two little rapscallions who came flying through the hedge to rap on the door. Galen wouldn't ordinarily have done it, but then his life was no longer ordinary.

He barely walked in from feeding the stock when Naomi met him at the door with a fresh shirt and told him to clean up, because the neighbors were expecting them. He knew she was enamored by the Schrock girls, especially the eldest one, Bethany. Galen didn't see the need for friends, but he understood that Naomi had a different point of view. "Hurry, hurry, hurry," she said, bossing him around like he was a child and she was the parent.

Next thing he knew, they were on their way to the Schrocks'. No sooner had they arrived, and Naomi and Bethany had put their heads together and twittered like little chickens.

Galen was relieved to see Jimmy Fisher, his new apprentice, at the house. Jimmy talked such a blue streak that Galen hoped he wouldn't be expected to say much.

A month or so ago, Deacon Abraham had dropped by to ask Galen if he might consider taking Jimmy under his wing.

"And why would I do that?" Galen had asked him. He knew Jimmy

Fisher, had known him for years. He was known as a fellow with a fondness for the ladies.

"I'm worried about the boy," Abraham had explained. "He's at a crossroads and I'm not sure he knows it." Jimmy's mother, Edith, had gone to visit her cousin in Gap while she happened to be in an off period in her on-again, off-again courtship with Hank Lapp. She met a widower in Gap and up and married him. Jimmy's brother, Paul, was finally engaged and would be taking over the family chicken and egg business. "Jimmy Fisher is a boy with a lot of potential, none of it realized."

"Why me?" Galen had asked.

"Haven't you seen that boy's love of horses? If you could give the boy some training, shape him, give him discipline, why, Jimmy Fisher might just amount to something."

It took Galen quite a long time to get his head around the thought of taking on an apprentice. Especially Jimmy Fisher. But you didn't say no to the deacon.

Galen had plenty of misgivings. Then he found out Jimmy had used firecrackers to flush out the snow geese from a wheat field and felt the first hint of interest in the boy. Most of Galen's work with horses was to train hot-blooded, just-off-the-track Thoroughbreds to buggy work, and that included desensitizing them to the unexpected. An apprentice who knew about firecrackers might be useful—assuming Jimmy Fisher had enough sense to know when and when not to use them. That was his main worry about Jimmy Fisher. Did the boy have *any* sense? Until Galen had confidence in him, Jimmy would be carefully supervised.

When he was seated at the Schrock table, Galen was faced with more choices to eat than he had seen on a table for quite some time. His gaze swept down the table and stopped at Rose.

"This is my vermin stew, Galen," Rose said, dishing a spoonful of vegetables for him.

"Oh?" he said politely. "What kind of vermin?"

Rose didn't miss a beat. "Whatever the boys caught today in their traps."

"It was a polecat," one of the little boys said. He seemed as full of mischief as his mother.

"Now, Luke, don't be giving away my recipes," she said.

"I happen to love polecat," Galen said, trying hard to be sociable. It was an unfamiliar labor, since he mostly worked at avoiding it. But he knew Naomi would be giving him the what for if he didn't at least try to be friendly. Besides, she had promised they could leave as soon as dinner ended.

He thought it might have ended abruptly at that awkward moment when Vera snapped at Rose and called her a future bishop. Vera Schrock was known to salt her speech rather freely with criticism. There was nothing hard about Rose—in fact, it was obvious to him that she was far too soft for what she had to cope with. She had tender expressions when she looked at her children, or at the stable of animals she kept. She could never quite get a lock of hair to stay fixed, and was always touching it nervously with one hand. "It won't behave," she would say, as if her hair were a child.

After dinner ended, Galen didn't get to his feet right away. The sense that he needed to hurry, which had been with him most of his life, had disappeared for a space.

# 8

The next day, Monday, responsibility descended upon Jimmy Fisher with a weight far beyond anything he had ever felt. He wondered what had possessed him to agree to work for Galen King, of all people, though he knew the answer to that. The work ethic of the Plain people was legendary, but Galen took it to another level. He never stopped working. He was a single-track man, all business. Jimmy held to a more leisurely philosophy about work.

Most people in the church were intimidated by Galen, but not Jimmy. Galen was perceived as a little unusual. He didn't say much, didn't socialize much, had a skill for avoiding various single women who did their best to lay a trap for him. The funny thing about Galen King was how hard he was to keep in scale. He wasn't a big man—in fact, was barely middle-sized—but when you walked up and looked him in the eye, it didn't seem that way. Jimmy was a few inches taller, but there was no way you could have convinced him that Galen was the shorter man. Galen had that effect on everyone. Jimmy had seen men straighten up when Galen walked past. He'd seen women tuck their hair in their cap. Even children quieted around him. Not that Galen had ever noticed he had such an effect on others. It would have meant losing five minutes off whatever job he had decided he wanted to get done that day.

By the time the sun was overhead, Jimmy had sweated through his shirt. The first breather of the day came when Naomi brought some gingered lemonade out to the barn. Early that morning, a new lot of horses had been delivered to Galen from Saturday's auction in Leola. Galen wanted to start buggy training them straightaway. Jimmy thought Galen should let them settle into their new surroundings. These two- and three-year-old colts came right off the racetrack in Kentucky and were skittish as foals. He said as much to Galen, but his helpful suggestion was ignored. It didn't bother Jimmy. He kept on making helpful suggestions and Galen kept on ignoring him. Jimmy would rattle off five or six different questions and opinions, running them all together.

After lunch, Galen led a chestnut mare, the one with white stockings and a blaze down her forehead, out of the stall and into the yard. Jimmy walked over to the fence to watch Galen work the mare. Galen considered her to be the prime of the lot he had just purchased.

Jimmy couldn't see why. "She's not the best-looking horse I've ever seen," he said.

"I'm not interested in her looks," Galen said.

She had her ears pinned and her eyes turned so she could watch him in case he got careless. "You ought to blindfold her."

"I want her gentled, not broke." Galen got her to accept the weight of the buggy shaft, but the minute the shafts touched the sides of her belly, the mare kicked as high as she could get. Jimmy got a big laugh out of that.

"There's plenty of fine horses to buy in this world, Galen. Why would a man like you want to waste time with a filly that ought to be hobbled and blindfolded?"

Again, Galen ignored him. The mare tentatively lifted the near hind foot with the thought of kicking whatever might be in range. When she did, he caught the foot with the rope and hitched it around a post. It left the mare standing on three legs, so she could not kick again without throwing herself.

"Look at her watch us," Galen said. The mare *was* watching them—even had her ears pointed at them. She was trembling with indignation.

"I wouldn't take it as much of a compliment," Jimmy said. "She's not watching you because she loves you." He didn't know why anyone would bother with such an ill-tempered horse.

"Say what you will," Galen said. "I've never seen a more intelligent filly."

"Maybe a little too smart for her own good."

"Like my apprentice."

Ouch. That stung. Jimmy had a love for horses that went bone-deep. Most folks assumed he was nothing but a flirt—but he took horsemanship seriously. There was a time when he toyed with racing and that ended badly. He learned his lesson. But he had never stopped loving Thoroughbreds. That's why he accepted Galen's out-of-the-blue offer to work for him. No one in Stoney Ridge knew Thoroughbreds like Galen King. It was part of his blood, his heritage. His great-grandfather had raised Percherons. The Kings were known far and wide for their horse-savvy, and Jimmy wanted to soak up everything he could from Galen.

Late in the afternoon, Sammy Schrock slipped through the privet to watch the horse training in action. Unlike Luke, Sammy was a silent, small boy. He stood apart shyly and stared at the mare. After a while he couldn't stand it any longer and his words wrestled their way through his shyness. "If you'll let me help, why, I'll do anything. I'll muck stalls, saddle soap harnesses, sweep the barn." He sounded hopeful, a boy who loved to be useful.

As Galen hesitated, Jimmy could see the boy's disappointment. "Give him a try, Galen. After all, the boy's only chance for learning how to gentle a horse is by watching me work."

Galen let that float off. "Sammy, you need to ask your mother if it's all right."

The boy ran home at once.

"Now, Galen, that was downright charitable of you. I wonder if you're getting soft."

Galen snorted. "His mother will say no so I won't have to."

Jimmy thought about that for a while, not at all sure Galen had called that right. Rose Schrock didn't strike him as a smother-mother type. He watched her the other night and she almost seemed too good-natured to be true. It was clear she was older—she had fine wrinkles around her mouth—but her skin was still soft and her face, as she bustled around feeding people, was quite lovely.

If he were only a decade or so older, Jimmy thought, grinning, then shook that thought off. Besides, Jimmy was finding himself besotted—yes, besotted—with Rose's stepdaughter, Bethany. As usual, love fell out of a clear blue sky—as fine a day as one could want, with the creek sparkling and sun shining and hints of spring in the air.

But even Jimmy had to admit to himself that he found himself besotted with girls on a regular basis. He reminded himself that he was turning over a new leaf and becoming a horse trainer. Getting besotted with ladies on a regular basis would have to be reckoned with. It was time to get serious about life.

No sooner had Jimmy taken one team in and brought another team of horses out to the yard, and Sammy was back, puffed up and proud. "She said yes! She said Luke could come too, if it's all right with you. Not today, though. He's in trouble and can't leave the house."

Galen was shaking his head, but he didn't look nearly as upset as Jimmy might have thought. "What's Luke got himself in trouble for?"

"Teacher M.K. told everyone it was 'No Complaining Day' and Luke complained about it."

Jimmy laughed, then he noticed that Sammy was bareheaded. Jimmy had brought his old black felt hat with him and put it in the barn. It was hanging on a peg, and he went back in and got it for the boy.

"Here, you take this," Jimmy said, surprised at his own generosity.

When Sammy put it on, his head disappeared nearly down to his mouth, which was grinning.

It was almost time to make supper and Rose was already a day behind in her tasks. She had linens to change in the guest flat, two pies to bake, and a pile of clothing to iron for Sunday church. Seated by the kitchen window, Vera watched Bethany walk back slowly from the mailbox, absorbed in a letter she was reading. "Bethany is spending too much time mooning over that boy."

The iron hissed as it slid over a dampened prayer cap that Rose was ironing, leaving behind a knife-sharp pleat and the smell of hot starch. "Jake Hertzler?"

"Yes. She fancies him far too much. He's Car Amish," Vera said, as if that explained everything. "What if she falls in love with him?"

Vera didn't seem to realize that Bethany already thought she was in love with him. At least, as in love as an impulsive, shortsighted nineteen-year-old girl could be. Rose set the iron upright on the ironing board to give herself time to think. She could only imagine what Vera would have to say if she heard that Jake Hertzler had pinned blame for Schrock Investments' downfall on Tobe, her precious grandson. Fur would fly! She still couldn't believe it herself. She didn't want to believe it—she preferred to think that Allen Turner's job was to be suspicious about everybody.

Vera coughed and Rose's thoughts returned to her ironing. She carefully lifted the freshly pressed cap off the ironing board and set it on the counter, then plucked a white shirt of Sammy's out of the laundry basket. "I don't deny that it's troubled me how devoted Bethany has been to Jake. Far more devoted to him than he is to her. I worry she'll end up with a broken heart."

"Then you should do something about this," Vera said. "Soon. Before that boy realizes what he might be missing and comes calling. Dean would have nipped this. Nipped it in the bud. You don't want grandchildren who aren't truly Amish."

Grandchildren who would never know Dean. That familiar sadness about Dean swept over Rose. It surprised her to realize that the sadness was only a visitor now. Not a permanent guest.

"A fish and a bird can't fall in love."

Rose sighed. It always, always circled back to this. Vera blamed Rose for the path Dean chose: leaving the Old Order Amish church to marry Rose, raising the children with the use of electricity and cars, pursuing higher education and getting his broker's license.

What Vera refused to believe was that Dean had quietly passed his GED and was taking accounting classes at the junior college—that was where Rose met him. At heart, he was not a farmer nor a craftsman. He was a man who liked to use his mind, not his hands. It was just a matter of time, he had told Rose, before he planned to leave the Old Order Amish church, especially after his first wife had abandoned the family. He couldn't re-marry if he stayed in the Old Order Amish church, even though he hadn't initiated or wanted the divorce.

To be fair to Vera, Rose acknowledged that Dean let his mother believe what she wanted to believe. It didn't bother him that Vera blamed Rose for everything. Or his first wife for everything else. One thing she had quickly learned about Dean—he wanted everyone to think well of him, especially his mother.

As she picked up the iron and started on Sammy's white shirt, she remembered a time, soon after they had bought their first home and didn't have much money to spare, when Dean volunteered to pay for a new roof for the church they had just started to attend.

Rose had been raised in an Old Order Amish home but had left, disillusioned, after an acrimonious split occurred in her church. Soon after—maybe too soon, she later wondered—she met Dean, was dazzled by him—he *was* dazzling!—and married him. As she navigated her new role of stepmothering, she knew it was time to return to church. Since Dean had been divorced and remarried, they couldn't return to the Old Order Amish church. They found a Mennonite church that welcomed them in.

One Sunday morning, Dean had stood up in church and said he would take care of the entire amount of the roof.

"Why did you do that?" she had asked him on the way home from church. "They were asking everyone to make donations. They never expected one person to pay for it all."

He shrugged. "I wanted to."

"But we don't have the money to make the next mortgage payment. We don't have enough to buy food for the week!"

He gave her a hangdog expression. "I know."

*How irresponsible!* she thought. *He did it to impress the minister. To deflect the unhappy fact of his first marriage.*

Then, softening, because there was something about Dean that always made her excuse him, she decided that he did it because he couldn't help it. He was a generous man and enjoyed making others happy.

She did not think at the time, though she did think it now: *He wanted the entire congregation to admire him. He wanted to be a hero.*

Through the kitchen window, she saw Bethany walking slowly, head tucked, engrossed in reading a letter. Was it from Jake? Oh, she hoped not.

"Our neighbor Galen King is sweet on Bethany," Vera said.

"What?"

"I've suspected for some time now that his feelings for Bethany went beyond neighborly interest." Vera smiled her crooked smile, delighted to upstage Rose with news. "The signs are all there—think how often he's been coming by. He shows up looking Sunday-scrubbed with a lilt in his step. He's happier than I've ever seen him."

Rose finished ironing Sammy's shirt for Sunday church and hung it over the back of a chair. "I think you're confusing him with Jimmy Fisher."

"Who?"

"Jimmy. He was here for dinner the other night." *And if you'd been paying attention,* Rose thought, *you would have noticed a change in Bethany.* She was glowing, awash in some internal light, wonderstruck, glancing in Jimmy's direction whenever she thought he wasn't looking—which was seldom.

"Oh! The one who kept waggling his brows. Well, handsome is as handsome does." As Vera mulled that over for a while, her eyes grew droopy and soon she nodded off.

Rose spread Mim's Sunday dress, a deep blue, over the ironing board to spray starch all over it. She didn't know what to make of the crazy notions that flitted through Vera's mind. The thought of Bethany and Galen was ridiculous. Bethany was a beautiful young woman, but in so many ways, she was still a child. Galen was a man who had never been young.

Vera might be talking about other people, but at its heart was always a concern for herself.

# 9

Spring had appeared violently, rain and sun and rain again. The earth was muddy and Bethany's feet sank into the front lawn as she walked back from the mailbox with Jake's brief letter in her hands. Her last letter to Jake had been returned with a red stamp on the envelope: OCCUPANT MOVED. NO FORWARDING ADDRESS. It upset her to no end because he didn't have a telephone or cell phone. Letters were their only means of staying connected—what would happen to them? To their future? So when she saw his handwriting on an envelope in today's mail, she was thrilled and relieved, delighted to discover that he had to move to another apartment and had forgotten to tell her. That was all. Perfectly understandable! Then her smile faded. There was no return address on the envelope.

"Is that true?" A voice spoke close to her ear. Startled, Bethany slid the letter into her dress pocket and turned around to see Jimmy Fisher.

"What? Is what true?" she asked.

"That," he whispered, pointing to the porch. "What your sister there said. Is it a fact? Pinching your nose makes you intelligent?"

Bethany looked at Mim sitting on the porch in the sunshine. She sat, holding her nose, reading. Beside her sat the little brothers, both holding their noses.

"My little sister knows nearly everything," Bethany told Jimmy. "And what she doesn't know she makes up."

For a moment they looked at each other in silence. Then each began to laugh. When she stopped, Jimmy kept smiling. He took a step closer to her and didn't disguise his frank examination of her face. "Where've you been all day? I've been looking everywhere for you."

She lifted her chin. "I don't know what you can be thinking, Jimmy Fisher."

"Are you going to quit your double life soon?"

Her smile faded. "Why do you always want to talk about that?"

"Normally, I have many other thoughts running through my fine brain. But when I get around you, I can't stop thinking about the first time I saw you working at the Stoney Ridge Bar & Grill in your fancy clothes. It's all I've got left in my head to work with."

Her mouth dropped open. It was just like Jimmy Fisher to say something she didn't expect to hear. "Why can't you just act like a normal fellow?"

"Normal is relative."

"So you consider yourself normal, do you?"

"Certainly," Jimmy said. "I never met a soul in this world as normal as me." He leaned toward her and whispered in her ear. "Maybe if you agreed to go on a picnic with me to Blue Lake Pond some fine spring day, I'd have more to talk about."

"I'll have you know that I have a boyfriend. Jake Hertzler."

Jimmy grinned. "Your imaginary boyfriend, you mean."

By the time she got her wits about her and tried to come up with a snappy retort, Rose was clanging the dinner bell and Jimmy had disappeared through the privet to Galen's. As she made her way into the house, she could hardly keep the grin off her face. *But no,* she thought as she opened the door, *why should I feel happier? There's no reason for it. It's ridiculous. What is Jimmy Fisher to me? He comes and he goes. You already have a fine young man waiting for you, Bethany Schrock.* She frowned. *Someplace.*

Jimmy Fisher had worked farms all his life and knew how hard the labor was, but it was different here at Galen King's. He had never worked like this before. He quickly established the habit of arriving in time so that he could start the day with a good breakfast, cooked by Naomi. Both for his sake and for hers.

He felt a little sorry for Naomi—her brother wasn't known for being much of a talker and all her siblings had married and moved away. Jimmy wasn't sure what the future held for a girl as shy and delicate as Naomi

King, though she was a first-rate cook. He supposed she might be able to attract another shy fellow, but who would ever start the conversation? Jimmy decided he would give the subject of Naomi's empty love life some consideration. He liked to help people. He was just that kind of a fellow.

Jimmy Fisher put three heaping teaspoons of sugar from the bowl on the Kings' kitchen table into the cup and stirred it and drank carefully. It was very hot and very sweet—the way he liked it. "Why did you put eggshells into the coffee?" he asked Naomi.

"It takes the bitterness away," Naomi said. "Doesn't it seem like the bite is gone?"

"With that much sugar in it, there wouldn't ever be a bite." Galen sat at the table and drank his coffee so quickly that Jimmy thought he must have a throat made of iron. He seemed to be swallowing steam. He gulped it down and bowed his head, signaling a silent prayer. Then he bolted out of his chair, nodded to Naomi, and headed down to the barn to take hay out to the horses. Jimmy swallowed the last of his sweet coffee, smiled at Naomi, and followed Galen.

The sun was just showing light in the east over a long green flat of pasture that led down to a small creek a hundred yards from the barn. Mist came up from the creek and layered the grass. The horses were making their way to the edge of the pasture. They already knew the routine—the morning hay would soon arrive.

Galen stood by the back door of the barn, one hand on the hay cart, watching the horses move through the mist as if walking on air.

"Well, look at that," Jimmy whispered as he walked up to him. "Never seen anything so pretty before, have you?"

"You talk too much," Galen said softly. "Just watch—you don't have to talk."

And so they stood and watched the horses head to their breakfast. Stood and wasted five or six minutes, and it was the first time working on Galen's horse farm that Jimmy had ever seen such a thing. His sullen boss, just standing when there was work to be done.

Imagine that. Galen King had a romantic streak.

Sammy was a continual worry, Mim thought. This morning at breakfast he asked if he could bring a friend for supper and of course her mother said yes. Maybe two friends, Sammy asked. And her mother seemed even more pleased. She was always encouraging Sammy to make friends. She worried he was too dependent on Luke. He asked Bethany, in his sweetest voice, if she wouldn't mind making her very excellent peach crumble for dessert. That was how he said it too. Her very excellent peach crumble. How could she say no to that? Then he went and got ready for school without being told. All during the school day, Mim kept an eye on him, wondering if he might be coming down with something. Cholera or the plague or dropsy.

Right at suppertime, Sammy came through the privet dragging Galen King by the elbow sleeve. Naomi followed behind. Galen looked all cleaned up, hair combed, face and hands scrubbed. He wasn't the smiley type, but his eyes seemed to twinkle when he said hello to her mother. When they were all in the kitchen, Sammy cleared his throat real loud, as loud as Bishop Elmo did at church, and said, "Bethany, Galen King has come to court you."

All heads swiveled to Galen. His mouth opened wide and his eyes quit sparkling.

Bethany dropped the excellent peach crumble right into the sink.

"What?" Naomi said. "Why, Galen, you never told me! You never even hinted!"

"How could he?" Luke yelped. "He never knew!" He started laughing so hard that he doubled over, holding his sides.

Mim's mother bent down and put her hands on Sammy's shoulders. "Son, sometimes we can get things confused."

Sammy looked up, eyes filled with hurt. "But . . . but . . . ," he sputtered, "Mammi Vera said the exact selfsame thing, and nobody yelled at her for it!"

"I never said any such thing," Mammi Vera said, waving those accusations away. "Nothing good comes of matchmaking. I'd just as soon poke a sleeping bear."

"You did! You said so!" He looked at Rose. "I heard her say it! In the kitchen the other night—she was talking to you about it. She said Galen was happier than he'd ever been." His head swiveled toward Bethany. "And she said that Bethany should stop pining for Jake. Cuz he's Car Amish.

And you agreed. You said you didn't think Jake was sweet on Bethany the way she mooned over him."

Mim saw Bethany flash a dark look at her mother and she felt a tight knot in her stomach. Sammy kept on blathering! On and on and on.

"Sammy," her mother said, "it's kind of you to think about others, but it's best to let folks do their own matchmaking."

Mim thought Luke was going to die of laughter. He was rolling on the ground, literally rolling, gasping for breath. Head held high, glaring at her mother, Bethany swept around him and bolted up the stairs. Luke just kept laughing, like a wild hyena. Sometimes, he was just appalling.

"Luke, if you don't get yourself up off that floor and stop acting like a silly fool," her mother said, "I'll get the switch and you won't be sitting down for a week of Sundays. And don't think I won't do it."

Luke stopped rolling back and forth, but he didn't get himself up, despite that threat. Finally, Galen picked him up under his arms and sat him on a chair. Luke quieted down straightaway, brought up short by Galen's firmness.

Then Galen said he was grateful for the offer of dinner, but perhaps another evening might be best and he tipped his hat and took his leave. Naomi followed behind him.

Dinner ended up being a sad and quiet affair. The kitchen clock ticked loud in the silence. Only Chase seemed unaffected, checking under the table like he always did to make sure there wasn't something left for him. Sammy didn't understand what he had done that was so wrong. "I was just trying to help!" burst out of him once or twice. Her mother said they could talk about it later, in private.

Without Luke's big ears and big mouth, was what she meant. Mim gave Luke a look of disgust and he returned it, crunched eyebrow to crunched eyebrow.

Bethany finally came down to eat but was, understandably, sulky. Sammy sat on the other side of Bethany, drawing up his small shoulders in a shrug as he sniffed back tears. Sammy meant well and Mim felt sorry for him. A few days ago, he had asked Mim a bunch of questions about courting. How did a fellow do it? What should he say? He was especially curious about the ages of people. Did they need to be the same age to court?

"No," Mim had said. "Dad was a lot older than Mom."

That knowledge was new to him and pleased him to no end. At the time, Mim thought he had a crush on Teacher M.K. A lot of the boys did. Not Danny, of course, but many others. Now she realized what was on Sammy's mind. She wished she could have set him straight before he embarrassed both Galen and Bethany. But then, it was hard for anyone to figure out the reasoning a boy follows.

One thing Mim knew, she would never let *anyone* know all the thoughts she had swirling in her head about Danny Riehl.

By Wednesday, the skies had cleared, leaving the air washed clean and the earth saturated from rain. Rose had been up most of Wednesday night. Her young mare, Silver Girl, had dropped her foal early and the colt was too weak to stand up. Rose was determined to save it if she could.

The sun was barely climbing in the sky when Luke ran to her in the barn stall, tracking in mud from his boots. The mare startled.

"Haven't I told you to walk up to horses?" Rose scolded.

"I'm sorry, Mom," Luke said, more excited than sorry. His eyes were fixed on the newborn colt.

"You were supposed to make up your bed before school," Rose said.

"I never did understand that," Luke said, eyes sparkling, "when I'll just be getting back into it tonight."

Rose frowned. "Seems like all you do is hang out the window looking for something to distract you from chores."

Luke wasn't paying her any mind. He had his palm laid out flat for the colt to sniff. The mare pinned her ears back in warning, not wanting him to mess with her baby, but Luke wasn't minding her, either.

His recklessness almost stopped Rose's heart at times—he was the kind of boy who would run out in the snow barefoot, bareheaded, oblivious to weather and risks. Sometimes, she feared for him, more than she ever did for Sammy. But she supposed most mothers shook their heads and worried about their sons. Boys seem to have to acquire common sense through bad experiences. The mare made a sudden move toward Luke and he stepped back, sticking his hands in his pockets. He looked like a ragamuffin under his shaggy head of hair.

It was hard to believe a little boy could catch a day's worth of play and dirty roughhousing by half past seven in the morning. "Luke, I need you to go get Galen next door. Tell him I'm having some trouble with a new foal." Before Luke disappeared, she added, "And then you've got to get yourself to school."

She heard Luke whistle for his brother as she walked over to the barn door. Sammy came flying out of the house, hatless, and raced to meet up with Luke to disappear through the privet. Sammy liked delivering messages as much as his brother.

A few minutes later, Galen arrived and eased his way into the stall, calmly and quietly, so the mare wouldn't spook. He looked the colt over. "I think you're going to need the vet."

Rose had feared that. She wasn't sure how she could afford it, but she didn't want to lose this colt.

Galen went down to the phone shanty to leave a message for the vet. When he returned, he let Chase into the barn, and suddenly an angry streak of gray burned across the center of the barn, tore past Galen, and disappeared in the yard.

"What was *that*?" Galen asked.

"That was Oliver," Rose said. "Fern Lapp gave him to Sammy. He's an old gray cat who hates dogs. He doesn't understand that Chase has no interest in cats whatsoever, even for chasing purposes."

"Well, I suppose a barn cat always comes in handy."

"Not Oliver. He's useless. He can't be bothered catching mice and rats. He's just a big sulking, gloomy presence." She watched the mare nuzzle her colt. "Not unlike Vera." As soon as the words popped out of her mouth, she wished them back. How could she have said such a thing? Thinking it was one thing, saying it was another.

She looked up, expecting to see Galen frown. Instead, she saw a big grin crease his face.

Galen returned home to finish feeding his stock, but later in the day he went back to check on Rose's little colt, half expecting it to be dead. But no—there it was, standing on its wobbly legs. Rose said the vet had brought along some bottles with nipples designed for colts that had trouble nursing, along with some powdered formula. He balked at first, but then, Rose said, he guzzled that formula like sweet cream.

For a woman who had spent part of the night in the barn nursing a newborn foal, Rose looked wonderfully fresh, bright eyed, and beautiful. Her face was relaxed in a way Galen had never seen it. The strain that always showed—the strain of holding a household together, he supposed—had disappeared, making her look like a young girl.

Right now, although he couldn't say exactly why, he felt uneasy.

Maybe he did know why.

He hadn't been able to stop thinking about Rose. It made no sense. He hardly knew her—just a few minutes here and there, as neighbors. He doubted all those minutes would even add up to hours. After those few hours with her, what could he know about her? It made no sense.

Random memories went flickering through his mind: the delight in her laugh, her grace as she crossed the grass, and even the way she had picked up and held that little colt in her arms this morning. He simply couldn't get her off his mind. What was happening to him? Now and then, he'd had a vague interest in a female or two, but he had never felt this way about a woman. This time it was different. Why was it different?

It was Rose. Rose in the rain.

He had a quick recollection of the first time he truly noticed her, as someone more than a neighbor. Last fall, a brief downpour had blown through Stoney Ridge without warning. Sheets of rain came pouring down, in biblical proportions, a nightmare on the roads. Someone was playing with the hose up there.

From his barn, Galen had seen Rose struggling with a flapping sheet on the clotheslines. Most women would have considered the wash to be a lost cause and run for the house, but not Rose. Her skirt was so wet it was plastered to her legs, and in the struggle, two or three pillowcases that she had already gathered up blew out of her hand and across the yard, which had begun to look like a shallow pond. Galen hurried to retrieve the pillowcases and then helped Rose get the wet sheets off the line.

Rose was soaked, as wet on the top as on the bottom, and the flapping sheets had knocked the pins out of her cap, causing it to come loose. The wash was as wet as it had been before she hung it up in the first place. She was taking sheets off the line that would just have to be hung back on in fifteen minutes, and it must have been out of pure stubbornness, since the sun was breaking through the clouds to the east of the storm. It baffled Galen as to why anyone would have a penchant to fly directly in the face of reason. Even worse, Galen was helping her do it as if it all made some sense.

In a strange way, he completely understood her logic. This woman would not quit. He had never met anyone with as much determination. As much as he had.

By the time he helped Rose finish pulling down those drenched sheets, the rain was diminishing and the sun was already striking little rainbows through the sparkle of drops that fell. Galen had walked on home, water dripping from the brim of his hat. He couldn't get that image of Rose struggling with the sheets out of his mind. He felt like a hooked fish, absolutely smitten. The thing was, Rose Schrock wasn't fishing.

The day finally came when Galen left Jimmy in charge. It was a weekday, which suited Jimmy nicely because it kept those little Schrock boys contained in the schoolhouse. Galen wanted to see some new horses brought in from Kentucky before they went to auction on the weekend. Jimmy did the chores with will and skill, whereas Luke and Sammy had marginal will and little skill. Sammy, Jimmy had to admit, tried his best. Luke—not so much.

Jimmy was determined to make a success of this day and prove to Galen that he could take on more responsibility. Just yesterday, he was helping Galen work a three-year-old gelding that was ready to be sold. "He's like me," Jimmy said, watching the gelding ignore all kinds of distraction that Galen was tossing at it.

"How's that?" Galen asked, waving a flag at the gelding. "Lazy, you mean?"

"Mature, I mean," Jimmy said. "He doesn't get excited about little things."

Galen rolled his eyes.

"When are you going to let me train a horse, start to finish?" Jimmy asked.

"When you're ready."

"I am ready."

Galen ignored him.

"Why are you so hard to convince?" Jimmy asked. "I can't seem to convince you of a single thing." His gaze was fixed on Bethany as she left Naomi at the kitchen door and crossed the yard, disappearing through the hole in the privet that led to Eagle Hill.

"That's not true. You've convinced me of one thing for sure," Galen said. "You're foolish about women. I expect Bethany won't have anything to do with you because she knows you're too fond of ladies. Now, would you mind getting back to work?"

Now *that* was not necessary. Three things bothered Jimmy about Galen. First, he didn't think Galen ever had any fun. Second, Galen didn't do a single thing that couldn't be predicted. Third, he wasn't easy to talk to. Jimmy didn't say anything more to him for the rest of the afternoon, though he didn't think Galen even noticed.

And then Galen did something that was both fun and unpredictable. He told Jimmy that he would be putting him in charge of tomorrow's training. *Nice!*

Jimmy was not going to let Galen down. The day had been going well, almost perfectly, up until the moment when that blasted filly Galen was so fond of took a nip at his hand and drew blood. After he led the filly into her stall, he looked through Galen's workbench to find some bandages. The day was only half done and he needed something to wrap his hand. He thought about going to the house and seeing if Naomi could help, but felt she might surely pass out from the sight of blood. She was *that* frail. Jimmy would rather leave chores half done than tell Galen that he had caused his sister to faint.

"Some horse trainer you are."

He whirled around and faced Bethany, standing by the workshop. He held up his hand. "That filly has an evil streak."

"I was visiting with Naomi and saw it happen from the kitchen window. You'd better let me see it."

That meant she'd been watching him. *Nice!* He held out his hand to her, unconcernedly, and told her it didn't hurt, which it did. She scolded him and insisted on bandaging up his fingers. "It's going to need some hydrogen peroxide. You'd better come with me over to the house."

Jimmy followed behind her, pleased. He had a new appreciation for that diabolical filly. That was the thing about Thoroughbreds—hot-blooded, strong-willed, feisty, moody, breathtakingly beautiful, poetic in their movement. Most preferred warmbloods or drafts—they wanted a horse they could depend on. Steady, solid, reliable. But for all of the problems of Thoroughbreds, Jimmy liked their unpredictable, high-spirited nature.

He grinned. He could have been talking about women.

In the kitchen in Eagle Hill, Bethany cleaned the wounds on Jimmy's hand and wrapped the fingers carefully.

"How do you like being an innkeeper?"

She kept her head down but glanced at him. "That's the very thing I was talking to Naomi about when that filly took such a serious disliking to you. It's not as bad as I thought it was going to be. Of course, we've really only had one guest. She is a grand lady, though. She taught me how to make genuine steeped tea the other morning. From loose leaves, not from a bag."

"Have you given any more thought to quitting the Bar & Grill and working at the Sisters' House?" Jimmy said.

She whipped her head around to see if Mammi Vera's door was shut. "Lower your voice. Stop talking about that!"

"All right, let's talk about something else. Have you changed your mind about going on a picnic with me to Blue Lake Pond?"

"I'd be delighted." She smiled at him and he smiled back. "We'd all be delighted. Me and Mim and Sammy and Luke and Rose and Mammi Vera."

His smile faded.

"You seem to keep forgetting that I have a boyfriend."

"I keep forgetting because I've never seen hide nor hair of him." He leaned back in his chair. "Now, what makes this bloke so much better than me?"

"Well, for one thing, Jake has ambition."

Jimmy raised his bandaged hand. "What do you think caused this?"

"I'm not talking about hard work. Jake has plans for the future."

"And I don't?"

"Nothing that lasts longer than five minutes." She tied the last bandage. A war whoop outside pulled their attention to the windows. "Luke and Sammy are home from school."

"Those brothers of yours need a firm hand," Jimmy said.

"Oh bother. What did they do now? No—never mind. I can't handle any more complaints today."

"That's another reason you need a new line of work. Customer complaints. Wouldn't happen if you worked at the Sisters' House. They're not the complaining type."

She frowned. "Stop talking about my line of work." She wrapped up the bandages. "Just how old are those sisters, anyway?"

"Pretty old. They've got their fair share of summer teeth."

"What are summer teeth?"

"Summer in their mouth. Some are elsewhere." Jimmy looked at her and made his eyebrows do that crazy up-and-down dance.

She covered her mouth but a laugh slipped out anyway.

"Maybe your brothers should work for the sisters. Maybe they could knock some sense into them." He picked up his hat off the table and grinned that mischief-loaded grin of his, when his eyes sparkled like he'd charmed the hair right off a cat. "They're wilder than the wind, and nagging them—especially Luke—does no good."

"Well, I try not to nag them," Bethany said, straightening her skirt.

"You nag," Jimmy said. "Galen and I can hear you all the way over at his place."

# 10

Rain began at midnight and continued until dawn and then on through the day. All evening, Mammi Vera was reminded of the terrible blizzard of 1993, when it took days to dig out and find the road. She told Bethany the story twice.

"You say the same things, over and over," Bethany told her, but her grandmother went right on repeating herself. Last night, reading to the older woman by the oil lamplight, Bethany held Mammi Vera's rough, aged hand—webbed with blue veins and brown spots. She had such a fondness for her grandmother. She liked older people better than babies. Older folks had interesting stories to tell. Babies only cried.

She thought about Jimmy Fisher's suggestion to work for the ladies in the Sisters' House. She wondered why Jimmy was steering her away from working at the Grill. He had said, more than a few times, that she was playing with fire.

That comment struck her as odd. Jimmy Fisher seemed to be the daring sort—the type who liked to play with fire. After all, the job he loved best, he said, was gentling wild horses. Her thoughts drifted to Jake. Where was he? The letter he sent was so brief and unromantic, filled with complaints about a minor misunderstanding with his cheap landlord. When would she hear from him again? Had he stopped loving her? For a moment Bethany wondered whether life was happier with men, or without them.

It was lightly sprinkling as Rose walked up the hillside behind the farmhouse, but she didn't mind the mist. She enjoyed these quiet moments as the sun started to light the sky. She liked walking apart from the farm, listening to the sounds over the area. A coyote howled, and another coyote answered back. The sound made her shiver. She hadn't given the sound of a coyote a second thought until she became a sheep owner. She knew what a coyote could do to a sheep—it lunged straight for the throat, so the last thing a poor little sheep saw was the spilling of its life's blood.

She stopped for a moment as she saw one of the eagles pass overhead and soar along the creek. It was still too dark to see if it was the missus or the mister. Sometimes she wished she could be such a bird, just for a short time. She wondered what they saw, high in the sky with their night vision, and she envied them their freedom. Maybe it wasn't as free as it seemed, she thought, when its sole purpose was to find food.

But her sole purpose lately didn't feel too far off from that. She ought to get back soon. She had bread to bake, clothes to wash, and a million and one other chores that needed to be done. And then, of course, there was caring for Vera. Rose sighed.

Looking over the horizon at dawn never failed to fill her with a sense of her smallness, contrasted to God's bigness. Her problems and worries seemed to shrink under the dome of the sky.

A twig snapped behind her and she whirled around. "Galen!" She smiled.

"No moon this morning." His greeting seemed quiet, intimate.

"What are you doing up here?"

"Checking traps. A coyote has been sneaking in and snatching Naomi's hens."

She looked around. "Did you find it? Or rather, did the coyote find the trap?"

"No. Too wily."

They walked along the path, silent companions, each with their own thoughts. There was only the sound of Harold, the rooster, crowing that morning had arrived.

"How is Naomi doing lately, Galen?"

He lifted one shoulder in a half-shrug. "Same cycle. She feels better, then does too much, and she'll get walloped with another headache and has to take to her bed."

She could see he loved his sister in his unspeaking way—continually warning her about her health or trying to keep her wrapped up from the cold. Naomi's migraines were a puzzle. Doctors couldn't quite pinpoint what triggered them or how to avoid them. They started when her parents had passed.

Galen was the eldest in his family of three boys, three girls. His parents died awhile back, first one, then the other, and Galen stepped into the role of patriarch. The other siblings had married, moved on, started families.

"What about Vera?" he said. "Any improvement?"

"None." Rose sighed. "If anything, she's getting worse. More confused, weaker on one side. She tries to hide it, but I'm awfully worried about her."

"She's blessed to have you."

"I wish she thought so."

He pretended to look serious, but his eyes gave him away. Sparkling green those eyes were, and crinkled at the corners. "One of my sisters used to say that every time she talked to Vera, she came away feeling like she's eaten a green persimmon. You know how they make your mouth pucker up?"

That unexpected comment made her laugh, and him as well. But the quiet that followed brought an awkwardness with it, as if they both felt wary of the closeness their shared laughter had stirred. "Galen, I don't know what we'd do without you. Teaching the boys about horses, helping me get the inn ready. You do a lot for us as a neighbor."

"A friend, you mean."

Down below, Rose saw the sheep wander in the fold, bleating. "I hope that coyote keeps its distance from my sheep."

"Remind me again why you want to raise sheep."

"I didn't set out to raise them. Someone drove up in a truck one day and asked if we'd take them off their hands. Said they were tired of them."

"And you said yes?"

"I . . . well. I was worried what might happen to them if I said no." She looked down the hill at the fold with five fluffy sheep. Sometimes, she just sat and watched them. They slowly munched and dozed their way around the pasture, passing the time in the way they loved best. "They're not the brightest, but they are sweet."

He stared at her in that intense way he had, and she could feel the color building in her cheeks. Then the creases around his mouth softened in a smile. "Well, everybody knows you are the lady to help people. And creatures." He gave her a curt nod and set off toward his farmhouse.

As Rose made her way down the hill, Galen's words came back to her. *You are the lady to help people.* It was pleasing to know what people thought of you, but worrying too. You couldn't help everybody—nobody could—because the world was too full of need and troubles, a wide sea of them, and no one person could begin to deal with all that. And yet, even if you were just one person, you could do one thing. You could say yes to five little sheep and give them a home.

Despite Bethany Schrock's opinion, Jimmy Fisher did have ambition that lasted longer than five minutes. But it was not to inherit his mother's farm to become a chicken and egg dealer like his brother, Paul, who didn't mind living his life in a groove etched out by their mother. Jimmy had different ideas for his life. He wanted to become a respected horse trainer, just like Galen King.

He listened carefully to Galen—though he knew his taciturn boss thought otherwise—and he had discovered that horses coming off the Kentucky racetracks were breaking down. Too many horses were bred for one quality—speed—at the expense of others. They were weedy and unsound.

Jimmy decided that he should help out mankind and create a superb Thoroughbred bloodline. He developed a plan: he would stop dating girls and start saving his money. And he would attend local spring mud sales held at county fire stations on Saturdays, looking for the perfect foundation stallion to start his superb bloodline.

Amazingly, he found the horse on the first Saturday at the Bart Township mud sale.

It was early. The auction wouldn't get started for a few more hours, but there was a crowd milling around a certain stall that piqued Jimmy's interest. He made his way through the crowd to get closer to the stall and see what folks were oohing and aahing over. Inside was the most striking-looking horse he'd ever seen—a chocolate palomino stallion with a flaxen mane. He tried to gather as much information about the horse as he could without having the owner notice him. Bright eyes, a long arch to his neck, thick cannons, hooves in good condition, sound teeth that revealed he was a young colt. And he was definitely a stallion. He could just imagine what Galen King would have to say if Jimmy bought a gelding as the foundation of his breeding plan. No thank you! He did not want to have to be on the receiving end of Galen King's disdain any more than necessary.

The owner noticed him and sidled over to him. "Beautiful creature," he said. "I hate to let him go."

"Then why are you selling?" Jimmy asked.

"I've got some bills to take care of." He rolled his eyes. "But . . . a man's got to do what he's gotta do." He stuck out his hand. "Jonah Hershberger."

"Jimmy Fisher." He shook his hand and noticed that it wasn't the palm of a typical horseman: calloused and rough. This was a man who didn't use his hands for a living. In fact, he looked like he didn't get outside much—he had pale skin, was small-boned and slender, blue eyed, with shingled mahogany hair. The indoor type. Mennonite, he guessed, with a name like Jonah Hershberger. Hard to tell his age but he didn't wear a beard so Jimmy assumed he wasn't married.

Jonah Hershberger nodded his head toward the horse. "You can check him out."

Jimmy ducked under the rope gate and walked slowly around the stallion. Perfect conformation—large eyes, broad forehead, knife-edged withers, sloping croup, lean body, good depth of girth, beautiful coat. Jimmy lifted each hoof and examined it. The horse was calm, at ease with handling. "Does he have a name?"

"I call him Lodestar."

Perfect. Absolutely perfect. He knew what that word meant: a guiding light. Lodestar bumped Jimmy gently with his nose and he was hooked. This horse was meant for him.

Jonah Hershberger looked around, then lowered his voice. "Look, I can tell you know horses."

Jimmy nodded. He did.

"I'd rather Lodestar go to someone like you, someone who would give him a good home, than let him go on that auction block."

"How much? How much do you want?"

"I haven't signed any papers with the auctioneer yet, so if you can get him out of here before the auction starts, I'll let him go for $1500."

Jimmy inhaled a sharp breath. "The thing is, Jonah, I don't quite have that much. Not yet. I could give you a deposit and make payments. I've got a steady job. I'm good for the money."

Jonah hesitated. "I don't know. Like I said . . . I got these bills to take care of."

"It would just be for a few weeks, maybe a month—I get paid on Fridays. I'm good for it. Ask anybody around here. They all know me."

"How much can you get me today?"

Just how much was in Jimmy's checking account? Last time he looked was . . . blast! He couldn't remember. He had never been much of a money manager—mainly because he just didn't care much about it. "I could write you a check for $500."

"Make it $750 and you've got yourself the finest stud north of Kentucky."

He looked over at Lodestar, who stretched out his neck now, lifting his head, looking calmly at Jimmy through big round dark eyes. What was it about the meeting of eyes that created a connection? He'd never felt such a bond with an animal before. It's like Lodestar was meant for him and they both knew it.

But he remembered Galen's constant refrains—*Never let your heart rule your head. You make a purchase with your stomach.*

Jimmy's stomach felt just fine.

"Okay," Jimmy said, grinning. "I'll be back in thirty minutes with a friend who has a trailer."

"Hold on," Jonah said, laughing at Jimmy's delight. "I've got a trailer hitched to my truck. Throw in an extra twenty-five bucks, and I'll deliver him right to your barn."

Jimmy's grin spread from ear to ear. "It's a deal!"

Later that afternoon, Jimmy confessed to Galen that he had bought a foundation stallion for his future stud farm. He braced himself for a lecture on impulsive purchases, but Galen surprised him with only interest. In fact, he wanted to go over to Jimmy's farm to meet Lodestar. As they drove the buggy down the road that led to the Fisher chicken and egg farm, the buggy horse pricked its ears, then started to speed up, prancing on the road. Not a moment later, a dark object came hurtling through the woods, leapt over a fence, blew past them, and disappeared into the trees on the other side of the road.

It took all of Galen's attention to keep his buggy horse from bolting. His fists were clenched around the reins so tightly that his knuckles were white. When the horse finally stopped straining, Galen relaxed his grip, little by little. He edged the gelding sideways over to the side of the road. "What was *that*?" he said, mystified.

"A horse, I think," Jimmy said, peering into the woods. He gave a snort. "Somebody's gonna be sorry they left a barn door open."

Wait. *What?*

"That was Lodestar!" Jimmy swung out of the buggy and ran into the woods, calling Lodestar's name. He stopped and listened, hoping to hear some sound that the horse was near. The woods were silent.

Slowly, Jimmy walked back to the buggy and climbed in.

"You're sure that was your new horse?" Galen said. "It blew past us pretty fast. I couldn't tell if it was a bear or a buck."

Jimmy hung his head. "I'm sure."

"Let's go to your farm and double-check." Galen clucked for the horse to move forward and drove down the road, turning into the Fisher driveway. Jimmy's eyes immediately went to the paddock where he had left Lodestar grazing just a few hours earlier.

Empty. The paddock was empty.

# 11

In the warm kitchen of Eagle Hill, Bethany washed dishes, suds up to her elbows. Mim dried and put the dishes away. Seated at the kitchen table, Luke was reading his essay to them.

"'Noah and his wife, Joan,'" he read, "'lived on the Ark for a long time.'"

"What makes you think Noah's wife is named Joan?" Bethany asked. "I don't remember reading what her name was in the Bible."

"Everybody knows that. Joan of Ark."

Bethany and Mim burst into laughter. Luke ignored them and went back to his essay. "'The ark came to its end on Mt. Error Fat. It is still up there, teetering on the top of the mountain, just waiting to be discovered by *National Geographic* magazine.'"

"Luke, where did you get that information?" Bethany asked, scratching her nose and leaving a spot of suds there.

"I made it up," Luke said, looking pleased. "What do you think?"

"Luke, you can't make up facts!" Mim protested. "You research facts. Facts are true. Made-up facts are not true."

"Unless you happened to have interviewed Mr. and Mrs. Noah," repeated Bethany, scouring out the soup pot, making Luke smile.

"Can I say I did?"

"No!" Mim and Bethany shouted.

After Luke and Mim went upstairs, Bethany finished up the last of the dishes. She was standing at the sink, her hands immersed in soapy water, when she noticed movement outside, half in the darkness, half in the square of light thrown out from the window.

Her heart skipped a beat. *Shootfire!* She smacked her hands to her cheeks. *Oh my. Oh my! He's come for me!* "Jake! Jake Hertzler."

He didn't hear her; he was staring in through a window now, as if searching the room. She waved a hand, signaling to him, and he startled, hesitated, then smiled.

She dried her hands before opening the kitchen door, and tried to appear calm as a cucumber, as if the arrival by night of Jake Hertzler lurking in the darkness was nothing unusual. As soon as she had closed the door, she ran into his arms. "You've come. You've finally come!" She was floating, lighter than air. She loved him, loved him so much! Her relief was so great, she felt dizzy with it. Jake had come for her!

Jake put his hands on her shoulders and gently pushed her back. "Bethany, I'm here for Tobe's sake."

Her chin jerked up. He hadn't even seen her in months and months . . . and he was worried about Tobe? About *Tobe?* "Well, that's a fine way to greet your girlfriend."

He glanced into the kitchen. "Keep your voice down. Tobe's in trouble. He needs our help."

"Have you seen him?"

"Yes."

"Where's he been?"

Jake took his time answering. "He's been with your mother."

Bethany's head snapped up. "WHAT?"

"Hush!" he clamped his fingers over her mouth. "There's something I need your help with. Tobe said he left something important in the basement. But when I looked in the windows—"

"You peeped in the basement windows? There's a paying guest in there!"

"Relax. She didn't see me. But obviously, stuff has been moved out of the basement. Where would it be now?"

She shrugged. She was still reeling over the news that Tobe was with their mother. She had no idea where her mother lived. Somehow, Tobe had tracked her down and was living with her? "I . . . I don't know. I could ask Rose."

"No!" Jake snapped. She stiffened and he noticed. His face softened as he added, "I don't want Rose to find out about this. It'll only make things worse for Tobe."

"But she should be told if he's in some kind of trouble. She'll know what to do."

"Legal trouble, Bethany. I'm trying to help him stay out of jail. We can't get Rose involved in this—not yet. Not with the SEC lawyer sniffing around. It puts her in a tight spot. She'd have to turn him in or she could be in trouble herself. You understand, don't you?" He wrapped his arms around her and pulled her to his chest. "I'm sorry, Bethany. I'm trying to do all I can to help your brother. Now I want you to think hard for a minute. Where would things be that were stored in the basement?"

She breathed in the familiar scent of Jake: Old Spice shaving cream and peppermint gum. He always smelled so good and looked so good—unlike most of the farm boys in Stoney Ridge who wore the barn on their boots. She wished she could stay in his arms forever. "What are you looking for, anyway?"

"Most importantly, two black books with red bindings."

"Books?" She pulled back to look right at his eyes. "Tobe didn't read."

"These are ledger books. For Schrock Investments."

"What's the next most important thing?"

He hesitated. "I'm looking for a key. But I'm not sure Tobe took it. I couldn't find it after the SEC cleaned the office out."

She tilted her head. "What kind of key? For a car?"

"No. Smaller than that." He shook his head. "Never you mind. The books are what I really need. What Tobe needs."

"Where will you be?"

"I'm on the road a lot—interviewing all over, trying to find a job. But everyone seems to have been an investor in Schrock Investments or their grandmother was—it ain't good. It's been tough, you know."

She rolled her eyes. "Tell me about it."

He softened at that, and leaned in to kiss her on the lips, gentle and sweet, then he jerked his head back and glanced in the kitchen windows when he heard the sound of the boys yelling to each other. "I'd better go." He kissed her again, before she could object. "Start looking for those books."

*Shootfire!* "Jake! Wait! You can't just show up and disappear like a spook. I want to know why my letter got returned!"

He grimaced, ashamed. "I hated to let the apartment go. Couldn't make the rent. I'm just staying on friends' couches."

"Well, how am I supposed to reach you if I find those books?"

"Good point." He took a piece of paper from his pocket and scribbled a number on it with a small pencil. "This is my cell phone number."

Her eyes narrowed. "When did you get a cell phone?" *And why didn't you bother calling me on it?*

He read her mind. "I got it for job interviews—but it's the kind with limited minutes. Call me the minute you find those books." He kissed her again. Then again and again, until the sound of her brothers' footsteps thundering down the stairs jerked him away. "Trust me on this, honey. You find those books and we can help Tobe clear his name." And he vanished into the shadows. She waited awhile, hearing his footsteps head down the driveway. In the distance, she heard a horse whinny and Silver Queen answer back from the barn. Then she heard the sound of Jake's truck drive off.

Honey. *He called me his honey!* Bethany hugged herself with happiness. He still loved her. Of course he did. Why had she ever doubted?

She inhaled the sharp night air, feeling a surge of pleasure. Then it passed and in its place rushed a thought that filled her with discomfort: Tobe has been staying with their mother. She wanted to know more, and yet she didn't.

On Monday morning, Jimmy Fisher woke up a determined man. He marched into Galen's kitchen and helped himself to a mug of coffee. "Where's Naomi?" he asked.

"She's not feeling too well this morning."

Jimmy pulled out the kitchen chair and dumped three teaspoons full of sugar into his coffee cup.

Galen finished buttering his burnt toast. "Any luck finding the horse?"

"No, no sign of him." He took a long sip of coffee. "But I am going to find Lodestar and get him back. Yesterday, I went to all the neighbors and told them to keep an eye out for him. If you can spare me for a few hours,

I'm going to staple posters on telephone poles and street signs. Someone's bound to have seen him. I was even thinking about taking out an ad in the paper, maybe adding a reward."

"Well, I hope you do find him. But there are other horses in the world."

"None like Lodestar. You haven't seen him. When you do, you'll know what I mean."

"If he's that fine a horse, someone will find him and keep him."

"Now, Galen, that's the difference between you and me. You're negative. I'm positive. You're pessimistic. I'm optimistic. You think people are all bad. I think there's good in them. Someone will find him and return him to me."

Jimmy snatched his hat off the wall peg and jammed it on his head. "I'm going out to look for him. I'll be back in a few hours." That horse was his destiny. He was going to find Lodestar. He was going to prove Galen King wrong.

Every few days, Rose stopped by the phone shanty to pick up her messages. She knew from experience that she couldn't handle it more often. At first, her message machine was filled with pleas from people who had invested with Dean's company. The first few months, after it all broke open, she would listen to the messages and her stomach would churn all day long. These people had trusted Dean with their life savings. So many people had been left penniless. Futures had been destroyed. Family homes had been foreclosed on. They begged Rose to return the money they had invested.

Didn't they understand there was no money?

She took down the information and wrote letters to each person who called, explaining the situation. She tried to include some cash in each letter—$5 or $10 or $20. There was a part of her that wanted to scold these people for trusting so easily, for getting tempted by high returns on their investment. What made them think that Schrock Investments could beat the market? In a brutal recession? It made no sense.

Today, she was relieved to see there were only a handful of messages. The calls were coming less frequently now and in a way, that made her sad too. They had given up hope of getting their money back. She wished she could tell each one, "I haven't forgotten! Just give me some time. I'm going to repay you, if it's the last thing I do." She picked up a pencil to take down notes from the messages. She had to listen carefully to the last one before it made sense. Then she listened to it again. As soon as her mind grasped what the message meant, she ran down the long driveway and pounded on the basement door. "Delia, something's happened! Something terrible."

Delia opened the door, an alarmed look on her face. "What's wrong? Come in. What's happened?"

Rose had to stop and take a deep breath after running from the shanty like that. "My first guest at Eagle Hill was a woman named Lois. Tony and Lois. She left a message that she had met you at . . . a gas station . . . and told you to come here. She had bright red hair—truly red, not orange-red—and orange lipstick."

Delia nodded. "Yes. Yes, I remember her. She helped me pump gas."

"She said that you seemed upset and looked like you needed a quiet place to be."

"That's exactly right. She's the one who told me about your inn. Has something happened to her?"

Rose sat down on the couch. She took a deep breath. "She said that your picture is all over the television. As a missing person. The news said your son reported you as missing . . ."

"My son? My son, Will?"

"Yes . . . that your son is on every news station pleading for some information about where you might be."

"Oh no." A trace of color rose under Delia's fair skin. "I should have called Will. I should have let him know. It's just that he's going through midterm exams and Charles didn't want to let him know about our . . . marital problems."

"Charles. Is your husband Dr. Charles Stoltz?"

"Yes. Why?" Then, impatiently, "Why?"

"Maybe you should sit down for this."

Delia sank to the sofa and Rose sat beside her. "Lois said she just heard on the news that your husband has been taken to the police station for questioning. She said that there's concern he might have something to do with your disappearance . . . that apparently he is having an affair."

She lowered her voice. "Lois said there is speculation growing that your husband killed you and has hidden your body."

"Oh my," Delia said. "Oh my." She covered her face with her hands, but for just a moment. Then she let them fall to her lap in a gripping fist. "I should get to a phone. I need to straighten this all out."

Rose bit her lip. "Lois already did. She said she called the police to let them know where you are."

Delia looked sick. "Please tell me this is a bad dream."

The sound of a siren was heard in the distance, getting louder and louder as it came up the road. Rose and Delia went to the window and watched a police car with a flashing red siren pull up the driveway. "As a matter of fact," Rose said, "I think you're wide awake."

Delia Stoltz spent the next two hours at the sheriff's office in Stoney Ridge, on the phone with the Philadelphia police, explaining that her husband was innocent—sort of, she wanted to add, but didn't think it would be wise to complicate the situation. It was already far too complicated. "My husband did not kill me and hide my body," she said in a wry tone. "I just didn't happen to mention to him where I was going."

As soon as the sheriff allowed, she called her son, Will. She felt terrible when she heard the relief in his voice.

"I'm coming down there," Will said. "Don't try to talk me out of it. I'm leaving now."

"No, Will—you've got exams to get through. I'm fine. I really am. I'll call you each day if you like. I can't get service out at the farm, but I'll drive into town. I'm sorry I didn't let you know where I was. But what made you think I went missing?"

"Dad called me, thinking you might have come to Ithaca. I started phoning your friends to see if they knew where you were. None of them had heard from you in weeks. You weren't returning any of Dad's or my phone messages. Dad said not to worry, but that only made me worry all the more. I mean, it's not like you, Mom. Dad is hard to get hold of, but you're always available. My imagination started rolling . . . too many CSI shows, I guess. So I called the police, thinking they might be able to locate your car or check with any hospitals to see if you might have been in an accident. Suddenly, it turned into a missing person's report, then I was interviewed for the evening news, then someone at Dad's office tipped off the police that Dad was having an affair with his attorney . . . and things got carried away."

Delia rubbed her forehead. What a mess. "I'm sorry to have caused you concern. I just needed a little time to catch my breath. So much happened, so quickly."

"Mom, I didn't know about Dad and this attorney bimbo."

"I just found out myself a few weeks ago. The day I found out about the cancer, in fact."

There was a long silence. "Wait. *What?* You have cancer?"

Delia squeezed her eyes shut. How could she have blurted that without thinking? She kept her voice calm and steady. "They found a lump in my breast and took it out. I'm sure they got it all." She wasn't at all sure.

"What did the doctor say? Were the margins clear? Anything in the lymph nodes?" Will's voice started to crack, which made Delia's eyes fill with tears.

"I . . . haven't gotten the results yet. I'm sure it's all fine." In fact, with each passing day, she felt a sense of growing dread about those results. She glanced at her wristwatch. It was too late to call today, but she would drive into town and call tomorrow.

"Does Dad know?"

"No. Not yet. I will tell him, Will." Her voice was firm. "Let me do that."

"So he's having an affair with his lawyer while you're recovering from cancer surgery." His voice was filled with disgust.

"To be fair to him, he didn't know, Will."

She heard Will call his father an unmentionable word and she cringed. She didn't want to become that kind of a woman—who told her son too much and turned him against his father. It wouldn't take much, she knew—Will and Charles always had a fragile relationship. "Listen—this is between me and your father. Not you and him. Nothing has to change between the two of you."

"Nothing has to change?" Will snorted. "Everything has changed! Dad destroyed our family. Life will never be the same again. Every holiday— Thanksgiving, Christmas—will be divided between parents. I've got plenty of friends from split-up families." He paused. "Look, Dad's . . . tomcatting . . . isn't as important as your cancer. You've got to find out the results of the surgery. I don't know when you're planning to come home, but you can't ignore this."

"You're right. I can't."

"I'll come down to Stoney Ridge. I'll tell my professors that my exams are just going to have to wait."

"Will, I'm going to be fine." She said it firmly, a mother to a son. "I can handle this. I won't have you jeopardizing your future because of me. You stay put at Cornell and I'll call you with the results. The minute I hear. Until then, no news is . . . no news."

She heard him exhale loudly. "Either way? You'll tell me the truth? The absolute truth?"

"I promise."

"Mom . . . do you think you and Dad can fix this?" Something in his voice reminded Delia of Will as a little boy, wanting a Band-Aid or a hug to make the hurt go away.

"Maybe. But I want you to know that I will be fine. And so will you. I love you. Now . . . go study."

Delia didn't leave the sheriff's office until he assured her that Charles had been released from questioning. She thought about calling Charles but knew he would be furious, and she couldn't take any more upset today. She still felt shaky from that call with her son.

Her mind drifted back to Will's question: Could this marriage be fixed? She was still trying to figure out when it had broken, and why.

Delia thought about a dinner she had at P.F. Chang's with Charles just last month. It was their favorite restaurant. He had left the table four times to make urgent phone calls and returned edgy, distracted. Delia had seen nothing unusual about it at the time. He was often edgy and distracted, though he had become far more so in the last month, since the malpractice suit.

Charles had a patient, a middle-aged woman, who had come to him with an enormous aneurysm pressing against her brain stem—a very dangerous situation. The brain could be surprisingly forgiving and tended to accommodate aneurysms or tumors as long as they grew slowly. Not in the brain stem with its tight pack of nerves. He explained all that and more to the patient, concerned she didn't understand how serious the situation was. The aneurysm had to be dealt with before it proved fatal. Charles persisted and she finally agreed to the surgery. The procedure was successful.

Delia remembered that evening—how satisfied Charles had been as he described wrapping coil after coil around the large aneurysm. She could tell he was pleased with himself. He had saved the patient's life.

And then the hospital called. Delia had never seen a look of fear on Charles's face until he hung up from that phone call. He didn't move for a long moment, and she heard him say, "Oh God, please no." The patient suffered a massive stroke and was having difficulty speaking.

The patient's husband ended up slapping a malpractice suit on Charles— his first. The husband insisted that his wife did not understand the risks of the surgery and that she would never have agreed to the procedure if she had known she might have ended up impaired. She didn't mind dying, he said, but she would mind living with such loss of function. And that was when Charles connected with Robyn Dixon, the attorney who represented him.

When Delia first learned of the lawsuit, she thought it might even be a good thing. Charles was so proud, taking on riskier and riskier surgeries. He thought he could do anything and do it well. He'd had very few failures in his career. He needed to remember that even he had clay feet.

Robyn Dixon convinced him to countersue, based on the fact—and it was a documented fact—that the patient had signed an agreement to have the surgery and therefore was duly informed of the risks. The countersuit claimed that the patient was causing him undue professional harm.

Delia had tried to talk Charles out of a countersuit. The poor woman and her husband had suffered enough.

Charles wouldn't hear of it. "It's never easy making decisions in matters concerning life and limb. Every surgery has its risks. She knew that. Bad outcomes are part of the medical profession. I'm only human."

If Charles really believed that, then why didn't he just admit he might have minimized any risk in his eagerness to have the patient agree to the surgery? He frightened the patient into thinking the aneurysm might kill her, but did he help her to understand that her life might never be the same, even with the surgery? In this situation, Delia thought his impatience and arrogance had interfered with his judgment.

But wasn't that the fatal flaw in Charles's character? He was never wrong, never at fault.

As Delia drove back to Stoney Ridge, she listened to her messages. There were quite a few from Will and Charles, increasingly frantic as they wondered where she was and why she wouldn't return their calls. She listened to two calm ones from Dr. Zimmerman's receptionist, asking her to call to schedule her follow-up visit, and then the voice mail said the box was full. She was just about to erase them all but decided to leave it full. She didn't want to hear anything more today. Not from anybody.

She pulled into the driveway and stayed in the car for a moment. Delia dabbed her eyes with an already damp tissue. Her face crumpled, and she started weeping softly.

Far above her flew the eagle couple, swirling in a courting ritual, skimming the distant trees, disappearing beyond the ridge. Their life was so simple. Why then did human beings not keep theirs simple too? Love, marry, till death do us part?

She was startled by a tap on her car window. Rose was waiting to speak to her. Delia didn't know what she was going to say. Ask her to leave, perhaps? She wouldn't blame her at all.

Until that phone message was left by Lois, Delia knew Rose had no idea why a stranger had arrived at Eagle Hill and collapsed like a rag doll. She was far too polite to ask, but now, it must have all become clear. She wondered what Rose told the family: Delia Stoltz's husband had left her for another woman. And a happenstance meeting with a stranger at a gas station convinced her to come here for her nervous breakdown.

Well, wasn't that the truth?

Delia opened the car door and stepped out.

"I need to take something over to the neighbor's," Rose said. "Would you like to come with me? Get some fresh air? It's a beautiful day. Not a cloud in the sky."

For the first time in hours, the tight, pained feeling in Delia's abdomen lessened a little. "I believe I would," she said with a hint of a smile.

So Rose and Delia took a loaf of extra bread over to Galen and stayed to watch him work his horses. They leaned against the top of the corral fence, transfixed by Galen's calm manner with very high-strung Thoroughbreds. Delia looked up. A dome of the lightest blue filled with air, with swirls and eddies of wispy clouds. She breathed in deeply, and felt the sweet air fill her with a buoyant optimism. Life, for just this moment, was good.

"I've been bringing fresh bread to Galen every other day, to thank him for tolerating the boys' help with his horses," Rose whispered. "Mostly, it's my excuse to spy on the boys and make sure they're behaving. But I do like to watch how Galen works with those prickly horses. He gets a look on his face as if he has a vision of what the horse will be like, once trained."

An Amish couple drove up in a buggy with a beautiful gelding tied behind them. Rose and Delia watched from afar as the husband explained to Galen that this horse had been a gift to his wife. The gelding had been a reliable horse, he was told from the previous owner, but now was behaving unpredictably in traffic.

The woman was quite upset. "I don't want to get rid of him. But I can't seem to get him to mind me. He bolts at the slightest thing."

Galen walked around the horse, stroked his neck. "The problem is you don't understand him."

"But I love this horse," the woman said. "I'm very kind to him."

"I didn't mean that you're mistreating him," Galen said. "Just the opposite. Horses from the racetrack are taught to go forward and run, no matter what. As long as they're headed in the right direction, forward, the trainers don't care how they behave. They don't want to kill the drive to win the race. So that's what the horse is trying to do now. Win the race."

The husband took off his hat and scratched his head. "What can you do to change that?"

"I need to work with him so he doesn't think running is the right choice. If he's in doubt or encounters the unexpected, he needs to pay attention to you."

The couple left the gelding in Galen's care. Delia overheard him tell Jimmy Fisher that most of the time the horse's training was just fine, and his job was about retraining the horse owners.

Delia wished Will could watch Galen work with these horses—he would find it fascinating, like watching a horse whisperer. Just being around Galen was very calming to the spirit.

She wondered what Rose thought about Galen. She was nice and polite to him, and he was as pleasant as could be to Rose, but now and then he seemed to look at her in a wondering sort of way. Why was that?

It was the kind of discussion Delia would have had with Charles over dinner, and he would vaguely answer as if he was listening to her, which he wasn't.

But there was the rub: there were so many things she wanted to tell Charles. Every day she thought of something new.

# 12

Call Jimmy Fisher what you will, but don't call him a quitter. He made a list of all of the spring mud sales that would be held in Lancaster County and decided to go to each one, every Saturday, handing out posters that described Lodestar. Someone, somewhere, must have seen his horse.

What he didn't expect was to find Lodestar at the very next mud sale of the season over at the Bird-in-Hand fire station. He had tied up his horse and buggy, picked up the posters he had printed, turned around and . . . there he was! None other than Lodestar. He dropped the posters back in the buggy, picked up a lead rope—something he had kept in the buggy in case he'd found Lodestar—and bolted to the stall where the horse was held. The chocolate brown horse looked healthy and cared for, which relieved Jimmy.

Jimmy stared at him, transfixed. This horse was regal—tall, elegant, confident. Jimmy held out his hand and the horse's ears perked up, thinking there might be a carrot. Lodestar edged his way over toward Jimmy and sniffed his open hand. With his other hand, Jimmy clipped the lead onto Lodestar's harness.

"Just what do you think you're doing?"

Jimmy spun around to face Jonah Hershberger. "You sold me this horse, square and fair."

Jonah tilted his head. "You're the one who didn't keep him in a place that could contain him."

"You put him in that pasture!"

"Temporarily. I was just doing you a favor by delivering the horse to you. Door-to-door service. It was your job to keep him from getting out. He's a stallion! All he needed was a whiff of a mare in season and he's out the door. If you're going to have a stud farm, you're going to have to pay attention to those kinds of things."

Jimmy frowned. That was a point he couldn't dispute. He hadn't given much thought to the mechanics of having a stud. Galen constantly chewed him out for not thinking into the future. "How did you find him, anyhow?"

Jonah looked at Jimmy as if his lantern seemed a little dim. "He found me. He's smart like that."

Dang! That *was* smart. Jimmy *had* to have this horse. "Look, I really need this horse."

Jonah sighed. "Then why did your check bounce?"

It bounced? Oh, boy. Jimmy was afraid of that. He wasn't exactly sure how much he had in his account when he had written that check to Jonah. He was hoping there had been enough. "I'll cover it."

Jonah looked at Lodestar. "You've put me to a lot of extra trouble." He rubbed his chin. "But there's something about you I like. I guess you remind me of me, a few years back. Okay . . . get me the deposit in cash this time, and we'll try it again." He stuck out his hand.

Jimmy looked down at it, looked over at Lodestar—what a magnificent beast!—and shook Jonah's hand. "Deal. I'll be back in an hour." He would get to the farmers' market and borrow the money from his brother, Paul. It was pretty generous of Jonah to give him a second chance, and to only ask for the deposit too. He was afraid he would want the entire amount, cash on the barrel. As he untied his buggy horse from the hitching post, he grinned. He thought about the large humble pie Galen King would be eating after Jimmy informed him that Lodestar was in his barn, safe and sound and ready to be the cornerstone of Jimmy Fisher's Stud Farm.

And if his brother was in a friendly mood and could be quick about lending him the cash, he might have time to stop in the Stoney Ridge Bar & Grill and check up on Bethany Schrock. He could tell he made her nervous—she always dropped or spilled something when he was around—and he got a kick out of that.

—☙ ◊ ❧—

As Saturday evening wore on at the Stoney Ridge Bar & Grill, Bethany felt more and more uncomfortable. First, she had told Rose she would be home by eleven and she wasn't entirely truthful to her about where she would be. She said she was taking a book over to M.K. Lapp's, which was the truth, though Rose gave her a funny look. Bethany should have thought of something besides a book. Everyone knew she didn't read much. And she certainly couldn't add on that she was working a late shift at the Grill.

What bothered her more than telling a half-truth was the group of men hanging out by the bar, drinking steadily, playing darts. Barflies, her friend Ivy called them. The Grill had a different clientele at night than during the day. On the wall was taped a full-page, full-length newspaper page of Osama bin Laden. "Go for the eyes," she heard them say as they threw the silver-tipped, evil-looking darts at the portrait. How awful!

Bethany steered clear of the bar as much as she could, but she had to walk past it to get in and out of the kitchen. One fellow, in particular, kept calling out to her in a slurry voice, "Hey, dollface, what's your hurry?" He sidled over to the end of the bar by the swinging kitchen door, trying to get her to talk to him as she passed by with a giant tray loaded with food for her table. "What time you get off tonight, sugar?" His comments took a turn for the worse as the evening progressed and his beer glasses emptied, and so did Bethany's temper. She had one more table to serve coffee, dessert, and collect the tab, then she would be done with her shift and could go home. But Slurry Voice made a critical mistake. He pinched her bottom as she walked out with a trayful of hot coffee mugs.

"Shootfire!" Bethany spun around, sending her tray toppling onto Slurry Voice. Hot coffee spilled over his shirt and pants.

"HEY!" Slurry Voice screamed, jumping back. He knocked into the man standing behind him, who shoved him away. Slurry Voice slipped on the hot coffee puddled on the ground and bumped into the back of someone else standing at the bar. A chain began of irritated barflies, overreacting, almost like a game of dominos—but it all seemed to be happening in slow motion.

At least, it seemed like slow motion to Bethany. Mouth agape, she stood frozen in the middle of the mess, staring at what was going on around her.

Someone approached Bethany from behind. Hard fingers dug into her arm and she was spun around abruptly, steered to the door. As she tried to slip out of this person's grip, he only hung on tighter. "You need to get out of here," an unpleasantly familiar male voice said. "I've got my buggy outside."

It was Jimmy Fisher, telling her what to do! What's he doing here, anyway? Outside by the buggy, she yanked her arm out of his grasp.

"I'm taking you home."

She glared at him. "What are you doing here?"

"I stopped in earlier today and found out you were working the late shift tonight. Had a hunch you might not realize what a Saturday night looked like at the Grill, so I decided to drop by."

She scowled. "How long have you been there?"

"Long enough to see what was going to happen after your shift ended."

"It hasn't ended! I still have customers in there."

"Doubt it." People were pouring out of the restaurant, eager to leave the chaos.

Bethany turned to him with a scowl. "You had no right to do what you did."

"What *I* did? How about pouring hot coffee down the pants of a customer and starting a brawl?"

She ignored that. "I could have handled the situation myself."

"Goodness, you're sassy. You beat any woman for taking the starch out of a man."

"I'm merely honest," Bethany said.

Jimmy practically lifted her into the buggy, then climbed in on the other side and snapped the horse's reins.

When a car passed by them, the headlights lit up the interior of the buggy. Her clothes! She was wearing her English clothes. She didn't even have on a prayer cap. Her Plain clothing was tucked in her cubby back in the restaurant. She would have to be as silent as snow as she entered the house. It was late, past midnight, but Mammi Vera was often awake during the night, prowling around the downstairs, fretting. Bethany hoped she might be sound asleep. Some things, she knew, were best left unexplained.

"Bethany, listen to me. I like excitement as much as anyone, maybe more than most. But you're way in over your head here. You need to quit."

In that instant, all her aggravation at Jimmy Fisher tumbled back. Here he was, telling her what to do again. She didn't speak to him the rest of the way home. Too furious. Too embarrassed, mortified at the thought of a creepy drunken man pinching her bottom. Too mad at herself. She never saw those things coming. They happened too fast. One minute, she's serving coffee, the next, she started a small riot.

If Jimmy hadn't been there . . . well, who knew how the evening might have turned out? She shuddered.

That was the thing about Jimmy Fisher. He had a way of making her feel as if her bonnet was on backward.

Jimmy Fisher was looking forward to church this morning as never before. He wanted to tell Galen that he was dead wrong about Jonah Hershberger. Lodestar was in a locked stall in the latched barn. And when he had stopped by the Stoney Ridge Bar & Grill and learned that Bethany would be working the late shift that night, he returned at the end of her shift . . . sensing she would need a little extra help. And he had been right—she was facing a very dicey moment. Best of all, he was sure she might be talked into going out with him sometime, if he ever had a little extra cash.

In the last twenty-four hours, he had made significant strides toward maturity and long-term thinking—two areas that topped the list of Galen's complaints about him.

He splashed cold water on his face and shaved so quickly that he nicked himself twice. He grabbed his shirt and took the stairs two at a time, stopping by the back door to jam his stocking feet into his boots. He hurried down to the barn, eager to check on Lodestar. As he came around the corner, he saw something that made his heart beat a little faster. The barn door was opened by about two feet. He gave it a push and walked inside. The sun was just rising on the horizon and cast a beam of light from the open door, down the interior aisle of the barn. Jimmy walked slowly down the aisle, holding his breath. When he got to Lodestar's stall, the door was wide open. The stall was empty.

The rising sun crested the tops of the hills that surrounded Galen's ranch. It had turned the clouds around it a coral pink and cast a pale yellow light over the fields that were just greening with the first shoots of spring.

Jimmy burst through the kitchen door of Galen's house and found him seated at the kitchen table, sipping coffee. Naomi was dishing up scrambled eggs by the stove and offered him a plate. He shook his head. Too upset.

"It happened again, Galen. I found Lodestar. Then he ran away again. I woke up this morning and he was gone. The barn door was open."

Galen chewed and swallowed a mouthful of scrambled eggs as if he had all the time in the world. "You latched the stall?"

He scowled at Galen. "Of course!" Of course he did. "I'm sure of it." He remembered latching it, then double-checking it. Didn't he? Could he have been so conscious of it that he neglected to actually do it?

"You'd be amazed at how wily some horses can be." Galen finished off the rest of his scrambled eggs. They were just the way Jimmy liked them—buttery, sprinkled with salt and pepper. His stomach rumbled.

Naomi brought over a plate of steaming waffles. "Didn't Dad have a buggy horse that could unlatch a gate with its lips?"

Galen laughed and helped himself to a waffle. "We had to get a combination lock, but that only worked until he learned his numbers. Finally wised up and got a key lock."

Jimmy wasn't listening. Deflated, he was in no mood for jokes. That must have been exactly what Lodestar had done. He should have spent the night in the barn, watching him. How could he have had that horse in his grip a second time, only to lose him? What were the chances he would get him back a third time?

"I'm going to get ready for church," Naomi said. Before she left the room, she turned and said, "Jimmy, if you change your mind about breakfast, you just help yourself."

Galen poured warm maple syrup over his waffle. "Where'd you find him?"

Jimmy watched the syrup run into the pockets of Galen's waffle. Maybe he should reconsider breakfast. Naomi was a fine cook and it was hard for a man to think straight on an empty stomach. "The trader had him. Said the horse had made his way back to him."

Galen froze, fork suspended in the air speared onto a bite of waffle. He put down his fork and made a small sighing sound, as if he'd heard this story before.

"What?" Jimmy took the plate of remaining waffles and poured maple syrup on top. Just the smell of the crisp waffle, smothered in melted butter and maple syrup, was lifting his spirits.

"Jimmy, you're never going to find that horse again. Even if you do, you'll never keep him."

Jimmy finished swallowing his bite. "What makes you say such bleak and gloomy things? This is why folks are scared of you, Galen."

Galen lifted his dark eyebrows. "You need to start thinking less like a man blinded by love and more like a horse trainer. There are plenty of other horses in the world."

"None like Lodestar."

"I'll help. We'll find another. Might take some time, but we'll get you a stud."

Jimmy finished off the waffles and eyed the bowl of scrambled eggs. He was definitely feeling more cheerful after eating something. If he had been smart enough to track Lodestar down a second time, surely he could find him a third time. "You are wrong, my friend, and I am going to prove it to you."

It was strange, thought Bethany, that you could go to sleep thinking one way, and awake the following morning thinking quite another. And so it was with her opinion about working at the Sisters' House. "I've changed my mind," she would say to Jimmy Fisher after church later today, if she could talk to him without anyone noticing. After all, she had her reputation to uphold. "I'll work for those old ladies."

Seated in a swept clean barn across from the men on wooden, backless benches, Bethany happened to steal a glimpse at Jimmy Fisher and was struck senseless by those blue, blue eyes. But as Bethany was here to worship God, she tried not to think about the color of Jimmy's eyes, or how he had rescued her last night from near disaster at the Stoney Ridge Bar & Grill and then acted like he was a knight in shining armor, which he wasn't. Then he caught sight of her peeking over at him a second time and gave her an audacious wink with a smile dipped in honey, which made her blush despite her best effort to keep her composure.

That Jimmy Fisher was no good and low down, with a bad character to boot.

He just sat across the room grinning like he always did, prouder than ever that he had made her flustered.

She lifted her chin a notch and turned her attention to the minister, who was preaching of days long ago, of a time when the Plain People suffered terribly for their faith. Sometimes Bethany listened to these old familiar stories. Sometimes she just let the words float around her while she drifted away on her thoughts. A barn swallow fluttered through a missing board to disappear into its nest in the rafters.

The minister was preaching now of how some of their ancestors had been driven from their homes and chased across Europe. Some had been burned alive, others whipped or stoned. Tongues were severed, hands and feet. She shuddered. She couldn't imagine feeling so passionate about something that she would be willing to be tortured for it, and that left her feeling guilty. Even today, the minister explained, there were hardships to suffer. Even in this land of plenty, the place where they had come to hundreds of years ago, to find freedom to worship God. Even here, there was pain, there was loss.

*That*, Bethany understood.

Her hands curled into a tight ball in her lap. Whenever she thought about her father, feelings of anger welled up inside. How could he? How dare he? He hurt so many people who trusted him. How could he have betrayed Rose and Tobe? And Jake too? All innocent people who cared about him. And then . . . he died. Rose insisted it was an accident, but Bethany had plenty of doubts. Death was an easy out. Her father was the very opposite of these martyred ancestors, who were willing to suffer for what they believed to be right and true. Her father . . . he was a coward.

So was her mother, for that matter. They both vanished when life took a sharp turn.

The minister's slow, singsongy voice was winding down to an end. Much time must have passed while Bethany's thoughts stayed on her father. She tried to shake off the unsettled feelings those thoughts left her with and push them away—that was why she didn't let herself think about him very often. Her gaze fell to her lap. She put a pleat in her apron with her fingers, then smoothed it out with her palm. She could smell the coffee brewing for the fellowship meal after the service. She listened to the chickens clucking in the yard through the open window, to the baas of the goats and the bleats of the sheep out in the pasture. During the silent and solemn moments of waiting for the minister to dismiss everyone, Bethany pulled her thoughts and feelings back together, like cinching a rope. It was much more enjoyable to think about Jake. Jimmy too.

After church, Bethany walked out of the cool darkness of the barn and blinked against the sudden wash of sunlight. Naomi waved to her to help serve tables. The women always served the men first. After the men had eaten, Naomi and Bethany grabbed a clean plate and sat next to each other at the end of the table. As Bethany spread church peanut butter over her bread, she asked Naomi if she had ever been kissed by a boy.

Naomi held her hands to her mouth, shocked. "Heavens, no!"

Bethany handed her the slice of slathered bread.

"Have you?" Naomi whispered.

She nodded.

"Oh, Bethany! Before you are married? Or even promised to someone? Oh my." She looked terribly concerned.

Suddenly, Bethany felt like a fallen woman. She often felt such pricks of conscience around her friend. Naomi was so pure and innocent and good and Bethany was so . . . tangled up and filled with doubts. "Well, it was the day I told Jake Hertzler that I was moving away. We were upset, you see, and didn't know when we would see each other again."

Naomi's face grew studious and she looked back at her plate. "Of course," she said at last, and sighed with relief. "Of course, it was a terribly emotional time. You were both overcome with sorrow. I'm sure it wasn't anything more than that. Just a heartfelt goodbye kiss."

Bethany nodded righteously, but she couldn't look her friend in the eyes again. She wondered what Naomi's reaction would be if she knew that she and Jake had kissed quite a bit, sometimes as passionately as if he was saying goodbye before heading off to sail the seven seas. As recently as a few days ago.

Some things, she decided, were best left unsaid.

# 13

Barn swallows darted in and out of the ceiling rafters. Galen had a mare's left rear hoof up on his thigh and was scraping caked dirt out of it with a hoof pick. Last evening, he noticed the mare looked a little lame and he wanted to check on her first thing this morning.

"Hello, neighbor."

Galen straightened up at the sound of Rose's voice. It was Monday, it was early, and he was in need of a shave. He wished he'd had a little warning that she was coming by.

Then he checked himself. Since when had he started worrying about what he looked like? Rose had seen him plenty of times looking pretty bad. Why did it suddenly matter? It shouldn't.

But it did.

He looked over the mare's neck at Rose and wondered how she was able to look fresh and pretty at this hour. He had a bunch of sisters—they sure didn't look like that at the crack of dawn. "Morning, Rose."

He could feel her eyes on him as he exchanged the hoof pick for a brush and began to run it over the mare's neck and withers. "Something on your mind on this rainy morning?"

"That coyote took down one of my sheep last night. An eagle was working on the carcass." She was trying to sound matter of fact, but Galen saw her shudder. It was a gruesome thing, what a coyote could do to a sheep. "I was hoping Jimmy wouldn't mind helping me move it before Sammy wakes up. It was his pet sheep."

Galen put down the hoof pick. "I'll take care of it."

"Isn't Jimmy here?"

"No. He's too busy chasing a horse he'll never catch."

"What do you mean?"

Galen straightened. "Two Saturdays ago, Jimmy decided he was going to be a horse breeder. He bought a colt off a trader that he thought would be his foundation stallion. Just like that." He clicked his fingers together. "No vet check. No paperwork about the colt's bloodlines. Not even a bill of sale." He shook his head. "My grandmother Jorie used to keep charts and graphs of her Percherons' traits, trying to find just the right match."

"Jimmy's learning a lot from you. Maybe it'll all turn out just fine."

"Oh, I don't think so. The horse is gone."

Her eyes went wide. "Gone? What happened?"

"Jumped the paddock and took off. That was the first time. The second time—he slipped out of his stall."

"Twice? The horse has gotten loose twice?"

"Twice." He lifted his chin. "Doesn't that sound a little fishy to you?"

"What do you mean?"

"There's an old scam called 'The Runner.' The trader sells the horse to a naïve buyer, but he's trained the horse to return to him with some kind of signal—a whistle or a clicker. Then he scoops the horse up in his trailer and sells him to the next easy target."

She looked at him, eyes wide. "Poor Jimmy."

Galen rolled his eyes. "Save your pity. That boy needs to learn everything the hard way. This is a lesson he'll never forget."

Disappointment showed raw in her face. "Galen."

"What?"

"He needs you. You could help him."

"What?" The word came out as a tiny squeak. He cleared his throat and tried again. "What? He hasn't been asking for my advice."

"Still, he's just a boy."

"He's twenty-two. Maybe twenty-three. Plenty of Amish boys have married by that age."

Her head snapped up. "You weren't."

Galen set his jaw at a stubborn tilt. "No. But I was entirely different—"

"Boys need time to grow up and become men." She ran a hand down the mare's long neck. "Jimmy reminds me of Tobe."

Galen gave a hard, short laugh, which caused Rose to give him a sharp look. Tobe Schrock? Jimmy Fisher reminded her of her stepson? If that were true, they might be waiting a very long time. Tobe Schrock had never impressed Galen. The last time he had seen him was a few days before he vanished into thin air. Dean Schrock had brought a goat home for the little boys but hadn't thought to buy feed for it, so he sent Luke over to borrow a bale of hay. When Galen reached the barn, he struggled to get the door open with the hay bale on his shoulder. Inside the barn was young Tobe Schrock, idle as usual, though there was plenty of work to be done. He sat on a wooden barrel playing a game of solitaire, using an upturned nail keg for a table. He glanced up at Galen, not even bothering to get off his duff to open the barn door. It evidently didn't bother Tobe to play while others worked, a fact that annoyed Galen. He was tempted to kick the barrel and send him sprawling. He hadn't, of course, but he had sorely wanted to.

"You of all people should be able to understand Jimmy. He lost his father when he was young, and his mother, well, you know what Edith Fisher is like. He's trying to become a man and he needs you in his life. You should be helping him find his way in the world, not feeling smug like he deserved what he got."

How was it suddenly Galen's fault that Jimmy did something stupid?

"Promise me you'll talk to him."

Galen wasn't about to make any such promise. Since when did the future of Jimmy Fisher become his responsibility? He was minding his own business when Deacon Abraham interfered—he hadn't even wanted an apprentice in the first place. And now Rose made it sound like it was his job to be a father figure to the boy.

"Sense gets wasted on people until they learn to ask for help. Jimmy has to learn. It's part of life," he said, knowing how callous his words sounded to her.

"I just don't understand you men. You won't listen to anyone's good advice, especially if it comes from a woman. You're all alike. Stubborn and proud and independent and unbending. Just like . . ." She seemed about to say more, but thought better of it and clamped her lips shut. "Sometimes," she added, "you have to keep talking until a person listens."

Her gaze met his over the horse's head. The silence between them took on a prickly tension, like a strand of wire pulled tightly between two fence posts.

As she turned to leave, Galen reached out and grabbed her sleeve. Her eyes were fixed on the hand that held her. In as gentle a voice as he could manage, he said, "I'll make sure that coyote doesn't trouble you again."

"It's part of life," Galen had told her.

What part? Rose wanted to ask. The part where a sweet little sheep had its belly ripped open by a vicious coyote, where a mother-in-law turned into a child, and a boy lost his dream of finding the perfect horse? How difficult did life have to get before someone stepped in? To come alongside and make it better. So much for living the Plain life, where one never needed to face life alone, never needed to be afraid.

Being Plain never meant being perfect, she could hear Bishop Elmo's voice say. Just yesterday in church, he had said it again. *Only God is perfect.*

She didn't expect perfection, but this hardness Galen had for Jimmy, for Tobe—it nettled her. How could Galen possibly understand? Rose thought. He wasn't married. He wasn't a parent. He hadn't raised a boy to become a man, only to discover that he had turned into somebody else entirely.

In many ways, Galen went out of his way to help her, as a neighbor, as a friend. But there was a part of him that remained aloof, separate, a little cold. It seemed nearly impossible for him to share his thoughts, his feelings. Sometimes, he seemed to her like a walnut that couldn't be cracked open with a sledgehammer. When she tried, like she just had, she saw the expression in his face change in a flash—surprised, confused, then annoyed—before he stiffened up like wet leather left in the sun.

It dawned on her that she didn't know how old Galen actually was, that he might be closer to Jimmy Fisher's age than to hers. Imagine that. Not all that much older than Jimmy Fisher. And yet, they were worlds apart.

On Monday morning, a day full of problems stretched in front of Bethany. First, she was going with Naomi to the fabric store to get some material for a new dress. Naomi went straightaway to the solid colors, but Bethany stopped by a lightweight fabric of bright blue waves. She stroked the printed fabric and was amazed at how soft it felt, as soft as the velvet nose on Rose's new colt. She felt a pang of longing.

Normally, Bethany didn't spend much time thinking about all the things she had given up after moving in to her grandmother's home: cell phones, cars, and lights that flipped on and off with a switch. There was usually a way to get the same thing done, even if it took a little longer. But it was another story entirely when it came to printed fabric.

Naomi came up behind her and said, "I can't imagine why any woman would wear a fabric like that. Men would stop seeing the real beauty of a woman if she were dressed in that."

Of course. Of course it would seem like that. Naomi would never understand why Bethany loved those prints. She was too good and pure and innocent. And she was right too. The Lord looked on a person's inside, but people—men, especially—looked on the outside.

Bethany wouldn't stay Old Order Amish forever. When Jake was ready to marry, she would return to the Mennonite church, become baptized, and be with him.

Just a little longer. Then she could wear all the prints she wanted to.

Bethany took a deep breath and walked over to the plain solid colors. She asked the shopkeeper to cut seven yards of a serviceable plum-colored fabric. As Naomi was getting her fabric measured and cut, Bethany walked by the wavy blue cloth one more time. What was it about that blue color that made her smile? The sight of it made her happy. Where had she seen it before? Then an image popped into her mind. It was the color of Jimmy Fisher's eyes.

Naomi dropped Bethany and her scooter off at the farmers' market and went home. Bethany waited until Naomi's buggy was out of sight, stashed her scooter behind the dumpster, and hurried to the Stoney Ridge Bar & Grill. Her friend Ivy met her at the door, eyes wide. "What on earth happened here on Saturday night?"

"Nothing!" Bethany said. "Well, other than a drunk fellow pinched me and I left early, but I had finished my shift." Almost finished.

Ivy seemed skeptical. "The manager wants to talk to you."

Bethany walked into the main room. Her jaw dropped when she saw the condition of the dining room. Chairs were overturned, tables were knocked on their sides. Ted, the manager, was bent over, sweeping up broken glass.

"It looks like a tornado swept through this room!" Bethany said, righting a chair.

Ted straightened to look at her. His voice turned to smoke. "An Amish tornado."

She swallowed. "Um, did this happen after I left on Saturday night?"

Ted gave her a look as if she might be one brick short of a full load. "Bethany, this job . . . it isn't right for you. Your paycheck is waiting for you up by the cash register."

Bethany could see the decision was made. She crossed the room to the cash register, stepping gingerly around broken bottles and stale puddles of beer, to find the envelope with her name on it. Ivy handed her a brown paper bag filled with clothing from her locker, then hugged her goodbye.

Bethany walked back to Ted. "What about my tip money from Saturday night?"

"Ah yes." He dug into his own pocket, pressed a tip into her palm, then closed her fingers around it. "Here it is." He turned around and went back to sweeping.

A one-dollar bill looked back at her.

Delia unpacked a few groceries in the little kitchen of the guest flat after she returned to Eagle Hill from a trip to the Bent N' Dent. She didn't want Rose to feel she needed to provide meals for her. Breakfast was enough.

As she tucked some apples in the fridge, she thought of the scene she had observed at the farmhouse last night. She had taken a walk up the hill behind the house to watch the sunset. As she came down the hill in the deepening dusk, her eyes were drawn to the only brightly lit room in the farmhouse—the rest of the house was dark. It was the living room, where Rose and the children were gathered around a board game at a table. Vera sat in a rocking chair nearby. Delia paused for a moment, touched by their pleasure over such a simple activity—laughing together, sharing a bowl of popcorn, eating sliced apples, having a wonderful time. Even Vera. A buttery glow from the kerosene lampshine in the room made the scene reminiscent of a Norman Rockwell or Thomas Kinkaid painting. It was so beautiful it hurt to look at it.

She couldn't help but compare what this farmhouse might look like if it were filled with a typical American family: every light in the house would be on and each adult or child would be in a different room, probably facing the cold glow of a television or computer. Maybe that wasn't a fair assessment of most Americans, but it would have been true of Delia's home.

Delia heard a knock at the door and went to open it, assuming it was Rose.

There stood Charles. His gray-green eyes looked icy cold. "May I come in?"

She took a deep breath and tried to keep her hands from shaking, told herself she could do this. She stepped away from the door.

Charles walked in and looked around the small room, then spun around to face her. "Did you realize the police hauled me off to the station for questioning? They accused me of doing away with you. Accused me of being a wife killer. *Me!*" He thumped his chest with his fist. "Did you think of that when you decided to vanish?"

She closed the door, then lifted her chin. "Of course I didn't. I should have told someone I was heading out of town. I never dreamed there would be such a fuss."

"And why here, of all places?"

"Why should that matter? Why should it matter where I've been?"

He narrowed his eyes. "Maybe it's a passive-aggressive way to try to get to me. Make a dig at my upbringing? Try to help me remember my humble roots?"

Charles's childhood was something he never discussed. He was raised Old Order Amish and left as a teenager to pursue college and a career in medicine. When she met him, he was a surgical resident. He told her he was estranged from his family—that they didn't believe in higher education and were ashamed of him for wanting more out of life than farming. Charles always said the word "farming" like it was a terrible disease—something to be avoided. Contact with his family over the years was minimal, despite

Delia's encouragement. He even attended his parents' funerals alone, insisting Delia and Will would be bored. She didn't push Charles on the subject. It wasn't worth it. Besides, it didn't make any difference.

"Do you realize that this was the town where Will interned for the game commissioner when he was kicked out of college? What were you thinking?"

She knew.

Maybe, subconsciously, that was the reason she had jumped so impulsively at Lois's suggestion. After Will had spent that spring on an Amish farm in Stoney Ridge, there was a change in Charles, a softening. He had even contacted his siblings to catch up on their news. That softening lasted until Will decided on vet school. Charles didn't think being a veterinarian would be enough of a challenge to his son. But Will's mind was made up, and Charles hardened again.

This time, Delia wasn't going to budge. She was going to hold her ground. "Sit down. I will explain, but I'm only going to say this once." Charles was a large man and tall, his stance a little threatening. She motioned to a chair but he didn't move to it, which didn't surprise her. "Not everything is about you, Charles." She sat in the chair by the window and folded her hands. Surprisingly, she felt remarkably calm. "I have breast cancer."

Charles sank slowly down in the chair.

"The day you told me that you were leaving me was the day I found out about the cancer. I was coming home to tell you, but your news trumped mine. Since then, I've had a lumpectomy. And I also found out that the . . . object of your . . . affections . . . is Robyn Dixon. I saw you in the car together, at the lawyer's office when we were scheduled to meet. That's the reason I left. I'm sorry it caused you a little inconvenience and bad publicity."

He seemed to be fighting to make sense of what she was saying. "Are the . . . were the margins clear?"

"I don't know. Dr. Zimmerman thought it was caught early, so I'm hoping so. I'll call in tomorrow and see if the results are in. I can't get reception out here, so I'll have to go into town."

She stood on wobbly legs and started for the door. "Now, if you'll excuse me, I believe we are finished with this conversation."

Charles didn't move. "Does Will know?"

She nodded. "We spoke on the phone."

He leaned forward in the chair and steepled his fingers together. "I'll call Zimmerman's office tomorrow. I want to see all the op notes and get the test results. There's a specialist in Boston I'm going to send you to."

"No. No, you won't. Dr. Zimmerman is an excellent doctor. You're no longer making decisions for me. I can take care of myself."

A muscle tightened in his jaw. "Don't be foolish, Delia. You have every reason to be upset with me, but—"

"I don't want you making any decisions for me. Not anymore."

He rose to walk toward her. She held up her hand as he opened his mouth to protest. "You must know why. I don't trust you, Charles. You have lied, you have cheated. You have destroyed our family. All that's left is mistrust. And sadness."

His throat moved up and down. For a moment, he looked away. On a shaky breath, he turned back to her. "I do have regrets, Delia."

"Regret." She gave a short laugh. "Like the regret you feel over the patient who had the stroke after the aneurysm surgery?"

Charles stared at her, his face settling into deep lines, and Delia stared back, her head held high, erect. "What does that have to do with us?"

She gave a short laugh. "Everything! You can't admit you make mistakes."

"I did not make a mistake in that surgery. But I do have regret for the patient."

"That's not the same thing as being sorry. Truly sorry." A flash of fury rose inside of her. "Has it ever occurred to you to apologize to that patient? Just to admit that you're sorry?"

"I said I had regret over that outcome!"

"No, your ego is bruised, but that patient's life is forever changed. So is her husband's life. You need to tell them how sorry you are. Sincerely sorry." She paused. "No, no. It's more than that. Not just a professional apology, without accepting any blame. You need to ask her to forgive you for not preparing her for the risks of surgery."

He looked at her as if a cat had spoken. "Do you realize what that would mean? What it could do to me, professionally? Legally? And it wouldn't change a thing."

"That's where you're wrong. I think that patient and her husband need something from you before they can move on with their life. I know you didn't intend to cause her any harm, but the fact is that she trusted you. She trusted you with her life. You need to ask for her forgiveness. You owe the woman that much."

For a moment Charles said nothing, and his mouth kept that tight, stern look. Then he sighed, rubbing a hand through his hair. "You're not being rational. I realize you're under a great deal of stress—"

"I believe we've both said enough," she said in a curt tone. She reached for the door handle and opened the door. "Please go."

She surprised him so, a stain of red flushed on his cheekbones. He looked at her now as if he'd never seen her before, as if she wasn't the Delia he had known for half his life.

Charles stopped at the threshold, reaching out a hand to Delia, but she flinched and he pulled it away. He headed out to his car. Before he climbed in, he gazed all around the farm. Then he gave his head a shake, as if he were dusting something off, and drove away.

As she saw the car disappear down the road, tears welled in her eyes. She had promised herself she wouldn't cry, but this was Charles and she had loved him so much. Her heart felt so bruised it was hard to breathe. *What happened to us, Charles? Our love was supposed to last forever.*

Maybe she shouldn't have said what she said. She shouldn't have blurted out that she had cancer, but the stunned look on his face was gratifying. She wanted to make him pay for the suffering he had caused. She wanted him to hurt.

She wished she could turn back time, to try to find the moment when they had started to lose each other, and to fix it.

More than anything, seeing him again, she realized she just wanted him back.

# 14

It was a beautiful afternoon in the first week of April, touched with a hint of spring. After Rose had helped Vera eat her lunch, she desperately needed some fresh air. It was strange how one person could change the mood of a room. Some could fill a room with excitement and energy. Jimmy Fisher was like that. Whenever he joined the family for dinner, which was happening more and more often, Rose noticed that everyone laughed more, ate more, lingered longer.

Then there were others, like Vera, who could drain off energy and joy, like siphoning sap from a maple tree. Her mother-in-law had a way of turning a sunny day into a dismally gray one. Well, she wasn't going to let Vera spoil this beautiful day.

Rose went out to the flower garden to pour clean water into the birdbath. Chase trotted behind her and ran off to chase a cottontail through the privet, the poor fool. He never caught a blessed thing, though he did his best. She noticed the "Inn at Eagle Hill" sign standing tall and stately at the end of the driveway. Galen had built it, Mim had painted it with her careful, deliberate penmanship, and Jimmy Fisher helped install it. It seemed so official to hang a shingle and the very sight of it brought delight to her.

She glanced over at the guest flat and noticed the curtains were still drawn. On Sunday, Delia Stoltz had a little spark back in her, but now, Wednesday, she seemed to be withdrawing into sadness again. Rose tried to ignore that spike of worry—the last thing she wanted to do was to grow attached to the guests.

But she just couldn't help it. She knew that Delia Stoltz needed Eagle Hill.

A few days ago, Rose saw Delia take a walk into the hills behind the farmhouse in the late afternoon. An unexplainable pity touched her heart as she watched Delia head up the path, head down, shoulders rounded, fragile and defeated. Yesterday, Rose walked next door to fetch the boys home for supper and couldn't pull them away until Galen had finished working with a jumpy horse. Galen displayed utter calm—a wonderful example for her sons to observe, especially Luke. When she returned home, Mim and Vera had informed her that Delia Stoltz had entertained a visitor in the guest flat. The male type—but he didn't stay long, they said. Vera commented on how fine looking the man happened to be, despite being English. Twice, she said it.

Rose had a hunch that fine-looking man might have been the doctor looking for his lost wife. She thought she should check on Delia, but the evening got away from her. Here it was a day later, nearly three, and she still hadn't had a moment to tend to Delia. Once the boys returned from school, the day was over.

Rose knocked gently on the guest flat door. When there was no answer, she opened the door and softly called Delia's name. The blinds were drawn to keep out the daylight, and it took a moment for Rose's eyes to adjust to the dimness. She found Delia curled up in a corner of the sofa, surrounded by a litter of crumpled, damp tissues.

Rose walked across the room to the window and pulled the cord on the window blind. Delia's eyes blinked rapidly as the bright noonday light streamed through the glass directly into her eyes. Rose's heart went out to her; she was a pitiable sight. "Delia Stoltz, you don't seem to me to be a woman without a backbone."

Delia remained still, facing her for a very long time, and then Rose saw tears well in her eyes and spill over onto her cheeks. "I know you want to help, but you don't know what I'm going through."

"You're right. I don't." Rose sat on the sofa, uninvited. "So tell me."

───◊───

Delia felt uncomfortable confiding in Rose, wondering if, behind that wide smile and those thoughtful gray eyes, she might be secretly judging her. But if she was, she gave no sign of it. After a few minutes, Delia felt more relaxed in her presence. She thought she might start crying again, but curiously, finally, she was out of tears.

Soon, everything spilled out. Drained and exhausted, she covered her eyes with one hand. "I'm alive. The cancer is gone, I hope and pray. I know I should be grateful for that, but I don't feel grateful. I feel completely lost." She opened her eyes, looking for answers in Rose's patient gaze.

Rose stood. For a moment, Delia thought she was going to put her arms around her and tell her it would be all right, and that would have made Delia furious. It wasn't going to be all right.

Instead Rose went to the little kitchen, picked up the trashcan, and started to fill it up with tissues. Then she went into the bedroom and made up the bed, tucking the sheets in so tightly Delia would have to pry them loose to get back into bed.

When Rose finished, she came back into the main room. She leaned against the doorjamb and folded her arms across her abdomen. "My husband had a knack for numbers and accounting. He started an investment company and, for quite a few years, he was very successful. More and more people heard about Schrock Investments. Dozens of our friends and relatives invested their life savings in the company. Then the recession hit and Dean had trouble keeping up those high returns. So he turned to riskier means to pay dividends. He was sure he could recoup the losses. But it all caught up with him. A year or two ago, everything started to fall apart. Everything.

"Dean had put our home up for collateral with bank loans and lost it. We had to move in here with his mother. The investors started to catch wind of Dean's problems and tried to pull their money out—but there was no money to pull out. It wasn't there. Dean declared bankruptcy. Not long after that, the police came to the house and told me Dean's body was found drowned."

Delia was stunned. "Your husband took his own life?"

Rose lifted one shoulder in a half shrug. "We don't know. We truly don't. He'd been having some racing heart troubles over the last year and refused to see a doctor about it. It was a very hot day, but why had he gone swimming in an unfamiliar pond? He wasn't much of a swimmer. The police declared it an accident—that he was a drowning victim, they said. I hope it was an accident."

"Didn't you have an autopsy? That might have answered your questions."

Rose looked down at the ground. "I refused it. Maybe that was a mistake. I don't know. Maybe I just didn't want to have my questions answered." She walked to the window and looked outside at the boys, pushing a wheelbarrow filled with hay toward the goat and sheep in the pen. "If Dean took his own life, our church believes he would lose his salvation. It's the ultimate way of turning against God. Of saying that God couldn't help a person out of a bad spot. I guess I felt it was better not to know why he died." She spun around to face Delia. "But then there's God's mercy too. Dean was stressed to the breaking point. I can't help but believe that God would understand. I pray so. I pray it every day."

Delia wasn't sure how to respond. She had never given suicide much thought other than pity. A terrible, terrible pity. She'd certainly never concerned herself about the afterlife.

"I was left to pick up all the pieces for Dean. I'm doing all I can to pay investors back what was owed to them. But this will follow me until the day I die. I want to make sure it doesn't follow my children." Delia saw her hands tighten into fists as she added quietly, "I will not let that happen."

"You have every right to be angry."

"Oh . . . believe me, I was. And I can be—it doesn't take much to flare it all up again. Whenever I get a call from that Securities and Exchange Commission lawyer with another twist and complication, I churn with feelings of anger all day long. But I know I can't live like that. I can't live on the precipice of anger. Husband or no, the world keeps on turning. I have children who need raising and a mother-in-law who needs tending to.

"So on those days, when anger returns, I go back to the beginning. I ask God to help me forgive Dean for not being all I wanted him to be, to help me forgive him so I can move on." Rose gathered a few dishes from the coffee table and put them in the kitchen sink. She turned on the hot water faucet and poured dish soap into the sink, swishing her hand to stir up bubbles. "Life doesn't always turn out the way we wish it would. Maybe we all have to get to the point in our lives when we face that fact. But I do know that God brings good things out of bad events. I've seen it, over and over. God doesn't waste anything. Not a thing."

Delia closed her eyes. "I don't know how to get there. How to get past the anger and disappointment. I wish I did, I wish I were more like you, but I just can't seem to do it."

Rose turned off the hot water and faced Delia. "For me, that's when I pray the prayer that always works."

"What's that?"

She lifted her eyes toward the ceiling and raised her soapy hands, palms up. "Help."

Two cars drove into the driveway, one right after the other. Rose rinsed off her hands and grabbed a towel as she went to the window. "The first car is our vet. She's coming to look at the colt. He's not eating enough. I don't know who is in the second car. A young fellow."

Curious, Delia rose from the sofa to join Rose at the window. "Why, that's Will. That's my son." It was the first time in weeks that she felt a genuine smile tug at her lips.

"Would you look at that," Luke said, excitement in his face. He had just arrived home from school and was delighted to see strange cars in the drive. He loved visitors.

The boys were standing in the doorway of the guest flat, watching Delia and her son embrace. Rose scowled fiercely at the boys until they backed off. She shooed them away to give Delia and her son a moment of privacy.

"Why's he crying?" Luke asked, as they walked to the barn.

"He's just unnerved—he's come a long way and I imagine he's just overcome at seeing his mother," Rose said.

"But he's a man," Sammy said. "Men don't cry."

"Men have tears in them, same as you," Rose said.

She went out to the barn to find the vet, a young woman named Jackie Colombo. Silver Girl's colt still wasn't thriving, so Jackie had come up with a few other remedies to help the little horse gain weight.

"He's just born a little too early," Jackie said. "Like a premature baby. I'll show you how to mix up some high-calorie meal for him." She carried a sheaf of hay to a worktable and took a knife to it, cracking and chopping that hay into baby-size pieces, almost like grain. Then she mixed it with some oats and a little molasses and a chopped apple. She held a handful out to the colt and he snorted over it suspiciously, but nibbled at it. He dropped more than half of it as he tried to chew it, but he went after the stuff he'd dropped. By the time Jackie was packing up to leave, his little sides were starting to fill out.

Sammy came bursting back into the barn. "Mom, something's wrong with the missus eagle!"

"What makes you say that?" Jackie asked.

Sammy turned to the vet. "She's screeching and screeching."

Rose's heart stopped. "Sammy, where's Luke?"

"He climbed a tree to get a close-up view of the eagles' nest."

The vet stuck her head over the stall door. "That nest must be forty feet high."

"I know!" Sammy said, proud of his brother's prowess. "He's up there!"

"Why would he try to get near the nest?" Rose said. "You boys know how dangerous eagles can be."

"We been watching them. They head up north during the day to hunt. They haven't been coming back to the nest by the creek till the sun starts dropping." Sammy's eyes were as wide as a dinner dish. "Luke said the nest was at least six feet wide and made mostly of sticks. Some of the sticks are bigger than me, he said. In the center of the nest is a soft spot made of grass and wool. Wool—from our very own sheep!" He took off his black hat, looking sheepish. "I almost forgot. Luke said he was having a little bit of trouble figuring out how to get down."

Even in the barn, they could hear the screeching sound of an eagle in distress.

"Something must be wrong with her." Sammy waved his arm at the vet. "It's good you're here. You can fix her."

"I wouldn't have any idea what's wrong with her," Jackie said.

"I do," said a man's voice. "She's defending her home. She's trying to warn you off. We'd better go get your brother out of that tree before she starts making a run at him."

They spun around and saw Delia's son standing at the barn door.

From her window, Delia watched Will escort the attractive young veterinarian to her car after the little boy was rescued from the tree. The two stood by the car, lingering. If Delia wasn't mistaken, she had noticed a spark or two between Will and the vet as they discussed the eagles. Of course, get Will on the topic of birds and he lit up like a Christmas tree. But wouldn't that be something—to have him find a girlfriend here, on an Amish farm? She smiled and dismissed the thought. Will always had a girl or two buzzing around him. Never anything serious, except for that one Amish girl, Sadie something-or-other, who had broken his heart. Delia only knew that because Will wouldn't discuss Sadie—he was pretty talkative about the other girls who had come and gone. Mostly gone. She hoped he would get serious about a girl someday. She was counting on grandchildren.

Earlier today, Will had finished a midterm exam and driven all afternoon to get here. For the first time, she saw not her son, full of boyish charm and mischief, but a competent and determined man.

Will told her he was going to stay with her until she was ready to return to civilization. "Even though you say you don't need my help, I want to hang around until you're back to your old self." He said the next part so firmly that she wondered if he was as confident about her recovery as he sounded. "You're going to get well, and I want to be there to help you do it. Is that such a terrible thing for a son to want to do? Help his mother, who's spent her whole life helping him?"

"No," she had said quietly. "Of course not, but I don't want you sacrificing the final stretch of your education just because of me. You're so close to the end. You need to finish and move on."

They agreed to a bargain. He would stay with her until she received the results about her lumpectomy. If the margins were clear, nothing in her lymph nodes, he would return to school. If they weren't, well, then they would decide together about next steps. She glanced at her watch. As soon as Will said goodbye to this lady vet, they should get into town so she could try to use her cell phone to call the doctor's office before it closed for the day. She finally felt ready to hear the results. It helped to have Will by her side.

She saw Rose herd those two boys up to the house. Rose moved lightly and quickly, Delia noticed, whether in the yard or in the kitchen. Often, she sang.

How she envied Rose. Just a week or two ago, if someone were to tell her that she would find herself envying an Amish widow, she would have laughed at the thought. Charles didn't speak much about his upbringing, but the truth of it was that she didn't ask about it. She wasn't interested. She didn't even ask Will many details about his spring on an Amish farm. If anything, it had embarrassed her to think her husband had been raised Plain, that he had looked like one of those little boys with black hats on. But there was something to this life, to these people. Maybe that's why Will had been so enamored with them. There was peace here.

Rose was a peaceable person. Delia repeated the word a few times. *I like that word peaceable,* she thought to herself. *It's what I would like to be.* She would try to be more like Rose.

Husband or no, the world keeps on turning, Rose had said. Add cancer to that list, Delia thought. Cancer or no, husband or no, the world keeps on turning.

During the rescue, for a few minutes or even longer, Delia had forgotten she had cancer. Forgotten that her husband had betrayed her. Maybe that's how emotional healing took place. Not all at once, but five minutes here and there. Hopefully, another minute each day. Perhaps by this time next year, she would hardly think about Charles.

As she pondered that, the strangest thing happened. A large news van with a satellite dish on top pulled into the driveway.

Will waved a hasty goodbye to the lady vet and came to the basement door. "That's another reason I thought it would be best if I come. The newspeople are still on this story about the disappearance of the doctor's wife. I saw a TV interview this morning with a scarlet-red-haired lady named Lois—she said you were tucked away at a charming new Amish inn in Stoney Ridge. She said you needed your peace and quiet, so everyone should leave you alone." He looked over at the news van. "So, of course, they came."

Vera sat at the kitchen window and watched Bethany hurry off to visit with that neighbor girl, Galen's sister. What was her name? Vera couldn't recall. She dismissed that hanging question and turned her attention back to her darling granddaughter. Even as a child, Bethany always did tend to flit through the house like a bird, too full of energy to sit still. Just like Dean had.

Vera adored Bethany, always had. She smiled, or at least she tried to smile. Her thoughts drifted to Rose, cruelly setting the washstand mirror near her bed this morning. Vera had turned and caught a glimpse of herself in the mirror. The image of the droopy side of her face mocked her and she burst into tears. Rose quickly took away the mirror—but it didn't lift the sadness weighing on Vera's heart.

She couldn't believe what Bethany—dear, dear Bethany—did next. She realized how upset Vera was. She rubbed Vera's back and said it was the most precious smile in all the world, crooked or not. That's what the sweet child said about her, right in front of those children and in front of that mean-spirited daughter-in-law.

*The most precious smile in all the world.*

Vera sat up straighter and sighed. "Nothing has worked out like I thought it would." One little comment in a letter—inviting Dean to come live with her after she learned that his house had been foreclosed—and things had started to happen, things Vera couldn't see the end of.

When Dean had told her they would accept her offer to move in, she thought it would mean no more worry. No more loneliness. Rose and Bethany and that feisty one could tend to her like daughters should tend to mothers and grandmothers.

But Rose and Bethany didn't tend to her like she thought they would. Rose didn't neglect her in any way that Vera could put her finger on, and the children were good to her, minding her when she asked, but there were many times when she felt left out of the life of her own household. Rose was completely absorbed with the constant demands of those children—and Vera didn't particularly like children. They were noisy and messy. Sweet Bethany immediately started working at that farmers' market. All day, nearly every day. She was sure that Rose was behind that. Rose worked those children too hard. Bethany, mostly.

When Bethany told her that she wouldn't be working at her job any longer, Vera was thrilled. When she expressed delight that Bethany would have time to tend to her, Rose said no. She said Bethany needed to find a job outside the house. *Insulting!*

It was a worry that Vera's tiniest suggestions were never appreciated. And then she had these awful strokes, and it seemed all she ever did was worry.

Rose would tell her there was nothing to worry about and then mangle Scripture in that way she had, quoting an English Bible when the Amish only used the Luther Bible: "'Do not worry about tomorrow, for tomorrow will worry about itself. Each day has enough trouble of its own.'"

Each day had trouble enough of its own. You didn't have to be a preacher to know that was true. But a thing may be as true as death and taxes and still be hard to put into practice.

But for today, Rose would remind her, they had enough. And enough was as good as a feast.

Enough. Enough to keep food on our table and a roof over our heads.

Wasn't that what Rose was trying to do with this notion of turning the farm into a . . . what was it? What did you call a place where you rented out rooms? Oh . . . it didn't matter.

What worried her most was that Rose was disgracing the family and didn't seem the least bit ashamed about it. And she just completely ignored all of those horrible reporters who wanted to know more about the doctor's wife. She'd like a minute or two with those reporters and tell them what she had to say on the subject: that doctor's wife should just scoot on home, that's what Vera thought.

No one in Stoney Ridge had ever run a—what was it? . . . a boarding-house?—from their home. She'd heard of such liberal Amish a few towns over, but never in Stoney Ridge. Vera shook her head. Dean's memory deserved far more. He would never have allowed his family home to become a . . . way station for travelers.

Vera struggled to find the word that Rose now used for this farm—the very farm where Vera had lived since she was born. Where her parents had been born. Bed and Bath? Bed and Butter? It was hard for her to remember so many things at once. It never was before. She stared at her right hand. Useless thing. *Come, now. Move. Open just a little.* Just the fingers, could she make a fist? What good was she without her hands? She couldn't roll out pie dough or make noodles. She couldn't pin hair. Sew, knit, garden— those were all lost to her. Such simple, everyday activities and things. How many hundreds of pies had she baked? How she'd loved to brush Bethany's long hair and pin it in a tight bun.

Vera stared at her right hand again. She noticed the half-done quilt tucked in a basket in the corner of the kitchen, where it had sat since she took sick. With that right hand, hadn't she knotted comfort quilts for sick folks and prisoners and orphans?

Rose had left the *Budget* out for her to read, turned to scribe letters from friends in Ohio and Indiana. Trying to determine what the newspaper said had nearly driven Vera crazy. The letters were all jumbled up for her. She'd read stories to Dean as a child. Now she would have to be like a child and have others read to her. Terrible!

Vera did appreciate what Rose did for her. She did. She had messed her bed this morning and Rose didn't say a word. She had brought her the mirror to distract her and quietly changed the sheets. Vera overreacted to the mirror because she was embarrassed about messing the bed. She knew that about herself.

She also knew that Rose was trying hard to find ways to keep the family together and solvent. But Vera couldn't let emotions cancel out her common sense. She refused to go soft over this terrible idea of turning their home into a Bed and . . . Brothel? No, no, that didn't sound right.

Besides, no one knew Rose like Vera knew her. They didn't hear the roof-raising argument Rose had with Dean on the evening before he died. Poor, dear Dean. Vera came from a generation of women reticent to argue with men. Vera always felt Rose was hardest on Bethany and the other one—the boy, that one who looked just like Dean. The one who ran away. Tobe! That was his name. He ran to get away from Rose, Vera was convinced of that. Why else would the boy have run?

Speaking aloud to the empty kitchen, she declared, "Why won't God heal me? Haven't I been serving him right along? Why me?" She no longer had anything to offer. And even worse, Rose wasted time to have to tend to her as an invalid. Vera had to ring a bell and stop everything if she needed anything at all. It was a terrible thing to have to be such a burden to others. A terrible, terrible thing.

Vera picked up the bell with her left hand and rang it as loud as she could.

Chase seemed to be patiently waiting for Delia to return from town. He greeted Delia and Will's car with his crooked dog smile, as if he knew what she knew. When Delia climbed out of the car, she reached down to pat Chase. The silly dog lifted his head to meet her hand and wagged his tail like a whirligig. Then he collapsed in a fury of friendliness.

Rose walked out on the porch of the farmhouse and waved.

Delia couldn't hold back her news. She cupped her hands around her mouth and shouted, "The cancer is gone! They caught it in time. It hadn't spread, not even to one single lymph node."

Will was grinning from ear to ear. "Rose, I think that sign of yours is spot-on."

Rose walked over to join them. "What do you mean?"

"That phrase, under 'Inn at Eagle Hill,'" Will said.

"What phrase? I haven't seen the sign close up yet—and now with those reporters, I don't want to go anywhere near the road." Rose turned to Mim, who had come outside to see what all the excitement was about. "Mim, what did you write underneath 'Inn at Eagle Hill'?"

Mim started blinking rapidly. "A Latin phrase: *Miracula fieri hic.*"

"Do you have any idea what it means?" Will said.

"No," Mim said, her face pinching with worry. "I read it in a book and liked how it looked."

Will grinned. "It means 'a place where miracles occur.'"

# 15

It was starting to become a habit for Jimmy Fisher to appear, magically, right at suppertime at Eagle Hill. Rose always invited him to stay and, of course, he always accepted.

Tonight, about the time Jimmy was due, Bethany pinched her cheeks for extra color. She peeked out the kitchen window and saw him approaching, one hand on Luke's shoulder and the other on Sammy's, steering them along the path from Galen's. Clearly, they had gotten into some kind of mischief over at Galen's. It was written on their faces. She hurried out to the porch and scowled at them before sending them in to wash up for supper.

"Those two boys are headed down a dangerous and slippery path," Jimmy said. "They pay me no mind."

"Join the club."

Jimmy had his eyes on the road where a news van was parked. The large satellite dish on the roof of the van was facing Eagle Hill. "What's going on over there?"

"Something to do with the doctor's missing wife, who was never missing in the first place. But never mind about that. I need to talk to you about something." She bit her lip. "Okay. I'll take it."

He gave her a sideways glance. "What exactly is the 'it' you're talking about?"

"That job at the Sisters' House."

"You're going to have to interview for it. I'll certainly put in a good word for you, but they're persnickety ladies."

Well, that was unsettling news. She thought she had the job if she wanted it.

He sat on the porch step and pulled off his muddy boots, one after the other. "I thought you were happy at the Stoney Ridge Bar & Grill."

She gave him her silkiest smile. "I was. I am. I'm just thinking of trying something new."

Jimmy rested the heels of his hands against the porch flooring and slanted her his superior look. "Liar."

Those blue eyes were much too perceptive. He was right, she was lying. She never lied! Well, hardly ever. Jimmy Fisher had a way of making her say things, do things, that were not herself. "Fine. I lost my job over that tiny little misunderstanding on Saturday night."

"From what I heard, it turned into a rip-roaring brawl."

Shootfire! How did he always know so much? "Are you going to help me get the job or not?"

"I'll do what I can, seeing as how you're so sweet and polite about it." Then he smiled at her, a sweet smile this time, and went inside the house like he owned the place.

Jimmy was an odd fellow, always good-natured and cheerful. His grin was like a flash of light. It was like the sun coming up at dawn; it changed everything.

When Rose woke early for her walk, she stopped abruptly as she came down the front steps of the porch. She was stunned to see that there was double the number of news vans out front than there had been last night. Hours after the first one showed up yesterday, Eagle Hill was crawling with reporters.

One reporter had walked right into the house while Rose and Bethany were scrubbing dinner dishes, reached into his black shoulder bag, pulled out a camera that he hung around his neck by a strap, took out a lined notepad, and laid it on the kitchen counter. He looked around the kitchen, squinting, and scratched his chin. "Somebody called the news desk and told him about your bed-and-breakfast. My editor thought it was a good human-interest story for the weekend section, so here I am."

Fortunately, Galen happened along to return Luke's forgotten hat, sized up the situation, and politely escorted the man off the property.

Then the game commissioner arrived, tracking the eagles that were building a nest on the farm. He shooed reporters farther away and ribboned the farm with yellow caution tape. The reporters camped out across the road and set up to film short clips for the evening news. The Inn at Eagle Hill sign featured prominently in the foreground.

Rose ordered her family to stay in the house. She was grateful to Delia's son for being willing to talk to the reporters and the game commissioner, whom he seemed to know. It was baffling—all that had happened in the last few days. When Monday morning arrived, she had thought she was facing a typical week. The children went to school. Vera complained about Rose's housekeeping. Luke came home from school with a note from the teacher that he had done something foolish. Nothing unusual in any of that.

Suddenly, her house was surrounded by predators. All because a woman with a famous husband needed a little time to herself.

Delia had offered to leave right away, but Rose wouldn't hear of it. God had brought her to Eagle Hill for healing. Rose was sure of that now, and she didn't want to see her leave until she was good and ready to go. No doubt, she told Delia, the reporters would move off as soon as another story broke.

But that was before one of the reporters translated the Latin saying about miracles that Mim had painted on the Inn at Eagle Hill sign. The story grew bigger. And bigger. It had been picked up on the internet, Bishop Elmo told her last night, when he dropped by with a brush and paint and politely asked her to remove that Latin saying. With every news account, the Inn at Eagle Hill became more peaceful, more beautiful. A place where miracles abounded. Ready for the picking, like ripe cherries on a tree.

On this morning, Wednesday, the reporters were still staked out on the road, so Rose went the other way, toward Galen's property. Usually, Chase liked to come along with her, but he was sleeping in Mim's room— probably curled up right on her bed—and she didn't want to disturb them. She took a hillside path that her boys had carved and stood at the top to take in the sight. The air was so crisp and clear that the rising hills in the distance weren't layered, but alone and separate.

Rose relied on these quiet moments. She needed to get off by herself and listen to the sounds of the country, to pray and to think. She was accustomed to feeling pressed from dawn till dark, bound in by the small but constant needs of others. Not until she felt fortified again—felt that she could lead the family—would she return to the farmhouse.

Here, high in the hills, she could relax and pay attention to other sounds. There were sounds, she thought, that belonged just to early morning. The country talked quiet: one human voice could drown it out, particularly if it was a voice as loud as Luke and Sammy. On a still day, those boys could be heard at least a mile, even if they were more or less whispering.

A mourning dove called in the distance, and somewhere in a nearby tangle of bushes, its mate trilled out a reply. The eastern sky was red as coals in an oven, lighting up the hillside. She watched the process happily, knowing it would only last a few minutes. The sun spread reddish-gold light over the trees, making them look like they were on fire. It would be gone soon, and the day would begin. A sunrise was tribute enough to the glory of God.

She saw Galen on the far side of the hill, rifle tucked under his arm. She waved and called out to him. "Any luck?"

At the sound of her voice, he turned, spotted her, waved, and crossed over to meet her. "He was in the trap."

What a relief! She would sleep easier without that mournful howl of the coyote. At least one thing in this day was starting out right. She tilted her head. "Galen, just how old are you?"

He looked surprised. "Thirty-one. What's that got to do with a coyote?"

She grinned. "Just wondered."

He took a step closer to her. "So how old are you?"

"Thirty-six. Thirty-seven come August."

He whistled two notes, one up, one down. "Practically ancient. Closing in on Vera's age."

Rose smirked. "Well, I hope I am not that ornery."

"No. There's a difference between strong coffee and bitter medicine."

She laughed out loud. "Galen King, you are a sore trial and a wonder. Both." Then he held her gaze and she blushed.

Galen was not as handsome as black-haired Dean, but there was something about him. In so many ways he was gruff and abrupt, but in his way with Rose, he was always gentle and she could always count on the truth from him. A true friend. "Remember when I told you the eagles' nest would be a blessing to us?"

He nodded.

"The police chased those reporters off the property and warned them to stay away because the game commissioner complained that they would disturb the eagles. So . . . blessing number one."

A corner of his mouth lifted. "Number one?"

"Yes. Something about those eagles choosing our home makes me feel blessed. A sign that God is with us."

"But God is always with us, Rose, whether we think it or not."

"Yes, but sometimes it's nice to have a reminder."

A blast of cold wind came over the ridge and Rose shivered. Galen reached out and adjusted the collar of her coat—Dean's old coat. Warm, callused hands brushed against her neck as he pulled up the collar and straightened it. "I won't let you chill." He rumbled the words in a soft, deep voice.

Rose lowered her gaze. "I'd better get down the hill in case Vera is ringing her bell." On the way down the hill, she pressed her hands to her fiery cheeks. How could such a simple gesture feel so intimate?

Galen felt uncertain. He exhaled a deep breath as he watched Rose hurry down the hill. He tried to reason out what had just happened. His heart was pounding like a teenager's, an odd staccato that echoed in his ears.

It troubled him that Rose skittered off just now like a frightened cottontail. He thought of what Jimmy Fisher had scolded him about recently—that the more he stayed apart, the more his presence made folks nervous.

"It's hard for normal people to relax around you, Galen," Jimmy had said. "You've never been relaxed yourself, so you don't know what you're missing."

The last few months, he felt as if he had been missing something in life.

His wants had always been simple. When his mother passed, and then his father was called home, he willingly took on the mantle of seeing his younger siblings to adulthood. He never resented that obligation. He was a man who felt responsibility keenly. He took great satisfaction in his work as a trainer of Thoroughbreds. It was challenging, interesting, and useful to the community. And sometimes, on a warm summer afternoon, he did like to catch a couple of cooperative fish, griddle size.

Was that enough? It had been. It used to be.

Sometime during lunch recess, when the students were playing a game of softball, Danny Riehl left a note in Mim's desk. It read "Be at the phone at 5 PM tonight. DR"

So Mim was at the phone shanty at 4:30. The phone call came in at 5:00 p.m. on the dot.

"Hello," she said, waiting to answer until the third ring. She didn't want to seem too eager. Bethany was always telling her that boys didn't like overly eager girls.

"Hello," Danny said. "You can see the moons of Jupiter tonight. Through my telescope. Around ten. I'll be there, at the hill behind the schoolhouse, I mean. Then I could walk you home. Or not," he added quickly.

Stargazing with Danny Riehl!

"Okay," she said.

"Okay," Danny said.

Then the phone went dead. Danny hung up without saying goodbye. As soon as Mim put the phone back in its receiver, the phone rang again.

She waited for the third ring. "Hello?"

"Goodbye," Danny said and hung up.

There was one bright spot about not having to work at the Stoney Ridge Bar & Grill: Bethany had more time to hunt for Tobe's books. She had searched the house through, but to no avail. The attic was all that remained. No one ever went into the attic, which probably meant the books were there, hidden beneath cobwebs. She shivered. She hated spiders. Hated mice. But then she cheered up—the books were in the basement up until a month ago, when everything had been shuffled around to make room for the inn. How many spiders could have found those boxes? Surely, not many.

She took the largest flashlight she could find and climbed the rickety stairs to the attic. Standing in the middle of the attic, she turned in a circle and shined the light on the walls and floor: old furniture, grimy trunks, dusty boxes that had been stacked in place for years. But then the light shined on boxes that looked new. They weren't dusty, and they had Rose's handwriting on them. Her heart beat fast. She ripped open the tape on the boxes. Inside were Luke and Sammy's baby clothes, shoes, some drawings Mim had made in school, a Mother's Day card signed by Tobe, the first nine-patch quilt square Bethany had made, which looked more like triangles. It was terrible! Why had Rose saved *that*?

In the last box was a bundle of letters tied in a blue ribbon, addressed to Rose, written by her father, dated before they were married.

Tears pricked Bethany's eyes at the sight of her father's graceful handwriting. She wouldn't cry. She wouldn't.

Taking care, she put the letters back in the box and folded the box top. In her mind, she crossed off one more room on her mental list. Tobe's books were not in the attic.

A beam from a thin moon streamed in the window. It fell across Mim's bed and onto the rug. She lay on top of her bed, fully dressed, until she heard the bongs of the grandfather clock in the living room hit half past nine, then tiptoed downstairs. The house was dark, silent. She grabbed the flashlight her mother kept by the kitchen door before she quietly slipped out, then hurried to the hill behind the schoolhouse. An owl hooted and she stopped short, then laughed silently at herself. She stood for a moment, listening to the saw of the crickets, the gentle purr of the creek, the soft soughing of the wind, and her heart felt full.

High on the hill behind the schoolhouse, she saw Danny stooped over the telescope, peering through it. She called out to him and he straightened, then waved.

When she reached him, he stepped back from the telescope so she could peer into it.

"What am I looking at?"

"Jupiter. You can see the four moons."

She squinted her eye and saw small dots of bright light all in a row and horizontal with the face of the planet. "I think I can see those moons. I actually can!"

"Those are the same four moons that Galileo saw with his first telescope five hundred years ago. Now scientists know that Jupiter has over a dozen moons, but I can only see the four with this telescope."

She stepped away so Danny could have a turn. He peered through the small lens and turned a few knobs on the long tubes of the telescope.

"All of the moons orbit the planet in the same plane, but at different distances and speed, so each night they're different. Tonight's a good night to see them."

She gazed up at the dome of the sky. "What's that bright spot. A star?"

Danny kept peering through the telescope. "If it's in the west and it's lying low, it's Venus." He straightened up to see where she was gazing. "Pretty soon, we should be able to see Mars coming up in the east. Mars looks red compared to the brightness of Venus."

Here, standing next to Danny in the crisp night air, with the black velvet sky dotted with diamonds, it was hard to feel as if anything could be wrong in the entire world.

Danny walked Mim all the way back to the end of her driveway, which she thought was very gallant. One more fact to add to her list about Danny Riehl. He was a gentleman.

They stopped to watch a little bat bounce through the air, taking bugs for his supper.

"Did you finish writing your vocabulary sentence?" Danny asked.

It was due tomorrow. Mim had been working at it all week, thinking of it nearly as often as she thought of stars and planets. And Danny. She recited it out loud to him: "The sibilant sound of the snake, eyeing the ort by the porch steps, was drowned out by the pother of my sudorific siblings, who refused to kowtow to danger."

"I like it," Danny said. "It's very clever and smart. And it succeeds at meaning nothing."

That was another true fact to add about Danny. He was incisive. A very incisive boy. It meant smart and insightful. Besides collecting facts, Mim collected words. In the very second when she looked toward him, he looked toward her. Then each turned away.

"I might be leaving Stoney Ridge," Danny said, scuffing the ground with the top of his shoe.

*Leaving?*

"Going where? When?" Mim wondered, her eyes bigger than her head. "You don't mean moving away?" *But . . . but . . . but . . . what about me?* She felt a pinch of panic in her tummy.

"My parents are talking about moving to a new settlement. Someplace in the south. My dad's cousins live there and said there's lots of good land that isn't expensive. They want us to come too. My dad wants to go, but my mom isn't sure." He bent down to tie his shoe. "One good thing is that it would be close to NASA. That's the headquarters for astronauts. You can see spaceships and moon rocks if you visit. I'd like to see NASA. My dad said that maybe we could go there sometime." He straightened and poked his glasses up on the bridge of his nose.

Mim felt another pinch in her tummy. Would Danny still want to be almost-an-astronaut if he saw moon rocks and spaceships? Or would he want to be a full-fledged astronaut?

Mim walked up the porch steps feeling very droopy, very down in the mouth at the thought of Danny going away. She felt like crying, and her mind was a pinball machine of exasperation with herself, with all of life. She tiptoed upstairs and flung herself into bed, but couldn't sleep. So she went to the window and opened it, propping her elbows on the sill. She looked out over the farm, listening to the sounds of night, letting her thoughts roam at random.

She tried to imagine what her mother would say if she told her that Danny, the boy she loved, was going away. If she knew that Danny wanted to be almost-an-astronaut. If he didn't come back from NASA headquarters, not ever. "You'll manage," she could hear her mother say. "Life will go on."

But Mim saw change coming, and that was always a worry.

# 16

Delia wondered if life was returning to normal for Charles, if he was proceeding with the legal separation. She told Will to go ahead and let his father know that her cancer was gone after he was back at school. She wondered what that news would mean to Charles. Relief from guilt, she supposed.

Trying to be more like Rose had not been going quite as well as Delia had hoped. She still wanted to wound Charles. She wanted him to hurt as badly as she hurt. She needed to work on this. Even though Delia didn't know her well, Rose didn't seem to harbor such evil thoughts toward her late husband. Or toward that sharp-tongued mother-in-law, either. Delia could hardly tolerate more than a brief encounter with Vera. She reminded her of a librarian who spent her days shushing people. Whenever Delia happened to see her in the yard or at the farmhouse, Vera would fling darts, such as, "Mercy, are you still here?" or "Isn't it time you scooted on home?"

Delia didn't want to scoot on home.

Before Will left, he had asked her how long she intended to stay in Stoney Ridge and she hadn't had an answer for him. She had the strangest feeling about this subject—as if she shouldn't leave. Not yet. She wasn't sure what it meant or where that gut feeling came from, but it felt as if a journey had begun for her and she still needed her travel documents. That sounded crazy, but that's how she felt. There was something she needed to get—to receive—before she left.

Delia had come to admire the genuineness of these Amish people. Their faith in God, especially. She had always perceived God as belonging in a compartment, like a piece of a pie that made up a life. Rose spoke about God as if all of life belonged to him. God was the piecrust, holding the pieces of life together. In fact, the strength of Rose's faith was part of why Delia had gone back to church last week. Rose seemed so happy and at peace even though she had been cast some serious blows. She hoped a little of what Rose believed would rub off on her.

When Delia was first getting acquainted with Rose, she seemed so calm and content that Delia honestly thought she might not be all that bright. She was embarrassed to admit it, but it was true. Most smart people she knew, including Charles, were forever complaining about the state of the world. They had all kinds of opinions on all kinds of subjects, but she'd rarely seen any of them do anything besides complain. As far as they were concerned, the world was bad and getting worse.

Rose didn't seem to trouble herself about the condition of the world. She was the kind of person who didn't discuss problems—she quietly set to work to solve them. And she had plenty of problems: her animals, her children, her cranky mother-in-law.

Rose was clearly a very intelligent woman. Delia's friends, no doubt, would have scoffed at the simplicity of the Amish life. After all, an eighth grade education? She could just hear the disdain drip from their voices. They valued higher education—the higher, the better. They would start to question the veracity of Rose's contentment—believing she was an oppressed woman who had no choices.

Rose was anything but oppressed. She spoke her mind and then some. It surprised Delia to see how she refused to answer those reporters' questions. She went about her business and acted as if they weren't even there—which, in a way, was worse than showing anger or upset. Being ignored was the very worst thing of all.

Of that, she had no doubt.

꧁ ◊ ꧂

On the way home from school, Mim would stop and get the mail from the mailbox. It was her job, hers alone, always had been, and she gave Luke and Sammy the what for if they beat her to the mailbox. Soon, Luke would be taller than her. Getting the mail first was one of the few ways she had to remind him she was older than him.

The mailman handed Mim a large bundle of mail, bound with rubber bands. She was astonished. Ordinarily, the mail contained a bill or two, a letter, a *Budget* newspaper, and some advertisements. As she walked up the driveway, she pulled off the rubber band and sifted through at least ten letters, addressed to Mrs. Eagle Hill Inn or Mrs. Miracle.

When Mim got to the house, she found her mother in the kitchen, washing the floor. She stopped at the threshold and waited until her mother noticed her.

"Where are the boys?" her mother said, a worried look on her face.

"They went straightaway to Galen's. Jimmy's setting off firecrackers today."

Relief covered her face. "Oh good . . . this floor will have a chance to dry." Half the floor was slick with soapy water.

"Is Mammi Vera awake?"

Her mother sloshed some soapy water on the floor and spread it around. "Not now. She's napping." Just then, a rat-a-tat sound came from next door. "Well, she *was* napping until Jimmy Fisher started his fireworks."

Mim helped herself to a chocolate chip cookie. Then she remembered the mail. She pointed to the bundle of letters she set on the counter. "Here's the mail. A bunch of letters are addressed to Mrs. Miracle."

Puzzled, her mother tossed the scrub brush on the floor and stood. She opened one letter, then another, then another. Then she shook her head and dropped the letters on the counter. She didn't even open the rest. "It's all because of those reporters." She pushed a lock of hair off her forehead. "I guess we can be expecting another visit from the bishop."

"What do the letters want? Reservations to stay here?"

Her mother bent down, picked up the scrub brush and dipped it in the bucket of soapy water. "No. They're asking for advice. They think the inn spits out miracles like a soda pop vending machine. They think we've got the solutions to all their problems."

Now *that*, Mim thought, was intriguing. "Are you going to answer the letters?"

"I should. I need to put a stop to them. I don't want folks to think of this inn as anything more than a nice place to stay. But with your grand-mother needing extra help, I don't know when I'll have the time to write them back."

Mim watched her mother slosh some soapy water on another section of the linoleum and scrub in circles. "Maybe I could help."

Her mother stopped scrubbing and looked up. "Really? Would you, Mim?" A big smile covered her face.

Mim loved her mother's smile. It was like the sun coming out and filling the room with light.

"All you need to tell people is that only God makes a miracle. That's all. You don't need to try and solve their problems."

Oh, but Mim loved to solve problems. "If I can use your typewriter, I'll answer the letters." She didn't think her own handwriting looked grown-up enough, though she did have the best handwriting in seventh grade.

Her mother beamed. "It's yours to use! That would be an answer to my problem, Mim."

Her mother was gazing at Mim, her head tilted in a question. "Mim . . . is there—" Mammi Vera's bell started to ring.

"I'm thirsty!" Mammi Vera called out in a creaky voice from her room behind the kitchen.

Mim's mother turned her head toward the back room. "Would you mind seeing to your grandmother so I can get this floor finished?"

Mim took off her shoes to tiptoe across the wet kitchen floor. The letters would have to wait. But as soon as Mim had finished tending to Mammi Vera, she slipped up to her mother's room, found the typewriter, and carried it straight to her room. She sat on her bed, cross-legged, to read through the letters. Fascinating! She felt as if she was peeking into people's lives, but not in a nosy way. With permission.

*Dear Mrs. Innkeeper,*

*I read about your Inn in the newspaper. My boyfriend forgot my birthday. Should I forget his?*

*Please write back.*

*Signed,*
*Forgotten in Delaware*

*Dear Mrs. Miracle,*

*I could sure use a miracle. Two years ago, I joined the Army so that I could see the world. I've seen it. Now how do I get out?*

*Sincerely,*
*Trapped in Tennessee*

*Dear Mrs. Innkeeper of Miracle Inn,*

*I have a new job, starting next week. But I will need to be late to work on the first day. Maybe the second day, too. When should I tell my new boss?*

*Very truly yours,*
*Rhonda from New Hampshire*

*Dear Mrs. Miracle,*

*I signed up for a class on "The Brain and Aging Well" at my community center. Then I forgot to go. They won't give me my money back! Any suggestions?*

*Sincerely,*
*Outraged in Harrisburg*

Problems, problems, problems. Her mother had told her not to try to solve these people's problems. But their problems were so easy to solve! And Mim hadn't actually agreed to what her mother had recommended, so technically, she wasn't doing anything wrong. She stared at the typewriter. Very carefully, she put in a fresh sheet of paper. She thought a moment, her fingers frozen above the keys.

She took a breath. And then, with two fingers, very slowly, she began to type.

*Dear Forgotten in Delaware,*

*I am sorry your boyfriend forgot your birthday. Here is my advice: wrap an empty box in gift paper and give it to him for his birthday. And then I think you should suggest that you will both do better next year.*

*Sincerely,*
*Mrs. Miracle*

This was fun.

*Dear Outraged in Harrisburg,*
*There is a lesson to learn in every circumstance. I think you are*
*missing your lesson. Do not worry about getting your money back.*
*The next time "The Brain and Aging Well" class is offered, sign up*
*for it again and be sure to mark it on your calendar. Take the class*
*again, Outraged. And again.*

> *Yours truly,*
> *Mrs. Miracle*

A door slammed. It was the exuberant sound of her brothers as they returned from Galen's. How much time had gone by? Mim rolled the last letter out of the typewriter. Carefully, she folded each one and tucked them into envelopes, addressed them, put a stamp on them, and put them safely in her pocket to mail.

It was already dark by the time Bethany had a chance to get out to the phone shanty to pick up messages. She'd told Rose she would check messages each day for her, seeing as how she was out of work, but she had a hope there might be a message from Jake. She called him as often as she dared—every other day, sometimes every day. She knew it wasn't considered proper to call too often and she never left a message—that would be far too bold. The call went straight to voice mail and she liked listening to his voice, but then she hung up so he wouldn't know she had called. She still hadn't found those books he wanted.

Today, to Bethany's shock, the message machine was full—people who wanted reservations at the place of miracles. She rolled her eyes. For days now, there had been all kinds of ridiculous newspaper articles about the Inn at Eagle Hill, starting with Delia Stoltz's disappearance and discovery, then the bald eagles' aerie. But details were always mixed up: one woman said she heard a lady's cancer disappeared while she was staying at the inn. Another one said she read that a marriage on the brink of divorce had been healed. The strangest one was a fellow who said he wanted to study the energy flows of the farm and see if that's why it produced miracles.

Energy flows? Miracles? Sheer craziness.

Bethany wrote down all the names and numbers for Rose, grateful these people weren't her problem. Delia Stoltz had certainly been a nice enough lady to host for the first guest, but Bethany still wasn't comfortable with the idea of strangers at the farm. Especially weird ones, like the energy flow man. Creepy.

Mim looked forward to getting to the mail each day, sifting through letters to Mrs. Miracle and tucking them up in her room before her mother saw them. Her mother had only asked her one time about the letters she was responding to—a few days ago when she couldn't find any stamps. "Have you used up an entire roll of stamps, Mim?" her mother had asked.

Mim froze. "Well, you said I could answer the letters."

"That's true."

"You said you felt concerned that people were looking to Eagle Hill to solve their problems."

"That's true. I did and I do. But I thought the letters had finally dwindled down. Seems like we haven't gotten any in a few days, have we?"

Just as her mother was about to ask her another question, Mammi Vera's bell started to ring and her mother's attention turned to see what she needed.

Crisis averted.

She did not want to be put in the position of lying to her mother. Lying was wrong. But she also did not want to stop receiving or answering the Mrs. Miracle letters. People counted on her to help solve their problems. She couldn't let them down. She felt important and that was a new feeling for her.

Today, she opened the mailbox and saw that the mail had already been picked up. Oh no! She hadn't anticipated that wrinkle. She ran down the driveway and into the house. Her mother stood by the kitchen table, sorting clean socks from a laundry basket. "Hello, Mim."

"Hello." Mim's eyes darted around the kitchen and landed on the stack of mail piled on the counter. She casually crossed the room to sift through the letters. She picked up three letters addressed to Mrs. Miracle.

Her mother was watching her. "You'd think they'd stop writing after a while, wouldn't you?"

Mim shrugged.

"It's not too much for you to answer those letters, is it?"

Mim waved that thought away. "No trouble at all. It helps me improve my typing skills. I'm up to 15.5 words a minute."

"You'd let me know, though, if it was getting to be too much. Wouldn't you?"

"Of course," Mim said, a little too happily.

Delia heard a knock on the door and opened it to find Rose, standing with a stack of stiff, sun-dried towels in her arms. She handed Delia the towels with a gentle smile and said, "Looks like it's going to start raining soon."

Delia put the towels on the table and motioned for Rose to come in.

"Have you told your husband that your cancer is gone?"

"My son was planning to tell him."

"I'm sure he'll be relieved."

Would he? She didn't know how Charles felt about her anymore.

Rose looked at Delia. "Do you think there's any chance for your marriage to be fixed . . . for things to be made right?"

Delia was quiet for a moment, thinking. "I know you mean well, but you make it sound easy, and it's not. At this point, I wouldn't even know how to begin to make it right."

"Sure you do, Delia. You begin with forgiveness."

"Forgive Charles for having an affair? For breaking up our family?" She crossed her arms against her chest. "Forgiving Charles won't bring him back, Rose. It won't change anything."

"I'm not saying it will, but I have no doubt you'll be surprised by what forgiveness can change." Rose walked over to the door and put her hand on the knob, then hesitated. She turned back to Delia. "I know what it's like to be married to a difficult man. A man who is too smart for his own good and hard to love because of it. I know what it's like to suddenly lose him. I know about regrets and grief that few would understand. But I also know that every marriage takes two people. I made my share of mistakes." A slight smile tugged at her lips. "Dean made more, mind you, but I made a few myself." She opened the door. "After you sort all that out, you can ask God to forgive you. And he will, Delia."

Delia curled up on the sofa after Rose left, mulling over her words. She had blamed Charles entirely for this affair. Was it possible that she played a part? She couldn't deny that they had been drifting apart the last few years, and the truth was, she hadn't really minded. As his work demanded more, she was happy to fill that space with activities that interested her. He had asked her to travel with him to some medical conferences, but they were so boring for her. Still . . . she could have gone to a few of them, especially when he was scheduled to speak.

Maybe . . . Delia could have tried a little harder to stay close, to understand the world of neurosurgery he lived in. It was so far beyond her understanding that she had stopped listening. Stopped trying.

But Robyn Dixon knew that world.

Delia leaned her head against the back of the sofa. It was clear that, somehow or other, Rose had found a peace with her circumstances that Delia hadn't. But still. It was a complicated issue.

Maybe that was the problem. Maybe it wasn't as complicated as she had assumed.

Delia decided to fix herself a cup of tea to ward off the chill of the rainy April afternoon. She filled the teakettle with water and set it on the stove. She turned on the burner and waited for the water to heat up, then poured the hot water through the infuser, watching the water change color and taste. Maybe that's what it was like with God—he infused a situation with love and forgiveness.

What was it Rose kept saying? That Delia just needed to ask for help. She set the infuser in the kitchen sink and held the teacup and saucer in her hands. What did she have to lose? She closed her eyes and said a silent prayer.

*God, I know there really isn't any reason for you to listen to me. I haven't done a very good job of listening to you these past sixty years, so a part of me feels hypocritical to come to you now, with a crisis. I wouldn't blame you a bit if you ignored me, but I pray you won't. Rose says I have to for-give Charles so that you can forgive me, and I want to. I'm just not sure I can, not unless you help me. Please, dear Lord, please help me. I've always thought of myself as strong, but I'm not strong enough for this. I just can't do it. Help me. Please help. Amen.*

Just as the "amen" was forming in her mind, she heard a car pull into the driveway. Her eyes flew open and she crossed the room to look out the window. Tea splashed into the saucer and the breath went out of her.

It was Charles!

# 17

Stop twisting my arm off." Vera flashed Rose a frustrated look.
Rose patiently continued exercising Vera's right arm. "Jehoshaphat, you're as prickly as a jar of toothpicks today."

Vera felt she could tolerate many things, but not having her moods waved away. She sat at the kitchen table, a truculent expression on her face. She had just completed reciting the litany of wrongs she felt Rose had committed as a wife to Dean, her dear boy Dean, starting with how she had tempted him away from his church to go to the liberals, which resulted in so many additional temptations, and ended with Rose being responsible for Tobe's running away.

She saved her best for last. "And what about Dean's passing? You've never admitted to the despair you drove him to. That despair led to his death."

A long moment of silence followed, Finally, Rose lifted her head and looked Vera right in the eye, giving her a stern look. "Vera, I know that your life did not turn out the way you hoped it would. I know that. But you need to get your mind off your troubles."

*Patronizing.* How dare Rose treat her like she was a child!

"As soon as we finish these exercises, I'll make you a cup of tea. Tea has a way of making everything seem better."

*Tea!* As if a cup of tea would cure what ailed her.

"Now try to work your shoulder," Rose said. "Up and down, side to side, and in circles."

Vera reached out, but her arm refused to budge. She tried to make her arm work, just a simple wiggle or twitch . . . yet nothing whatsoever happened. The weakness was getting worse. *No. Oh no. Father, don't let this be real.* Her eyes filled with tears as she tried and tried to move her arm.

Rose stood behind her and started to gently exercise her shoulder. "Vera," she said softly, "we will find ways to make things work. I'm going to do everything I can to help you get back to where you used to be."

Vera knew exactly what Rose was referring to—leaving her to fend for herself, like she'd had to do since Dean had up and married Rose and gone off to the liberals. She'd be alone again.

*What will I do if Rose decides to leave? What will happen to me then?*

As shakes started to overtake her, Vera couldn't say whether it was from anger or fear. Both!

Delia opened the door to Charles but didn't say a word.

"I came by to . . . to talk to you." Charles took a deep breath. His voice was shaky and she noticed his hands were trembling. "Will called me. He said the margins were clear. Is it true?"

"Yes. You didn't need to drive all the way out here."

"Well, I couldn't get anything out of that idiot Zimmerman."

Delia stiffened. "He's not an idiot. He was respecting my wishes."

The wary, belligerent expression came back to Charles's face, and he drew back a little, taking on that stance of his that always reminded Delia a little of a prizefighter. She knew that look so well. She started to close the door in his face.

"Wait! Delia, just give me five minutes. I just need five minutes. Hear me out, then I'll leave and I won't bother you again."

The sooner it was over, the sooner he would be gone. "Come in," she said, half order, half request.

He walked into the large room and sat on the sofa, eyes fixed on the ground. His hands were clasped together on his lap; now she saw them tighten involuntarily. "It's not easy for me to talk about some things."

"I've always known that about you," Delia said. "That's why I've never pressured you to talk."

She watched his body change—from ready-to-snap tension to dropping his chin on his chest. And to her total surprise, Charles began to cry. Huge sobs and heaving shoulders. The works.

Charles . . . was . . . crying! She didn't know what to think or what to do. He sat on the sofa, weeping. Her authoritative, in-control-of-every-situation, brilliant neurosurgeon husband was crying so hard that she had to keep feeding him tissues. "I'm scared, Dee, for the first time in my life, I'm really scared. I just feel . . . adrift, I guess. That's it. It's like I woke up to find myself sitting in a boat in the middle of the ocean. I've got no sail, no oars, and no idea where I am. I don't know what kind of man I've turned into."

Just an hour ago, she would have danced a jig to see Charles's remorse, but she didn't feel that way anymore. She wasn't interested in exacting revenge or placing blame. How astonishing! Rose had reminded her that, even in the midst of tragedy, it was possible to find unexpected blessings if you only asked for God's help. Hers had been exactly that, a newfound ability to let go of the past and the bitterness she'd harbored toward Charles.

They sat there in the basement of an Amish farmhouse while Charles told her he was miserable without her.

But . . . she wasn't to be fobbed off so easily. "And so you decided to come back to what was familiar—to a time when you knew who you were?"

"Yes. No! Dee, it was a mistake. Robyn, moving out of our home. I'm sorry. I understand now what I put you through. And I'm just so sorry. When I was suddenly faced with losing you . . . I think that's when I started to realize what I'd done. What kind of man I'd become."

She was doing the very best she could to be empathetic, compassionate yet detached. After all, tears didn't wipe out the damage that had been done.

"I drove all the way here to tell you I've ended things with Robyn. It's over. And I want to ask if we could get back together. I'd like things to be the way they were before."

She drew in her breath sharply; she had *not* expected this. She was listening intently, her heart lifting with every word. These were the very words she had wanted to hear. The very words. But the truth was, she didn't want things the way they were before. Everything had changed. She had changed. She recovered her poise quickly. "I don't want to go back to a marriage of two ships passing in the night."

Charles stared vacantly out the window, though it was impossible to see anything through the rain and fog that clouded the glass. "I guess I can't blame you, Dee. But I just want you to know I meant what I said. I'm sorry for everything. I don't expect you to forgive me."

And to her surprise she said quietly, "This isn't just your fault, you know. There were things we both could have done differently. I'm sorry too."

"Well, maybe, but when the going got tough, I was the one who called a lawyer, not you."

That was true.

"Delia, I thought about what you said—about the difference between having regret and being truly sorry. Before Will called to let me know your test results—I spoke to the patient who was suing me for her stroke. I apologized to her. To her husband too." Charles's voice choked up. "That was all they wanted to hear. That was it. They dropped the malpractice suit."

Delia was stunned. Never, in her wildest dreams, could she have imagined such a conversation. Never.

"I don't know when you're planning to return home—"

Delia stepped in quickly. "I don't know that, either."

"Maybe, if it would be all right with you, I could come out and visit you. We could go out to dinner and just . . . talk. Would that be acceptable?"

She smiled. "Entirely acceptable." They were a long, long way from reconciling, from becoming a family again. But it was a step in the right direction. Then something occurred to her, out of the blue. "Before you go, could I ask you to pay a house call on Rose's mother-in-law?"

Outside, rain fell softly, nourishing Rose's recently planted strawberries in the dark, wet garden earth. She hardly noticed. Vera was having a bad spell, and when a knock came on the door, it startled Rose. When she opened it, there was Delia, looking pleased, with a man by her side. A fine-looking man. Her husband.

"Rose, this is Charles. I thought it might be a good idea if Charles were to meet Vera."

Rose stepped onto the porch, pulling the door closed behind her. Charles put his hand out to shake Rose's. She looked down at his hand before taking it, then she didn't release it.

"It's not a good night for visitors." Rose lowered her voice. "Vera's having a bad night."

"That's why I wanted Charles to meet her," Delia said. "As a doctor."

Rose turned and opened the door and let them both into the kitchen. Vera sat in a chair, hiccupping, tears streaming down her face in misery.

Charles turned to Rose. "Has she had medical attention?"

"Yes, of course. The doctor said she was having mini-strokes."

"What medication is she on?

"Coumadin."

"Does she get episodes of singultus very often?"

Rose looked at him. "Single-what?"

"Swallowing disturbances," he said.

"Hiccups," Delia clarified. "And yes, she does."

Rose nodded. "More and more. For longer and longer stretches. And the weakness in her right side is spreading."

Charles crouched down by Vera and tried to straighten out her right hand. "Do you have a tingling sensation in your hand?"

She nodded.

"Dizziness? Headaches?"

"Some."

Charles patted Vera's hand reassuringly in a way that was touching to Rose. From the way Delia had described him, she would have assumed he was a stern man, but here he was, tender and kind, to a complete stranger. "I'd like you to get an MRI to help pinpoint the problem."

"What's that?" Vera asked.

"Magnetic Resonance Imaging. It's a technique used to take pictures of soft tissues in the body."

"But why?"

"Strokes can be misdiagnosed. There are many other things that share symptoms of strokes, but they aren't strokes." It seemed like a stone had fallen into the room. No one moved. No one breathed.

Vera stared hard at Charles. "Such as?"

Rose saw Delia and Charles exchange a glance.

"We can talk about it more after the tests are concluded," Charles said.

"What else could it be?" Vera said, in between hiccups. "What else? Do I have Old Timer's Disease? I do, don't I?"

Charles looked confused. "Old Timer's?"

"She means Alzheimer's," Rose whispered.

Distress clouded Vera's face. "That's what you're thinking, isn't it? That I'm losing my mind!" She started to wail.

Charles hesitated, but the look on Vera's troubled face couldn't be ignored. "No. I doubt it would be Alzheimer's. It's more likely to be operable—maybe a brain tumor—"

Those two words were like the crack of doom.

Vera wailed louder.

Jimmy Fisher must have gone right to work. A day later, Bethany received a written invitation from the Sisters' House, asking if she would come for tea to discuss the opportunity to work for them. There was a postscript at the bottom of the letter: "Do you have a steady eye and good aim? Do you like rituals?"

Bethany marched right over to Galen's barn and found Jimmy in the workshop, repairing a harness buckle. She waved the letter at him. "Are these sisters truly sane? Am I safe going over there?"

Jimmy roared with laughter and said yes, the sisters were both safe and sane. A little eccentric, perhaps. "You should go. If nothing else, you'll have a great story to tell."

None of that prepared Bethany for what actually happened. The Sisters' House was two-story, framed and old, in need of fresh paint, surrounded close in by a small picket fence that was also in need of paint. The grass in the yard needed mowing as well—or would as soon as the weather warmed up.

The sisters met her at the door, five of them lined up in a row, all in their eighties. You never saw such an elderly group of ladies, and Bethany thought Mammi Vera, at sixtysomething, was ancient. Very prim and ladylike, with white hair piled like swirls of whipped cream at the back of their heads, tucked under their gossamer prayer caps.

"I've been expecting you," Ella, the eldest, said. "Right on time . . ." She spoke in a quiet, intelligent voice, but right away Bethany noticed she had the habit of dropping off her words in midsentence, as if she had forgotten what she was going to say.

"She always claims she knows when a person is coming," Ada, the second eldest, whispered to Bethany. "She claims she knows everything."

Lena, the third eldest, led Bethany into the living room. Bethany felt stunned by the condition of the room. It was filled with furniture, stacks of books, overflowing boxes. Every nook and cranny was steeped with some kind of clutter: newspapers, books, boxes filled with quilting material, baskets full of yarn, junk mail, bills. Even the walls were covered, floor to ceiling, with old calendars. Most Plain families had . . . well, plain homes. A rug, some perfunctory furniture, maybe a calendar or two on the wall. Sometimes a picture of a bird. But walls were mostly bare. This home looked like nothing Bethany had ever seen.

One of the sisters—Sylvia, the youngest—caught the look of shock on her face. "It might seem a wee bit disorganized, but we know where everything is."

Ella bobbed her head. "We do."

"We're facing a bit of a sticky wicket, you see," Sylvia said. "We're supposed to have church here and some of our relatives said they would help us clean things out. But we don't want them to help. Last time they helped, we couldn't find anything for weeks."

"Months," said another sister.

"Years," said another.

Bethany exhaled. "When are you scheduled to host church?"

The sisters looked at each other. "Whenever we can get the house tidied up, I suppose," Sylvia said. "Deacon Abraham said we didn't have to rush. But he'd like us to take a turn. It's only fair, he said."

"That's true," Ella said. "It's only fair."

Bethany looked around. Tidied up? That was an understatement. This house was buried in clutter. It was drowning.

They emptied stacks of old *Budget* newspapers off the sofa and sat down to tea—excellent tea, made by Fannie, the fourth eldest, which Bethany thought even the oh-so-proper Inn at Eagle Hill guest would approve of.

"Can you make a good cup of tea?" Fannie asked. "We don't drink coffee. But we do love our tea. Real steeped tea. Not the cotton ball type."

"As a matter of fact, I can." Delia Stoltz had shown Bethany how to make tea one rainy morning after she had brought down the breakfast tray. At the time, Bethany listened politely to the tea steeping lesson, but inside, she was thinking, my lands, Delia Stoltz was a grand lady. Now, she was grateful.

"And have a prune," one of the sisters said, thrusting a bowl of wrinkled prunes at Bethany.

Another sister nudged her. "Never pass up a chance at a prune."

Bethany swallowed hard.

Then things took an odd turn. Or rather, even more odd. The sisters sat along the sofa, in order of their age, and peppered Bethany with questions, one after the other, right down the line. "Do you have fine penmanship? Are you trustworthy? Are you punctual? Do you get nervous if you're confined in small, dark places? Can you keep a secret?" Bethany's throat went bone dry. These ladies might be certifiably crazy. She barely put her teacup down when Ella said, "Sisters, I believe she will do . . ." Then her voice trailed off, distracted by something in her head.

Ada peered at Bethany over her spectacles and picked up where Ella left off. "I believe you're right, Sister." The three other sisters nodded in agreement, capstrings bouncing up and down, along with their chins.

Bethany was still very unsure of what exactly they were proposing.

Sylvia, the youngest, was the only one who seemed to sense Bethany's confusion. "We'd like to offer you the job. Of course, take all the time you need to make your decision. A minute. Two minutes. Whatever you need."

While Bethany's head went round in perfect circles, the sisters assumed her silence meant acquiescence. As they walked her to the door, she was told to return in a week's time—because it would take them that long to get used to the idea of having someone in their employ—to wear work clothes, and to not be late.

# 18

Why her? Why did bad things always happen to her? Vera lay in bed early on Sunday morning, startled by the sound of a door shutting. That would be Rose, slipping off to watch the sunrise. It was a habit of Rose's and an annoying one, considering Vera's bedroom happened to be on the first floor.

Last night, after the guest lady and her doctor husband finally left, Rose pointed out that Vera and the guest happened to be about the same age. "Well, I might look like her if I didn't have the troubles I do," Vera snapped back.

Her mind drifted back to her troubles. The doctor's words. Why did doctors always circle-talk and cross-talk and use hundred-dollar words? Why didn't he just come out and say she was dying?

Because she was. She knew she was. She had been old since she was thirty-five, when her dear husband died after a fall off the roof. She'd been teetering at death's doorstep since she was forty-seven, when her first daughter-in-law abandoned dear Dean and their two babies. Then at fifty, she took a step through the threshold when her son left the Old Order Amish church to take on a second wife and faced excommunication. She just hadn't gotten around to the actual dying part yet. When she stood over her Dean's coffin, she clutched the coffin rim and said, "Mine will be next. I'll be the next box they shovel the dirt on."

Deacon Abraham chastised her for saying such a thing. "Only the Lord knows the future," he said. True, but Vera had a gift for prophesying doom. And she was rarely disappointed.

What was the point of having another medical test? Besides, that test sounded like something out of a nightmare. Imagine getting rolled into a big tin can and have magnets turned on? There was no way in the world she could tolerate something like that. She must have looked like she just found out they were going to drop her in a pot of boiling lard, because the doctor hastened to add the test should only last for ten minutes. Ten minutes too long! She heaved a stretch-to-the-limits sigh.

If Dean were still alive, he would let her pass in peace, dignity intact. The very thought of Dean made her sadder still, if that were possible. Why had God taken Dean, but left her? It wasn't right for a mother to outlive her child. "Therefore shall his calamity come suddenly, suddenly shall he be broken without remedy," the proverb read. That was true. She was left broken without a remedy.

A little later, Vera locked eyes with Rose the minute she stepped into the kitchen from her morning walk. "I'm not going through with it. No matter what you and your fancy English friend say. I'm not doing it."

Rose crossed the kitchen floor to start the coffee. "I assume you're talking about the MRI." She measured scoops of coffee into the filter, then set it on the stovetop. "It's your choice, Vera." She walked up to Vera, seated at the kitchen table, and wrapped her arms about her. "You know that we need you around as long as the Lord sees fit. I need your help raising those children. I don't know what we'd do without you. Why, there's no telling what those two little rascal boys would turn into without their grandmother's fine influence."

"So true. So very true." Vera closed her eyes, squeezing them tight for a long moment. "Bieg der Baam wann er yung is, wann er alt is, kannscht nimmi." *Bend the tree while it is young, when it is old, it is too late.*

"Mim is just starting to turn into a young lady. She needs a grandmother to help her with that. And you don't want Bethany to end up with a liberal like Jake Hertzler, do you? When you've got someone like Jimmy Fisher buzzing around? And then there's Tobe. I haven't given up hope that he'll be home one day."

Vera chanced a look at Rose. "You'll mess it all up without me."

Rose kissed the top of her head. "I truly would."

—◌ ◊ ◌—

A bird screeched, followed by a chorus of frantic cries. Rose hurried outside to see several birds in flight, along with a flock of crows excitedly beating their wings. Obviously they'd been disturbed by someone or something. As she turned away from the window, she caught sight of Mister or Missus Eagle—she couldn't tell which. It soared elegantly in the distance, circling the farm. For once, the word "awesome" seemed apt. Its beauty and grace were stunning. Hypnotic to watch. It didn't take long to realize there was no love lost between the eagle and the other birds.

Luke and Sammy came barreling outside to join her. They had heard the bird racket too. She hushed them and pulled them close to her. "Watch with your eyes, not your mouths."

The three of them stared at the sky until the eagle flew off. "Mom, did you hear there's an egg in the aerie?" Luke said.

Rose frowned at him. "How do you know that? Were you climbing trees again?"

"No!" Luke said. "Some of the bird-watchers told us so."

There was an avid group of bird-watchers that set up their scopes morning and night to watch the eagles hunt for food in the creek.

She grinned. "Well, that's good news. When do you think it might hatch?"

"Mim said it takes thirty-five days," Sammy said. "So that would be . . ." He started counting on his fingers.

Luke couldn't wait for Sammy's slow accounting. "In a few weeks."

"We'll have to mark that birthday on the calendar," Rose said.

"Don't get your hopes up," Mim said, standing by the kitchen door. "The chance of a baby bald eagle surviving its first year of life is less than 50 percent. That's a fact."

Luke's and Sammy's faces crumpled.

Jimmy knew that asking Galen for a cash advance wasn't going to be warmly received, but he didn't expect to hear Galen's churlish opinion about his judgment.

Earlier this morning, Jimmy had located Lodestar at the Bart Township mud sale. Jonah Hershberger was brushing him down in a makeshift stall. As soon as he spotted Jimmy, he threw the brush down and lit right into him, giving him a lecture that felt like the ones his mother used to give him—causing the very hair on the back of his neck to stand up straight.

"What's the matter with you, son?" Jonah bellowed. "Don't you lock your barns up at night? He's running loose all over the county! You've been awful lucky that Lodestar's a one-man horse. He can track me like a flea on a dog. But you—" he pointed his finger at Jimmy's chest—"you don't deserve a horse like Lodestar."

"But I do! I really do. I must have left the barn door open."

Jonah narrowed his eyes. "What kind of horseman leaves a barn door open?"

"It'll never happen again. You can count on me."

Jonah squeezed his eyes shut. "This goes against my better judgment." He opened his eyes and let out a puff of air. "But I've got to get this horse sold. Look . . . get me cash for the rest of the money you owe me and I'll give you one more chance." He stabbed his finger against Jimmy's chest with each word: "Last chance, Fisher. I mean it this time. Do. Not. Lose. That. Horse."

Jimmy promised to bring Jonah the remaining seven hundred and fifty dollars by noon—but that meant he would need to ask Galen for the cash. His brother Paul had made it clear that he was not Jimmy's bank.

An hour later, he pulled his buggy into Galen's yard and couldn't find him in the barn or paddocks. He ran to the house and Naomi let him in, pointing to the living room where Galen worked at his desk.

"Galen, I need to get an advance on a few weeks' salary. Cash."

Galen put down his pen and leaned back in his chair. "What do you need it for?"

"Can't you trust me?"

"No."

"I found Lodestar. I need to get Jonah the balance that I owe him."

"Jimmy, when are you going to learn?"

"I've learned my lesson. This time, I will keep the barn door shut. Locked!" He frowned at Galen's reluctance. "Why can't you just give me a little credit?"

"I'll tell you why, since you're finally asking questions and not just yapping your jowls. Have you ever heard of the Runner Scam?"

Jimmy shook his head. "What is it?"

As Galen explained the scam, Jimmy's head rocked back a little, as if he'd just been slapped.

"You've been swindled."

Jimmy shook his head. "You don't know that. How could you possibly know? You've never seen the horse. You've never met the trader. Maybe the horse just has a knack for getting out of tight spots. I'd do the same thing, if I was a horse."

Galen rolled his eyes, disgusted. "Everything you described about it fits the Runner Scam. A trader sells the same horse a half-dozen times over. As soon as folks get wise to him, he disappears."

Jimmy paced the room, back and forth, then swung around to face Galen. "Maybe you're right, maybe you're not. But I'm not letting this chance slip through my fingers. That's the difference between you and me. You're always watching life from afar . . . you never take any risks yourself. You let chances slip through your fingers all the time. You're crazy about Rose, any fool can see that, and yet you—" He stopped himself abruptly. He was crossing the line and he knew it by the warning look that covered Galen's face. He glanced at the clock on the desk and realized he needed to get back to Jonah by noon. "If you're right, you're not out any money. I'll work for you without pay."

Galen didn't move or make a sound, but Jimmy could feel something change in him. He finally stood, walked to the kitchen, opened a cupboard door, and took out a coffee can. "How much?"

The wind had come up hard in the night and Jimmy woke with a start when a door banged shut. For a split second, he wasn't sure where he was, then he remembered—he had slept in the barn on a cot in the saddle room—determined to keep Lodestar contained. A gust of wind banged the door shut again. Jimmy grabbed his flashlight and bolted down to the horse's stall. It was empty, the door wide open. Out of Jimmy's mouth burst an unrepeatable word that he saved for emergencies.

He heard something. He flung himself out the door so fast he bumped his shoulder on the jamb and cried out in pain. Outside, he scanned the farm, hoping to see Lodestar. It was a moonless night, pitch black, and he had to wait for the sough of the wind to still—but he was sure he heard something. There! He heard it again—the squeak of hinges as a trailer door shut tight and then the sound of a car pulling away.

He covered his face with his hands. He wasn't sure what hurt more—the fact that he had lost Lodestar for a third time or the fact that he was going to have to tell Galen he had been right all along.

Jimmy, a young man who considered himself unsusceptible to hood-winking and swindling, had been hoodwinked and swindled.

"Mom, Mom, Mom!" Sammy came flying into the house, tears stream-ing down his face. "The baby eagle died! It died, Mom!"

Rose wrapped her arms around her youngest son. The bird-watchers had made the discovery and told Luke and Sammy the news as they went to school. It rankled Rose that those bird-watchers didn't think about the hearts of a little boy. Couldn't the news have waited?

After Sammy had finished his cry, she washed his face and walked him to school through the field, so they didn't have to talk to the bird-watchers. When they went into the schoolhouse, she noticed that Luke was slouched at his desk, looking sad. She also noticed that Luke's desk was exactly one stretched-out arm away from the teacher's desk. It surprised Rose that Mim hadn't informed her Luke's desk had been moved. Mim usually kept her abreast of Luke's crimes.

"I'm sorry Sammy is a little late today," Rose told the teacher, who understood there had been a crisis without needing an explanation.

As Rose walked back through the fields, she went up the hillside to watch the eagles. Missus Eagle was on the edge of the nest, her white feathered head bowed. Mister Eagle was at a distance in another tree. That was typical—it was rare to spot the two eagles together. Usually one protected the nest while the other hunted, then they would switch roles.

"I just heard."

Rose turned and saw Galen approach her. "What do you think happened? Do you think another bird attacked the eaglet?"

"Eagles don't have any predators. They're at the top of the chain." He stood beside her, watching the mother eagle on the side of the nest. "More likely, they're just inexperienced parents. They messed up. Maybe left it alone too long. It was cold last night. It might have chilled. Or starved."

"Do you think the eagles will leave the nest and not come back?"

"Maybe, but maybe not. Time will tell."

"I know I shouldn't give human emotions to birds, but doesn't she seem sad to you?"

"She does. She truly does."

At that moment, Mister Eagle flew next to Missus Eagle on the nest and tucked his head against her neck. It seemed as if he was trying to give her comfort. Heartbreaking! Rose turned away, buried her face in her hands, and her shoulders shuddered.

Galen moved so his chest grazed her back and wrapped his arms around her. Turning her chin slightly, she said, "How can the world be so beautiful and yet break the heart?"

Galen drew in his breath. There were moments in life when something had to be said, or be left unsaid forever. It wasn't the best time for it—he knew it wasn't—but he had to speak.

Twice, he opened his mouth to say the words; both times, words failed him. For a moment, he lost focus. He never lost focus. Never, though earlier, he'd lost his breath when he saw Rose coming toward him on the hillside, the hazy morning sunlight casting a glow about her. Sometimes out of nowhere the sight of her could snatch his breath and make his chest hurt. She was beautiful. Graceful and beautiful. He wanted to protect her from all the sadness in her life. The emotions shimmering in her tear-filled eyes tore at him, so he wound his arms about her, pulling her into the shelter of his very being. Finally, he said, "There are sad times, but there are good times too. Like . . . now."

She pulled away from him and turned to face him, puzzled. "Now?"

"Yes. Now." He cleared his throat. "This very moment. This is a good time. For me, anyway."

She turned her deep-gray eyes on him, calm and penetrating. "Galen, what are you trying to say?"

He had yet to take his eyes off her. "Rose . . . I . . . care about you. And what I want to know is this . . ." He cleared his throat again. "Would you let me court you? Sometime? Soon?"

She looked surprised, her mouth formed a small, tight O. Her eyes popped, then mysteriously, filled with tears. Were these sad tears, happy tears, angry tears, outraged tears, a little of each? He couldn't tell. He was relieved she wasn't leaping down the hill.

The moment stretched between them until finally she spoke. "Galen, I have children to raise and a farm to run, and I've got to make money to pay back those investors, and a son who seems to be facing serious legal problems."

He swallowed hard. "You take a lot of chances, and you stand up to them all. Why not take a chance on me?"

"Because . . . well, for one thing, because of our friendship. It means so much to me. I don't want to lose that."

"Why would we lose it? It's our foundation. I want to build on it."

She didn't speak for a long moment. "Galen, my husband broke my heart and then broke it again."

"But I'm not him."

She studied him. Indecision played across her features. At long last she set her jaw and lifted it, and his heart missed a few beats. To his surprise, she took his hand. He felt it, cool in his own, believing, for a moment, that she might love him the way he loved her.

"Do you mind if I wait a little while before giving you my answer?" she asked gently.

He did mind. He had hoped she would say yes at once. But he remembered his manners and took a step back. "Of course not. Take all the time you need."

Rose could hardly bear to see the pained expression on Galen's face after she told him she needed time to think. His voice had gone flat, no longer throaty, warm, inviting. He waited, but there was nothing more to say. She was not going to say yes on a whim. She had to go home and ponder his question. The silence fell heavy between them, thick and cold, and after a moment too long of it, he turned and left.

He had shocked her when he told her he wanted to court her. Shocked her . . . and yet . . . it hadn't shocked her at all. Their friendship had been deepening. Hardly a day went by when they didn't see each other, talk to each other. She counted on him in a way she didn't count on anyone else. Did she love him? Was this love? Did he love her? He looked so devoted, she felt almost weak. What had she done to deserve all this love?

Would she like to be courted by Galen King? *Well, why not?* A part of her answered back. *Really, Rose, why not? He's kind and caring and he's the best friend you've ever had. And he loves you. You know he does. You've known it for some time. You've seen it in his eyes.*

But then the practical part of her brain kicked in. Galen was much younger than she was. His life could be—*should* be—just starting with a young woman. Hers was inching toward the midline. His life was fairly uncomplicated. Hers was a big tangled spool of thread and she was just starting to figure out where the thread began. She had no idea where it would end.

Besides, there was a reason Galen had remained single. Hadn't she learned her lessons about independent men?

No. She should definitely not entertain any thought of being courted by Galen. Put those thoughts right out of her head. Banish them now.

On Monday three bad things happened. First, Mim received a B on last week's vocabulary sentence. Teacher M.K. thought she hadn't tried hard enough. Second, a horrid sixth grade boy, whom Mim considered to be a blight on humanity, told her she looked like a chipmunk in glasses. The glasses part didn't bother her as much as the chipmunk part. She was very sensitive about her teeth and took excellent care of them. Excellent. She did not want to be toothless when she was older, like so many of the people in Mammi Vera's church. Third, Danny didn't even look her way at church yesterday. Or today at school. Not once.

Mim wanted to talk to someone about Danny Riehl. Was it significant that he didn't look her way? Was it possible that he thought she looked like a chipmunk too?

She thought about asking her sister, but Bethany thought of Mim as a little girl. She would tell her to stop wishing she were older than her years.

She thought about talking to Naomi, but lately Naomi had been so enthralled with Bethany that she hardly knew Mim was there. It wasn't like that when they first moved to Stoney Ridge. Naomi spent equal time with both sisters, which was only fair because, she acted like she was right between them in age. But when she turned eighteen, she seemed to think she was much closer to Bethany's age than to Mim's. She would only spend time with Mim if Bethany was at work.

Mim checked herself. What kind of advice would Naomi give to her? First, she would be shocked that she was even thinking about being in love with a boy. Second, she would tell Galen, straightaway, about Mim spending time on a hillside with that same boy. At night and unchaperoned. She wouldn't understand that it was perfectly innocent and they were only stargazing.

And what would Galen do? Mim smiled. Probably listen to his sister and quietly dismiss it. That's one thing she liked about Galen. Unlike most of the people in her life, he did not overreact.

She had a mental list of whom she would *not* talk to about being in love with Danny Riehl: any girl at school. Mammi Vera. Her brothers.

That left her mother.

Her mother was the one person Mim did want to talk to about Danny. Her mother would not overreact and she would not think Mim was too young to be in love. This afternoon, she was going to find a window of time alone with her mother and ask her about love. She reached home ahead of the boys and went right into the kitchen. It was empty. There was a note on the kitchen table:

*Mim, Luke, and Sam,*
    *I have taken Mammi Vera to Lancaster to get the MRI test. Delia Stoltz drove us over. We won't be home until late. Mim, start supper. Luke and Sam, feed goat, chickens, sheep, and horses. Boys—Mim is in charge until Bethany gets home. Mind your sister!*
        *Love, Mom*

The boys burst in behind Mim, tossed their hats on the bench by the back door, and started hunting for a snack in the pantry. It was like a pack of wild dogs descended on the kitchen. They stuffed cookies into their coat pockets and headed back to the door.

"Where do you think you're going?" Mim said.

"Eagle spying," Sammy said. Luke was already out the door.

She held up the note. "Mom wants you to feed the animals."

"We will!" Sammy said, his mouth filled with cookie. It was disgusting. "After the eagle spying." The door slammed behind him.

Mim looked around the empty kitchen. Everyone was gone. The house seemed eerily quiet.

Under normal conditions, Jimmy Fisher could snap out of a funk. But being a victim of a scam was not a normal condition. When he discovered that his initial check to Jonah Hershberger had indeed cleared—which meant he had paid for Lodestar one and a half times—he felt stupid, he felt duped, he felt angry. Mostly, he felt grief over losing that beautiful horse. There was something about that horse he just couldn't forget . . . or get over. Galen kept telling him there were other horses, but none were like Lodestar.

After Galen and Naomi went into town to run an errand, Jimmy put the horse he was exercising back in its stall and took a break. He pushed a chair in the sun, tucked his hat back, and started to whittle on a piece of wood.

"You aren't getting anywhere very fast, are you, young feller?"

When Jimmy looked up and saw Hank Lapp walk up the driveway, he snapped shut his whittling knife and dropped it into his shirt pocket, then hopped up to greet his elderly friend. There was no law against whittling, but he didn't want to get a reputation as an idler. Hank Lapp was Amos Lapp's uncle, a confirmed bachelor, a quirky, lovable character who ruffled everyone's feathers at one time or another. "What brings you around here, Hank?"

"MY BIRTHDAY PARTY, of course! I'm coming to invite you."

"Why, Hank, are you a hundred yet?"

"I'm crowding it, boy." Hank eased himself into the chair that Jimmy had just vacated. He leaned back and tugged his hat over his eyes. "Jimmy, do you know what men who live in glass houses should do?"

Oh no. He wasn't in the mood for one of Hank's lame jokes. "What should they do?"

"Change in the dark!" Hank chuckled so hard his hat fell in the dirt. He reached down to grab it, slapped it on his knee to dust it off, and plunked it back on his head. "Any luck finding that mystery horse of yours?"

"No." Jimmy threw the piece of wood on the ground. "Galen thinks I've been scammed."

"He's probably right. Galen's seen 'em all."

Jimmy was disgusted. "The two of you don't give me enough credit. It's like you think I don't even have a handle on life."

Hank yawned. "I used to have a handle on life, but it broke." He pushed his hat back and sat straight up. "I nearly forgot! I want you to put on a fireworks show for the end of my birthday party. It's a paying gig."

"Yeah? How much?"

"All you can eat. Tell Galen he's invited too. We're going to have fun."

Jimmy snorted, amused by the comment. "Galen never had fun in his whole livelong life. He wasn't made for fun. That's my department. That's why he needs me."

"Yes, but what's far more interesting to me," Hank retorted, "is why you need Galen King."

# 19

What a difference a week made.

Delia drove Rose and Vera to Charles's office to find out the results of the MRI. Charles had arranged for the test to be done at a local facility in Lancaster, then had the results sent to his office. Delia could see that Vera had never been so frightened in all her life. Getting an MRI had terrified her. Usually, an MRI took about ten to fifteen minutes. For Vera, it took nearly an hour. She had a fit of claustrophobia and needed to be pulled out of the machine, then she sneezed and that slowed it all down. She complained about everything—claustrophobia, the noise of the vibrating magnets. She had to wear earplugs, then earphones over the earplugs. And she had to be absolutely still—that meant no talking. A terrible thing for Vera to endure!

Rose stayed by Vera's side through it all. Delia knew Vera was grateful, though she would never let on. Even she could also see the decline in Vera since she had arrived at Eagle Hill. Her physical weakness and confusion were escalating, and whenever she felt stressed, real or imagined, the hiccups started up again.

Delia was so focused on Vera and Rose that she hardly thought about the fact that she would be going to Charles's medical office for the first time since they had separated. She knew the office staff—had known them for years—and was warmly welcomed by them, but her mind was preoccupied with Vera.

When the receptionist asked them to wait in Charles's office, Delia assumed she would stay in the waiting room. "Please, come with us," Rose said.

So Delia followed behind them and went into her husband's office. On the desk and in the bookshelf were pictures of her and Will. When Charles came in, his eyes met Delia's and softened. He greeted Rose and Vera, then he sat at his desk and turned on the computer monitor to show Vera the picture of her brain.

"It turns out that you didn't have a stroke after all, Vera, just like we had discussed at your farm. But you do have a brain tumor." He turned the computer screen around and showed her the picture of her brain.

"I don't see anything," Vera said.

"It can be hard to see," Charles said. He ran a finger around the outline of the small tumor. "The tissue is one texture. The tumor is a different one."

"All I see is a gray blob."

"That's the tumor. It's grayer than the gray of your brain. It's called a primal tumor. Symptoms mimic a stroke so similarly that about 3 percent of primal brain tumors are misdiagnosed as stroke victims. In a way, you're very fortunate. Most brain problems don't give warnings. Aneurysms, for example, can hide in the brain like a ticking bomb."

Too much. He'd said too much. Delia could see Vera gasp at the words "ticking bomb."

Charles saw it too. "But lucky for you," he hastened to add, "your symptoms of aphasia and singultus and weakness have given us a heads-up."

Vera and Rose swiveled in their chairs to look at Delia for translation. "What's he saying?" Vera asked.

"*Aphasia* means having trouble with word recall," Delia explained. "Tip-of-the-tongue-itis. *Singultus* means . . . hiccups."

Vera's face pinched in fear. Her hands worked in her lap. "I knew it! I knew it. I'm dying!"

"No, no," Charles said, hastening to reassure her. "The brain tumor is located in a part of your head that is very accessible. I believe we can remove it."

"Brain surgery?" Rose said.

"I don't want my head split open and have people rooting around in it like a pumpkin," Vera said. "Tell him, Rose."

Rose reached over and held Vera's hand. "Let's find out more before we decide anything."

"Charles, is it benign?" Delia asked.

"We won't know until it's been removed and sent to the lab, but I'm cautiously optimistic that it's not malignant."

"What do them hundred-dollar words mean?" Vera whispered to Rose.

"Cancer," Rose whispered back and Vera shuddered.

Charles turned off the computer monitor. "Vera, I recommend we take care of that tumor. Soon. Very soon. I have every confidence that the tumor can be removed."

Vera fixed her gaze at him. "Can you guarantee that? One hundred percent guarantee that?"

Charles and Delia exchanged a look. She wondered if he was thinking about the malpractice suit. "No, of course not. No surgery is without risks."

"Then I don't want it."

Rose sighed. "What would happen without the surgery?"

Vera sat up straighter in her chair. "Maybe I can wait. Maybe it'll go away on its own. Like Hank Lapp's toothache."

"Hank had that tooth pulled," Rose said.

Charles looked like he was starting to run short on patience, which, at best, was never a leisurely path. "The tumor will continue to grow and eventually affect other regions of the brain. And then . . ."

"And then I'll die." Vera clapped her hands together over her chest. "I am ready to meet my Maker."

"Vera, before you do, let's hear more about the option of surgery." Rose turned to Charles. "If the surgery is successful, will her symptoms disappear?"

"Most should. And if it's benign, then she won't require any treatments—just follow-up scans. Physical therapy will help her regain her confidence in her strength and balance."

Rose turned to Vera. "I think we should consider it."

Vera huffed. "And how are we going to pay for this brain surgery? Have you thought of that?"

Rose, normally so capable, seemed at a loss for words. "Well, I . . . I'll speak to Deacon Abraham. I'm sure the church will help. We'll manage somehow."

"Charles will volunteer his services," Delia blurted out. Charles's eyebrows shot up. "He does it all the time. Bona fides. It means free. He's generous like that." She studiously avoided Charles's stare, but Vera did calm at that news.

Rose walked back and forth in the room. "When do we need to decide?"

"Right now," Charles said. "There's an opening for tomorrow morning. We had to postpone a patient's surgery because his blood pressure is too high. Delia can drive you over to the hospital now and get you settled in."

"You're going to do it?" Vera asked, the first, tiniest glimmer of hope crossing her eyes.

"My specialty is with vascular neuropathy," he said. "My job is to cut off the blood supply that feeds tumors and allows them to grow. The surgeon I have in mind for you is excellent. He's available tomorrow because of the canceled surgery."

Vera flashed a look of panic at Rose, who turned to Delia. Delia could see this was a new wrinkle. Possibly, a deal breaker. If Vera was going to agree to this, it hinged on Charles's performing the surgery. "But Charles, you have done this surgery. Hundreds of times."

"Yes, but . . ."

"And you've always said that every single brain surgery is unique. There are no two situations that are exactly the same when it comes to brain surgery. You've said that the reason you're such a good neurosurgeon is that you're prepared for every possible scenario. You've kept your skills current. I've heard you say that, dozens of times."

"Yes, but . . ."

"So you are familiar with this type of surgery?" Rose said.

His eyebrows shot up. "Of course. As Delia said, I've performed open brain surgery more times than I can count. But, just to be clear, I'm a specialist for an even more complicated type of brain surgery . . ." He looked at Rose, then at Vera, who looked back at him with eager anticipation. "I . . . but I . . ." He looked at Delia. She saw his expression slide from disbelief to confusion to acceptance. She knew him well enough to know what he was thinking. He hadn't expected this turn of events—but he was pleased, nonetheless. Charles had a great deal of confidence in himself and knew he was an excellent surgeon, but he was not immune to others' appreciation for his skills. In other words, he could be bought. "Yes . . . I could perform the surgery. Assuming Vera gives her consent."

Then all eyes turned to Vera, waiting for her to agree to the surgery. She sat quietly as she considered all that Charles had said to her. "Why? I don't understand why this is happening. Why would God do this to me? Why would he let me down?"

Rose crouched down beside her chair. "Vera, I know one thing. I know that God has never let us down. Not even when Dean passed. He has never abandoned us. It's not possible. God is good no matter what circumstances you're facing. We need to remember that, and to keep declaring that God is good, no matter what. That we know it to be true."

Vera nodded in agreement. "I need more faith."

"Then borrow mine," Rose said.

Those three words felt like an electric shock to Delia. Was that even possible? To borrow someone's faith? She'd been leaning heavily on Rose's faith since she arrived at Eagle Hill. Or maybe Rose meant that a person's faith could be inspired to grow just by observing the depth of another's faith.

Whatever Rose meant by that, it seemed to do the trick. Doubt and blame seemed to be pushed away, and peace rolled in. Vera turned to Delia. "Is he any good?"

"Vera, if I had to have brain surgery, I would insist that Charles perform the surgery." Delia looked at Charles. "He's the best, Vera. The very best."

Charles didn't even exhale when she said this. It was as though he was holding his breath, waiting to hear Delia's response to Vera. Then he let out a breath and turned his attention to Vera. "I have the skills to help you, Vera, and I love using those skills. I want to try to help you so you can get on with the rest of your life. But I can't guarantee a perfect outcome. No one can. All I can promise is that I will do the very best job I can."

Vera rose, a little wobbly. "Let's get this over with."

As Charles held the door for them, Delia was last out the door.

"Bona fides? I think you meant to say pro bono. That means free. Bona fides means in good faith."

She lifted one shoulder in a half shrug. "Same thing." She turned to him. "Charles—this family, well, I can't explain it, but they have become a very special family to me."

His eyes softened again. She had forgotten how he used to look at her in that special way. A just-for-her way. How long had it been? "We'll figure something out," he said.

"Thank you for agreeing to perform the surgery. I think that made all the difference to Vera."

He lifted an eyebrow. "I'd forgotten how the Amish can be surprisingly stubborn."

She arched an eyebrow back at him. "I hadn't."

Delia took Rose and Vera over to the hospital to get Vera checked in. Charles's office had called over to smooth the path—and still, it was daunting. She wasn't sure how two Amish ladies could have navigated the complexity of hospital administration without this kind of streamlining help. She could barely wade through it all herself.

As a nurse settled Vera into her hospital room—a private room, which she knew Charles had arranged—Delia spoke quietly to Rose. "Tell me how I can help. Would you like me to drive you home tonight? Or would you be willing to stay at my house here in town?"

"I think I should stay at the hospital tonight," Rose said. "Vera is frightened. This is all happening so fast." There was a pull-out bed in the corner. More like a padded bench.

"I can call the farmhouse and leave a message."

Rose frowned. She wasn't sure if the children would remember to check the messages for her. "Maybe you could call Galen. He has a phone in his barn. There's a better chance of getting through."

"Rose, would you like me to drive out tonight? I could let everyone know what's happening."

Relief flooded Rose's face. "Oh, Delia, would you? Then they could pray. And that would put their minds at ease."

Delia would have worded it differently. If she had information, then her mind would be at ease. And then she could pray. Information felt like control—but it really wasn't. Rose had it right. Prayer came first, then the peace. "Why don't you give me a list of things you and Vera will need for a few days."

"How long do you think she'll be in the hospital?"

"I don't know. Tomorrow will answer a lot of those questions." Assuming there was a tomorrow for Vera. Brain surgery was risky. "I'll go now. I'm just going to drop by my house and pick up a few things, then head out to Eagle Hill. I'll return first thing in the morning." At the door, she turned to Rose. "Maybe you should call Galen anyway. I think he'd like to hear about all this from you."

Later, as Delia drove west along I-76, she called her son Will.

"Isn't it amazing, Mom?" Will said after she had explained all that had happened in the last week.

"What?"

"The circumstances."

"Yes, your father definitely made this surgery possible for Vera."

"More than that. You're a big part of this. What about the fact that you happened to be at that particular Amish inn, and Dad happened to have met Vera. I mean, what are the chances? Seems like it's all part of a master plan. Like God is orchestrating all of this."

She hadn't thought of the last few weeks like that, but as soon as Will said it, something clicked into place for her. It *was* God's orchestration! She felt it deep in her bones—a feeling of love and well-being washed over her. God was involved in all of this, down to every detail. He loved prickly Vera, he loved strong Rose, he loved her—flaws and all. He probably even loved Charles. Tears welled in her eyes. She had to blink them back.

"It's kind of you to help them, Mom. A few weeks ago, they were strangers to you."

"They've become friends. Rose, especially."

"If anybody would have told you, a month ago, that you'd be moving heaven and earth to help an Amish family whom you just met, well, wouldn't that surprise you?"

She grinned. "I suppose you're right."

"You've changed. You used to be so determined not to let anyone get close. You're different now."

Delia hesitated, not sure how to respond. But Will was right, something had changed her. Or Somebody. This entire experience had affected her, and for the better. Uninvited and unwanted, cancer had barged into her life—as another woman had barged into her marriage—and turned it upside down. Thank God.

"Mom, years ago when I was in Stoney Ridge, living at Windmill Farm—I came away with a belief in God. I've let it sort of get crowded out. Gone dormant."

Crowded out. Dormant. That's exactly what she had done with God. Kept him there, but pushed off to the side of life. She hadn't needed God . . . until now. "Me too, Will. It's time to change that. I don't think God wants to be a bystander."

Will laughed. "Amos Lapp told me one time that if you weren't paying attention to God, then God had a way of getting your attention."

Wasn't that the truth? Hadn't this last month been a wake-up call for Delia? Awful events—yet, she wouldn't change a thing. If cancer and Charles's affair were what it took to feel this close to God, to have these kinds of conversations with her son—it was all worth it.

"By the way, if you happen to see that vet who was treating the colt, would you get her phone number for me?" He cleared his throat. "I have a question or two for her . . . about one of my classes."

She grinned. She *thought* there was a spark between those two! "I'll see what I can do."

# 20

————————

Breakfast was scorched scrambled eggs, orange juice with frozen lumps that hadn't dissolved, and undercooked pancakes. There were rumblings of thunder and lightning, which meant the boys had to remain inside until school started.

And that meant that Mim couldn't concentrate on her book. Luke and Sammy were stomping around their bedroom, which was next to Mim's. They were like a hurricane, Mim thought. Those two would never stop joshing each other and trying to outdo each other. Finally, downstairs, Bethany had enough of the big thumping sounds. She told them to clean up their rooms and throw their collections out. Usually, Bethany barked commands that nobody obeyed. But she was serious about getting rid of those collections. She complained they were stinking up the whole upstairs and she couldn't stand them one more minute. Those boys collected all kinds of things—anything useless. Birds' feathers, pebbles, eggshells, snake skins, the skeleton of something that might be a bat. They were regular packrats.

The boys burst into Mim's room without a knock. "We need you to make a sign for us," Luke announced. Sammy nodded.

"What kind of a sign?"

"We want to sell stuff."

"That's ridiculous. No one will buy your useless stuff. It's junk."

Luke was insulted. "They might."

She put down her book. "I'm all for you cleaning out your collections and I'm all for you making money, but you need to find a way to make your things desirable to someone else."

Sammy brightened. "Like . . . buried treasure?"

She laughed. "Oh sure! Just tell folks you're selling rare antiques and your junk will sell like that." She snapped her fingers in the air. She was joking.

The boys looked at each other, then their faces lit up like firecrackers and they vanished back into their bedroom.

"I was joking!" she called out.

Later that night, Mim lit the small oil lamp on her desk. There were definitely moments when she missed flipping a switch and having electric lights, but she couldn't deny that there was no pleasanter light than the soft glow of an oil lamp. She read once that whale oil gave off the nicest flame, but she didn't know where a person would buy whale oil.

She couldn't sleep tonight, not with her mother away in Philadelphia in a hospital with her grandmother. Too many worries bounced through her mind. Tomorrow would be a very big surgery for her grandmother. She might die. Mim hoped she wouldn't die, but she might. In such important matters, Mim always felt it was best to prepare for the worst.

She uncovered the typewriter and polished her glasses. Then she set to work on answering Mrs. Miracle letters. She found the questions about love to be the trickiest to answer. Love was a mystery. How could she try to explain the shaky-excited feelings she got whenever she was in close proximity to Danny Riehl?

*Dear Mrs. Miracle,*

*My boyfriend cheated on me. Should I cheat on him to teach him a lesson?*

*Signed,*
*Angry in Arizona*

*Dear Angry,*

*I am sorry to hear that your boyfriend had such bad judgment. But no, you should not cheat on him to teach him a lesson. Two wrongs don't make a right. However, I do think you should break up with him and find a new boyfriend. A faithful one.*

*Very truly yours,*
*Mrs. Miracle*

Satisfied, Mim pulled the letter out of the typewriter with a flourish and folded it. She typed the address on the envelope, put the folded letter inside, licked it, stamped it, and set it on her nightside table. Time for the next letter:

*Dear Mrs. Miracle,*
 *I would like to know, according to all your experience, if love can overcome everything.*
 *Lonely in Love*

*Dear Lonely,*
 *If love is true, it will overcome almost everything.*
 *Sincerely,*
 *Mrs. Miracle*

Mim stopped and stared at the page. Wasn't that the answer to her own dilemma? If Danny were her true love, then even if he moved away, that wouldn't change anything, would it? She smiled. Mrs. Miracle had solved her problem. She took out a blank piece of paper, rolled it into the typewriter, and started typing . . .

*Dear Mrs. Miracle,*
 *My mother doesn't see me. She doesn't hear what I say. She thinks she does, but she doesn't. She is busy with my grandmother, my sister, and my brothers. I would welcome your exceedingly wise counsel.*
 *Very truly yours,*
 *Miss Invisible*

Mim pulled the paper out of the typewriter and held it up. To see a problem in black and white made it seem less like a conundrum and more like a situation waiting for a solution. Almost like a math formula. Not quite, but almost. No wonder she was so inspired in her new role as Mrs. Miracle.

◌ ◊ ◌

Rose felt such a shock at the sight of Vera getting wheeled out for surgery that she had to steady herself against the wall. The pre-operative area was a large, busy room. Nurses and doctors were rushing here and there, machines beeped, worried families gathered in clumps and murmured quietly, gurneys slid by with patients on their way to surgery. One of those gurneys held Vera. Seeing her mother-in-law with head shaved, tubes going everywhere, a big IV bag filled with saline by her side—the sight made Rose's stomach twist. For Vera's sake, she tried not to let on how she felt. It was no time to be weak. She squeezed Vera's hand as she walked alongside the gurney.

The orderly stopped the gurney at the operating door and gave a nod to Rose. "This is as far as you can go. Wish her well."

Rose leaned over and brushed a tear leaking down Vera's cheek. "I'll be praying the entire time and I'll be here when you get through it."

Vera squeezed her eyes shut. "Dean's the lucky one. He's missed a lot of heartache."

"He's missed a lot of joy too."

Vera opened her eyes. "I wish I could be as strong as you."

"Why, Vera, you're the strongest person I know," Rose said, in a gentle tone. "I couldn't manage without you. We've weathered all kinds of storms together. We'll get through this one too."

"Rose, I don't really think you're the worst daughter-in-law in the world."

"I know you don't."

A sharp little spark lit Vera's eyes. "The first one Dean brought home—she was the worst."

Rose sighed.

As the orderly pushed Vera's gurney through doors that led to the operating room, Rose decided to try to find a quiet place, maybe a chapel, to pray. To pray away some troubles that just weren't willing to leave.

Trust, from Galen, came slowly. When Delia Stoltz asked him if he would like to drive to the hospital with her, he hesitated. His mind raced through all the potential disasters that could occur in his absence with Jimmy Fisher in charge. He knew he kept Jimmy on a short tether—he thought the boy had a talent for horses, but he also knew his tendency toward the lazy when unsupervised. And if Bethany happened by, Jimmy couldn't keep his mind on the task at hand.

But Galen did see glimmers of maturing in Jimmy. In fact, he was learning so quickly and developing into such a skilled hand that Galen felt a little guilty for holding him back from more responsibility.

Still, leaving Jimmy Fisher in charge of his Thoroughbreds for an entire day? The boy couldn't even keep track of the one horse he had bought.

It was Delia who said just the right thing to convince him to set aside his worries and go to the hospital. "I think Rose might need to have a special friend like you by her side."

Galen looked at her sharply but didn't answer right away. He had never so much as mentioned Rose's name to anyone—how could Delia know Rose was on his mind? It was disturbing to him to have one's thoughts suddenly plucked out of the air. Women could smell feelings as a dog could smell a fox.

Would Rose be glad to see him? He wasn't really sure. But he knew he needed to do this.

A full day of waiting stretched out in front of Rose. To wait and wait. She hadn't eaten breakfast and was starting to feel a little weak, close to tears, as the what-ifs crept into her mind. What if Vera's brain was damaged in the surgery? What if the tumor was cancerous? What if she didn't survive the surgery? Vera may not be the easiest person to live with, but she was family. She was loved.

Sitting on that uncomfortable chair in the sterile room, Rose felt so alone. Tears welled in her eyes, and her throat ached. A deep sense of loss rose up in her, so forceful, woven of so many memories. Vera had a saying: Oh, das hahmelt mir ahn. *Calling to mind poignant memories with such vividness that they brought pain.*

Such scenes rolled through her mind: Dean's happiness on the day he brought Rose home to meet Vera, Tobe, and Bethany. The children's small faces, so hopeful as they looked at her, eager to have a new mother. Luke and Sammy as toddlers, wrestling like two bear cubs. Serious Mim with her arms filled with books. The children's shocked faces as they stood by their father's graveside, newly turned earth, the raw wind cutting through their coats—Mim hated wind from that day on. Bethany's stoic face—she never shed a tear for her father. Not that day, not since. Someday, Rose knew those tears of hers would need to spill.

But after the funeral . . . they all buried their grief and carried on. Got back to the business of living. That was the way of things.

Too much. Sometimes, it was just too much.

The whoosh of the automatic doors startled her and she raised her head. She hadn't known she was crying until she felt the air from the outside cool the wetness on her cheeks. In strode Galen King with his black hat on, coming through the doors as if he walked through that hospital door every day of his life. In one hand was a cup of coffee, in the other was a brown bag.

"Are you all right?" he asked, peering at her with concern. "Are you okay, Rose?"

She nodded, still not quite trusting herself to speak. The truth was that she had never felt so glad to see anyone. All her nervousness and sadness squeezed right out of her. "Galen!" she said at last, whispering the words. "How did you get here?"

"Delia Stoltz drove me in. She dropped me at the door and went to park. She's going to go see if she can find out how the surgery is going." He handed her the coffee. "We thought you might need a little moral support."

She took a sip of the coffee. A dollop of cream, just the way she liked it. "I'm glad you're here, Galen. I have to admit I'm scared of today's outcome."

He looked at her with one of those quiet smiles that touched only his eyes and said, "You always seem as calm as a dove."

"That's on the outside," Rose said. "On the inside, I'm a bundle of raw nerves."

He sat in the chair next to her and stretched out his legs, crossing one ankle over the other. "There's no outrunning fear. It comes on you and you have to face it."

She just looked at him, then, taking her time and thinking. He held her eyes, then looked away, as if embarrassed. He lifted the brown bag. "Delia stopped by a store and bought a package of one-bite doughnuts."

He opened up the bag of cinnamon sugar one-bite doughnuts and offered one to Rose. She found them amusing. Delicious too. As Galen filled her in on the news from Stoney Ridge, she found herself feeling weepy again. She knew what it had taken for him to give up a day of work just to sit here with her. He was not a man who sat and kept vigil.

She wasn't sure what the end of the day would bring, but she decided that from now on, she would savor sweet moments, like this one, as much as she could. Like one-bite doughnuts.

Galen and Rose had gone for a walk outside to get some fresh air. Delia stayed in the waiting area, flipping through an old copy of *People* magazine. They had invited her to walk with them but she said no. It was an ideal opportunity to give them time alone. There was precious little of that in their lives.

Delia had a sense about matchmaking and she could just see that there was more to Galen and Rose's relationship than friendship. She didn't think they realized it yet—certainly not Rose—but Delia could see it clearly. Galen and Rose spoke the same language, thought the same thoughts. True, he was younger than Rose, but in all the important ways, he seemed older.

As they drove in this morning, she had expected it to be a silent drive, but Galen was surprisingly talkative. Granted, she peppered him with questions, but he didn't freeze up like she thought he would. He answered her questions about his horse training business, Naomi's headaches, his other sisters and brothers who had married and moved away. The very fact that he steered any and all conversation away from Rose only led Delia to believe that he was in love with her.

Time passed in an instant. The last thing Vera remembered, she was fighting back tears as her hair was getting shaved off. She had never had her hair cut. Not once in her entire long life. And this morning, it was all shaved off.

An instant later, she woke up in a recovery room, feeling like a hen caught in the middle of a killing neck twist. What had happened? Her head was bandaged in gauze like a foreigner's head wraps. She saw such a thing once on a bus trip she took to Sarasota, Florida, to visit her cousin. What was the word for it? And underneath the gauze that was wrapped around her head were staples and glue. Staples!

There was one bright spot she hadn't expected: brain surgery was relatively painless. The nurse explained that even though there were many nerves in the brain, they were nerves that thought, not nerves that felt. "You'll be off those pain meds by tomorrow," she told Vera. "And I think you'll like the effects of the steroids the doctor will give you to control swelling. They'll make you happy and hungry. You might even like our hospital food."

Vera opened one eye to peer at the tray she had brought. "Doubt it," she mumbled. "That would take more than drugs." Who ate blue Jell-O? Before she left this hospital for home, she might try to get into the hospital kitchen and show the cook a thing or two about how the Amish managed to cook for big crowds.

Then that fine-looking doctor came in and asked her to count backward from one hundred. She couldn't. Each moment of silence that passed caused Vera's fears to grow. She had never been good at arithmetic. He asked her what day it was and who the president of the United States was right now. How should she know? She never voted. Rose did, but she never did.

Tears started to fill her eyes. The doctor's hand clasped hers and squeezed. "Right now there's tissue swollen from the surgery," he explained. "As the swelling goes down, everything will improve. It's too soon to worry, but I'm not expecting significant implications from the surgery."

It was never too soon to worry, Vera thought bitterly. How infuriating to have this invasive, frightening surgery, only to have it do nothing for her! She was in worse shape than she was before she had it. She should have never agreed to it.

The doctor wrote down a few things on her chart and told her he would be back later in the day to check on her. Then he sailed out of the room and left her alone with beeping machines.

A turban. *A turban.* That's what the gauze on her head felt like.

She remembered!

After the surgery, Rose was allowed into Vera's intensive care room for ten minutes. No longer. Vera looked peaked and drawn, but there was some fire in her too. "Get me out of here," she whispered to Rose.

"Not quite yet. As soon as Dr. Stoltz says you can go home."

Amazingly, that could be as soon as a few days, he had said, when he came into the waiting room to tell Rose that the surgery had been successful. He had walked through those swinging doors in his blue scrubs, a big grin on his face, and stopped abruptly. In the waiting room was not just Rose, but seven Amish people from Stoney Ridge, a crowd, peering at him with concerned faces under their black hats and bonnets. "Everything went very well, better than expected," Dr. Stoltz told the group, sounding satisfied. "We won't know more until she wakes up. I'm hopeful for a complete recovery as the swelling recedes, but, of course, I'm not the ultimate healer."

"I believe that position is already taken," said a woman's voice from the back of the Amish crowd. It came from Fern Lapp.

Fern had organized a Mennonite driver to take a few church members into Philadelphia and stay with Rose during the surgery. At the sound of her voice, Dr. Stoltz's dark eyebrows shot up and his entire countenance changed. That serious, extremely confident man suddenly seemed like a small boy who'd met up with a stern librarian with an overdue book in his hand.

But then, Fern Lapp—thin as a butter knife, wiry and active—had that effect on nearly everyone, with one exception: Vera. Those two women tried to outdo each other in everything: quilting, cooking, baking, gardening.

Fern offered to stay the night at the hospital so Rose could return home and rest. The driver was waiting in the parking lot for Galen and the others. "I'll stay the night so you can go on home," Fern said, after Dr. Stoltz made a hasty exit. "You look terrible. Awful. Like something the cat dragged in."

Rose hadn't slept a wink—partly because of that awful padded bench, but mostly because Vera kept hollering out things through the night she wanted Rose to know about . . . just in case. In case she died, she meant.

"Write this down: The farm goes to Tobe. I promised him!"

"Yes, Vera."

"Make sure Bethany gets *A Young Woman's Guide to Virtue*. She loves that book."

"Yes, Vera."

"My mother gave me that book. It was her book. Did I ever tell you that?"

"Yes, Vera. Try to sleep now."

But of course, Vera didn't want to sleep. As far as she was concerned, it might be the last night of her life on earth. Why spend it sleeping? she told Rose. Finally, Rose turned on the light and read the Bible aloud to her. Psalm 23, then 139. Vera quieted at those ancient words of comfort. Soon, she was snoring loud enough to rattle the windows. Rose closed the Bible, turned off the light, and tried to sleep.

After such a long night, the thought of Rose's own bed sounded heavenly, but she knew Vera needed her. "Thank you, Fern, but I'll stay."

Later, trying to get comfortable on the awful chairs in the waiting room for the ICU floor, she regretted that decision. Tomorrow night, if Vera continued to improve, she would take Delia up on her offer to stay at her house for the remaining nights until Vera was released. She spread a gray blanket over her that a nurse had brought out. Its color mirrored the reflective mood Rose was in. She thought of the kind and considerate friends who had waited with her all day in the hospital. Of Fern Lapp, who said she would take a meal over to Eagle Hill for tonight's supper. Of Delia Stoltz, who was staying at her own home tonight and promised to check in first thing in the morning. Of Hank Lapp, who kept everyone entertained with the box of dominoes he had brought with him.

Her mind traveled to Dean. His chief focus, especially in the last few years of his life, had been on making more and more money, but did money bring any greater happiness than friendship? She thought not.

Then she thought of Galen. He had given up a day of work to stay by her side, and she knew what that meant to him. And she had ended up hurting him.

Before Fern and the others had arrived, she and Galen had gone outside to get some fresh air. They stopped at a bench, blanketed in sunshine, and sat down. Out of the blue came the question, "Rose, have you given some thought about letting me court you?"

She had been dreading this conversation. "I've thought about it. I've thought about it plenty." The smile she gave him came a little shakily. "Can't things just go on between us the way they've been going? As good friends?"

"You don't know what you're asking of me. You might as well tell the grain to stay green. The way we are now might be fine for you, but not for me. I want more, Rose."

"I'm not right for you, Galen."

"What you really mean is . . . I'm not right for you."

She raised her head. Those piercing green eyes were looking down at her under the brim of his black hat, searching her face, trying to see into her heart. "Yes," she said softly. She felt him stiffen beside her and look away. It pained her to say those words to him—nearly as much as she knew it pained him to hear them, but it was the truth.

Slowly he turned back to her. His face was flat and empty, but a muscle ticked in his cheek and she could see the pulse beating in his neck, fast and hard. "I'll go see if there's any word about Vera." He walked to the door that led to the hospital waiting room, half turned at the door, then swung back. "The hard truth is that I'm not the one who's too stubborn and independent and unbending. You are. You won't let anyone help you. You don't mind having people rely on you, but you don't want to need anyone. If that's not pride, I don't know what is."

He waited, but there was nothing more she had to say to him, or at least she hadn't within her the words he wanted to hear. The silence hung between them, waiting for someone to act—but then they heard someone call Galen's name. They turned and saw a group of Amish church friends, climbing out of a Mennonite taxi at the curbside, who had come to help stand vigil. Galen walked over to meet them.

Pride? *Pride?* He thought she was prideful?! Rose was stung.

It was unfortunate that Bethany's first day of work at the Sisters' House happened to fall on the day Mammi Vera ended up having surgery. In a way, though, it helped Bethany to keep her mind from fretting about her grandmother. She couldn't do any good by just walking the walls of the hospital, anyway.

Early that morning, Bethany was met at the door of the Sisters' House by Ada. She led Bethany into the living room and told her to start from one corner and go from there. "Use your own judgment about what to keep or what to get rid of."

"Are you sure?" Bethany asked. "I don't really know what you might need." Not that there was anything worth salvaging, in her mind. Maybe a box of fabric for quilt scraps. A ball of yarn. Everything else? *Out!*

"Maybe you're right," Ada said. "We do use everything, sooner or later. I just hate that feeling of when you throw something out and—" *snap!* she clicked her knobby fingers—"next thing you know, you're looking high and low for it."

Bethany looked around the room. "I need three boxes," she told Ada. "One for things you want to keep, one for things you want to donate, one for things to discard."

Twenty minutes later, Ada returned with four boxes. "I thought it might be wise if we leave one for things we can't decide about. Just in case."

All right, Bethany told her, and soon regretted it. One sister after another would mosey in and start weeding through the Donate and Discard pile and quietly move things into the Keep and Undecided boxes. By lunchtime, they had undone all the morning work Bethany had done.

Okay, this wasn't working. She decided to take a break and eat her lunch on the front porch. It was a pleasant day and she couldn't work with the sisters in the same room. Since there were five of them, they acted like slippery barn cats, oozing their way in and out of the living room, making off with something from the discard pile. When she finished her lunch, she went back inside and found Ada bent over the Undecided box, rooting through black sweaters. So many sweaters! All black.

"Maybe I'll just go tidy up the kitchen," Bethany said. Stick to the dishes, she decided.

Ada was thrilled by that suggestion which, Bethany knew, was because she worked too fast and made her nervous. Too many treasures ended up in the wrong boxes.

By day's end, Bethany was exhausted. She stopped by the phone shanty to check messages—hoping there might be word about Mammi Vera from Rose. And maybe a word from Jake.

She tried her very best not to call Jake every single day. She knew, from reading chapter 13 in *A Young Woman's Guide to Virtue*, that she should restrain herself. But each day, she found a reason or two to slip around the hard and fast rules of the book. Today, she wanted to talk to him about her grandmother's surgery, about losing her job at the Bar & Grill and taking the job at the Sisters' House. She hoped he might feel disappointed that she had committed to a new job, even if it was part time and very casual. She hoped he had plans for the two of them. But, like always, he didn't pick up. Before she thought twice, she left a message that she needed to talk to him and hung up.

As she was closing the door to the shanty, the phone rang. She lunged for the receiver. "Hello?"

"Bethany! Did you find the books?"

Not even a howdy. "No."

"You said you needed to talk to me. I thought it was about the books."

"I do need to talk to you, but I haven't found them yet."

"Are you looking?"

"Of course I'm looking! I've gone through the entire house, top to bottom. Mim mentioned that a lot of Mammi Vera's junk was hauled out to the hayloft, so I'll start there soon." She shuddered to think of spending hours in the dusty hayloft. She hated mice with their beady little eyes and long skinny tails. Hated them. "I do have other obligations, I hope you know." Like, a job with five certifiably crazy old ladies.

His voice softened. "I wish I could help. I'm sorry to leave this job to you."

"So . . . why can't you help?"

"Bethany—I told you. If your family were to see me, if Rose were to know about Tobe's problem, it puts her in a terrible spot." He let out a sigh. "Besides, I'm miles and miles away, looking for work."

The discouragement in his voice made her feel a tweak of guilt. It didn't seem right to talk to him about her new job at the Sisters' House when he had lost his job and couldn't get hired anywhere else—all because of her father.

"Honey, what did you need me for, then?"

She loved it when he called her honey. "I . . . just wanted to hear your voice."

"That's sweet. I sure am missing you. As soon as you can find those books, I will hightail it back to Stoney Ridge. Once we get Tobe cleared . . . then . . ."

She held her breath. *Then what?*

". . . everything else will come together."

She let out her breath.

"I need to get going. Bye for now, honey."

For a long while, she stared at the receiver before she set it back in the cradle. She loved it when he called her honey. Loved it!

# 21

In every human heart, Rose thought, even the most forbidding, there was a place that could be touched. The difficulty was finding it; there were people who carefully concealed that place. Sometimes, though, their guard slipped for a moment or two, and the way to a heart lay open. She saw such a moment today. She thought of such things as miracles, though she knew Bishop Elmo would disagree. But to Rose, unexpected moments of healing and happiness pointed people to God. Wasn't that a miracle?

That moment came when she saw Charles and Delia Stoltz talking to each other in the hospital corridor. Standing close, listening carefully to each other. They didn't strike Rose as a couple who were heading to divorce court. They looked like they were finding their way back to each other.

Other unexpected miracles occurred today too. When Dr. Stoltz pronounced Vera ready to go home—four days after the surgery. Rose thought it might be a little premature, but it seemed the hospital staff was particularly eager to have Vera released—she was *that* bossy and critical.

Delia drove Rose and Vera back to Eagle Hill. They arrived home to find the table set for dinner, the animals fed and tucked away for the night, the house tidied up, and a beautiful dinner waiting to be served. That felt like a miracle to Rose.

Rose tucked Vera straight into bed, promising her plenty of time for catch-up talks with the family in the days ahead. She tried to keep everyone quiet, but Vera said not to bother—that the sounds of family at the dinner table filled her with happiness. Soon, the house was a jumble of noise and confusion and joy. Another miracle!

Delia and Jimmy Fisher joined the family for supper. Rose sent Luke and Sammy over to invite Galen and Naomi and was disappointed when they declined. She wanted things to be as they were. Why couldn't Galen understand that life wasn't as simple for her as he made it out to be?

She was prideful, he told her. *Her!* That from a man who kept himself apart from others. Who only took on an apprentice because the deacon insisted. Well, if that's how Galen wanted things to be between them—all stiff and stern—that was fine with her. Just fine.

During the meal, Rose looked around the table with overflowing gratitude. It had always done her heart good to watch people eat the food from her kitchen, especially her own family and friends. To some, it might seem like such an ordinary thing. To her, it felt like a healing balm. All would be well.

Miracle number five.

Whenever a chore around the farm needed tending to, Luke and Sammy quietly slipped out of sight. Today, Saturday morning, Bethany had enough of their disappearances. She was tired of feeding chickens and sheep and a goat. She marched down to the roadside where they were trying to sell their junk. "You two get up to that barn and take care of your animals."

"Can't!" Luke said. "Saturday morning is our peak selling time."

"Who would buy your junk?" Bethany said, annoyed with their flimsy excuses.

"Tons of folks. We've been making a boatload of money."

Sammy nodded solemnly. "A boatload."

"What do you two have that anybody would ever want?"

"It's all in the selling," Luke said. "Mim was right. If we call something an antique, it sells."

Bethany's eyes grazed over the cardboard table with disgust: old amber bottles, rabbit feet, rusty lanterns, blue jay feathers, a baseball cap the boys had found on the roadside that cars had run over a few times, jigsaw puzzles with missing pieces, some black books, galvanized milk pails, . . . wait a minute. Black books? Two black books with red bindings. Heart racing, she grabbed them and leafed through them. Pages and pages of names, dates, numbers. Tobe's books! "Where'd you find these?"

"In the bottom of a box in the hayloft," Sammy said. "Why?"

She hugged the books to her body. "Hallelujah and never you mind!"

The next day was bright and sunny, already warm by midmorning. Mim was watering the strawberry patch with a makeshift watering can that Luke had rigged up: a plastic jug of Tide laundry detergent with holes poked in the cap. Nearby, two bluejays were having an argument. Mim wished Luke would come along with his handcarved slingshot to silence them, but he and Sammy were down by the road, trying to sell their junk. Her mother came out of the kitchen and stood at the edge of the garden. She watched quietly for a long time as Mim watered the rows of green little plants with delicate white flowers.

"Won't be long until we can make strawberry jam."

"I don't think it will be much of a crop," Mim said. "Not unless we get more rain."

"How does Mammi Vera seem to you?"

Mim gave that some thought as she refilled the Tide water bucket. When Mammi Vera had come into the house last night, she looked like she'd wrestled with a black bear and lost—her head was bandaged and she had dark circles under her eyes. But then she started complaining about how dirty the house was—it wasn't—and how noisy the boys were—they were—and Mim knew she would be fine. Her face got all soft and sweet when she saw Bethany. Her eyes shimmered with tears of joy—and then came the best part. No hiccups!

"She seems the same. A little better. But it might be too early to tell if she's fixed."

"How did the game of checkers go this morning?" The nurses at the hospital had told Vera to play a lot of board games and do puzzles. It was good exercise for the brain, they said. Luke, Sammy, and Mim set up a schedule to take turns playing games with her.

Mim straightened up. "Well, she cheated. But she always did cheat at checkers."

Her mother grinned. She walked over a few rows and cupped Mim's cheeks with her hands. "Mim, I do see you. I do hear you. I know this last year has been overwhelming at times, but I never want you to feel as if you're not important to me. You are."

Mim gave her mother a look that in half a minute went from anger to worry to sadness to resignation. "The letter. You read the letter." Bethany had kept everyone so busy getting ready for Mammi Vera's homecoming that Mim had completely forgotten to pick up yesterday's mail.

Her mother nodded. "I went through the mail last night before I went to bed."

Mim squinted her face. "How did you know it was from me?"

"How many typewriters have a letter *A* that is slightly crooked?"

Mim hung her head. She hadn't thought of letter *A*.

"I wondered if you might like to take some early walks with me this summer after school lets out? I'd like your company."

Her mother had never invited anyone on a morning walk, not even her father. Mim took off her glasses, polished them, and replaced them. "I suppose. I suppose I could do that."

Her mother smiled. "Let's plan on it, then."

Bethany felt bewildered, disoriented. She slammed the rolling pin down onto the ball of biscuit dough. She pushed hard and the dough flattened. She pulled and pushed the heavy wooden pin, pulled and pushed, rolling out the dough with such vigor that flour floated in a white cloud around her.

She stopped pushing the biscuit dough and stood in stillness a moment, bent over the table, her hands gripping the rolling pin. She straightened, dusted her hands off on her apron, and laughed at her silly nervousness. Wedding jitters. Every bride felt them. *A Young Woman's Guide to Virtue* said to expect them.

Bethany had called Jake to leave a message and tell him about the books and was surprised when he answered his phone. When she told him about the books, the phone went silent. Then he let out a huge sigh of relief. "Just in the nick of time. I'll be there tonight."

"What time? I have to be at a birthday party for a neighbor."

"Where's the party?"

"At Windmill Farm—just a few miles up the road from Eagle Hill."

"I'll be down at the end of Windmill Farm's driveway at 8 p.m. tonight. Be there with the books."

Now she was silent.

"Bethie?"

"What does that mean . . . just in the nick of time?"

"I've got a job opportunity in Somerset County. A good job. I've held off as long as I can. Because of you, because you found those books, I'll be able to help Tobe and get to that job."

"So will Tobe be coming home soon?"

"No doubt, honey. All because of you."

"What *about* me, Jake? You're just going to disappear again, aren't you?"

In the silence that followed, Bethany felt the air about her crackle and tremble, like the pause between lightning and thunder—something had to happen. She couldn't live this way any longer—waiting, waiting, waiting for Jake. If she was going to lose him in the end, better to face it now. "I'm no good at waiting."

In a raspy voice, almost choked up, Jake said, "Then come with me."

What?! She lurched to grab the counter so she didn't lose her balance. Weren't those the words she'd been longing to hear from him for over a year now? But now, faced with the reality of them . . . she wasn't sure if she was ready for them. "I don't know . . . I'm not sure I can leave my family . . ."

"Bethany, your family is doing fine. You told me so yourself. Everyone has adjusted. They don't need you now like they did. It's your time, honey." He paused again. "So . . . come with me."

She drew in a deep breath and then another. "You mean, as your wife?" she had asked. "Because that's the only way you'll ever have me, Jake Hertzler."

He had laughed then and asked her what kind of a low-down excuse of a man did she consider him to be? Then he said he needed to go, but he would be at the foot of Windmill Farm tonight at eight o'clock. And he told her he loved her.

He had never spoken of love to her before. As she hung up the phone on the cradle, she hugged herself with happiness. Jake loved her! He was coming to get her. They were going to be married and live happily ever after. She had dreamed of this day.

So why was her stomach twisting and turning?

If only Jake had asked her to marry him a year ago, before everything bad happened, then it all would have been so much easier. They could have had a proper church wedding, and her family would've embraced Jake as a son. Her father had already thought of him as a son.

She squeezed her eyes shut. That was then and this was now. Her father wasn't here any longer.

After moving to Stoney Ridge, Bethany had known that if she married Jake, it would come down to this: eloping. There were too many complications surrounding them—the messy problems of Schrock Investments, their different churches, her family. Her grandmother's heart was set on the grandchildren becoming Old Order Amish. Set like stone. She wasn't sure how many times her grandmother's heart could break and mend.

She took a deep cleansing breath, in and out. It would be fine, she reassured herself. Everything would be fine. Mammi Vera was well again. Tobe would be home soon. Like Jake said, it was her time now.

She laughed again, feeling light-headed all of a sudden. Everything would be fine.

Delia woke up feeling better than she had in a long time. She actually hummed as she went into the bathroom, turned on the faucet to get the hot water going, which, she had learned, could take several minutes, and started brushing her teeth.

As she rolled up the tube, trying to coax the last bit of toothpaste out, she thought about the conversations she'd been having with Charles. They had spent more time talking the past few days—about truly important things—than they had in years.

Just a few weeks ago Delia was so downhearted and depressed that she couldn't face the idea of even getting out of bed, and now, here she was humming to herself, cancer free, and ready to return home.

Home. Yes! She wanted to go home, she decided as she spat a white stream into the sink and filled the cup with water to rinse her mouth. She reached behind the curtain to test the water. Almost hot enough. Another minute should do it.

Best of all, she thought, as she noticed the steam coming over the top of the plastic curtain, she was going home as a different person. Stronger, yet weaker. No—not weak. Humble. That's how she felt. She was a humble person learning to rely on a strong God. Somehow, that awareness made all the difference.

After she had dressed and started to pack, she spotted Rose on her way to the barn and hurried out to talk to her. "I hope this doesn't seem too sudden to you, but I'm ready to head back home."

Rose smiled. She understood. "Do you think your husband will be joining you?"

Delia looked thoughtful. "We're a ways from that. But I think we're heading in the right direction." She laughed. "I have Eagle Hill to thank for that."

"We can give the glory to God for bringing you here, right when we needed you. Imagine if your husband hadn't seen Vera that evening."

Delia nodded. "Did I ever tell you that Charles was raised Old Order Amish?"

Rose's head snapped to face Delia and her eyes went wide. "No, you never did. I think I would have remembered that particular piece of information."

"I'm ashamed to say that I have rarely asked him much about his upbringing. He never volunteered much about it and I wasn't all that interested. But now I am. And he's finally willing to talk about it."

Rose smiled. "Sounds like you're off to a fresh start."

"A fresh start. I like that. I hope you're right. Not just with my marriage. Also with my faith. Thank you for encouraging me, Rose. I hope to come back to Eagle Hill. Often."

Rose smiled. "You were our first guest. Our first blessed guest."

So true! Later, as Delia zipped up her suitcase and gave the guest flat one more lookover to make sure she hadn't forgotten anything, she rolled Rose's words around in her mind: a blessed guest.

She had come here on a whim and stayed for over a month! She took her suitcase out to her car and put it in the trunk. Her heart was suddenly too full for words as she let her gaze roam lovingly over the Inn at Eagle Hill:

over the lofty barn and the large white clapboard house tucked against the hill. The creek that wove like a ribbon from the hill down to the road. The green pasture that held that silly goat and four sheep.

"Rose just told me. She said you're leaving today."

Delia turned to find Bethany watching her. "What you have here, Bethany, it's so special. So rare." Delia's gaze lingered on Bethany a moment and then shifted to the end of the driveway, where Sammy and Luke sat behind a cardboard table. "It's days like this that are worth the remembering. A day like this can stay with you, can settle down to live on in your soul forever."

"Maybe you should think about buying a farm."

Delia turned to her. "A farm? I didn't mean the land—though it is a beautiful property. I meant—" she lifted her palm and made a wide sweeping arc—"I meant your family. Your neighbors. Your church and community. Most people look for this their entire life and never find it. It's so . . . special. Never, ever let it go."

Her words fell into an empty silence.

When Delia spun around to look at Bethany, she was surprised to see the girl's eyes had filled with tears. Delia took a step toward Bethany, then another. She reached out her hand to touch her shoulder.

"Why, Bethany, whatever is wrong? Did I say something to upset you?"

Bethany covered her face with her hands, but just for a moment. "Don't mind me. I'm just having an emotional day." Her voice was shaky as she backed up a few steps. "I'm glad we met, Mrs. Stoltz." She turned and ran to the farmhouse.

Puzzled, Delia watched until she disappeared into the house. She felt as if she had gotten to know Bethany. Whenever Bethany had brought breakfast to the basement, she would linger for a chat. Delia had even taught her how to make tea the right way—real English steeped tea. But the girl sounded as if she thought they'd never see each other again.

She saw Galen lead a horse from the paddock to the barn and walked over to say goodbye to him. She found him in his workshop, starting to repair a harness. "I've come to say goodbye."

He stopped unbuckling the harness and gave his hat brim a tug. "Godspeed to you."

She hesitated, wanting to say more. In the hospital, she couldn't help but notice the way Galen and Rose interacted. There were times when Rose let her eyes linger on his face in a way that made Delia wonder if her feelings for Galen were quite as platonic as she claimed. Delia had asked her once if she thought she would ever love again, and Rose had seemed surprised by the question. "I never thought of it," she had told her. Delia understood why, but never was a very long time. Rose was a lovely young woman and Galen was a very special, very kind, very patient man. The type of man who would deserve someone like Rose.

Delia weighed her thoughts back and forth as Galen grew increasingly uncomfortable. He wanted to get back to work. Finally, Delia decided to just say what was on her mind. "I hope you don't mind if I speak in a forthright manner."

Galen's eyebrows lifted.

"I hope you will rouse yourself and propose to Rose. Soon."

Galen's eyes went wide with astonishment.

"You must not be a sissy about this."

He cleared his throat. "A sissy?"

"Galen, you love Rose. You know it. I know it. Rose is the one who doesn't know it. There. I've said what I've come to say."

His gaze drifted around the workshop, alighting everywhere but on her. "It's not quite that easy. I've tried. She's said no."

"You'll have to keep on trying."

"She doesn't see me that way. I'm just a friend to her. A neighbor."

"You can change that. She deserves someone like you."

He looked very unsure. "I don't know . . . what else to do."

"Well, for starters, did you happen to know that she wants a porch swing?"

Delia found Mim waiting patiently by her car with a wriggling puppy in her arms. "Why, Mim, what's this?"

"Mom said you're leaving today." She held the puppy out to Delia. "I brought you something. You don't have to keep it if you don't want to."

Delia took a step toward her. The puppy was yellow, with long ears, curly hair, and a small, black button nose.

"Oh Mim! He's adorable." She took the puppy from Mim's arms and cradled it in her own. The puppy looked up at her with big brown, liquid eyes that seemed to beg for a home.

"Puppies are nothing but trouble," Mim warned. "That's a fact. I'll take him if you don't want him."

Delia smiled up at Mim. "What kind of dog is he?"

"A male, one of Chase's puppies. Apparently Chase had paid a call to a certain female yellow lab over at Windmill Farm. Fern Lapp's dog. She's named Daisy. Chase is quite taken with Daisy. He has good taste—she's a pretty girl. This puppy is definitely not purebred, so if that matters—"

"If he's part of Chase, it doesn't matter to me at all."

Mim reached over and scratched the puppy's ears. "I picked him out myself. He seemed like the calmest and smartest of the litter. He hasn't had his shots yet."

"My son can take care of that."

Mim went to the house and brought back dog food, a water bowl, and a towel for a bed. "This will take care of you for a while."

"I've never had a dog," Delia said, grinning as the little puppy sniffed around the car.

"Never? I can't remember ever not having a dog. Seems like everyone needs a good dog."

"I already love him. Thank you, Mim."

"You'll have to choose a name for him."

The puppy wandered around the yard, sniffing, running, stopping, then bolted after a butterfly. "Maybe I'll name him *Miracula fieri hic* and call him Micky for short. To remember the miracle of being here."

Mim's face lit with a smile. She gazed at the puppy. "Hope you'll still feel that way after you've had him for a few days."

# 22

❦

Mim, Luke, and Sammy arrived at Hank Lapp's birthday party at Windmill Farm just as a softball game got under way on the front lawn. Galen dropped them off so they could join their friends, then he went to fetch the sisters at the Sisters' House. Bethany had walked over earlier, to help set up for the party, she said, and Mim was glad she had left the house because her sister was in a weird mood today. Teary one minute, snapping at Luke and Sammy in the next minute, humming with happiness the next.

Mim happened to notice that Danny Riehl was at bat, so she hurried to the team her brothers were on. She and Sammy were sent to the outfield. Luke was sent to cover first base. Jimmy Fisher was pitching. Hank Lapp was umpire. He was always the umpire. He said it was because his arthritis was acting up, but Galen said it was mainly because he had the loudest voice of anyone. Jimmy lobbed a ball to Danny and he hit it sailing, sailing, sailing, right to Sammy. The ball dropped out of his mitt and Luke let out a large groan. Then Sammy overthrew it to Luke when he should have thrown it to second base. By the time Luke retrieved the ball from the BBQ pit, Danny had made a home run. Luke glared at Sammy. That boy Luke, Mim decided, was getting too high and mighty.

But then Mim watched Sammy miss every ball that came his way, even ones where he didn't have to move an inch. Unexpected tears stung her eyes. He needed a father.

When it was time for dinner, Mim helped the women serve the food out on the picnic benches. She was filling glasses with iced tea when she spotted Galen King seated next to Jimmy Fisher. She reached around Galen for his glass and took her time filling it. "You should, you know," she whispered as she set his glass next to him, "teach Sammy how to catch a fly ball."

Surprised, Galen looked up. Before he could speak, she was gone.

One hour to go. Jake had said he would pick Bethany up at eight at the end of the driveway—just as it grew dark. She was feeling feverish inside, all shaky and sweat-sticky and cold. And she kept forgetting to breathe. *I must do this. I must.* If she didn't go with him tonight, she would lose Jake forever.

At seven thirty, she walked nervously around the yard, taking in the sight of her brothers and her sister, forcing it to her memory. How tall would her brothers be the next time she saw them? What about Mim? She was just on the threshold of becoming a woman.

Before she left for the party tonight, she had tucked a letter under each person's pillow, telling them she loved them and always would. Her grandmother was sleeping when she had to go, which was a relief. She knew she would burst into tears if she tried to say goodbye face-to-face. She slipped in and kissed her bandaged forehead.

She watched the five ancient sisters from the Sisters' House, sitting in lawn chairs on the grass, like little sparrows on a telephone pole. She had only worked for them one week, but she was growing fond of their quirky ways. She had left a letter for them under Rose's pillow, explaining that something important had come up. She hoped Jimmy Fisher would find someone special to work for them.

She saw Jimmy serve a volleyball—what was it about the sight of him that made her start to grin, even when he wasn't trying to be funny? There was just something about him . . .

*I must do this. I must.*

Fighting tears, she slipped quietly down the driveway, retrieving the ledgers she'd hidden behind a fence post. She tucked them under her apron and waited for Jake.

While she waited in the dark, a panic gripped her chest so tightly that she thought her heart had stopped beating.

Jimmy saw Bethany head toward the road and he tossed the volleyball to Sammy, who missed it. That boy needed a little work. He swooped up the volleyball, delivered it into Sammy's hands, tapped him on the head, and hurried after Bethany. What was she doing, heading down that way in the dark? She had seemed a little strange tonight—quiet and sad and nervous—and he thought she might be feeling poorly. He saw her about halfway down the driveway, arms crossed against her middle like she had a stomachache.

"Bethany?"

She spun around, her hands flew to her face. Her eyes looked wild.

"What's wrong? Are you sick?"

"I can't do it! I can't go. I can't leave them. I thought I could but I can't."

"Can't leave who?"

"I thought I loved him. And I do! I thought I did. But not enough. Not enough to leave my family. Not like this, anyway."

"What the Sam Hill are you talking about?"

"Jake Hertzler. He's coming for me. He wants me to run off with him. I said I'd go, but I can't. I can't leave my family. How will I tell him? He'll be devastated." She looked up, eyes shimmering with tears. "Will you stay here with me? Will you help me? Jake can be very persuasive. I don't trust myself to not cave in."

"Of course."

"Please, Jimmy. I need you to stay nearby because I'm not tough at all. I act like I am, but I'm not. Not really."

He had already known that about her. He wrapped his arm around her shoulders, bumping hips with her, clumsy and yet tender. He stood there for a moment, holding her, and it was like he didn't want the moment to ever end.

Then they saw the beam of two headlights in the distance and Bethany froze. A truck pulling a horse trailer stopped at the end of the driveway. The window rolled down. "Let's go, honey!"

Bethany took a sharp breath. "Promise you'll stay right here, Jimmy."

"You can count on me."

Bethany walked down to the truck and spoke through the open window. He could hear their mumbling voices, then Jake Hertzler's voice grew louder. And louder. He was spitting mad, Jimmy could tell that, even in the dark. Jake started hollering at Bethany, saying ugly things and calling her unrepeatable names.

Wait a minute. Wait just a minute. Jimmy knew that voice.

Hank Lapp's party guests were starting to make noises about heading home, but he wouldn't let anyone leave without a final surprise. He wanted Jimmy Fisher to put on a fireworks show, but no one could find him. A short while ago, Mim had seen Jimmy head away from the gathering on the front yard and down the long driveway. She ran to tell Hank Lapp and the two of them walked over to see if they could find Jimmy.

They were about halfway down the driveway when they spotted Jimmy Fisher behind a tree, standing in utter stillness. Jimmy motioned to them with his arm, holding a finger up to his lips. Hank Lapp made a lot of noise, even walking. Jimmy pointed down the hill. It was getting dark, but Mim could hear Bethany arguing with someone in a truck on the road. "Mim, get Galen. Be quick about it. Don't let anyone know. Hank—stay with me. And for heaven's sake, man, be quiet."

She'd never heard that tone in Jimmy's voice. It didn't have the teasing sound that was never far away. It was . . . it was the sound of a grown man. Something was terribly wrong. She flew up the hill so fast that her hair was flying every which way out from under her prayer cap and she was panting hard from all that running. She found Galen over by the barbecue, spreading the red hot coals with a stick so they'd cool down. "Come with me!" She grabbed Galen's elbow, dragging him back down the hillside to meet Jimmy. Along the way, he kept asking what was wrong and all she could say was, "Jimmy needs you."

By the time they reached Jimmy, Hank Lapp was nowhere in sight. "Galen," Jimmy whispered. "I think the fellow Bethany is talking to down there is the horse trader who's been scamming me."

Mim strained her ears. "Why, that's Jake Hertzler!"

"Also known as Jonah Hershberger," Jimmy said. "Horse swindler. First-rate con-artist."

"Why is Bethany crying?" Mim said.

"She's saying goodbye to him."

Jake had just grabbed something from Bethany's hands and was shouting at her. "He's not liking it." Mim started to feel frightened.

Galen's gaze went from Mim to Jimmy, then down to the end of the road. "Well, Jimmy, have you got a plan?"

"Always." Jimmy turned to Mim. "You stay put. If anything happens, you run to Amos and get help." Then he nodded his head to Galen. "Let's go."

Mim watched as the two men walked down to the end of the driveway, cucumber calm. Jimmy approached Bethany as Galen slid around to the driver's side. Mim took a few steps down the hill, scared, worried about Bethany, but not wanting to miss what was being said. Where did Hank Lapp go, anyway?

Jimmy put his hands on Bethany's shoulders and moved her away from the truck, then leaned against the window edge. "Well, well, Jonah Hershberger. We meet again."

"Jonah?" Bethany said. "What are you talking about, Jimmy? Are you crazy?"

"Jonah Hershberger. The fellow who keeps selling me the same horse."

"What?" Bethany said. "Jake is the horse trader?"

Jake pulled back from the open window. "Bethany," he said, nearly growling, "for the last time, get in the truck."

"She's not going anywhere," Galen said from the other side of the truck.

Jake's head whipped around, then back to Bethany.

"We've got a little business to discuss," Galen said. "You owe my partner here a sizable amount of money. Plus a horse."

With that, Jake flipped the ignition, revved the engine, and stepped on the gas. The truck sped off down the dark road and into the night.

But the trailer remained. Hank Lapp stood in front of the horse trailer. The trailer was slightly hitched up, the unplugged electrical cords dangled. "IS THAT WHAT YOU WANTED ME TO DO, BOY?"

Jimmy grinned. "It was, Hank. It was, indeed."

# 23

~~~⚬⟡⚬~~~

Hank Lapp's birthday party would become the talk of the town for days afterward. The story would become bigger and more dramatic with every telling—all but one piece of it. Jimmy Fisher would omit the part that Bethany was planning to run off with Jake. No one would know. He would tell no one.

But Rose figured it out that night.

While the party was going on, Rose had found Bethany's goodbye letter on her nightstand as she came upstairs to look for a book to read. She read it through, twice, heart pounding. There was a second letter addressed to the sisters at the Sisters' House.

Rose wished she could run through the privet and ask Galen his opinion, but she couldn't. Mainly, because he was at the party, but even if he weren't, there was a strain between them. She had come outside when he arrived to pick up the children and he hadn't even come down from his buggy. He wore the pain she had given him in his eyes.

It hurt so much that she was the one to look away.

On a hunch, she had gone to Mim and the boys' bedroom and found letters left on their pillows. Then she tiptoed into Vera's room and grabbed the letter on the nightstand, grateful Vera hadn't seen it yet. If Bethany did leave with Jake tonight, she didn't want Mim or Vera or the boys to read her goodbye letters before going to bed. Morning would come soon enough. Such news could wait.

She thought about what Galen would say if she were to tell him she found

228

the letters Bethany had left, informing everyone she was leaving home. What would he say if she were to tell him she wanted to stop Bethany from making the biggest mistake of her life? She could practically hear Galen's deep voice: "What good would it do to try and stop her if she wants to go? Bethany has her own life to lead, including making her own mistakes." And then he would remind her, "God is faithful, even when we are not."

Galen was right, of course. Just like he was right about Rose being unbending and stubborn. It *was* a hard truth, but it was the truth. In a way, it was prideful to be unwilling to ask for or receive help. It was prideful to think she could handle everything on her own. She blew out a puff of air. How she missed him. She missed her friend.

So Rose sat at the kitchen table with a cup of tea and her well-loved Bible and prayed like she had never prayed before. She prayed for a miracle to intervene in Bethany's life. She prayed for something unexpected to occur. She prayed for Bethany's well-being, and her future. She prayed for heaven's protection over her beautiful, impulsive stepdaughter.

An hour later, when Galen's buggy pulled into the driveway, Rose nearly flew outside. She let out a gasp of silent thanks when Bethany tumbled out of the buggy and hurried past her into the house. "We had a little excitement tonight," Galen said. "I'll let Mim and the boys tell you all about it."

As he drove away, Mim and Luke and Sammy took turns talking over each other to tell Rose the news: Jimmy's horse swindler was their very own Jake Hertzler! Rose listened carefully, asked a few questions, and pieced together the story until she had a pretty good idea what had happened. When she saw Bethany had come downstairs, Rose sent the children up to bed. Bethany stood with her back against the wall, pale and sad, hugging her elbows tight against her body the way she did when she was a little girl.

Rose handed her the letters. "Are you looking for these?"

Slowly, Bethany reached out and took the letters from her. Then she tore them into pieces and threw them in the garbage can under the sink. She balled her hands into fists, her voice shaking. "I'm such a fool."

Rose crossed the room and looked into Bethany's face, so young, so beautiful, so filled with incomprehensible misery. She reached out and gently unfurled her tight fists. "Only if you don't become wiser through this."

A few tears trickled out of the corners of Bethany's eyes, and she wiped them away with her sleeve. "Rose, how could he have left like that?"

Rose shrugged. "Jake had everybody fooled. Myself included."

"Not Jake." She shook her head and the tears splattered. "Dad. How could he leave us like he did, just let his family go? I couldn't do that! I tried and I couldn't." She squeezed her eyes tightly shut, trying to hold back the tears. But they came faster and faster, until she couldn't stop their coming. "Tobe is the lucky one. He took the easy way out."

"There is no easy way out of this." Rose pulled her into her arms as she started to sob—deep heaving sobs, finally subsiding into a few shudders. "Go on, now. Get your cry out," Rose said, rubbing her back in small circles. Sadness had a way of piling up inside a person until there was nothing for it but to let it all out. "Cry it all out."

On Monday afternoon, after she finished readying the basement with fresh linens for the next guest who was due to arrive any minute, Rose called Allen Turner of the Securities and Exchange Commission. She told him that Jake Hertzler had turned up and left with the company books. They had been hidden on the farm all this time. All this time! "He's been horse trading around the county, using another name: Jonah Hershberger," Rose said. "He said he had a job opportunity in Somerset County, but I don't know if that was true."

Allen Turner was silent for a long moment. "He's probably halfway to Canada or Mexico by now. But then again, he's pretty bold. Could be he's sticking around, like a bad penny. In the meantime, we're still looking for your stepson."

"Jake said Tobe had been staying with his mother, but I don't know where she's living. I don't know anything about her except her maiden name: Mary Miller."

"Mary Miller?" He groaned. "Could there be a more common name among the Amish?"

She said goodbye, hung up the phone, and walked over to Galen's. She found him in front of his barn, tossing a softball back and forth with Sammy, back and forth. He looked up at her and smiled when he saw her.

There was something about the smile that touched her; as if he had been hoping she would come by.

"Is something wrong, Rose? Is Vera all right?"

"Vera's fine. It's me—I'd like to ask you something."

"Sammy," he said. "Go take that hay out to the horses in the far pasture. Scatter it around this time. Don't just leave it in a clump."

Sammy threw the ball back to Galen, but it went sailing over his head. He hollered out an apology as he ran to the wheelbarrow filled with hay and started to push it down the dirt path to the pasture. Galen picked up the ball and walked to Rose. "If he could just remember to plant his feet when he aims at something, he might stand a chance as an outfielder."

"Could I see this horse that Jimmy paid for a few times over?"

"Of course. He's in the barn in a double stall."

She followed behind Galen. The barn held a mixture of sweet and pungent smells, summer hay and the sour tang of manure, the ripening sunlight pouring through the open door. She took in a deep breath, feeling almost dizzy.

Galen continued down the aisle and stopped at a stall. He turned and gave a puzzled look at Rose, still by the door.

She walked to the stall and peered in at the stallion. She gasped when she saw its flaxen mane. "That might be the most beautiful horse I've ever seen."

"That he is. He's a fine stud. Jimmy actually knew what he was talking about."

"Jimmy said you're going to stable him here."

"For now. We have to break his Houdini habit. Keeping him in such a big stall will help."

She chanced a glance at him. "Did you really call Jimmy Fisher your partner?"

Galen groaned. He moved a pitchfork out of the way and opened the top half of the Dutch door of the stall. "He's crowing about it all over town, I suppose."

"He is. Seems pretty pleased about it."

Lodestar stuck his head over the stall door. Galen reached out to stroke the horse's nose.

Rose looked at Galen's hands—beautiful, capable hands. Scarred, strong, deft. Hands that had the power to control a hot-blooded horse but the gentleness to caress its velvet nose. Hands she trusted.

"Would it be such an impossible thing for an independent fellow like you? Having a partner?"

His gaze met hers over the horse's head.

"Makes a lot of sense, you know. The Bible teaches us that 'two are better off than one, because together they can work more effectively. If one of them falls down, the other can help him up. Two people can resist an attack that would defeat one person alone. A rope made of three cords is hard to break.'"

He had yet to take his eyes off her. He didn't seem to be breathing. "Are we still talking about horses?"

She stroked the horse's blond forelock. "Why haven't you ever married?"

"I've never met anyone I wanted to marry. Not until you came along."

Her throat was hot and tight, full of the things she wanted to say. "Galen, I'm carrying a very big burden. I feel such deep shame over all that happened with Dean and his company. I need to pay people back for the money he lost. I can't ask you to share that burden. That's why I've kept you at a distance. That's why I keep pushing you away. Maybe you're right. Maybe it's pride. Stubbornness. I need to learn to ask for help. Help is a gift."

There was quiet—complete quiet.

And on and on the silence went, not a word out of Galen, not a sound. He stared at her for what seemed like an endless amount of time. A stain of color spread across his sharp cheekbones. "I would move heaven and earth for you."

"I know. I know you would." She laid the back of her hand against his cheek. "The problem, you see, is I've also been too stubborn to realize how much I care for you."

Galen's gaze traveled gently over her face, in that loving way he had of looking at her, and stopped at her lips. And then he dropped the pitchfork and it clattered to the concrete floor in the quiet of the barn. He reached around Lodestar's big head and grabbed Rose up in his arms. He swirled her around and around in a big circle and set her down again, then bent over and cupped her face in his hands. He leaned closer and brushed his mouth across hers, almost reverently. He started to pull away, but she reached up and wrapped her arms around his neck, holding him until he reached down to kiss her.

The next day, Mim found a note tucked inside of her desk when she arrived at school. "Super Moon. Tonight. 8 PM. Same place. DR"

She bit on her lip to keep from smiling. She would not look at Danny Riehl. She would not, would not, would not.

She looked.

She saw his eyes flit her way for a second and her stomach did a little flip-flop. After finding such a note, how could a girl ever concentrate on her schoolwork?

That evening, she met Danny on the hill behind the schoolhouse right at eight o'clock sharp. Danny wasn't even peering through the telescope. "You really don't need a telescope to see the night sky—just a dark night and your eyes." His head was tilted back, looking with awe at the full moon, the color of rich cream, so beautiful and round and low on the horizon. "It's called a perigee moon. Perigee means that it's at its closest point to the earth. An apogee moon is when it is farthest away."

Perigee. Apogee. Two new words for Mim to collect.

"The perigee moon occurs once a year. The orbit of the moon brings it about sixteen thousand miles closer to the earth. NASA said this super moon appears 14 percent bigger and 30 percent brighter than other full moons." He pushed his glasses up on the bridge of his nose. "I read those facts in a magazine for future astronauts."

Mim had always been fond of the moon. To her it was a more interesting thing to observe than the sun, which did the same thing every day. The moon changed, it moved around the sky; it waxed and waned. She had read that the moon moved the seas, but she hadn't been able to get her head around that. How could a moon move an ocean?

On a night when the moon rose, shining so brightly, like tonight, it seemed so close that she could almost climb a tree and step right on it. Even on nights when the moon was just a little white thumbnail, she tended to lose her worries when she gazed at it. Sometimes, she would sit by her window and imagine sitting on that hook, peering around the universe, untroubled about all that was happening on the little blue and green earth. She wondered how Danny would react if she shared those thoughts with him. Would he laugh at her? He might be shocked. He might expect her to stick to facts. So she said, "Is this what they call a blue moon?"

"No. That happens when a full moon appears twice in one month. A blue moon only occurs about once every three years." He stepped toward the telescope, peered into it, and twisted some dials. "The size of the moon is about the same size as the continent of Africa. Some people think it's flat, but it has valleys and craters and basins and mountains on it."

She would have to remember to tell Sammy these moon facts.

They took turns looking at the moon through the telescope, then stood side by side, heads craned back, to study the moon without any device. It was . . . glorious. Resplendent. Majestic.

"We're not moving away after all," Danny said quietly. "My mother said no."

Mim froze. Her heart sang with happiness. Goose bumps danced all over her arms. Her toes wanted to tap.

She cut a sideways glance at Danny at the same moment that he looked at her. They smiled, then they both looked away.

Later tonight, she thought she might have to write again to Lonesome and tell her that "Yes, true love can definitely make everything better."

Rose's plan this morning was to walk to her favorite spot and watch the sun rise. Her plans changed when she saw how hard the rain was coming down. She steeped a cup of tea, à la Delia Stoltz's style, and took the mug outside to sit in the new porch swing. Chase followed along and curled up by her feet. The scent of summer was in the air, a whisper of promise. She loved this time of year, when the earth seemed to be warming up from within. She took a deep breath. A handful of memories were tied to the scent of the rain, damp grass, and mist. Good memories. The kind that filled you with peace and happiness and satisfaction.

She could think of Dean now without the crushing burden of grief. Remember the good times and smile, grateful for the life they'd shared. She was thankful for the incredible gift of her children. She'd loved her husband, faults and all, and his death had badly shaken her world and her sense of self.

Lately, the only thing she'd been able to count on was that things change. But they had made it through the worst. Vera was under a doctor's care and her condition was stable. Bethany had turned an important corner into adulthood. Mim and the boys had their ups and downs, but they were adjusting. And she always had a hope that Tobe would return.

And then there was yesterday's news: at Galen's urging, she had gone to the bishop to let him know she was trying to pay back investors. She surprised the bishop so, his face flushed red above his gray beard. "Rose, Rose," he said in his kind voice. "Why would you think you were all alone in this? That was a burden God never meant for you."

He told her a group of Amish and Mennonites had formed a committee to handle the settlement of claims outside the court process. They would use donations from Amish and Mennonite communities nationwide to reimburse those investors, the Plain people, who wouldn't be using the court process.

Those people—all those sad, sad letters—they would be paid back. She still couldn't believe it! She simply couldn't believe it.

She told the bishop about Tobe's involvement, about the elusive Jake Hertzler. At first, she wondered if knowing about Tobe might change the committee's mind about reimbursing people. But no, Bishop Elmo said that revelation had no bearing on their decision.

"The Lord doesn't ask us to judge how or why needs occur," Bishop Elmo told her, his spiky gray eyebrows drawing together. "He only asks us to take care of those in need. We all have need, Rose. Each one of us."

On the way home from the bishop's house, she was a little sorry that he had wanted that phrase removed—"*Miracula fieri hic*"—from the bottom of the Inn at Eagle Hill sign. Miracles did occur, every day. Maybe they weren't the kinds of miracles that could be scrutinized for scientific proof, but how could you ever test for a change of a heart? Or a healing of an emotional wound? Or the power of forgiveness? Miracles meant that God was at work.

Her thoughts drifted to the letter she had from Delia yesterday. She said that her son, Will, might be moving to Lancaster County in the fall to head up a new Wild Bird Rescue Center. "He has had some wonderful offers from veterinary clinics but thinks he will be turning them down," she wrote. "I think it might have something to do with that lady vet he met at your farm." Then she added that Charles had agreed to go to marriage counseling with her. "Things can get good again," she had written and underlined it twice.

*Yes, they can,* Rose thought to herself. Corners could be turned. The pendulum would swing. Everything could change. As it would again, and again, and again.

She smiled, running a hand along the smooth arm of the white porch swing that Galen had made for her as a surprise. He called it their courting swing. Dear, kind, faithful Galen. She knew that he hadn't been good to her because he expected anything in return but because he was who he was—a man with a genuine desire to help fix what was broken. He was good at that.

She felt a hard band let loose around her ribs and took in a long breath. This place, Eagle Hill, was her home. Soon, the cares of the day would creep in. She would need to rouse the boys and get the day started. There were new guests in the basement and she liked to bake her blueberry cornbread for first-time guests. Blessed guests.

But first, she'd just sit here, listen to the rain, and be thankful. Be thankful for the new day.

# Rose's Blueberry Cornbread

| | |
|---|---|
| 2 | large eggs |
| 1 | cup buttermilk |
| ¼ | cup butter, melted |
| ⅔ | cup all-purpose flour |
| 1⅓ | cup cornmeal |
| ¼ | cup sugar |
| 1½ | teaspoons baking powder |
| ½ | teaspoon salt |
| 1 | cup fresh or frozen blueberries, rinsed |

In a bowl, beat eggs, buttermilk, and butter to blend. In another bowl, mix flour, cornmeal, sugar, baking powder, and salt.

Stir flour mixture into egg mixture just until evenly moistened. Gently stir in berries. Spread level in a buttered 8-inch square pan.

Bake in a 375 degree oven until a wooden skewer inserted into the center comes out clean, 25 to 35 minutes, depending on your oven. Let cool 10 minutes, then cut into 9 squares.

# Discussion Questions

1. This story begins and ends at moments when Rose Schrock meets the sunrise. The rising of the sun contains all sorts of symbolism. What does it mean to Rose?

2. How were concerns for family different for each of the characters? Rose Schrock? Her mother-in-law, Vera Schrock? Delia Stoltz? Even Galen King, Rose's neighbor?

3. Several kind people end up playing significant roles in the Schrocks' life. Who is your favorite and why?

4. Delia Stoltz tells her husband, Charles, that a sincere apology, even if the committed wrong was accidental, helps the victim get on with his or her life. Do you agree with her? Why does Delia believe that an apology holds that much power?

5. Vera Schrock believes that her family has finally returned to the right church. Rose has a different point of view—she feels that she can worship God in any church. What are your thoughts?

6. Bethany has to learn a hard lesson: Jake Hertzler wasn't the person she thought he was. Name someone in your life who has surprised you as you've gotten to know him or her—in a good way or a bad way. What has that experience taught you?

7. The reader never learns the truth of how or why Dean Schrock died. What do you think—was it an accident? Or did Dean take his own life?

8. In this first in the series, that uncertainty over Dean's death lingered over many characters' heads: Rose, Tobe, even Vera. What is the significance of living with unanswered questions?

9. One theme in this story is that God works through all things for good (Rom. 8:28). When have you seen his hand in your life, where something bad turned into something good?

# Acknowledgments

With each new book, my appreciation for the Revell team continues to grow. It's quite astonishing to realize the care they take to get a book right—its cover, scenes and characters, grammar—and then the marketing and promotion too. Each person goes above and beyond to get a book ready for the shelf and into the readers' hands. Special thanks to Andrea Doering (aka ACFW 2011 Editor of the Year); to Barb Barnes (Grammar Queen), Michele Misiak, Janelle Mahlmann, Robin Barnett, and Twila Bennett (Marketing & Publicity Geniuses), Cheryl Van Andel and Paula Gibson (Cover Artists Extraordinaire) for your keen eye with all the details. To Amy Lathrop, for being so much more than a publicist.

As always, my gratitude extends to Joyce Hart of The Hartline Literary Agency. The only agent who was willing to take me on! I hope I've made you glad for that fateful decision, Joyce. I know I couldn't be in better hands.

A smile to my family, who has a way of keeping a healthy perspective about this writing gig—bumping into my chair as they pass by on the way to the washer and dryer, texting me with grocery lists during my radio show, using my computer to check their Facebook updates when they *know* they are not allowed to touch it. Sigh. Where would I be without all of you?! Without 3-D characters, that's where.

My heartfelt appreciation goes to my first readers, Lindsey Ciraulo, Wendrea How, and Nyna Dolby, for being such a huge help with that critical first draft (and second draft too!). A thank-you to Chip Conradi, who took time to give me excellent legal insights. He helped to make the downfall of Schrock Investments as credible as possible. And to my husband, Steve, for sharing his know-how in the world of accounting and investments over coffee at our favorite little coffee shop. Steve doesn't even like coffee.

A thank-you to Jeff Camp for answering questions about brain surgery. Jeff said he was particularly grateful for excellent care from the neurology staff at the University of California, San Francisco. A big hug to AJ Salch for answering equine questions with me. And one last thank-you to Lindsey Bell and Melinda Busch, my crackerjack Latin translators, for helping me with the phrase, *Miracula fieri hic*. Miracles are made here.

And to the Author of all miracles . . . how can I ever thank you enough? You've blessed me in ways I never imagined and never deserved. To God be the glory, amen.

# The
# Calling

Dedicated to
my youngest son, Tad,
who spent days during Christmas 2012 reading through
the messy first draft of this manuscript,
and nights walking and rocking his newborn niece to sleep.

# 1

As far as Bethany Schrock was concerned, this summer was hotter than a firecracker lit on both ends. A little rain would certainly be welcome, she thought, as she untied her stiff prayer cap strings and tossed them over her shoulders, but the heat wave held Stoney Ridge tightly in its grip. All the more reason to set to work in the cool of the basement of the Sisters' House.

At the bottom of the basement stairs, she held the lantern up to gaze around the dusty, cobwebby basement, and blew out a puff of air. If it were even possible, there was more clutter down here than in the rest of the house. She'd been steadily trying to organize the Sisters' House for weeks now and had barely made a dent. Sylvia, the youngest of the five elderly sisters of the Sisters' House, had told her she was doing a fine job and they didn't know how she worked so quickly. "You are a doggedly determined young lady," Sylvia had said.

Bethany had smiled, pleased that Sylvia was so pleased. She had always considered doggedness to be a rather unappealing characteristic, but it had been valuable at the Sisters' House. "Thank you," she told Sylvia. "It's easy when you know how to organize things."

The sisters, on the other hand, did not know how. They were in desperate need of someone with dogged determination after the deacon had gently reminded them they were overdue in taking a turn to host church. Overdue by years and years. They needed to get their house tidied up first, they told him, giving him their sweetest smiles. And that's where Bethany came in.

Jimmy Fisher had done the sisters a very great favor by suggesting they hire Bethany to organize their house. If it wouldn't cause his big head to swell even bigger, she might even tell him so one day.

But she wouldn't tell him how much she needed to work, to keep busy, to get her mind off the near shipwreck she had made of her life. It still galled her to think that just four weeks ago she was *this* close to running away with Jake Hertzler, only to find out he wasn't the man he said he was. Not even close. He was a no-good, low-life skunk, that's what he was.

In the end, as her stepmother Rose often reminded her, she hadn't run off with Jake. Something deep down in her knew better, Rose insisted. Her grandmother, less forgiving in nature, had left a 1948 edition of *A Young Woman's Guide to Virtue* on Bethany's pillow, a not-so-subtle poke about her disastrous judgment in men. Bethany thought she might use it to start a fire.

Bethany carefully pushed and pulled boxes so she could carve a path to the small window. She needed fresh air in this stuffy, musty basement. Hands on her hips, she looked around and wondered where to begin.

The sisters had left for a quilting at Naomi King's house this afternoon, which suited Bethany just fine. She much preferred working without them anywhere nearby. Just this morning, her younger sister Mim had asked if she minded working for such ancient ladies.

Mim was right about them being old. Ella, the eldest, was in her 90s. Sylvia, the youngest, was in her early 80s. Fannie, Lena, and Ada fell somewhere in between. But they were lovable sisters, spinsters, who had lived together all their lives.

No, Bethany didn't mind their ages. What she minded was that they were so extraordinarily messy. Yes, it gave her a job to do and, yes, the sisters paid her well. But it was not an easy job. These old sisters saved everything. Everything!

The cleanout and organizing of the Sisters' House could have gone faster but for two reasons. First was the sisters' involvement. They were constantly rummaging through Bethany's system of three boxes: keep, throw, give away. The sisters were particularly interested in the giveaway box. Somehow, nearly everything Bethany tossed into it was quietly removed and slipped into the keep box.

The second reason the cleanout job moved slowly was Bethany's doing. There was prowling to be done, especially in the basement. Being her share of nosy, she took her time examining wondrous things she had never seen the likes of—treasure chests overflowing with fancy old clothes, ruffled parasols, lacy unmentionables. Who knew that these ancient sisters had an exotic past? How thrilling! How worrisome.

She took care to hide the unmentionables in the bottom of giveaway boxes. It would never do to have such things end up at a Sisters' House yard sale. Word might get out that the sisters were fallen women. Unrepentant jack-a-dandies. She could just imagine the dour look on her grandmother's face, sorting through a box of ladies' whale-boned corsets. Next thing you knew, the old sisters would end up on the front row of church, kneeling for confession before the entire congregation, promising to mend their ways. How awful!

Well, never mind. The old sisters' secrets would stay safe with her.

It was fascinating to sift through the lives of these eighty-plus-year-old women. There were old newspapers and musty books, boxes of clothing, old quilts, even an old diary. One box held little bottles filled with liquid. Bethany hoped the bottles might be perfume, that she had found another delightful secret about the fallen sisters. But when she opened one, it smelled like medicine. Evil smelling, strong and sickly sweet.

She came upon a soft black leather trunk, packed underneath other boxes at the bottom in a corner of the basement. It looked like it hadn't been touched in years. The leather straps were cracked and dry, the brass nails that held it together were black with tarnish. She tried to open it but the latch was jammed, so she found an old iron fireplace poker and pried the lid open. Bethany peered into the trunk and stood with a start. A coppery cold moved along her spine and the perspiration on her skin turned to ice. She'd never had a sensitive bone in her body, unlike her friend and neighbor Naomi King, who'd imagined seeing ghosts and angels and demons her whole life. But this . . . this!

*Shootfire!*

She backed toward the stairs, trembling. It would take a raging river to wash from her mind the sight of what was in that trunk. Human bones, including two skulls, with their empty sockets looking back at her. She hurried up the basement stairs, thinking of all the things she had to say to Jimmy Fisher to singe his tail feathers.

The day was so hot that Jimmy Fisher waited until the sun wasn't directly overhead to do some needed training exercises out on the road with Galen King's newly purchased sorrel gelding. The blacktop was hot enough to fry an egg, and they wouldn't last long out here, but he wanted to expose this gelding to a few passing cars or trucks.

In the afternoons, his employer and partner, Galen King, gave Jimmy conditioning exercises to do with a few of the horses. At first Jimmy was nervous when Galen watched him work a horse. Galen's silences had a way of making him lose track of his thoughts—some of which were perfectly good thoughts, in their way. He felt Galen might be watching because he was doing something that needed correcting. But one afternoon after another passed by, and Galen merely observed.

Today, Galen had left him with instructions to walk the gelding onto the road to start conditioning him to traffic. Most of the racehorses were accustomed to the unexpected—loud noises, distracting movements—but their response was to run, hard and fast, to the finish line. That wouldn't do for a buggy horse, which was Galen's and Jimmy's main objective: take young and retired racehorses and train them to become buggy horses. Today was the first time Galen wasn't hovering and Jimmy didn't want to mess up. He walked the gelding up and down the road for nearly half an hour, hoping a car or truck would come by. Naturally, there was nothing. Just as he thought about heading to a busier road, he saw Bethany Schrock come zooming toward him on her scooter, mad as a wet hen.

As she drew close to him, she jumped off the scooter and let it drop to the ground with a thud, startling the sorrel gelding. She came at Jimmy with a pointed finger, aimed at his chest. "I should have known! Whenever someone talks fast and fancy like you do, I should have known better than to listen. You were just trying to pass off a skunk as a swan."

*Beautiful.* She was beautiful. She might be the prettiest thing he'd ever seen. With that crazy tumble of pitch-black hair, as shiny as a child's, that never stayed put for long under that pinned and starched prayer cap. She had high, wide cheekbones and a dainty, pointed chin that gave her face a Valentine's shape. Her skin was like freshly skimmed cream. Her body was lean and long-limbed, but not at all delicate. She exuded confidence and strength, even arrogance.

After a pause, Jimmy spoke. "Okay. I'm not following."

"Those sisters! They're nuttier than loons! They have a box of bones down in the basement. Human bones! Are they killing people and stuffing them in trunks? Why would you get me a job at a crazy house? It was pure meanness on your part. Is this your idea of a big joke? Because it's not funny, Jimmy Fisher!" Her hands were on her hips, her brows knitted in a fierce frown.

Jimmy tried to make sense of what she was saying, but he kept getting distracted by sinful thoughts that would require some confession on his part before the day ended, stirrings in places he shouldn't even be thinking about.

Bethany Schrock intrigued him. Quite a bit. But there were plenty of attractive girls around Stoney Ridge. If that was what appealed to him, all he had to do was show up at a youth gathering. Any number of good-looking girls were eager for his attention.

Why her? Why this feisty, hot-tempered girl? Why now?

He didn't have the answers to those questions any more than he knew how to draw traffic along the road right now to condition this horse to unexpected noise.

It was something in her eyes, he decided. Deep, dark, intense. Yes, she was attractive, but it was the intensity in her eyes that spoke to him. There was some kind of fathomless depths to those eyes, and in them, something vulnerable. It quivered around the edges of her all the time, something a bit lost, lonely. Confused, maybe.

It wasn't as if Jimmy didn't have a few reservations about pursuing Bethany. He had plenty. Mainly—she'd been planning to run off with Jake the Snake, and though Jimmy had a quick-to-forgive nature, he wasn't about to let himself be runner-up in any girl's estimation. It was true—Bethany did refuse Jake—but Jimmy wanted a girl's whole heart. Not the leftovers.

"Simmer down, now," he said, his voice what's-the-weather-today calm, trying not to stare at her rosy lips and deep blush. "I'm sure whatever is bothering you is just a misunderstanding."

That made her all the more upset. For just an instant, he pressed his fingers against her mouth, but she pushed him away, furious. "I am not one of your horses! You can't speak to me with soft words and think you'll win me over, just like that!" She stamped her foot fiercely and that set the gelding dancing on its lead.

Jimmy held tight to the lead and stroked the horse's back, whispering sweet words to it. After the gelding settled, he turned his attention back to Bethany. "Calm down and start from the beginning." He tried to keep his voice even sounding, yet firm. The same way he spoke to this skittish gelding.

She had been watching the gelding, but with those words, she swung around on him so fast her capstrings bounced. She flashed her dark eyes at him with one single, pointed glance, a glance that managed to be both accusatory and frightening. "You try calming down after opening up a trunk and finding a skeleton staring back at you! With *two* skulls. *Four* empty eye sockets!"

The gelding pinned its ears back at Bethany's loud voice and Jimmy tightened his hold, keeping one eye on that horse. One more shout from her and his horse would bolt to kingdom come.

Bethany shuddered. "I will never sleep again." She was furious, shoulders rigid, chin tilted at that arrogant angle.

But at least she wasn't shouting anymore. "Maybe there's a reasonable explanation. Did you ask the sisters about the trunk?"

"No, of course not. They weren't home." She crossed her arms. "They're hardly ever home. I don't know what they do with their time, but it sure isn't spent cleaning their house." A little laugh bubbled up in her throat. "Besides, why would I want them to know that I knew they were killing people and stuffing them in trunks? I'm not stupid." She gave him one last look of utter disgust and marched back to her scooter.

The gelding pointed its ears at Jimmy. He stroked the horse along its neck and spoke to it softly. "Did you understand a word of that?" The horse stood as if planted to the ground. "Me either. Well, Bethany may not have been a passing truck, but she does have a way of creating a maelstrom. I think she took care of your conditioning exercises for today."

For the past three summers, Miriam Schrock's twice-removed third cousin from York County had invited her to come along on a vacation to visit relatives in Maine with them, and each time she thanked them and thanked them, then said no.

Her older sister, Bethany (her half sister—same father, different mothers—to be precise, and Mim valued being precise), couldn't get over this. A free trip to Maine! Weeks of swimming and lobsters and hiking and fir trees. No chickens to feed. No stalls to muck. No goat to stir up trouble. All that sounded nice, but Mim didn't want to go. She just wanted to spend the summer in Stoney Ridge—to watch Galen King and Jimmy Fisher train Thoroughbreds, play with her younger brothers if and when she felt like it, and read piles of library books. What if she were to get sick while she was away? She had never been away from home without her mother, and she wasn't about to start now. Her mom needed her. Ever since her father had died suddenly in a drowning accident last year, Mim just wanted things to be safe and familiar.

Besides, who would visit with Ella at the Sisters' House? Ella was the oldest of the five ancient sisters who lived together in an even more ancient house. Mim tagged along now and then when Bethany worked at the Sisters' House trying to organize their enormous accumulation of clutter. Mim did odd jobs for the sisters and had become rather fond of Ella. She was round and short, warm and steamy like a little teapot. She always smelled of fresh-baked gingerbread. Whenever Mim would stop in at the Sisters' House, Ella would look up from her crocheting or quilting or newspaper reading, pat the chair next to her so Mim would sit down beside her, and say, "So tell me everything."

Ella said she considered Mim to be the granddaughter she never had. Mim wished Ella *were* her grandmother. That had to be a private wish, though, since she already had a grandmother. Mammi Vera. Well, Mammi Vera was just Mammi Vera. Mim thought she was born old and cranky.

Yesterday, Mammi Vera said that Luke, Mim's brother, who would soon be eleven, was full of the devil. He had memorized a Bible verse to a snappy tune and taught it to Mammi Vera. It was one of those tunes that got stuck in your head. A neighbor named Hank Lapp stopped by to say hello and heard her humming it. He asked her about it, so she sang the

Bible verse. Then Hank laughed so hard tears rolled down his leathery cheeks. Turns out Luke had been singing Bible verses to a radio jingle for fine-tasting filter cigarettes. That was when Mammi Vera said Luke was full of the devil.

The devil seemed to be lurking around Eagle Hill on a regular basis, in Mammi Vera's mind, and she was often warning Mim, Luke, and their eight-year-old brother Sammy with strange proverbs from the Old Country: "Speak of the devil and he will flee."

Awhile ago, Mammi Vera caught Mim peering into a mirror. In a loud voice she said, "Wammer nachts in der Schpiggel guckt, gucket der Deiwel raus." *When you look into the mirror at night, the devil peers out.*

The thought scared Mim so much she didn't look in a mirror for an entire month. She even took down the mirror in her room, just in case she happened to forget and glance at it during the night. Finally, she discussed Mammi Vera's saying with her very good friend Danny Riehl and he thought it didn't sound at all logical. Why would the devil only look at you in the night? That's the kind of thinker Danny was. Logical. He made everything easier to understand.

Mim was so touched that Ella thought of her as a granddaughter that she nearly confided in her about her great devotion for Danny Riehl. In her diary, she had filled the margins with versions of her name connected to Danny Riehl: Mrs. Daniel Riehl, Miriam Riehl, and her very favorite, Danny's Mim.

Mim had never told a soul how she felt about Danny. Although she shared almost everything with her sister Bethany, she had never mentioned Danny to her, because sometimes, oftentimes, her sister could be a little insensitive. If Danny found out, even accidentally, about Mim's deep feelings for him, it would be the most humiliating thing she could ever imagine.

Today, as Mim ran to get the mail, she was glad she had turned down her York County cousin's invitation and for an entirely different reason than Danny or Ella. Nearly every day, there was a letter in the Inn at Eagle Hill mailbox addressed to Mrs. Miracle from someone who direly needed an answer to a problem.

A few months ago, when Mim's mother, Rose, had first opened the Inn at Eagle Hill, she had asked Mim to paint a sign for the inn. Mim was known far and wide for her excellent penmanship. Excellent. She worked long and hard on the large wooden sign, penciling the letters, painting them in black with a fine-tipped paintbrush. At the bottom of the sign, Mim had added a little Latin phrase she had found in a book and liked the way it rolled off her tongue: *Miracula fieri hic.* At the time, she didn't realize what it meant: Miracles occur here.

A newspaper reporter, who happened to have taken five years of high school Latin, he said, translated the phrase and said *this* was the story he'd been looking for. There was a human-interest angle to spin from the Latin phrase—it spoke to a longing in everyone for a place that fed their soul and spirit. He wrote up an article, weaving in truth and mistruths, about the miracles that occurred at the Inn at Eagle Hill. The article was picked up by the Pennsylvania newspapers, then the internet, and so on and so forth. Soon, the inn was considered to be a place where people could practically order up a custom-made miracle like a hamburger. And then people started to write letters to Mrs. Miracle. Buckets and buckets of letters. They kept pouring in. Mim's mother, overwhelmed by the quantity, was relieved when Mim offered to answer the letters. But she told Mim what to say: "The Inn at Eagle Hill couldn't solve their problems. Only God could provide miracles."

Mim believed that part about God and miracles, but after reading a few letters, she thought she could help the people solve their problems. Most of the problems were pretty simple: injured feelings, sibling rivalry, how to cook and clean. All of that she had plenty of experience with, especially with the sibling rivalry. Her two little brothers couldn't be in the same room without some kind of fuss and tussle. So she decided to answer a few letters, offering advice, posing as Mrs. Miracle. Then a few more and a few more, until she finished the big pile. She knew she hadn't done what her mom had expected her to do, but it was just a small disobedience, a slight adjustment to the truth, and for the best of reasons. She was helping people, and hadn't she been taught to help others? Plus, Mim was sure the letters from people seeking advice would dwindle down as the Inn at Eagle Hill miracle story blew over. After all, with this heat wave they'd been having, the inn had been getting cancellations for reservations as soon as people discovered there was no air-conditioning. If they really thought the inn could dish out miracles, they wouldn't let a little hot weather stop them, would they?

Maybe, maybe not. But letters addressed to Mrs. Miracle kept coming. Mim made a point of meeting the mailman each day so her mom wasn't made aware of this interesting development. Each afternoon, she listened for the squeaky mail truck to come down their road and bolted to the mailbox when she heard it. So far, so good. The letters continued to arrive, stealthily, and the problems in the letters were still pretty simple to solve. She hadn't been stumped yet.

In today's mail was a letter from the local newspaper, asking Mrs. Miracle if she would like to have a regular column in the *Stoney Ridge Times*. Mrs. Miracle would be paid five dollars each time the column ran. Five whole dollars! Mim would be rich!

There was just one glitch. The letter from the newspaper stated she needed to be over eighteen and they wanted her signature and birth date on the W-2 form. Mim was only fourteen. She didn't mind bending the rules for a good cause, and this was definitely a worthy cause. But she would need help. First, she thought about asking Naomi King, her friend and neighbor, who had turned eighteen recently. But then she dismissed that notion. Naomi followed rules the way she quilted: even, straight, tiny, perfect stitches. No mistakes. Keeping a secret like Mrs. Miracle's true identity might cause Naomi to unravel.

Then she thought of her sister Bethany, who had just turned twenty and didn't mind bending rules at all. But the tricky part was catching Bethany in just the right mood to ask for a favor. It all depended if Bethany was feeling friendly or not. Anticipating Bethany's moods lately took skill—often, she seemed pensive and just wanted to be left alone. It was all because of Jake Hertzler. He was Bethany's ex-boyfriend, a charming fellow who had worked for her father at his investment company. When Schrock Investments went belly up, Jake Hertzler, along with Mim's oldest brother Tobe (again, to be precise, Tobe was her half brother), went missing.

On a cheerier note, this newspaper column was a wonderful opportunity for Mrs. Miracle. It was disappointing that Mim needed to keep this opportunity top secret—her mother, and *especially* her grandmother, must never find out! The way Mim rationalized it, it was only a tiny breaking of all the rules her church was so fond of and she was helping all kinds of people and that was worth keeping a secret or two. But if her grandmother found out—oh my! Then Mim would be full of the devil.

As soon as Geena Spencer arrived at her church office this morning, the elder board of the New Life Church of Ardmore, Pennsylvania, had called her into a meeting and told her, gently and firmly, that they were very sorry but things weren't working out the way they had hoped and they had to let her go. They had already found another interim youth pastor, an enthusiastic young man fresh out of seminary, to fill in for her. Starting today. They thanked her for her service, said they'd provide a glowing letter of recommendation, and asked if she needed any help cleaning out her office.

Stung and ashamed, Geena bent her head, and went to her office.

Objectively, she could see that they were right. The elder board had wanted a youth pastor who could preach the paint off the wall and act like a magnet for the youth of Ardmore. They had a plan to triple the size of the youth group, thereby drawing parents into the main sanctuary. Geena had a way with people, especially teens, as long as it was one-on-one, but as hard as she tried, she was a terrible public speaker. That was why she'd been passed over for so many positions. She only received the church in Ardmore because her favorite seminary professor, who happened to be her uncle and a good friend of the head elder, had called in a few favors and promised Geena would improve with time and practice.

Also, no other candidate accepted the call.

It had been an opportunity for Geena to prove herself, but after only six weeks, the elders started to pay her Monday morning visits with what they considered to be helpful suggestions: "Don't read your notes. Make eye contact. Speak up. Slow down. Speed up." Their feedback only made her all the more nervous. During youth group each Wednesday night, a handful of elders would come and sit in the back of the room. She would glance out at the sea of young faces, then at the back row of old faces, and feel a startled jolt, a deer in headlights, as if she were preaching to a room full of dour seminary professors.

Geena knew she wasn't a gifted orator, but she thought by now the church might have developed an appreciation for all she did do well: She'd been told she was a "2 a.m. pastor"—the kind families wouldn't hesitate to call in a crisis. During spring break, she organized a youth group trip to help on a Habitat for Humanity building project in Kentucky. She started weekly Bible studies—one for the boys and one for the girls. While the youth group wasn't exactly tripling—not by a long shot—she was discipling a core of committed teens. She tried to equip them so they could influence their peers in any situation—at school, in sports, or just hanging out. She never forgot anyone's name. And she loved them, every single one of them.

But obviously, all that wasn't enough.

It was humiliating to suddenly be let go, released. Fired. As she took books off the shelves and placed them in boxes, she kept telling herself to pull it together, to find a way to get over this, to stop being a big baby. But it wasn't working.

She felt sorry for herself. It was hard not to. She thought this was "it"— the job she'd been waiting for all her life. At long last she could set down roots. She'd been Head of Children's Ministry for five different churches since she graduated from seminary—hoping one or the other might turn into a youth pastor position. Each opportunity seemed promising, until the Sunday morning came when Geena was given a chance to fill in for the senior pastor. It was customary for the ordained staffers to preach on low attendance Sundays—after Christmas, after Easter. When the congregation heard her preach, everything went south.

No call ever came, not until the one from this church in Ardmore.

The call to ministry was a strange thing. It was exactly that—a calling, a thing you responded to not because you wanted to but because you had to.

Stranger still to have the call and not get a call.

As Geena opened her top desk drawer, her eyes fell on a gift certificate from grateful parishioners, a quirky, big-hearted couple named Lois and Tony. They had given it to her a month ago, after she had come to the hospital when their granddaughter had been involved in a car accident. She stood vigil with them until the doctor brought good news, and they were appreciative of Geena's calming presence during those troubling hours. The gift certificate was for two nights' stay at an Amish bed-and-breakfast in Lancaster County.

Impulsively, Geena called the Inn at Eagle Hill and asked if there was an opening for tonight. A woman answered the phone, her voice as soft as chocolate. "Actually, I happen to have a week's opening because of a cancellation," she said. "The heat wave we're having is discouraging fair-weather visitors. I have to warn you, we don't have any air-conditioning."

Geena jumped at the chance to leave town. "I don't mind the heat. I just need . . . a place to take a break and do some serious thinking for a few days. I'll take the whole week." Boy, did she ever have thinking to do. Like, her entire future.

"Well, then, it sounds like you'll be coming to the right place."

Two hours and one stop at Sonic for a double cheeseburger and fries later, Geena had exited I-76, driven along the Philadelphia Pike, then followed her GPS to the country road that wound to Stoney Ridge. She noticed a siren in her rearview mirror. She pulled over, hoping the police officer just needed to pass by. Her heart sank as he stopped his patrol car behind hers. He walked to her passenger window, leaned over, and growled, "License and registration."

Geena handed him the paperwork and waited while he returned to his car. After a few more long moments, the officer reappeared at her window. "What brings you to Stoney Ridge, Ms. Spencer?"

"Reverend. Reverend Spencer. I'm a minister." She was slightly ashamed to play that minister card, but . . . it often worked in the clutch.

He didn't bat an eye.

"What brings me here? Just a whim." She shrugged. "I needed a little vacation."

He nodded slowly. "Well, I'm sorry your vacation is starting off on a sour note," he said as he scribbled on his pad, "but as fast as you were going, I really don't have a choice." He tore the ticket off the pad and handed it to her. "You'd better start slowing down, Reverend Spencer. You're in another world."

# 2

It was the silence that woke Geena on the first morning after her arrival at the Inn at Eagle Hill. She had never heard such silence. Now and then, a horse would neigh to another horse, an owl would hoot, or she'd hear the clip-clop of a horse and buggy travel along the road. Mostly, though, all was still. Utter quiet.

She tried to go back to sleep—after all, how many times in her life could she sleep in?—but finally gave up and decided to take a long walk into the hills that lined the back of the farmhouse. Rose Schrock, the Amish woman who ran the inn, the one with the voice as soft as chocolate, checked her in last night and told her about a trail that would take her to the top of the ridge.

Rose also mentioned that breakfast would be delivered at her door at seven in the morning and hinted at something about blueberry cornbread. Geena had heard glowing stories about Amish cooks and wasn't about to miss breakfast. Her father always said she had the appetite of a professional football player—unusually impressive for a five-foot-one, one hundred-and-seven-pound woman.

Yesterday, as Geena got out of her car at Eagle Hill, the sour manure smell from the cornfields, mingled with the humidity of a prolonged heat wave, pinched her lungs hard enough that she coughed like an old lady to get air. Today, her nose felt a little more accustomed to the unique aroma of an Amish farm. She walked to the middle of the front lawn and turned in a slow circle, taking in a full panorama: the red barn, the mare and her colt in a fenced pasture, a goat sticking his head through to another pasture to find better grass, the soft green canopy of shade trees, the four little sheep down by the creek. Her heart missed a beat when she caught sight of an eagle pair soaring over the ridge. Eagle Hill, she decided, looked exactly as an Amish farm should. Pristine, cared for, safe for all creatures, peaceful.

It was good that she had come.

It was bad that she had been fired.

What hurt her most about being let go was that she had tried so hard to meet the needs of the congregation. Once she even returned from a vacation when she learned that a fire swept through the home of a teen in her youth group. She dropped everything and helped organize a donation drive to provide for this family. How could the church turn its back on her?

She shook her head. *No wallowing, Geena.*

She had come to Eagle Hill to stop, take a breather, absorb the blow, and think about what to do next.

The first fingers of sunlight tipped over the eastern edge of the ridge that framed the farm. The light was a delicate pale butter, washing the hills with a soft brush, hazing the edges of the trees. The very top leaves of the trees were illuminated, almost glowing. Birds whirred and whistled. A pair of squirrels chased each other around a tree trunk.

When had she last stopped and noticed the delights of God's handiwork in nature? Really, truly noticed?

There was *something* about this farmland. It was so drastically different from the city. Not a freeway or high-rise in sight—only wide open rolling hills that whispered history and serenity. Rose had told her that by mid-August, the land would look entirely different. The farmers' corn, now ankle high, would tower above any man. "You won't be able to see the hills like you can now," she told Geena. "You'll have to just come back and see for yourself how this area changes through the months." Geena wondered where she would be, come mid-August, when that corn grew taller than her.

For the first time since she was a teenager, she questioned herself. What if she wasn't meant to be a youth pastor after all? Maybe she'd misunderstood the call. What was that old joke her father used to tell? "If you get the call, you have to answer. But then again . . . you might just let it ring."

Geena's father was a well-known, beloved pastor, a leader of one of the largest congregations on the East Coast, and particularly revered for the delivery and punch of his sermons. Her uncle, too, was the dean of a highly regarded seminary. They were so proud of Geena for finally getting a call to a position. How could she tell them she'd been fired?

*No wallowing, Geena. And maybe, for just a little while, no thinking about your future.*

She forked off on a trail that ran behind the hill, pondering how she wanted to spend the rest of her day. Yesterday, as she drove through the small downtown section of Stoney Ridge, she was glad to see there wasn't a tourist shop in sight. Not an inch of neon on Stoney Ridge's main street. Not a single billboard. This was a place where you could walk to town, where you could buy a quart of milk or a packet of shoelaces in the village. It was easy to completely forget she was only two hours away from Philadelphia, to forget that society even existed, let alone a society brimming with traffic, hustle and bustle, and stress. She felt her soul start to settle, relax, let go.

She had always loved to hike—had loved the feeling of being alive under the sky, feet touching the earth, being wholly herself. Thinking. Walking. Praying. On the trail, she had always been able to leave her troubles behind. Here there was only room for wind and sky and sun and communing with God.

The early morning silence, broken only by the faintest of crickets somewhere out in the fields and the crow of a rooster, fell on her like a quilt. It had texture and depth, a velvety weight to ease her jangled nerves, her weary brain. *Everything will be all right*, was what she heard.

She knew that nearly audible voice. Knew it well. It came to her when she least expected but when she most prayed for it. The words were always short and to the point; clear, concise directives. Nothing confusing, nothing vague. And the message was always accompanied with peace. Bone-deep peace that couldn't be explained and wasn't dependent on circumstances.

She turned around and headed down the trail back to the farm. As she neared the farmhouse, the smoky scent of frying bacon reached her nose and she picked up her pace. She made a shortcut through the yard, along the side of the henhouse, then stopped abruptly. A man emerged through the privet bushes that ran between Eagle Hill and the neighboring farm.

Geena had never seen an Amish man before; she had imagined them to be portly, flush-cheeked, ragged old hippies. But the man who came striding across the yard from the neighbor's farm was tall and fit, young and very deeply tanned, weathered in the way of an outdoorsman. And the look on his face as he saw Rose come out of the kitchen door with an overflowing laundry basket in her arms, well, it was a sight to behold.

Geena leaned against the henhouse. She knew she should turn around and leave—good heavens, she was a grown woman—but she found herself mesmerized by what was going on between them. The man's eyes met with Rose's, a quiet greeting that lasted a good long minute.

Rose's face was bright, as if with happiness. She set the laundry basket on the ground and waved. "Good morning, Galen."

A big golden retriever spotted Geena and bounded toward her. She was sure he'd bark and give her away, but when he reached her, he sat in front of her, shifting from paw to paw, considering her. It was as if he was asking, "Well, now, who are you?" and regarded her with the gentle expectation of a wise old teacher waiting for a student to come up with the answer. Geena bent down and stroked his thick fur through her fingers, eyes again glued to the Amish couple.

The man—Galen—walked over to the clothesline. As Rose's gaze settled fully on him, her eyebrows drew together in a slight frown. "What's the matter?"

Galen hesitated for a moment, as if he was gathering his thoughts. "Rose, I want to tell you something," he said, "only I don't really know how to say it properly. Words can't—" and he made a small, helpless gesture.

"Well, try."

"I love you, Rose. I love you. That's all. That's all I have to say."

From where Geena squatted, against the side of the henhouse, absently stroking the big dog, she could see Rose's face go blank, utterly expressionless. She wondered why the man had felt the need to express his feelings like that, right now, on a summer morning. The silence became painful—he was getting nothing back from her. Nothing. Poor guy.

Then a smile began, starting in Rose's eyes, until it covered her entire face. "I'm taking the boys for a swim later today, at Blue Lake Pond. Would you like to join us?"

Suddenly, the mood lifted, as real as if sun had broken through gray skies, and the two grinned foolishly at each other. "I'd like that." He touched the edge of his hat and strode back to the hole in the privet, slipping through and disappearing. The golden retriever bolted after him, tail feathers wagging like a flag.

Hiding like a schoolgirl, eavesdropping on an Amish couple, Geena knew she should be ashamed of herself. And yet, it was such a charming moment! So unexpected. She felt a delight at such a surprise—who would have thought she'd stumble upon a tender moment of expressed love on an Amish farm? She grinned. Such surprises were good. A tiny glimmer of well-being wisped through Geena, the first she'd felt since arriving at the church office yesterday morning. Coming here had been a good idea.

Everything would be all right.

After Mim had taken a breakfast tray down to the new guest in the guest flat, she looked everywhere for Bethany and finally found her outside, beside the henhouse, tossing cornmeal from a tin pie plate to a flock of hens pecking the ground. "For a tiny little lady, that preacher sure does like to eat. I asked her how many pancakes she wanted and she said six. Even Luke can only down five."

Bethany flung her arm out wide, and the wind caught the cornmeal and sent it swirling in a yellow cloud. "I like a girl who's not afraid to admit she's hungry."

A good sign. Bethany seemed to be in a good mood. Mim tiptoed across the chicken yard, carefully as she was barefooted, and stood closer to her sister. "I need your help with something."

Bethany tossed another handful of meal at the hens. "If the goat has wandered off again, I'm not going after it. If he doesn't have enough sense to get himself home, I say good riddance."

"No. It's not the goat. It's something personal. But first I need your promise that you'll keep it to yourself, even if you decide not to help me."

She scattered the last of the cornmeal for the hens. "All right."

"You promise?"

"I told you all right, didn't I?"

"Do you remember the letters that came to the house after I had put that Latin phrase on the bottom of the Inn at Eagle Hill sign?"

Bethany squinted her eyes, trying to remember.

"The newspaper reporter translated it to mean 'Miracles occur here.' Then he wrote a newspaper story saying that our inn handed out miracles."

Bethany shrugged. "I don't remember."

Was she serious? How could Bethany not remember *that*? Because she was mooning over Jake Hertzler, that's why. Just like she was now. Mim tried not to look as disappointed as she felt. "Well, it was a news story that other newspapers picked up, then it was on the internet . . . then Bishop Elmo came by and asked us to paint over the Latin phrase."

Bethany let out a laugh. "That doesn't surprise me." She turned completely around. "That's the problem with being—"

"Funny you should mention that, because it underlines my need for secrecy." Mim had to cut Bethany off, straightaway, and reroute her back to the topic at hand. She knew just where her sister was going with this. Ever since Jake Hertzler had come and gone, she'd been complaining about being Amish. Everything started with "That's the problem with being Amish . . ." as if there was just one thing. Bethany had a long list of complaints: she thought she should be able to have print fabric for her dresses, shorter church services, telephones in the house, a computer might be nice. On and on and on. *Blah blah blah.*

Mostly, Bethany was just "in a mood." The moods changed—sad, teary, angry, snappish—but rarely happy, like she used to be. It seemed to Mim that Jake Hertzler stole something from everybody: he stole a horse from Jimmy Fisher and he stole happiness from Bethany. She wasn't sure, but she had a feeling that her brother Tobe's running away had to do with Jake Hertzler. So, in a way, Jake stole her brother away from them too. How could one person hold so much power over others?

"I haven't got all day," Bethany said.

"Letters started coming to the inn. Addressed to Mrs. Miracle. Asking for help with their problems. Lots of them."

Bethany tilted her head, mildly intrigued.

"Mom didn't have time to answer them. It happened around the time when Mammi Vera was ailing, then she ended up having brain surgery. So

Mom let me answer the letters. She told me to say that only God makes miracles and that we couldn't solve their problems . . . but . . ." She hesitated.

"So . . ." Bethany urged, surprisingly interested.

Mim tried to sound nonchalant. "I didn't exactly do what she said to do. I wrote the people back and solved their problems."

"You *what*?"

"I pretended I was Mrs. Miracle and solved their problems. Most of their problems were pretty easy to solve. And the ones that weren't—I think those were people who just wanted to be listened to." She bit her lip. "You won't say anything to anyone, will you?"

"Verzaehl net alles as du weescht?" *Tell not all you know?*

"Something like that."

"And Rose doesn't know about this?"

Mim shook her head. "The letters kept coming. More and more and more. It hasn't stopped. I hurry to the mailbox every day so I get the letters first. So . . ."

"So . . ."

"The features editor from the *Stoney Ridge Times* wrote and asked if Mrs. Miracle would write a weekly column for the newspaper. But he thinks Mrs. Miracle is an old lady."

Bethany's eyes went wide with astonishment, then she burst into laughter. That tears-rolling-down-her-face kind of laughter.

Mim was horrified. She hadn't confided in Bethany to be laughed at. She took her role as Mrs. Miracle very, very seriously.

"Oh Mim!" Bethany finally said, gasping for air, "this is the funniest thing I've heard in a long time."

Mim was crushed. She had made a serious mistake and now Mrs. Miracle's future was in jeopardy. What if Bethany told her mom?

Bethany wiped tears from her face. "Well, it's a humdinger of a chance for Mrs. Miracle, and it sure beats feeding chickens. Just tell me what you want me to do." She grinned. "But remember this, Mim: Loss dich net verwische, is es elft Gebot." *Don't get caught is the eleventh commandment.*

❦ ◊ ❧

The afternoon sun's piercing glare gave Naomi King a headache, making her feel as if a red-hot poker had been stuck through her head. She had woken with a mild headache and tried to ignore it, hoping it would ease up as the day went on. She even went to her quilting, since she was good for little else. It soothed her head a little, and the soul, as well, freeing her of self-pity. She loved quilting more than just about anything, and the twice-a-month quilting bee was an event she looked forward to.

She wouldn't have missed the Sisters' Bee for all the tea in China, and she loved tea. She'd rather quilt than eat, any day of the week. The Sisters' Bee was named because it was originally the quilting group of the five sisters from the Sisters' House. They added Edith Fisher, Jimmy's mother, and years later, they invited Naomi to join. Naomi wasn't really sure why she was included in the Sisters' Bee but on the day she turned fifteen, she was swept into the circle. It happened to be the year the group had volunteered a quilt to be auctioned off to help the Clinic for Special Children in Strasburg and Edith Fisher had chosen a pattern that was beyond anyone's piecing skills. Suddenly, Naomi found herself to be a highly valued member of the group.

Last night, she had stayed up late to finish a quilt top for today's bee: it was a Sunshine and Shadow pattern—bright reds and yellows and shiny gold.

As the women nibbled on Naomi's lemon cookies, they oohed and aahed over the quilt top. "This is the best you've done yet, Naomi!" and she agreed.

Which wasn't vanity. She had made her first quilt, a doll blanket, when she was seven, and she'd been making them ever since. She was a devoted gardener, a cheerful cook, but only a true expert at this one thing. When it came to fine, intricate stitches, she couldn't be beat. She took twelve stitches to the inch whereas most of the women took eight. She had a talent for working out complicated patterns, and an eye for piecing colorful swatches together in surprising ways.

Naomi thought her gift at piecing might be because of her headaches—they gave her plenty of time to quilt and think and dream. And sometimes, those strange bright lights that flashed in her head, those disturbing auras, gave her ideas for color and pattern variations. Sometimes, she saw strange things. Or rather . . . she *felt* them. Warnings, hunches, presentiments. The old sisters called it a gift. Naomi didn't consider it a gift. To her, it felt more like a burden. And she was of a mind that everyone had such intuition, but few paid attention to it.

Today, the quilting bee was held at Naomi's house. They were welcoming back Edith Fisher, who had just returned to Stoney Ridge after the untimely and unfortunate passing of her brand-new husband. It was true that no one was overly fond of Edith Fisher, but Naomi always felt her bark was worse than her bite. Edith had never said a mean word to Naomi, though she had never said anything kind, either. She was a big sturdy woman without much softness.

Earlier this morning, Naomi had dropped off a loaf of banana bread to Eagle Hill and mentioned that Edith Fisher had returned to Stoney Ridge. As Vera Schrock took a slice of banana bread, she said, between bites, "Edith can be as sour as bad cider when she wants to be, that one. Words out of that woman's mouth fade like snow in a fry pan."

Those observations struck Naomi as ironic, seeing as they came from a woman who was more than a little cold and sour herself.

"Say what you will about Edith," Rose Schrock said, "but her son Jimmy Fisher is a credit to her."

Even Vera didn't dispute that, and she disputed nearly everything her daughter-in-law Rose had to say.

Jimmy had been working for Naomi's older brother, Galen, for a few months now and considered himself a partner in the horse-training business. Galen rolled his eyes at that, but Naomi thought he was quietly pleased by Jimmy's dedication. His hard work too. If Galen wasn't pleased, Naomi supposed, he would have sent Jimmy packing. He could be like that—once he made up his mind about a person, that was that.

Most girls in her church were green with envy that Naomi got to see Jimmy Fisher nearly every day. For breakfast and lunch and often dinner, which he showed up for on a regular basis. Naomi liked Jimmy. She liked him quite a bit. But she wasn't in love with him and knew she never would be. Jimmy was a fine-looking man, of a good build and height—not tall, but he held himself very straight as if to make the most of what he had—with hair like the stubble left in the fields after haying, and eyes as luminously blue as agates. When he smiled, the right side of his mouth curved up more than the left. He was fun-loving and lighthearted and charming and downright adorable. But she wasn't in love with him, nor he with her. They weren't at all right for each other.

Naomi had a sense about these kinds of things. She had predicted her brother Galen's romance with Rose Schrock long before it was obvious to others. She saw how her brother stilled whenever Rose was nearby, or the way his eyes lingered after her. She was hoping Jimmy might have those same sweet feelings for Bethany, though it was true that Jimmy Fisher liked most girls and even more girls liked Jimmy Fisher. But maybe it was finally time for Jimmy to settle on someone. At least, his mother thought it was high time.

Since Edith Fisher had returned to Stoney Ridge, her first objective, she made clear, was to get Jimmy married. Paul, her older son, had tied the knot during Edith's brief marriage and then surprised everyone by moving off to Canada with his bride right after Edith, unexpectedly widowed, returned to Stoney Ridge.

Edith was indignant! She was counting on localized grandchildren, she said, and now it was all up to Jimmy. And she made it no secret that she had selected Naomi King for him. No thank you! Jimmy Fisher might be adorable in every way that mattered, but he was not right for Naomi. Besides, her heart belonged to another, but that was a secret she guarded carefully.

Naomi had a hope that once her friend Bethany was done with her melancholia for Jake Hertzler, she might wake up to the fact that Jimmy Fisher was perfectly suited to her.

Naomi adored Bethany. She was fond of Mim, the younger sister, but being with her was like looking into a mirror. Naomi and Mim did things exactly alike, and sometimes Naomi knew what Mim was going to say before she said it. Bethany was a real live wire, and it was exciting to be around her. She made life interesting.

Naomi knew Bethany was hurting after the Jake Hertzler disaster, and she had a plan to help. She was sure that if she could bring Bethany into the quilting group, gently nudging her toward Jimmy Fisher while wooing over his mother, those wounds would heal.

Naomi stopped to examine the seam she was stitching. She picked up a pair of scissors and trimmed a loose thread. She was waiting for just the right moment to bring up Bethany's name, to test the waters and see how

Edith Fisher would react. Anyone wanting to marry Jimmy Fisher was going to have to win over Edith Fisher. Wasn't there a saying for that very thing? Wann'd der Sohn hawwe witt, muscht dich mit der Mudder halde. *She that would the son win must with the mother first begin.*

Not that Bethany was interested in Jimmy. Not yet. But Naomi was going to do her best to light that spark between them she was sure was there. Almost sure.

When there was a lull in the conversation, Naomi casually said that she thought it would be nice to include her friend Bethany in the quilting bee. Naomi finished her stitch at the instant she looked up at Edith and caught the look of disapproval on her face, which made her run the needle into her finger. When she glanced down, she saw a little drop of blood on the place she was stitching around and put her finger into her mouth.

The five elderly sisters stopped their sewing but kept their heads bowed, the edges of their capstrings dancing on the quilt top. They didn't say a word. Not a peep. Naomi glanced nervously around the circle.

Unfortunately, whenever Naomi felt nervous, she babbled. Her brother Galen grew quieter and she grew more talkative. Their mother used to say they evened each other out. As she realized the women were staring at her, she started a long tale about how she had known Bethany for years and years, and what a fine cook she was, and how she was sure they'd all enjoy having her in the circle. She spoke faster and faster, jumping from topic to topic, making very little sense, all the while wishing her mouth would just snap shut. She sped right on: "And Bethany said she doesn't like to sew." She cringed and clamped her mouth shut.

What possessed her to say *that* when she was trying to snag an invitation for Bethany to a sewing group? It was true, but why did she have to say so? Just yesterday, Naomi had mentioned to Bethany that she quilted because it was the most comforting thing to do. Bethany said the reason she quilted was because it kept her from biting her fingernails.

Edith Fisher squinted at Naomi through her thick spectacles until Naomi blushed and looked down at her piecing. "I've never met a woman who didn't like to sew."

Sylvia, the youngest of the elderly sisters, finally spoke. "Bethany's a more modern girl, Edith. She has other things to do besides sew with old ladies."

Sylvia forgot that Naomi wasn't an old lady. All the women forgot. There were times when Naomi wanted to point out that she wasn't a spinster quite yet, not at eighteen. They'd never thought to wonder if Naomi King had feelings, dreams, desires of her own. She knew they considered her to be a frail thing, someone to be pitied and fussed over. That might be how she seemed on the outside, but on the inside, Naomi felt strong and brave. At least, that was how she thought of herself when she wasn't plagued with one of those dreadful headaches.

Then Edith Fisher cleared her throat, determined to take charge, and Naomi wondered what everyone was in for. "Speaking of modern and worldly ways, I understand those Schrocks have a preacher staying in their guest flat now." She pursed her lips as if tasting a sour lemon. "A lady preacher."

"A youth pastor," Naomi said quietly but firmly.

"Same thing," Edith said.

"Now, Edith," Fannie said, a smile wobbling at the edges of her mouth, "your halo always did fit a little too tight." Fannie was second from the bottom of the five sisters, the polar opposite of her younger sibling, as full figured as Sylvia was petite and as opinionated as Sylvia was soft-spoken.

"How did you hear that, Edith?" Sylvia asked.

Edith paused while she threaded her needle. "Oh, well, people talk. You know."

People do talk; Edith certainly did.

"Mark my words. Those Schrocks attract trouble like molasses draws flies. They're just like those Amos Lapps over at Windmill Farm. No difference at all. And I don't mind telling them so right to their faces."

Something out the window caught Naomi's eye. Up the walk came Hank Lapp, former suitor to Edith before she spurned him for her now-dead brand-new husband. And that was when Naomi's headache took a turn for the worse.

Jimmy was in the cool of the barn, wrapping his prize horse Lodestar's leg before he exercised him so the horse wouldn't knick his forelegs with his hoofs.

"JIMMY FISHER? WHERE ARE YOU?" The horses in the barn stirred and lifted their heads at the sound of Hank Lapp's bellow.

Jimmy popped his head up over the stall. "Hank, how many times do I have to tell you to keep your voice low and calm around these Thoroughbreds?"

Hank Lapp was a one-of-a-kind older Plain man in looks and personality. Wiry white hair that stuck out in all directions, a wandering eye that made a person unsure of which eye to look at, a fellow with his own way of thinking about things. Most folks had trouble tolerating him for a multitude of reasons, all reasonable, but Jimmy was fond of him. For all his bluster, Hank had a good heart.

"Well, you could have warned me that house was filled with cackling hens."

"And just how was I supposed to know you were looking for me?" Jimmy bent down to finish wrapping Lodestar's foreleg. "How was Ohio?"

"It was fine. Just fine. Julia and Rome are trying to talk us into moving there with them."

"No kidding? Is Amos considering it?"

Hank shrugged. "All depends on Fern. She's from there, you know." He picked up a currycomb and examined it. "Women run the world," he muttered. "You could have warned me that Naomi had her quilting bee today."

"Now, how could I have warned you when I didn't even know you were back in Stoney Ridge?"

"Well, you should tack a sign up on the front door. Give a fellow a little heads-up." He lifted his hands in the air, drawing a sign: "ENTER AT YOUR OWN RISK."

"When did you get back?"

"Yesterday. Thought I'd better grab you for some afternoon fishing before someone beats us to all the good ones."

"I'd like to, Hank, but Galen's at an auction and I need to get a few things done before he gets back."

"Now, see? Galen had enough sense to go missing from the farm on quilting days." Hank scratched his neck. "Did you know your mother is up there in that henhouse?"

So *that's* what was nettling Hank. "Yup. She returned to Stoney Ridge a few weeks ago. You probably hadn't heard since you were in Ohio. Her new husband passed."

Hank took off his hat. "Well, I'm sorry to hear that." He put his hat back on. "Not too terrible sorry, though. I never did understand why she up and married him so fast after she spurned me." He leaned against the stall wall. "Women are a mystery."

"They are at that." As Jimmy wrapped Lodestar's other foreleg, he made sure the wrap would stay tied. Galen was always chiding him for babying this horse, but Lodestar wasn't just any horse. Jimmy didn't want a single scar on his forelegs to mar his appearance. He had plans for Lodestar—this horse was going to be the anchor of his breeding business. He checked the ends one more time, then straightened up.

Hank picked up a piece of straw and chewed on it. "You still trying to get Bethany Schrock to pay you any mind?"

Jimmy frowned. "Getting girls' attention has never been hard."

"No, not most. Just hers."

"If I really wanted Bethany Schrock, I could get her."

Hank let out a rusty laugh. "Well, I never thought I'd see the day when a Fisher boy couldn't get a girl!"

Hank Lapp had just sailed past friendly and arrived at annoying.

"You're just like your brother. Always shopping, never buying."

"Paul *did* get married," Jimmy said, teeth gritted. The Fisher boys' reluctance to settle down was a constant source of amusement for Hank— ironic commentary from a dedicated bachelor. It deeply annoyed Jimmy to be compared to Paul. He wasn't like him. He wasn't. "I will, too, when I'm ready to pick the girl."

"Unless that girl happens to be Bethany Schrock!" Hank roared. "You'll have to chase her till she catches you!"

What irked Jimmy was that Hank spoke the truth. He wasn't accustomed to not being taken seriously by a woman. Most girls loved any attention Jimmy threw their way. Bethany acted as if she could take him or leave him. For example, if they happened to be talking, she was always the first to say goodbye. That bothered him. He liked to be the first to say goodbye. He thought it left a girl wanting more.

But it was time to change the subject. "Hank, why would you suppose someone might have a trunk of human bones hidden in a basement?"

Hank pulled off his hat and turned it in a circle, thinking hard. "Well, there could be all kinds of explanations."

Now, that was just one of the reasons Jimmy tolerated Hank Lapp better than most. When Hank grew irritating, which he inevitably did, Jimmy could steer him off in a different direction. Hank didn't mind exploring odd trails of conversation. His entire life was a giant trail of loose ends.

"Could be a real simple reason." Hank scratched his wooly white hair. "Not sure what it might be, though."

Jimmy thought about that for a long moment. "You just gave me an idea." He closed Lodestar's stall and locked both sections of the door with a keyed lock and hung the key on the wall. This beautiful stallion had escape on his mind at all times. "Coming with me?"

"Where are we going?"

"Just up to the house." Jimmy grabbed his hat. "I have a question or two I need to ask the sisters from the Sisters' House."

"NO SIR! I'm not going back up there. The way your mother glared at me—I felt as doomed as a chicken laying its head down on the chopping block." He scowled at Jimmy with his good eye. "I'm going fishing."

"Suit yourself," Jimmy said, grinning.

Bethany sat in the air-conditioned waiting room of the *Stoney Ridge Times* office, holding a paper cup of amber-colored lukewarm tea. She'd been waiting over thirty-five minutes for the features editor to get out of a meeting so she could hand him the signed paperwork to set up Mrs. Miracle's new column. She glanced at the wall clock again. Forty-five minutes.

*Shootfire!* She was already tired of the newspaper business.

Bethany leaned back in her chair and took in a deep breath, then let it go. Offices had a unique smell: ink and paper and waxed floors. A wisp of yearning wove through her chest. The scent reminded her of her father's office at Schrock Investments, and that reminded her of Jake Hertzler. She felt very unsettled today, almost like a storm was heading in, but it wasn't.

Time. Things took time to heal.

Rose had reminded her of that very thing after Jake's abrupt departure. Maybe she should write it on an index card and stick it in her dress pocket.

How could it still sting so much, even as the weeks flew by? It was embarrassing how much she thought she had loved Jake. Humiliating how she had played right into his hands, swept along by his charm. Horrifying when she learned he had tried to cheat Jimmy Fisher out of that pretty horse with the flaxen mane.

Where would Bethany be right now if she had run off with Jake like they had planned? Most likely, he never intended to marry her.

She knew she should feel grateful that she had enough sense to have refused, in the end, to go with him. In a way, she was grateful. But she was also steaming mad at Jake. It wasn't easy to be steaming mad at a person who had vanished . . . where did all that madness go? Stuffed down deep, that's where it went.

Most everyone thought Jake had broken her heart in two when he left, and she let them think whatever they wanted to think. She doubted Jake's heart was broken when she refused to go—but then, she wasn't even sure he had much of a heart. No, breaking up with Jake wasn't the cause of the lingering sting she couldn't shake off.

She still couldn't get her head around that piece of information that Jake had told her months ago when he appeared suddenly in Stoney Ridge—that her brother Tobe, who had gone missing, was with their mother. A fresh wave of anger washed over her. *Bethany* wanted to be with their mother. *She* wanted to know her, to find out why she had left. She knew so little about this mysterious woman who had given Bethany life, then vanished.

Her father would never discuss their mother. Mammi Vera would turn red in the face with rage if the subject came up. And so it didn't.

Why had her mother left? Why? Bethany would never understand. As long as she lived, she'd never understand it. How could a mother desert her children? How did her mother walk away, knowing it would mean she would never see them sing at a Christmas program or wear a wedding dress or hold her grandbaby? Whenever Bethany looked back on all the moments of her life, both trivial and wondrous, her mother was always missing.

Rose was a wonderful stepmother, a truly caring, loving surrogate. But how could anyone take the place of a mother? Why was finding her mother so important to her? It was all she could think about since Jake had told her about Tobe. Bethany could hardly remember her, except in the barest fragments.

She swirled the tepid tea in the cup, mesmerized by the whirlpool it created. Something floated up from the back of her mind, a wisp of a memory—

*She closed her eyes, a rush of water swirled around her. Then there was a woman's scream and someone lifted her up. Bethany opened her eyes and saw a woman, dressed in blue. "Don't be afraid, Bethany," the woman said.*

Jolted by the sudden blast of memories, Bethany put the cup down and shook her head slightly, as if to shake off that image. What was happening to her lately? Strange, disjointed memories kept floating through her head, like steam from this teacup.

Someone cleared his throat. "Mrs. Miracle, I presume?"

Bethany snapped her head up to discover a heavyset man leaning on the doorjamb, looking at her with a very bored look on his face. She rose to her feet and tossed the paper cup into the trash can, giving him her most charming smile. "I'm as close as you'll ever get."

# 3

Mim rode her scooter to the Bent N' Dent to buy some baking soda for Mammi Vera, who preferred it to toothpaste. She had hoped Bethany would go, seeing as she had a surfeit of free time on her hands now that she wasn't going back to the Sisters' House because of the risk of getting murdered. But Bethany said it was too hot to go anywhere and Mammi Vera said she agreed with that. But Mammi Vera didn't think it was too hot for Mim to go.

As she was searching on the shelves for baking soda in aisle four, she heard a deep voice whisper her name. "Hello there, Mim."

Mim looked up to catch Danny Riehl peering down at her, and for a moment she felt absolutely bewildered. She hadn't seen him in well over a month and he had grown a foot or two. His shoulders were wide, and if she wasn't mistaken, there was some peach fuzz on his cheeks and under his nose. Why, he hardly looked like the same boy who finished eighth grade in May. He was on the old side for his grade, but still. He practically looked and sounded like a grown man.

Mim pushed her glasses up on the bridge of her nose at the exact same moment that Danny did. "Hello," she said, trying to sound casual and nonchalant, but everything inside her was on tiptoes. "Are you back from visiting your cousins in Alabama?"

He nodded. "We got back last week. I've been meaning to stop by, but . . ."

"I've been very busy," Mim said. "Hardly home." That wasn't at all true. She was home 97 percent of the time, but Danny didn't need to know that.

"Did you get my postcard from NASA?"

Did she ever! She floated on air for a week after receiving it. And now it was tucked under her pillow. "Yes. Thank you. Did you see any moon rocks?"

A big grin creased Danny's face. "I did. I saw rocket ships and moon rocks and an astronaut suit."

Mim wondered what Mammi Vera might say if she overheard Danny's excitement. Her grandmother was always pointing out the dangers of too much book learning. Je gelehrter, no verkehrter, she would say. *The more learning, the less wisdom.*

Mim didn't agree with Mammi Vera about book learning, and she definitely didn't think Danny was losing wisdom. Just the opposite. Danny's mother was Mattie Zook Riehl, and everyone knew those Zooks were overly blessed with wisdom. Danny's mother was the most respected woman in their church. Everyone went to her with problems. Mim liked to think that someday she would be thought of just like Mattie Zook Riehl. It was one of the reasons she took her job as Mrs. Miracle so seriously. Training for the future, she hoped. Training to be Danny's Mim.

"I was just getting a few things for my mother," Danny said, holding up a small basket filled with some spices. He cleared his throat. "Are you heading home?"

Mim snatched the baking soda off the shelf. "Yes."

After paying at the cash register, they walked down the road and Danny told her about a special chart his father bought him at NASA that displayed the constellations. Once Mim's father had taught her how to identify the Milky Way—like a swirl of milk in a cup of black coffee. "I used to think that the Milky Way was like a big curtain in the sky," she said. "If you pulled it back, you could see Heaven." She felt her cheeks grow warm. "Not logical, I know."

"Not logical, but a nice thought," Danny said.

"Do you think logic can always find answers?"

"No. Some things are just mysteries. Like Heaven." He slowed down a little so she could keep up with him. "I saw your sister in town yesterday. She didn't see me. She was heading into the newspaper office."

"Oh?" A stain rose on Mim's cheeks. Most of the Amish didn't read the

*Stoney Ridge Times* because they thought it was too liberal, which was a relief to Mim. She wasn't sure how many might have even heard about the story claiming there were miracles to be had at the Inn at Eagle Hill, but the fewer Amish who knew of Mrs. Miracle, the better.

Danny was waiting for an answer from her. About why Bethany was in the newspaper office.

Diversion. That was how Mim handled topics she'd rather not discuss. "My sister has a mystery. She was cleaning out the basement at the Sisters' House. She opened a trunk and found human bones. Skulls, too. She thinks the sisters might be killing people and stuffing them in the basement. She thinks she is next on their list. She's afraid to go back to work."

Taking a moment to adjust his eyeglasses, Danny seemed in deep thought. "The old sisters don't strike me as ruthless murderers."

"That's just what I told Bethany."

"Why would she think the *Stoney Ridge Times* could help explain a trunk full of bones?"

*Oh, boy.* So much for trying to derail Danny. "That's an excellent question."

"Has Bethany asked the sisters about the bones?"

"Of course not. She's not very logical."

"That seems like the best place to start. Certainly better than the newspaper."

Mim nodded. *Phew.*

"Let's go ask."

"Really? Now?" She never liked to miss opportunities to talk to the sisters, especially Ella. If it was a good, clear day for Ella, Mim found she often gained insights to use in her important role as Mrs. Miracle.

Danny nodded. "We're not far from the Sisters' House. Let's go."

So Mim and Danny turned down a road that led to the Sisters' House and asked to speak with them about a very private concern. All five sisters came to the door, curious looks on their wrinkled faces. They invited Mim and Danny to come in for tea. That did slow down the investigation considerably, but Danny didn't seem to be in a hurry. "It's best not to alarm them," he whispered to Mim. "Just in case they *are* murderers."

Mim had been going to the Sisters' House with Bethany since school let out in May, but she was still amazed by the clutter. Every horizontal surface was covered with . . . stuff. Bethany could have a job here until she was an old lady herself, which was good news because she had said those sisters paid well.

When the tea was finally served, all five sisters sat on the living room sofa and waited for the very private concern to be explained. Mim decided she would try to keep her eyes open for what didn't sound right, to see things from the sides of her eyes.

"Go ahead, Mim," Danny said.

*What?* She thought he was going to be the one to talk. She took a deep breath. All five sisters smiled serenely at Mim, capstrings bouncing.

"Of course you know that my sister Bethany has been cleaning out your house."

More smiles.

"Two days ago, she was down in the basement and opened a trunk and found . . ." Mim squinted her eyes shut.

"My thimble?" Ella said. "I've been looking everywhere for my thimble."

"Now, Ella dear," Sylvia said. "Your thimble would not have been in the basement."

A confused look covered Ella's face.

"You have plenty of thimbles," Fannie said, mildly irritated.

"I'm looking for the thimble Mama gave me," Ella said. "It had a band of roses around the base."

Fannie rolled her eyes.

"Honey, we'll get you a new thimble," Sylvia said.

Danny nudged Mim with his elbow and whispered, "Better say something or we'll be here all day."

"Bones! Skulls!" Mim blurted out. "Human bones and human skulls. That's what Bethany found in the trunk."

The sisters looked at each other, startled, eyes wide. "Glory be!" Lena, the middle sister said.

"Oh mercy!" said another.

"Is that why she didn't come to work today?" Sylvia asked.

Mim nodded. "She's frightened. She thinks you're planning to kill her."

"Oh my goodness," Ada, the second oldest sister, said. "That poor child."

The sisters assured them that they had no intention of killing Bethany and hoped Mim and Danny would agree, which they did. But none of the sisters had any idea what a trunk filled with human bones was doing in their basement. And could Mim please ask Jimmy Fisher to come over immediately?

The sun was coming up hot again on a new day when Jimmy knocked on the kitchen door of Eagle Hill. He breathed the fresh morning air deeply, happy to be alive and not at home where he was subject to his mother's relentless henpecking. He grinned when Bethany answered the door—he was hoping she would. "You can unglue that scowl from your face, Bethany. I know you're not happy to see me. But you will be, when you hear my news."

"What news is that, Jimmy Fisher?"

He tried not to get distracted by the blue-black ringlets that escaped from her tightly pinned bun and framed the nape of her neck. He diverted his eyes and noticed that she held an empty egg basket in her hands. "Hey," he said. "If you need eggs, all you gotta do is sing out. That's one thing I have plenty of. Fisher Hatchery at your service, ma'am."

She glanced down at the basket. "Usually, we have plenty. But Luke and Sammy started tossing them at each other and then the day's supply was scattered over the lawn. They're spending the morning in their room, contemplating their actions, in case you wonder why they're not over at Galen's."

Those two little brothers of hers were a passel of trouble, especially Luke. Sammy was less impulsive by nature, but Luke talked him into all kinds of mischief. Luke reminded Jimmy of himself, back in the day when he was young and immature. *Not so long ago*, echoed Galen's voice in his head, *like last week*. Jimmy frowned. Wasn't it enough that he worked alongside of Galen every livelong day? Did the man have to fill his head with advice and warnings? He shook off that thought and focused his attention back on Bethany. He tried not to grin at the sassy look on her heart-shaped face.

"So what news are you talking about?"

"The mystery. I solved it."

She tipped her head to the side. "What particular mystery are *you* talking about?"

"The bones in the trunk."

She narrowed her eyes. "What about them?"

"I've been back and forth to the Sisters' House lately, asking them a few questions. More than a few. It takes quite a lot of work to keep them on task. Especially Ella. Have you noticed?"

She gave him a look that made him realize he had gone off track just like Ella. Maybe it was contagious.

"Just what are you getting at? Did you tell them about those bones, because if you did—"

Jimmy erased that in midair. "Actually, Mim and Danny Riehl had already told them." Bethany's eyes went wide and her mouth became a round O, then settled into a tight line. Jimmy hurried to his main point. "I'd been going about it in a gentle way, asking them roundabout questions without actually saying they had a trunk full of bones in their basement. Then your sister pays a visit and just bursts out with it—telling them you think they're murderers. Scared those sweet little ladies to the hereafter and back again."

"Shootfire! How could Mim do such a thing!" Bethany spun around to go find Mim and give her the what for, but Jimmy grabbed her arm.

"Hold on. Before you go off half-cocked, there's more to the story."

Bethany gave him a suspicious look, but she did stay put.

"It occurred to me that those old bones might belong to the previous owner of the house. The sisters have only lived in the house for some sixty-odd years." He snapped his fingers. "Bingo! As usual, I made a clever deduction."

Bethany rolled her eyes heavenward.

"A doctor used to live there. In fact, his office was in the basement—which, by the way, the sisters want you to finish cleaning out as soon as you have recovered from your shock."

Bethany shuddered.

"One of the sisters remembered the doctor. They said he taught anatomy over at the college in Lancaster. They think he probably used the bones for his classes and forgot all about them." He grinned, pleased with himself. It had not been bad work, thanks to his quick thinking and even quicker logic. He believed in giving credit where credit was due, and he was due some. "Well?"

She shielded her eyes against the glare of the morning sun. "Well, what?"

"Aren't you going to thank me for solving this mystery? Now you can go back to work and not worry about getting murdered by five frail and wobbly eighty-year-old women." He took the hem of her sleeve and held it gently between his thumb and forefinger and didn't let go. A quiet spun out between them. She tried to look outraged, but he could see the smile tugging at her lips.

"I'll thank you once you get rid of that trunk with the bones in it."

He let her sleeve slide from his fingers. "Done. Took care of it last night. The sisters want you to come back as soon as your nerves have settled, they said, so you can all have a good laugh about it." He held her gaze until she looked away, a stain of pink rising in her cheeks, and flounced back inside the house in that unique Bethany-flouncing way. As he slipped through the privet to Galen's, he noticed the eagle pair that nested at Eagle Hill soaring high in the sky, in tandem, and his buoyant spirits lifted even higher, if that was possible.

Bethany had stopped by Naomi's to ask her how to fit together some tricky quilt pieces and discovered, to her dismay, Edith Fisher in the kitchen. It was a small kitchen with little in it, and Edith Fisher's large presence made it seem far smaller.

"Naomi," Edith said, "has a little headache and shouldn't be disturbed." She proceeded to show Bethany what she had done wrong with the quilt pieces.

*That* woman surely needed some castor oil. There wasn't a thing Bethany could put her hands to that she didn't have a hard word about. It befuddled her how a sharp-tongued woman like her reared a son like Jimmy.

Despite all Jimmy Fisher's faults, plus his bad character, he had been kind to her and to her family. Far too patient with her little brothers who buzzed around him like horseflies. Sweet as whipped cream to Mammi Vera, and Bethany knew her grandmother was no Sunday picnic to be around. Helpful to Rose, attentive to Naomi, a hard worker to Galen. It was a shame that his reputation was so low and irreparable. And why did he have to be so handsome?

As Bethany walked through the privet, she saw a woman in jeans and a jacket and a bandana heading to the porch of Eagle Hill with a tray in her hands.

"Hello," the woman said. "You must be Bethany, right?"

"Yes. That's me. I'm Bethany Schrock." She took the breakfast tray out of her hands. "And you must be the lady preacher."

"Not much of a preacher, actually. More like a youth pastor. Not much of a youth pastor, either." She waved a hand in the air to dismiss the topic. "Just call me Geena."

Bethany looked into the pleasant, beaming face of a small woman with olive skin, brown hair, and chocolate brown eyes. "Are you comfortable in the guest flat?"

"It's fine."

"Hot, though. We're having a terrible heat wave."

"The flat stays pretty cool."

"Rose said you were from the Philadelphia area. Are you planning on staying long?"

Geena looked up at the sky. "I'm not sure. I . . . well . . . to be perfectly honest, I was fired from my church."

"Fired?" Bethany asked, amazed. "For the Amish, only God fires ministers. And that only happens when they pass."

Geena smiled. "I guess you could say that's true for the non-Amish too. But the day jobs might switch up a little more often."

"It must be hard to be a preacher. Preachers make me nervous. Whenever I'm around them, I always think about things I shouldn't have done but did and things I should do but haven't."

Geena's eyes went wide for a second, then she burst out laughing.

Why was that so funny? Sometimes, the sense of humor of English people struck Bethany as very odd.

Geena spent the morning walking around the farm, watching the sheep in the pasture, the horses grazing in the field. A field of white linen draped across the yard—sheets on a clothesline wafting in the summer sun. It was so peaceful here, so quiet . . . until a high-pitched shriek came from the direction of the barn. The door slid open and two little boys burst out of it, little one chasing the bigger one, with the golden retriever at his heels. The little boy was hollering in a language Geena couldn't understand and running so hard to catch up with the bigger boy that he lost his hat. But both boys stopped abruptly at the sight of Geena.

"You're the lady preacher!" the big boy said. He had dark hair, nearly black, and twinkling eyes, and she knew this cute boy was going to be trouble in a few years. "I'm Luke Schrock and this is my brother Sammy." The younger boy resembled his mother, Rose. Softer, with round cheeks, a headful of wavy curls, and rather sizable ears.

"I'm Geena." Two sets of brown eyes gawked at her curiously. "Something going on, boys?"

"We've never met a lady preacher before," Sammy said.

Geena laughed. "I'm a youth pastor, not a preacher. But I didn't mean me—I meant, whatever caused you both to come flying out of the barn like it was on fire."

"Oh, that," Sammy said.

Luke gave his brother a warning frown, but too late. Sammy, oblivious to undercurrents, blurted out, "Luke bet me a dollar to ride the goat backwards and I did, and now he won't pay up."

Luke jabbed him with his elbow. "You didn't stay on it longer than five seconds! I bet you for a full minute."

"That backwards stuff is harder than it looks!" Sammy complained.

"Luke made a bet?" someone said stonily.

The boys whirled around to discover their grandmother, Vera Schrock, had appeared on the porch steps and overheard Luke's bravado. Geena watched the boys exchange a glance. She knew boys well enough to know their instinct was to bolt and run, but these two knew better. They turned to face their accuser.

Quick as a whip, Luke said, "Why, Mammi Vera, your hearing must be going bad. Sammy and I were just introducing ourselves to the new guest and telling her to be careful of the goat."

That drew a stern look right out of the book of grandmothers. She wasn't buying this boy's wide-eyed, butter-wouldn't-melt look for a minute. "Wer eemol liegt, dem glaabt mer net wann era a die Waahret secht." She glared at Luke and pointed to the house. Head hanging low, he trudged inside. Sammy, wisely, stayed behind. Before Luke went into the house, he turned and balled his fist to pantomime an uppercut at his brother.

"What did your grandmother say to him?" Geena whispered to Sammy.

"He who lies once is not believed when he speaks the truth." The kitchen door slammed shut. "And about now she's getting warmed up for a long lecture about the devil and lies."

Sammy turned and headed to the barn—a sanctuary from lectures and grandmothers and bullying brothers. Geena grinned. Set aside the buggies and bonnets and beards, and she could have been observing any family in America.

# 4

Bethany arrived at the Sisters' House with a new plan of attack. She tucked a strand of curly dark hair behind her ears as she continued to shuffle through things, sorting them into three piles: keep, give away, throw away.

Books and magazines: give away.

Two sets of binoculars with broken lenses: throw away.

Bags and bags of fabric scraps: give to Naomi for her quilting group, which, by the way, Bethany still didn't want to join.

Threadbare rugs: throw away.

The keep pile was empty . . . until one sister after another would wander into the room and pull things out of the give away and throw away piles and move them into the keep pile.

Since there wasn't any rain on the horizon, Bethany planned to empty out the living room so she could wash the windows and sweep and scrub the floors. She sighed, gazing around the cluttered room. Most every Amish family in Stoney Ridge practiced upkeep. The sisters practiced downkeep. Spiderwebs clung to the corners, a thick layer of dust covered every horizontal surface. There was collective clutter and then there was individual clutter. The sisters called it all functional clutter.

Bethany had created a mental list of considerable length. She had noticed that whenever she started to push the sisters to make decisions about getting rid of things, they would send her off to another room. So far, she had made a dent in practically every room, but not much more than a dent. Well, this house was in for the cleaning of its life, no matter how long it took. The deacon had asked them to take a turn hosting church, but fortunately, he hadn't given them an actual date. Cleaning out this house might take over a year.

Bethany had gone back to work at the Sisters' House today, as soon as Jimmy Fisher had come by to let her know the trunk of human bones mystery was sorted out—and she and the sisters and Jimmy actually did have a good laugh over it. Jimmy, especially, but she thought he found most everything amusing. Especially when she looked to be the fool. She did her best not to get riled at him for laughing at her and she didn't say anything about his bad character. Hardly much at all, anyway.

But Jimmy Fisher was a man of his word. He had hauled the trunk of bones away and donated them to the college in Lancaster.

This morning, to her surprise, the sisters asked her to stop working inside and start on the outbuilding that once housed the buggies. They were heading off for the day—and after the bones in the basement fiasco, they didn't want to leave her alone in the main house. She wasn't sure if they were worried she would find more creepy things, or if she would toss out too much without their knowledge. Both, she presumed.

She didn't mind working outside for a while, especially on such a hot summer morning, and hoped the carriage house would be cooler than the house. At least she'd get some fresh air. She needed to air out her brain too—her thoughts felt all jumbled up.

She wished she could talk to her brother Tobe. Where was he, anyway? Was he still with their mother? How had he found her? Where had she been living all these years?

Bethany mulled over all the questions she'd harbored about her mother. What was she like? Did she ever ask Tobe about Bethany? Then there was the biggest question of all . . . why did she leave in the first place?

All those thoughts were scrambling through Bethany's head instead of the one thought that should have been there: *Get to work!*

She opened the door to the carriage house and took a deep breath. There was barely room to walk. The sisters didn't keep horses any longer, but there was a dusty old buggy, leaning against the wall. "I don't know where to begin."

"It is a bit of a pickle." Sylvia, the youngest sister, had come up behind her and stood by the doorjamb. Ella joined her, then Fannie and Ada. The women peered into the cluttered space, hands on their hips, taking it all in. "It's all Lena's doing," Fannie said. "She's crazy about tag sales. Brings home all kinds of worthless junk."

That wasn't the whole truth, Bethany knew. So far, Fannie blamed the clutter problem on Ella, who blamed Ada, who blamed Lena, who blamed Sylvia, who blamed Fannie. Bethany thought all the ladies had clutter problems, but who was she to say? She was paid handsomely for sifting through all kinds of interesting things. Even the trunk full of bones was interesting. Frightening, creepy . . . but interesting.

"Mim, maybe you can keep a look out for my thimble," Ella said.

Fannie drew in a chest-heaving sigh. "This is Bethany, Ella. Mim's sister."

Ella gave her head that little shake. "Where's Mim?"

"She had something she had to do." Something to do with Mrs. Miracle. Bethany had brought a cardboard box from the house and set it in the shade of the carriage house. "What would you like me to do with all the things in the discard boxes?" She was trying to be as diplomatic as possible. "I thought we might plan on having a yard sale of your own."

"What a good idea!" Sylvia said. "But we'll have to discuss it first."

Of course, of course. Everything was decided by committee in this household. A long, endless committee of indecision.

Ella and Fannie and Ada walked over to join Lena by the front door. They were heading off somewhere—they always had places to go and Bethany didn't know where.

Only Sylvia remained. "It will be nice to have this place cleaned out. Papa would have been so pleased. He always intended to clean out this carriage house."

*Oh, great. That's just great.* That meant this carriage house hadn't been cleaned out in at least thirty years. What might be crawling around in here? Several generations of mice and snakes and spiders. Bethany looked around the dusty carriage house, at the thick cobwebs clinging to the corners, at the smudged windows. She shuddered.

"We're off, then," Sylvia said. "Won't be back until after three. Ella needs her afternoon nap."

Ella, the eldest sister, was ninety-two and never without a sweet smile on her face. Sylvia said she put her love in things beyond herself, and that kept her spirits high.

Bethany nodded. "Have a good day."

Then Sylvia leaned close to Bethany and placed her wrinkled hands on her arms, peering at her with mortal seriousness. The top of her head only reached the tip of Bethany's chin, but there was no shortage of stature in Sylvia's tone when she spoke up like this. "You mustn't blame yourself or look back—not any longer than it takes to learn what you must learn. After that, let it go. The past is past. But you're still here," she whispered urgently and exerted a gentle pressure on Bethany's arms. "And I'm glad. You be glad too."

Tears sprang in Bethany's eyes. How did Sylvia know how troubled she'd been feeling this summer? She'd never said a word.

Sylvia gave the carriage house one more look-over and waved her hand. "Oh goodness—this old carriage house can wait another week. What would you think about helping us today? We could always use an extra pair of hands, especially at the end of the month."

Bethany wiped away a tear. "I'm all yours."

"Excellent!" Sylvia said. "The more the merrier for this project." She pointed to two little red children's wagons, filled with food, waiting on the front walk. "You can help us pull those wagons."

"Where are we going?"

"To the Grange Hall. To make lunch."

Bethany was about to ask why, but decided against it. She'd find out soon enough.

Like any town, Stoney Ridge had good areas and not-so-good areas. The Sisters' House, one of the oldest in the area, was in the not-so-good area. As the town grew, the original area became run-down and neglected. The Sisters' House was only a block from the main road. The Grange Hall stood at the corner. On one side of the Grange was a vacant lot. On the other side of the Grange was a group home for wayward teenage girls. The entire block looked tired and worn-out and neglected.

As the women pulled the wagons past the Group Home, Bethany looked at the house more carefully than she ever had. No one tended the grass.

There were no flowers in pots, no curtains on the windows. A television screen, always on, could be seen from the road.

Hopeless. That's what the house looked and felt like. It seemed a little disturbing to Bethany, as if the house had a personality of its own—which was ridiculous—but the sisters just waved to the wayward girls and walked right on by it. Only one of the wayward girls waved back.

When they got to the Grange Hall, they went around back and parked the wagons by the kitchen door. "We'll need to take a few trips to get all that food inside."

"That's an awful lot of food for lunch for you," Bethany said.

"It's not for us." Sylvia walked up the three steps and unlocked the kitchen door. "We run a soup kitchen for the folks in Stoney Ridge who are a little down on their luck."

Fannie put a large bottle of Dr Pepper at the base of the door to hold it open. "A few years back, when the recession hit head-on, we sisters kept seeing a need in this town. So we talked to the fellow who had the keys for the Grange and he told us we could use the kitchen to serve the hungry. Once a week, everybody in Stoney Ridge who's in need gets a hot meal."

*That*, Bethany thought, would be a very small group. She didn't know a soul in Stoney Ridge who was in need.

Lena read her mind. "Child, look out the window."

Bethany turned to see what she was talking about. She could see into the backyard of the Group Home. Five or six girls sat at a picnic bench, a few of them smoking. "You mean, you feed *them*?"

"That home is for girls who are in trouble, or their parents are. There's a woman whose job is housemother. She does her best with what the county gives, but it's not enough to stretch the week."

"So how many people come for a lunch?" Bethany asked. "Those five?"

"Anywhere from twenty to thirty-five," Fannie said. "Busier at the end of the month when food stamps run out."

Ada handed Bethany a bag of onions. "And we send out five meals to the homebound. Can't forget them."

Bethany was shocked.

"We cook most things from scratch," Fannie added.

"A good cook starts from scratch and keeps on scratching." Ella chuckled at her own joke while Fannie gave her a look like she was sun-touched.

"We haul the wagons over here and do the cooking and serve it up," Lena said.

"You pull those wagons all the way here and cook all those meals?" How had Bethany never noticed? She'd been working for the sisters, three days a week, for over two months. She had no idea this was where the sisters went on other weekdays. You'd think she would have noticed something. Or asked. She felt ashamed of herself. And yet it was baffling to Bethany too. How could the sisters live in a home of such clutter and chaos, yet have the wherewithal to plan and execute such a purposeful event, once a week, week after week?

Sylvia read the look on her face and answered her question as if she had asked it. "We'd rather be out, doing things for others, than fussing with a silly house."

"Sometimes, it takes two trips to get the wagons to the Grange Hall kitchen," Sylvia said. "But it's good exercise for us. It's a long day. We usually get here by nine and spend the morning chopping and cutting and cooking. The kitchen opens up from twelve to one, then there's cleanup."

"But why hasn't anyone been helping you?" It was the Plain way for neighbor to help neighbor. It was what they did best.

From the look on Sylvia's face, the thought never crossed her mind. "It started small enough that we could manage ourselves. And then, as it got bigger, we kept finding new ways to manage. Besides, it's summertime and farming families are busy."

"Where do you get the food?" Bethany asked.

"We get most from the Lancaster County Food Bank," Sylvia explained. "Some things, like this pork butt, are donated by the butcher on Main Street. The Bent N' Dent gives us their canned goods that are too bent and dented to sell. The Sweet Tooth Bakery gives us their day-old pastries. Some things are from our own garden."

The sisters had a system for getting things in the kitchen from the wagon. They lined up along the stairs like an assembly line and passed items along. Ella had a little canvas chair and put things in the chair, then dragged the chair with her cane across the threshold and into the kitchen. She used her cane to prop open the refrigerator. Remarkably resourceful, these ladies were.

Today, Bethany took care of the lifting. The Grange Hall kitchen was starkly clean. A whiff of Clorox lingered in the air—Bethany could see the tile floor had been recently swabbed. Utensils were neatly hung on hooks. The pots and pans, battered and sturdy, in every imaginable variety, were stacked below the countertop and on the shelves around the room.

Sylvia had a system for everything. She had gone through a certification process with the Board of Health so she knew what she should serve and how to keep the kitchen sanitary. Bethany realized that she must've started this soup kitchen when she was in her late seventies. Amazing! Mammi Vera was only in her mid-sixties and acted like she needed full-time tending.

Soon, the kitchen was humming. On the stove in big pots were sautéed onions and green peppers. In another pot was the pork butt in a braising liquid. As Bethany chopped onions, she glanced out the window now and then at the girls from the Group Home, sitting in the shade at the picnic table. They seemed so . . . apathetic.

By noon, they had set tables with plastic spoons and forks and napkins, stirred up the sugary punch the sisters had created and added Dr Pepper to it, and Sylvia opened the doors.

In walked the girls from next door, the five from the picnic bench and four more. The two knots of girls sat far apart from each other. A handful of old men walked in, a few families, and a single mother with three toddlers. There were the homeless, of course, wearing too many layers of clothes, none too clean, and young drifters and runaways, pierced and tattooed, their eyes hungry.

Bethany had no idea there were so many down-and-outers in need in Stoney Ridge. How had she not noticed? It wasn't easy for her to see them or to smell them. The musty scent of unwashed bodies nearly choked her. After a while, she grew used to it, though now and then a whiff of someone sorely in need of a bath and a bar of soap hit her hard, and she turned away by faking a cough. It shamed her, but it was the truth. She wished for hot showers and soft beds for them.

After everyone found a seat, Sylvia insisted on a word from the Lord. "Jesus gave you this day," she said. "He didn't have to do that, but he did.

So now we are going to hear his words." Everyone bowed their heads as she read a few verses from the Sermon on the Mount.

"Amen!" an older black man shouted out, after she read that the poor would be blessed. "Amen for that blessing, Sister Sylvia! Praise the Lord!"

Accustomed to the man's enthusiasm, Sylvia gave a nod to Bethany to start serving the paper plates. She liked to control the portions, so each plate received the same amount of food: two slices of pork, mashed potatoes, green beans, a slice of watermelon. People could have seconds, she said, if they asked.

Bethany took plates to the table of girls from the Group Home. They looked at her with blank stares and took the plates without even a thank-you. Do you realize how hard these old sisters are working? she wanted to ask them. Do you even care?

Bethany felt the eyes of someone on her. She turned and was startled by one girl at the end of a table, staring at her. Her fiery red hair was long and tangled, as if she had not combed it at all, and she eyed Bethany with a hard-edged hostility. Angry eyes. Bethany looked back, and even from this distance she could feel the radiating resentment, so fierce and terrible.

By three o'clock, Bethany was exhausted. The five sisters kept at it, making sure everything was spick-and-span in their careful, deliberate way. Each pot had been scrubbed, rinsed, and returned to the shelf. The kitchen was spotless, just the way it had looked when they arrived. And nothing at all like the kitchen in their own home.

It was Sunday morning. The summer heat lay heavy over the barn, blending the air with barn smells of horse and cow and hay, along with Sunday smells of soap and starch and brewing coffee. Seated on hard backless benches on one side of the large barn were the men and boys, across from them sat the women and girls.

As much as Jimmy Fisher tried to keep his mind on the sermon, his gaze swept across the room to a checkerboard of pleated white and black prayer caps. Seated along a row of young women, white shawls and white aprons and crisp black prayer caps to mark their maiden status, with them, and yet somehow apart from them, was Bethany Schrock.

She sat with her shoulders pulled back, and a look on her face as if she was supremely interested in the minister's lengthy description of the plagues of Exodus. She appeared utterly pious but Jimmy knew better. His gaze fell to her lap, where she was gripping and releasing, gripping and releasing, small handfuls of apron.

Bethany Schrock didn't have the hands of a typical Amish girl, Jimmy noticed, not big, blunt-fingered hands. They were slender, delicate hands. He tried to push those thoughts away, to keep his mind on the suffering of the Israelites, but one thought kept intruding—what was Bethany thinking about that made her hands so tense? What was running through her mind?

It was unfortunate that Katie Zook happened to be seated next to Bethany. Each time Jimmy chanced a look at Bethany, whose eyes stayed straight ahead, Katie assumed he was making eyes at her and she would start to brazenly blink her eyes rapidly and her lips curled into a pleased smile. His interest in Katie Zook had come and gone like a summer rain burst, but her interest in him was more like a coal miner staking a claim. He would have to give some thought as to how to go about dropping her kindly. Katie was the persistent type, cute but clueless.

He listened to the chickens cluck and scratch outside the open barn door, to the horses moving around in the straw in their stalls, to the bleats of the sheep out in the pasture. The minister was preaching now of how persecuted the Israelites had been as slaves to the Egyptians, how many hardships they suffered. The familiar words rose and fell, rose and fell, like gusts of wind. This was the first of two sermons preached, testimony given, prayers and Scripture read, more ancient hymns sung—and the whole of it would last for over three hours.

Plenty of time to ponder how to face Katie Zook's blinking eyes and let her down easy, so gently she'd think it was her own idea. Plenty of time to ponder how to capture and hold Bethany Schrock's interest.

Bethany had perfected the art of appearing deeply attentive during church while her mind drifted off in a thousand directions, especially during the long and silent moments between sermons and testimony and Scripture reading. The only part she could say she enjoyed was the last five minutes.

If there was any exciting news, that's when it would be announced. The grim and somber hymns that told the stories of the martyrs through the ages were her least favorite part of the service. Most of these hymns were written in dark and damp prison cells, four hundred years ago, and while she did have a healthy respect for what her ancestors had endured—what Plain person wouldn't?—it was hard to fully appreciate it all on a beautiful summer day.

After the benediction, the church sat and waited. Bishop Elmo rose to his feet in the middle of the barn, straightening his hunched back. He raised his head and his gentle gaze moved slowly, carefully, over each man, woman and child. First he faced the women; slowly he turned to face the men. Then he began to speak. "Two of our young people want to get married."

Instantly, Bethany came back to the world. Among the Lancaster Amish, weddings didn't usually happen until the fall when the harvest was in. She wondered which couple might be getting engaged. This was the most exciting moment in a woman's life. She searched the rows of prayer caps, trying to see which of the girls might be blushing—giving away the secret. She wasn't alone in her curiosity. All the women were looking up and down the rows. All but one.

Mary Kate Lapp had her head bowed, chin tucked against her chest.

Bishop Elmo cleared his throat. "The couple is Mary Kate Lapp and Chris Yoder. The wedding will take place in late August so they can move out to Ohio. The church there is in dire need of a buggy shop and Chris Yoder has been asked to come." Then Bishop Elmo sat down and the song leader announced the last song. Everyone reached for their hymnbook and opened it to the page, singing a mournful hymn as if nothing unusual or thrilling had just happened.

As soon as the song ended, Mary Kate and Chris rose and walked outside. By the time church was dismissed, they had driven away in Chris's buggy. They were off to address invitations to their wedding.

Bethany felt a combination of delight for her friend, sorrow that M.K. was moving away, and, if she were truly honest, jealousy. M.K. and Chris seemed to have it so easy. They met, fell in love, were getting married, and would live happily ever after. End of story.

That's what Bethany had wanted too. But she had the bad luck of falling for that crooked lowlife Jake Hertzler, who had everybody fooled with his easy charm and winning smile. She shuddered. She would never let herself fall in love with anyone, not ever again.

As she put the hymnal back under the bench, her sister Mim slipped over and stood in front of her, her face filled with worry. "Who is going to teach school next term? When Teacher M.K. gets married, who will take her place?"

Bethany lifted one shoulder in a half shrug. "I don't know, Mim. But they'll find someone. They always do. Some poor unsuspecting soul who has no idea what's about to hit her."

On Sunday afternoon, Mim suggested a picnic out at Blue Lake Pond to escape the stuffy house, and Mim's mother was delighted. Naomi, Mammi Vera, and Bethany were invited, but Naomi needed to rest and Mammi Vera said it was too hot and Bethany said she was in no mood for mosquitos. Mim thought that mosquitos or not, Bethany always seemed to be in a touchy mood lately, but she was disappointed not to have her company, touchy mood and all. Her little brothers caused chaos and turmoil, even if they just stood still.

Those boys wouldn't be doing any standing still at Blue Lake Pond. It was their favorite place to be on a summer afternoon. The buggy hadn't even come to a stop before the boys jumped out and hightailed it for the blackberry vines drooping with ripe fruit. Galen lifted old Chase out of the buggy as he was getting too arthritic to jump, though not too old to run after the boys. He loped behind them, tail wagging so fast it looked like a whirligig. Galen tied the horse's reins together and fastened them to a tree so it could graze while they picnicked.

Mim inhaled a deep breath. So sweet. The summer air smelled of sun-baked pine needles and lake water and freshness. She spread a blanket under the shade of a tree and set up the picnic.

Her mom pointed to those blackberry vines and said, "Mim, we could have great fun making jam."

*Oh, boy.* Mim knew what the week ahead was going to look like: picking berries, pricking fingers, scratches on arms from thorns, followed by hours in a hot and steamy kitchen with pectin, Mason jars, wax, sugar, cheesecloth. *Fun?*

Galen sat with his back against the tree and tipped his hat brim over his eyes. Mim liked that Galen was the kind of person who could sit and not fill every second with chatter the way Mammi Vera did. Sometimes, her head hurt from Mammi Vera's ongoing commentary of Mim and her brothers. Of course, it was always critical. Her grandmother would stand tall and draw in a deep breath and pucker her lips like she was sucking on a lemon and . . . watch out! So unlike Galen, whose words were few and soft, in that deep, gravelly voice, and when he spoke, others always listened.

Her mom nudged her gently with her elbow and whispered, "Now there's a sight you don't see too often." She pointed to Galen. His hat cast his face in a shadow, and his whole body looked relaxed and lazy. He was the hardest working person they knew, and that was saying a lot for a Plain man in Stoney Ridge. Mim pushed her glasses up on the bridge of her nose and smiled at her mom. It was a peaceful moment and she was glad she'd thought of coming to Blue Lake Pond.

Then suddenly the boys were upon them, jerking Galen out of his all-too-brief nap. Juice ran down their faces and onto their shirts.

"You're more the color of berries than boys," her mom said. Sammy smiled, his teeth white in his purple face. She gave him a cake of Ivory soap. "Get in the lake and scrub the stains off. Luke, watch your brother."

The boys dove into the lake in their berry-stained shirts. When Luke came to the surface, he let out a whoop that echoed off the trees. He went under again and stayed down a long time before coming up in the middle of the lake. Sammy, not as skilled a swimmer, stayed in shallow water with the bar of soap in his hand and watched his brother rise up and down in the water like a whale.

"I don't think Luke's got stain scrubbing on his mind," Galen said.

The three of them sat side by side in the quiet, watching the boys as they swam. "Jimmy Fisher's been teaching the boys to swim this summer," her mother said. "Trying, anyway. They exasperate Jimmy. Luke, especially."

Galen glanced over at Mim. "Notice anything different about Jimmy lately?"

"Like what?"

"He's . . . distracted. Off his feed." Galen stretched one ankle over the other. "The kind of work we're doing with Thoroughbreds—he has to keep his mind on the job." He looked directly at Mim. "Anything you're aware of going on with Jimmy? A new girlfriend?"

Mim had a pretty good idea what was nettling Jimmy. "Naomi said his mother's back in town."

Galen's dark eyebrows lifted. "I hadn't thought of that. I saw her at church this morning. She came to visit Naomi last week."

"She's moved back," Mim's mom said, brushing some leaves off her dress. "Her new husband passed and she decided to return to Stoney Ridge. And her older son Paul moved with his new bride to her family's home."

"That's awful sudden," Galen said.

"Quite," Mim added, though her mother raised an eyebrow at her. It was true, though. Tongues had been wagging about it all week. "I heard that the last straw was when Edith Fisher starched and ironed Paul's underwear. The next day, they said they were moving."

"Mim, don't tell tales."

Galen stretched out his legs. "I suppose I'd move on too, real quick, if someone were to starch and iron my underwear."

"When it comes to a mother-in-law and a daughter-in-law, it's never just about the starched underwear."

Mim's head popped up like it was on a spring. For days, she'd been puzzling how to answer a letter to Mrs. Miracle. Her mom had just crafted her the perfect response.

Galen's mouth lifted in a slight smile. "Edith Fisher always did cast quite a shadow on her boys." Then he became silent again and their attention turned to the boys splashing around in the water. After a while, her mother insisted they come out of the water and dry off.

"Are you hungry?" Mim's mother asked, spreading a feast out on the blanket.

"Always," Galen said.

Out of a basket, she pulled fried chicken, deviled eggs, macaroni salad, watermelon, and her special blueberry buckle for dessert. The boys, wrapped in towels, pinned down the edges. Chase was banished to the outer perimeter, watching hopefully for any scraps that might be dropped.

A few hours later, after they had returned home and the remains of the picnic basket were put away, Mim slipped up to her room and pulled out the typewriter. She took out the manila envelope of letters to Mrs. Miracle that she kept hidden under her mattress.

*Dear Mrs. Miracle,*

*Last night, my husband and I had our first fight. It was over the silliest thing: whether to have eggs scrambled or fried. It's been four days and we still can't agree.*

*What should I do?*

Thanks to her mother's keen insight, Mim knew just how to answer:

*Dear What Should I Do,*

*It's never about the eggs . . .*

*Sincerely,*
*Mrs. Miracle*

# 5

For no reason, between one stride and the next, Jimmy Fisher's prize stallion, Lodestar, suddenly rolled out of his easy gait into a flying buck. Jimmy had been exercising Lodestar on a lead rope, relaxed and calm, but somehow this horse had sensed that he had his mind on other things. He bucked, then reared, and as the rope slipped out of Jimmy's hands, Lodestar took the opportunity to jump the fence and gallop off into the woods.

*Aggravating!* This horse was conditioned by his former owner, the slippery Jake Hertzler, to be a "runner" and it was taking all of Jimmy's efforts to break him of that habit. In a way, Lodestar's independent streak pleased Jimmy—he had never cared for totally docile horses. He liked an animal that was as alert as he was—or, in this stallion's case, even more alert. Jimmy had been aware of his own preoccupations, whereas he had had no inkling of Lodestar's intentions. He had no doubt the horse would try bolting again and again.

Jimmy jumped the fence and grabbed a bucket of oats he kept handy for Lodestar, then ran into the woods, whistling for him. He knew the horse wouldn't go far from the barn—he always exercised Lodestar right before feeding time for that very reason. That horse may like his freedom, but even he wouldn't pass up a bucket of oats.

As he walked into the woods, his thoughts drifted back to all that filled his mind. The last few days, something was rolling around inside Jimmy Fisher, making him tense and snappish. He could do nothing with Lodestar lately.

299

Horses took on his mood, and Galen had taught him that those weren't the days to do the work of training. Galen's spirit was quiet and calm and the horses sensed that. Jimmy had worked with Galen long enough to know that if he could mirror that calm, the horses calmed too. Those were the days he made progress in training. Especially with Lodestar.

All week, Jimmy Fisher had been working from sunup to sundown at Galen King's and he was happy to do so because he didn't want to go home. His mother had moved back to the family farm at Stoney Ridge and his new sister-in-law lasted only a week. He had overheard the argument between Paul and LaWonna.

"It's been two days," LaWonna was telling Paul, "and your mother has told me I do everything wrong, from the way I fold your shirts to how I spread jam on bread. Every blessed thing! Paul, I can *not* live under your mother's thumb for the rest of my life! I just can't do it. No woman could!"

The following day, Paul told his mother and Jimmy that he'd been given a wonderful opportunity to manage LaWonna's parents' farm in Canada. And they'd be leaving immediately.

For the first time in his life, Jimmy was the sole focus of his mother. Paul was no longer the buffer between them. She wanted Jimmy to give up the horse breeding business and take over the full management of the hatchery. That hatchery was supposed to be Paul's life work. Jimmy's life work was going to be all about horses.

Be a full-time chicken farmer? No thank you.

And then there was his love life. His mother was working overtime to encourage Jimmy to court the girl she had picked out for him: Naomi King. Now, Naomi was a sweet girl, and in a certain light she might be considered pretty, but Jimmy liked fire in a girl. There wasn't even a spark in Naomi. He saw her every day, and she was a good friend to him, but all he knew about her was that she suffered from terrible headaches and she liked to quilt. What kind of life would that be?

His thoughts slipped off to Bethany Schrock, which was happening quite a bit lately. That girl was maddening, hot-tempered, and feisty . . . and entirely fascinating to him. One minute, she would hardly pay him any mind, the next minute she would bat her eyelashes at him and send a look his way that would make his heart turn over. He could never quite tell if she was flirting with him or not. It was a contest . . . and Jimmy loved a challenge.

His mother must have caught wind that he had his eye on Bethany Schrock and she was doing everything she could to redirect his attention to Naomi. She kept dropping by to visit Naomi and inviting her over for meals, cultivating the relationship with her intended future daughter-in-law.

In the distance, Jimmy saw a buggy coming up the road with a horse following behind. In the buggy was Galen. Trailing with a rope was Lodestar, which made Jimmy feel better and humiliated, all at once.

He walked to meet Galen and took the rope from him. "Thanks."

"Wouldn't keep happening if you kept your mind on your work."

Galen headed up the road to the farm. Jimmy and Lodestar followed along. In the barn, Jimmy led Lodestar to his stall and gave him a slap on the rump as the big horse crossed the threshold. He was a magnificent horse but he took every ounce of Jimmy's attention. Jimmy tossed two slices of hay over the top half of the stall door and reached over to grab the water bucket to fill it.

As Jimmy walked down the middle of the barn aisle to fill up the water bucket, he suddenly heard the unmistakable sound of Lodestar's hooves clip-clopping on the concrete and spun around. Lodestar's stall door was wide open and the horse was heading toward the open barn door. "Galen! Close the door!"

In the middle of pitching hay into a wheelbarrow, Galen stabbed the pitchfork into a hay bale and made a lunge for the door. He grabbed Lodestar's halter just as the horse reached the threshold and led him back to his stall, scowling at Jimmy.

"I know, I know." Jimmy lifted the water bucket. "I was filling the bucket."

Galen shut the hinges on both parts of the door. "What is the problem with you lately?"

Jimmy sat down on a trunk and crossed one ankle over the other. "My mother wants me to give up the horse breeding business."

"Ah," Galen said.

"She wants me working full-time with the chicken business. And she wants me to think about getting married . . . to the girl she's got picked out."

"Who's that?"

Instantly, Jimmy regretted bringing that topic up. There was no way to talk about Galen's sister Naomi and come out on the right side of that discussion. If Jimmy disparaged her—admitting that he could never imagine himself with her—he would find himself tossed out of the barn on his rump. On the other hand, if Jimmy were to compliment Naomi, he would also find himself under Galen's constant surveillance. It was a no-win situation and Jimmy wanted none of it. Galen was very protective of his little sister. Unless a fellow was happily married, Galen didn't want him anywhere near Naomi.

Jimmy pitied the poor fellow who would ever try to court Naomi. Galen would be watching that fellow like a duck watched for waterbugs. He glanced at Galen and realized he was waiting for an answer. "You know my mother. She's got a short list of acceptable females that meet with her approval."

"Someone who'll kowtow to her."

Jimmy nodded. Then he slapped his hands on his knees. "I do not want to be a chicken farmer and I do not want to have my mother pick my bride."

Galen picked up a broom and started sweeping the hay that had dropped from the wheelbarrow. "Didn't Hank Lapp have a fondness for your mother?"

"Yeah, but he courted her for more years than ticks on a mule. She got tired of him dragging his heels about getting married."

Galen set the broom against the wall and crossed his arms against his chest. "Well, seems as if even your mother might have trouble if she had too many pots boiling on the stove."

"What do you mean?"

Galen closed his eyes briefly, and it seemed to Jimmy that under cover of his lids, he rolled them. "You've got a brain. Use it." He picked up the handles of the wheelbarrow and started for the door. When he slid it open, both Galen and Jimmy saw Bethany Schrock flounce across the yard to head to the house to visit with Naomi. "I doubt Bethany Schrock would be on your mother's short list."

"No. She's got something against those Schrocks. Doesn't matter, though. Bethany doesn't take me seriously. She thinks I'm nothing but a flirt."

"She's right." Galen grinned. "Now, Bethany Schrock is a girl who would go head-to-head with your mother. I sure wouldn't mind having a seat in a tree when those two come together."

"I'm having enough trouble getting Bethany to go out with me. I sincerely doubt having my mother impress her opinions would endear her to me." He gave Galen a sideways glance. Since Galen was courting Rose, he knew Bethany pretty well. "Any suggestions?"

Galen belted out a laugh. "Women have always confused the daylights out of me. Let me know when you figure out how to understand what a woman means when she says something." He strode off to the closest pasture, where five horses hung their heads over the pasture fence, eager for their meal to arrive.

Jimmy leaned against the doorjamb. *Interesting.* Sometimes—often—Galen saw things before he did. Since Jimmy had been promoted to Galen's partner in the horse breeding business, things had become easier between them. More and more it seemed Galen was a man he could have a comfortable word with from time to time. His mother turned every word into an argument about his future. Galen was different. Galen observed things. Rarely would he volunteer advice, but when asked, his advice was always to the point. Jimmy admired him greatly.

Maybe . . . if Jimmy could get Hank Lapp to start buzzing around his mother again, she'd be too distracted to manage Jimmy's life. He took a deep breath, feeling his bounce return to him.

Bethany was coming out of the house and hurrying back across the yard. She had her usual look—the look of a woman whose mind was somewhere else. It gave her a distracted beauty.

"Hey, Bethany," Jimmy called out and jogged over to her. "Wait up for a second."

She stopped and turned, cocking her head in that saucy way, as if to say, "Why should I bother waiting for the likes of you, Jimmy Fisher?" Those vivid eyes were looking straight back into Jimmy's.

"How's about letting me take you home after a Sunday singing sometime?"

She lifted her chin and flashed him a bright smile. "Well, seems to me you might want to take Katie Zook home like you've been doing lately."

It was true—Jimmy had dallied a little with Katie Zook. Just a little. He couldn't help himself. He was a natural dallier. Unfortunately, Katie had misunderstood his dallying and taken it for serious courting. But how in the world had Bethany heard about it? Was there to be no end to the humiliations of this day?

He tried to think of a way to explain about Katie Zook; he tried out what he wanted to say to her in his head, but everything he came up with made it all seem worse. His mouth had suddenly gone dry. Bethany was already slipping away, walking with fast, sure strides toward the privet hole, soon to disappear. He threw his hat on the ground. Was he losing his touch?

Bethany Schrock was as taxing and exasperating as a girl could be.

And yet the feeling made him strangely light-headed, the same way he felt as he dove into Blue Lake Pond on a hot summer day and the cold water gripped him like a fist and pulled him down, down, down.

Bethany put a red-checkered napkin on top of the breakfast tray to keep the food hot while she walked it over to the guest flat. Coffee in a thermos, cream in a small pitcher, six blueberry pancakes, syrup, four strips of bacon, two halves of a grapefruit, one bowl of cereal, and a large glass of orange juice. One thing she had learned quickly about this little lady preacher—she had a sizable appetite. Each morning, the tray was returned empty. Practically licked clean.

Bethany barely knocked on the door and Geena opened it with a big smile. Bethany set the tray on the little kitchen table. "What are you planning to do today? Most of our guests go over to Bird-in-Hand or Intercourse to shop. Those towns are more touristy than Stoney Ridge."

"Already been. To each and every town along the Philadelphia Pike. I'm kind of tired of being a tourist and thought I'd do more hiking in the hills. I do need better hiking shoes. Any chance there's a shoe store nearby?"

"Only if you happen to be a horse."

Geena turned half around to her and smiled. She poured some cream into her coffee and stirred, took a sip, and got a look on her face like she was instantly transported to Heaven. "I don't know what you do to the coffee, but it is delicious."

"Broken-up eggshells. I add them to the grounds. Takes the bitterness out."

"Everything is so good, Bethany. You and Rose are excellent cooks."

Bethany was pleased. Not all the guests were easy to delight. A few were fussier than Mammi Vera and that was saying a lot. Last week a man stayed at Eagle Hill and knocked on the kitchen door one morning. He told Mammi Vera he'd like to show her the proper way to make a poached egg. She scolded him in a rapid stream of Penn Dutch and thoroughly confused him so that he tucked tail and hurried off to the guest flat.

"Well, I'm due at the Grange Hall soon. Serving lunch to the down-and-out of Stoney Ridge," Bethany said as she walked to the door.

"Need any help?

Bethany spun around. Was Geena serious? "Well, sure. The sisters who run it could always use an extra pair of hands. But I'm leaving in ten minutes."

Geena was already seated, napkin in her lap, fork in her hand. "I'll be ready."

The sisters were delighted to meet Geena and very curious about her—they had never met a lady preacher before, they said. Geena explained she was a youth pastor, not a preacher, but they didn't seem to think there was a distinction. They were quiet, watching her carefully, but Bethany could see they were itching to ask Geena something. Like an avalanche that began with a pebble, Ella asked one thing first, then Fannie, and soon, all five sisters pummeled her with questions.

What did she preach about? All kinds of topics from the Bible. Did she wear long black robes? No. Were folks nice to her? Mostly. Did they accept having a lady preacher? Again, she explained she was a youth pastor. What did she like best about being a lady preacher? Serving God by caring for the youth. What did she like least? Well, preaching.

It seemed no time at all before they had arrived at the Grange Hall, the kitchen was unlocked and the groceries were stacked on the countertop. Geena seemed to know how to help without being asked. She walked right into the kitchen and pulled open the dishwasher. It was full of clean dishes, so she put them away, opening cupboard doors and quickly getting familiar with the layout of the kitchen. In no time at all, soup was simmering on the stove, the tables were set, bread and butter were on the tables, and the down-and-outers were lining up outside.

Bethany didn't mind making meals for the down-and-outers. She was getting to know each one and understand why they were where they were; each one had a story. She liked keeping busy and she loved to cook, but her pleasure dissipated when the wayward girls from the Group Home arrived. Those girls made her uncomfortable, especially that red-haired girl.

When the red-haired girl walked inside, she looked all around the room like she owned the place, then swaggered over to a table. The other girls followed behind her and sat around her. The red-haired girl stared at Bethany without friendliness. She met that girl's dark eyes, standing her ground. Inside, though, Bethany felt a chill run up her spine.

Geena walked right up to the wayward girls' table and introduced herself. Once, Bethany even heard her laughing—Geena had a very distinctive low-sounding laugh—and she wondered what was so funny. The red-haired girl, she noticed, acted like she didn't care if Geena was there or not.

That was the thing about those girls. None of them seemed to care.

Mid-afternoon, after the kitchen was cleaned up, the women started back down the road that led to the Sisters' House with empty wagons. As they passed the vacant lot between the Group Home and the Grange, Bethany looked at it more carefully. Trash and tumbleweeds blew into the lot, catching on junk of various kinds—discarded tires, plastic grocery bags, sawed-off tree limbs, a couch where two girls sat smoking . . . something small that didn't look like a cigarette. One of those girls was that red-haired girl.

"I just have to say," Bethany said, "that lot is an eyesore and I think something should be done about it. Who owns it, anyway?"

"I think it belongs to the Grange Hall," Sylvia said.

Fannie raised her eyebrows. "Bethany, what would you like to be done with the lot?"

"I don't know," Bethany said. "I haven't thought about that. I wish those girls had something to do besides just sit around and stare at people."

Lena nodded. "They're bored."

"Sylvia, didn't you say there was a housemother at the Group Home? Can't she make those girls do something?"

"Mrs. Green? She does her best but she's old and tired."

Bethany had seen Mrs. Green. She was at least thirty years younger than the sisters. Maybe even younger.

"When school starts in the fall, the girls will be busy during the day," Fannie said.

Bethany glanced at the girls on the abandoned couch. "Seems like they could be gardening on that lot or mowing grass or washing windows at the house. Something."

Geena stopped for a moment to look it over. "Maybe the yard could be turned into—a big garden! Or better still, lots of little garden plots. It gets plenty of daylight, all day long." She turned to Sylvia. "Wouldn't that be something? A community garden."

"It would indeed." Sylvia inclined her head, a quizzical expression on her brow. "Do you think it's possible?"

Geena turned to Bethany. "I'm a city girl. What would it take?"

"I guess we'd have to build raised beds and bring in topsoil. That dirt is no good."

Sylvia nodded. "I think that's a splendid idea, Bethany. You need a project and it needs you."

Bethany stopped. "Wait a minute. I didn't mean *we* as in *me*. I meant it in the generic sense."

Sylvia smiled. "'We' doesn't always mean somebody else."

Oh no. Bethany did *not* need another project. Cleaning out the Sisters' House was more than enough for anyone—and it was not a job for the faint of heart.

"Imagine that!" Fannie said, clasping her hands in delight. "Bethany and the lady preacher want to start a community garden! Plots for each family in need. Maybe a few for the Group Home. That would keep those girls busy and teach them skills too! It's a wonderful idea."

*Me?* How did one tiny suggestion get carried away? "It's already the end of June," Bethany pointed out. "Too late for planting." The Eagle Hill garden had been planted weeks ago. Same with Naomi's. Strawberries had already come and gone.

"No—not necessarily," Sylvia said. "Amos Lapp has plants in his greenhouse, year-round. He could help us by providing starts. Tomatoes, cucumbers, zucchini, even corn. And then there's fall planting too—swiss chard and spinach and lettuce and carrots. All kinds of things could get in the ground before the first frost hits in October."

Bethany thought of the vacant lot, the hostile girls, and then Sylvia's description of the gardens. In that instant, she caught the vision. She saw the garden in full summer, corn tasseling, pumpkins sprawling, those bored-looking girls plucking tomatoes they'd grown themselves.

She realized she hadn't thought about Jake Hertzler or her brother Tobe or her mother or father or any other unsolved problem for at least an hour, maybe more. Maybe she did need a project. She turned to Sylvia. "We'll look into it."

Geena woke before dawn and couldn't go back to sleep. Too much was swirling through her mind. She tiptoed to the kitchen to warm some milk for hot chocolate. The milk in the pan frothed and Geena poured it into a chocolate powder she had spooned into the bottom of the mug. She stirred it and took the mug to the sofa, the one by the window, where the soft morning light was just starting to fill the room. Bethany had showed her how to light the stove, but she wasn't quite sure she could manage lighting a kerosene lamp without supervision. She was sure she'd blow up this Amish farmhouse.

Her Bible was in her other hand. Her comfort, her solace. It was leather-bound and well loved, a gift from her father when she graduated from seminary. Its binding had broken and its pages thinned to onionskin. She had always felt that if a fire swept through her belongings, this is the one thing she would grab. Everything else could go, but not this Bible.

Geena burrowed deep in the couch and gently opened the Bible to the center. *Ah. There.* The book of Psalms. They were like old friends, the Psalms, each with a word to address her needs—some for wisdom, some for thanksgiving, some for sorrow. This morning, she sought guidance and direction. She'd been at the Inn at Eagle Hill for eight days now. Rose told her there had been another reservation cancellation and she could stay on through the weekend. She wanted to. But she also knew she had to start facing the inevitable: what to do next.

Psalm 27. She read aloud, softly. "Hear my voice when I call, Lord; be merciful to me and answer me. . . . Do not hide your face from me, do not turn your servant away in anger; you have been my helper."

How audacious. How wonderful! To think David spoke to God in such a familiar way and yet God called David a man after his own heart. The wonder and the mystery of a loving, holy God.

Her finger scrolled down to a verse she had underlined. *Teach me your way, Lord; lead me in a straight path because of my oppressors.*

Who were her oppressors?

Fear. Insecurity. Self-doubt. Anxiety about her future.

Her eyes traveled to the end of the psalm. *Wait for the Lord; be strong and take heart and wait for the Lord.*

Geena leaned her head back and closed her eyes. *Wait for the Lord.* The words swirled around her mind, reminding her, bringing comfort and peace. Surely the God who set the stars in the sky would let her know when and where her next church would be.

*Wait for the Lord.*

Of course. She would wait.

It was a good thing Edith Fisher slept like a hibernating bear. It gave Jimmy time to sneak out of the house early in the morning and sneak back in late at night. He took his meals at Galen's. He was doing his very best to avoid any confrontation or conflict with his mother, because any interaction with her meant a healthy dose of both. Few would guess that Jimmy disliked conflict, but he did. He never minded stirring things up, but he didn't like to stick around long enough for the aftermath.

Long ago, he had learned that the best way to get along with his mother was to go along with her. At least on the surface. Under the surface, he quietly went about his own business. On this morning, he was tiptoeing down the stairs in his stocking feet when his mother met him at the base of the stairwell, arms akimbo.

"Have you spoken to Galen King yet?"

He stiffened. "About what?"

"About quitting that silly horse business and managing these chickens, full-time. That's what. I've been talking about nothing else for weeks."

And that was the truth. His mother had a way of having one-sided conversations and Jimmy was used to being on the quiet end.

"Now, Mom, we've been over all this. The chickens don't need full-time management."

"Maybe not right now, but that cornfield is going to need cultivating in another month or so. Harvesting a month after that. And if it doesn't get harvested, then it doesn't get ground for meal and then my chickens don't get fed. And Fisher Hatchery goes—" her arms shot up to the ceiling— "belly up."

"Now, now, that's a little dramatic. Don't you think I've been working on a plan? But you see, there's only so many hours in a day. I'm working at Galen's, I'm helping Naomi—" He said that to try to derail his mother's line of thinking and it usually worked. Since she had returned to Stoney Ridge, her favorite topic was the courting of Naomi King.

She cleared her throat, puffing out her cheeks. "Mostly, I hear you're spending time fluttering around Bethany Schrock."

Where did she hear that? It was true, but where had she heard it?

"That's another thing I wanted to talk to you about. Jimmy, you've always been too softhearted for your own good."

He sidled around her to get to the bench by the door. "What are you talking about?"

"You're taking pity on those Schrocks."

He sat down and reached for a boot. First one, then the other. "Now why would I be taking pity on them?"

"Because of all the trouble that family has caused folks. Poor innocent people."

"The women didn't have anything to do with Schrock Investments," he said emphatically. "That had everything to do with Dean Schrock and his son Tobe and that no-good employee of theirs, Jake Hertzler."

"How do you know that? How do you know Rose and Bethany weren't in on it?"

He couldn't explain it to his mother, but some things you just knew.

"Apples don't fall far from the tree."

"Meaning . . ."

"I've never said anything about your flittering around other girls—"

It was too early in the morning for this kind of a conversation. "Well, then, let's just leave well enough alone, all right?"

"—but this time I am stepping in. I'll say it plainly. I don't want you cozying up with Bethany Schrock."

Jimmy bristled like a cat in a lightning storm. "What have you got against Bethany? And don't try to tell me it's about Schrock Investments. You've got something in your craw about her."

"I want someone better for you, that's all. What's so terrible about that?" Her voice was controlled and quiet, but there was an edge of steel in it, the way it got when people tried to talk her down on the price of her eggs.

"I think I'm old enough to make those decisions for myself," he said. "Decisions like becoming a horse trainer."

"Your father—God rest his soul—started this chicken and egg business to pass on to you boys. Paul left. Now it's all up to you. You're all I've got. I'm doing it all alone."

Jimmy sighed. "I know," he said, feeling guilty for snapping at her. His mother really did mean well, but she was so . . . insistent. He softened his tone. "I do agree with you, Mom. About the chickens needing someone part-time."

He stilled, an idea taking shape. *In fact . . . I have just the person in mind!* He jumped off the bench and grabbed his straw hat off the wall peg. Windmill Farm wasn't far from the Fishers' farm, but it would take at least an hour to get Hank Lapp woken up, talked into showering, shaved, changed into fresh, clean clothes, and over to the Fisher farm. "I'll be back soon with our new part-time employee."

He flew out of the house and into the barn to hitch the horse to the buggy before his mother could object. Fifteen minutes later, he was rapping on Hank's garage apartment above the buggy shop at Windmill Farm. "Open up, Hank! It's Jimmy. Come on, wake up!" He kept knocking until the door finally opened.

Hank squinted at Jimmy with his good eye. "WHERE'S THE DADGUM FIRE?!"

Jimmy winced—both at the loud sound of Hank's voice and his appearance. The sight of Hank Lapp, first thing in the morning, was not for the squeamish. "Hank, my mother asked for your help."

Hank straightened hopefully, then eyed Jimmy suspiciously. "I find that a little hard to swallow. She was awful mad at me when she last spurned me. Then she up and married that other fellow. Then she returned, widowfied, and looked at me like it was all my fault."

"Well, that's water under the bridge. That temporary husband of hers is pushing up daisies on his own accord. A lot has happened since he up and died—no one's blaming you. Paul moved and left me with Mom . . . I mean, left the chicken business to Mom to run. She needs your help, I tell you. Wants to hire you part-time." He clapped his hands twice. "Now. Pronto. Lickety-split."

Hank's good eye lit up. But there were two things in Stoney Ridge that couldn't be rushed: the weather and Hank Lapp. He took his sweet time showering, singing at the top of his lungs—so loud it could break glass. While he showered, Jimmy hunted around the garage apartment for a fresh set of clothes. By the time Hank was done with the shower, Jimmy had a clean shirt and pants waiting for him. "Come on, Hank. You're wasting precious time. Galen's waiting on me."

Hank scowled as he wrapped a towel around his privates. "You've got me as nervous as a turkey before Thanksgiving. You go on ahead. I'll get there."

"Not a chance. I'm hand delivering you."

Another hour and a half later, Jimmy pulled the buggy into the drive-way of the Fisher farm. He jumped out and called to his mother to come outside. "I brought your part-time help, Mom. Someone who has a way with chickens and is eager to please."

Edith came out of the house, wiping her hands on her apron, and stopped short when she saw someone come around the other side of the buggy. Hank took off his hat, held it against his chest, and walked over to Edith.

Their eyes met.

# 6

On Wednesday, Bethany planned to head to the Sisters' House early in the morning even though they didn't expect her. She packed up the cookies and the buttermilk and most of what else they had left in the refrigerator, telling Mim things were going bad so fast in this heat that giving them to the soup kitchen would save her from having to throw them out later.

She didn't want anyone to think she'd gone soft.

After thinking it over, Bethany had decided to help the sisters serve lunch to the down-and-outers of Stoney Ridge on a weekly basis. She liked most of the down-and-outers and looked forward to seeing them—all except those ungrateful girls from the Group Home. And she worried about the sisters, lugging those little red wagons filled with food under the hot sun and working so hard to make a good meal.

When Mim found out what her plans were for the day, she asked to go along and Bethany agreed. After all, if Bethany could help Mim with the secret of Mrs. Miracle's true identity, then Mim could help with the soup kitchen. When Bethany picked up the breakfast tray in the guest flat, Geena offered to come too. So the three of them, morning sun blazing hot on their backs, headed over to the Sisters' House.

The five elderly sisters were delighted to see them walk up the front steps. They happily passed off the wagon handles to Bethany and Mim, and the eight of them started up the road to the Grange Hall.

Within the hour, Bethany and Mim sliced and diced big yellow onions on the countertop of the kitchen at the Grange Hall to make a chili soup for lunch. Despite the heat wave, ingredients to make chili soup had been donated by the local Bent N' Dent, so chili soup it was.

Bethany was blinking away onion tears when Jimmy Fisher walked in with his dazzling grin. "Why don't you just admit, Bethany, that I have a powerful effect on you?"

Slicing an onion in half with a big knife, Bethany gave him a look. "Same effect as a pungent onion." But she couldn't help but return his grin. Jimmy's smile was like the sun breaking through the clouds. "Just what brings you to the Grange Hall on this steamy summer morning?"

"I waved him in," Sylvia said, opening a bag of paper napkins. She handed the napkins to Mim to start setting places at the table.

"I was heading to the hardware store in town to pick up some nails for Galen," Jimmy said. "We're fixing a fence that borders Eagle Hill and Galen's back pasture, on account of a certain goat that seems to have a lack of respect for boundaries."

"That goat!" Bethany said. "I wouldn't mind if he wandered off and never returned."

Sylvia walked into the kitchen with something on her mind. "We have a wonderful plan to create a community garden."

Jimmy jumped up to sit on the countertop. "What are you talking about?"

"It was all Bethany's idea," Fannie said, coming over to get a box of plastic forks for the table settings.

Jimmy glanced at Bethany in disbelief. "It was, was it?"

*Of course it was.* Bethany tried to ignore his look of shock but a blush warmed her chest and rose to her cheeks.

"We're planning on putting the garden over there, in the vacant lot." Fannie pointed out the window.

Bethany did a double take—if she wasn't mistaken, it seemed that Fannie was batting her eyelashes at Jimmy. *That* boy had a strange and particular effect on women of all ages.

Jimmy craned his neck to peer out the window. "The lot between the Grange Hall and the Group Home?"

Sylvia's dark eyes glittered. "That's the one."

Jimmy jumped off the countertop and crossed the room to look out the window. "It'll take a ton of work to clean it up. It's littered with everything from broken glass to old tires."

Sylvia smiled. "That's where you come in, Jimmy."

Swift as anything, he looked at her over his shoulder. "Me?"

"Yes. You. You can gather some of your friends and organize a work frolic to get that lot cleaned up."

Jimmy turned back to look out the window, crossing his arms, thinking. "We're going to need a dumpster for all that trash."

"I thought it would be best to have individual raised beds," Bethany said, still slicing and dicing the onion.

Jimmy gave Bethany a sideways glance. "You did, did you?" but he sounded as if he still couldn't believe she had thought this up on her own.

She gave him her sweetest smile. "You could make those too."

"We could probably use the old fence wood that Galen had me tear down last week. A lot of the boards could be reused to make the beds." He yanked off his hat and worried it in a circle. "Topsoil will have to be brought in. Amos Lapp and Chris Yoder might donate it. I'm sure I can talk Hank Lapp into pitching in."

As he spoke and spun his hat, Bethany took Jimmy's measure. He was a fine-looking young man by anyone's standard. His forearms showed roped muscle, born of a hundred farm tasks he undertook. Then there was his thick blond hair and mesmerizing blue eyes. Those blue, blue eyes, nearly aquamarine. She shook that thought off and tried to replace it with her diced onion. She scooped the onions up with her big knife and dumped them in the big pot to sauté.

"So, you'll help?" Bethany said. "We sure do need it. And you love to be helpful." Sylvia was pretty crafty, she thought. Having Jimmy be a part of this project would ensure any number of young women from the church would be happy to volunteer in the garden.

"It's just dirt, water, and sun," Fannie said.

"And paying attention," Ella pointed out. "Don't forget that part. That's the most important part of all."

"So, then, you'll help?" Bethany repeated. Jimmy flashed one of his charming, easy smiles, and she caught her breath. That grin gave him a dangerous boyish look that she didn't buy for a moment.

He wiggled his dark eyebrows. "What else you got cooking today?"

The onions! Bethany hurried to stir the pot before they burned. The onions were completely translucent. "Chili soup." She scooped up a pile of papery onion skins and dumped them in the trash.

"Save me a bowl, will you? And I'll stop by later to sketch out a plan." He flipped his hat up in the air to land squarely on his head.

"Jimmy . . ." Bethany swallowed and looked at him doubtfully. "You sure?"

"Of what?" he asked with a slow grin. "That you need the help or that you'll have enough chili to spare me a bowl? Answer B is up to you—I love chili, even on a broiling summer day. Answer A is 'absolutely.' You've bitten off a big job, but . . . I'm willing to give it a try." Once again, Jimmy wiggled his eyebrows at her, then headed to the door.

Bethany added ground beef to the big pot and stirred it until it browned. Then she poured in four quarts of beef broth from big cans. She hoped it was beef broth, anyway, because the cans were missing their labels. She added six dented cans of diced tomatoes, stirred, then waited for the liquid to come to a boil. When the soup reached a full, rolling boil, she added four cans of red kidney beans, turned down the heat, added a bay leaf, cumin, chili powder, oregano, salt and pepper, and celery tops.

"Do you think we might be taking on something too big with that community garden?" Bethany asked Sylvia when she came to check on the chili soup.

"It is a big project, but it's a good one. You're the one who realized those children at the Group Home needed a project." The chili soup was so thick that Sylvia added some water to the pot. "It will give them a sense of purpose." She left the kitchen to help Mim and the sisters set the tables.

Bethany stirred the water vigorously into the chili mixture. "I wish I felt that," she said to no one in particular. "A sense of purpose would be nice."

Geena took the empty cans and dumped them in the recycling box. She turned and inclined her head. "You need only ask God for it, Bethany. He is all about purpose."

What would it be like to stumble onto your future and recognize it so clearly? Was it really as simple as opening a door and seeing it before you?

Then what? "But then watch out, right? What if I get called to do something like becoming a lady preacher, like you did?" Bethany was joking.

"Youth pastor," Geena corrected. "And I love serving these people." She put a hand on her heart, unaware that Bethany had been teasing her. "Serving gives life meaning, and shape, and purpose. I am honored God would call me to this work. That's how it works." She picked up a knife and grabbed a loaf of day-old bread from the Sweet Tooth Bakery.

Geena sliced the bread and put out sticks of butter on paper plates while Fannie, Ella, Lena, and Mim poured juice into paper cups. Sylvia stood by the door, waiting for the clock to strike twelve to open the door. A line had gathered, out of thin air, right at noon, and in filed an odd assortment of people.

It was easy for Bethany to ladle up the chili soup for these down-and-outers, feeling something warm like kindness or goodness fill her chest. At least, she did feel a pleasant glow until the teens from the Group Home, filled with bravado, pushing and jabbing each other, came in knots of two and three. Bethany followed Geena's lead and spoke to each one as she brought out the bowls of chili soup on a tray. "Good afternoon" and "How are you?" and "Would you like chili?" Most didn't answer and kept their eyes down, but the angry red-haired girl met her eyes, almost in a hostile challenge—*Do you see me?*

*I'm trying,* Bethany thought. *But you make it so difficult.*

A few spoke in return. "I don't like onions," said one, holding the chili soup bowl up in the air. "Can you take them out?"

"No," Bethany said in a no-nonsense tone she had learned from Fannie.

"You're new," said another, a girl with hair dyed as black as coal. She looked Bethany up and down. "You in some kind of trouble?"

She was a big girl, at least fifteen or sixteen years old, with arms that were tattooed from wrist to shoulder. Bethany couldn't help but stare. The girl noticed Bethany's gape, laughed, held out her arms so she could see the drawings. "They're called sleeve tattoos. They tell the story of my life."

Bethany was horrified. Rose called tattoos "permanent evidence of temporary insanity." What kind of permanent story could fill up both arms when you were only fifteen?

There were others, too, whom Bethany would not have expected. There were two painfully young mothers with toddlers on their hips, washed and humble, waiting for bowls of chili soup. Sylvia said to hold on, just wait until the end of July if she really wanted a surprise: Families of all shapes and sizes and colors. She said they were especially busy the last week of each month because people on public assistance had run out of food and money and wouldn't get any more until the first.

In that moment, Bethany realized she hadn't thought about her problems all day long. It was happening each time she helped at the sisters' soup kitchen—she forgot all that troubled her, for a little while anyway. She turned to serve the next girl, a round girl with acne and thick glasses, who smiled at her. This felt . . . good. Really good.

There were three things Mim liked about helping the sisters with the soup kitchen. First, she liked any excuse to be near Ella, the oldest sister. She stuck to Ella like glue. Today, a mouse came running through the Grange Hall kitchen and Mim chased it away with a broom. Afterward, Ella was feeling a little wobbly-kneed so she sat on a chair, pulled a tissue from her dress pocket, and dabbed at her forehead. "There's just something about a mouse," she said, and Mim had to agree.

The second thing she liked was that as soon as the kitchen was cleaned up and the sisters returned home with their empty wagons, Mim and Bethany set off to the *Stoney Ridge Times* office. Bethany went into the building and returned with a large manila envelope of mail for Mrs. Miracle. As soon as they turned the corner, Bethany handed Mim the mail pouch.

"What are you going to do with the money you're making?"

"I'm not sure," Mim said. "It's only five dollars a week." Mostly, she needed to buy paper and envelopes and stamps. She might try to save enough money to buy Danny a new telescope that didn't need to be held together with black electrical tape, but she had no idea how much telescopes cost. Plus, she wouldn't want him to think she was sweet on him. She was, but it was better not to let a boy know such a thing. She had read that very thing in Mammi Vera's book *A Young Woman's Guide to Virtue.*

The third thing Mim liked about volunteering at the Grange Hall was that she and Bethany passed by Danny Riehl's home on the way home to

Eagle Hill from downtown Stoney Ridge. If Mim walked slowly enough—if she had to stop and tie her shoelaces, for instance, like she did today—there was an excellent chance Danny would be doing chores in the barnyard and spot them. And when it happened, he waved and talked to them for a few minutes.

She liked that best of all.

Later that day, Mim sat cross-legged on her bed, unsure of what to do. Mrs. Miracle's response to *What Should I Do* ran in Tuesday's edition, and by this afternoon, Wednesday, when Bethany picked up the mail pouch at the *Stoney Ridge Times* office, there was already a responding letter to Mrs. Miracle's wise and witty wisdom.

> *Dear Mrs. Miracle,*
>
> *I showed my husband your column in which you said that our arguing really wasn't about the kind of eggs we have for breakfast. We talked and talked about it . . . racked our brains over it . . . even went to an emergency counseling session with our pastor over it last night . . . but discovered it really was about the eggs!*
>
> *So our pastor suggested that we compromise: scrambled on Mondays, fried on Wednesdays, sunny-side up on Fridays. He also suggested that I not ask you for marital advice.*
>
> > *Sincerely,*
> > *Now I Know What to Do*

Oh, boy.

As usual, life moved faster than Hank Lapp intended it to. Jimmy had hoped that working part-time at the Fisher Hatchery, in close proximity to his mother, might rekindle their on-again, off-again romance. The plan completely backfired. Hank had a love of talking and an aversion to hard work—two qualities his mother had no patience for.

Though loyal and good-hearted, Hank had never displayed the slightest ability to learn from his experience, though his experience was considerable. Time and again he would walk into the yard of the henhouse, knowing there was a protective rooster lurking about, and then look surprised when the rooster came flying at him, claws first.

Young Luke Schrock did the same kind of thing over at Galen's. He would walk up on the wrong side of a horse that was known to kick, and then look surprised when he got kicked.

When Jimmy thought about it, he wondered if there were some people in this world who were destined to make the same mistakes over and over. They simply could not learn from experience. Or maybe they just had no common sense.

Jimmy saw Hank walk up the driveway three hours after he was due for the chickens' first feeding. There was no point in losing any more time. If Hank was not of a mind to be serious, nothing could move him. Jimmy needed to fire Hank before his mother insisted on it.

"HELLO THERE!" Hank hollered when he saw Jimmy in the distance.

Jimmy walked down the hill to meet him. "Hank, you're late. Ridiculously late."

"Not for the fish at Blue Lake Pond! We had a pre-dawn appointment today. My oh my, they practically leapt into my boat, Jimmy. You shoulda been there."

"Hank, you would exasperate a preacher."

"Well, I always figured preachers needed a little exasperating."

Jimmy yanked off his hat and swiped at the drops of sweat that clung to his forehead. "The thing is, Hank, the chickens can't wait until you get back from fishing. They need to eat at a specific time, or they get stressed. If they get stressed, they stop laying eggs. If they stop laying, Fisher Hatchery goes under."

"Good thing them chickens have you looking after them."

"That's the thing, Hank. The very thing. I was hoping *you'd* be looking after them so I could keep my job over at Galen's. You've been late four out of four days this week."

"Now wait just a minute. I was only doing you a favor—minding those squawking hens. I don't even like chickens. And I hate roosters. Always have." Hank stiffened up like wet leather left out in the sun. "You know—you used to be a whole lot more fun. You're turning into a crotchety old schoolmarm."

Jimmy sighed. "I'm sorry, Hank. I shouldn't have pressured you into working here in the first place. I need to let you go."

Edith Fisher came out of the house, hefting a heaped laundry basket on a practiced hip, and crossed the yard to the clothesline.

Hank noticed. In a split second, the expression on his face changed from a frustrated frown to a brilliant smile, like the sun appearing from behind a cloud. "DON'T FRET, BOY!" He winked at Jimmy. "Being in between jobs gives me a little more time to come calling on your sweet mama." He brushed past Jimmy and went up the hill. "LET ME HELP YOU CARRY THAT HEAVY BASKET, MY LITTLE BUTTERCUP!"

What was even more shocking was the mildly pleasant look on his mother's face as she saw Hank approach.

Jimmy shook his head in wonder. Maybe his plan hadn't backfired quite as badly as he thought. Maybe he shouldn't have fired Hank. No . . . that was definitely the right thing to do. His chickens would have perished under Hank's care.

*His* chickens? Since when did he think of those pesky hens as *his* chickens? Never! He felt just like Hank did about poultry. Couldn't stand them.

What was going on with him lately? Hank was right—he wasn't fun like he used to be, if you considered fun to be stealing a nap by the pond when he should have been at his chores or playing a prank on an unsuspecting someone. Someone like the bishop, who could be easily tricked and was never the wiser for it. Jimmy didn't even tilt his hat at a rakish angle anymore.

But why? Why was he suddenly acting like . . . a man? A responsible man? He never expected such behavior of himself. It wasn't comfortable—making a hard decision like firing his old friend Hank. It felt like he was wearing a pair of stiff new shoes. The newly mature side of him pointed out that maybe the shoes just needed breaking in. But the old side of him asked, why? The old shoes were pretty comfortable.

The thing that made Jimmy least comfortable of all was that, deep down, he knew the reason for his newfound maturity. He never lied to himself. It had to do with Bethany Schrock. He was falling for her.

The feeling had started even before he knew his mother didn't want him courting Bethany, though he wouldn't deny his mother's vehemence made him all the more determined. He had started falling for Bethany from the first second he'd laid eyes on her, and a little deeper every moment he'd spent in her company since then.

A few weeks back, he took Katie Zook home from a Sunday singing, and even kissed her a few times, just to see if he could be distracted by another girl, if being around another girl made him feel the same way he felt when he was around Bethany. It didn't. It was yet another experiment that backfired on him.

At night he thought of Bethany, and wondered if she ever thought of him. During the day, if he caught sight of her coming or going from Eagle Hill, he watched her, whenever he thought he could do so without her noticing. Her eyes were mysterious to him—often she seemed to be amused by him, at other times irritated. Sometimes her eyes seemed to pierce him, as if she had decided to read his thoughts as she would read a book. It didn't stop the longing he felt for her. He imagined them raising horses and children together. In a strange and wonderful way, he knew she was the girl for him. In a way he couldn't quite explain, even to himself, he knew she needed him.

No one had ever needed Jimmy before, not really. Not the way Bethany did.

# 7

Shootfire! Not another word of excuses!" Bethany pointed to the house. "You boys get right up to your rooms and think about how'd you feel if you were that goat!" Sammy and Luke climbed the porch stairs in tandem, with her watching all the way.

To Bethany's annoyance she saw Jimmy watching her from the hole in the privet with an amused grin on his face. "Sorry," she said, trying to make light of it.

"Don't be," Jimmy said. "I'm glad to see that you lose your temper with other people as well as with me." He walked toward her. "What did those two do now?"

"Look for yourself."

Over by the patch of grass along the side of the house was the billy goat with a push lawn mower harnessed behind him. "I told them to mow the lawn and this is what they came up with."

Jimmy grinned. "I tried that once myself. Didn't work. The goat didn't budge." He walked toward her. "You have to give them credit for creativity."

"Lazy. That's the only thing they get credit for. I'm about fed up with those two. If I give them any slack they run headfirst into trouble. You can never guess what may be going on in the minds of boys—"

"Usually not much. Speaking from personal experience."

"—but it doesn't pay to let them out of your sight very long."

"Aw, Bethany, they're just being boys."

"They're savages, I tell you. Savages. They don't give anybody a moment's peace from dawn to dusk."

Right under the open window of the boys' room, Bethany could hear Sammy and Luke arguing about something. She looked up at the house and frowned.

"My father used to say that sometimes there wasn't any better music than two brothers bickering." She looked back at Jimmy. "He should have told that to Mammi Vera. Her favorite saying about those two is 'Buwe uffziehe is so leicht as Eise verdaue.'" *Raising boys is as easy as digesting iron.* "Just this morning, she gave them something to chew over for breakfast: 'Sand and sin are one and the same. Tolerate a little, and soon it'll be a lot.' Then they come up with a trick like roping the goat into mowing the lawn. They can't learn a blessed thing without getting in trouble, those two."

Jimmy stared at her for what seemed like forever. She could almost feel his gaze moving over her, like the touch of the wind, before it shifted to the poor goat stuck with a lawn mower roped to its harness. Then came one of those unexpected and dazzling smiles. "Come with me a minute." He went over to the goat to unbuckle the harness and untie the rope that held it to the push mower. Then he took hold of the goat's harness and locked the goat in the fenced yard. He led Bethany over to Galen's yard and pointed to a large wagon, where tools and wood were stacked. He jumped easily onto the wagon bed. "Rakes, shovels, chicken wire for the base of the beds, nails, hammers. Everything we need for the community garden. Practically a fully outfitted hardware store."

She walked around the wagon, examining everything inside of it. "This is terrific! Where'd you get all the tools?"

"The hardware store provided nails, Galen King provided wood from a fence he was replacing, Amos Lapp is delivering topsoil. He told Chris Yoder to donate vegetable starts from the Lapp greenhouse. Even the Sweet Tooth Bakery is offering pastries for the frolic." He wiggled his eyebrows. "Day-old, of course." He jumped off the bed and stood beside her.

Her delight amused him, and once again that slow grin claimed his face.

Bethany looked at all the supplies, thought of all the work he'd done, the time he'd spent, and put a hand on his arm. "I don't even know what to say. You've done so much. Thank you, Jimmy. You're really . . ." He looked at her, and Bethany didn't turn away, wondering if something might be blooming between them. "Thank you," she said simply.

He covered her hand with his. "So, then, how about letting me take you home from Sunday's singing?"

The warm wind kissed her face and rustled the ends of her capstrings. A sense of anticipation skittered over the top of her skin, traveling up her arm, brushing her elbow, tickling the back of her neck. His eyes were shaded by the soft brim of his hat, so their color was a simple dark blue, and his mouth was very still. He leaned forward, bringing his face close to hers. Too close, so that she wanted to pull back from him, but she didn't.

"You know you want to say yes," he said, giving her one of his cat-in-cream smiles. "And I know a place we can talk privately." The wind blew between them in a gush of warmth.

She narrowed her eyes. "Said the spider to the fly."

"I mean it. I'd like to get to know you better."

There was such a sweetness in his voice that she almost got lost in the sound of it. Maybe, she thought, this was something possible. The thought made her smile.

Then the kitchen door opened and Naomi came out of the house with Katie Zook at her side, and Jimmy's head jerked in their direction. He waved and gave the girls his best grin.

His best grin. The one she thought he saved just for her. Bethany tried not to let her disappointment in him show, but she knew her eyes would give her away. Her father used to say that her eyes were like a weather vane for her feelings. "Save all your charm for the other girls," she said, sounding a tad more haughty than she intended. She softened, just a little. "I like you just fine without all that embroidery."

He looked surprised. "But I do want to spend time with you! I meant it."

She nodded and started back to Eagle Hill. "I'm sure you always do," she tossed over her shoulder.

Jimmy hurried to catch up with Bethany before she disappeared into the house and before Katie Zook could trap him. She was dropping by more and more often, to see Naomi she said, while cornering him in the barn.

The lady preacher drove in the driveway and Bethany stopped to say hello, giving Jimmy just enough time to reach her. The woman got out of her car and waved. "I saw you at the Grange Hall the other day but I don't think we officially met," she said. "I'm Geena Spencer."

"I know. You're the lady preacher everyone's talking about," he said.

"Actually I'm a youth pastor."

"His name is Jimmy Fisher," Bethany said in a schoolteacher's voice.

Geena shook Jimmy's hand. "What are you two up to?"

Jimmy grabbed his chance. "Bethany and I were just heading over to the Grange Hall with donations for the community garden."

"I never said anything about going with you," Bethany said, frowning at him.

"But you were thinking it."

Flustered, she jerked her gaze away from his.

"Is there room to store everything in the Grange Hall?" the lady preacher asked.

Jimmy half shrugged his shoulders. "Won't need to. Saturday is the day set for the frolic."

"Frolic?" Geena said.

"That's what we call a work party," Bethany said. She glanced over at Jimmy. "Mim and I have started to spread the word."

"Wait a minute," Geena said, confused. "Saturday? *This* Saturday? You came up with the idea for the garden on Monday, and you're going to start it on Saturday? Don't you need work permits? Time to coordinate volunteers?"

Bethany and Jimmy exchanged a look. "If there's a need, we just get to it," Jimmy said. "As for volunteers—like Bethany said, we just spread the word around the church. And we're not just starting on Saturday. We're ending on Saturday too. By the end of the day, the gardens should be built and planted."

"But . . . that's so fast!"

"Well, it's already the first week of July," Bethany said. "We can't wait any longer if people want any produce this summer."

Geena tilted her head, amazed. "Count on my help. I'll be staying in the guest flat through Sunday. Longer, if the heat wave continues and someone else cancels their reservation." She went back to her car to unload some groceries.

"I sure hope this hot spell breaks," Jimmy said, trying to keep Bethany's interest. He had spotted Katie Zook, popping her head over the privet, watching, waiting for him, and he wanted to stay clear. "This is one summer I won't miss. Galen and I can't even work the horses like we want to—they get too overheated. I want to get Lodestar out on the roads but the blacktop feels like it's melting." He sidled a half turn to keep Bethany from noticing Katie at the privet.

"How's it going with that horse?"

Jimmy squeezed his eyes shut in disgust. "Bethany, he's not *that* horse. He's one in a million." Lodestar was Jimmy's pride and joy. He was a stallion that Jimmy had bought, several times, off that swindler Jake Hertzler. *Never mind.* Despite how he had ended up with Lodestar, the horse was worth every penny. Jimmy had plans to start using Lodestar as a stud horse, just as soon as he broke him of his bad habit of running off. It would never do to deliver his stud to a mare for a few days' work, only to have him disappear.

"So sorry," she said, feigning her apology. "How is your one-in-a-million horse behaving?"

"We're making progress. Patience is required, you see, when you're a serious horse trainer." And when you're serious about a certain girl. He gave her his most charming grin. "So let's get back to the important matter. What about Sunday's singing? How about letting me take you home?"

She lifted her chin in that saucy way she had. "Well, you'll just have to keep practicing your newly found patience. I haven't decided yet."

He watched her head back to the house. Before she went inside, she turned and gave him a grin. All he could think when she gave him that grin was that he wished he were a better man.

Then his smile faded. Katie Zook was still waiting for him by the privet hole.

Mim bent down and put her eye to the lens. It was a very good telescope, with powerful magnification and a sturdy tripod, even if it was taped together with electrical tape. When she looked through it, the stars popped vividly forward, with one glowing brightly in the middle. "So majestic," she murmured, then stepped away and looked straight up to the sky, crossing her arms over her chest.

Then Danny came over to bend down and take a look in the telescope. "Amazing, isn't it? I never get over the night sky."

"Do you know the names of those constellations?"

"Some." He straightened up and craned his neck to look at the sky. "That's Cassiopeia, right there," he pointed, "and the Big Dipper, of course, and Gemini."

She tried not to think of how close Danny was standing to her, of how he smelled of bayberry soap, and how good and kind and smart he was. She tried not to think about sneaking out of the house to join Danny tonight and how much trouble she would face if Mammi Vera were to find out where she was and why. Instead, she tried to focus on those beautiful sparkling stars, diamonds on black velvet, and soon she fell into the vastness of the darkness, the far-away-ness of the stars, the possibilities of so many stars lighting so many systems. "So many stars," she murmured. "Millions upon millions."

Danny nodded. "Each star has a place in the sky, a purpose to fulfill."

As usual, whenever she was with Danny, he said something that was so profound, so hard for her to grasp, that she found herself falling in love with him all over again. She tried to rein in her feelings and focus on the stars. Thinking about the stars sent her mind traveling to another baffling letter to Mrs. Miracle from this week's mail pouch. She didn't know how to solve this person's problem:

*Dear Mrs. Miracle,*

*Do you think life is fixed? Like the stars are fixed in the sky? My mother is in jail for shooting my father. I wish I could say I cared but I hardly remember either of them. My mother had all kinds of rage issues and my father was an alcoholic. Will I live the same kind of life that my parents did? It seems I already am. Sometimes, I get so angry . . . I want to hurt someone.*

*Signed,*
*Stuck*

She had no idea how to answer Stuck's letter. But . . . Danny, with his infinite wisdom, might know. "Do you think a person's life is all his own to live? Or do you think that the way he grows up, or the kinds of DNA he has, shapes a person's life?"

"Nature versus nurture, you mean?"

She nodded.

"That is a conundrum." He glanced at her. "Do you know what that means?"

"Of course. Of course I do!" She had no idea.

"It's an interesting question. Nature certainly does play a role in the way a person thinks or behaves, just the same way your hair is dark and wavy like your mother's."

Mim's hand flew to her prayer cap. He had noticed her hair?

"Certainly, there's a nurture factor. If a person had never received love as a child, how could he grow up to know how to love?"

Maybe that was the problem with Stuck. It seemed as if she had never known love.

"That's what makes it such a conundrum. A difficult problem to solve."

*Ah!* So that's what conundrum meant.

"But you can't leave out the most important factor: God. The Bible says we become a new creation."

"Where? Where does it say that?"

"Second Corinthians 5:17." He looked up at the sky as if he were reading the words written on the stars: "'Therefore if any man be in Christ, he is a new creature: old things are passed away; behold, all things are become new.'" He started to fold up the telescope. It was time to head home. "So I guess the answer is that while some people might have a harder time than others to break patterns and habits, nothing is impossible for God."

That was just the answer she needed for Stuck! She would write back this very night. She might even say a prayer for Stuck too. It had never occurred to Mim to pray for the letter writers. But Mrs. Miracle had never received a letter like Stuck's, either.

—⁓ ◊ ⁓—

Bethany was checking messages in the phone shanty when a battered old car coughed and sputtered its way up to the house and stopped. She thought it might be someone who was lost and needed directions, so she closed up the phone shanty and walked toward the car.

"Bethany!" the driver hollered.

Then there was her brother Tobe, of all people! Swooping toward her and picking her up in a bear hug. His face had matured a little in the . . . how long had it been? Ten months? No, closer to a year now.

"Oh Tobe," she said, laughing, "I'm so glad to see you!"

Tobe's attention shifted to the two little boys who were racing each other from the house to greet him. He opened his arms wide and scooped up Luke and Sammy as they barreled into him. "Who are these two giants? What happened to my little brothers?"

The boys squealed and hooted. "We have so much to show you and tell you!" Luke started, then the boys started talking at the same time, both at once, telling him bits and pieces of the news—only the news that pertained to them—the eagle pair that nested on a tree high above the creek, Galen's horses, a new fishing hole Hank Lapp promised to show them before school started in August.

Tobe laughed his deep, hearty laugh, like nothing had happened in the last year. "Where is Mim? And Rose and Mammi Vera?"

Bethany shooed the boys up to the house to find Mim to tell her that Tobe had come home. She filled the short span between the car and the house telling Tobe details about who was where and when and updating him about family news. "Mammi Vera had some surgery a few months ago. She's doing better now. Not one hundred percent, but she's much better than she was before the surgery."

"Did they fix her crankiness?"

Bethany laughed and clapped her hand to her mouth. "Don't say things like that out loud, even if you think it. But no, since you asked, she's as cranky as ever." They stopped at the porch steps and she took a minute to gaze at her brother. A year of living hand-to-mouth had taken a toll. He was thin, like he needed some good home cooking. A haircut too. His black hair fell in a glossy swath across his forehead. He had large hazel eyes that could be sympathetic or furious or inscrutable. His clothes were English—a washed-out T-shirt, khaki shorts, flip-flops. But when he grinned, he was the same old Tobe: amiable, funny, handsome, charming as ever.

She could hear the chickens fussing in the coop. Mim hadn't fed them yet, Bethany could tell. "Where've you been, anyway?"

"Here and there."

"I heard you were with Mom."

He stopped abruptly, glanced at the house, then lowered his voice. "Where'd you hear that?"

"Jake Hertzler."

Tobe's eyes widened, and Bethany couldn't quite tell what was behind that—curiosity? No . . . no, it was alarm. "Jake is here?"

"Was. Gone now."

So it *was* true. Jake Hertzler, Bethany's ex-boyfriend (and her mind exaggerated the EX part), was the one who had told her Tobe had been with their mother, and he was full of lies. She wanted to know more, and yet she didn't. Not yet. So she changed the subject. "You heard Dad passed, didn't you?"

A flash of anger sparked in his eyes, then he softened. "Of course I heard."

"But you couldn't trouble yourself to come to his funeral?"

He stiffened. "Things aren't as simple as you'd like to believe, Bethany."

She let out a short, derisive laugh. "Shootfire! You can say that again. Like you showing up, out of the blue, after disappearing for a year without a trace." She was pushing him too far and she knew it. She made her voice as gentle as she could manage. "What matters is that you're home now, Tobe. I'm glad you're here. I truly am."

# 8

When Rose and Mammi Vera arrived home from the Bent N' Dent to find Tobe, sitting at the kitchen table like he always had done—one leg stretched out, one elbow resting on the back of the chair—Rose was so stunned she nearly dropped the groceries in her arms. She said she had never stopped praying that he would return home someday, but she didn't know when that someday might ever come.

And Mammi Vera, why, she practically fainted at the sight of her favorite grandson. Wasn't it a tonic for her? To have Tobe home—what better medicine could there be for someone recovering from a major surgery?

It wasn't long before the house was a jumble of noise and confusion and happiness. As Tobe began to settle in to Eagle Hill, he looked more and more like his own rumpled self. Bethany was struck by how much he resembled their father—the same hair, black as starlings' wings, and slender build. So much like their father that Bethany kept getting goosebumps on her arms.

In the midst of the reunion, Galen and Naomi came over to see what the commotion was all about. When Galen saw Tobe, he shook his hand and welcomed him home. Galen's voice was happy sounding, but his face was curious and stunned and then his eyes sought out Rose.

A little later, Bethany was getting butter out of the refrigerator for dinner. As Galen helped get a wooden salad bowl from an overhead kitchen cupboard, she heard him whisper to Rose, "So the prodigal has returned. What do you make of that?"

"I'm not sure what to think," Rose whispered back. She picked up a garden carrot and cut the greens off, then started to peel it. "I really don't."

"Well, his coming will be good for Vera," he said as he set the bowl next to her on the countertop.

Mammi Vera had been pleased to see Tobe, but the excitement exhausted her and Rose had tucked her straight into bed, promising her plenty of time for catch-up talks in the days ahead. She tried to keep everyone quiet, but Vera said not to bother. The sounds of family at the dinner table filled her with happiness.

*That*, Bethany thought, was a wonder right there. Usually, Mammi Vera squawked at the boys to hush up during dinner.

During dinner, Bethany saw the look on Galen's face go from puzzled to amused to wary when he noticed Tobe sit next to Naomi and strike up a conversation. Usually, Naomi was shy as a hummingbird, but she was all lit up as she talked to Tobe, giggly and sparkly. Galen looked at Rose, and lifted his eyebrows, and she did the same back.

Later, after Galen and Naomi had gone home and the boys had been sent to bed, Bethany and Rose put away the last of the dinner dishes and hung the wet dishrag over the faucet to dry. Rose turned and saw Tobe standing by the door, a newspaper tucked under his arm. "I didn't realize you and Naomi had known each other so well."

So, Rose had noticed sparks flying too.

"The three of us—me and Beth and Naomi—we played together when we were younger." Tobe's mouth lifted in a grin. "Ain't she turned into something sweet and fine?"

"Naomi?" Bethany had never thought of her friend like *that*. She'd always been frail, gentle Naomi. But Tobe was right—her gentleness gave her a certain appeal. And tonight, she was positively beaming.

"This inn you've started sure has gotten a lot of attention." Tobe looked up. "Since when have you started calling the farm Eagle Hill?"

"Just a few months ago," Rose said, "after we started the inn. It got its name because an eagle pair has a nest on the property. I'm sure Sammy and Luke will want to show it to you tomorrow."

"First thing, they said." He grinned. "I like the name. And I like the idea of turning the farm into a moneymaker." He wandered over to the refrigerator, swung open the door, stood staring into it for a moment, then grabbed the milk, opened the container, and took a few swigs while holding the door open. "I read in the papers some news about miracles on the farm. That a lady's cancer was cured. And someone else's marriage was saved from divorce court. Is any of it true?"

Bethany saw her stepmother stiffen. Rose discouraged the inn's reputation as a miracle maker.

"No, not really," Rose said primly. "It was the same guest, Delia Stoltz. She had surgery for cancer before she arrived, so that was already cured. As for her marriage, well, I do think a miracle saved it. But it wasn't because of the inn. It was God." She turned to Bethany. "I think it's starting to stop—all that nonsense about miracles at the inn. Don't you, Bethany?"

At the sink, Bethany stilled. How could she answer that without lying about Mrs. Miracle? Fortunately, Tobe didn't wait for an answer.

"Rose, you're looking at it all wrong. You can't buy that kind of publicity for any money. You don't want it to stop. That publicity will put the Inn at Eagle Hill on the map. People from all over the country will be coming to Stoney Ridge. Eating, shopping. Why, every business in downtown Stoney Ridge should be thanking you."

Bethany looked at Rose and wondered what she was thinking, why she had such a serious look on her face. His measure of delight in the inn's reputation seemed to push Rose in the other direction. Bethany had nearly forgotten how Tobe had always added some slight, raw element of strain to the family.

"Seems like this is a golden opportunity," Tobe continued. "I think we could be taking better advantage of it."

Rose had been spooning ground coffee into the coffeepot's filter to ready it for tomorrow's breakfast, but stopped abruptly at that comment and made an about-face. "You sounded like your father right then. It's something he might have said."

"What's wrong with that?"

She turned back to finish spooning the coffee into the filter. "Tobe, he was always chasing rainbows." Her voice was gentle, sad, but firm.

Bethany could see Tobe was just about to object when Rose closed the lid of the coffee can and held up a hand. "Son, it's late, and I need to get up early and start breakfast for the guest in the guest flat. We can talk tomorrow." At the doorway, she turned. "It's good you're home."

"Wait. Rose, before you go, I want to ask you one more question."

She leaned a shoulder against the doorjamb.

"From what I've read, it seems like everything is going to work out. With Schrock Investments, I mean. I read in the newspaper that donations from the Amish and Mennonites will reimburse the Plain investors. As for the English investors—they've filed claims with the SEC, so they'll be reimbursed from the liquidated assets."

"That's all true."

"So . . . everything is working out. We've got a fresh start."

Was that why Tobe had returned? He assumed that the slate had been wiped clean? Even Bethany, who didn't know every detail about Schrock Investments' collapse and sure didn't want to, even she was stunned at his naïveté, absolutely stunned.

Rose took a few steps toward him and spoke in a clear voice, gentle but firm. "A lot of people have lost money, Tobe. Families are losing their homes. Parents who scrimped and saved to provide for their children's future are realizing they're going to have to keep working for years to come—"

"I understand that! I do. And I feel terrible about it, but it's not my fault."

Rose shook her head sorrowfully and continued, ignoring his interruption. "It's not over, Tobe. Not even close."

Bethany was afraid Tobe might disappear if Rose told him more. This was his home, where he belonged. She forced herself to smile, hoping it looked natural. "Late at night isn't the time to discuss anything more."

"Bethany's right," Rose said. "There will be time for talk."

But Tobe wasn't ready to drop it. "Rose, you always said that God is in the business of fresh starts."

She hesitated. "And I do believe that. But sometimes the best thing to get off your chest is your chin."

Naomi glanced at the kitchen clock. Galen was out feeding the horses and would come in from the barn soon, hungry for breakfast. She started a pot of coffee brewing and put away some dishes that were drying in the rack. She set a pan of water on the stove to boil, and as soon as the bubbles formed, she stirred in the oats. You couldn't rush oatmeal, just like you couldn't rush a quilt.

Quilting was always on Naomi's mind. She was either working on a quilt pattern or thinking about one. It took a long time to sew a quilt block, to make tiny stitches that would stay tight and secure for years to come, a lifetime even. When she was faced with a pile of scraps, it could be hard to see how it was all going to come together, how each patch would fit with the others and how the colors and patterns would play against one another. She always started with a pattern in mind, but she never really knew how the block would turn out until it was finished. Now and then she had to go back and swap out a color or rip out a seam. More often than not, everything turned out better than she could have imagined.

When she finished a quilt top and held it up, everything looked so right together, the connections so obvious, the points so precise, that she wondered why she hadn't been able to see it from the beginning. But when she started on the next quilt she found that she was just as confounded as she was the time before.

Maybe that's the way it went with life too. Circumstances came into a person's life that were hard to make sense of, like a bag of quilt scraps, but often things ended up turning into something better than anyone could imagine.

When the oatmeal was the perfect consistency, she took it off the stove to cover it and keep it warm for Galen. The brown sugar jar was empty, so she went into the large pantry to refill it. As she scooped, she heard her brother's voice in the kitchen and realized someone was with him. Rose Schrock.

"Galen," she heard Rose say, "I need some advice about Tobe. I'm wrestling with something."

"Hold on," Galen said. "I need to fortify myself with a swig of coffee first."

Naomi froze. Had something happened? She knew quite a bit about the problems of Schrock Investments—she'd followed news reports with great interest. Anything that involved Tobe Schrock was of great interest to her. She was torn between wanting to know more and thinking the right thing to do was to make her presence known. Still . . . Tobe wasn't just a neighbor's son to her, like he was to Galen. This was Tobe. She set down the sugar scoop and carefully closed the door to a crack.

Galen crossed the kitchen and took two coffee cups out of the cupboard. Naomi held her breath. He was just a few feet away from the pantry. She heard him pour the coffee, then add a scoop of sugar to one, just the way Rose liked it. She heard the scrape of two kitchen chairs being pulled out from under the table, then the sound of Rose and Galen sitting at the table, and she let out her breath. Eavesdropping was a terrible thing to do . . . truly terrible . . . and surely revealed an immature character. Now would be the time to come out of the pantry with the sugar jar and no one would think twice about it. Now!

But the moment passed. She couldn't help herself.

"Okay," Galen said to Rose. "Now I'm ready."

Rose sounded pensive. "There's a fellow named Allen Turner from the Securities Exchange Commission who has been looking for Tobe for months now. He wanted me to let him know if I heard from Tobe." She was quiet for a long moment. "I can't stop that inner tussle—should I call him? Or not call him?"

"Why does this SEC lawyer want to talk to Tobe?" he asked.

"He said Tobe adjusted figures at Schrock Investments so that the accounting numbers looked more positive than they really were."

"Do you believe it?"

"I don't want to. I want to believe Tobe would never do such a thing. But what if it's true? What if Dean had known? He didn't tell me everything. When the bank got involved in Schrock Investments—after checks started bouncing and it was apparent there was no money—Dean was under tremendous pressure. There's a part of me that wonders if they both had been tempted to do something dishonest."

"Even a saint is tempted by an open door," Galen said.

*Zing!* Naomi cringed. She should definitely reveal her presence and let them know she was eavesdropping.

But then Rose's voice dropped to a whisper and Naomi strained to hear. Ever so carefully, she leaned closer to the open crack of the door.

"Do you think that I should call Allen Turner and let him know that

Tobe has returned? How can a mother do such a thing? Even though I'm not his mother, I *am* his mother."

"Rose, if Tobe has nothing to hide, then wouldn't it be better to be up-front about the fact that he's returned?"

*Good thinking, Galen!* Because Naomi was absolutely, positively sure that Tobe had nothing to hide.

"Yes. No." Rose sighed. "Is everything always so clear to you, so black and white? It seems to me that there are shades of gray worth considering."

"Whenever I'm struggling with a decision, I find it's best to whittle it down to the basic principle. In this instance, the principle is: Do you want the truth?"

"Maybe that's the heart of what I'm struggling with. I still feel such a sense of shame over Schrock Investments. Such a deep shame." The room was quiet for a long moment before Rose added, "I want to find out if or how those records, the ones the SEC confiscated, were falsified. I want to find out if Tobe has done something illegal. I suppose I want to know if Dean had discovered that Tobe had done something, if that knowledge might have driven him to take his own life and drown himself in the pond that day. But even more important than getting answers to those questions, I want Tobe to straighten out and get back on track. By coming home, he's made a step in that direction. It's a start. At least, I hope it is."

*Oh, it is, Rose!* Naomi thought. *Believe in Tobe! Believe in the best of him.*

"So far," Rose said, "nothing in Tobe's words makes it seem like he's moving forward. So, Galen, what should I do?"

"You're not going to like what I have to say," Galen said.

"Go ahead."

"What you *really* need to do is to tell Tobe about Allen Turner. Then let him make that phone call."

"Maybe I should just talk to Allen Turner, first."

"Rose, it doesn't do to sacrifice for people unless they want you to. It's just a waste. As painful as it can be, you have to leave people to their own life."

"I just don't know if Tobe could do it. It would make sense for him to call Allen Turner, but he's . . . never been overly blessed with good sense."

*That isn't right! Tobe just has his own way of thinking.*

"Sense is wasted on some people," Galen said.

Naomi couldn't argue with that, but she was aware that Galen was hard on people. Maybe too hard. She knew that Galen had never thought highly of Tobe. He had known Tobe since he was a young boy and was convinced he had a lazy streak. Compared to Galen, everybody had a lazy streak. People could change. Tobe could change, if he wanted to. Take Jimmy Fisher. At first, Galen didn't think much of Jimmy Fisher. He only took him on as an apprentice horse trainer because the deacon asked him to. But after a few months, Jimmy had earned Galen's respect and now he hardly flinched much when Jimmy called himself a partner.

"It's time for Tobe to start making his own decisions," Galen said. "The decisions he makes now will determine the person he's going to be. He needs to set his own course."

Until that moment, it hadn't occurred to Naomi that this time—returning home, settling up with his past—was a crossroad for Tobe.

"Rose, you would be robbing that opportunity from him if you overstep now."

She hesitated. "Well, I thought I should give him a little time to get settled."

"Time for what?"

"Meanwhile," Rose said, ignoring Galen's pointed implication, "I was hoping . . . you might ask Tobe to work for you. You don't have to pay him. Just let him help you around the farm."

Naomi practically dropped the lid to the sugar jar. *Oh, what a wonderful idea!*

"No." Then, more softly, Galen added, "He doesn't have the temperament for horses."

"You said similar things about Jimmy Fisher and look how well he has developed into a horseman."

"But Jimmy had the love of horses to begin with. Tobe doesn't love anything."

"You're judging him from how he was as a young teenager."

"There's another reason. I don't want him around my sister."

Naomi straightened like a rod. What did *that* mean?

"Just because he was flirting with her last night? Is that so bad? Maybe Tobe's good for her. I'm sure she'd be a wonderful influence on Tobe."

"What makes you think he'd be any good for Naomi? He's a fence jumper—"

"Galen, that's not fair. If you'd only give him some time . . ."

It was a good thing that Naomi was hiding in the pantry because she was thoroughly flustered.

It took a lot to get Galen riled up, but she could tell by the tenor of her brother's voice that he was annoyed. "And what happens when Tobe finally gets around to calling the SEC lawyer and finds out he's in a little more trouble than he had expected? Have you even told him about the SEC lawyer?"

Silence.

There was a rattle of a cup and saucer, which seemed like Galen's version of ending the conversation. "Rose, you're interfering with that boy's path to adulthood. Like it or not, he has to face consequences. He runs away from too many responsibilities. Once you start running, you can't stop."

A chair clattered. Galen was on his feet, then Rose. Naomi heard their muffled voices as they walked to the door but couldn't make out what they were saying. She waited until she knew they had left the house before she peeked her head out of the pantry. The coast was clear. She took the brown sugar jar and went to the stove to stir the now stiff and pasty oatmeal, pondering all she learned from overhearing that conversation. No wonder eavesdropping was considered to be a sin—it was dangerously delicious. And so very helpful.

# 9

Tobe fed hay to Silver Queen and her colt as Bethany filled their buckets with water. Caring for the animals had always been his job when he was growing up. She and Tobe had many good conversations while they worked, side by side. She smiled to herself, thinking how wonderful it was to have him here and how easily they settled into their old routines.

"Tobe, I want to know more about Mom. No, I don't. Yes. I do."

He straightened up, startled by her question.

"You couldn't have taken me with you to see her?"

"It never crossed my mind." He pitched some hay into the stall. "One thing I will tell you, Bethany, she's not what you'd think."

"I don't think anything. I have no idea what she's like. I hardly remember her." She gave him a sideways look. "Do you? Remember her, that is."

Tobe leaned against the stall door. "Probably more than you do. I remember once or twice when she and Mammi Vera had words. Mom seemed to feel poorly, and slept a lot."

"Tobe, why did she leave?"

He turned and held his hand out to the colt to sniff. "I don't know."

"Yes you do. Why won't you tell me the truth?"

He didn't look at her. "Some things are best left alone. This is one of them."

"Did you even ask her why she left?"

He shook his head. "We didn't talk much."

"Did she ask about me?"

He shook his head.

341

"I want to see her. I want to meet her for myself."

He tilted his head, shaking it. "Bethany, I don't think that's a good idea."

"Shootfire! Why not? You got to be with her. How'd you find her, anyway?"

"Jake Hertzler. He knew where she was."

"But . . . how?"

"I guess he poked around Dad's old records. He showed me their divorce certificate, and I copied down the return address on the envelope."

"Was she glad to see you?"

"I wouldn't say . . . glad."

"What would you say?"

"Let's just say it gave me some peace of mind to see her."

"That's what I want too. Peace of mind."

"Bethany . . . you can't unsee a thing once it's seen, or unknow it once it's known."

"What does that mean?"

"Just leave it alone. Remember her the way you want to remember her."

Well, that was the problem right there. She couldn't remember her mother. The images were so mixed up they never made much sense, strange thoughts and feelings that flickered and were gone like moths darting at a lamp. She remembered someone humming a song. She remembered a black-and-white dog sleeping on her bed. She remembered playing checkers with another child—Tobe?—in a room that was dimly lit. She wanted to know more. "Would you at least give me her address?"

He shook his head. "I'm trying to protect you as best as I can."

"I don't need protecting. I need answers." She put the water bucket down. "I just feel so mixed up inside. I'm trying to make peace with things—Jake, Dad's death—but I feel like I can't move forward, not in anything, until I get some things sorted out."

Tobe was silent for a long, long time. "I'm sorry, Bethany. Like I said, some things are just best left alone."

*Shootfire!* Everybody seemed to think they knew what was best for her.

Mim had responded to Stuck's letter by telling her just what Danny had said—that a life could be transformed by God, if a person were only willing to ask for help. The newspaper didn't want to run something so overtly religious, Bethany said, after a brief meeting with the features editor, whom she thought was small minded and unimaginative, so Mim went ahead and mailed Mrs. Miracle's response to Stuck to the return address on the envelope.

The features editor did tell Bethany one interesting thing: the column was getting a lot of attention and he was thinking about expanding it from once to twice a week. Bethany said she smiled at him and took full credit. "Here's this week's mail pouch," she said as she tossed the manila envelope on Mim's bed.

It was twice the size of last week's batch.

"I bought more stamps for you while I was downtown." She handed Mim a roll of first-class stamps. "You're not going to make any money if you mail letters to people. Just because the newspaper isn't printing them, it doesn't mean you have to answer them."

"I know. I just want to."

Bethany sat on the bed. "What are these poor saps writing to you?" She put a hand out to reach for the manila envelope, but Mim grabbed it.

"You're being mean. Don't call them poor saps. They're just people. All kinds of people. And you can always read the column in the newspaper. It's not a secret."

Bethany tilted her head. "Isn't it?" She jumped off the bed and crossed the room to the door. "Sure hope you know what you're doing, Mim. You could get into a heap of trouble for this if anyone catches on that you're masquerading as Mrs. Miracle." She closed the door behind her.

Masquerading? How insulting. People needed to write to Mrs. Miracle and she felt compelled to write back. She turned the manila envelope upside down on her bed and let the letters spill out. She picked up a letter and opened it:

*Dear Mrs. Miracle,*

*My name is Peter and I am in the sixth grade. When I talk, I stutter. Yesterday I tried to order a large coke at the movies. I said to the counter guy I would like a lllllllllllllllllarge coke. He looked at me as if he thought I was mental. It was very embarrassing. That kind of thing happens a lot to me and I take a lot of teasing.*

*Sometimes it feels that my mouth is stuck in a traffic jam and nothing can move.*

*Will my stutter ever go away?*

> *Yours truly,*
> *Peter*

Mim remembered a boy with a stutter from her old school. She could still see the pain on his face as he tried to get some words out, with children snickering all around him. This boy grew quieter and quieter, until a new teacher arrived in the middle of the year and put a stop to the teasing. She came up with all kinds of strategies to help this boy. Mim remembered a book report he read on the last day of school . . . without a single stutter. She would never forget the look on that boy's face when he finished the report—like he had scaled Mt. Everest. Mim tapped her chin with her pencil . . . what were those strategies the teacher gave to that boy? Oh yes! She remembered.

She pulled the typewriter out from under her bed and set it up on her desk. Then she took a fresh sheet of paper and fit it into the roller.

*Dear Peter,*

*I have some tips that might help the next time you are in a situation that makes you feel anxious, like ordering a large coke at the movies or giving a book report in school.*

*1) Say the words in your mind before you say them out loud.*

*2) If you have to give a talk in front of your class, avoid looking at any one particular person. Look above the heads of the other students and focus on something in the back of the room.*

*3) Take up singing. Stutterers normally don't stutter while singing. It will help you build confidence.*

*4) Try not to put pressure on yourself. One of the things that makes stuttering worse is anxiety.*

*I hope those ideas might help you, Peter. And I also hope you will not let anyone's teasing cause you to stop talking.*

> *Sincerely,*
> *Mrs. Miracle*

Mim pulled the letter from the typewriter and scanned it for typos. She was a stickler for typos. Satisfied, she carefully folded the paper in three sections and placed it in the folder to be returned to the *Stoney Ridge Times*.

Being Mrs. Miracle was a wonderful job.

Mim glanced at the alarm clock on her night table. She had time for one more letter before she needed to go to bed. She was waking up extra early this summer so she could join her mom on pre-dawn walks up in the hills. It was their special time together, just the two of them, and she loved to have those moments with her. She flipped through the pile of new letters and saw one with Stuck's unique scrawl. She ripped it open.

*Dear Mrs. Miracle,*

*It was nice of you to send a letter to me but I am sorry to say you are dead wrong about God. He doesn't exist. If he did, my mother would not have killed my father. She would not be spending her life in jail. If there were a God then someone on this earth would care about me.*

*Don't bother praying on my account. It's just hot air hitting the ceiling.*

*Signed,*
*Stuck*

Oh, boy. Being Mrs. Miracle was a difficult job.

When Sammy and Luke galloped past Bethany as she hung laundry on the clothesline, she hollered at them to stop. "Where's Tobe?"

"In the barn!" Sammy said.

"Hunting for something," Luke added. Then they both vanished through the hole in the privet.

Galen King, she thought, was a saint to put up with those boys underfoot.

Bethany finished hanging her dress on the clothesline—a blue one—and she stopped for a moment, watching the dress flutter in the gentle breeze. She was always drawn to the color blue and she couldn't say why. The color gave her a feeling of calm and safety. One of the eagles flew overhead and caught her attention, silhouetted against the sky. Maybe she loved the color blue because it had something to do with the vastness of the sky. Endless, permanent, predictable.

She still had bedsheets to wash and hang on the line to dry, but she wanted to talk to Tobe while no one was around. She walked down to the barn and, once inside, was hit with a blast of pungent moist air: hay and horses and manure. She blinked; it took a moment for her eyes to adjust to the dimness and she heard footsteps above her head. She found Tobe in the hayloft, amidst a sea of opened boxes, dusty old trunks, broken furniture waiting to be repaired. "Tobe, I've given this a lot of thought. I want the address for Mom."

He looked up at her. "You're not going to get it from me."

Bethany crossed her arms over her chest, furious. "Shootfire! You seem to be keeping a lot of information to yourself these days!"

"My thoughts exactly," Rose said, as she emerged up the hayloft ladder. "I have two questions for you, Tobe, and I'd like the answers." She climbed to the top and leaned against a haystack. "Why did you run off last year, and why did you come back?"

Tobe didn't answer her, but his eyes looked a little frightened when Rose asked him those questions, or perhaps only surprised. Like a cottontail caught in a sudden beam of a flashlight.

Rose walked closer to Bethany and Tobe. "Tell me what you're looking for."

He kept his eyes fixed on the ground. His hands were clasped together; Bethany saw them tighten involuntarily. "Just something I left behind. Bethany said that most of the things in the basement got moved up here when you started the inn."

Rose looked around the dusty hayloft. "That's right. The inn has kept me so busy, I haven't had time to organize anything. It's on my to-do list." She brushed some hay off a barrel top. "Tobe, are you looking for something that has to do with Schrock Investments?"

"Maybe I should leave," Bethany said.

"No," Rose said firmly. "Bethany, it's time you understood the bigger picture." She turned to Tobe, who had turned his attention back to the barrel. "I want an answer: are you looking for something that has to do with Schrock Investments?"

Head down, he stilled. "There's nothing more to be done with the business."

"No, that's not true."

He snapped his head up to look at Rose. "The Amish Committee is paying people back. The other investors have already gotten their money from claims. It's going to be okay."

"But that doesn't answer the question of why the business started to fail in such a fast and furious way."

He shrugged and started to go through the contents of the box in front of him. "It was the economy."

"It was more than the economy. You know that . . . don't you?" It wasn't really a question Rose was posing. "Tobe, if you're in trouble, I can help."

He startled. "What makes you think I'm the one who's in trouble?"

"You disappeared for a reason. My guess is that you were frightened. Maybe you thought something was going to be discovered. Something you had done wrong. So you panicked and left."

"Is that true, Tobe?" Bethany asked. She had assumed he had left because he felt like she did, tired of the whole business of failure.

He turned away from Rose and Bethany and opened up another box. "I left because the business was going under and there was no reason to stay."

Rose slapped her hand down on a trunk so hard the dishes inside it rattled. Tobe jumped. Bethany's eyes went wide. "No! That's a lie!" she said. "You need to stop lying to me! You and Jake Hertzler did *something* to Dad's business. This isn't going to go away, just because you hope it's all over. It's not. Life doesn't work that way. You're in serious trouble with the law, Tobe." The words echoed and echoed, into the barn rafters.

She surprised Tobe so that his face flushed. He looked at Rose now as if he'd never seen her before. "What makes you say that?"

"There is a lawyer with the Securities Exchange Commission who wants to talk to you."

"There's no reason! I haven't done anything wrong. I haven't." Tobe stared at Rose, silent, then his chest shuddered with a deep sigh. He slid to the ground, his back against a pole, and covered his face with his hands. He started to cry. Rose crouched down on the floor with him and held him in her arms, the way she held Sammy and Luke when they were little, until he pushed her away. "It wasn't my idea," he protested, his voice breaking on the last word so that he sounded as guilty as he seemed. "It was Jake's. He falsified bank statements so it looked like we had money when we didn't."

Bethany heard the words but it was her brother's anguished face that broke her heart. A panic gripped her chest so tightly that she thought her heart had stopped beating. She kept discovering new things about Jake that seemed impossible to believe. "How? Why? Why would Jake do such a thing?"

Tobe rubbed his eyes with the palms of his hands. "He said it was to help Dad out. He said that if Dad and I could just keep getting new investors, there wouldn't be any problem. He kept reassuring me that everything was okay."

"How did you find out he falsified bank statements?" Rose said.

Tobe wiped his face with both hands. "Jake usually deposited the checks at the bank. One time, Jake was at the dentist so I deposited for the day. I checked on the balance and saw that it had dwindled down to practically nothing. That was when I first thought that something fishy was going on."

"Then why didn't you tell Dad?" Bethany asked.

Tobe looked up and his hard gaze met hers like a blow. "I was going to! I wanted to. But when I went back to the office, Jake was there, so I showed him the bank balance and asked what he knew about it. He told me that he knew all about it—there was less money in the bank than Dad thought there was, but he knew Dad was having heart problems. He didn't want to worry Dad, so he just changed the statements that he showed him. He said not to tell Dad, not to put him under any more pressure, that things were going to be fine."

"And you believed him," Rose said, but in sadness, not anger.

"I was worried about Dad. Jake said he had enough stress. I wanted to believe him. You remember how tense Dad seemed, and he never slept, and how his heart was beating too fast."

Bethany remembered. She used to hear her father's footsteps downstairs as he paced in the middle of the night.

"Jake wanted Dad to concentrate on getting more investors. He said it could be a very short-term cash flow crunch, if we could only go out and get more investments. Jake had a way of explaining things that made it seem like a good idea. So I went along with him." He picked up a piece of straw and rubbed it between his fingers. "Then the house was foreclosed on and we had to move to Mammi Vera's. Things kept getting worse, not better. So Jake told me he had figured out a way to buy a little more time until the economy improved."

Rose was stunned. "Did you not realize he was setting up a pyramid scheme?"

Tobe shook his head. "Jake kept saying it was a short-term solution. Just to buy some time." He dropped his chin to his chest. "It was the simplest thing. Strangely simple. Jake just whited out the address and account number, using other investors' statements, typed the right address and account number, and then made a copy so you couldn't see that it had been changed."

"And Dad had no idea?" Bethany asked.

Tobe shook his head. "It gets worse." He crumpled the straw and tossed it away. "Checks started bouncing right and left. As word leaked out, shareholders started to try to liquidate, which only made everything spiral out of control. Dad was advised by the bank to declare bankruptcy so they could try to control the implosion and figure out what had happened. That was when Jake showed me that he had been keeping a second set of books. He had given Dad the cooked books. Jake had the real books, the real story—Schrock Investments was running out of money."

Rose rubbed her face. "Then the ones Dad handed over to the SEC were falsified books?"

Slowly, Tobe nodded. "That's right. I was in the office on the day the subpoena was delivered to Dad. He was told that shareholders had organized a lawsuit against Schrock Investments. That was when I started to panic. I took the second set of books and I hid them in the basement. I just needed to get away for a few days, to think. To figure out a plan of how to tell Dad what Jake and I had done." He put his forehead on his knees. "And then Dad died. I couldn't come back. I just couldn't. So I ran. I ran as far away from here as I could get."

"Es is graad so weit hie as her," Rose said. *It's just as far going as coming.*

Tobe squeezed his eyes shut. "I was only trying to protect Dad. He must have known what I had done. He must have figured it out."

"Probably so," Rose said. "He was very upset the night before he died.

He left the house and said he was going to go fix everything. I didn't know what he meant by that. The next thing I knew, the bishop and police arrived to let me know Dad had drowned."

At the mention of her father's death, Bethany suddenly felt aware of how hot and stuffy it was in the hayloft. She felt as if she was having trouble getting a full breath of air. She walked over to the open hayloft window and tried to get some fresh air.

"So," Rose said, all calm and matter-of-fact, "you only came back because you heard that the Amish committee was going to reimburse people for what they lost?"

"Yes." The word had come out of Tobe almost like a gasp. "I thought it would be safe. I thought it was all over."

"Are you looking for ledger books? For the accurate books?"

"I've looked everywhere! I've been combing this hayloft for two days. I can't find them anywhere."

Bethany's head snapped up. "I gave them to Jake."

Tobe stared at her. "You *what*?"

"He was here a few months ago. Jake told me you were in trouble. He said you needed those books. I thought I was doing something to help you."

He let out a short, bitter laugh. "Jake scores again."

"Tobe, we need to talk to the SEC lawyer," Rose said. "Allen Turner is his name. He's been looking for you for the last year."

His head shot up in panic. "You would turn me in?"

"I'm not going to tell Allen Turner anything. You're going to tell him. Everything." Out of Rose's pocket, she pulled Allen Turner's business card and handed it to Tobe.

His face crumbled. "I can't do it. I can't. You don't understand."

"I understand that life doesn't give you many moments like this. You have a very long life ahead of you. But how you handle this situation will decide the man you're going to be from now on. The man God wants you to be."

He fingered the card. "God has forgotten about me."

Rose shook her head. "He hasn't," she whispered. "You must never think that. His love is always there, Tobe, always there. We're here too. Your family will always support you. That's what families do."

Tobe listened, but said nothing.

"You heard me, didn't you, Tobe?"

Tobe nodded. "I heard you." He wiped his eyes and held up the business card. "I'm going to be different from now on. You'll see. I'm going to be different."

"In what way?"

"In every way. I am going to be a different man."

Bethany looked at her brother. For all his faults—and she had to admit they were manifold—he had a good heart. And as much as he could be frustrating, he could also be amusing and generous and appealing.

"Don't change too much," Rose said gently. "We love you the way you are."

She stood and walked to the hayloft ladder, then swiveled around to face Tobe. "I understand that cash inflow from new investors could be used to pay other investors' dividends. I understand that returns on investments had diminished. But what I don't understand is where all the principal money went. Where is all *that* money?"

Tobe shrugged. "The recession. Plus Dad made some bad investments. Some real estate properties went belly up."

Bethany looked back out the hayloft window. She thought about Jake's new truck with all the bells and whistles he was so proud of. About his new horse trailer. About his cell phone. About the fancy restaurants he took her to. His overly generous tips. It never crossed her mind to ask where that money came from. It never crossed her mind.

And she had trouble getting a full breath of air again.

With all Tobe had revealed in the hayloft, Bethany couldn't shake the feeling that life was spiraling out of control. She had to grab something to hold on to, something to help her feel as if she could find her own way.

Later that day, while Tobe was taking a shower, she sneaked into his room and riffled through his wallet. Tobe kept everything important in his wallet. She noticed exactly how everything was before she took it out so she could be sure to put it back the same way. She went through old receipts, a piece of gum, a few dollars—ah! no wonder he came home when he did—and a folded-up paper from a Schrock Investments' memo pad. She opened it up and squinted, barely able to make out the faded penciled writing:

*Mary Miller Schrock, 212 N. Street, Hagensburg, PA*

Bingo!

That had to be it. Tobe had said she wasn't too far from here. She heard the shower turn off, so she scribbled down the address on a piece of paper, put the papers and gum back in the wallet, and tiptoed out of Tobe's room.

All day, Bethany kept fingering the paper with her mother's address on it. She wasn't even sure how to get there, or if she even wanted to.

Yes she did.

No she didn't.

# 10

This afternoon, Geena's mind was mainly on dinner. Earlier today she had bought a juicy strip steak at the butcher shop in Stoney Ridge and thought she might ask the Schrocks if she could use their grill. The Amish, she was told, loved to barbecue. And it was still blistering hot, which she didn't really mind because it meant more canceled reservations and her stay could extend at Eagle Hill. The longer she was here, the longer she could put off the inevitable job search.

As she walked out the guest flat toward the house, she spotted Bethany near the clothesline, a mound of wet bedding in her arms. Of all the Schrocks, she found herself most drawn to Bethany: feisty, opinionated, strong—probably stronger than she knew—yet with an undercurrent of pathos. She wondered what that undercurrent consisted of. Where did it come from?

As she approached Bethany, she could see that something was wrong. Bethany's hands were trembling. "Are you all right?"

Startled, Bethany said, "Of course. Of course I'm all right."

"You're sure?"

Bethany's eyes filled with tears. "I don't know." She looked away. "Maybe not."

"I see." Geena leaned forward. "Would you like to talk? Life gets complicated sometimes. It can help to talk things out."

Bethany shook her head, splattering tears, then ducked her chin in embarrassment. "Shootfire!" she said fiercely. "I'm sorry. I'm never emotional like this. Hardly ever."

Geena patted her back. "Come inside and let's chat."

In the small living room of the guest flat of Eagle Hill, Bethany poured out her life story: her mother's disappearance, her father's untimely passing, her brother's reappearance, and all the pieces in between. "I just want to know why. Why did she leave? Did I do something to make her go? Did my father? I feel as if I can't stop wondering about her—maybe because my father has died. I'll never know anything more if I don't track her down now."

When Bethany had finally finished with her long story, with her tears and deep breaths, Geena encased Bethany's hand like a sandwich between her own and looked deeply into her face. "Maybe you should go find your mother and get some answers to your questions."

"I don't even know how to get to Hagensburg. Buses, I guess."

"I could drive you there. I could go with you."

Bethany's head snapped up. "I didn't mean to ask—"

Geena held up a hand. "You didn't ask. I offered."

"Maybe my brother is right. Maybe it's best to just let sleeping dogs lie."

"Sometimes it is best to leave things alone. But sometimes, a person can't move forward until she faces what's holding her back."

"What if I find out something I don't want to know?"

"I guess that's something you need to decide for yourself."

"I want to know about my mother," Bethany said. "But I don't."

"Sometimes the past can cling to us like cobwebs, getting in the way of the future." Geena patted Bethany's shoulder. "If you want to go, just let me know when and I'll drive you over there."

From the guest flat window, Geena watched Bethany walk back to the clothesline and her heart felt sad. She hoped it had helped for Bethany to talk to her, though the way her shoulders were slumped made her think she had only added to the poor girl's confusion. She would have loved to have dropped everything and driven Bethany right over to Hagensburg, right now, and get answers to those burdensome questions. But going, or not going . . . that had to be Bethany's decision.

Geena wasn't surprised that Bethany had shared personal information with her even though they had only known each other for a short time.

People had always told her their stuff, even before she was ordained. Maybe she was easy to talk to. She hoped so. Sometimes people just needed a safe place to unload their troubles. An objective listener. Her counseling classes at seminary had taught her that the best way to draw someone out was just to listen.

But to whom did a minister go to share his or her stuff?

Early Friday morning, Tobe called Allen Turner of the Securities Exchange Commission. The lawyer told him to sit tight, that he would be there in a few hours.

Bethany had heard the name of Allen Turner for over a year. She had an impression of the kind of man he might be: old, balding, with thick glasses, wearing a detective's overcoat that brushed his ankles, and carrying a fat briefcase with papers sticking out of it. The real Allen Turner turned out to be youngish, sort of. In his mid-forties, she guessed, with a full head of blondish hair and a rather kind-looking face. Not looksome like Jimmy Fisher, sort of a craggy face, but not bad for a middle-aged English man. His smile was kind, lighting up the sadness in his eyes. That was what surprised Bethany the most—his eyes. They weren't the eyes of a ferocious lawyer. They were fatherly eyes.

"This is one case I'm determined to solve," he told Rose and Bethany as they met him at the car and walked to the house.

"Is it still considered to be a case?" Rose said.

"Yes, ma'am, it is."

"It's naïve, I suppose, to hope that there's enough information to clearly show that my husband and son had done nothing wrong with Schrock Investments. Nothing intentionally wrong."

"Yes, ma'am. That would be naïve."

Allen Turner sat at the kitchen table of Eagle Hill, opened his big briefcase—that was one part of him that did fit the image in Bethany's mind—and started to pull out thick files. She had to fight a powerful urge to stand up and fuss with the food or do the dishes, start some coffee. Women, Rose had once said, had to do something with their hands in times of crisis. Boy, was that right. She had to sit on her hands to keep from fidgeting.

Rose sent Mim over to Naomi's to tell Tobe that Mr. Turner was here. And she asked Mim to stay over there, to keep an eye on Luke and Sammy. Bethany was pretty sure Rose wished she could send Mammi Vera away for this conversation too. Her grandmother was hovering in the kitchen, glaring at Allen Turner as if she were a mother lioness and he was threatening one of her cubs. Which, in a way, was true.

When Tobe returned from next door, his face was flushed and not from the heat. Even Bethany was aware this was a significant moment in his life. Tobe shook Allen Turner's hand and sat down at the table.

Bethany caught Rose's eye and nodded her head to the door.

"Would you like us to leave?" Rose said, setting a pitcher of iced tea on the table with two glasses and a plate of cookies. "We can give you some privacy."

"I'm not going anywhere," Mammi Vera announced, seating herself at the table.

Allen Turner took a glass and filled it with iced tea. He took a long sip and set it down, then wiped his forehead with a handkerchief. The room felt like an oven and it was only eleven in the morning. "Please stay, all of you. I have questions for you too. We've got a lot to wade through." He set a tiny tape recorder on the table and looked up. "I hope you don't mind if I record our conversation." He turned it on without waiting for anyone's permission. "Tobe, start by stating your name and age."

"My name is Tobias Schrock. I'm twenty-two years old . . ."

Tobe answered Allen Turner's questions for over two hours, while Rose and Mammi Vera and Bethany sat at the table, patiently listening. There was nothing new in what Tobe had to say, not to Rose, but something new did occur. Allen Turner pulled out two black ledgers and set them on the table. "Do you recognize these?"

Bethany pressed her backbone against the hard chair. Those were the two books that she had given—searched for and handed over!—to Jake Hertzler, just two months ago. She felt that strange feeling start again in her chest, like she couldn't get a full breath of air.

Comprehension stilled Tobe, but only for a moment. "Those are the actual ledgers for Schrock Investments. Those show the real story. That we were running out of money."

"This case has been pretty unusual for me. Without any computers, there's no paper trail. Everything boils down to these ledgers." Allen Turner opened one of them up. "Maybe you knew that." He lifted his eyes to observe Tobe's response.

"I've never worked with computers. I wouldn't know any difference. That's just the way Schrock Investments kept their records." Tobe bit his lip. "How'd you get those?"

"They arrived at my desk, sent anonymously. A note inside said they belonged to you."

Tobe squeezed his eyes shut. "The entries were made by Jake Hertzler. You can compare handwriting and see that's the truth. But I took the books and hid them on the day the subpoena was delivered and my father was told there was a lawsuit forming against Schrock Investments."

"Why did you hide them?"

Tobe shrugged. "I panicked. It was stupid. I just thought I could protect my father."

"These ledgers only reveal part of the story. Schrock Investments was in trouble but it wasn't only because of poor returns." Allen Turner reached out and took one of Rose's cookies. He took a bite, then a few more. The room had grown quiet, the crunching of the cookie sounded like a cow in dried cornstalks.

"I'm sure there's a perfectly good explanation," Rose said quietly, but she clasped her hands so tightly, the knuckles turned white.

"Quite right, Mrs. Schrock," Allen Turner said, talking around bites of cookie. "Someone was siphoning money from the company."

Tobe jerked his head up. "It wasn't me! I would never have done such a thing."

Allen Turner flattened his palms on the table. "No one's accusing you, son. We think it was Jake Hertzler. He was skimming off the company from the start."

"How did you discover that?" Rose asked.

Allen Turner pulled out another file, with a picture of a man on top. Jake's picture. "It's taken me awhile to piece it all together. Jake Hertzler, aka Jack Hartzler, John Hershberger . . . he's got a number of aliases. He's a con artist. A clever one. He dabbles in all kinds of money laundering scams."

Quietly, Bethany added, "Horse trading too."

Allen Turner looked over at her as if he just realized she was there. "Wouldn't surprise me. Anything he can get his mitts into, he finds a way to turn a fast one."

Mammi Vera slammed her fists on the tabletop. "That Jake Hertzler always did strike me as slicker than a pan full of cold bacon!"

Allen Turner grinned, a first. "Well, his luck is running out. He got greedy with Schrock Investments and caught the SEC's attention on this one. I'm going to nail this guy." He looked at Tobe. "And if you want to avoid some jail time, you're going to help me."

"Jail?" Tobe asked, color draining from his face. "Why would I have to go to jail?"

"Son, you broke the law," Allen said, his eyes both weary and wary. "You committed felonies."

"How?"

"Concealing records. Withholding information. You're facing jail time. A lot of it . . . unless . . . we can prove Jake Hertzler's involvement as the mastermind behind this pyramid scheme."

"But he was!"

Allen lifted an eyebrow. "Then help me prove it."

"How?"

"You'll need to come back to Philadelphia with me."

Tobe looked at him suspiciously. "So you can throw me in jail?"

"I'm going to do what I can to keep you *out* of jail. But there are people you're going to have to talk to first. And I need to have your full cooperation to build this case against Jake Hertzler. We need your testimony."

"I'll do anything I can to pin Jake down." A shadow crossed over his eyes. "Anything."

"Tobias Schrock!" Mammi Vera snapped. "Revenge is not an option." She tapped a finger on the tabletop. "Don't forget who you are."

Tobe looked over at her. "Jake should pay for what he did. Is wanting justice so wrong?"

She narrowed her eyes at him. "God decides those matters. Justice belongs to him. You were raised to be a Plain man. You can't toss that away like an old hat."

Allen Turner leaned forward in his chair. "Son, is there something else you know? Something you're not telling me?"

Tobe hesitated. He kept his eyes on the tabletop. "I know he falsified bank statements. I saw him do it."

"Yeah," Allen Turner said. "I figured that out."

"What else, Tobe?" Rose said. "Do you know something else about Jake Hertzler that you're not telling us? Are you frightened about something? Is that why you disappeared?"

Everyone stilled, all eyes on Tobe. He ran his finger along a spot on the oilcloth that covered the table, then finally lifted his head. He didn't back down. If anything, his jaw hardened. "I told you what I know for sure."

Bethany knew her brother well enough to know he was lying. Tobe knew something else he didn't want to say. But what?

Rose must have had the same sense. "I'm going with you to Philadelphia," she said.

Tobe's head jerked up. "No you're not. I got myself into this and I'm going to get myself out of it."

"I'm coming too," Mammi Vera added. She looked right at Rose. "Don't even try to talk me out of it."

Rose opened her mouth, then clamped it shut with a frown. Both women ignored Tobe, talking over his objections as if he weren't even there.

"I'm due for a three-month checkup with that Dr. Stoltz anyway. I'll just move it up a little. We'll stay at Delia Stoltz's house. She stayed here plenty long." Mammi Vera waved a hand at Rose as if shooing a cat. "You call her today and let her know we're coming."

Rose sighed. It was decided. "Then we'll have to take the boys too. Bethany and Mim have enough to do with the inn and their work at the Sisters' House."

"You can leave them, Rose," Bethany said. "We'll trade off watching them. Tobe needs you right now."

Rose hesitated, nodded, then turned to Allen Turner. "We can't leave for a few days, though. There's a work frolic tomorrow to help build the community garden."

Allen Turner had been watching the family interaction with a stunned look on his face. Bethany thought everything about Schrock Investments probably stunned him. "Mrs. Schrock, this isn't a vacation. Your stepson is under investigation for criminal charges."

Rose lifted her chin. "My *son* is innocent." She didn't like to use the word "step" when referring to her relationship to Bethany and Tobe. As far as she was concerned, they were a family. Period. "And my son is not going to Philadelphia without me. We need Tobe tomorrow for the frolic. And then there's Sunday church. So we can't leave until Monday. You can come back for us then."

"Nooooooooo," Allen Turner said, drawing the word out for emphasis. "I am not letting Tobe Schrock out of my sight. I've been trying to catch up with him for a very long time."

"So have we," Rose said firmly.

Bethany nearly grinned, despite the seriousness of the matter. Rose could be surprisingly stubborn.

"Another day or two won't matter in the grand scheme of things," Rose said. "You'll just have to sit tight. You're welcome to help with the frolic. You can stay here, at Eagle Hill."

"Frolic? Under the circumstances, that hardly seems like an appropriate use of time."

Rose's face softened into a faint smile. "It means a work party."

Allen Turner rubbed his forehead. "This is highly unorthodox."

"You have our word, Mr. Turner. We will leave with you on Monday morning."

"Do any of you have an idea where Hertzler might be?" Allen Turner asked. "Favorite places? People tend to do predictable things even when they're in trouble, maybe even more so then."

Tobe shook his head. "Jake won't do anything predictable."

"True, but it's also true that an animal run aground usually finds a way to reproduce the familiar." Allen Turner turned to Bethany. "How did you contact him when he was in Stoney Ridge?"

"I had his cell phone number. I still have it."

Allen Turner's eyebrows shot up. "Well, why didn't you say so in the first place? We might be able to trace his location."

"His phone isn't on very often," Bethany said. "Usually, I just left messages for him."

Allen Turner turned over his yellow pad of paper to a fresh page. "That's because he knows to keep it off so it can't be located. And if he's smart enough to take the battery out, we can't trace calls at all."

"Jake is freakishly smart," Bethany said.

Tobe scratched his chin. "How can a cell phone be traced?"

"Mobile phones work by hopping from one tower to another. As you drive out of one range, you hook onto another. Each of these towers have a certain range, and the cellular provider can use triangulation and calculate the time it takes for the signal to get from the tower to your phone and back to calculate distance from that point." Allen Turner tapped his pencil on his pad of paper. "So do you have the number?"

"It's up in my room. I'll go get it." As Bethany passed the front door, she saw Geena Spencer come up the steps with her breakfast tray. She hurried to open the door to let her in. "I forgot all about your tray."

"No problem. I'm heading into town so I thought I'd drop it off." Geena handed the tray to Bethany, then looked quickly around the table. Her smile faded at the sight of Allen Turner. She backed up against the pistachio-colored wall, a look of astonishment on her face.

Allen Turner stared at her for a long moment. Then the craggy lines of his face softened in a smile. "Hello, Geena. Long time no see."

Of all the people in all the world over, Geena thought, as she made a hurried return to her guest flat, she would not have expected to find Allen Turner on an Amish farm. She hadn't seen him in years and years, not since the day she had told him she wouldn't marry him.

No—that was only part of it. She wouldn't give up the ministry for him. That was what he wanted from her and it was more than she could give him. She had hoped that Allen would reconsider and discover that he couldn't live without her, but that wasn't the way he was wired. He loved her but wasn't willing to share her with a church. She loved him but wasn't willing to give up the ministry for him. And so they parted ways.

A year or so later, news trickled to Geena that Allen had married. It was for the best, she knew, and she had prayed for Allen and his bride to be blessed. But she'd never gotten over feeling a bit of a sting whenever she thought of Allen.

At that moment the subject of her thoughts knocked on the guest flat door.

"Do you mind if I come in for a moment?" Allen said as she opened the door. He was big, blond, and had the kind of angular face that some might find handsome. She did. The added lines in that virile face had only given him character. His was the kind of presence that filled a room. "I'm going to be staying up in the farmhouse for a few nights. Three, to be exact."

"Did they invite you?"

"Sort of." He wiped the back of his neck with a handkerchief. "This heat wave is really something. No air-conditioning anywhere."

"It's an Amish farm, in case you hadn't noticed."

He grinned. "I did, in fact. Geena, I'd like to ask you a few questions."

She raised a palm toward the sofa. "Well, then, why don't you sit down." She sat across from him in a chair. "I take it this is legal business?"

He nodded.

"I don't know anything, if that's what you're wondering. I've only been here a week and a half."

Allen leaned back and raised an arm against the top of the sofa. "What brings you here, of all places?"

"Someone in my church gave me a gift certificate and I finally had time to use it. The inn has been booked up for months, but this heat wave brought some cancellations. So . . . I was in luck. At least until the heat wave breaks, anyway."

"It is hot. I'll never take air-conditioning for granted." He picked up a magazine and started to fan himself. "So, have you been able to get to know the Schrock family? The Amish tend to be utterly private people."

"They've been very welcoming to me. Very pleasant. I've gotten to know Bethany, in particular. She's the oldest daughter."

"Has anyone mentioned a fellow named Jake Hertzler to you?"

"No. And Allen, even if she did, I would consider it to be a confidence."

He nodded. "The privileges of the priesthood."

She bristled. How strange. Twenty years had passed and they were automatically in the roles they had left behind. She stood. "If there's nothing else, I have an errand to run in town."

"Wait, Geena. I'm sorry. I didn't mean that the way it sounded. Really.

It was a careless comment. I just meant it as it was—you have the right to hold confidences. Please, sit down. I'd like to catch up with you."

She slowly sat down again. "There's nothing much to say."

"Are you still working at the church in Ardmore?"

How did he know where she was working? "I'm . . . in between jobs right now."

"Is that why you're hiding out here, on a remote Amish farm?"

*Okay. That was enough probing.* She glanced at her watch. "I really need to head into town to get an errand done." That wasn't entirely an untruth. She had planned to go to the Sweet Tooth Bakery where she could get wi-fi and update her résumé on her laptop. And get a cinnamon roll. "If you'll excuse me, Allen." She went to the door to open it.

He rose and walked to the door. "Maybe I'll see you tomorrow."

"I don't think so. I'm going to help the Amish build a community garden tomorrow."

He smiled. "So am I. Wherever Tobe Schrock is, there I will be. See you tomorrow, Geena."

# 11

On the day of the work frolic, Jimmy Fisher came to Eagle Hill just after breakfast to pick up Bethany. She was waiting on the porch step, shielding her eyes from the bright sunlight that bleached the blue right out of the sky. "Looks like another scorcher."

"Not hardly," he said, drawing out the words teasing and lazy. "Won't be truly hot until the water in the creek gets to boiling." He handed her some drawings. "Last night, I figured out how much lumber we had and drew up some plans for the garden plots. See what you think."

She looked over his detailed sketches. "Why . . . they're excellent. Jimmy, you did a fine job."

He shrugged, as if it was nothing, but she knew it wasn't. He must have spent hours laboring over those plans. And then there was the recruiting he had done to talk dozens of people into volunteering a few hours for the community garden, despite the week's record heat. She handed the sketches back to Jimmy. "Why are you doing all this?"

He looked at her as if she might be sun-touched, then shook his head. "How could anyone in their right mind refuse an opportunity to spend a day slaving like a dog in ninety-five-degree weather with one hundred percent humidity?"

She lifted her chin and tried not to grin. "Excellent point."

By eight o'clock, dozens of Amish had arrived and stood in a large clump, under the shade of the Grange Hall roof, listening to Jimmy Fisher explain how the garden plots would be laid out. By midday they would all be sweltering beneath a blanket of gummy, heavy air. And yet, the heat hadn't stopped anyone from coming.

As Jimmy spoke, Galen stood with his arms folded, until Bethany saw him gesture to someone in the crowd. Then she spied her two brothers, sneaking through the rows of people, tiptoeing with exaggerated silence toward the platter of day-old pastries from the Sweet Tooth Bakery. Galen shook his head. They halted, making gestures of protest. He pulled his brows together and pointed to the edge of the crowd, far from the table of snacks. Deflated, they slunk away.

Jimmy had organized the day quite efficiently. Within minutes he started a group of men measuring and building raised wooden beds. Young boys were given the task of wheeling in barrows of topsoil and dumping them into the beds. Clumps of girls and women planted the vegetable starts that Amos Lapp had donated. Hank Lapp pounded in small wooden placards in front of each one, to identify whose garden plot was whose.

Allen Turner, the SEC lawyer who was investigating Tobe, worked alongside the Schrock family. For a lawyer, he was surprisingly capable with a saw and hammer. But he was never far from Tobe who was never far from Naomi. Bethany knew Allen Turner didn't want to let Tobe out of his sight—the man was sleeping on the lumpy couch in their living room, which made Mammi Vera furious. But he didn't let Mammi Vera's cold stares bother him. He seemed to Bethany like a man on a mission and that mission was Tobe. Or maybe, in the end, it was Jake Hertzler.

But it was Geena who impressed Bethany the most. She had a pleasant way of getting everyone involved in a task. No one was left out, especially children.

Despite everything that weighed at the back of her mind, Bethany felt it was quite an astonishingly wonderful morning.

After a simple lunch of ham-and-cheese sandwiches had been served by the sisters of the Sisters' House, most of the Amish families went home. The bulk of the work had been done. All who remained were those who wanted to grow and manage a garden plot. Geena had heard about the community of the Amish, but seeing it up close and personal—it was something to behold. They arrived early and slipped seamlessly into a role, as if they all knew where they fit best.

To Geena, it felt like watching Paul's words in action from his letter to the Romans: "We have different gifts, according to the grace given to each of us. If your gift is prophesying, then prophesy in accordance with your faith; if it is serving, then serve; if it is teaching, then teach; if it is to encourage, then give encouragement; if it is giving, then give generously; if it is to lead, do it diligently; if it is to show mercy, do it cheerfully." Watching Bethany, Jimmy Fisher, Galen King, Amos Lapp, Hank Lapp, Rose Schrock, and Naomi King spread out among the newly built plots and teach people how to care for the gardens . . . Geena went suddenly all soft inside with choking that was so close to tears. Every church in the world, she supposed, had a little knot at its solid center. The goodness, the simple honest goodness in some people!

Geena knelt by the Grange Hall garden plot, gloves on her hands, looking at the soft open space with fierce intent. She picked up a handful of dirt, smelling the heady dampness of it. With her spade, she made a row and tucked some pea starts into the dirt every few inches, then patted the earth around each little start. Sammy and his dog Chase appeared at her side.

She held up a handful for him to examine. "This is good earth," she told Sammy. "See how dark it is?"

He nodded seriously, and smelled it when she did, his big eyes always taking everything in. The sun sparkled over the top of his head. "I still don't like peas, though."

"Maybe you'll like them better when they're fresh and you pick them yourself."

Sammy looked unconvinced, then heard Luke call to him, and he ran off, his dog loping at his heels.

"How are you doing?"

Geena had to squint to look up at Allen, and he noticed and moved around to the other side. "Sorry about that."

"Doing fine, thank you. Getting the peas in on this end. That end will be tomatoes. Maybe pumpkins in the middle, where their vines can sprawl over the edges." She picked up a packet of pumpkin seeds and shook it.

The big seeds rattled inside. "Might be a little late to plant these, but we'll give them a try."

"You've done this before, I think." His blue eyes had the gleam of a blue pearly marble she'd had as a child. Such clear eyes seemed as if they could see too much. "Are you going to go back? To the ministry?"

"Of course. I . . . just have to figure some things out." How could he possibly understand how deep her calling to ministry went? To her very marrow.

"It must be hard to be a person of God. When you were trying to eat lunch, I saw that you kept getting interrupted by people who wanted a word with you."

Just one or two. Maybe three. Now that she thought about it, she hadn't had a chance to finish her lunch. No wonder she was still hungry.

"It brought up memories," Allen said. "I remember how mothers always wanted to talk to you, anytime they were worried about something. Doesn't it drive you crazy, people needing you constantly like that?"

Geena thought, with longing, of the way children, teens, even parents from her church would look in her direction when she arrived at their home, or to the waiting room of a hospital, or once at a county jail. When they realized she had come to help them, their upturned faces were expectant, hopeful, grateful. "No." She took a breath. "I love it. I love being needed."

"I guess that's the nature of your job, isn't it?"

Geena didn't know how to answer him.

"You seem happy, Geena. Really happy."

"I am." And she was. Even if, at the moment, she was a youth pastor without a church, she was happy. She knew who she was and what her purpose was.

"You're very lucky." He strolled off before she could say another word.

Geena watched him walk through the middle of the lot, looking at all of the garden plots, smiling at the other gardeners, who smiled back. The sound of happy voices and laughter filled the air. Children chased one another through the pathways between plots, and a few dogs trotted along behind them, the Schrocks' golden retriever Chase among them. He spied Geena and came loping toward her, tongue lolling.

"You look thirsty, ol' boy. C'mon, let's find some water for you, shall we?"

In the kitchen, she found a dented, old stainless steel bowl and carried it outside. She filled the bowl and put it down in the shade and whistled for Chase, who came racing and dove into the water with eager slurping.

Geena went back inside the Grange Hall to wash her hands. A little sunburn gave her cheekbones some color. She took a moment to try to tame her hair and wash the dirt streaks off her face. Even with a big garden hat on, the sun had kissed her. She looked rested and healthy.

Thinking of how lovely Bethany looked even after hours of hard work, she peered into the mirror, wishing she had fuller lips or a bit more chest, or darker eyelashes, or some extraordinary feature, but she was honest with herself. Her eyes were an ordinary brown, her mousy brown hair too frizzy, her cheekbones too broad to ever be considered pretty.

She plucked a few more curls from her ponytail, let them frame her face a little, fall down her neck. Better.

In the mid-afternoon, Bethany sank down at the picnic table under the shade of the Grange Hall roof, took off her gloves, and slapped the dirt from them. Her hands were shaking and she realized she hadn't stopped to eat since breakfast. Geena walked over and brought her a sandwich and a glass of sweet, cool lemonade—just what she needed.

"Look at this," Bethany said, satisfied. "Look what you started, Geena. It was your idea to turn a crummy old vacant lot into a garden." Each plot had small vegetables growing in it: tomatoes, carrots, radishes, lettuce, zucchinis, cucumbers, beans, peas, onions, eggplants, corn shoots. It wouldn't be long at all before those plants started to sprawl, covering up the entire beds with thick green vines and leaves.

"It is beautiful," Geena said, gazing around the garden. "But an idea is one thing. Doing it is something else. This community garden was everyone's doing."

"Mostly Jimmy Fisher, I think. He's spent a lot of time on this." Bethany's eyes had often sought Jimmy out and her chest tightened with a sweet longing. He seemed to be everywhere at once, handing people tools, wheeling in a barrow full of dirt, carrying boxes of Amos's plant starts, scooping up the leftover messes.

Her gaze followed Jimmy as he attached a hose to a spigot at the back of the Grange. Luke and Sammy sneaked up from behind to jump on him, but he must have heard or sensed the imminent attack. He spun around, hosing them down with water. The boys screamed and laughed. They adored Jimmy. He was always surprising people, Jimmy was. Bethany, mostly.

Speaking of surprises, Bethany's little sister seemed to be filled with them. She watched Mim walk slowly along the garden path with Ella, holding the old woman's elbow to keep her from falling. Mim had become Ella's keeper. She shadowed her, helping her along, answering questions, making sure she stayed safe. Ella's safety was a growing concern. But who would have thought Mim would become someone's caregiver? She had to be asked to spend time with Mammi Vera.

There was more to Mim than Bethany had thought—or maybe she just hadn't noticed. Mim didn't know this, but Bethany had started to read the Mrs. Miracle letters that were published in the *Stoney Ridge Times*. Not always, but often, Mrs. Miracle revealed a surprising depth, a startling wisdom. Of course, Bethany wouldn't share that thought with Mim, but she was impressed.

Then Bethany's gaze traveled to a group of wayward girls from the Group Home, clumped together, watching everyone else work. "What do you think those girls are thinking about?"

Geena turned to see. She sighed. "They probably haven't seen people work together like this before. And I think they're watching families work together and feeling great self-pity. Their version of family is nothing like this."

"We're doing this for them, but they won't help." They were invited to pitch in—Bethany had overheard as Geena asked them. And a few seemed willing, until that red-haired girl said no and the rest of them followed her lead. They wouldn't lift a finger to help today, though they did eat lunch when offered.

The red-haired girl was the obvious ringleader. There was something about her that irritated Bethany. She had a permanent look of contempt on her face. Under her breath, Bethany muttered, "That red-haired girl shouldn't be allowed to intimidate the other girls."

"True, but more importantly, why does she feel the need to?" Geena turned around to face Bethany. "Until we walk in someone's shoes, we really can't judge what makes them do the things they do." She patted Bethany's hand. "The garden is the first step toward making a difference in those girls' lives. But the garden needs time to grow and we need to allow God time to work in the girls' hearts."

Time. Bethany had never been one for patience. "Do you know anything about that girl?"

"Her name is Rusty but I don't know anything else about her." Geena slapped her hands on her thighs. "I'm going to find out." She walked over and sat on the ground next to the clump of girls.

Bethany's curiosity about Geena Spencer continued to grow and grow. She was easy to talk to and didn't seem anything like a lady preacher, not that Bethany knew what a lady preacher should be like.

"Anything left that's sweet to eat?"

Bethany turned to see Jimmy Fisher leaning against a support post that held up the Grange Hall roof, one booted foot crossed over the other, his hat dangling from his fingers, gazing at her with an inscrutable look. Flustered, she spied a dish at the end of the row. "One piece of Rose's famous blueberry buckle is left. You want it?"

"Split it with me?"

"I'm already full," she said, leaning over to scoop up the lone square of cake. She put it on his plate. He'd just washed up, for the ends of his hair dripped water and he smelled of Ivory soap. "You've worked hard on this project. Everyone appreciates it."

"Everyone?"

She blushed. "I appreciate it." She looked from his eyes up to the sky, then back to his eyes again, judging which were bluer. His eyes were definitely bluer than the sky.

He leaned toward her, though he was careful not to touch her, cautious about who might be watching them. "So, what do you say about tomorrow night? Will you let me take you home from the singing?"

For one little moment, that vine twined around them again, binding them together as he looked at her. His blue, blue eyes twinkled, but there was also something solid and real there.

"Jimmy! Oh Jimmy Fisher!"

He whirled his head around. And there was Katie Zook, waving to him to come help her carry a tray of seedlings.

Bethany shook her head in disbelief. *That* girl surely needed a copy of *A Young Woman's Guide to Virtue.*

"Be there in a minute." He turned back to Bethany, but it was too late. She'd had enough and was already brushing past him to head into the Grange Hall to help Sylvia with lunch dishes.

Sunday morning was quiet at Eagle Hill. Geena had watched the Schrock family pile into a buggy and head off to church. Last evening, Rose had brought fresh sun-dried towels down to Geena and said that another inn reservation had been canceled due to the heat wave, so she would be able to stay two more nights in the guest flat. She was thrilled. She had no reason to return home. Not yet.

Geena planned to go to church in town later in the morning, after a hike. As she stepped out into the light from the coolness of the guest flat, the sun fell on her skin like a skillet, heavy and hot. She paused for a moment, closing her eyes, letting the early morning heat sink deep into her bones. Unlike most people, she loved warm weather. Maybe she should look for a youth pastor position in Florida or Arizona. Or Texas?

She spotted Allen, leaning against a fence, sipping coffee, and walked over to join him. "You're up early."

"They're early risers, these Amish folk." In the freshness of the morning, the weariness in his face was erased, and she saw only the kindness. He had always been kind.

"I'm a little surprised you let Tobe out of your sight for the morning. I figured you'd accompany him to church."

"Three hours in a sweltering barn, listening to preachers in a foreign tongue—I figured Tobe was pretty safe for the time being."

Geena grinned. "Well, then, want to go hiking? Then we can go to church."

"Hike? Church?" He looked at her as if she'd suggested bird watching. "I suppose so." He tossed the rest of the coffee on the ground and set the mug on a fence post. He unfolded the stems of his sunglasses, the motion deliberate, and slipped them on. They walked side by side for a few hundred yards until they reached a part of the trail that required single file. He let her take the lead. "I was watching you yesterday. You have a real gift for ministry."

"I miss it," she said honestly.

"So why aren't you . . . ," he paused, searching for the right word, "ministering?"

"It's a long story."

"I have time."

She picked up her pace. "From what I remember, you were always too busy with work to listen."

"From what I remember, you were always talking to other people, not to me."

She spun around, facing him off. "That's not fair. That's what being a good minister is all about. Being available to others."

His face became gentle. "I know that. And you were—you are a good minister."

The fight drained out of her. "And you were—are a good attorney."

"Truce?" He held out his hand to her.

She looked down at it, remembering how big and strong his hands were. Not the kind of hands that belonged to a pencil pusher. It was a hand she had loved once, a hand she had trusted. She reached out and shook it. "Truce."

They started up the hill again, Allen trailing behind Geena. "So you never married."

She shook her head. "I guess I'm married to my work." She glanced back. "I think I heard that you married."

"My wife's name was Alyssa. We were very happy."

Geena felt a strange swirl of jealousy. Where did *that* come from?

"Until she left me."

She stopped and made a sharp about-face. "I'm sorry, Allen." She truly was. Divorce was a terrible thing. "Do you have children?"

"One. A son. He's thirteen now."

"Do you see much of him?"

"I do. We share custody." He was huffing and puffing and his face was turning red. Clearly, the man didn't exercise much. "So why aren't you ministering right now?"

She went ahead of him to reach the top. "I told you. I have a few things to figure out right now," she tossed over her shoulder.

"So you're adrift? That doesn't sound like the Geena I remember."

At the top of the hill now, she ignored him and looked down over Eagle Hill. The pastoral scene took her breath away. She sat down on a rock and he fell beside her, breathing heavily. Slowly, she tipped her head back and let herself be drawn up, up, up into the bright morning sky, the endless and empty sky.

"A body could get lost up there if she isn't careful."

She ducked her head, suddenly shy, aware he was watching her. Down below, the sheep were grazing, milled in a bunch. Just then one of them startled at something, jumping stiff-legged and sideways, and landing with a loud bleat. It spooked the rest of them so they scattered in the pasture.

Geena and Allen laughed at the sight of the silly sheep, and their laughter—his mellow and deep, hers light and airy—wove together. A killdeer trilled sweetly and a chickadee burbled as the wind gently swayed the tops of the trees. "Isn't it lovely?" She turned to face him and caught the look on his face. He stared at her with such intensity that she could almost feel it, like a warm gust of breath on her face.

"You didn't answer my question, Geena. Why are you drifting?"

*Hmmm* . . . she thought. *Only you would ask that question.* "Allen, are you ever *not* a lawyer?"

He laughed, eyes crinkling at the corners. "Funny you should ask. I'm giving some thought to leaving the SEC. My son needs more of my time. He's a good kid, but when you're thirteen . . ."

"The world revolves around your friends."

"That's true. Exactly right. You always did have a knack for understanding kids."

"You get a lot of experience when you're in youth ministry." She stretched her legs out and put one ankle on top of the other. "So what will you do if you're not an SEC lawyer?"

"Not sure yet. I need to finish up this last case involving Schrock Investments."

"This case seems awfully important to you."

"It is." His gaze shifted down to the quiet farmhouse. "A number of innocent people have been hurt. I'm going to see this through."

She stared at his profile, a face that she had once memorized. "It seems more than that. It seems . . . like there's something personal for you in this case."

He kept his gaze on the sheep, far below them, as if watching them eat was the most fascinating thing in the world. "Anything personal would be a conflict of interest."

Now *that* sounded like the Allen she knew. He loved the law like she loved the church. But something about the determination in his voice seemed a little unusual to her. "Unless the SEC wasn't aware of why it was so personal to you."

He turned abruptly back to her, lifting his eyebrows in surprise. "So, Geena . . . you never answered a question I have tried to ask you several times and still am waiting for the answer. Why are you hiding on an Amish farm?"

*Ah, changing the subject. A diversion tactic.* "I'm not . . . hiding. I'm just taking a breather."

"Yesterday, you were really in your element."

"What do you mean?"

"You were just tireless, and everybody looked to you for help and advice."

"It's funny how a day like yesterday just"—she made a circle in front of her heart—"pulls me in. Everybody working together for a common good. A day like yesterday makes me feel like I'm a much better version of myself." Before she could stop them, words came pouring out of her mouth. "But I love being a youth pastor. I love working for a church, being part of a whole." Below, the wooly sheep had moved under the canopy of a weeping willow. "I love church, period."

"So why aren't you working?"

She sighed. He wasn't going to let this go. So like the Allen she remembered. "My church fired me. They felt I didn't have the preaching skills, not enough charisma, to match their plans for growth and development. They hired me with expectations to triple the size of the youth group within a year's time." She tossed a pebble against a tree. "Obviously, it didn't."

He wiped his forehead and neck with his handkerchief. "Sounds more like a business plan."

She laughed softly. "Sometimes, it did seem that way."

"So you're 'in between' youth pastoring."

"I miss my work," she said. "I don't know who I am without it."

"Do you have any plans?"

"Not yet." She spoke her own truth. "I have absolutely no idea of where I'll go next. Or what I'll do."

"You say that like it's a bad thing."

"Well, it is. And please don't give me any platitudes. You know it's a difficult question."

"It is that and I don't have the answer for you."

She closed her eyes. "I have to figure this out."

"Yup, you do."

"It's just that . . . I do feel called to be a youth minister."

"Yeah, sure, I understand that. But not called to be perfect."

# 12

Bethany would never have agreed to go to the singing had Tobe not pleaded with her. He just wanted an excuse to shake off Allen Turner for the evening. She was in no mood to listen to girls' silly chatter and she still was on the fence about going home with Jimmy Fisher. It wasn't that she didn't think he was something special, but that he thought he was something special, and so did most every girl in Stoney Ridge.

Yesterday, she nearly allowed herself to be swept away by Jimmy Fisher's considerable charms. His leadership at the work frolic was impressive—many commented on it. Somehow, in his lighthearted way, he had the whole thing organized like a well-run clock. Yes, she was nearly caught under his spell, but stopped herself just in time. One thing for sure, she wasn't in the market for a boyfriend. Not now, maybe not ever again.

Tobe hitched up the buggy and then hurried next door to get Naomi while Bethany waited in the backseat. As Tobe and Naomi crossed the yard, Bethany was startled by how comfortable they were with each other—heads close together, laughing over something.

Then Naomi remembered Bethany as they reached the buggy, glanced at her, and did a double take. "What's wrong?"

"Why does everybody keep asking me that?" Bethany said, sounding a little more snappish than she intended to.

Naomi looked concerned. "You have dark circles under your eyes."

"Nothing is wrong. I'm just tired."

Tobe and Naomi exchanged a glance. "She's been touchy all day," Tobe said.

Bethany shrugged. "It's the heat. It's getting to me."

"Oh, I can understand that," Naomi said. "This morning I took a stick of butter out of the fridge and it melted on the way to the countertop."

Bethany relaxed. Naomi was a good friend.

It wasn't the heat that was bothering Bethany. She had woken in the night with her heart racing like a drum, gasping for breath. In her dream, she was under water, down, down, down, bubbles coming up all around her. And then there were two hands hauling her up out of the water. She was shivering violently, crying. Crying. Someone held her against her chest. Someone in blue. "I've got you. I've got you. Don't be afraid. You're safe."

She couldn't fall back to sleep for hours. What was happening to her?

She headed to the barn where the singing would take place and where the girls had already gathered, expecting Naomi to follow her. At the barn door, she turned back and saw Naomi and Tobe, still standing by the buggy. Naomi was laughing at something Tobe had said, looking all bright and sparkly as she gazed at him. *Oh Naomi,* Bethany thought, feeling sorry for her gentle friend. *Be careful. I love my brother dearly but he'll just break your heart. That's what men do best.*

In the cool of the barn, Bethany sat at the end of a long table on the girls' side. On the boys' side, she was surprised to see Danny Riehl, Mim's friend, laughing with the other boys and having himself a grand time. She asked the girl sitting next to her why Danny was here and was told he had just turned sixteen. Old enough to attend youth groups.

If Mim knew Danny were here, having so much fun without her, it would make her sad. Mim tried so hard to hide her interest in Danny Riehl. Bethany knew, though. Where had Mim's sudden passion for astronomy come from? It didn't take a genius to put two and two together. But she kept Mim's secret and didn't tell Rose about the stargazing on moonless nights. She might not be the most patient and understanding sister, but who was she to point fingers about boyfriends?

She wondered if she should tell Mim that Danny was here. After giving it some thought, she decided to leave it alone. After all, Danny wasn't doing anything wrong. But he sure was having a good time. He sure was.

Someone announced the first song and everyone started to sing. Now this—*this* was worth coming for. The sounds of harmony were pure heaven to Bethany. In church, they only sang the old hymns, slow and sad, in one voice, no harmony lest any one stand out. But at singings, they could sing different parts and Bethany loved it.

She watched as the girls passed around a glass or two of water, filled from the pitcher that stood in the middle of the long table. On the other side, the boys also had some water glasses to share. A little later they passed a saltshaker around the table. Anyone who was beginning to get hoarse from singing sprinkled a little into the palm of his hand and licked it, like a cow at a salt lick. The first time Bethany had seen that, she thought it was disgusting. Now, it seemed perfectly normal.

Two hours of hymn singing later, one of the boys announced the closing hymn and Bethany realized she had forgotten to tell Tobe they needed to leave right away. Jimmy had glanced at her once or twice and wiggled those dark eyebrows, but she tried to ignore him. She didn't want to give him any reason to think he had her in his pocket. That would have been the worst thing for a boy like Jimmy. He was already far too self-confident.

Where was Tobe, anyway? In fact, where was Naomi?

During the closing hymn, she slipped out of the barn. Tobe and Naomi and the buggy were gone. *Shootfire!*

Bethany knew she could wait for Jimmy to give her a ride home, but she decided against it. She kept her chin tucked to her chest and walked down the driveway quickly, hoping no one would notice she had left.

She almost made it.

"Hey! Hey, Bethany!" Jimmy called to her from the top of the long driveway.

For a moment, Bethany thought about breaking into a run, pretending she hadn't heard him, but then she thought twice. That was a pretty stupid plan. She took a deep breath, let it out, and reminded herself that she was not interested in getting tangled up with another charming fellow. Why was she always falling for the wrong type? Surely something was seriously wrong with her. She would not encourage him, but she could be friendly without being friends. It was just a matter of being polite and keeping her distance.

She pasted a smile on her face and turned around. "Hi, Jimmy."

He was puffing. He'd run down the driveway to catch her. "I thought I was going to give you a ride home. What do you say?"

"Some other time. I just want to be alone tonight." That was sort of true. With everything that was on her mind lately, she wasn't good company. "Jimmy—you and me—I just don't think it would be a good idea."

That part was the absolute truth.

"Look at me, Bethany."

She lifted her head.

"I know you think I'm just playing. But I'm playing for keeps."

And then Jimmy was gone, striding away from her and toward the buggy. The cant of his shoulders made Bethany feel suddenly cold, as if summer had turned to winter in the blink of an eye, though it was a humid and sticky evening. She took in everything as he swung onto the seat: his muscled forearms clutching the reins, his cheeks, clean-shaven in the morning, now shadowed, his gaze, set resolutely ahead. He drove the buggy right up to her. "Hop in."

*Shootfire! There he goes, telling me what to do again.* Just as she was feeling a little softhearted toward him, he went and ruined it all.

"Bethany, Eagle Hill is over five miles away and your brother left with Naomi hours ago."

"Well, fine," she said as she let him help her up. "But this doesn't mean a thing, Jimmy Fisher."

He slapped the horse's reins to get it moving. The horse snorted and broke into a trot. The buggy creaked and rumbled and clattered over the wooden bridge that spanned a small creek at the bottom of the driveway. Tenderly, Jimmy nudged her shoulder. "You okay?"

She looked up at the brilliant stars in the moonless sky. "I'm fine. Never better."

They weren't far down the road when he pulled up on the reins and turned the buggy to the side of the road. "You want to tell me what's bothering you lately?"

She turned toward him. "What makes you think something's bothering me?"

"Let's see . . . you're jumpier than usual, prickly as a cactus pear, you look like you haven't had a good night's sleep in a while—"

"Enough. I get your point." Why did he have to be so good-looking? She was touched by his concern, despite herself. Bethany hesitated. "Look, Jimmy, there's a lot on my mind right now and I need to get a few things figured out."

"Like what?"

"You wouldn't understand. It's not the kind of thing you're accustomed to."

"There you go again. Thinking that I'm just a one-trick pony. Try me, Bethany. I'd like to help you, even though you're too stubborn to accept it." Jimmy reached out to touch her hand and she nearly jumped out the window. He turned in the seat. "When are you going to realize how much I care about you?"

"Me and everyone else in Stoney Ridge who wears a dress. Naomi says you go through girls like potato chips."

"She said that? How insulting." Though he didn't seem a bit insulted.

She looked out the window. "The last time I let someone affect me . . . well . . . it was . . . Jake Hertzler."

Jimmy groaned. "I thought he was ancient history."

"He is." She glanced at him. "I'm not the right one for you, Jimmy."

He crossed his arms over his chest defensively. "Wow. That's a pretty smooth brush-off. What comes next? Are you going to tell me you just want to be friends? I'm not playing games with you, Bethany. Maybe you're the one playing games."

She wasn't going to take that from anybody. She stood her ground. "That's not fair, Jimmy. You've done a lot for me, but I never asked you for anything. I've been trying to keep our relationship friendly rather than romantic."

"I see," he said sharply. "Well, you can go on pretending there's no spark between us, but we both know it isn't true. Challenges don't scare me. They just make me more determined." Their gazes met and lingered, then parted. He gathered up the reins and started them on their way again. Finally, in a kinder voice, he said, "Bethany, whatever it is that's troubling you, just remember you're a lot stronger than you think you are. Whenever you figure things out, I'll be here, waiting for you. I'm not going anywhere. Not going after anyone else, either." He grinned in that slow, charming way that made her heart pound. "I don't even like potato chips."

———◦ ◊ ◦———

Despite herself, as Naomi watched Tobe drive the buggy away, her heart swelled with hope. Maybe, just maybe, her dream was going to come true.

It was a dream that began years ago, when Naomi was eight and Tobe was twelve. He and Bethany had spent a few weeks of the summer visiting their grandmother and the three of them played together each day, as soon as their chores were done. They rode ponies over to Blue Lake Pond, picnicked on the shore, hiked up in the hills. Those summer visits were happy memories for Naomi.

But it was three summers later that things drastically changed between Naomi and Tobe—at least the way she felt about him. Her mother had died during the winter. Just when school was out for the year, her father had been badly hurt in an accident with a horse. He lingered for over a week, then died suddenly of complications. Everyone had treated Naomi with kid gloves, assuring her that her father would be all right, that he would rally.

All but Tobe.

She had asked him if he thought her father would survive and he had said no, he didn't think so. He said he hoped he was wrong, but to get prepared, just in case. It was the day of her father's funeral that Naomi experienced her first migraine. She couldn't even attend the service for her father. She remained in her darkened bedroom, with curtains drawn because the light hurt her eyes so much.

Tobe shimmied up the rose trellis and onto the roof and knocked on her window to keep her company while the service was going on. He sat on the floor, back against the wall, and read to her, using a small flashlight to see by. The sound of his soothing, calm voice eased the pounding in her head. By the time the worst of the headache had passed, Naomi was thoroughly smitten.

By the age of fourteen, she was crazy about Tobe.

By sixteen, she was head over heels in love. Loving Tobe was as familiar to her as breathing.

But Tobe Schrock had a reputation, even as a teenager, even though he only came to Stoney Ridge in the summers when he visited his grandmother. Naomi wasn't sure how much of his reputation was deserved and how much was inflated, but all her friends warned each other about falling for Tobe Schrock. He was too good-looking, they said. He was unreliable.

Lazy as a man could be, her brother Galen often noted. So Naomi kept silent her feelings for Tobe, but she soaked up every mention of his name over at Eagle Hill. His absence hurt her the way it did Rose and Vera and Bethany, so much so that she tried to talk herself out of love with him. She told herself he would never return.

Until this week, when he did return.

Seeing him in the kitchen of Eagle Hill that first night, looking and acting like he'd never left, ruined her resolve to stop loving him. Instead, images rolled in her mind, unsummoned, memories of growing up together. She knew every inch of that beautiful face, the scar across his left cheekbone that he'd received when he and a friend were skipping rocks at Blue Lake Pond and his friend threw a wild pitch that hit Tobe in the face. The heavy dark brows that could signal wrath or disapproval or amusement with the slightest shifts; the prominent eyetooth.

A young Tobe running through the privet, calling for her to come out. Tobe as he grew into a young man, broad shouldered and handsome. Tobe leaning against a wall, watching Naomi struggle to fasten the shafts to the buggy, muscled arms crossed over his chest, wanting to help but holding back because he knew she wanted to do it herself; of Tobe laughing, and frowning, and listening, and telling her the truth no matter what, and the way she felt when he entered a room. She could never stop smiling whenever Tobe was around, though she knew she didn't have the same effect on him.

Until this time, coming home, when Tobe smiled back at Naomi. For the last few days, he courted her carefully, cautious to avoid Galen. She had quietly followed him up to Blue Lake Pond one afternoon, stumbling on him sitting on a log as if she was always at the pond in the afternoon. He invited her to sit down. It was awkward at first, but soon they started to talk and talk and talk. Later that night, long after midnight, he had tossed pebbles at her window until she went to see what was making that noise. She thought it was a bird and was shocked to see Tobe down below, waving to her to join him. "Come on down," he whispered. She had never dressed so quickly in her life.

Each night after that first one, Tobe would toss pebbles at her window and Naomi would hurry down. They walked in the moonlight, up the ridge, to connect to a shortcut to Blue Lake Pond that only he knew about.

Tonight was one of those nights bright with untold numbers of stars. After Bethany left to go to the barn for the singing, Tobe quietly asked Naomi if she would mind skipping the singing and go for a ride. She jumped back in the buggy, quick as a whip, before he could change his mind. They drove to Blue Lake Pond and sat on their favorite log. It was a windless night and the water was so still and calm it looked like a mirror, reflecting the stars.

Naomi stared at it so long that Tobe asked what she was thinking. "The stars are almost like a pattern," she said, pointing to the water. "Can you see it? I'm wondering if I could design a quilt top to match it."

Tobe smiled. "Why do you like to quilt so much?"

It was a question no one had ever asked her before and yet it was such an important one. "To me," she said, "piecing a quilt top seems to be evidence of how God works in this world."

He tilted his head at her in that adorable way he had, his way of encouraging her to keep talking.

"I take all these scraps and leftovers and odds and ends, and turn them into something beautiful. Something useful and purposeful. It just seems like that's what God is always doing, all around us. Taking our jumble of mess and transforming it into something wondrous."

Tobe stared at her for a long, long time. And then he started to confide in her all he knew about Schrock Investments and all he had seen and heard. Every detail.

She listened carefully, trying to understand, careful not to judge, though she felt shocked by what he revealed. His eyes were so weary, so sad. Eyes too old for such a young face. Naomi's heart broke for him.

"I'm leaving in the morning with the SEC lawyer," he said after he finished the long, sad tale. "I don't know what's ahead for me."

The news of Tobe's departure wasn't a surprise for Naomi. Bethany had told her Monday was the day and Naomi had tried to push it out of her mind. Tried not to think of having to say goodbye to him again.

He took her hands in his. "Naomi . . . I know I'm not much of a catch."

"You're the only catch I want," Naomi said eagerly and Tobe grinned in that boyish way he had. Then he reached out and drew her close to him, and kissed her. Tobe's lips were soft, but his kiss was hard, slow, almost lazy, and so assured. His arms rested at steep angles across the small of her back and the blades of her shoulders.

She melted into the circle of his arms, leaning in, lifting up, softening her mouth. For a few sweet moments, everything felt right to forget and safe to remember.

It was her very first kiss and it was perfect. Absolutely perfect.

On Sunday evening, Geena was finishing up a book an elder from her church had given to her: *Help! I've Been Asked to Preach. Don't Panic: Practical Help to Keep Your Sermon from Sinking* by Maylan Schurch. She took notes as she read, wondering if the elder thought her sermons sank or stank. A knock on the door interrupted her. "Come in."

Rose popped her head in. "Do you have a moment?"

Geena happily put away the book. "I do. Please come in."

"Do you need anything? Towels, fresh sheets, extra shampoo or toothpaste?"

"No. You've provided everything I could possibly use."

Rose held her hands behind her. She seemed ill at ease, as if she had something to say but didn't know how to say it. "It looks as if the heat wave is going to break by Tuesday."

"Oh. Oh!" Now Geena realized what Rose was trying to say. "Your reservations! I'll leave, then."

"Actually, I have a favor to ask. I'm going to Philadelphia tomorrow with Tobe and my mother-in-law. We're not really sure how long we'll be gone."

Geena was well aware that everyone was leaving in the morning. She and Allen had spent all of Sunday together, hiking, church, a brunch afterward, wandering through the small towns and shopping, then dinner together because Tobe went to a church youth gathering. Before Allen said goodbye, he asked her what she might say if he were to call her sometime. Maybe to go out for dinner. "That would depend," she told him, "on how much you can help Tobe Schrock stay out of jail."

"I'll do all I can," Allen had promised. "He's not the one we're after. I want Jake Hertzler."

There it was again. The feeling she got that there was something personal about this case for Allen. "Still," Geena said. "Promise me you'll keep Tobe out of jail."

But Allen wouldn't promise. He did say he would do his best, and if she happened upon any information that might prove useful, please call him. He gave her his business card and kissed her on the cheek. When had she last been kissed on her cheek by a man who wasn't a senior citizen? Years and years and years. It was, she couldn't deny, very nice.

But none of that pertained to Rose Schrock, standing in the middle of the guest flat living room, looking embarrassed. "Geena, I wondered . . . if you're not in a hurry to return . . ."

"I'm not."

Rose glanced up at her, a shy look on her face. "Would you be willing to move into the house and stay with my daughters? Just in case they needed extra help with the boys while they're working and managing the new guests?"

Geena was pleased to be asked. Grateful, too. She wasn't ready to go back to Philadelphia to officially start job hunting. She knew it was waiting for her and she dreaded it. "Consider it done. I'm glad that you feel comfortable asking me."

"Well, I have a confession to make. We're going to be staying at the home of someone who was our first guest at the inn. She has become a good friend. Her name is Delia Stoltz."

"Aha. Now I see." Delia Stoltz attended Geena's church. Her husband, Dr. Charles Stoltz, was new to church attendance but very vocal about his feelings that Geena should be replaced with someone who was a more dynamic preacher. "So, you're probably aware that I was fired."

Rose nodded.

"Don't feel badly. It's not a secret. I told Bethany about it." Geena grinned. "But now you can understand why I have a surfeit of spare time."

"I certainly wouldn't charge you for staying at the house. You'd be doing me a favor."

"I'm happy to be of help, Rose. In fact, I couldn't be more delighted. It's been good for me to be here."

Rose looked at the title of the book on the kitchen table. "Delia mentioned that the problem wasn't with your pastor's heart, it was with your preaching."

"That's about right." Geena rubbed her forehead. "I try so hard to preach well. I try to be just like my father—that's what everyone expects. My father is a wonderful minister. I've been trained by the very best. I prepare detailed notes and put in hours of research . . . and still, something in the delivery goes badly. I bore myself!"

Rose picked up the book and flipped through it. "I don't know much about being a minister, but one thing our preachers don't do is to use notes. They let God's Spirit guide them."

"No notes? None at all? That would have given heart attacks to my seminary professors. Sermon preparation was a major focus. It even has a fancy name: *homiletics*." She pressed her palms together. "They trained us to deliver a nice, tight sermon. Tight. Sixteen minutes long would earn you an A. Studies have found that's the attention span of the congregation."

Rose looked confused. "But how can God's Spirit lead when a minister has it all planned out?"

Geena hadn't thought of it that way. "But don't your ministers ramble and go off on bunny trails?"

"Some do. Some are long winded. But some get right to the point. Those are the ones you can tell have forgotten about themselves—they're just trying to share the word of the Lord because they love it so much. They talk from the heart." She put the book back on the table. "Maybe . . . you shouldn't try to preach like your father. Maybe you should just try to be yourself." She threw her hands up in the air. "Listen to me! What do I know about preaching?" She shook her head. "Thank you for your help this week. I'm glad you came to Eagle Hill, Geena. You've been a blessing to us."

# 13

On Monday morning, Bethany made pancakes for Sammy and Luke while Rose finished packing for the trip to Philadelphia. Allen Turner stood patiently by the open trunk of his car, waiting for suitcases to appear. Mammi Vera stood beside the car, frowning at Allen Turner, standing vigil. She didn't like him or trust him, but that was only because she thought he was creating trouble for Tobe. She couldn't understand that he was trying to help him.

Rose was bustling around the kitchen, giving Bethany and Mim last-minute instructions for the inn.

"We'll be fine, Rose," Bethany said. "Besides, as long as this heat wave continues, we're not going to get any new guests."

"The weather is supposed to cool down," Rose said. "I told Geena she could move into the house while I'm away if she'd like to stay longer."

"Mammi Vera did not like hearing that!" Mim said, grinning. "She said Mom is turning Eagle Hill into a boardinghouse."

"Allen Turner paid us for staying for the weekend," Rose said, scribbling down some instructions on a piece of paper. "He insisted." She glanced at Bethany, then stopped writing and straightened up, looking at Bethany for a long moment. "You look exhausted. Didn't you sleep well?"

"Better not ask her that," Luke said. "I told her she looked terrible and she snapped my head off."

Bethany frowned at her brother. "I'm ready for this heat wave to break."

Rose nodded. "It's supposed to rain Tuesday or Wednesday. Here's the phone number to reach me at Delia Stoltz's. Leave a message and I'll call back." She put down the pencil and looked out the window. Tobe had returned from saying goodbye to Naomi, escorted by Galen, and went to wait by the car.

Galen came into the kitchen to say goodbye. "Better get going, Rose, if you want to beat traffic." He looked at the boys wolfing down pancakes at the kitchen table. "You two, finish up with breakfast. I've got some fence repairing that's waiting on you."

The boys let out a whoop. Luke and Sammy were always glad to have something to do that involved hammering and making noise. Luke rolled up the last pancake, shoved it into his shirt pocket, and shot out the door so fast he made Bethany blink. Sammy followed, a little slower.

Rose smiled as she watched the boys run through the privet to Galen's. She turned back to Bethany and Mim. "Listen, girls, we'll try to get back to Eagle Hill as soon as we know what's going to happen to Tobe."

"Mom, do you think he'll have to go to jail?" Mim asked.

Bethany saw Rose and Galen's eyes meet over Mim's head. Rose's eyes said, *This is so complicated. How do I answer?*

Galen stepped in. "Tobe says he's telling the truth. He's confessing to any wrong he might have done. The rest is in God's hands. God's good hands."

Rose shot him a grateful look.

It was strange, that wordless communication between a man and a woman who loved each other, the silent signal of caring, the way they checked in with each other. Would Bethany ever have *that* with someone? Or was she destined to make terrible choices? Like her father did. Like Tobe still was. Maybe it was a Schrock family trait. Fixed.

A few minutes later, Bethany and Mim waved to everyone in the car as it drove down the driveway. Galen went back to his farm. Watching the car turn onto the road, Bethany stroked Chase's thick fur, trying to stamp down the worry she felt over Tobe.

"Bethany? Are you listening to me?"

She startled. She hadn't even realized Mim was still beside her. "What?"

"I said I'm going to be up in my room working on my Mrs. Miracle column. It's due for Tuesday's edition and I'm way behind because of the community garden work. You can still drop it by the newspaper office, can't you?"

"Yes, sure, I'll take care of it. By the way, I'll be gone tomorrow."

"Where are you going? I thought you had to work at the Sisters' House."

"They canceled me for tomorrow—they have the Sisters' Bee at Edith Fisher's and it makes them nervous when I'm working in the house and they're not around to supervise."

"I thought Naomi wanted you to join that quilting bee."

"I haven't decided yet. Besides, I'm going on an errand with Geena tomorrow." She hadn't actually asked Geena yet, but she was hoping it would be all right. "I'll be gone most of the day. You'll be okay, won't you?"

Mim looked a little worried. "All day? Watching Luke and Sammy all day long?" She scrunched up her face. "*Luke?* All day long? He doesn't pay me any mind."

"Galen and Jimmy can be in charge of those two." She frowned. "Don't you have a column to write?"

Mim ran up the porch steps and disappeared through the kitchen door.

Chase nudged Bethany's hand, then stood there staring up at her with a worried look in his big round eyes. She bent down to rub his ears, his favorite thing. "Try not to fret, old pal. Tobe will be home soon." But she wasn't sure of that at all. She chewed on her lip, thinking. What if Jake went free and Tobe ended up in jail? Wouldn't that just beat all?

Again the thought of Jake Hertzler filled Bethany with such a huge prickling of red spikes that she almost couldn't catch her breath. She still couldn't get her head around the news that he had stolen money from her father's company. How could he *do* such awful things? Her family had been good to him. Anger added to anger.

It seemed to Bethany that a chain of actions, of people offering trust to Jake without expecting him to earn it, had resulted in the trouble they were facing. She should never have introduced Jake to her father . . . her father should not have given Jake access to so much of Schrock Investments before he knew him well—he had left the cat to guard the cream. Tobe shouldn't have accepted Jake's rationale about the diminishing money at the bank when he sensed something wasn't adding up. Jimmy Fisher should never have trusted Jake so easily when buying a horse from him . . . and of course she was at fault for falling prey to Jake's charms. The start of it all was Jake Hertzler.

All her life, Bethany was taught to love her enemies. Jake had become her first true enemy. How could she forgive him? It wasn't over—Jake kept on hurting the people she loved. She hated him, even though she knew she wasn't supposed to hate, that it was a sin. And she hated herself for harboring such darkness.

Standing there with the morning sun pouring down hard on her head, Bethany had half a mind to stomp to the phone shanty and call him. Why not? Why shouldn't she? She would! She would call him and tell him just what she thought of him.

Hands shaking, she dialed the number for Jake's cell.

As she waited to see if the number still worked, if it would connect, the first wave of doubt floated along. Maybe it wasn't smart to call Jake and tell him off. Maybe she should hang up. *Tell him off. Don't tell him off.* Back and forth she went, a battle between anger and good sense.

But the call connected and clicked right over to voice mail. She took a deep breath and banished those niggling doubts. "Jake, this is Bethany. Bethany Schrock. My brother Tobe came home. He told us what you did to my father. To all of us. He said you were trying to frame him by giving those books I found for you to that SEC lawyer."

She felt a surge of fresh anger, invigorating anger. "How *could* you? How could you be so cruel to people who trusted you? My father, my brother, all the investors—and then Jimmy Fisher and that horse." She was on a roll. It felt good to tell Jake just how she felt. She never had before. It felt so good! "You're not going to get away with this, Jake. It's catching up with you, but fast. People like you think they can do anything to Plain people because we won't defend ourselves. Well, you're wrong. Tobe's going now to tell that SEC lawyer everything you've done."

She stopped and sighed, the fight slipping away from her. "Shootfire! What's the point? I'm just wasting my time. You don't care about anybody but yourself." She slammed the phone down and marched out of the shanty. She was officially *done* with Jake Hertzler.

If Mim had more time, she would ponder what was going on with her sister lately. One minute Bethany was fine, the next minute she was distant and preoccupied, the next—she was stomping mad. But there was no sense in stewing over Bethany's mental state. At least not at this moment. Mim had to get her Mrs. Miracle column prepared for today's deadline. Just saying the word filled her with a secret delight. She had a deadline!

Under her bed, she kept a box of the Mrs. Miracle columns that she cut from the *Stoney Ridge Times* newspaper. It wasn't easy to collect them because her family didn't subscribe to the newspaper. But . . . the sisters at the Sisters' House did. They loved to read, anything and everything. Whenever Mim was over at their house, she would tiptoe around the house, hunting for the latest edition of the newspaper—which was never in the same place twice—tear out Mrs. Miracle's column, fold it carefully, and tuck it into her dress pocket.

A few days ago, Ella came up behind her and caught her in the act. "Do you need scissors, dear?"

"Uh, no," Mim said, cheeks burning. "Just something I wanted from the paper. I didn't think you'd mind."

Ella was looking right at the Mrs. Miracle column in Mim's hand, *right* at it! Then she gazed at her for a long, long moment with an inscrutable look on her face. "Well," she said at last, "we are a reading household. Papa always wants us to have good reading material. But I don't suppose he'll miss one column."

How strange, Mim noticed, for Ella to talk as if her papa was nearby. He must have passed decades ago. Then the wave of guilt hit—Mim hadn't realized the sisters ever actually read the paper, only collected them, and she certainly never meant to lie to anyone, especially Ella. *That*, she decided right then and there, was the last time she would take the column from the sisters. She'd find another way to collect those columns. Maybe she could ask Bethany to get them from the receptionist at the newspaper.

In her bedroom, Mim pulled the manila envelope out from under her mattress and set the typewriter up on her desk. She dumped the letters on her bed.

*Dear Mrs. Miracle,*
*I have been happily married to "Phillip" for ten years. We have a nice-sized farm where we grow beets.*
*Last spring, a neighbor lady, recently divorced, asked if Phillip would*

*teach her how to use a tractor. At the end of each day, Phillip goes over to give her tractor lessons. It has been three months and he is still teaching her to drive a tractor. Each time I mention that the neighbor lady has had enough time to learn how to drive the tractor without help, he says she is a slow learner. He comes home late and is very tired. I am starting to feel suspicious that more is going on than driving lessons.*

> *Gratefully,*
> *Beet Farmer's Wife*

*Dear Beet Farmer's Wife,*
  *If your neighbor lady hasn't learned how to drive a tractor by now, she should consider getting a horse. It would be much easier for her.*

> *Sincerely,*
> *Mrs. Miracle*

*Dear Mrs. Miracle,*
  *Nancy and I have been best friends since we were girls. We've never kept secrets from each other. Recently, I found out that Nancy's husband, who is a dentist, is having an affair with his dental hygienist. Should I tell Nancy? Is it ever wrong to keep a secret?*

> *Signed,*
> *Wringing My Hands*

*Dear Wringing,*
  *Would you want Nancy to tell you if she knew your husband were having an affair?*

> *Sincerely,*
> *Mrs. Miracle*

Mim was particularly proud of that answer. It was inspired! She had no experience with marriage or affairs and didn't want to mislead anyone. This answer put responsibility for the decision back on Wringing. Yes, that was an ideal answer, and she felt it would prove beneficial to her many readers. She always tried to choose letters for the newspaper column that many readers could relate to.

She opened another letter to read:

*Dear Mrs. Miracle,*

*I thought I had something special with my girlfriend, but then she broke up with me.*

*I stayed in bed. I fought with friends who meant well. Once, I got into a fist fight that I knew I would lose just so I could feel a different type of pain, but nothing hurt more than my broken heart. It's been seven months and I still have not moved on. I think I'm ready. I finally shaved. But my heart still races with anxiety when I think of losing my girlfriend. I mean, I was really in love.*

*Just Wondering What to Do Next*

Mim felt stupefied by the letters about broken hearts. She thought she understood love—after all, she loved Danny Riehl and planned to marry him one day—but she did not understand what brokenheartedness felt like and she hoped she never would. It sounded awful. It sounded like a person's heart had been ripped open, without anesthesia, and was bleeding inside his chest. Mim couldn't imagine how dreadful it would be to have a truly broken heart. She set Just Wondering's letter aside, unsure of how to answer.

She read through the stack of letters from last week's pouch and placed them into piles on her bed: Answer, Don't Answer, and I Have No Idea How to Answer.

She almost missed a small envelope at the bottom of the pile. It was from Stuck.

*Dear Mrs. Miracle,*

*Sometimes I feel like leaky dynamite—just waiting for the spark to make it explode.*

*Yours truly,*
*Stuck*

Mim leaned back against her bedframe, holding the letter in her hand. How in the world should Mrs. Miracle handle *that*?

# 14

Early Tuesday morning, Bethany wiped her feet on the mat before stepping into the guest flat's bright living room. It was hard to believe this was the same dreary space, filled with old junk, that it was a few months ago. Rose had transformed it and she'd done it on a shoestring budget. Now it was a cheerful space with buttery yellow painted walls, white woodwork, a large window that let in bright light. The window overlooked Rose's flower garden near the barn. The transformation was amazing. The guest flat was much cooler, too, than the house above it. "Geena?"

"In here!" Geena was in the bedroom, packing up. "You're just in time to give me a hand. I thought I'd move my things up to the house so I can clean the guest flat when we get back later today."

"You don't have to clean anything," Bethany said. "You're our guest. Mim and I have it down to a routine." She plumped a pillow. "Besides, if the heat wave doesn't break, I'm sure those folks will cancel."

"Supposed to rain tomorrow." Geena looked around the room and grabbed her purse. "Well? Ready to go meet your mother?"

Bethany took a deep breath. "As ready as I'll ever be."

An hour or so later, they were driving into Hagensburg. "At the next street make a right onto the bridge," droned the GPS in Geena's car.

"Almost there," Geena said.

This might be a huge mistake, Bethany realized. Over the years she had learned to live with her mother's abandonment. Why did it need to change now?

Bethany felt her stomach lurch. Coming here had been a bad idea. A really bad idea. And she found herself simply wishing she could talk to . . . not to Geena, not to Rose, but to Jimmy Fisher.

Where had that idea come from? Why would she feel a longing for the counsel of Jimmy Fisher, of all people? What might he say to a complicated situation like this, anyway? What could he possibly know?

A ridiculous notion! But she could almost hear his voice: *You've gone this far, Bethany. Don't lose courage now. You need to get your answers if you're ever going to get through this gray stretch in your life.*

The car stopped in front of an old but cared-for house with wooden ramps leading up to the front door. Bethany took in a deep breath. This was it. This was where her mother was. An eerie sense of something lost moved through her chest, cold and hollow.

Geena turned off the ignition. "Let's go get your answers."

They pressed a doorbell button and waited until someone came to the door. An older woman, skin like chocolate and hair like a salt-and-pepper Brillo pad, looked Bethany up and down as if she recognized her.

"We're here to see Mary Schrock," Geena said at last. "She might go by the name of Mary Miller."

The woman was still eyeing Bethany. "Didn't expect you folks till the end of July."

Bethany was confused. "I've never been here before."

Now the woman looked confused. "Who are you?"

"I'm Mary's daughter. I'd like to meet her."

The woman rolled her eyes and sighed. "Oh Lawd—jez like that boy that come 'round here awhile back."

"My brother, Tobe."

"Child, whatever you're looking for, you ain't gonna find it in your mama."

*Shootfire!* Everywhere Bethany went, she hit the same brick wall. Everybody thought they knew what was best for her. "I'd like to decide that for myself."

Geena put a calming hand on her shoulder. "Ma'am, this is Bethany Schrock. She'd just like the chance to meet her mother. That's all. Seems like a daughter should be able to meet her mother."

The woman fixed her gaze at Geena, as if she just noticed her. "And who are you?"

"I'm the Reverend Spencer. A friend of the family's."

Something changed instantly in the woman as soon as she learned Geena was a minister. It was like a free pass. She opened the door wide. "Mary's in her room."

Bethany and Geena followed behind the woman. They went through a room where a few elderly women sat on the couch, watching television. Only one noticed Geena and Bethany and stared at them.

"Mind if I ask," Geena said, "what kind of home is this?"

The woman stopped and turned toward Geena. "It's a home for ladies with mental health issues."

"What kind of mental health issues?"

"Bipolar, manic depressive, clinical depression, psychotic, schizophrenia, paranoia—"

"So my mother runs this home?"

The woman looked at Bethany as if she had a loose bolt. "Say what?"

"I thought you were taking us to her office."

The woman's face softened in understanding. "Oh, baby. No, no, no, no, no. She ain't running the place. She's a patient. She's been here for a long, long time. Longer than I've been here."

Everything went upside down. A funny tingling feeling traveled through Bethany, starting with her toes. By the time it reached her head, she felt she might faint. The room started to spin and she dipped lower, as if her knees might give way, but Geena grasped her around the shoulders.

"Are you okay?" she whispered.

Bethany nodded. She had to be strong. She just had to. She took a deep breath. In, out.

Geena turned to the woman, still holding Bethany's shoulders. "Why is Mary here?"

The woman's back went up. "'Cuz it's better than an institution. We try to make it homelike. Most of the staffers have been here for years and years. They know all these patients. They treat them like family."

"I meant . . . what's the diagnosis?"

"I can't tell you that."

Geena held her gaze.

"It's them stupid HIPAA laws." The woman pressed her lips together. "I could lose my job."

"Please," Bethany whispered.

The woman looked at Geena. "You really a preacher? You ain't wearing a collar. You don't look much like a holy roller."

"I can assure you . . . I am an ordained minister."

The woman hesitated, wavering. She turned to Bethany. "Your mother is a chronic schizophrenic."

"What is that?" Bethany asked, confused. "I don't know what that means."

"Her brain is sick, baby."

"It's a mental disorder that makes it hard for the patient to tell the difference between what's real and what isn't," Geena said.

"I don't understand," Bethany said, her voice gravelly and dry. "How does someone get schiz . . . schizo . . ."

"Schizophrenia," Geena finished.

"Was my mother born that way? Had she always been sick?"

The caregiver glanced up and down the hall, then lowered her voice. "From what I heard about your mama, it started with acute schizophrenia when she was in her late teens, then it went on to chronic schizophrenia. She's on some heavy antipsychotic meds. They help her with her hallucinations, long as she stays on it—and she can be tricky that way—but even on her best days, she can't take care of herself and she can't live on her own." She started walking down the hall again and stopped in front of a door. "Baby, you look awful pale. Why do you want to do this?"

Bethany followed behind her. "I need to."

"You sure you're up for this?"

Bethany closed her eyes. Was she? She heard Jimmy's voice: *You've come this far. And you're stronger than you think.* "Yes."

The woman opened the door. "Mary, honey, you got some company."

Bethany hesitated before she stepped toward the open door. It was a small room with a single bed, a nightstand, and a chair in the corner next to the window. Curled up in the chair was a small woman, staring out the window, her long dark hair pulled back severely into a ponytail.

As Bethany crossed the room and stood beside the chair, she could feel her heart pounding. There was a salty, bitter taste in her mouth that she recognized as fear. Her gaze searched the woman's face, then went slowly over the rest of her. She was small boned and fine featured and her skin was so pale that Bethany could see the blue veins on the insides of her wrists. Eyes shaped like Tobe's—half moons with those thick lashes that Bethany had always envied—but these eyes seemed flat and empty.

Bethany groped for a thought, something she could say. How did a person introduce herself to the woman who gave her life? "My name is Bethany. Bethany Schrock." She enunciated each word slowly and carefully.

The woman—this was her mother!—blinked her eyes rapidly, but looked at Bethany without recognition.

She tried to clear the gritty feeling out of her throat. "Do you remember me? I'm your girl. I'm Bethany. Your daughter." She reached out to touch her arm, but the woman flinched. "Tobe is my brother. Dean Schrock was my father. Your husband."

The woman clutched and unclutched her hands. The lines at the corners of her mouth pulled deeper.

Bethany crouched down so she was face-to-face with the woman. "I came because I wanted to see you." She tried to sound calm but couldn't quite keep the quiver out of her voice. "I've missed you. My whole life, I've missed you. I've never stopped missing you."

"No," her mother whimpered. She drew her legs up tight against her chest and started to rock back and forth, her arms tightly around her knees, her eyes squeezed shut.

Bethany noticed her hands. She held her hand up next to the woman's. "Look. Look how similar our hands are. Even the nails. Tobe always teases me that my hands are small. They're just like yours."

The woman responded by balling her hands into a fist and ducking her chin to her chest. "He said not to give it to anyone."

"Give what?" Bethany asked. "Who said such a thing to you?"

"No, no, no, no, no." Her whole body was so rigid it shook.

The caregiver stepped in and put a hand on Bethany's shoulder. "She's getting agitated. Maybe you need to come back another time, baby. This isn't a good day for her. Don't feel bad. Even before you came, I knew it wasn't a good day for her."

Bethany reached out a hand toward the woman's shoulder, then dropped it so it hung limply at her side. Slowly, she rose and walked toward Geena, waiting by the door, then turned back for a final look. The woman was sucking in great gasps of air, breathing, breathing, breathing frantically, as if she dared not stop even for an instant.

This was her mother. This was her *mother*!

Tobe was right. She should have left it alone. Once you know something, you can't unknow it.

Bethany turned and stumbled toward the door, fumbling for the tissue she put in her dress pocket. She squeezed her eyes shut against the burn of tears, but they came anyway.

The caregiver told them to wait for her in the hallway while she tended to Mary. "Any doubt if she's actually your mother?" Geena asked. "There could be a mistake."

Bethany shook her head, splattering tears. "No doubt." Those eyes, that hair, even the shape of her fingernails. There was no mistaking the family resemblance. She dabbed at her eyes with the tissue, then lifted her head slowly and glanced upward. "All my life, I assumed my mother was living a grand life somewhere, happy to be rid of us, never giving us another thought. I never ever imagined her life to be . . . to be like . . . *that*."

The caregiver came out of the room and walked them to the front entrance.

"Can you tell me anything more?" Bethany asked. "How long has my mother been here?"

"Don't know. I started here about six years ago. All I know is that she's been here a long, long time, and her bills are paid for every month, right on time. That's all I know."

Geena tilted her head. "When we first arrived, you said something about not expecting anyone until the last day of the month. What did you mean by that?"

"That's when the ladies come to visit her. Three or four of them, like clockwork. They pretty her hair and fuss over her. The last day of every month, rain or shine, unless it's a Sunday. Then they come on Monday."

"What made you think Bethany was part of that group?"

The caregiver looked Bethany up and down. "Well, because she's dressed the same—with them little bonnets."

"They're Amish?"

The caregiver nodded. "They sit and quilt with Mary. It's her best day. She's always real calm after they visit."

Bethany leaned forward. "Did you say they quilt?"

"Yes. They're a quilting group, they say. Call themselves the Sisters' Bee."

# 15

Jimmy," Naomi said, resting her forehead in her hand as she talked, "for the tenth time, I don't think you did anything wrong."

"But I told Bethany I'd take her home from the singing. She didn't say anything about having to leave early. I did end up giving her a ride, but she was mostly quiet. She's never quiet. Usually, she's complaining about my bad character. She even wore that lavender dress that I like so much. She looked beautiful. A little tired, though. Did you notice?"

"I did." Naomi sighed. Jimmy was her friend. So was Bethany.

"I just don't understand what's happened," Jimmy said. "At times, I think she's genuinely interested in me, you know? And other times, she acts like I'm invisible."

"I don't think you should be worried. She went to the singing, didn't she? If she wanted to avoid you, she wouldn't have even gone."

"That girl flashes hot and cold faster than I can keep up." He worried his hat in his hands. "Doesn't it seem like something's bothering her lately? More than her usual fiery temper?"

It did seem so to Naomi too, but she had no idea what exactly was troubling Bethany. "Maybe there's just a lot on her mind with her brother's coming, then going." Tobe was certainly on the top of Naomi's mind.

Jimmy wiggled his eyebrows up and down. "By the way, you and Tobe sure did make a fast getaway at the singing."

Naomi froze. "Did anyone else notice?"

He grinned. "Your secret is safe with me." Then his smile faded. "So do you think you could talk to Bethany?"

"If there's a chance to talk, then I'll try. No promises. I'm your friend, not your matchmaker." That wasn't entirely true, Naomi did enjoy matchmaking and thought she had a talent for it. But she hadn't had any time alone with Bethany for quite some time now. She didn't even know where she'd gone today.

Naomi looked out the window at Sammy and Luke, racing behind her brother Galen as he led a horse into the ring for training exercises. Those two boys never seemed to walk in a straight line. Instead, they ran in zig-zags. What would it be like to have that much energy?

"I'd better get out there before Galen wonders where I've gone," Jimmy said. At the kitchen door, he stopped. "Hank Lapp told me the other day that there were only two women in Stoney Ridge who could ever manage me on a full-time basis—Mary Kate Lapp, who spurned me for Chris Yoder, and Bethany Schrock. Think he's right?"

Naomi grinned. "Let's just say I think you and Bethany are perfectly suited."

"Me, too. I just need to convince her of that." He fit his hat on his head. "Thanks, Naomi. You're a good pal."

The ride home from Hagensburg was a silent one. As they drew closer to Stoney Ridge, Geena glanced at Bethany and wasn't surprised to see tears pouring like hot, silent rain over her face. She fished a small package of tissue out of her purse and handed it to Bethany. "Do you want to talk?"

Bethany pulled a tissue out of the package and wiped her eyes and cheeks. "All these years, as long as I could remember, I was so angry with my mother, so angry that she'd torn our family apart. How could I even have thought such a thing? If I could, I'd take them all back. Every resentful thought, every hateful word. I feel riddled with as many holes as a wormy apple." She blew her nose.

"You didn't know," Geena said kindly. "You had no idea what had happened to your mother. Is that typical of the Amish? For your father to not tell you the truth about your mother?"

"I don't know if he knew the truth. Knowing Dad, he might have sugarcoated my mother's illness, but he wouldn't have lied." Then the tears started again. "How can God ever forgive me for being so hardhearted? At times, I hated her," she whispered.

"But he does forgive, Bethany. He does." Geena turned off the highway onto the back roads that wound toward Stoney Ridge. "Sometimes," she said softly, "we have to make decided efforts to let go of the past. Not so that we pretend hard things didn't happen, but so that the power of hard things is lessened. In the Bible, Isaiah talks about forgetting the former things and not dwelling on the past."

"It's not that easy."

"No, it's not. 'The past is not a package one can lay away.' Emily Dickinson said that."

"Who's that?"

"She's an American poet. Lived in the 1800s."

"Well, no wonder I've never heard of her if she's passed on."

Geena swallowed a grin. At times, Bethany seemed wise beyond her years. Other times, she seemed so young, so naive. "Are you going to tell the sisters from the Sisters' Bee that you know they're visiting your mother?"

Bethany turned toward the window. "I don't know. I just don't know what to do about that piece of news. I'm still stunned. I've been working for them for months now and they've never said a word about my mother. Though, not long ago, I discovered they were feeding lunch once a week to thirty people. They are a puzzle, those old sisters."

"Mind if I give you some advice?"

"Please."

"Don't do anything about it for a while. Just give yourself some time to wrap your head around what you found out about your mother today. After all, the only thing you know for sure about the sisters is that they visit your mother once a month. That's not such a bad thing."

Bethany glanced at her from the corner of her eyes. "Keeping it a secret is."

"Bethany, just pray long and hard before you talk to the sisters. Make sure God is the one leading you to talk to them, if you do it at all."

Bethany nodded. "Now *that* is some advice I could've used recently. Any time I get all puffed up and self-righteous, I make a mess even bigger."

Laughter broke through her self-pity. "I need a nap. It's been an emotional day."

Geena patted Bethany's arm. "In a good way."

Bethany closed her eyes and Geena drove past rolling fields, farmhouses with clotheslines flapping, horses hanging their heads over fences. The weather was changing—gray clouds were moving in from the north and the wind was picking up. Geena rolled down her window. The air was at least ten degrees cooler now than it was when they headed to Hagensburg this morning.

She was glad she had gone with Bethany today. She wasn't sure if the caregiver would have been as forthcoming with information had Geena not slipped into the conversation that she was in the ministry. Finding the truth today was much harder than she expected, but she couldn't help but feel it was necessary for Bethany to come to peace about her mother.

For the first time in months, perhaps in years, Geena had a sense that she was right where she was supposed to be.

A headache came over Naomi in the afternoon that was so painful she had to come inside the house to rest her eyes from the bright sunshine. She brewed a cup of tea from the spearmint leaves that Sadie Smucker, the local herbalist, had given to her. Sadie had recommended that she distract herself from the pain, rather than lie in bed and dwell on it. So Naomi sat in the living room and tried to put a binding around a quilt, a Basket Garden pattern she had just finished.

Sitting quietly and sewing the bright green binding inch by inch to the border, covering all the uneven edges and raveled threads with a smooth band of green, seeing all those different bits and scraps of fabric come together, stitch by stitch, into a neatly finished whole, did help lessen the pounding in her head, just a little.

She had made this quilt with all kinds of scraps from her piece bag, and the scraps brought up happy memories of her siblings when they still lived at home. There were five brothers and sisters in between Galen and Naomi—they were the bookends, their mother had called them. They were the most alike too. Quiet, thoughtful, introspective, and frequently underestimated by others. Her sisters, now married with families of their own, had invited Naomi to come live with them, but she didn't want to leave Galen. She understood him. She wondered when he would get around to asking Rose to marry him and what that might mean for her. Knowing Rose, she would want Naomi to remain with all of them. One big happy family.

And that was tempting, especially when Naomi considered Tobe, which she did quite a lot.

She wondered how the week was going for Tobe and hoped he was being completely candid with that lawyer. She had encouraged him to tell everything, to not hold back anything. Tobe seemed skeptical, but then she reminded him that he had spent most of the last year hiding from the truth and where had that gotten him? Honesty, she said, was always the best way.

Even if being honest might open up a Pandora's box of troubles? he had asked her.

Even then, she said.

Naomi had been stitching around a corner, which took careful attention to set the tucks just right, when the headache took a severe turn. She put down the fabric pieces and rubbed her temples.

Outside, the sun disappeared as if someone had popped a lid over it. She went to the window and saw the weather was changing—no wonder she had such a headache. Whenever the barometric pressure in the air changed suddenly, she felt the pressure in her head. She watched streaks of lightning light the sky, muted and hidden by low-lying clouds. Not rain clouds, just those empties. "Always threatening, never delivering," Galen called them. She saw Galen and Jimmy lead some horses from the paddock into the barn. No more training would happen today if lightning flashed in the sky.

Finally, she went down to the darkest part of the basement to curl up and rest on a cot. The basement was usually her last resort, but the quiet and the darkness often helped to alleviate the headaches. Sometimes she felt as if tiny men were inside her forehead, pounding on it with little hammers. She closed her eyes and tried to sleep. The lightning was closer now, with large cracks of thunder quickly following. The sound filled her with such tension that she didn't think she could endure it. If it went on much longer, she felt it would twist her like a wire.

A gust of wind rattled the basement window and she shivered. For no reason she could have named, Naomi felt a ripple of foreboding. In her mind flashed images—bright lights, like a spinning police siren. She smelled freshly turned earth, then saw a shovel and . . .

Naomi's eyes popped open and she was on her feet. Something terrible was about to happen.

Jimmy listened to Naomi's vision and didn't know what to make of it. Sometimes, when Naomi had a fierce headache, she would have these . . . visions or dreams or second sights . . . and while they often turned out to mean something, just as often they didn't. He wished Galen were here, but he had gone into town to pick up some liniment for a horse's lame leg. Jimmy appeased Naomi by saying he would check every horse on the entire King farm.

"It's not here," Naomi said, trembling. "The trouble isn't here."

"Then, where?"

That . . . she didn't know. Jimmy saw Hank Lapp saunter up the driveway with a fishing pole in his hand and waved him into the kitchen. Maybe he could make sense of Naomi's vision. At this point, Jimmy wasn't sure what else to do. Hank listened carefully to Naomi, asking details as if she were a witness to a crime and not just dreaming the whole thing up. He suggested they check over Galen's livestock first, so he walked with Jimmy through the barn, then out to the pastures, but the horses were all accounted for and nothing seemed awry. "I'm not sure what to do to appease Naomi, Hank," Jimmy said, walking back to the house. "Those headaches can make her a little . . ." He whirled his finger around his ear.

"Her vision might not be real," Hank said, "but it's real to her."

And then Mim came flying through the hole in the privet hedge. "Jimmy— we have to get to the community garden! I just got a call from Bethany. Something's going on down there."

Jimmy fetched a buggy horse from the barn and Hank hitched it to the shafts in record time. Mim jumped in the buggy and Naomi came out of the house to join them, but Jimmy discouraged her from coming along by promising to stop by later with news. He could almost see the headache pain radiating from her eyes. He climbed into the buggy, slapped the reins on the horse, and started to take off, when Sammy and Luke ran through the privet. "We're coming too!"

"HOP IN, BOYS!" Hank bellowed.

Jimmy stopped the buggy and let them climb into the backseat. He glanced at Mim. "What exactly did Bethany say?"

Mim's hands were gripping the sides of the buggy. "She and Geena were driving past the community garden on their way home and saw that the garden had been trashed."

"What?" Jimmy glanced at her. "By who?"

"She didn't say. It was a quick call."

"Where were Geena and Bethany coming from?" He hadn't seen Bethany all day, and he'd been looking.

"I don't know."

No one said a word for the rest of the ride. Jimmy detoured down a road for a shortcut, across a fire path in a field, and pulled the horse to a stop at the back of the garden, behind a fence. He jumped out of the buggy, tied the reins to a tree, and helped Mim down. The boys raced around the fence corner. Then they stopped abruptly, stunned. Jimmy, Hank, and Mim joined the boys; the five of them stared at the gardens with blank expressions.

Here was Naomi's warning.

It looked like cattle had stampeded through, trampling the new and carefully tended plots. Plants were smashed, dirt was scattered, leaves and blossoms lay in clumps, gravel from the pathways was churned up. Some of the wooden boards that held the plots were smashed into splinters.

They were ruined.

Rage rose in Jimmy as he strode through the gardens. Nearly every plot had been damaged, but it was capricious, like a tornado. Some gardens had been trampled and yanked up badly. Others had only sustained wounds. A handful of others had taken a hit, with broken plants, footsteps in the middle. He started counting. Two very badly damaged plots. One of them was the Grange Hall's kitchen plot. That was better, he felt, than if it had belonged to a needy family or the Group Home. He picked up a stake, shoved the support in the ground, tenderly knelt and propped up a listing tomato cage. Within, the tomato plant had a few broken arms which Jimmy pinched off, but its main stem was intact. It would survive.

The wanton destruction trailed off toward the far end of the gardens, as if the vandals had been chased away. Or interrupted.

He heard a slight moan and turned around to see Bethany, standing with her fist clenched against her mouth. He walked up to her. "This is unbelievable," she said.

"Mim said you and Geena were driving by when you saw that the gardens had been wrecked. Did you see anyone?"

She pointed to the back of the garden. "In the shadows back there, I saw some figures moving. Two, maybe three people. When Geena pulled over, they ran off." Something fierce crossed her face. "How could anyone do such a thing? Why? This is food! They're gardens. They're only meant to help people."

He looked around the plots, teeth clenched together. "I don't know. I just don't know." Then he turned to face Bethany. "But we're not going to let them think they've taken something away." He peered at the sky. "It might rain soon, but until it does, we're going to start fixing things."

"Now?"

"Now."

Mim had been standing nearby, listening to their conversation. "I'll go to the Sisters' House and let them know." She took off running.

"WAIT FOR ME, MIM!" Hank called. "I'll use their phone to start the Amish telegraph." Mim waited for him to catch up and the two hurried off together to the Sisters' House.

"Jimmy," Bethany said, "who is capable of this kind of violence?"

"It doesn't matter," he called, walking backward toward the Grange Hall to get tools from the shed. "What matters is that the garden keeps growing."

Soon the word spread and church members started to arrive. Everyone surveyed the damage, faces masked with shock and sadness. "Why would anyone do such a thing?" Amos Lapp asked, lifting a smashed zucchini plant. He tried to brace the broken boards of a raised bed, but they kept falling over again.

"I have no idea," Bethany said. She must have said it over and over. She still couldn't believe what had transpired here today.

A few girls from the Group Home drifted over and Geena set them to cleanup tasks. Bethany admired how easily Geena related to those girls. Bethany avoided them, was intimidated by them, but Geena always went right up and drew them into conversation.

Sammy stood by the garden plot Bethany had planted for the sisters' soup kitchen. He was peering at his pea shoots, which had been twining up a trellis he had made out of stakes, and made a roaring noise. "Someone wrecked my peas!" he cried, hurt crumpling his face, and Bethany wrapped her arm around his shoulder.

"No, Sammy, look," she said, bending down to examine the plants. "Some of the pea vines are broken, but not all. They'll keep growing. Peas are hardy things." She spied some stakes and reached out to grab them and put them back in the ground. "I think if you leave those peas alone, they'll survive."

Luke ran over to see the plot, a scowl pulling at his face. He jammed his fists on his hips and jutted out his chin. He whipped his head around to Bethany, his eyes flaring brightly. "Until they do it again." He stomped off down the garden path.

Sammy's mouth trembled. "What if it happens again?"

Gently she brushed the hair out of Sammy's eyes. She hardly had to reach down to do so anymore, he was getting that big. He would be nine years old come fall. Before long, he'd be growing past her, like Luke already was. "There's no point in worrying about what-ifs. Let's see what can be salvaged."

Kneeling, she plucked leaves from an eggplant and removed a crumpled stem of a sunflower. The carrots and potatoes and onions and garlic would be fine, tucked deep under the earth. A swath of corn shoots was crushed. She tried to appear calm, for Sammy's sake, but as she tossed the ruined plants aside, she saw that her hands were shaking.

Jimmy walked over to where she and Sammy were working. "Sammy, Amos Lapp brought some flats of mixed bedding plants from his greenhouse to help replace those that had been lost. Run over and see if there are some plants he'll let you have." As Sammy ran over to Amos's wagon,

Jimmy examined the two boards of the raised bed. He pulled out some nails from his pocket and hammered the corners together. "That'll hold for now. I'll get corner latches on it tomorrow."

Bethany still couldn't imagine who would have done this. She glanced over at the Group Home and saw Rusty and her friends on the porch, watching others clean up the gardens. Maybe she *could* imagine whom. But why? What could cause those girls—Rusty, if she were honest—to commit such a reckless act? "What would make her do something like this?"

Jimmy raised an eyebrow. "Why'd you say that? Why'd you say 'her'?"

Bethany didn't know for sure that Rusty had done it. If so, she certainly would have needed help from her friends, but that wouldn't have been too difficult. Rusty said jump and they asked how high. "Just a hunch."

"Well, you might be on to something." He glanced over at Rusty. "The only plot that wasn't damaged was the Group Home's."

"We were just trying to do something for the community, to make things a little bit nicer." She wiped at some dirt on her cheeks. "People think they can do anything to us because we won't fight back."

"I know," Jimmy said quietly, not looking away. "But we shouldn't stop trying to do good. Things are damaged, but most of it is fixable."

Geena walked up to them. "Whoever did all this has been damaged too, or they wouldn't choose to do this kind of destruction."

"Well, we probably can't fix them, but let's see what we can do about this garden." Jimmy reached down and picked up his hammer and extra nails. "Where've you been all day, anyhow?"

Bethany stilled and her eyes pricked with tears. She glanced at Geena for help.

"Taking care of some old business," Geena volunteered. "Jimmy, you're absolutely right. Let's see what we can do about this garden."

# 16

In less than a week, Bethany's missing brother had returned and was being investigated by a big city lawyer, her church had built a community garden, she had discovered that her mother was mentally ill, and to top it all off, the brand-new community garden had been trashed . . . and rebuilt.

Still, the sun rose on Wednesday morning and Harold the Rooster crowed and new guests were due at the inn this afternoon. It was strange how time moved along, like a river rushing to meet the ocean. Nothing could stop it.

Right after breakfast, Mim and Bethany scrubbed and cleaned the guest flat, washed the windows, changed the sheets and towels, and prepared the rooms for new arrivals. Now the sisters were expecting Bethany to help serve lunch at the Grange Hall. As she put on her bonnet to walk to the Sisters' House, Chase greeted her at the door, barking his big, deep bark, wagging the whole back half of his body. "You want to come with me, don't you?" Chase tilted his head toward her for a nuzzle. She scratched his back, rubbed his ears. "You're the best." She didn't know how anybody could get along without a good old dog.

The rain from last night had stopped, but the air was thick with it, dense to breathe, smelling of damp soil. Now and then a slight whiff of horses wafted through. Geena invited herself along and they walked to the Sisters' House, Chase trailing behind, sniffing and baptizing every bush along the way.

On the way, Geena asked how she was processing through all of yesterday's events. "As I thought about it last night, I realized you probably have more questions than answers. And most likely, the sisters have the answers. Some of them, anyway."

"I've thought of little else." Bethany blew out a puff of air. "I had to bite my tongue last night when I saw the sisters at the garden—I wanted to ask them what they knew about my mother. Wanted to but didn't. I'm not sure I can handle knowing anything more. I doubt it's good."

"Wait for God's timing on this, Bethany."

Bethany glanced at her, a little annoyed. "I told you—I didn't say anything."

"Waiting on God doesn't mean forgetting or ignoring. It means you pray for God's timing. Ask him to let you know when the time is right. Don't act until you sense God's leading. Waiting on God isn't passive. It's very active."

"Then what happens? Should I be on the lookout for a burning bush or something?"

Geena laughed. "I don't think you'll need something quite that dramatic. For me, it's more like a knowing, deep inside. The more I pray, the more familiar I've become with getting direction from God. I try not to act until I get his prompting."

It never crossed Bethany's mind to pray the way Geena prayed—asking and expecting and asking some more. She had no idea a person could talk to God like that. No idea at all. She'd been in church all her life—different churches too. Amish and Mennonite. Never had she heard that prayer was a two-way conversation. Was it that her churches didn't encourage that kind of praying? Or had she just not paid attention?

As they turned onto the road that led to the Sisters' House, Geena brought up Naomi's warning. "Does she get those . . . presentiments . . . often?"

"She thinks of them as intuition. Gut feelings. And she thinks everyone has intuition but people don't listen to it enough. But I've noticed they seem to be related to her migraine headaches." Bethany kicked a stone off the sidewalk. "Naomi is an interesting person."

"Her voice reminds me of a librarian, hushed and refined. She seems like a gentle soul."

"That she is. She does generous and loving things without even a second thought. But she's stronger inside than she might seem on the outside."

Geena grinned. "That's the opposite of the girls from the Group Home. They look tough on the outside, but inside, they're still little girls."

"Why do you like those girls so much?"

"I've always been partial to teens," Geena said. "That's why I love being a youth pastor. If I were running that Group Home, I'd start a weekly Bible study for the girls. And I'd try to organize a mentoring program for them, so they could be matched with people—" she held her palm out to Bethany "—people like you, who have so much to teach these girls."

*Oh no. No thank you.*

"I guess the thing I like about teens is that they're less jaded than adults, more vulnerable, more willing to believe."

"But you're going to look for another youth pastor job?"

"Oh yes. I like supporting teens during their impressionable years—to make them feel part of the church, to listen without lecturing them, all while pointing them toward God's highest and best."

"But what if a church wasn't in a building?"

Geena opened her mouth to say something, closed it, opened it again, closed it. She seemed flustered by the question, yet it seemed so obvious to Bethany.

Sylvia was in front of her house and called out to them when she saw them coming up the road. "Turkey Rice Soup on the menu today." She was filling a little red wagon with jars of homemade turkey stock.

"It's the first time all summer that serving a hot meal sounds good," Bethany said. She and Geena took the wagons on ahead to the Grange Hall while Sylvia gathered her sisters.

Chase wasn't allowed in the Grange Hall kitchen, so he moseyed over to the community garden to visit with a few gardeners working on their plots. Geena unlocked the kitchen and started to unload a wagon. Bethany stopped for a moment to gaze at the gardens. It was amazing to see that the garden didn't look all that different today from how it looked on Saturday afternoon—neat and tidy and full of promise.

"REMARKABLE SIGHT, AIN'T IT?"

Bethany flinched at the loud sound and spun around to find Hank Lapp standing a few feet away from her. "Morning, Hank. What are you doing here?"

"Thought I'd give some help to the gardeners."

"That's nice of you."

"Well, some of them are new at this. That family there—" he pointed to a mother with two little girls—"they're planting onions next to beans. That'll stunt the growth of the beans." He shrugged his shoulders. "If you haven't been raised Plain, you don't know about gardens."

Well, that might be stretching things a little, but it was true that the Amish passed their know-how from generation to generation. Bethany picked up a sack of flour, glad to see it. She'd ask Sylvia to see if she could get some flour so she could start making biscuits for lunches. That store-bought white bread had no taste at all. She glanced at the Group Home. She wondered if those girls ever had a homemade biscuit before, hot from the oven, topped with a pat of cold butter. Maybe today, if she could get started soon.

Hank shielded his eyes, looking over the garden plots. "You'd never know this place had been such a mess."

In her other hand, Bethany picked up a big jar of broth. "When I think of what happened last night to the gardens—yes, it is remarkable."

"I wasn't talking about last night. I was thinking about how it looked just a week ago. The whole lot was a mess."

She smiled and handed Hank the jar of broth, then another. If he had time on his hands, she had things for him to do. "I suppose you're right."

"Takes a pretty determined woman to have seen all that through."

She looked at him in surprise. "You mean me? Oh no. I was just a small part of it. These gardens were a community effort."

"Look at this," he said, spreading his free hand to encompass the garden. "Do you remember what a wreck this was? A less determined woman . . . a less stubborn woman would have given up before she even started. Not Bethany Schrock."

She grinned. "Stubborn—now that label most of my family would agree with."

"There are worse things than being stubborn."

Chase noticed a few girls from the Group Home in the garden before Bethany did. He went flying over to greet them. To her surprise, Rusty bent down and rubbed his head all over.

Hank was watching the interaction too. "I think we should call it 'The Second Chance Gardens.'" He handed the jars of broth back to Bethany and sauntered off to help the mother and her children in their garden plot.

She watched him walk down the garden path. When she first became acquainted with Hank Lapp, she thought of him just like everybody else did: an odd fellow who made church a little more interesting. She remembered countless Sundays when Hank would fall asleep during the sermons, snore loudly, then jerk awake. He would look around the room, startled, blinking rapidly like a newborn owl, oblivious to the disruption he had caused. Another time, his stomach growled so loud that the minister stopped preaching and looked right at him. "Die Bauern haben gern kurze Predigten und lange Bratwürste," Hank told him in his usual loud voice. *The belly hates a long sermon.*

Hank Lapp had always been amusing to Bethany, but that was all.

After Jimmy started to work for Galen, Hank dropped by Eagle Hill and the King farm often and she discovered other sides to him: his kindness, his good intentions, and his love for the Plain life despite his stubborn streak. He had a good heart, Hank Lapp did. She held the kitchen door open with her foot and motioned to Geena to start the assembly line to unload the little red wagons.

By the time the sisters arrived, the wagons were unloaded, the biscuit dough was resting, and Bethany was chopping vegetables for the soup. Geena stood next to her, staring at the cutting board as Bethany took the last onion, made six quick, deep cuts into the flesh, another six crossways, then chopped through the onion.

"The speed that you cut an onion is amazing," Geena said.

"No man is his craft's master the first day. That's a saying my grandmother likes to quote. In other words: do enough of anything and you'll get good at it."

"Except for preaching," Geena said with a grin.

Just then the girls from the Group Home slipped in early—something Sylvia didn't normally allow. She thought Sylvia or Fannie might shoo them out but they were preoccupied with taking turkey meat off the carcass and chopping it up for the soup. Lena, Ada, and Ella, setting the tables, were too softhearted to ask them to wait outside.

Bethany would have liked to give those girls jobs to do to help get lunch ready—set places, sweep the floor, fill glasses with that sugary Dr Pepper and juice drink—but when she brought it up once, Sylvia disagreed. She said it wasn't time yet. Bethany didn't know what she meant by that—as far as she was concerned, there was work to be done and those girls needed to work.

Geena left the kitchen and went over to talk to the girls from the Group Home. She pulled out a chair and sat next to Rusty. They talked awhile—sadly out of Bethany's earshot. Geena patted her on the shoulder. Why? Rusty didn't seem like the type to pat much.

Bethany had been watching Rusty since she came in. Inside her battled a war: her basic nature was to be confrontational and she knew, she just *knew*, Rusty had something to do with the trashing of the community garden. But she also knew it was wrong to accuse others. Hadn't it been drilled into her for as long as she could remember? What right did she have to accuse another of a sin when she was a sinner herself? And she was.

Still, wasn't it important to be held accountable for one's actions? To face consequences. Isn't that what Rose was trying to get Tobe to understand? But then . . . Rose wanted Tobe to take responsibility for himself. That was the rub, right there. Bethany wanted someone else to hold Rusty accountable. She could feel the pointed finger of judgment brew within her, and that was where pride gained hold.

"It's good of you to show interest in those girls," Bethany said when Geena returned to the kitchen.

"It's always illuminating to me," Geena said. "It really boils down to the fact that the girls want to feel understood, accepted, and heard even while they struggle to understand, accept, and hear others. I guess it's not that surprising when I stop to think about it. That's what everybody wants and what everybody finds so hard to do."

Bethany took a pan of biscuits out of the oven. "I guess that's the difference between the Amish and the English. Being English means you struggle to find your place. Being Amish means you belong."

Geena found a spatula in a drawer and scooped the hot biscuits into a basket. "Don't forget these girls are on the extreme side of your definition of being 'English.' Most of them have never been wanted by their families; they've never belonged anywhere. I remember something one of my seminary professors had said: 'Most people are in way more pain than anybody knows.' That is so true." Geena carried the dirty spatula to the sink and rinsed it off. She put the spatula away in a drawer.

Bethany started to ladle out the soup into empty bowls set on the countertop. "I guess I haven't thought about why the girls were the way they were. I've only noticed how they act. Like they're always pushing people away from them."

Geena set the soup bowls on a tray. "What I've come to learn is that hurt people push others away because they want someone to come and get them, to say they haven't forgotten about them, to show how much they're wanted and needed."

Bethany fit three more bowls on Geena's tray. "Maybe if those girls made a little effort in the right direction, it might be easier for people to want and need them." There it was again: judgment. It was gaining a foothold. "Don't listen to me. I'm still frazzled from yesterday."

"It's been a big week for you, Bethany. It's a lot to process. Give yourself time." Geena squeezed her arm before she took the tray to the dining room.

*Process.* Geena had used that term before. She made it sound like thoughts and feelings were in motion and maybe they were. Bethany felt like she was trying to sort things through and put them where they belonged. It was as if her cluttered mind was a version of the Sisters' House and she was trying to get it organized.

Bethany ladled out more bowls of turkey rice soup and put them on a tray to take to the table of Group Home girls. They always sat in the same place—the farthest table. One clump on one side, one clump on the other, as if they didn't like each other and, probably, they didn't. She tried to focus on what Geena had mentioned—that these girls, including Rusty, were hurt souls, longing to be loved and valued. Noticed.

With a sigh and a prayer, she took the tray over to the table and set it on the table. One by one, she served a bowl of soup to each girl. She forced herself to smile and make eye contact. Then she came to Rusty. The two of them locked eyes almost like clockwork.

As Bethany reached across the table to serve the bowl to Rusty, she slipped

Bethany a note. She put it in her dress pocket. When she went back into the kitchen, she pulled it from her pocket and read it. A chill moved through her, tickling down her spine.

*Yesterday was just a warning. Tell Tobe to leave it alone.*

It was in Jake Hertzler's handwriting.

# 17

*Shootfire!* When it came to Jake Hertzler, Bethany made mistake after mistake after mistake. She was the one who had introduced him to her father, years ago, on a Sunday morning at church. She mentioned to her father that Jake had accounting skills and was looking for a job. She had done it intentionally—she thought Jake was charming and handsome, and he was. But he was also crafty and cunning and shrewd . . . and now she had discovered that he could be threatening.

Her anger evaporated as she realized, *It's all my fault.*

Why had she called Jake and left that message, tipping him off to Tobe's whereabouts? She was ashamed of her action, embarrassed by it, unsure of what to do about the note from him. What had she done? What did Jake mean—warning Tobe to "leave it alone." Leave *what* alone?

Why did she always seem to underestimate Jake?

She knew why. She was raised to believe the best in others—it was ingrained into her. How many times had she been told that if you search for the best in people you're bound to find it?

But what about people in whom there was no best?

Chase had been following her from room to room as she paced through the farmhouse, never leaving her side for longer than he absolutely had to. She sat at the kitchen table and he slumped under her chair and gazed at her, a worried expression on his furry face. Then his tail began to wag. She bent down and stroked his ears. She knew she needed to start dinner soon, but her thoughts couldn't leave that note.

She looked at it again. It was definitely Jake's distinctive handwriting. Rusty must have some involvement with Jake—which made it all the more likely that she had played a role in trashing the garden. Bethany thought back to those three figures she had seen at the back of the garden. She didn't think any was a man, but Jake had a slight build. Maybe one of those had been Jake, along with Rusty and one of her friends.

She wished she could talk to Rose. Or Galen. Geena? Should she call Allen Turner? Rose had left his business card on the kitchen countertop. But if Tobe heard about this, he would clam up and stop talking to Allen Turner. And then, without realizing the ramifications of clamming up, he would end up taking responsibility for the illegal things Jake had done to the business. She knew her brother's nature. He would avoid conflict at all cost. Why else had he disappeared for nearly a year?

She folded up the note. She just didn't know who to talk to or even how they could help. She tried to think straight and gather facts.

One fact in particular stared back at her: Jake was nearby.

Each afternoon, around five-ish, Mim waited at the phone shanty, hoping for a call from Danny Riehl to go stargazing. If he did happen to call, which wasn't often, it would be around that time of day. He would have finished his evening chores and be checking phone messages for his father before he'd be expected back at the house. She didn't really think he would call because there was a full moon tonight, round and creamy. Beautiful for the soft light it shed on the fields but too bright for stargazing. Those were the thoughts that were running through Mim's mind as the phone rang. She took a startled step backward, then lunged for it, sure it was Danny.

Instead, it was Rose, Mim's mother. "How's everything going, Mim?"

"Everything's fine. Well, at Eagle Hill, anyway. Bethany moved into my room so Geena Spencer could stay in her room. There's a new couple staying in the guest flat. They seem nice, but they're not around much. Turns out the lady is allergic to horses so she runs from the guest flat to her car with a pink handkerchief over her mouth."

"I wonder why she came to an Amish farm if she's allergic to horses."

Mim had the same thought. "And she needs her food to be gluten free.

We've been giving her scrambled eggs and applesauce for breakfast and told her they're gluten free."

"Mim—those things have always been gluten free."

"We know. But the lady seemed impressed so we decided not to say anything more."

"Do you think Geena will stay on for the rest of the week?"

"I hope so. She helped clean up the mess at the community garden."

"Wait. What? Why was there a mess?"

"Someone trashed the gardens on Tuesday afternoon."

"What? Why? What happened?"

"Nobody knows."

Silence. "I'm sorry about that. You've all worked so hard on those gardens."

"No kidding. But everybody has. And the same people helped clean it all up. It almost looks as good as it did on Saturday afternoon. Almost."

"What else have you been doing?"

"Me? Um . . . I . . ." She'd been sifting through letters for Mrs. Miracle and hoping to go stargazing with Danny Riehl, but she couldn't tell her mom any of that. "The usual. Chickens, horses, goat."

"Are the boys behaving?"

"Same as usual. Galen keeps them so busy that they fall asleep early."

Her mom laughed. "Good for him. That's pretty smart."

"How's Mammi Vera holding up?"

"She's sticking close to Tobe whenever we're at Allen Turner's office."

"Mom, is everything going to turn out all right for Tobe?"

"I . . . don't know yet. I hope so. He's spending a lot of time in depositions."

Mim knew all about those. She read up on depositions after a letter to Mrs. Miracle mentioned them. "But he'll be coming home soon, won't he? Won't all of you be home soon?"

There was a long pause. "I'll know more in a day or two. Are you managing by yourselves? Do you think Geena might stay until we return?"

"I can ask her. She doesn't seem to be in a hurry to get home."

"You can ask Galen for help too."

"I know. He stops by each day."

"Is Bethany doing all right?"

"She's been awful quiet." Mim wasn't sure where Bethany had gone on Tuesday, but she had come home a different person. Quiet, defeated. Another reason she was glad Geena was staying.

"I guess we're all shaken up by Tobe's return. Give her time, Mim." Mammi Vera's voice was calling in the background. "Your grandmother needs some help. I'll call again when there's news. And feel free to call Delia's house. The number is on the kitchen countertop. Bye, Mim."

Mim hung up the receiver and walked to the house, up to her bedroom, and back to her secret role as Mrs. Miracle. She wished she could talk to her mom about a problem that was brewing for Mrs. Miracle. Bethany had brought over the mail from the *Stoney Ridge Times* office and the envelope was bursting at the seams. Nearly every letter was about Mrs. Miracle's advice to "Wringing My Hands." Readers had all kinds of opinions about whether it was right to meddle in marriages. Four to one ran against Wringing My Hands telling the truth to her friend, Nancy. But what distressed Mim was the actual response from Wringing My Hands. She had absolutely no idea how to respond back to her:

*Dear Mrs. Miracle,*

*I took your advice and thought about whether I would want Nancy to tell me if my husband were having an affair. I would be grateful to my friend for the courage to tell me the truth and not let me remain a fool. So I told Nancy that her dentist husband was having an affair with his hygienist.*

*Nancy didn't believe me and said she will never speak to me again.*

**Really** *Wringing My Hands*

Mrs. Miracle's sterling advice might not have been quite as wonderful as Mim had thought. Then another letter completely baffled Mim:

*Dear Mrs. Miracle,*

*Have you ever noticed that you often answer a question with a question? Why is that? Are you trying to avoid giving an answer?*

*Cordially,*
*Wants an Answer*

Oh, boy. What could she say to that? Then she realized she had just done the very thing Wants an Answer accused her of doing.

She pulled out the next letter.

*Dear Mrs. Miracle,*
*    I messed things up. And now I don't know how to fix them.*
                        *Sincerely,*
                        *Stuck*

Mim chewed on the inside of her cheek. Now *this*, she thought she knew how to answer. For years, her mom had disciplined her two little brothers in just this way and it always worked:

*Dear Stuck,*
*    You can do two things:*
*    1) Apologize (sincerely).*
*    2) Do something that helps someone else.*
                        *Sincerely,*
                        *Mrs. Miracle*

On Thursday, after Bethany and Mim had spent a few hours tackling another corner of the Sisters' House, they walked into town to take care of a few errands. Chase had tagged along with them to the Sisters' House, where the sisters kept slipping him snacks, and then trotted behind the girls as they walked to town. When they reached Main Street, Mim handed Bethany the envelope that contained next week's Mrs. Miracle column. She was proud of herself for being ahead of her deadline.

"Be sure to ask for my paycheck," Mim said.

"You mean, *my* paycheck," Bethany said. "Don't forget that it's made out to me."

Mim frowned. "I'm going to get something at Pearl's Gift Store. Come on, Chase. We'll meet you back at this end of Main Street in ten minutes." Chase's ears pricked up at the mention of his name. Tongue lolling, tail wagging, he trotted behind Mim.

Bethany went into the *Stoney Ridge Times* office and asked the woman at the receptionist's desk for the envelopes for Mrs. Miracle. She wasn't the usual receptionist and peered curiously at Bethany as she handed her the manila envelope. "I'm Penny Williams. I'm a new hire. Just started today. You can't be . . . you aren't . . . Mrs. Miracle?" Her voice was hushed in awe.

"No," Bethany answered truthfully. "Her true identity is top secret."

"Of course you couldn't be Mrs. Miracle. She's got to be an old woman! Please tell her I love the column. It's getting a lot of buzz—everyone thinks Mrs. Miracle gives such comforting wisdom."

Bethany had to bite hard on her lower lip to keep from bursting into laughter. What would Penny Williams say if she knew Mrs. Miracle was a fourteen-year-old!

As the receptionist went to get Mrs. Miracle's paycheck, Bethany heard the sound of tires screeching, then a blood-chilling scream that sounded like Mim. Bethany dropped the column on the receptionist's desk and bolted to the door. She ran all the way down Main Street. Her bonnet blew off and a car had to stop short to let her cross the street.

There, lying in the middle of the street, was Chase. Mim was beside herself, shrieking that he'd been hit by a car, tears running down her face as she hovered over the poor dog. Bethany lifted Chase's head, and his eyes opened but he didn't even whimper. Between Mim's sobs she could hear him breathing hard. He was still alive. A crowd of people started to gather and suddenly beside her was Jimmy Fisher. He knelt down and put a hand on Chase's chest. He looked up at Bethany. "Go get my buggy. It's in front of the Hay & Grain." She hesitated, not wanting to leave Chase. "Go now."

She ran to it and drove the buggy over to where Chase lay. "Hurry, Jimmy. We can get him to the vet."

But Jimmy didn't hurry. His hand was still on Chase's chest. A soft look passed over his face. "I'm sorry. He's gone."

Bethany looked at Chase, feeling utterly helpless. Sweet old Chase lay dead. She would not let herself cry, not now. She needed to be strong for her sister. Mim held her hands in tight fists against her mouth.

Jimmy took over and lifted Chase in his arms. "I'll take him to Eagle Hill and bury him." Bethany spread a buggy blanket on the floor of the buggy and gently laid Chase on top. As Jimmy guided a stricken Mim into the buggy, Bethany remembered her bonnet and walked down the block to look for it. She found it in the gutter and bent down to pick it up. When she looked up, she noticed Rusty from the Group Home, about one hundred yards away, standing against a tree, watching the whole thing with an unreadable look on her face. Bethany locked eyes with her, until Rusty did a sharp about-face and walked away.

Back at the buggy, Bethany asked Mim if she had seen who had hit Chase. "No. It happened so fast. I was crossing the street and Chase was behind me. The next thing I knew, I heard the sound of a big thump, then a car rushed off."

"Did you recognize it?" Jimmy asked. "Or the driver?"

Mim shook her head, tears spilling. "I can't remember the car at all. It happened too fast. All I could think about was Chase, lying there on the ground." She put her face in her hands. "I should have been watching him more carefully."

"It's not your fault, Mim," Jimmy said. "These things happen."

"But Mim—"

"Bethany, not now," Jimmy said sharply. "Hop in." He helped Mim and Bethany into the buggy, then climbed in and drove them back to the house. He took the dog out, and Chase drooped in his arms, which started Mim sobbing all over again. "Bethany, where's a shovel?"

"I'll get it." Bethany went to the barn and brought back a shovel. She would not cry. She would not.

Sammy and Luke bolted out of the house, Geena following behind. When they saw Chase in Jimmy's arms, they stopped abruptly on the porch stairs. It was Luke who pierced Bethany's heart. Understanding settled over him first, she saw his face go utterly stoic—a strange look on an eleven-year-old boy. His head was up and slightly tilted, his gaze focused on Jimmy, and something about him seemed like their father in every way.

"What's wrong?" Sammy said, his forehead puckered with worry, his eyes too wide and bright. "What's wrong with Chase?"

"He's dead," Luke said coldly. Sammy burst into sobs. His whole heart shone on his face.

Tears prickled Bethany's eyes and she bit her lower lip to hold them back. *Not now. Not now.*

Geena joined them as they walked to the hill beside the house. Mim said Chase loved to sit on that hill and watch the sheep in their pen, so Jimmy chose a beautiful tree with a large canopy and started to dig. He laid Chase gently, ever so gently, in the hole, then put a big handful of dirt in the boys' hands. Geena said a few reassuring words about what a good dog Chase was and sang a hymn that no one else recognized, but they liked it. Then they dropped their dirt on the little grave, and made a great ceremony of filling it and piling rocks. By the time the funeral was over, the afternoon was nearly past.

Geena and Mim walked down the hill with Jimmy and Bethany and the boys trailing behind. "I don't know how I'll tell Rose," Bethany said, about halfway down the hill. "She adored Chase."

Luke spun around and glared at Bethany. "It's your fault!"

She stared at him, trying to understand him. "That's not true, Luke. It's not true and it's not fair."

"With Mom gone, you were supposed to take care of us!"

"Wait a minute!"

Luke's eyes flashed, and he started to protest, but Bethany wouldn't let him interrupt. He shook his head as she came up to him.

"Listen to me," she said. "This was just a terrible accident. It was no one's fault."

"It's your fault!" Luke shouted as he lifted his face. Angry tears filled his eyes. "You should have been watching out for him. You should have stopped this!"

"Luke, I—"

He didn't wait for her answer. He lurched around and ran back up the hill, disappearing over the ridge.

Bethany worried so about Luke. She knew he was edging up to manhood, his heart sore and lonely with grieving for their father. He'd taken to doing and saying things he'd never have dared to try to get away with when their father was alive. She started to follow, but Jimmy grabbed her arm.

"Let him go. It wasn't your fault."

A wave of guilt crashed over Bethany. She was sinking beneath it. "Luke's right. If I'd been paying attention . . ."

"Don't think like that. It wasn't your fault, understand?" He turned her so she had to look at him. "Bethany, did you happen to see that pickup truck that hit Chase?"

"No. I was in the newsp—I was in a store." She looked up. "You must have, though, if you knew it was a pickup truck."

"I can't be sure . . . and I only saw it once before, at twilight. Months ago. It was at Windmill Farm, at Hank Lapp's birthday party."

Bethany stilled. *Oh please, no.*

"It looked like the same black pickup that Jake Hertzler drove."

Another warning from Jake.

Later that night, Bethany tiptoed into Luke's room and sat on his bed. She rubbed his shoulders to soften the ache she knew was there, and to comfort him. "I'm sorry about Chase, Luke. So very sorry."

Luke wiped his eyes with his pajama sleeve. "There'll never be another dog like Chase."

"No. Chase will always be special. But there will be another dog to love. Chase wouldn't want you to stop loving another dog just because you loved him so much. He'd want you to honor his memory by loving again. We'll find you a special dog."

"Chase came to us. We didn't go to him. That's the way it is with the best dogs. They find you."

"Then we'll be waiting."

They stayed like that a long time, just listening to Pennsylvania night sounds through the open window—the soft hoot of a great horned owl and the harsh squawk of a Northern Mockingbird and, now and then, the steady clip-clop of a horse pulling a buggy—each of which had their own way of giving comfort.

# 18

After the long sick worry of a week, Bethany helped Naomi sew a binding on a quilt top on Friday evening and found it strangely calming. As soon as they finished, Naomi wanted to drop it off at the Sisters' House so it could be wrapped and taken to a fundraising auction in the morning. A full moon cast eerie shadows all around Bethany and Naomi as they drove home from the Sisters' House in the buggy.

The more time Bethany spent around the sisters, the more amazed she was at their quiet and purposeful lives. Now she understood why their house was a mess—they had better things to do with their time than clean and tidy and iron and dust. And they didn't just talk about doing things—they did them. They even cared for Bethany's own mother.

She still didn't know the story behind that, but she was taking Geena's advice to sit on it and pray about it. Geena said she would know when the time was right, but so far, nothing. She hoped Geena was right. This praying and expecting and waiting for an answer to come was new to her. She would prefer a burning bush.

"I'm glad for the chill in the air," Naomi said as Bethany turned the horse down the road. Bethany stopped and looked both ways when they reached the intersection, although she knew there wasn't a car in sight. She tugged the horse's reins and murmured, "Tch, tch," to urge him forward.

All of a sudden, Naomi grabbed her arm. "Look out, Bethany!"

She pulled back on the horse and slammed on the buggy brake, stopping no more than a yard in front of something lying across the road. If

428

Naomi hadn't spotted it in time, the horse would have tried to jump it and the buggy could have been wrecked. "Shootfire! That was close. What's in the road?"

"I don't know."

They got out of the buggy together and walked to a large tree limb that was lying crossways in the road. "How in the world did that get there?" Bethany looked up. "There aren't any big trees hanging overhead."

"Maybe it fell off a truck," Naomi said. Bethany leaned down to pick up one end of the tree limb and was about to ask Naomi if she would pick up the other when Naomi said, "Something's not right here. Quick, Bethany. Get back in the buggy. We can go back down the way we came."

"Why? That'll take a lot longer to get home."

"I can't explain it. I'm just getting a funny feeling."

"I thought you only got those when you had a headache."

"Hurry! We need to get out of here!"

She straightened up to see what Naomi was so anxious about, and just as she did, a man emerged out of the cornfield. She opened her mouth to ask for his help, but before she could utter a word, it dawned on her that tree limb wasn't there by accident. The man came toward her, slow and deliberate, and stopped just as he reached the buggy headlight. He took a step closer, moving across the beam of the headlight off the buggy, and she saw who it was.

Jake Hertzler.

He walked right up to her and smiled, but his eyes showed no warmth, only a cold, hard gaze. "Hello, Bethany."

She stood like a statue, frozen to the spot.

"Bethany, who is he?" Naomi asked in a trembling voice.

"I'm Bethany's boyfriend, Jake Hertzler. Bethany, honey, I've come for you." Jake's voice was soft and charming, like always, and there was the faint scent of Old Spice aftershave lotion, like always, but he didn't look the same and he didn't act the same. He had a strange look on his face that scared her. Something had changed, something essential, deep down. Even then, Bethany thought it was odd that she'd noticed such a thing.

"What is it you want, Jake?" Bethany practically spit the words. "You killed Chase. You ruined the gardens. What more can you take from my family?"

Jake sneered and his eyes narrowed slightly in the way of a man study-ing a mildly perturbing question. "I need to talk to Tobe and I think it's best if you're with me."

"She doesn't want anything to do with you," Naomi said boldly. "No-body does."

Jake waved his hand at Naomi, as if he were brushing away a pesky fly. He kept his eyes on Bethany.

"I'm not going anywhere with you," Bethany snapped. "You keep away from me!"

He gave her a slow look over, up and down, in a way that made her feel filthy.

"Don't you touch me," she said, teeth chattering. She didn't want him to see how cold she was. She was shaking with it, she was feeling so cold. She took a step back.

Jake lunged toward her and grabbed her wrist. "You know you don't mean that. You know you belong to me."

She tried to yank her hand away, but he slapped her across the face with the back of his hand, then hit her again with his palm. She tried to get away, but he held on to her wrist tight as a trap.

By now Jake's cool exterior had vanished; he was seething. She looked into that face, into eyes that were relentless, ruthless.

"What's the matter, Bethany? Aren't I good enough for you anymore?" Jake put his hand on her throat and moved it down over her body. She began to shake all over even while she was trying so hard to be brave.

"Leave her be, Hertzler." A voice spoke out calm and clear in the dark. Jake stilled.

"Hertzler, I told you to leave her alone," the voice said a little louder. In the beam of the buggy headlight stood Rusty.

Jake dropped Bethany's wrist as if it were a hot potato and spun around. Bethany's legs gave out and she fell into the dirt. Naomi ran to her side.

"Run along, kid," Jake said. "You've been paid for your work."

"You can keep your money," Rusty replied in the same calm voice and pulled out a handful of crumpled bills from the pocket of her jeans. She threw them at Jake's feet. "Leave the women alone." Bethany realized she had never heard Rusty's voice before. She spoke as quietly as a person in a library. "They won't fight you, being Amish, but I will."

Jake laughed at Rusty, sizing her up and dismissing her. He turned back to Bethany and grabbed her arm. "Get up. You and me are going for a ride."

Rusty pulled the buggy whip from its socket and whipped it, like a flash, against the back of Jake's hand so that he released Bethany. "I told you to leave her alone."

Jake gripped his stung hand. Then he swung at Rusty, but before he could land a single punch, she kicked him in his privates. He bellowed out with pain and she kicked him again so that he dropped his hands to the front of his pants and doubled over. Rusty pulled something out of her back pocket and held it up high, in front of her, so Jake would see it in the beam of the buggy headlight. In her hand was a six-inch knife. It looked familiar, like the knives that belonged to the Grange Hall kitchen.

"Now, why don't you just get along back to that rock you live under," she said, still in that calm, quiet voice.

Strangely authoritative, Bethany realized, and wondered why her mind was working though her body wouldn't budge.

Jake turned to run and Rusty kicked him in the small of this back. He made a *whoomp* sound and limped off into the dark.

Rusty watched, making sure he was gone for good, before she turned to Bethany, her breath coming as easy as if she'd been out for a walk. "You all right?"

"Where did you come from?" Bethany's voice was high and shaky, and she cleared her throat.

"Just heading back to the Group Home."

"Thank you," she whispered.

Rusty nodded, shifting from one foot to the other. "I'll move that tree limb out of the road. Then I'll be getting on."

"No!" Naomi cried. "What if he comes back?" She was as pale as a ghost.

Rusty hoisted the tree limb and shoved it to the side of the road like it was a feather pillow. "I don't think so. Not tonight, anyway. He'll be hurting for a while."

"I can't drive the buggy," Bethany said. "My hands are shaking too much." Naomi was trembling even more.

"I'll drive you," Rusty said. She hopped right into the driver's side of the buggy. Naomi helped Bethany in, then got in and sat in the backseat. Bethany wanted to know more about Rusty, to ask how she happened to be right there when they needed her, how she knew Jake, why she was willing to fight him off. And how did she know how to drive a buggy? But Bethany's cheek was smarting where Jake had hit her and her teeth kept chattering and she wasn't sure she could get the words out in any order that made any sense. Rusty didn't volunteer any information—she just drove the buggy down the road like she'd been doing it most of her life.

When Rusty pulled up to Naomi's house, Jimmy came out of the front door. "Galen was just wondering where you were, Naomi." He stopped short as he realized there were three in the buggy. "What's happened?"

From the backseat, Naomi poked her head out the buggy window. "Bethany needs help."

Jimmy jumped the porch rail, landing near the buggy.

"We just had a scare, that's all," Bethany said.

"The scare of our life," Naomi added.

Jimmy yanked open the buggy door, and Bethany slid out and fell into his arms.

"Let's get her inside," Naomi said, hurrying to climb down from the buggy.

Jimmy wrapped his arm around Bethany and helped her up to the house. Her legs still felt shaky—she couldn't have walked to the house without his help. They reached the porch steps before she remembered Rusty and turned back to the buggy.

"Rusty!" she called, but there was no answer in the darkness.

Galen opened the door. "I'll put the horse and buggy away . . . ," he started to say, then stopped when he saw the bruise on Bethany's face. "Do you want me to get a doctor?" he asked.

"No," Bethany said.

Jimmy set her in a chair as Galen grabbed a sweater hanging on the wall and wrapped it around her.

"I'll get a cold rag for your face," Galen said.

"I'll start some tea," Naomi said, her voice sounding stronger. "Tea always helps everyone calm down." She filled the teakettle with water and put it on the stove to boil.

Jimmy knelt down in front of Bethany. "Are you all right?"

Bethany nodded, her eyes on her lap, where her hands twitched.

"Look at me, Bethany," Jimmy said.

She raised her head as slowly as she could, glancing at him, then turning to the stove where the teakettle was starting to sputter.

He covered her hands with his. They were so warm and she was so cold. "Are you sure you're all right?"

"Yes," she said in a squeaky voice. "He didn't . . . he tried to make me go with him . . ."

"Who?"

Bethany kept her eyes on her hands that were tucked under Jimmy's. She took too long to answer, so Naomi spoke up. "Jake. Jake Hertzler."

"Oh no . . ." Jimmy grabbed Bethany out of her chair and hugged her so hard she could hardly breathe.

"I'm all right, Jimmy. Truly I am."

The teakettle started to whistle, so Naomi filled a teapot with hot water, then dipped four teabags into it. The cinnamon scent of the tea filled the air, calming Bethany's racing heart. Galen brought a cold rag and she held it up against her cheek to keep the swelling down. Every few minutes, without saying anything, he took the rag and refolded it so it would be cool, then put it back against her face.

Naomi set the teapot and four mugs on the kitchen table, then sat at the kitchen table and poured tea for everyone. Bethany looked up and saw Naomi gazing at her with concern, handing her a mug of hot tea, and she felt so lucky to have such good friends that tears came to her eyes.

As Naomi's nerves settled, she was able to start at the beginning. Bethany filled in parts she missed, so that soon Galen and Jimmy heard every detail, including the rescue by Rusty.

When the girls had finished, Jimmy hit the table with his fist. "I'm going after him!"

"No!" Naomi said. "No. You can't catch him. You shouldn't even try."

"Naomi's right," Galen said, "but we should call that SEC lawyer. He needs to hear—"

"No," Naomi said firmly. "We should let God alone deal with this."

Bethany looked at Naomi. "What else did you see tonight?"

Hesitating, Naomi kept her eyes fixed on her tea mug. "Jake Hertzler cast two shadows. I saw it in the moonlight, plain as day."

A chill traveled down Bethany's spine. Jimmy and Galen exchanged a look.

Naomi's hands were wrapped tightly around the mug. "That man is possessed."

Early Saturday morning, Jimmy arrived at Galen's to start work. Galen was in front of the barn, waiting for him, a tight, serious look on his face.

"I thought I'd stop over at Eagle Hill before the day begins and see if Bethany's doing all right after last night's scare."

"Hold on a minute, Jimmy."

"What is it, partner? You look like someone has died. Naomi's all right, isn't she?"

"She's fine. Jimmy, when I got up early this morning, I noticed that the barn door was wide open. Someone had been in there during the night. But I never heard a thing."

Jimmy snapped to attention. "What's happened?"

Galen rubbed his chin. "It's Lodestar. He's gone missing."

Bethany sent Luke and Sammy outside with a basket to gather eggs in the henhouse because Jimmy said he wanted to talk to her privately. He pulled out a kitchen chair. "Bethany, sit down. There's something I need to tell you before your brothers find out."

At the kitchen sink washing breakfast dishes, Bethany wiped her soapy hands on a dishrag and sat at the table. She could hear the drip of water in the sink as she waited for Jimmy to say what was on his mind: *plink, plink, plink.*

He cleared his throat. "Lodestar was stolen."

Bethany's shoulders shivered faintly. She squeezed her hands together into tight fists. "Jake," she said in a deadly quiet voice.

"Probably. Can't prove it but probably so."

Bethany sat there fuming for a few seconds, then she slammed her palms on the tabletop. "It isn't fair. It isn't right! He takes everything we love."

She shook her head as if trying to shake off an image of Jake. As quickly as it came, the fury drained out of her and a ripple of hope crossed her face. "Do you think you can find Lodestar?"

"I don't know." He lifted his hands, showed his palms. "Maybe . . . it's for the best."

"How so?"

He leaned back in the chair so the front two legs lifted. "My mother has been after me to manage the chicken and egg business, full-time."

"But you hate chickens."

"I do indeed. But she's my mother and I do love her. And maybe I've been making too much of being a horse trainer. It's created nothing but tension with my mother. I left Paul alone to handle the chicken business and that wasn't fair, either. Sometimes, the things we love can turn into our glory. My sense of purpose, my significance—I put it into something finite. Maybe horse training has become too important to me."

Bethany pressed the heels of her palms into her eyes. "Jimmy," she whispered, wiping guilty tears with the back of her hand. "I'm just so sorry . . ."

He crossed his arms over his chest. "Why? You didn't do anything."

"If I hadn't introduced Jake to my father in the first place, he wouldn't have swindled all those people, and you wouldn't have lost Lodestar."

Jimmy's mouth split into a grin and he shook his head. "Boy, you sure think a lot of yourself, Bethany. I'm perfectly capable of making my own mistakes, thank you."

"But . . ."

"I'm the one who was dazzled by Lodestar and bought him from Jake without getting a bill of sale. I did that all by myself. Maybe I've lit too many firecrackers in my day," he said, rapping his head with his fist. "Or maybe I'm just stubborn. Probably that. But whatever I am, whatever I've done, I've done myself. So quit trying to hog all the credit, will you? Besides, I'm glad things happened the way they did."

Seeing her open mouth, he laughed. "Don't look at me like that. I mean it. I'd been thinking about all this even before Lodestar went missing. I've ignored my mother's need for help with the chicken farm. I think maybe God had to shake me to get my attention."

"You think God arranged for Lodestar to get stolen?"

"Well, I don't think God opened the stall door or anything like that, but I do think he used the situation to shake some sense into me. Galen said once that the hardest choices in life aren't between what's right and what's wrong but between what's right and what's best."

He leaned forward to brush tears from her cheeks. "And who knows? With that horse's penchant for running, maybe I won't have to find him at all. Maybe he'll come back to me."

She tried to smile, but it came out all wrong: sad and pitiful.

"So, think you don't mind being courted by a chicken farmer?"

Bethany's back went straight up. "And who said anything about courting, Jimmy Fisher?"

He wiggled his eyebrows up and down. "When are you going to admit you're crazy about me?"

She gave him a sly look. "You want me to turn into a quiet, timid little Amish girl."

Jimmy grinned. "Not hardly."

"Let me tell you something, Jimmy Fisher, I am not the kind of girl who cares about silly things, like whose cobbler tastes best at Sunday potlucks or what anyone might be saying about an early winter or an early thaw or if the wheat might blight this year due to heavy rains."

"I want you just the way you are. Spitfire and all." He scooted his chair closer to her. "You know you're sweet on me, Bethany."

"Maybe I am, but that's beside the point."

"What is the point?" He scooted his chair even closer to her, his gaze fixed on her lips. "The only thing on my mind is kissing you."

"You need more on your mind, Jimmy Fisher." She turned her chin away, trying not to think about being kissed by him, so of course all she could do was think about it. His fingers were brushing her hair from her neck and then his lips fell there, on her nape, which made her shudder. He noticed. "Look at me," he said quietly.

And as if her body belonged to someone else, that's what she did. She turned to face him and he kissed her. Sweetly at first, full of tenderness. Gentleness. She felt safe here, in his arms.

Luke and Sammy ran past the kitchen windows, holding a basket between them full of freshly gathered eggs.

"Bethany!" Luke shouted. "Open the kitchen door. The basket's heavy and we're hungry!"

Jimmy released her. "What happens if we give it a try, Bethany? This relationship thing?"

She only looked at him.

Jimmy smiled his slow, wonderful smile and plopped his hat back on his head. "I'll talk to you soon."

# 19

Geena had been right to encourage Bethany to wait before asking the sisters about her mother. She felt better prepared to hear the truth than she had last week, when it was fresh. Painful. She had needed time to "process," as Geena would say.

But the time had come to find out more. Bethany had woken up on Monday morning with a strange inner knowing that it was time. Could it be she was finally sensing the intuition that Naomi said belonged to everyone? Or maybe it was the prompting from God that Geena had said would come, in good time. And here it was.

Over the weekend, Bethany had confided in Naomi, telling her everything she knew about her mother, and Naomi had repeated her standing invitation to the quilting bee. "Come to the quilting bee on Monday," Naomi said. "Come and ask."

Bethany hadn't given Naomi a definite answer, but all morning long, she kept getting a tug she couldn't ignore. More like a push. At noon, she appeared at Naomi's front door. "I'm going to go."

Naomi smiled, as if she knew all along.

The Sisters' Bee was meeting at Edith Fisher's house. A Log Cabin quilt top, pieced from purple and blue fabrics, was stretched onto a large frame in the living room, with chairs positioned around the frame. The women were just finding their places as Jimmy Fisher darted in and handed his mother a bag of lemons. His eyes locked on Bethany's and he made his eyebrows do that crazy up-down dance, which always made her grin as

438

hard as she tried to squelch it. Edith Fisher caught their look and glared suspiciously at Bethany, who ducked her head in embarrassment.

Edith held up the bag of lemons. "I'll put the teakettle on. I'm serving my shortbread," she announced as if it were a surprise.

"I'd hoped you would," Naomi said kindly.

Bethany had hoped she would not, but fat chance. She was amazed that Naomi—who was a fine baker—could be so charitable about Edith Fisher's rock-hard shortbread. A person could chip a tooth on it.

The ladies chatted to each other in a mingling of Penn Dutch and English. For a moment Bethany closed her eyes, letting the harmonious sound of the two mingled languages fill her. The best sound, she thought. Like music.

"Has anyone seen my favorite thimble?" Ella asked Bethany and Naomi. "I've misplaced it."

More and more, Bethany felt a spike of concern about Ella's with-it-ness. She was always looking for that one lost thimble, the one with the band of roses around its base, though she had plenty of other thimbles.

When the women had settled in their seats and pulled out their needles and thread, Bethany took a deep breath and blurted out, "I have a question to ask and I would like an answer."

Heads bobbed up. The sisters looked curiously at Bethany.

"I want to know the truth about my mother."

Hands stilled. Chins dropped to chests and eyes riveted to needle and thread. All but Naomi. She kept her head high. Bethany was so glad she was beside her. "I went to Hagensburg. I saw my mother. I know she's schizophrenic. I also know that some of you visit her once a month." She hoped someone in the room would speak, but it was as quiet as death.

The ladies peeked around the circle at one another, avoiding Bethany's eyes; then each turned to Edith Fisher, just as they always did when there was a difficult decision to make. It was remarkable how much authority Edith possessed. She would have made a fine deacon, Bethany thought, and wondered why in the world she was thinking such a stray thought when she was waiting to hear the truth about her mother.

"What's that you were saying?" Edith Fisher said stonily.

"I said I wanted to know the truth about my mother."

Sylvia let out a deep sigh and set down her needle. "I always thought we should have told her, right from the beginning. Do I have your permission, sisters?" She looked around the circle for approval. "Edith, is it all right for Bethany to know our secret about Mary?" Everyone waited.

Bethany looked at Edith Fisher. She shrugged her big shoulders up and down, but at last, she muttered, "I suppose we knew this day would come, sooner or later."

Sylvia picked up her needle and thread and set to work. "Bethany, your mother started this quilting bee," she said. "When she married your father, she moved here to Stoney Ridge and asked Ella to teach her to quilt. Ella has always been known for her fine quilting and for her bottomless well of patience." She nodded at her sister.

Ella seemed pleased with the compliment. "Patience is a virtue."

"That it is, dear," Ada said. "And in short supply today."

*Oh no.* Once the sisters veered off topic, it was never a short trip back.

"She called us the Sisters' Bee, your mother did. And soon a few others joined in who weren't good quilters. Edith, for example."

Edith's sparse eyebrows lifted.

"It's the truth, Edith," Fannie said. "Your stitches were long as inchworms."

"They never were!"

"Knots the size of flies," Lena added.

Edith's lips flattened into a thin line of disgust.

Lena waved that away. "It wasn't your fault, Edith. You just hadn't learned right. You've made a lot of progress over the years."

Bethany cleared her throat to remind them of the topic of her mother.

Sylvia picked up on Bethany's cue. "Your mother was a pretty girl, just as pretty as you. She and your daddy made a fine pair. But your mama was awful young when they married. And she started showing signs of the sickness before Tobe was born."

"What kind of signs?" Bethany asked.

"She grew fearful," Ada said.

"Oh yes, yes," Fannie said, nodding her head. "I remember that now. She thought someone was after her. She wasn't always sure what was real and what wasn't. But she had good days, when she seemed right as rain. We all thought the sickness would go away after the baby came."

The sisters nodded. "We did think that," Sylvia said. "But after Tobe was born, the sickness came on her and didn't leave. It hit her hard. We all tried helping out—sometimes new mothers get the baby blues."

Fannie shook her head. "This wasn't the baby blues."

"No, it wasn't," Sylvia said. "It was something we didn't know how to handle. Our church was different back then. We had a different bishop—it was after Caleb Zook's time—"

Ella spoke up. "Caleb Zook would have known how to help her. He was a fine, fine bishop."

All five sisters nodded. Even Edith gave a curt bob of her head. Just one.

"Our bishop at that time was hard on Mary," Ada said. "He convinced her that she was being punished for her sins."

Sylvia poised her needle in the quilt, then looked up. "Poor Mary got sicker and sicker—strange, strange behavior. That doctor gave her some medicine, but she didn't like the way it made her feel. She slept almost around the clock."

"All day and all night," Ella echoed.

"And they didn't know as much about mental illness twenty-some years ago," Sylvia said. "Mary couldn't tolerate those drugs, sleeping all the time, not with a little toddler running around. Your daddy took her to more doctors and tried more medicines. One doctor said she would need to be locked up before she hurt herself. Then your daddy heard about a *Braucher* in Ohio and they paid him a visit. When they came back from the faith healer, they threw away her medication. They both thought she was healed. Your daddy—" she sighed, "well, the need to believe things were going to be all right was a powerful one. And for a little while, she did seem better." She looked around the room at her sisters. "Remember that?"

Capstrings bounced in agreement.

"Then she became in the family way with you," Sylvia continued. "And the sickness came back to her and wouldn't leave. One of us took turns staying with her, all the time."

A hot, crushing sensation sharpened in Bethany's chest. "What happened then?"

The sisters exchanged a glance, then their eyes settled on Edith Fisher.

"It was a hot summer day and I was on duty with her," Edith said.

"Tobe had fallen outside, so I ran out to see if he was hurt. Your mother was resting, and you were in your cradle, sound asleep. But when I came back in, I found her . . ." She stumbled on the words, then stopped. She puffed air out of her cheeks and looked away.

Whatever Edith was trying to say, it was hard for her.

She turned back to look straight at Bethany. "I found her trying to drown you in the bathtub. She said you had a demon in you."

What did that mean? The heat of the afternoon made Bethany feel like she might faint. She opened her mouth to speak, then stopped. The hot spot on her chest grew hotter and larger, spreading up her neck to her cheeks. This truth . . . as it settled in, it was searing her heart.

"So we packed Mary up and took her to that little house for sick ladies," Sylvia said. "And we never told your daddy or anybody else where she'd gone."

Bethany's breaths came in rapid pants and her throat was so dry. "You did that? You let my father, all of us, think she had run off? Just abandoned us?"

"We did," Sylvia said gently, firmly, "and we'd do it again."

"But . . . why? How could you do such a thing?"

"We were afraid your father would go get her and bring her back and then we didn't know what she might do. To herself, to you, to Tobe. We couldn't risk that."

Bethany dropped her hands in her lap and looked hard at Sylvia. "But that wasn't fair! It wasn't right. Not to my father, not to the rest of us. To not know where she'd gone or why."

"It might not have been fair," Sylvia said, "but it was better than the alternatives."

"How could you put someone away without their will?"

"It wasn't against her will," Edith interrupted impatiently. She'd let Sylvia be in charge long enough. "This was all Mary's idea. She had asked us to help her, begged us, if there came a point when she couldn't take care of you or Tobe. We loved her. We did what she wanted. We even helped with the divorce papers even though it went against our beliefs."

"Against everything we believed in," Fannie said.

"We didn't think it was the right thing to do. If the bishop knew, we would've been in hot water ourselves."

"Terrible hot water," Ella echoed.

"Kneeling on the front bench," Ada added.

"We tried talking Mary out of it," Edith said, "but she was adamant."

"But . . . you helped her get a divorce? My father would never have divorced my mother, no matter how sick she became."

"That's true," Sylvia said, "but he also wasn't willing to protect her. His need to believe everything was all right was stronger than the facts."

Bethany felt a chill run down her spine. Hadn't she heard Rose say the same thing to her father as Schrock Investments imploded?

"I know this is hard for you to understand," Fannie said, "but your mother was desperate. She had moments of clarity that horrified her and she knew the sickness was getting worse. Your mother needed help and your father wouldn't get it for her. He could never accept what her sickness was doing to her. He refused to believe that she was as sick as she was. We felt desperate too, Bethany. That was when the Sisters' Bee had a talk and we agreed to do what Mary asked us to do. We didn't know how else to help her. I suppose we thought this was her only chance to keep herself safe—for her own sake, for others, to give her some peace of mind."

Edith rose. "We never abandoned Mary. We still take care of her. We rotate a schedule and visit her every month."

Sylvia gave Bethany a sad smile. "This is why we keep quilting. We raffle off our quilts at local auctions and pay Mary's monthly bills."

Bethany tried to steady herself, tried to breathe, as she absorbed this news. "I need to think about it all. I want—I just—" She stood, hoping her knees wouldn't buckle. "I can't take it in." She headed for the door, then stopped and turned around. "How did you know she would never get well? How could anybody predict that?"

The question hung in the air as they all grew quiet again, eyes on Edith. There was something more, a final part of the secret.

"I knew your mother as a girl," Edith said. "We were childhood friends. I introduced her to your father." There was a tremor of sadness in her voice. She looked down at her hands, then lifted her head and looked straight at Bethany. "Mary's mother had the sickness too. She knew what her future looked like."

Bethany grasped the top of a chair. She felt a blow, as real as if someone had kicked her in the stomach. And that was when it hit her. It was genetic. Her mother's sickness was hereditary.

"So *that's* why you don't want Jimmy to court Bethany," Naomi said in a quiet voice.

Edith spoke right to Bethany. "Die Dochder aart der Mudder noh." *The daughter takes after the mother.*

"Edith! That's an awful, awful thing to say," Sylvia scolded.

"It's the truth," Edith huffed.

Sylvia crossed the room and reached for Bethany's hands, covering them with her own hands, wrinkled and speckled with brown spots. "We kept this secret because we didn't want you to grow up with such a burden hanging over your head. Not you or your brother Tobe." She squeezed Bethany's hands and held them close to her heart. "Just remember one thing, Bethany. Your mother loved you. Don't you see? She loved you and your brother and your daddy enough to give you up."

Bethany had to get out of that house, that stuffy room, away from the looks of pity on the sisters' faces, relieved Naomi didn't follow her. She spotted Jimmy in the cornfield and skirted quickly around the chicken hatchery to reach the road, hoping he hadn't seen her. She desperately needed to be alone.

As soon as she reached the shady tree-lined road, she slowed. She gulped in air and tried to find words to pray, but she couldn't find them. Her thoughts were on her mother as a young woman—about how she must have walked down this very road when she was Bethany's age—when she felt her heart start to race and she had trouble taking a full breath of air. Her stomach cramped. A tingling sensation ran down her arms to the ends of her fingers. She stopped on the side of the road and sat on the grass under a tree, hoping it would pass. What was happening to her?

After a few long moments, her heart stopped racing, she could breathe again, and she was left with a wave of exhaustion. A sort of oppression settled over her—weighing her down, stealing her energy. This wasn't the first time she felt like something might be wrong with her. Each time, it felt different. A few days ago, her hands couldn't stop trembling. Another time she woke in the night in a cold sweat, convinced she was suffocating. She hadn't slept more than two hours at a stretch in the last week. Was she too young to have a heart attack? Her father had heart trouble.

Or . . . was she going crazy? Like her mother? It wasn't the first time she had thought such a thing. After meeting her mother last week, the worry had been lurking at the back of her mind. All summer long, she had been turning into all moodiness and distraction. She tried not to think she was losing her mind, but that was like trying not to think about a cricket that was chirping. The more you don't think about it, the louder it gets.

Schizophrenia could be inherited. Hadn't Edith Fisher just admitted as much?

She had to go talk to Jimmy Fisher.

"You're breaking up with me?" Jimmy's mouth opened wide and his eyes quit twinkling. "And we haven't even started courting yet?"

"I've given it a lot of thought since we talked, Jimmy," Bethany said, trying to sound clear and strong and brave. No wavering. "It's for the best. It's good that nothing's gotten started yet. It'll be easier. We were friends before and this way we'll remain friends." It hurt too much to look in his eyes so she didn't.

He grabbed her shoulders and made her face him. "What have I done wrong?"

*Tell him. Don't tell him.* "Nothing. It's nothing like that. It's just . . . I'm just not right for you." To her horror, tears sprang to her eyes and she bit her lip, trying to make them stop. It had been such a long afternoon and she was dangerously emotional, teetering on a breakdown.

"Whatever I did, I'm sorry. If you'll just tell me, I promise I won't do it again."

That pulled her up short. Sympathy was the last thing she expected, or deserved. *Tell him. Don't tell him.* She turned her head away and looked at the chicken hatchery in the distance. "You wouldn't understand."

He gave her shoulders a gentle shake. "Then help me to understand. Why are you suddenly going cold on me? Usually, you're only mad if I've done something stupid."

His face looked so sad, she wanted to hug him, but of course she didn't dare. "I'm not mad at you. I'm not."

His shoulders slumped. Just as he was about to say something, she stopped him. "Please. I just need to be left alone. Can't you understand that?"

He shrugged, but not in a good way, as if he accepted what was coming and was bracing himself for it. "Yeah, sure. Absolutely." He let her go and took a step back, then his eyes turned to a snapping fire for a second and his mouth broke into one of those reckless smiles that made her feel as if her heartbeat missed a hitch. "Don't you worry none about me, Bethany," he said, the words clipped, hard. "I'll get along just fine."

But then she never doubted that and it was hardly to be wondered. Him with his mighty faith, so strong and solid. It was herself she doubted. "I know. I know you will."

He gave her a probing look, one she couldn't read. "Just answer me this . . . what are you so afraid of?"

She turned her head from his hard gaze and felt burning tears flood into her eyes, causing her to sniff like a baby. He just wouldn't leave well enough alone and made her look at him square in the face. "Tell me."

She hesitated for a moment before giving him the only possible answer. "Of making a terrible mistake."

# 20

Early Tuesday morning, Mim found some sheets of used, slightly wrinkled wrapping paper and tape in her mom's desk and sat at the kitchen table to wrap the present. She had never been so excited to give someone a gift before.

"What have you got there?" Bethany asked as she came into the kitchen with an apronful of gathered eggs.

Mim spread out the wrapping paper and ran her hand along it, trying to smooth out the wrinkles. "I found a thimble for Ella. She's always looking for her thimble so I thought I'd get her one."

One by one, Bethany put the eggs into a bowl and set them in the refrigerator. She came over to the table and picked up the thimble. "Mim, it's sterling silver."

"I know," Mim said, pleased. "Look at the band of wild roses around the base. Just like the one Ella keeps looking for. The one her mother gave to her."

Bethany held it up to the light. "It's dated from the 1890s."

"I know."

"Where did you find it?"

"At Pearl's Gift Shop on Main Street. I saw it in the shop window and knew I had to get it for Ella. That's what I was looking at the day . . . when Chase got . . . hurt."

"But Mim . . . this must have been expensive."

447

Mim smoothed out a few pieces of tissue paper and tried to figure out how to wrap up such a tiny thimble. If she wrapped it too tightly, Ella's arthritic, knobby fingers couldn't open it. "That's why I wanted you to get my paycheck from the newspaper. I wanted to use my Mrs. Miracle money."

Bethany handed her the thimble and sat down in a chair. "You realize that Ella will probably lose this thimble."

Carefully, Mim cut out a piece of wrapping paper. "No she won't."

"Oh Mim, don't you see? Haven't you noticed how forgetful Ella is? She's always losing things."

"Everybody loses things. Luke can't keep track of a hat for longer than a week."

Bethany blew a puff of air out of her cheeks. "This is a different kind of forgetfulness, Mim."

"No, it's not." She set the thimble in the center of the square and folded the paper up around it. "Ella lost her thimble and she needs a new one. That's all. Stop being mean about her."

"I'm not being mean. I'm just trying to help prepare you—" She stopped and gave Mim a look that she couldn't understand—sweetness and sadness, all mixed together. "Hold on. I might have a box you could fit the thimble in. That would make the wrapping go easier." Before she left the room, she gave Mim a kiss on the top of her prayer covering.

No girl had ever broken up with Jimmy Fisher before—he'd always been the one to cut ties. Was this how it felt? Was this the pain he had inflicted on so many girls? Most recently, Katie Zook? It felt like he had been sucker punched. Left for buzzard pickings under a hot sun. Like someone tore his heart out of his chest with a dull kitchen knife.

Jimmy had hooked the team of horses to a cultivator and was working the soil between the rows of corn, taking out most of the weeds, but not all. Some of them were particularly stubborn and had to be hand pulled.

The horses had done this many times and knew what to do. They walked evenly without stepping on the corn. The rain last week had loosened the soil so the chisel teeth of the cultivator turned the spaces easily: new upturned earth, thick and black against the green stalks of corn. Jimmy kept at it steadily all afternoon, up and down the field, as his mind spun in circles.

For the umpteenth time, he reviewed everything Bethany had said to him as she crushed his heart. Then how, to his shock, she had walked over and put her head against his chest. She put her arms around him and held him tightly. It was so surprising that he almost lost his balance. He put his arms around her to steady himself. She didn't raise her head for what seemed like minutes. He could feel her body trembling and could smell her hair—a scent of vanilla. Then she stepped back from him as abruptly as she had come to him, though she caught one of his hands and held it a moment. Her cheeks were wet with tears.

Bethany's expression had been so full of pain. Why was that? A flare of hope burned through his mind. Maybe it wasn't that she had stopped caring about him. Maybe there was something else that was causing her to be so hot and cold with him.

Naomi. She would know.

He looked at the sun and the corn in the field and decided he had done a good day's work. Fair, anyway. If he hurried, he might be able to talk to Naomi while she was making dinner.

He found Naomi in the kitchen, just like he thought he would, a warm smile on her face. The scent of supper enveloped him, onions and pork and something sweet. She had become, he realized, the sister he never had. "I need some advice."

He sat at the kitchen table as Naomi brought him a cup of coffee, and spilled the sad tale of the breakup. He looked for answers in Naomi's patient gaze.

Letting his head droop, he heaved a melodramatic sigh and pretended to beat his head against the table. "This is pathetic." With his head still on the table, he mumbled, "I hate this."

Naomi rose and set three places of silverware at the table, working around Jimmy. "I'm sorry."

He jerked his head up. "You should be. This is all your fault. You're the one who thought we were meant for each other. You're the one who encouraged me to pursue her. I should never have listened to you. Now I can't get her off my mind." He peered glumly into the bottom of his coffee cup, annoyed that she wasn't giving him anything but sympathy. He was sure she knew more. He was putting her in a hard position, he knew that, but he was desperate.

She set a platter of steaming pork tenderloin, smothered in onions, in the middle of the table. "Bethany has so much on her mind right now. Be patient with her. She just needs some time."

Jimmy kept his eyes on the platter of food. He loved pork and onions more than a cat loved sweet milk. "Or maybe she's just not that interested in me. Not like I thought she was." He forced himself to stop looking at that steaming pork. "Can't you do something? Talk to her or something?"

"No, I can't. You're twenty-three years old. You're acting like a moonsick fifteen-year-old." She rolled her eyes.

"I am moonsick. And that girl makes me feel like I'm fifteen." He dropped his head into his hands. "Pathetic. I'm just a pathetic case."

She caught sight of something out the window and said, "Galen's on his way in. Would you like to stay for dinner?"

Jimmy lifted his head and smiled. "That, I could do."

Bethany felt as if she were living underwater. People said things to her but the words were muffled in her mind. She was going through the motions, doing what she must, stupidly and slowly, as if trying to wake from a deep sleep, to shake off a bad dream that refused to end.

She hadn't called Rose to tell her about Jake's attack or about Chase's death. Or that Lodestar had gone missing. She thought about it, quite a lot, but Naomi's vision of two shadows stopped her short. She hoped Rusty was right—that Jake was gone for now.

She didn't want to give any credence to Jake's "warnings." If Tobe knew of them, she was pretty sure he would stop talking to Allen Turner. That was the way it was with Tobe—if he could avoid difficulty, swerve from facing bad things, he'd find a way. And then Jake would win again.

Whatever Tobe was telling Allen Turner, whatever was taking so long, needed to be said. She had a strange feeling that Tobe's time in Philadelphia was pivotal, though she didn't know why or how.

Late Tuesday evening, she couldn't sleep. The wind was blowing hard through the treetops, rattling the leaves and branches against the windows. Bethany shivered. It was a warm night, but the wind made it sound cold. She went downstairs to make some chamomile tea and found Geena at the kitchen table, scribbling away at her yellow pad.

Geena looked up when she saw Bethany. "Do you know anything about résumés?"

"Not a thing," Bethany said. She filled the teapot with water and set it on the stovetop. "Would you like some tea?"

"No thanks." Geena took her glasses off and rubbed her eyes. "I'm trying to update my résumé and jazz it up. Give it a little punch. It's hard, though, to figure out how to word the fact that I've been fired from my last job. I have to make it sound like a positive thing."

Bethany was half listening, but her gaze fell to her hands. As she waited for the teapot to boil, she was gripping and releasing, gripping and releasing, small handfuls of her nightgown. She made herself stop. "Getting any idea about what to do next?"

Geena shook her head. "I've asked God, but haven't gotten any word back yet. Not a single word." She grinned. "But I'll keep asking till I get my marching orders. 'Ask and ye shall receive.'" She stretched her arms over her head and rolled her neck from side to side to get out the kinks. "Does your neighbor Galen ever talk much?"

"He's not particularly chatty. Why?"

"He brought the boys over, pointed to the hose, shook his head, and walked away."

"By any chance were Sammy and Luke covered in mud?"

"They were! Head to toe."

"That explains the trail of mud up to the bathroom." The teapot whistled, so Bethany turned off the burner. "I'm sure they're sorely trying Galen's patience while Rose is away. Luke, especially. He's the ringleader for mischief."

Geena rose and walked over to the stove. "How are you doing?"

"Fine." Bethany got a tea bag out of the cupboard and put it in her mug, then filled it with hot water. She put her hands around the mug.

"How are you doing, really and truly? You hardly said a word at dinner tonight."

Bethany paused for a moment, lifting her eyes to the ceiling and blinking. Her throat had been getting tighter and tighter, as if a hand had wrapped around her neck. She was desperate to talk—she felt she might explode if she didn't get this out—and Geena might just be the right person. Everyone else was too connected to the problem. She needed someone neutral. Geena had an objectivity that no one else did—not Rose, not Jimmy, not Naomi. But she wanted to get through this without losing her composure. She hated tears, they made her feel weak and frightened, and she wanted to be strong. She always wanted to be strong.

Bethany took a deep breath. "I think . . . I'm going crazy . . . just like my mother." Out spilled yesterday's revelation by the sisters, all she knew about her mother as a young woman. The coming of the sickness, her father's refusal to accept the illness, the near drowning, the Sisters' Bee intervention. "I'm about the same age—maybe even a little older. I found out my grandmother had the sickness too. I've been waking up in the night frightened, scared to death . . . and I don't know why."

She swirled the teabag in the water, watching the dark color seep out of the bag and infuse the water. She would not, would not, would not look at Geena's eyes. If she saw eyes filled with pity, she thought she might scream. She needed help, not pity.

"Do these episodes only happen in the night?"

Bethany's head snapped up, surprised at the matter-of-fact tone in Geena's voice after hearing such a sordid tale. "No. Sometimes it happens when I'm just walking down the road. It must be the beginning of schizophrenia."

"Any other symptoms?"

"My heart races so fast it feels like it's going to explode. I have trouble getting a full breath. My palms get sweaty."

"How long has this been going on?"

Bethany kept slanting looks at Geena, expecting to see more than mild concern on her face. Didn't she realize all she was confiding in her? Didn't she care? But Geena was only considering her with a detached professionalism. This, Bethany realized, must be the ministerly side of Geena. Up until this moment, Bethany had viewed her as first a guest in the inn, then as an interesting woman, then as a friend. "Two weeks. At first it happened every few days. Then last week, every day. I had the worst one of all this afternoon."

"Are you having bad dreams?"

"Terrible."

"So when it happens in the daytime, have you ever noticed what you were thinking about?"

Bethany tilted her head. "Today, it happened right after I'd been at the Sisters' Bee and heard what they had to say about my mother. I was thinking about how my mother might have walked down that same road when she was my age. That's when I started to feel dizzy. Confused."

Geena nodded. "There could be all kinds of reasons you're having those episodes. It would be a good idea to have a physical exam—just to rule out anything like—"

"You think I'm going crazy, don't you?"

Geena smiled. "I was going to say, like low thyroid. Anemia. There could be a lot of physical reasons you're having those episodes."

"But you think I'm getting schizophrenia, don't you?"

"I'm not a doctor. I've had a few counseling classes in seminary, but I really can't make a diagnosis—"

Bethany squeezed her eyes shut. "You do. You think I have the sickness." She thought she might start to cry and she swallowed hard a few times. Only a few tears trickled out of the corners of her eyes, and she surreptitiously wiped those away with her sleeve.

Geena sighed. "I don't think you're describing mental illness. I think you're describing panic attacks. Frankly, that makes a lot of sense, given all that's been going on in your life lately."

Bethany's eyes popped open. "Panic attacks?"

"Yes. Just like it sounds. They're very real. And very frightening. But they can be managed too. Panic attacks typically begin suddenly, without warning. They can strike at almost any time—just the way you've described. Waking up in the night or walking down the road. Symptoms usually peak within about ten minutes, and you can be left feeling worn out. Exhausted." She put her hands on Bethany's shoulders. "Look, I shouldn't be diagnosing you. But I will help you find a good counselor, if that's what you need. A counselor can give you coping tools. First, we need to get you to a doctor. That's the best place to start. You may just be run-down or needing vitamins or something simple like that."

"What if it's not simple? What if I'm going to get the sickness?"

"Then we'll deal with that. There's lots of treatments now, Bethany, much better ones than when your mother was diagnosed. If you were showing signs of schizophrenia, and I truly don't believe you are, but if you were, you would be at the earliest stages of the illness and at the most treatable point."

A breath eased out of Bethany in an odd sigh.

"Can I give you one piece of advice?"

She nodded, but she couldn't quite meet Geena's eyes.

"I know it's been a hard week, a hard summer . . . well, just a hard year for your family. But you need to hold on to what is in front of you, not spend your life looking for what's been lost or what might never come."

She gripped Bethany's shoulders firmly to make her look at her. "You do not have to live the life your mother lived. Or your grandmother." She softened her grip, then dropped her hands. "Don't start going down that worst-case path. Just put it out of your mind for now."

If only it were that easy to put things aside. To send it to the back of Bethany's mind like she sent Sammy to bed when he was tired. If only life were that simple. "So . . . what should I do?"

"Pray," Geena said, then immediately closed her eyes and lowered her head.

Geena was going to pray here? Now? Out loud? Prayers were said in private silence, as was the Plain way, unless it was the Lord's Prayer. Feeling awkward, she followed Geena's lead, closed her eyes, and ducked her head down.

Quietly, in everyday language, as if Geena were speaking to someone she knew well and respected enormously, she thanked God for Bethany, for bringing things to light so that Bethany could deal with them and not be frightened by them. She asked for guidance and direction to help her get answers for why she was having these episodes and the support she needed so that she could keep doing the good work she was doing—helping her family, the community garden, and the soup kitchen.

"Amen," Geena said, and then looked up at her and smiled. "There. That wasn't so hard, was it?"

Bethany shook her head. "No. Not hard. But a little casual, considering you're addressing the Holy Maker of the Universe."

"Yes! Isn't it amazing?" Geena clapped her hands together in delight, like a child. "That a wondrous and majestic God would want us to talk to him like we're talking to our own father! And he does. Says so in Galatians 4:6."

Bethany didn't know how to respond. She had lived her life attending church—observing traditions, obeying rules, following guidelines—and yet there was so much she didn't know about God. She wanted to know more. Geena made faith sound easy, enjoyable, fortifying. Exciting. Geena's faith gave color to the way she viewed the world and those around her, like strong coffee. Bethany's faith . . . well, if it colored anything, it would be a mild tint, like weak tea.

"God will answer. Trust me. 'I call out to the LORD, and he answers me from his holy mountain.' Psalm 3:4. It's a promise."

"Okay," Bethany said, but doubtfully. If talking to God and getting answers back were really as easy as Geena made it sound, she would have liked sky writing or a booming voice, or maybe a parting of the Red Sea. Some dramatic, no-questions-about-it sign. Some kind of guarantee from God that she wasn't going crazy.

The air was soft and warm after the morning rain shower. Naomi walked over to Eagle Hill as soon as she saw Geena's car drive into the driveway. She'd been watching for it all afternoon after Bethany told her she was seeing a doctor today, sure she was going certifiably crazy.

By the time Naomi slipped through the privet bush, Bethany was out of the car, beaming ear to ear.

Naomi felt a wave of relief. "What did the doctor say?"

"Geena was right! I'm having panic attacks. I'm not getting the sickness!"

Naomi beamed. "I knew it! I was sure you weren't getting it. But I'm so glad that you know it for certain."

"The doctor sent me right over to talk to a counselor in his practice. She gave me some strategies to cope, next time I get a panic attack." Bethany sighed happily. "But at least I don't have the fear attached to it that I'm coming down with schizophrenia like a bad cold."

Geena laughed and reached into the backseat for a bag of groceries. "You two talk. I'm going inside to start dinner."

The girls went up to the porch. Naomi sat in the swing that Galen had built for Rose. She kicked off the swing with her two feet so that it gently swayed. "What was it like to talk to a counselor?" More and more, she heard of church members who were getting counseling and it seemed like a good change. Everybody needed help now and then.

Bethany leaned against the porch pole. "She was so easy to talk to. She told me all about panic attacks and how to discern between true fear and anxiety, and gave me some books to read."

"What *is* the difference?"

"True fear is a constructive emotion. Like . . . do you remember last winter when Sammy and Luke were wrestling up in the hayloft? And I saw Sammy start to fall and ran to catch him before he fell onto the concrete down below."

Naomi nodded. She and Bethany had just walked into the barn and heard the boys overhead. Suddenly, Bethany was at the hayloft ladder, arms cast wide, as Sammy tumbled down the opening, headfirst. She caught him before he hit the concrete floor.

"I moved so quickly—yet it felt like it was all happening in slow motion. I've never moved that fast in all my life and doubt I could again. But fear made me move like that—constructive fear. It was helpful. Anxiety is nameless and vague, and doesn't provide anything constructive. That's what I seem to be experiencing in those panic attacks."

Naomi stopped the swing from swinging so Bethany could sit on it.

"The counselor also agreed with what the doctor said—that there was nothing in my symptoms to indicate a presentation of schizophrenia."

Naomi let out a breath. "What a relief to hear that."

"It doesn't mean I'm immune to it, but the doctor didn't think it was likely." She pushed off so the porch swing started swaying again. "He said that one in five are affected by mental illness. One in five! It shouldn't make me feel better to know that, but somehow, I don't feel quite so alone."

"Speaking of alone, Jimmy Fisher came to talk to me," Naomi said. "He's terribly upset that you broke things off with him." She glanced at Bethany. "Maybe you'll reconsider, now that you have a better idea of what's been troubling you."

"It was hardly a breakup. We'd only talked of courting for about five minutes."

"So, you'll reconsider?"

Bethany looked at Naomi, eyebrows lifted. "Since when did you become such a matchmaker?"

Naomi just smiled. "Only when I get a certain feeling. Like with Galen and Rose. Or you and Jimmy."

"What about you and Tobe? Do you have a certain feeling about that?"

Naomi looked away, feeling a blush warm her cheeks. "Don't be silly. Your brother would never be serious about someone like me."

"Don't sell yourself short, Naomi. Any fellow would be lucky to have you. I mean that. But as much as I love my brother, he's a ways off from being serious about someone."

Naomi grew somber as the smile swept away from her eyes. "What makes you say that?"

"Tobe spent a long time trying to be what my father wanted him to be. And then he spent a long time running from that. I think he needs time to figure out who he wants to be. He still has a ways to go." She grinned. "But I won't deny that he noticed you. Even better was the look on your face when he was around."

"I don't know what you're talking about . . . yes . . . I do." Naomi covered her face. "How embarrassing."

Bethany reached out and covered Naomi's hand with hers. "I just don't want you to get hurt."

"Duly warned. Enough about me. Maybe you should try noticing how Jimmy Fisher looks at you."

"How does he look at me?"

"Well, I wouldn't want to spoil it for you." She smiled her old-soul smile. "He's the one, you know."

"The one?"

"Yes. The One. The one you've been waiting for. The reason you didn't run off with Jake. Deep down, you knew God had someone better in mind. He's the One."

"We'll see."

She nodded. "You'll see. I know."

# 21

Mim waited on the porch for the taxi to arrive. Her mom had left a brief message that they were heading home this afternoon. She wished for her brother Tobe, with his easy laugh. She even wished for her grandmother, all pinch-mouthed. Most of all, she wished for her mom. She searched the road, straining to hear for an approaching car, needing to see her mom's face. She thought if her mother hadn't left, most of the bad things from the week might not have happened. There was something about her mom that felt like a shield.

Close to five o'clock, the taxi drove up to Eagle Hill. Her mother opened the car and helped Mammi Vera out. Mim ran over to meet them. "Where's Tobe?"

"Geduh is Geduh." *What is done and past cannot be called again.* Mammi Vera walked up to the house, slower and older and a little hunched over, different than she seemed nine days prior. Luke and Sammy barreled out of the house, Bethany behind them.

While the taxi driver got the suitcases out of the trunk, Mim's mom dipped her head into the back of the taxi and came out with a six-month-old golden retriever puppy, wiggling and squirming in her arms. Luke and Sammy lunged for the puppy. "Wait, slow down, boys. Let him get used to you."

Holding on to the blue nylon leash, she set him carefully on the ground and let the puppy sniff. "Mim, this is the puppy that you gave to Delia Stoltz on the day she left Eagle Hill. Turns out her husband is not fond of having a dog in the house, so when Delia heard about Chase, she thought it would be best to return him to us."

Mim bent down to pat the puppy. "She called him Micky, right?"

Mim's mom laughed. "That's right. Short for *Miracula fieri hic*."

Tears sprang to Mim's eyes and she blinked them away, keeping her head bowed. "Remember, Luke? This pup's father was Chase. His mother is Daisy, from the Lapps over at Windmill Farm."

Sammy bent down immediately, nose to nose with the round-eyed pup. Luke didn't utter a word. He just watched the puppy, almost reverently, as he made his way sniffing around the suitcases. Then Luke hugged his mother, hard, and took the leash from her. "Let's go show him around, Sammy."

Bethany, Mim, and their mother watched the two boys and the puppy in a footrace down to the barn.

"How did you know about Chase?" Bethany asked.

*Uh oh*. Mim had called Delia Stoltz's house each afternoon, around five or so, after she was sure Danny wasn't going to call to go stargazing—which he hadn't, not in a while—and left long phone messages for her mom. She had told her mother everything, but she accidentally-on-purpose neglected to tell Bethany that she had called. Bethany had said she didn't want to worry her mom or Mammi Vera, but Mim couldn't help it. She couldn't hold all that worry inside her. Besides, Galen had called and talked to her mom each day too. Bethany didn't know that, either.

Before her mother could answer, the taxi driver wanted to be paid and Galen and Naomi came over to welcome them home. Mim saw Galen exchange a look with her mom that seemed like married people who sent messages without talking. Their eyes met. His asked: You okay? Hers answered: I'm okay. Not great, but okay.

"Where's Tobe?" Mim repeated.

"Tobe isn't coming back for a while," her mom explained. "He ended up pleading guilty to withholding evidence and was given a light sentence. He'll be transferred soon to a federal prison camp in central Pennsylvania to serve out the sentence."

"He did the right thing," Naomi said firmly.

Galen gave her a look that was a mixture of surprise and confusion.

"Well, he did," Naomi said, her chin lifting a notch. "He showed courage."

Mim looked at Naomi and realized she had changed from a young girl to a woman this summer. Naomi seemed whole and strong and complete inside herself in a way she never had before. How did people change so quickly?

"Rose," Bethany started, "Jake Hertzler—"

"There's a warrant out for Jake Hertzler's arrest." Rose looked at Bethany. "Tobe got a light sentence because he agreed to provide evidence about Jake Hertzler."

"Rose, Jake is far more sinister than we ever realized."

"I know, honey." Her mother's eyes filled with tears. Mim had never seen her mom cry before. Not ever. Her voice choked on the words. "Mim told me all about it."

"You what?" Bethany glared at Mim.

"Don't blame your sister. She was worried about you. But after I told Tobe what Jake had done to you—what he had tried to do—he pled guilty and self-surrendered that very day."

"But why?" Bethany asked, her eyes filling with tears. "Why would he do that?"

"I don't know. I just . . . don't know." She held out her arms and Bethany sank into them.

Bethany arrived at the Grange Hall early on Wednesday morning, though the sun was already searing the morning sky with a blinding light. The sisters weren't expected for hours, but Bethany thought if she could get the bread rising early enough, it would be baked in time for lunch. Just as she pulled the flour bag out of the cupboard and up on the countertop, she heard a knock on the door. When she opened it, no one was there but a note was taped to the door.

On it were scrawled only two words: *I'm sorry.*

Bethany saw Rusty kneeling next to the garden plot of the Group Home, thinning radish starts. She was wearing jeans that were too short and a ratty-looking brown sweater that was much too big. Sunlight streamed on her tangled bird's nest of long red hair, making it seem as if it had caught fire.

Bethany stood a few yards away for a while before letting Rusty know she was there, and looked at her, truly looked at her, as if she were seeing her for the first time. She looked beyond the angry eyes and tough-girl attitude, and saw a young, mixed-up teenager.

A purple martin darted between them, flapping its wings in sudden terror. Bethany spotted a cat slinking toward them on a garden path. She smiled. Jimmy's purple martin houses were attracting all kinds of creatures. She sat on the edge of the wooden garden bed. "How'd you like to learn how to bake bread?"

The funniest expression crossed Rusty's face—wariness and calm and hope, all mingled together. Then she dropped her eyes and tugged on her cutoff jeans. She shrugged. "Beats weeding, I guess."

"Good. Put your tools away and meet me in the kitchen in the Grange."

A few minutes later, Rusty joined Bethany in the kitchen. Bethany pointed to the sink. "Wash your hands. Then wash them again. Get the garden grit out from under your fingernails. Scrub them like a surgeon heading to the operating room."

Rusty scowled at her—which didn't surprise Bethany because she knew Rusty didn't tolerate anyone telling her what to do—but she went to the sink and started to scrub.

Bethany stirred a packet of yeast into a jar of warm water and set it aside. She measured flour into a big bowl, created a well, and added a tablespoon or two of oil. Then she picked up the yeast, now stirred to life—thick and bubbly—and dumped it into the well.

Rusty peered over her shoulder. "That gray stuff is alive."

Bethany laughed. "It is. It's a living organism. When water is added to yeast, it wakes it up." She picked up a sturdy wooden spoon and stirred it together, stirred and stirred, until it was a thick, lumpy blob of dough. She scattered a layer of fine white flour across the surface of the countertop, divided the dough into two pieces, one for each of them, and gave half to Rusty. "It's going to be sticky to start with, but just keep kneading and it will get better. If it's too sticky, dust it with a little more flour."

Rusty pounded it with her hands.

"Whoa! Keep it steady. Watch me. Do what I do." She pushed the heel of her palm into the dough and it squeezed upward, cool and clammy. "You knead dough by folding it, and then pressing the heel of your hand into

461

the fold, like this." She folded, pressed, folded, pressed. Bethany loved the way it felt, spongy and cold, and how it started to change under her palm as she kneaded it.

"Why do you have to knead it so much?"

"You're releasing the yeast into the flour and water and salt. It's a miracle, in a way, to think of delicious bread coming out of such simple ingredients." She glanced over at the sticky lump in Rusty's hands. "Add a little bit of flour as you go so it doesn't stick to your hands."

"How do you know when it's done?"

"The more you bake bread, the more you'll just know, but until then, there are a couple of ways to know for sure: If it holds its shape when you lift the ball in the air. If you poke it and the hole fills in." She grinned. "Or if your arms get tired." She stretched her ball of dough and pounded it down on the countertop. "It's not ready until it's not sticky. It should seem like a smooth, firm ball. Good thing is you can't knead it too much. Not like pastry dough."

Rusty crinkled up her face in confusion and Bethany realized this girl knew absolutely nothing about cooking. She probably had never tasted a homemade piecrust before, buttery and flaky. "When the ball is elastic and doesn't stick to you at all, it's time to let it rise for a few hours. Then we pound the air out of it, knead it some more, let it rise again, and bake it."

"That's a ton of work for a slice of bread. Why don't you just buy a loaf of Wonder Bread from the store?"

Bethany gave her a look as if a cat had spoken. "Later today, after you eat a piece of this bread right out of the oven, with butter melting on it, then I'll ask you the same question." She watched Rusty push and pull the dough, a serious intent on her face, and thought she might just be enjoying herself. "But if what you're really asking is why anyone would bother to go to all this work—I love to bake bread. I love to cook from scratch."

"Why? It's simpler to just buy stuff."

Bethany was surprised. Rusty was easier to engage in conversation than she would've expected. Almost as if she was just waiting for someone to show genuine interest in her. Geena, no doubt, had probably discovered that right away. "I get a lot of pleasure out of nourishing and feeding people. It makes me happy."

Rusty mimicked Bethany's movement: pressing the dough with her palm, then rolling and pressing it again.

Drumming in Bethany's head was Geena's prophecy about being a mentor to these young girls. It gave her a shivery feeling down her spine, like how she felt after one of Naomi's visions came true.

As they pushed and pulled at the dough, Bethany said, almost whispering, "Rusty, do you have any idea where Jake Hertzler is now?" She had told herself not to ask Rusty about Jake. Told herself, yet out it blurted. She didn't want to talk about him, to think about him, but in the back of her mind, she had a hope that Rusty might be able to help the police find him.

Cornered and knowing it, Rusty pressed her lips together and stilled. "No," she said at last. "I haven't heard from him since . . . that night."

"I'm not judging you. I know Jake can be a smooth talker. But I wondered how he found you in the first place."

A tiny shade of relief passed over Rusty and she started to push and pull the dough again. When she had her words lined up, her voice dropped to that calm tone she used on the night of the attack. "I've known him for a while. He used to get drugs and stuff for me and my friends. He drove by the Group Home and recognized me. Paid me a bundle to destroy the gardens." A combative light came into her eyes as she looked squarely at Bethany. "But I didn't hurt your dog. I wouldn't do that. That was all Jake. I didn't know it was you he was after."

"I'm grateful for your help that night." Back and forth with the dough, back and forth, pushing and pulling.

"He'll be back. Your brother's got something he wants."

Bethany froze. "What? What could it be?"

"I don't know. I don't know if it's a thing or if it's information. I just know he's determined to get something. I'd tell you if I knew anything more." Rusty jammed her fist at the dough. "He's a bad one, that Hertzler. Bad through and through."

*That he is.* Bethany hated the man, hated the man with such force she shuddered with it and felt no shame for it. She should, though. It shamed her that she felt no shame.

Rusty didn't offer up another word about Jake and Bethany was fine with that. She didn't think she could stand one more fearful thought about Jake Hertzler. "So what's new at the Group Home?"

"Old Biddy Green is leaving."

Bethany looked up. "The housemother? She's leaving?"

"Yup. Her mother is about to kick the bucket so she's gonna go take care of her."

"When is she leaving?"

"As soon as they find some sucker to take her place."

Bethany grinned. "Mrs. Green wasn't so bad."

Rusty rolled her eyes. "She spends most of the day on the couch watching soap operas."

Bethany shaped the bread into balls and put them in a large wooden bowl, then covered it with a damp dishcloth and set it near the oven. *Someone to take her place.* She glanced over at Rusty, an idea starting to surface. With a sense of sudden purpose, she said, "You might be surprised. Mrs. Green's replacement could be an ideal match."

Geena woke in the middle of the night and somehow knew, without a doubt, the time had come to leave Eagle Hill. Rose and Vera had returned, the Schrock family didn't need her help any longer, and she sensed that inner prompting she was always listening for. It was time. "I get the message, Lord, but what am I going home to?" She waited for an answer, eyes on the ceiling.

Nothing.

"I'd really prefer to get the full picture, Lord, if you don't mind. I've never been good at that step-by-step thing."

Nothing.

"Well. Fine, then. I'll head back to my apartment in the city and wait for further orders."

Nothing.

In the morning, Geena stripped the sheets off the bed in Bethany's room and packed her suitcase. She looked around to make sure she had left the small room the way she found it. She would leave, but not until after breakfast. She wasn't about to miss her last Amish breakfast. She thought she smelled the sweet scent of freshly baked blueberry cornbread all the way up in her room. It was the Inn's specialty and always served at the first breakfast for new guests.

When Geena went downstairs, she found Bethany alone in the kitchen. The kitchen clock chimed softly while she helped herself to a cup of coffee. "You're up earlier than usual."

"The new guests in the guest flat are bird-watchers. They wanted breakfast at 4:30 a.m. so they could go birding at dawn."

"And you accommodated them?"

Bethany smiled. "Not me. Rose did. She likes birds, herself."

Geena sat at the kitchen table and set her mug down. "It's time I head back to Philadelphia."

Bethany glanced up, disappointment on her face. "So soon? Do you have a job? Do you know what you're going to do?"

"No. God hasn't told me that part yet." Not yet. Soon. She felt confident of that. Each day, she went to the Sweet Tooth Bakery for coffee and a cinnamon roll, then spent a few hours in the corner of the bakery using the wi-fi. She had emailed dozens of résumés and sent emails to colleagues. She had received one answer back from a church that showed mild interest. They were looking for a youth pastor, though she would have to move to a remote section of South Dakota. She was willing. She would go anywhere God called her. Even South Dakota.

Bethany turned off the burner at the stove and set down the spatula. "Geena, would you consider applying for the job as housemother at the Group Home? Mrs. Green can't leave until she finds a replacement, and Sylvia told me just yesterday that there haven't been any qualified applicants. Being housemother probably doesn't pay much money and you'd be doing more counseling than preaching. I know it's not quite what you had in mind, but you're so good with the girls. Would you consider it?"

The suggestion caught Geena by surprise, so much so that she hesitated a moment before answering. "Thanks, Bethany, but I'm committed to serving in churches."

"But who's to say what kind of church? Isn't serving God what you want to do? You're wonderful with those girls. And being a housemother is a position that plays to your strengths. You've said that was important."

Geena managed a kind smile and hoped it didn't look as patronizing as she felt. It was sweet of Bethany to worry about her, but how could an Amish girl possibly understand what it was like to be a trained seminarian? Just as Bethany opened her mouth to say something more, Geena cut her off. "Breakfast sure smells delicious."

Bethany clamped her lips shut. A loud clunk hit the ceiling and her eyes rolled upward. "I hear those boys stirring upstairs. I'd better finish up."

An hour later, Geena had said her goodbyes to the Schrock family with promises to return, and drove away from Eagle Hill. She passed by the Sisters' House, the Grange Hall, the community garden, the Group Home. As she turned the corner onto Main Street, she heard the voice of God. It said gently, *Stop. Go back. Feed my sheep.*

Instead, she headed down Main Street and noticed the Sweet Tooth Bakery. She loved that little shop.

She heard the voice again: *Geena, make a U-turn. Watch over my flock.*

She checked her GPS for the road that would lead her east on I-76. To Philadelphia. She clicked on her blinker.

Again, she heard the voice: *Go to the Group Home and care for those girls.*

As soon as the words formed in her head, she understood. She had been asking the wrong question: *Which church should I serve in?* Surely the answer was to look around and see the church was everywhere. She hesitated. And she almost went back. Instead, she stopped at the Sweet Tooth Bakery and bought a cinnamon roll. She loved those cinnamon rolls.

Then she went back.

# 22

School started on a gray mid-August morning with a rainstorm due at any moment. The wind had picked up, the sky had darkened. As a few drops started to fall, then more and more, Teacher M.K. rang the bell to call everyone into the schoolhouse a little early. For a moment, everything felt normal to Mim. She had been worried Teacher M.K. wouldn't be here this term, but there she was!

Teacher M.K. had an odd look on her face as she welcomed the class back for another term. Happy and sad, all mixed up together. "I have some news," she said at last, and Mim's hands started to feel cold and clammy, even though the air in the schoolhouse was heavy and humid from the warm summer rain. Mim never did like change and she sensed change was coming.

"Since I'm going to be getting married and moving to Ohio, I won't be able to teach this term."

Mim hung her head. She had been holding out a tiny glimmer of hope that maybe Teacher M.K. would keep teaching or postpone her wedding. Just one more term—then Mim would graduate and it wouldn't be a problem if the new teacher were awful.

"The school board has been looking for a replacement for the last few weeks and, so far, hasn't found anyone. In the meantime, they have decided on a substitute teacher. This is someone I recommended to the school board. This person is the smartest student I ever taught. And even though he's a little bit younger than most teachers, he was born to teach. I am counting on each one of you to support him." She was staring right at Luke when she said that.

The door opened and all heads turned to see who was coming in. First, all they could see was a big black umbrella, dripping with rain. Then it dropped to the floor and there stood Danny Riehl.

Mim's heart soared.

Danny shadowed Teacher M.K. all day. Mim stuck around after school let out, hoping they might walk home together. Hoping he might ask her to meet him on the hill behind the schoolhouse and stargaze. After the rainstorm that swept through Stoney Ridge this morning, the skies were clear, the moon just a sliver of a thumbnail, and it would be a perfect night to observe Orion. But Danny didn't look at her, not once, and he stayed close to Teacher M.K.'s desk, peppering her with questions about teaching.

It was getting late so Mim quietly slipped out the door to head to Eagle Hill. As she reached the road, she heard Danny call to her. Her heart soared again as she waited for him to catch up with her.

"I need to go back in and work with Teacher M.K."

She nodded. She understood.

He pushed his glasses up against the bridge of his nose. "I just found out about substituting a few weeks ago. The school board has been look-ing for teachers all summer and couldn't find anyone. No one wanted it. That's why they finally came to me. I wasn't supposed to tell anyone."

"That's all right."

He looked down at the tops of his shoes. "The thing is, Mim, I want to do well in this job."

"Of course," she said. She twirled her apron corner around one finger. "Of course you do."

"So . . . I . . . won't be asking you to go stargazing anymore. In that . . . I'm your teacher now."

Oh. *Oh!*

"And I need you to do me a favor."

"What?"

He kept his eyes on the waving cornstalks that rustled in a gentle breeze. "You should call me Teacher Danny." For a brief moment he met her gaze. "You called me Danny a couple of times today. I think it would set a good example to the younger students."

She tried to look casual and nonchalant, but she knew it probably looked weird and tight and forced. Her disappointment was massive and she had never been good at hiding her feelings. If she didn't leave soon, she would start to cry and that would be mortifying. She had to swallow twice before she could speak. "I understand perfectly. I'd better get home. Mom will be wondering where I am." She turned and hurried down the road.

"Mim," Danny called.

She stopped but didn't turn back.

He walked up to her. "I'm sorry."

Mim started for home, feeling halfway sad and blue, halfway stupid. As tears slipped down her cheeks, she thought now she could finally answer questions for Mrs. Miracle about love and broken hearts.

Summer was slipping away. The air had gone quiet, falling into the purple hush of dusk as the sun slipped suddenly behind the ridge that framed Eagle Hill.

A hummingbird buzzed through the air, paused to stare at Bethany as she turned on the garden hose, and then settled on the edge of the watering can. It dipped its little bill into the water three or four times and watched her again. A glistening drop of water perched on the tip of its beak. She stopped moving to see what the tiny bird would do, but it flew away. When she turned around, there was Jimmy Fisher.

She walked up to him. "Hello, Jimmy. I haven't seen you around." Now that he wasn't working at Galen's any longer, she hadn't seen him in quite some time.

"You said you needed some space. I've been trying to give it to you."

The expression on his face was so full of pain. She couldn't bear him being hurt. She simply could not bear it. She had to look away. "I guess I owe you an explanation."

He stilled.

She raised her head. He was looking down at her with those spectacular blue eyes of his. A muscle ticked in his cheek and she could see the pulse beating in his neck, fast and hard. "My mother has a mental illness. That's why she left Stoney Ridge the way she did—she disappeared when Tobe and I were little and we grew up thinking she had abandoned us. I didn't know the truth until just recently. I tracked her down and visited her, and I met her." She had a hard time talking around the knot in her throat and her voice cracked a little. "But she didn't seem to know me at all. She's . . . in bad shape. Though she's in a good place. I mean, she's well cared for."

A sadness welled up inside Bethany, choking off the words. She shut her eyes and pressed her fingers to her lips. She hadn't wanted to cry and didn't think she would, but in the next instant scalding tears pushed against her eyes. She buried her face in her hands, but just for a moment. Then she let them fall to her side, curled into balls.

She swallowed and drew in a deep breath. "Turns out, my grandmother had the same sickness. I thought . . . well, lately, I've felt so confused and upset and moody—I might be getting the sickness too. That's why I ended things with you, before they got started."

"You didn't even give me a chance." He said the words simply, his voice low and flat.

His comment surprised her. She wasn't sure what she expected him to say, but not that. "I know." She looked down at her hands, which were now twisted up into a knot with her apron. With a deliberate effort she unclenched her fingers, smoothing out the bunched material. She lifted her head. "I'm not sure you can understand this, but I felt so scared, Jimmy. I was sure I was getting the sickness. I broke things off with you because I couldn't bear the thought of tangling you in this sickness. I even went to a doctor, and now I'm seeing a counselor. I've been having panic attacks and she's helping me." She bowed her head.

"You didn't think you could tell me any of this?"

"I'm sorry. My mother's situation . . . well, it's complicated. And messy." She shook her head, splattering tears. "Shootfire! If I told you, it would scare you to kingdom come."

His expression grew quite sober. "Think you're the only one with skeletons in your closet? We Fishers have plenty of our own. Let's see, there's old Rufus, who had six toes on each foot. My father passed on at an early age because of high blood pressure . . ."

"Jimmy, those are physical things. Mental illness . . . that's another beast."

"Okay, then. Okay." He bit his lip, as if he was weighing whether or not to say something. "My mother's father lost his mind. I don't know what kind of sickness he had—he died before I was born—but I know it was pretty bad."

"Your mother's father? He was mentally ill?"

"She won't talk about it. Not with anyone."

Edith Fisher, she was discovering, was very good at keeping secrets.

"Bethany, life comes at you like a hurricane, and you do what you can with whatever it blows into your hands, good and bad. I don't think we have any idea about what we're going to be faced with in life."

"Do you really believe that? You think that fate is lying there like a snake and it'll take you no matter what you do to try to stop it?"

"No, no. That's not what I meant at all. What I'm trying to say is that we don't know what the future holds, only God does, and there's no point in trying to avoid trouble. Like . . . genes. They're a mystery. Who knows what makes us the way we are? Or what triggers an illness? Nobody knows, Bethany. It's amazing how fast life can turn its course—"

"On a nickel and give you some change."

He nodded. He bent over and took her face in his hands, his thumbs lightly tracing the bones in her cheeks. "The only thing I'm sure of," he said, in a voice so loving that it brought fresh tears to Bethany's eyes, "is that I'd rather have you, just the way you are, than never have you at all."

Then, just as suddenly, he turned away abruptly to head down the driveway.

If she'd been holding on to any illusions about how much she cared about Jimmy Fisher, that last speech would have clinched it. And suddenly she was completely aware of this exact moment—the sweet smell of fresh-cut grass, the sound of horses neighing to each other in the pasture, the bleating of the four little sheep, the clatter through the open kitchen window of Rose putting dishes away—because as she watched Jimmy head through the privet hole, she realized that she loved him. Whatever happened, as much as she had tried, she couldn't un-fall in love with him.

On the way home from school one afternoon, Mim stopped to pick up the mail in the mailbox before she walked to the house. There was a thick envelope addressed to her in Ella's spidery handwriting. She dropped her lunch box and sat down under a tree to read it.

*Dear Mim,*

*The silver thimble you gave me is very special. I will treasure it. Sylvia is holding on to it and only letting me use it during our bee time, so it doesn't get lost.*

*You might have noticed that I have days when things are right as rain, and days when life seems very foggy. Today is a very good day. Clear as glass. But I am becoming more forgetful, and it is possible that one day I might not know where I am or who I am or, even more important, who you are. So I wanted to say a nice, clearheaded thank you while I still do have my wits about me, or at least some of them.*

*You are simply the best young woman in the whole world. Never forget that. The real me, inside here, remembers you well . . . as my little Mrs. Miracle.*

*Fondly,*
*Ella*

One tear, then two, leaked from the corner of Mim's eyes and splattered on the envelope. She brushed them off and felt something else in the envelope. She pulled out four newspaper cuttings of Mrs. Miracle columns, from the last month, ever since Mim stopped nicking the columns from the Sisters' House.

It seemed to Bethany that she had always been worried about something. Now suddenly, her worries had evaporated into bright air.

Could people change? Bethany thought so.

She felt like a different person. She had come to Stoney Ridge to help her family get settled and she ended up having her heart settle. She prayed now, often. When she began to pray it felt awkward, forced, like those stumbling, start-and-stop conversations you have when meeting someone for the first time, full of uncomfortable silences as she racked her brain for the right way of saying things, just so.

Then one day, while she was kneading wheatberry bread dough, she started praying the way Geena prayed. Like she was talking to someone she admired and respected, yet knew well and felt comfortable around. She prayed for Tobe and Rose, her siblings, Galen, Naomi, Jimmy, and for all her doubts and worries, as well as all things she was grateful for. She had even started praying for her enemy Jake Hertzler. *Shootfire!* Lord knew he needed prayers most of all.

Somehow, as she was praying, pushing and pulling and stretching the lumpy dough, warming it as she kneaded, back and forth, over and under, the stiffness melted away. Words flowed from her, easily, in a way that matched the way she was kneading: simple, rhythmic, forgetting to be worried about the outcome, focused only on the dough, waiting for that moment of elasticity when she knew the yeast and salt and water and flour were no longer separate ingredients but fully blended and the dough was smooth and springy. At that moment she pulled her gaze back to discover the bigger picture, to see what had developed through the kneading of the dough and the sheer honesty of her prayers—and she liked what she saw. She poked the bread and the hole sprang back. Good to go.

As the bread was rising in the Eagle Hill kitchen, she walked down the road to pay a visit to Edith Fisher.

When Edith opened the door, she stiffened. "Jimmy isn't here."

"I know that," Bethany said. "He's over at Galen's. I came to see you."

Edith opened the door and led Bethany to the living room. They sat on opposite sides of the room, very awkward. "I assume this is about your mother." Edith shifted her weight, putting a strain on the chair, whose joints squeaked in protest.

"Not really. It's about your father."

Edith Fisher's mouth went hard. Bethany hated to say bitter, but that's how she seemed, all tight and vinegary and hard. She had the coldest, stoniest look on her face she'd ever seen on a woman. For that matter, a man, either.

"Jimmy told me about your father. That he was mentally ill."

The color drained from Edith's face. "I suppose you told him what I did for your mother." Her lips clamped in a thin, silent line.

Bethany shook her head. "No. That's your secret, Edith. All he knows is that my mother had a sickness. He needed to know that much, but only that much."

Edith relaxed a little. She rose and walked over to the window. "My papa was a wonderful man. He used to call me his 'little ray of sunshine.'"

Bethany couldn't imagine Edith Fisher as a little anything.

She chewed on her lip for a moment, staring ahead. "He loved to travel. He used to send me postcards from places. Years later, I found out that he was sending them to me from a home for the mentally ill."

Bethany rose from the chair. "The same one where my mother is?"

"Yes." She turned to face Bethany. "That's how I knew what the future looked like for your mama. They had the same sickness. And that's why I don't want you and my Jimmy together. Too risky. The chance of your children getting the sickness is too high."

Well, Bethany knew that wasn't necessarily true. The doctor had given her all kinds of information about schizophrenia. But she doubted she could convince Edith of that and she decided she wouldn't bother. "It's too late. Your boy Jimmy is in love with me. And I love him." The words came into her mind out of the blue, without any thought on her part, as if she had practiced a speech, but she hadn't at all.

"Edith, there are so many unexpected things that happen in this life. You know that better than anybody. Goodness, you just started to live a new life with a new husband, and poof! It's over." She crossed the room to face Edith. "You can be happy about us or you can be miserable about us, but it won't change how we feel about each other."

Edith turned back to the window and crossed her arms over her chest. "I know that. Jimmy told me."

"He did?"

"His eyes flashed with a hard, dark expression I've only seen once or twice in him. When he looks like that, I know he's made up his mind and nothing on earth is going to get him to change it."

Bethany's eyes prickled with tears. Jimmy was so many things that were fine, but the fact that he had stood up to his mother about Bethany was the moment she realized he loved her, truly loved her.

Edith did a sharp about-face. "You are one bold girl."

She nodded. "That's true."

Bethany clasped Edith's her hands. "I don't remember much about my mother—nothing specific. But I do remember you, Edith. The bathtub—I remember you holding me, telling me not to be afraid. You wore a blue dress. I do remember that." She squeezed her hands. "Thank you for that. Thank you for all that."

Edith's mask cracked slightly but her lips didn't move one tiny bit. It was her eyes that gave her away. They glistened with tears.

As Bethany walked home in the afternoon sun, she thought again about her mother, walking down this same road when she was Bethany's age. She said a prayer for her mother, like the counselor had suggested she do whenever she started to think about her. Then she took a deep, deep breath, in and out, in and out. Then she waited and, slowly, she grinned. There was no hint of a panic attack.

Since school had started, Mim had stopped taking early morning walks with her mom. There were too many chores to do before school and she was staying up later than usual to keep up with the demand for Mrs. Miracle's advice. But after two more days of Danny acting so high and mighty in his new role as temporary teacher, she knew she had to talk to her mother.

When her alarm went off at 4:30 a.m., she woke with a start and nearly changed her mind. Another hour of sleep sounded sweetly tempting. But then she thought of yesterday, when Danny organized a spelling bee for the schoolhouse and paired Mim with a sixth grader named Arthur Zook. Nobody ever wanted to be paired with Arthur Zook. It wasn't fair—most eighth graders were paired with much younger grades, so they could be bossed around. Arthur wouldn't listen to anybody and mixed everything up. Sure enough, despite the fact that Mim told him exactly how to spell the word *isosceles*, Arthur spelled out "e-y-e-s-a-u-c-a-l-e-e-z."

They were the first pair—the very first!—to be sent back to their desks. Mim glared at Danny for the rest of the afternoon, but he never paid her any mind. He virtually ignored her. She was nothing more to him than another student. Less so, she thought at times. He didn't always call on her when her hand was raised in the air. And once, when he was called outside by a farmer one afternoon, he asked seventh grader Betsy Miller to watch over the class. A measly seventh grader! Worst of all, he had given Mim a C+ on a book review she had written, with a note that she could do better. She hated him! And she loved him.

Her mom was surprised to see her downstairs, waiting by the door. "Mim, what are you doing up so early?"

Mim shrugged. "Just happened to be awake." She stifled a yawn. "Thought I'd go out with you today."

"Well, I'm glad to have your company. I've been missing our talks since school started."

Mim followed her mom outside and onto the trail that led up the hill behind the house. The full moon, lying low, cast large shadows along the path. Her mom slowed to walk alongside her. "How's school going this term?"

"So-so."

"Must feel a little strange to have Danny as the teacher."

"It's . . . awful."

Her mother nodded.

"It's just that . . . he's trying to act like he's all . . . grown up."

"Imagine how hard it would be—to suddenly be a teacher to the very students you played softball with a few months back."

Mim hadn't thought about Danny's point of view.

"I know he didn't want to take that substitute teaching job. His mother told me the school board paid quite a few visits to their farm over the last few weeks. Finally, Bishop Elmo had to get involved."

Mim didn't know that. She thought Danny would have jumped at the chance to teach. He was a natural teacher. "It's just that . . . I thought we were friends. And now he acts . . ."

"Like there's a big wall between you?"

Mim nodded. They had reached the top of the ridge and were able to look down on both sides. Eagle Hill shared a border along the ridgeline with the Riehls' farm. It was impossible to get to the Riehls' farm from the hill, though—their side was a steep decline. As she walked to the edge, she could make out the creek that bordered the Riehls' farm. And if she squinted, she thought she could see someone carrying a lantern light from the house to the barn. Maybe that was Danny, doing early morning chores before he left for a day at the schoolhouse. "He told me to call him Teacher Danny."

"So stargazing is on hold?"

Mim took in a sharp breath. She had never told anyone—not *anyone*—that she stargazed with Danny. "You knew?"

Her mom put her arm around Mim. "I knew. And I also know you're fond of each other."

Mim's cheeks burned with embarrassment. She had tried so hard to hide her feelings. "Is it that obvious?"

"No, not really. Certainly not to others. But I'm your mother. Moms pick up on those kinds of things." She smiled. "You have fine taste in men, Mim. But you always did have an abundance of common sense."

Mim dropped her head. "Everything's changed. Danny's changed. I don't think he likes me anymore."

Her mom was quiet for a long time. "You need to take a long view. This is just a short period—until the school board finds another teacher."

Mim knew that wasn't going to happen anytime soon. And she could tell Danny loved teaching.

"I know it's hard to do when you're a teenager, I know everything seems so important and so serious, but there's a much bigger picture to consider."

"What's the bigger picture?"

"Right now, Danny has a job to do. It's not an easy one, but he took it on. Instead of feeling overly concerned about yourself, or about how this job is affecting your friendship with Danny, think about Danny. Think about how to support him. Encourage the other children to respect him."

Mim didn't. Just yesterday, during noon recess while Danny was inside, Arthur Zook mimicked him. He pushed his glasses up on the bridge of his nose the way Danny did—and Mim joined in the laughter. She should have been a better friend to Danny. He was a good teacher, a fine teacher, even if he did act all high and mighty.

"Mim, you have a job to do too."

Oh no. Had her mom found out about Mrs. Miracle? She didn't subscribe to the *Stoney Ridge Times*. Hardly any of the Amish read the local newspaper. She thought her hidden identity would be safe. Had Bethany told? Had Ella?

"You're helping Bethany with the community garden. You're finishing your last year of school. The sisters want to pay you to be a Saturday companion to Ella. You have plenty of things on your own plate."

Relief flooded Mim. Mrs. Miracle's secret identity was still safe. So far, so good.

"Time is your friend, Mim. You're only fourteen. Danny's only sixteen. If you're meant for each other, nothing will get in the way of that."

"But . . . what if we're not?" That was the question, deep down, that plagued her.

"Then that means there's someone God has in mind who is better for you too. Not just Danny."

Harold the Rooster let out his first crow and her mom laughed. "That's our signal. Time to head back down the hill and start the day." Just then, the eagle pair soared over their heads. "I thought they might leave us, after their baby died last spring. But they've stayed. Maybe next year they'll have another baby. Maybe two." She looked at Mim. "Life can get good again."

She started down the trail and Mim waited a moment to watch the eagles circle low over the creek, hunting for breakfast. Then, feeling like she had dropped a heavy stone, she ran to catch up with her mom.

# 23

～∽◦∾～

"L adies, the quilt's waiting for you," Edith Fisher announced as everyone took their places and began to stitch the green sashing. They all murmured their approval at the intricate Star of Bethlehem pattern, made up of blues and yellows and greens.

"It's pretty. Awful pretty," Edith Fisher said.

Naomi stopped sewing and looked at her. So did Bethany. Edith Fisher had never in her life said anything was pretty.

"Well, it is," she sniffed.

"Did you all hear that the lady preacher who was staying at Eagle Hill took the job as housemother at the Group Home?" Fannie said.

"Where'd you hear that?" Edith said as Naomi and Bethany shared a secret smile. Not only did they already know that piece of information, but Geena had already roped Bethany into volunteering to teach cooking classes for the wayward girls from the Group Home. Next summer, Geena wanted the girls to help out at the soup kitchen. She had even given the soup kitchen a name: The Second Chance Café.

"I heard it from her this very morning," Fannie said, looking pleased she knew something before Edith did. "I saw Geena Spencer in the Sweet Tooth Bakery wolfing down a cinnamon roll."

"Well, that's just dandy," Edith Fisher said. "Teach all those young innocents how to be women's libbers." Now she was her old self again.

Ella was following things better that afternoon than she had in a long time. "I heard that folks throw a cat on top of the quilt as soon as the last stitch is in. If the cat jumps into your lap, then you're the next to get married."

Fannie snorted. "*Now* you remember the secret to catching a beau, Ella. Should've told us that sixty years ago." The women all got a big laugh out of that and started vying to have the cat fall in their lap. All but Naomi.

She leaned close to Bethany and whispered, "I wish the sisters would remember that I'm not in my eighties."

Bethany grinned. "I have an announcement to make," she said. Her eyes moved around the ring of faces, starting with Sylvia and ending with Edith. The room was so quiet, they could hear Naomi's needle go through the quilt. The needle squeaked as she pushed it through the cotton with her thimble.

"I'd like to visit my mother," Bethany said. "On the rotation schedule. I'd like to go with you. Each month. She's my mother, even if she's sick. I want to help take care of her. The caregiver said my mother's best days were when the quilting ladies paid her a visit."

For a long moment, no one said a word.

"Me too," Naomi piped up. "I'd like to go too."

More silence. And then Sylvia smiled. "Of course. Of course." She looked at Edith. "That's a fine plan, isn't it, Edith? It's the best plan of all."

Everyone looked to Edith. "I suppose."

"Then count on me," Bethany said, and her heart was suddenly too full for words as she let her gaze roam lovingly over these women: the ancient sisters whose hearts were so large; Jimmy's mother Edith, who wasn't nearly as tough as she liked others to think; Naomi, her loyal and kind friend. It was a wonderful place to be, nestled in the heart of these good women.

They sewed quietly for a long time, no longer feeling a need to talk, until at last, Edith Fisher stuck her needle into the quilt and took off her thimble. "Somebody tell me where's the time gone. I forgot all about refreshments." She placed her hands on the side of her chair and hefted herself up. "I'll put the teakettle on. Tea always hits the spot after an afternoon's sewing. Did I tell you I've got shortbread?"

She took a few heavy steps toward the kitchen before stopping to place her hand on the back of Bethany's chair and leaning over to examine the quilt in front of her. "Well, lands sake, those are real nice stitches. You're coming along just fine."

She looked at Edith and smiled, and, in her own stiff way, Edith smiled back.

Summer had a few days left to run, but here and there, spots of yellow and pale orange on the trees made it clear that fall was fast approaching. A gust of wind in the branches made a rustling sound, as if the leaves were made of paper. The sun shone bright and clear in a sky of brilliant blue.

Bethany was on her way to Eagle Hill after another session of cleaning out the Sisters' House. Today, she thought she might just be making headway in the de-clutter process. A person could walk through the living room now without having to swerve around stacks of books or bags of quilt scraps. The sisters were still a long way from being ready to host church, but it was on the horizon. The far, far distant horizon. Especially now that the sisters had asked Bethany to supervise the Grange Hall Second Chance Café and she had said yes.

*Shootfire!* How did that happen, anyhow? One minute, she's lugging the little red wagons over to the Grange Hall just to help the sisters. The next thing she knew, the sisters smiled their sweetest smiles at her and suddenly she's in charge of the soup kitchen. But how could she say no? What would happen to all those down-and-outers if something happened to the sisters? They weren't spring chickens, after all. A slow grin lifted the corners of her lips. Those sisters could talk the birds right out of the trees.

Bethany had one foot on the porch step of Eagle Hill when she stopped, spun around, and strode over to Naomi's. She wanted to see how Naomi was faring after a fierce headache that kept her sequestered in the basement all weekend.

As Bethany walked through the privet hole, she noticed Galen standing by the far edge of the barn, talking to someone, slapping shoulders the way men do when they're glad to see each other. She stilled, realizing it was Jimmy to whom Galen was talking.

She hung by the privet, watching the two from afar. She thought of the first time she had seen Jimmy, at the farmers' market, and he was just a stranger, handsome and amusing, eyes with a fiery sparkle that caught girls under his spell. Not Bethany, of course, but most other girls. He was still a boy, she had thought then, in a man's body. But Jimmy seemed different somehow, taller and older than just a week ago when he had come to talk to her at Eagle Hill.

She could hear the rumble of his laugh from where she stood. She loved that laugh of his, so kind and warmhearted. When he laughed, he reminded her of a feisty horse you couldn't help but be fond of, full of life and spirit. With a start, she realized she had never felt happier than she did at that moment. No, wait. It wasn't happiness she felt. It was joy. Something deep down that couldn't be stolen.

Just then Jimmy caught sight of Bethany and snapped to attention. Galen noticed and politely absented himself, disappearing into the barn.

She waited for Jimmy to stride across the yard to come to her, as recommended by *A Young Woman's Guide to Virtue*. A girl must never chase after a boy.

Jimmy did cross the yard, but he stopped a few yards away from her. Merriment sparkled in those blue, blue eyes. "Something on your mind?"

"Why yes, there is." A voice that she was surprised to realize was hers said, "Jimmy Fisher, I love you." Her heart beat faster. "That's all I have to say. I honestly and truly love you."

Jimmy looked at her intently for a long moment beneath his hat brim, then his blue eyes twinkled. "I know. I knew it all along. But I'm glad you finally got around to figuring it out for yourself." A slow smile, homey and unhurried and sweet, like syrup over pancakes on a Sunday morning, spread across his face.

Naomi was right. No one had ever looked at her the way Jimmy did. It was the look of a man in love.

He opened his arms. "Come here."

She walked toward him and he met her halfway, their lips meeting at the same time. It felt like home to be in his embrace, familiar and safe.

# Rose's Blueberry Buckle

| | |
|---|---|
| ¾ cup | sugar |
| ¼ cup | soft shortening |
| 1 large | egg |
| ½ cup | milk |
| 2 cups | sifted all-purpose flour |
| ½ teaspoon | salt |
| 2 teaspoons | baking powder |
| 2 cups | blueberries (fresh or frozen) |

Preheat oven to 375 degrees. Mix sugar and shortening, then add in egg. Stir in milk. Sift together and stir in flour, baking powder, and salt. Carefully blend in berries. Grease and flour a 9" square pan. Spoon batter into pan. Put on crumb topping before baking. Bake 45–50 minutes, depending on your oven.

### Crumb topping:

| | |
|---|---|
| ½ cup | sugar |
| ½ cup | flour |
| ½ teaspoon | cinnamon |
| ¼ cup | soft butter |

Blend together with fingers and drop mixture on top of batter, spreading evenly.

# Discussion Questions

1. Finding a trunkful of human bones in the basement of the Sisters' House might seem amusing, but it actually kicked off a theme of "skeletons in a closet." Has there been a time in your life when you were faced with some unfinished business from your past? (By the way—finding a trunkful of human bones in an attic of an Amish farmhouse was a true story!).

2. Which character did you identify with the most? Why?

3. How were the concerns different for each of the characters: Bethany Schrock? Mim Schrock? Geena Spencer? Jimmy Fisher? Naomi King?

4. Sylvia, the youngest of the ancient sisters, gave this advice to Bethany: "You mustn't blame yourself or look back—not any longer than it takes to learn what you must learn. After that, let it go. The past is past. But you're still here," she whispered urgently and exerted a gentle pressure on Bethany's arms. "And I'm glad. You be glad too." When might you have needed such advice?

5. How did Bethany's view of herself change throughout the story? What contributed to that change?

6. All families face strife from time to time, just as Jimmy and his mother did. What were your thoughts when Jimmy decided to set aside his passion for horse training and return to the Fisher Hatchery to help his mother?

7. In spite of her headaches, Naomi is peaceful in her spirit. In what ways, surrounded by a troubled world, can we cultivate a spirit of peace?

8. Did you pick up on any clues that Stuck, who wrote letters to Mrs. Miracle, was Rusty? How did Mrs. Miracle affect Stuck/Rusty?

9. A person cannot change his or her past actions, but can they make up for the hurt they've caused by helping others? Does the good that Edith Fisher did for Bethany's mother make up for the years of keeping her whereabouts a secret?

10. What did Ella's lost thimble symbolize? How were other characters searching for something from the past?

11. How did reality measure up when Bethany met her mother?

12. Bethany obviously feels respect for Geena. How does Geena share the same high opinion for Bethany?

13. Another theme in this book is coming to grips with one's past so one can move forward. Bethany longed to find purpose, Geena was seeking purpose, even Mim was looking for purpose with her secret identity of Mrs. Miracle. How did all three find purpose through serving others?

# Acknowledgments

As the saying goes, writing is a lonely business.

It would be impossible to get books out into the world without a solid network of help and support. My circle is rich, and they deserve the small moments of attention here.

I could never get anywhere without the saintly team at Revell, welcoming the characters of Stoney Ridge with open arms. And deepest thanks to my editor Andrea Doering, for helping me find my best work, over and over again, and challenging me to be better than I think I can be.

Special thanks to my agent, Joyce Hart of The Hartline Literary Agency.

The Grange Hall soup kitchen is based on a true story. There is a woman in the San Francisco Bay Area, Mother Williams, who started a once-a-week soup kitchen while in her early eighties. She is nearly ninety now and still going strong. A remarkable and inspiring woman. It took five sisters in this story to match the energy and determination of one Mother Williams! Grateful to you, Becky Blakey, for filling in some details.

And last on the page, but not in my heart, thanks to my readers. The circle is not complete without you, so thank you from the bottom of my heart. I love hearing from you and listening to your stories. Find me online at www.suzannewoodsfisher.com or send me an e-mail at Suzanne@suzannewoodsfisher.com.

# The
# Revealing

To my son, Gary,
who has a special knack
for encouraging others
to be originals

# 1

This secret life was doing her in.

At times, Naomi King wondered how in the world she had become so secretive. She used to be the type who would answer any question, talk to anyone about anything. No longer. Maybe years of enduring dreadful migraines that had kept her pinned home so much of the time, waiting for the worst to pass, had made her more reticent and reclusive. Maybe it was because she'd never had a reason to keep a secret of this magnitude. Most likely, it was because she didn't realize what she was missing until now. It was as if she had come out of the shadows and into the real world.

And it all had to do with Tobe Schrock.

Tobe was serving out a sentence at FCI Schuykill in Minersville for withholding evidence about wrongdoings in Schrock Investments, his late father's investment company, from the Securities Exchange Commission. Minersville was a one-hour-and-thirty-one-minute bus ride from Lancaster, plus another twelve-minute bus ride from Lancaster to Stoney Ridge. Naomi had it timed to the second.

Except for today, when the bus to Stoney Ridge had run late.

As she walked down the lane, she unrolled a half-eaten pack of Tums, chewed two tablets, and tried very hard to do nothing but take deep breaths and think about Tobe. It helped a little, but not enough. She found herself nervously twirling the strings of her prayer cap and forced her hands down by her sides. Stubbornly, she wrestled against the anxiety. If Galen were already home and asked where she had been, she wouldn't lie to him. *I will not lie.* She had never once lied to him, though she didn't tell him everything, either.

So what would she tell him? The band around her chest cinched tighter and her pulse picked up speed. She would say that she had gone visiting a friend on a Sunday afternoon, which was true. And yet it wasn't. Tobe wasn't just a friend. He was much, much more than that. But Galen, her dear, intrusive, overprotective brother, could never understand that.

She heard a horse nicker in the darkness and another one answer back, and panic swooped down and seized her from head to toe.

She took another Tums and chewed fast.

She couldn't keep this up. She couldn't keep the secret about Tobe much longer. Today he had promised her that the time was coming soon when everything would be out in the open. He said he would be released from prison soon. Any day now.

But until then? Her hands were trembling and her stomach was churning and her heartbeat thundered. Galen *must* be home by now. The horses would need to be fed soon.

Unease tightened in her stomach. She took three more Tums out of the package and chewed them, fast and hard.

Oh . . . where had she left that bus schedule to Minersville? *Where, where, where?* If her brother found out she had been to see Tobe Schrock . . . at a federal prison . . . She cringed.

Naomi and Tobe were an unlikely pair, she knew that. He had been born Amish but spent his growing up years in a Mennonite church and remained unbaptized. Uncertain. Worldly. She was sheltered, overprotected by her brother. Her life was on the horse farm that her brother managed. Her work was to care for their home and be a part of the Amish church, and she loved her life.

Her brother did not think well of Tobe Schrock. It wasn't just because of the recent troubles the Schrock family had with their investment company imploding—his disdain went farther back. He considered Tobe to be lazy and selfish, an opinion based on Tobe as a young teen. But Naomi saw past that and found so much more in Tobe. She believed the best about him. There was a fine man in there, a diamond in the rough, and she was desperately, hopelessly in love with *that* man.

She took a new pack of Tums out of her dress pocket, chewed two tablets, and swallowed so fast she didn't even taste the chalky cherry flavor, turned down the wooded driveway of the King farm, and stopped short. There, in front of the house, was her brother Galen. He stood with his arms crossed against his chest, deep in conversation with Bishop Elmo and Deacon Abraham.

Lightning split the sky, followed by a great clap of thunder and a torrent of soft raindrops. There was a sweet smell in the air on this gray Monday morning, the mulchy smell of wet earth. Spring was but a promise, but a promise was better than winter.

Rose Schrock crossed the yard to the henhouse with an empty basket in her arms, hardly aware of the rain that was falling, mindful of all she needed to do before the children returned from school. The guest flat needed to be cleaned, aired out, fresh sheets and towels brought in. She just received a message on the machine in the phone shanty from a woman who wanted to reserve the guest flat for an extended stay. The woman said she needed a quiet place to "reinvent herself"—whatever *that* meant.

Rose felt relieved to have someone stay in the guest flat during the off-season. The inn had provided a far more steady stream of guests than she could have imagined, mostly because of the mistaken notion of Eagle Hill as a place where miracles occurred. But the stream of visitors drizzled in December and came to a complete stop in January, February, and March. It was a worry. This was her first year as an innkeeper. She didn't know if it was normal to expect a seasonal dip or if it meant an inevitable decline, but she did know she counted on that income to help make ends meet for her family.

Something on the road caught her eye and she stopped for a moment. It was a truck, following a buggy, and it looked as if they were turning into the vacant property across the road. She'd heard that a new Amish family was moving into the district. Vera, her mother-in-law, who rarely left home but knew the business of everyone, said that the recently widowed father was a minister. He had bought the Bent N' Dent grocery store, looking for a fresh start for his brood, and Rose certainly understood that. A fresh start sounded delightful on days when life's complications seemed to hold her by the ankles.

The chickens fussed and clucked as she entered the rickety henhouse. She let them out into the yard and gathered the eggs in the nest boxes, taking care with Harriet, the old hen who refused to leave her nest and pecked with a vengeance. When the basket was full, Rose hurried outside and latched the door behind her. As she turned, she found Galen King, her particular friend and neighbor, waiting for her with an odd look on his face.

"Rose, there's something I need to talk to you about." His voice was both soft and gruff, very, very bass, like rumbling thunder from the next county. She loved the sound of it.

He paused, shifting from one foot to another as if he had a pebble in his shoe. He coughed, and Rose saw a bead of perspiration trickle down his temple under his black felt hat. She looked at him, wondering if he wasn't coming down with a fever and thinking that standing here in the rain couldn't be good for him if he was. "Come inside for a cup of coffee."

He glanced toward the house. "Vera's inside, isn't she?"

"Yes. In the kitchen."

He cleared his throat and met her eyes at last. "Then, no. I'd rather say what I have to say in private."

"Well, could we at least get out of the rain?" She walked over to the porch and spun around to face him, a tad impatient. He followed behind, glancing nervously at the kitchen windows to see if Vera was peering out them. What did Galen have on his mind? It was cold and her feet were wet. She was in no mood for a mystery. "Is something wrong?"

"No, no, nothing's wrong. Well, actually, maybe there is. Did something happen to trouble Naomi yesterday?"

"Nothing that I know of. Why?"

"Bishop Elmo and Deacon Abraham dropped by yesterday afternoon to ask if I would take on another apprentice, since Jimmy Fisher is busy with the chickens."

That didn't surprise Rose—she knew Galen had more work than he could manage—but she held out a hope that he might wait for Tobe, to apprentice him after his release. Beyond Galen, Rose noticed a porch gutter was clogged with leaves, causing the water to spill over the gutters. The droplets fell to puddles on the ground with uneven *plips*. She looked at him, not sure what an apprentice had to do with Naomi. It wasn't typical of Galen to circle around the block before getting to his point. "So . . . about Naomi . . . ," she urged.

"Naomi walked up the driveway like she'd seen a ghost, then shot past us and into the house. Acted as twitchy as a cow's tail at fly time all evening long."

Rose shivered in the damp air. "I can ask Bethany if she knows something, though I'm not sure she'd tell me." She started to move past him.

He reached out to stop her, his hands on her arms. "But Naomi's not the reason I stopped by." He glanced over her shoulder to the kitchen windows. Satisfied Vera wasn't peering out at them, he looked straight into Rose's eyes, took a deep breath, and said, "I think it's time we moved things along."

She glanced around the farm and saw all the things that needed moving along—a pasture fence that needed repairing, a barn door that kept falling off its track, a sagging clothesline that was threatening to fall over in the next big windstorm. She was surprised it had lasted through the winter. In May, they were due to take a turn hosting church at Eagle Hill. The to-do list was endless. Where to start?

But Galen's face had such a strange look on it, uncomfortable and shy, not like a man who was creating a to-do list. A blush began to creep up his face. Slowly, his meaning began to dawn on her and she was astounded. "Galen!" she exclaimed. "Are you asking me to marry you?"

His eyes flew open wide, and he swallowed hard. "Doesn't it sound like I am?"

"Well. Sort of. Maybe. Not quite." The more she said, the sillier she felt. But at the risk of embarrassing him even further, she knew she'd better make her position clear. She wasn't ready. Her husband Dean hadn't been gone two full years and things were still unsettled, unfinished.

Galen took another deep breath. "Yes. Yes, I am. I am asking you to marry me." He took her two hands in his. "Rose, there will always be obstacles. I want us to face those things together. I want us to get married. Soon."

"I . . . I don't know what to say."

"Just say yes." To Galen, everything was simple.

But it wasn't a simple question. The very thought of getting married was ridiculous. It made no sense. Frankly, their entire relationship made no sense! She was older than Galen by more than a few years. She had a family—two stepchildren, three children, plus a very cranky mother-in-law; he had never married. She was still trying to unravel the mess of her husband's investment company gone awry. Tobe, Dean's son, was serving time in jail. Jake Hertzler, a key player in the downfall of the company, charged with all kinds of terrible crimes, hadn't been found. Getting married was the furthest thing from her mind.

And why now, on a rainy Monday morning, would Galen blurt out something like asking her to marry him? Why not yesterday, when the sun was shining as they had picnicked up at Blue Lake Pond?

Yet such an unrehearsed proposal was so like him. Words were few with Galen, but when he did speak, they were impactful. He was a man of action instead of words, purpose rather than intention. So different from her first husband, who could stir up a dust cloud with his fancy way with words.

Rose remembered the first time she had noticed Galen—truly noticed him. It was a sunny afternoon, sometime after the foggy period when Dean had passed, and Galen had offered to teach her how to drive a buggy. She had been raised Amish but had left the church over a dozen years ago. She hadn't been near a horse in as many years and it was high time she grew comfortable with them again. As she was climbing into the buggy, the horse pranced sideways at a scurrying mouse, and Rose leaped back with a screech, startled. Immediately Galen stepped forward, taking the bridle, rubbing the mare's forehead, and the horse soon quieted. But Rose's reaction must have been so unexpected to Galen that his eyes went wide.

"I take exception to mice," she explained, feeling color rise in her cheeks.

Then Galen broke out in a rich laugh. Never having seen him even smile before, she was unprepared for the impact. The sight was incredible; it completely changed him. She had not known his eyes to sparkle in such a way, his jaw to be so perfect, his throat so tan, his mouth so handsome. It was the first time she saw all that he could be.

An embarrassed laugh left her throat, then a second, and soon her laughter joined his and she suddenly found herself feeling happy. Happier than she had felt in a long, long time. He had held out both his hands to her to help lift her into the buggy and she felt an unexpected jolt of excitement. As they sat together in the small buggy, she was as close to him as she'd ever been and the thought made her light-headed.

Each time she saw him after that buggy ride, there was a knife-edgy feeling in the pit of her stomach. Galen was so quiet and composed that she had no idea he felt the same way. It was months later that he admitted he had fallen in love with her.

With the rain falling behind him, Rose looked at Galen. He had a rugged, capable face. Firm features, determined jawline, placid eyes. She saw the great kindness in his expression, and she saw his wisdom, which was well beyond his years. She saw compassion in those green, green eyes. She saw love there.

It made no sense to marry now. No sense at all.

But . . . the thing about love was, once started, it couldn't easily be stopped. A voice that she was surprised to realize was hers said, "Yes, Galen. I believe I would like to marry you."

# 2

Bethany popped up in bed again and stared at the window. For one crazy moment she thought Jimmy Fisher might have come calling. He certainly needed to do something to make amends to her after totally deserting her two nights ago. He had told her that he wanted to take her home after the youth gathering on Sunday night, and so she expected him to be there, but he never showed up.

She ended up going home with Simon Glick, a thoroughly awkward young man. So tall, his elbows and knees seemed to stick out at angles and she felt that if he fell he might break into small pieces. And yet that was a little unfair, because he wasn't all that clumsy—he only looked as if he might be. In fact, he was more talkative than she expected. He even made her laugh once or twice. Nothing like the way Jimmy made her laugh, but it would serve him right if she started going out with Simon Glick.

She shifted on her bed to try to get more comfortable and shut her eyes. She tried to think of nothing, but crazy thoughts kept shooting through her mind.

Bethany picked up her pen and wrote "Mrs. Jimmy Fisher" on the page of her journal. Not that she wanted Jimmy Fisher to propose, but she wondered if he might. And when.

She must have dozed off because, a short while later, she was startled awake when her room filled with light. A broad beam of light swept the wall and the ceiling, circling again and again. She came up on her elbows, heart pounding, crawled out of bed, and knelt at the window. At first she could see nothing; then Jimmy Fisher removed his hat, waving furiously at her, and the moon bounced off the crown of his hair.

She should ignore him and go back to bed. She knew she should. But of course she didn't. She slipped into her clothes, wrapped a shawl around her shoulders—it was only March and the air was brittle—and hurried out to meet him.

She would scold him, of course, for dragging her out on a night as cold as this one, with off-and-on rain, but then she'd climb in the buggy with him, hidden at the end of the driveway, and they'd go to one of their favorite spots to talk. And hug. And cuddle. And kiss. And when things got a little heated, she would act indignant and insist he take her home again. On the way back, she would let her shoulder bump up against his now and then to know that she didn't mean it.

It was a game they played, and one that Bethany hoped would entice Jimmy to think about how nice it would be not to have to say good night. To get married and live happily ever after. *Shootfire!* Was that too much to ask?

Jimmy was waiting with the flashlight, which he turned off the minute he saw her framed in the doorway. Once Bethany walked outside, he caught her in his arms and tipped his forehead against hers. She could feel his breath, his words, falling onto her. He tilted his face so that their mouths came together.

She wedged her hands up between them to set her distance. "And where were you on Sunday night, Jimmy Fisher? You can't just show up like I'm at your beck and call and think I'm available for kissing."

She looked at him, daring him to say he was sorry. Instead, he said, "My mother was so distraught . . . you know . . . after you dumped her out of the wheelchair—"

"Dumped is a strong word. I prefer to think of it as tipped." Edith Fisher was recuperating from bunion surgery, and Bethany wheeled her outside after the fellowship lunch at church to get some fresh air and a little sunshine. There was a ramp, after all, and the air was unusually warm, almost springlike.

But Bethany had never taken a wheelchair down a ramp. As she guided Edith backward, the wheelchair started to gain momentum. Edith's weight, plus the wheelchair's, surpassed Bethany's. At the bottom of the ten-foot ramp, the wheelchair flipped sideways and dumped Edith out, facedown on the grass.

Naomi, Edith's favorite girl, ran for a wet rag to hold against the scrapes on her forehead and a towel for a pillow. Edith, furious and humiliated, wouldn't accept Bethany's profuse apologies. Jimmy ended up taking his mother home early.

"—after I finally got her settled down, I fell asleep on the couch and when I woke up, it was morning."

"Did you happen to hear that Susie Glick and Tim Riehl have an Understanding? And Elizabeth Mast and Eli Miller do too." She squeezed his hands. "Eli said he'd like to marry before spring planting starts." That's exactly what Bethany would like to have now . . . a formal Understanding. She would like to know where she stood with Jimmy Fisher.

"Hmmm," Jimmy said, nuzzling that tender spot on her neck that he knew she liked.

"It's nice, isn't it, when a couple has an Understanding? When the fellow steps up and makes a decision to move forward."

"Mmm-hmm."

"Folks say that weddings always come in threes."

"Yup."

"You haven't heard a word I've said, have you?"

"Mmm-hmm."

Bethany's temper went up like a March kite. She broke away from him and thrust her hands on her hips. "Ever since you've been taking care of those chickens full-time, you have turned right back into the boy I first met. As immature as can be."

Enjoyment fled Jimmy's face. He sighed and met Bethany's gaze. "I know. You're right. There's something about those birds that makes me feel like I'm thirteen all over again. It's those chickens. They're running me ragged . . ." His voice trailed off. "You know, I've hated chickens for as long as I can remember. They stink, they squawk, they peck at me. They make me stink and squawk and act peckish."

He was always griping about those chickens and she was tired of hearing about it. It wasn't just the chickens. It was living under his mother's thumb. As Galen King always said, Edith Fisher cast a long shadow on her boys. She sucked the joy of life out of them. And when Jimmy was away from his mother, like now, he acted like a silly schoolboy on summer break. Nothing on his mind whatsoever. She walked a few steps away from him and looked up at the clouds gliding past the moon. He followed behind and slipped his arms around her waist.

"Jimmy, the solution is simple. You need to find someone to work for your mother."

"It's not that easy." He sounded a million miles away. Miles from Bethany and from Eagle Hill.

"You'd better figure it out. And you'd better start making noises about our future together, Jimmy Fisher, because if you don't take me more seriously—"

Spinning her around to face him, Jimmy put a finger to her lips, reached for her hand, and pulled her out of the moonlight and into the shadows. "I take you plenty seriously! You're my best girl, Bethany."

Immediately her temper sizzled. "I'd better be your only girl, Jimmy Fisher!" She knew her voice had risen an octave and sounded sharp, and she regretted it. But he was always saying they would get married someday, and someday never seemed to come. Perhaps the rainbows had gone and the glow had dimmed for Jimmy. If so, she'd rather know it now.

He lifted his eyes. "That's what I meant. You're my only girl. My best and only girl." He took his hat off. "Aw, Bethany, what's the rush? We're young. We have our whole lives ahead of us."

"Maybe you do, but I'm not about to waste my life on a fellow who hates chickens and won't do anything about it. I only agreed to go out with you because I thought you were a fellow with some plans for himself."

"I did have plans! I did. Good ones. But without Lodestar as the cornerstone, my entire horse breeding business fell apart."

She rolled her eyes. "There *are* other horses."

He cut a smile in her direction. "None like that horse."

She let out a big sigh. "Have you looked for him?"

"Every chance I've had. That's what I've been doing on Saturday afternoons." So *that's* where he'd been when he was supposed to be stopping by Eagle Hill.

"What about Galen? Have you asked him to look for you?"

"He's no help at all. He told me I needed to let that horse go and stop making excuses for being a man." He rubbed his chin. "I'd like him to have a week living with my mother, then he can tell me all about being a man."

"So you're saying that if you had Lodestar back, your life would be back on track. You'd have your future mapped out."

His dark eyebrows lifted.

"Did you hear me?"

"I heard you." He cleared his throat. "If I could ever get Lodestar back, I think everything else will fall into place."

"Like . . . our future."

Jimmy ran his finger around his collar and smiled at her ruefully.

Lately, Jimmy Fisher had begun to feel something like . . . the word "panic" crept into his head, but he pushed it away. He didn't do panic. He just felt . . . unsettled, that was it.

As he had left Bethany last night, all the emotional jumble inside him came together in his stomach. He was crazy about Bethany Schrock. Her smile, when she turned it on him full force, was numbing. It made his bones turn to butter. She was the girl he saw himself growing old with. She was everything he'd ever wanted. Why was he scared to death to ask her to marry him? Was old Hank Lapp's prediction about him true? "Always shopping, never buying." He frowned, hearing Hank's loud voice echo in his head.

No. It wasn't that. There were just too many unsettled things in his life right now.

He adjusted the brooder lamps, checked the feeders, muttering away about how much he hated chickens, and walked over to the workbench to get a Band-Aid for his finger. He kept a big box of Band-Aids in the pullet barn, on the ready. There were a couple of hens who had it in for him. He was convinced they waited for him to enter the pullet barn, then sent a secret signal down the line of the nesting boxes so they would all come flying at him, beaks and claws sharpened. Today, one of them drew blood from his hand as he refilled the water trough.

He glanced through the open barn door and smiled at the sight of Honey, grazing in the pasture. She was a fine little mare, almost like a pet. He would take carrots from the garden and feed them to her by hand. He delighted in her so much that he always gave her a brushing before he harnessed her. He kept a little horse brush in his back pants pocket just for that purpose. This was the mare he had hoped to breed with Lodestar. The perfect complement to Lodestar. She was the one.

Galen King had given him Honey as a sorry filly and wouldn't take a dime for her. "Not fast enough to race," he told Jimmy, "too small for a full day's work, not strong enough to pull the team." But as smart as Galen usually was about horses, he wasn't thinking about Honey as a broodmare. And he certainly wasn't factoring in Lodestar's fine genes. A sorry filly, indeed.

If only Jimmy could find Lodestar's whereabouts. He was sure everything would work out once he had Lodestar back in his stall, locked up good and tight because that horse had a streak of Houdini in him, and his breeding business could begin. Bethany was right. Once Lodestar was back with Jimmy, everything else would fall into place. He swallowed past a knot the size of a goose egg in his throat. Even the part about Bethany Schrock.

The air smelled of lightning, and the breeze from the south carried a scent of heavy rain. All the signs were good that rain would arrive soon.

As soon as Naomi saw the barn door slide shut behind Galen, she pulled out her box of stationery from the kitchen desk and sat down to write a letter to Tobe. If she hurried, she could get it into the mailbox before the postman drove by.

*Dear Tobe,*

*When I arrived home on Sunday afternoon, there, on the kitchen table, was the bus schedule. Just what I was afraid of! But you must have been praying: although Galen had beat me home, he hadn't gone in the house yet. The deacon and the bishop were waiting for him in the yard. They had a few suggestions for an apprentice for Galen's horse work, but he turned them all down. You know how finicky he can be about anyone around his horses. Anyway, I was able to dash into the house and hide the bus schedule before they all came in for coffee. My hands shook as I poured coffee in the bishop's mug. Shook like a leaf!*

*How much longer, Tobe? I can't keep this up. We need to tell him. Them. All of them.*

*Love,*
*Naomi*

—⁖ ◊ ⁖—

The storm that blew through Stoney Ridge this morning split two trees near the creek that ran alongside Eagle Hill. Water flowed over the road like a river. Behind the farmhouse, a trail that led up the ridgeline had turned into a small waterfall.

To Bethany Schrock, there were few displays on earth more thrilling than a thunderstorm. Her friend and neighbor, Naomi, felt quite the opposite. She was sure Naomi had passed the whole of the storm with a shawl pressed to her eyes.

By the time the rain was letting up, Bethany was on her way to the Sisters' House, where she worked a couple days a week for five elderly sisters. Once a week, she and Naomi made lunch for the down-and-outers of Stoney Ridge at the Second Chance Café held in the Grange Hall, but that was volunteer work. She'd been volunteered for it by the sisters. Her main job was the Sisters' House.

Her job entailed cleaning out and organizing the ancient sisters' home so they could take a long-overdue turn at hosting church, but it was an endless task. She loved them, though, each one. Ella, the eldest, insightful, kind. Ada, sensitive and cheerful. Lena, the middle sister, tender, a peacemaker. Fannie, efficient, determined, bossy. Sylvia, the youngest, capable, creative.

Today, Sylvia met her at the door and waved a letter in her face. "We have exciting news, Bethany! You have to stop your downstairs organizing and start right away on the guest bedroom."

"The second-floor guest bedroom," Fannie clarified.

"Yes. That's the one," Sylvia said. "I haven't been up there in years and years."

Bethany took off her bonnet and tried to find an empty wall peg by the door, frowning because she had just emptied those wall pegs of umbrellas and old bonnets and a man's straw hat a few days ago, and they were completely filled up again. "Are you expecting company?"

"Yes!" Sylvia said. "A relation. He's come to Stoney Ridge to investigate the family tree. It's very exciting."

As they walked into the living room, Bethany nodded to Ella, Lena, and Ada, all seated in their favorite chairs.

"It's terribly exciting," Lena said, looking up from her knitting project.

"He told us he was hitting brick walls," Ada said, engrossed in a crossword puzzle in an old copy of the *Stoney Ridge Times*.

Ella, a woman with a soft fan of wrinkles beside each eye and curly gray hair that peeked from under her prayer cap, looked from sister to sister. "That sounds painful." At ninety-three, she was easily confused.

"I don't think he meant it literally, Ella," Fannie said. "It's genealogy lingo that means he is stumped."

"How do you happen to know about genealogy bingo, Fannie?" Lena said.

"Lingo," Fannie said in a brisk tone, "not bingo."

As Lena paused to ponder her response, Bethany knew she had to jump in and veer the sisters back to the original subject quickly or it would be lost forever. It often happened. Most of their conversation ended up on little bunny trails that led nowhere. "How close a relative is he?"

The sisters looked at each other blankly.

"Distant," Fannie said.

"Fourteenth cousin twice removed," Sylvia said. "He's coming soon, he said. By week's end. You can manage, can't you?"

Bethany sighed. If the second floor looked anything like the first floor, basement, and carriage house, her week had just taken a dismal downhill turn.

Five hours later, Bethany stopped by Naomi's house before she headed home to Eagle Hill. She was exhausted. Discouraged too. That upstairs bedroom was going to take her all week to clean out. And where would she put things? Managing that Sisters' House took every spare ounce of energy she had.

She was eager to show Naomi the quilt top she had finally finished last night and also to share a letter from her brother, Tobe. Under Naomi's tu-telage, Bethany was finishing her first quilt for her eventual-but-not-official wedding to Jimmy Fisher. She'd started plenty of quilts over the years but abandoned them because she hated to sew. But Naomi was adamant that she needed to finish *something*. She gave her assignments to do and checked up on her tasks: cut, trim, sort, sew. Then: undo, rip out, redo. Bethany had hoped the quilt would be finished by now, but Naomi kept insisting it had to be perfect.

Good thing Jimmy Fisher didn't seem to be in a rush to get married, because this quilt wasn't making much progress. She frowned. *Shootfire!* What *was* taking Jimmy Fisher so long to propose? Just once she'd like him to behave the way she expected, but the fact that he never did was one more reason she couldn't seem to get enough of him.

As Naomi opened the door, Bethany inhaled a sweet scent of cinnamon and nutmeg floating in from the kitchen. "What did you make?"

"A new recipe for pumpkin cinnamon rolls," Naomi said. "I thought I'd practice the recipe before serving them at the next Sisters' Bee. Want to try one?"

Bethany nodded. Baking was her favorite thing in the world. Her younger sister, Mim, preferred to read or write. Naomi would rather quilt. But Bethany would rather be in the kitchen than anywhere else. As she grabbed a fork and sat down to eat, she slid Tobe's letter closer to Naomi and watched her reaction. Naomi stilled as she saw the thin gray envelope, addressed in Tobe's sloppy handwriting. Then she snapped to attention and went back to stirring sugar into her tea. "You brought the quilt top for me to see?"

"Yes, and I brought Tobe's letter for you to read, if you might be in-terested."

Naomi took a sip of tea. "Any news?"

"He hopes he'll be released soon. But no date yet. That lawyer is trying to pea bargain for him."

"I think you mean plea bargain," Naomi said.

Bethany pushed the letter closer to Naomi. "You can read it for yourself."

"No need," Naomi said breezily. "You've told me what's in it. Now, let's see about that quilt top."

Bethany was sure Naomi was sweet on Tobe, just *sure* of it, though she could never get her to admit it.

And wouldn't you know that Naomi insisted she rip out the last row of the quilt top just because a few corners didn't match up? "Why should it matter?"

Naomi sighed a deep sigh. "Bethany . . . imagine adding a tablespoon of salt into a recipe when you were only supposed to add a teaspoon. It would matter a great deal. Same with quilting." She held out the quilt top. "You need to redo the binding before the next Sisters' Bee. We had planned to help you quilt it."

Naomi was turning into a bossy hen, that's what she was.

Bethany took the quilt top back and examined it. She'd only been going to the Sisters' Bee for a few months and she was already tired of the quilting business. But she loved Naomi and she loved the old sisters and she was even feeling a twinge of affection now and then for Edith, Jimmy Fisher's mother. Nothing more than a twinge, but at least she wasn't frightened of her anymore. She might not be Edith's choice for a future daughter-in-law—everyone in Stoney Ridge knew her favorite girl was Naomi King—but at least she was accepting that Jimmy and Bethany had an Understanding.

At least, she thought they did, until last Sunday's unfortunate incident.

Bethany sighed. The wheelchair tipping might have set back her and Jimmy's Understanding.

After finishing the pumpkin cinnamon roll, she gathered up Tobe's letter—which Naomi never even bothered to read—and her quilt top with the unaligned border corners and went on her way.

Naomi snipped off the end of a piece of thread with her teeth. Last evening, Bethany had brought over her re-sewn quilt top and together they had spread it across the frame, over a layer of white batting and the backing to the quilt. She had promised Bethany she would help quilt it, but she was regretting that promise. It pained her to see the mismatched corners, the triangles with missing points, the crooked seams.

Naomi idly threaded a needle and bowed her head over a quilt square, making small, even stitches without the benefit of a ruler or a machine.

She remembered what Tobe had said once about her stitches: "They're so tiny, they almost seem to disappear."

Her thoughts wandered to their brief time together last summer, when he had finally returned home after being a nomad for over a year. They spent every minute they could snatch together after that first time, when she had chanced upon him at Blue Lake Pond, sitting on an old log. He moved over to make room for her and she sat down, but he didn't say anything and neither did she. Somehow, she seemed to understand his need for silence. Instead, she had fixed her gaze out over the lake. It was so calm, not a ripple. A perfect summer day.

Naomi considered Blue Lake Pond to be one of the best things about living in a place like Stoney Ridge. A small town on the edge of a big natural pond. It wasn't much of a pond, considering other lakes in Pennsylvania, but it was a very nice one by any standards, full of little creeks and inlets, shaded by tall pine trees. It froze over in winter and transformed into an ideal skating rink. On that day, a hot August afternoon, stick bugs skittered over the surface of the water, while dragonflies buzzed in lazy circles.

A cottontail came and peered at them, looking curiously from one to the other before he hopped away. They laughed at the rabbit, which broke the tension between them, and soon they found they could talk to each other easily.

"Isn't it beautiful here?" she said. "Thinking out problems gets easier here at the lake."

He let out a snort. "I guess it depends on the problems. The problems I have—well, there's no one I can think them out with. Certainly not my family. And I really don't have any friends left."

She suddenly remembered a proverb her mother used to say: To be without friends is a serious form of poverty. "Hush." She spoke to him as a child. "I'm your friend. I'll listen."

He seemed to take a long time deciding and she wondered what he was thinking. She wanted to touch his hand, to squeeze it, to encourage him to confide, but she didn't. When he finally spoke, he refused to meet her eyes, but kept them fixed on the lake. "I just don't know how much to reveal about Jake Hertzler and Schrock Investments. Or whom to tell."

Once he started to talk, he was like a pent-up dam. He described his anguish over his father's death and the burden of guilt he felt, but what could he have done to prevent it? Tears rolled down his face as details of that unforgettable day spilled out. They sat for hours as the summer afternoon light came in patches between the hickory and beech trees that surrounded the pond.

Countless questions popped into Naomi's mind, but she held back and merely listened. She was surprised by what he confessed, and yet not at all surprised. She had always known there was more to the story of Dean Schrock's death. When he had run out of words, Tobe asked her what he should do.

"I think," she said, choosing her words carefully, "that you need to take responsibility for your part in it, and let God handle Jake Hertzler."

Tobe's eyes widened in shock. *"What?"* His lips clamped, his head came down with a snap, and he shot her a cautious side glance.

"Trust the Lord to carry out revenge, Tobe. He is a just God. He'll do what's right. Most likely, we won't."

The shadows grew longer as they sat on the log at the pond and talked. That was the day that began their dependence on each other—for him, it was the knowledge that she was the only person who understood the pressures, the pain, and the indecision he had been living with for the last few years. And for her, she had someone who viewed her not as fragile and timid but as strong and bold and wise.

They met each afternoon on the log, but their meetings had to be conspiratorial so no one, especially Galen, was wise to their rendezvous. There wasn't time to tell each other all the things still to tell, but by the end of the week, Tobe had agreed to speak to Allen Turner at the SEC and tell him about what had gone on, illegally and with intent, at Schrock Investments. "Almost everything," he said.

Naomi wondered what that meant, but from his demeanor she decided that it was best left alone for now.

Night after night, Naomi lay alone in her bed remembering that day Tobe had cried and she had held him in the woods. She could remember the way his body shook and how she could hear his heart beat against her. She could bring back the smell of him, of pine soap and coffee. She could remember the way his hair had tickled her neck and how his tears had wet her cheeks. And she remembered that final evening, when he had kissed her.

She had never imagined that a kiss could be so sweet, so natural, and so very easy. When they said goodbye to each other, they both had tears running down their faces, and he told her that he felt like a fool. "I should be strong and courageous for you, Naomi, not cry like a baby."

She smiled. "Rose says that men have tears, same as women. They just don't know that it's good to let them flow now and then."

After that week, Naomi King felt like a new person. She was able to do more than ever before. She could scarcely remember the days when a headache pinned her down and time had seemed long and hung heavily around her, waiting for it to lift. Now there weren't enough hours in the week for all that had to be done.

But when the postman arrived and she bolted to meet him before her brother, hoping he wouldn't notice how terribly interested she was in the mail, or when Bethany spoke of Tobe and dropped hints that she thought Naomi was sweet on him—those were the times when her stomach tightened into knots of stress and she had to chew Tums like they were M&Ms.

She sighed and wondered how much longer this was going to last. She wasn't cut out for living a secret life. It was all wrong.

But it was so right too.

# 3

Now and then, Mim Schrock would stop by the Sisters' House on her way home from school to help her older sister Bethany with the endless task of organizing the elderly sisters' home. Bethany was quicker, but Mim was the one who hung about, who found excuses to have meaningless little conversations with the sisters, to try to find out more about the life they led in the white clapboard house with the lilac bushes and the tall hollyhocks that guarded the fence. It was a house filled with true stories from another time.

Her favorite sister was Ella, the eldest, who had good days in which she remembered all kinds of interesting details about her childhood and told her amusing stories about the people of Stoney Ridge, and bad days when she lived in a fog and got questions all mixed up. Last week, Mim had asked Ella if the gout in her big toe had eased up at all.

"Not bad," Ella replied. "Though it got away after I tried to wring its neck."

Mim tilted her head, puzzled. "Wring whose neck?"

Ella gave Mim a look as if she might be sun touched. "The chicken's!"

The sisters didn't have any chickens.

That was a bad day for Ella. Today, though, was a good day. Bethany had already finished organizing for the day and hurried home, but Mim stayed anyway to have a visit with Ella. She had all kinds of stories to report about the fourteenth cousin twice removed, who was soon to arrive and was, according to Ella, quite dashing and worldly and exciting. Mim often wondered if Ella had ever loved a man, if any of the five sisters had ever known the kind of love she felt for Danny Riehl.

The afternoon was cold as Mim set off for the Bent N' Dent to pick up a few things for her mother before she went home. The March sun shone weak in a pale sky, trying to break through the gray clouds to warm the air, then it would disappear again and Mim would feel a chill. "Come on, spring, hurry up," she whispered aloud. For a while she walked behind an Amish couple she recognized from church. The woman walked serenely at her husband's side, nodding to those he nodded to along the road, smiling at those he smiled at, head cocked to hear his every word. Even the sun seemed to cooperate and shone down on them, scattering and dispersing the clouds left over from the morning's storm.

*That could be me with Danny Riehl,* Mim thought with envy. And she watched until they crossed the street and disappeared down a long lane. Walking backward, still thinking about Danny Riehl, Mim tripped over something and fell hard onto her rump. The something proved itself to be the long legs of a red-haired boy of fourteen, fifteen tops, who sat with his back against a fence post, eyes closed, soaking in the sun.

The boy's eyes popped wide open, eyes that were as round and brown as currant buns. Mim peered up at the boy: hair orange as a carrot peeping from beneath his black felt hat; a big smile that showed more spaces than teeth, and a face beslobbered with freckles, forehead to chin, ear to ear.

The irritation, the sting of her bottom, and the red-hot scrapes on her palms loosened Mim's tongue. "How dare you trip me!" she said as she picked herself up and brushed muck off her skirts. She gave the bow of her bonnet a straightening tug and smoothed out the now wrinkled skirt of her apron.

"I didn't," he said calmly, an ankle crossing a knee. "You were the one who was daydreaming and not watching where you were going."

Mim thrust her chin into the air. "Daydreaming? You were taking a nap without even worrying to see whose way you were in."

The boy shrugged. "I'm just passing the time, waiting for my sister," he said, gesturing toward the Bent N' Dent. "Enjoying the sun shining on my face." He radiated mischief, amusement, and mockery too.

"I've never seen you around Stoney Ridge."

He lunged to his feet. "My name is Jesse Stoltzfus." He introduced himself expansively, as if his name alone should bring her pleasure. "Nor have I seen you before. A girl with eyes as gray as a raging storm cloud, cheeks like Georgia peaches, and hair as dark as a black-crowned night heron."

Mim stared at him. She felt a blush creep up, no matter how hard she tried to stop it. She knew her face was turning the color of red raspberries. For some inexplicable reason, out of her mouth spouted something her grandmother would say: "The lowly woman and the meek woman are really above all other women, above all other things." She had just read that very thing in her grandmother's favorite book next to the Bible, *A Young Woman's Guide to Virtue*, published in 1948 and still as relevant as ever. According to Mammi Vera, anyway.

Jesse considered her words solemnly. "Then might I say, 'Never have I seen a girl with such beautiful meekness'? Or perhaps 'I am overwhelmed by your lowly spirited, meek-minded, lowly hearted, meek-looking humility, which meekly shines . . .'?"

Mim was staring at him with her mouth open. She knew it and she couldn't help it. It was the most ridiculous thing she had ever heard.

Jesse Stoltzfus doffed his hat and flourished it before him as if he were going to sweep the floor. He had wiry hair that grew upward from his head. It was sticky-up hair. When he straightened, he said, "No doubt we shall meet again. The glow from your jubilant meekness will lead me to wherever you are. Also your stormy gray eyes." He smiled as brightly as a full moon. "No doubt it was God's plan that we meet today."

Mim thought God might have better things to do than to concern himself with a chance meeting in the parking lot of a grocery store. Jesse Stoltzfus winked at her and strode off, whistling, toward a buggy his sister, another redhead, was loading with boxes of food. The girl looked over at Mim and waved in a friendly way.

Mim gave a halfhearted wave back to her and frowned at Jesse's back. *That* boy, she decided, thought he was *something*. She watched their buggy leave the Bent N' Dent and then she pulled a strand of hair out from under her black bonnet to look at it closely. Like a black-crowned night heron, he had said. It must be a bird, she thought, though she'd never seen one.

Whatever it was, it had a crown as black as her hair, and she almost smiled as she skipped up the steps to the store. Almost.

Rose hadn't had a chance to talk to Galen since he'd asked to marry her. This morning, she caught sight of him striding across the yard and stopped what she was doing to watch him. She studied his familiar walk—the efficient steps, his long legs, the way one shoulder was a little lower than the other, the way he tapped his fingers against his thighs as he walked when he was puzzling over something.

He spotted her and walked toward her, meeting her by the privet. His hat brim hid his eyes, but there was a slight smile to his lips. "I was going to come over today. I've got a little spare time and want to get working on Silver Queen's training. It's time she learned how to be a buggy horse."

Rose smiled. She knew that Galen King didn't know the first thing about spare time. He worked. And worked and worked. Sunup to sundown, he never stopped. She knew he was just looking out for her. Her buggy horse Flash was long past retirement age and could only be used for short trips around town. He couldn't even stand and wait during church with the other horses because it made his joints too stiff.

"Now's as good a time as any," he said.

Side by side, they walked to the barn, the morning frost crackling beneath their shoes. Galen stopped by the oats bin and scooped up a handful, then slid open the door to Silver Queen's stall and offered her the oats. With his other hand, he stroked the horse's long neck and absently combed his fingers through her mane. That was one of Galen's ways, Rose realized. He taught a horse to trust him by giving her what she loved best: a handful of honeyed oats and a loving touch. In return, the mare gave him her best.

In the stall next door, Silver Queen's colt pricked up his ears, whinnied and stamped his foot, snorted, then tried to wedge his nose between the stall bars, eager for attention. Or oats. Or both. Rose stood by the colt's stall and let him nuzzle her hand.

Galen looked up. "Soon, it'll be time to get that one started."

"Oh, but he's young yet. Scarcely a year."

Galen slipped a bridle over Silver Queen's head. "Too young to pull weight, but not too young to condition to traffic."

Rose ran a hand over the colt's velvet nose.

Galen tossed the lead line over Silver Queen's neck and came back outside the stall. "Rose, I'd like to talk to the bishop. Make it formal, set a date for our wedding."

She looked at him in surprise. "I thought we could wait until Tobe is released from jail. It shouldn't be much longer."

"Why do we need to wait?"

"There's so much that needs to get figured out first."

"Like what?"

She could feel his gaze. She glanced at him and found him watching her with concern from beneath the brim of his black hat. "Where we'll live, for one. If we live in your house, what should I do about the inn? A guest is due in tonight. And I'm starting to take reservations for the summer. And who will care for Vera?" She took a few steps away. "But if we live at Eagle Hill, then what about your house? What about Naomi?"

"Naomi has a lot of options. Besides, the houses are only fifty yards apart. Hardly a difficult thing to navigate."

"Then there's Bethany. She's counting on Jimmy Fisher to propose soon."

"Really?" His brows lifted. "He hasn't said a word to me."

They looked at each other, sharing a mutual thought. Jimmy talked a blue streak about anything and everything. If he were going to propose soon, wouldn't he be crowing about it? "I thought, perhaps, Tobe might be interested in running the inn."

A moment passed, then Galen dropped his chin to his chest. "You're expecting too much of Tobe."

"Maybe you don't expect enough of him." Rose spoke the words and knew them to be true, and the thought behind them was true, and yet she was sorry she'd said them aloud. She found herself always defending Tobe, although she understood Galen's assessment. Understood . . . and even agreed with him. But unlike Galen, she wouldn't give up on Tobe. She held hope that he was becoming a new man. His letters, though infrequent, certainly seemed to be showing evidence of maturity. "Tobe is broken, Galen. You saw that when he was here last summer. He's lost. Sincerely lost. He needs us."

Galen made a small sighing sound, as if he'd heard this before. "I just don't think we should arrange our plans around Tobe."

Just then the wind kicked up hard, blowing through the open barn door, slapping her skirts and rattling the loose shingles on the eaves. The weather had turned cold again, with no hint of spring at all. She wrapped her arms around herself, feeling deflated. "I just need a little more time, Galen. To sort things out."

He walked up to her, put his arms around her, and gently pulled her against his chest. She could hear his heart beating, so steady, so sure. "Then take all the time you need," he said softly.

The temptation to pull the covers over her head and never get up was so strong that it frightened Brooke Snyder into dropping her legs over the side of the bed. Cold linoleum met the soles of her feet. She made her way across the bedroom to a utilitarian bathroom. Although small, it had been modernized. Perhaps this Amish inn wasn't quite as run-down as she'd imagined it to be when she arrived late last night. And it was thoughtful of the innkeeper to leave the guest flat open for her and a small kerosene light burning, though the hiss of the light took getting used to.

She stared at herself in the mirror, then her fingers constricted at the edge of the sink. Her face was haggard, gaunt, drawn. She looked like she had aged a decade in the last few weeks. She splashed water on her face, trying to detach herself from her bleak situation so she could make a new plan. She stared glumly down at the soap dish. Right. As if any of her big ideas had worked lately.

She showered, wrapped herself in a towel, and returned to her room, where she slipped into a pair of jeans and a comfortable sweater. She sat cross-legged in a chair and opened up a notebook, brainstorming ideas for a new life. She scribbled down a few, reviewed them, then tore out the page and balled it in her fist and threw it at the wastebasket. All the ideas she jotted down were awful. She was getting the uneasy feeling that she didn't know how she was going to get herself out of this mess. She closed the notebook, wondering when breakfast might be served. For now she simply wouldn't let herself think about her messy life. Maybe if she didn't dwell on her upsetting circumstances, they'd disappear.

And maybe not.

She walked over to the window and pushed back the curtains. A shower of lemony light drenched her. It streamed through the window as if it had been poured from a bucket, rays so intense she had to close her eyes for a moment. When she opened them, she saw the rolling hills of Lancaster County lying before her.

"Oh, my . . ." She rested her arms on the windowsill and took in the red barn, the pastures with horses and sheep milling around. And was that a billy goat? She wanted to see more, and she turned away from the window, then stopped as she saw how the light had changed the character of the room. Now the butter-colored walls were beautiful in their sparseness, and the simple furniture spoke more eloquently of the past than a volume of history books. She moved through each room, opening the curtains. The living room, which she'd barely glanced at the night before, felt cozy and homey.

The door opened and a woman in her sixties walked in. She had a dumpling figure, doughy cheeks, small dark eyes, salt and pepper hair that was primly twisted into a tight bun and capped with a white covering. Brooke had heard the Amish were known for their friendliness, but this woman didn't look at all friendly.

"You must be Rose Schrock," Brooke said.

"No." The woman set a breakfast tray on the kitchen table. "I'm Vera Schrock, Rose's mother-in-law."

"Denki." Brooke liked to demonstrate her exceptional mastery of the Penn Dutch language. She considered herself a whiz at foreign languages.

The woman didn't seem at all impressed. "Leave the tray outside the door when you're done."

"Do you happen to have a newspaper?"

"No. You'll have to go into town to get it yourself."

Vera opened the door, then stopped and looked back at Brooke. "If you don't eat everything, don't throw it out. We don't waste food around here."

Got it. Eating was serious business with these people.

Brooke looked past Vera at the door and saw a road curled against the hills in a pale, smoky trail. This beautiful place! To think that only yesterday she wasn't even sure she wanted to be here. The woman's dark mutter broke the peaceful mood, and she startled, realizing the woman was waiting for her to respond. "I'll do that. Thank you."

Even the dour expression of the woman couldn't detract from the enchantment of this quiet, peaceful location, and the knots inside Brooke began to loosen.

Finally, something had happened to ease her discouragement. She started the day with a much lighter heart. She walked to the window to gaze up at the sky. The high, fluffy clouds looked as though they should be printed on blue flannel pajamas.

It was a beautiful Sunday, and she wouldn't let even a surly Amish grandmother spoil it for her.

Mim and her brothers arrived at school just as Danny rang the bell. He had asked her to call him Teacher Danny like the other children, but she refused. Instead, she never addressed him at all. She hurried to put her lunch on the shelf in the back of the schoolroom and slipped into her seat. As she took out her books from her desk, she noticed a buzz of conversation in the classroom. She felt a gentle tap on her shoulder and turned to discover the horrible boy who had tripped her was seated next to her.

"Remember me, Miss Humility?"

Mim gave him the stink eye, a look usually reserved for her brothers.

"You never told me your actual name."

She turned forward in her chair, ignoring him.

"I'm Jesse Stoltzfus," he whispered loudly. "We moved in across the road from your farm. My father bought the Bent N' Dent."

Something red caught her eye and she realized there were more students in the schoolhouse. All redheads. Carrot tops. All with that same sticky-up hair. Her gaze traveled across the room as horror set in. There were so *many* Stoltzfus children! Were they all as awful as Jesse? "How many of you are there?"

"Six. I'm the only manchild. It's a sore trial." He motioned toward the teacher's desk. "She's the oldest. Katrina. Dad sent her to get us registered for school. She's seventeen, nearly eighteen. I'm fourteen. Nearly fifteen."

Standing next to the teacher's desk was that girl who had come out of the Bent N' Dent after Jesse tripped Mim. Danny was listening carefully to the girl, then laughed at something she said.

Jesse leaned across the aisle. "Boys go crazy over Katrina. They always have."

Katrina was beautiful, delicate yet curvy in all the right places. She had perfect teeth, and her neck was long, like a gazelle. She had a face like an angel. Mim, she hated her.

As soon as school let out that afternoon, Mim hurried home, ran to her room, and locked the door. On the top shelf of her closet, too tall for snoopy Mammi Vera to find, she had hidden a hand mirror that she bought at a yard sale last summer. She took it out and examined her face in the mirror. It was a perfectly reasonable face. Why then was she lacking sparkle, like Katrina had? It wasn't a lively face. It looked flat somehow.

She turned to Luke's big dog, Micky, who was staring at her with a soulful look on his face. "What do you think, Micky?"

His tail thumped once, then twice. He seemed pleased. He stretched his big creamy limbs in front of her door.

"Move, Micky. I need to go downstairs."

She found her mother in the kitchen and grabbed an apple from a bowl on the table. "Mom, do you know anything about those Stoltzfuses?"

Her mother stopped chopping vegetables and looked out the window toward the Stoltzfus farm. "I know that their father is a minister, David Stoltzfus, and he comes trailing clouds of respect."

"I've heard he's a man to be reckoned with," Mammi Vera added.

Mim would not mind having David Stoltzfus for a neighbor. She was less sure about his son, Jesse, who both irritated and intrigued her. "His son Jesse is abominable."

"That's a very unchristian attitude," Mammi Vera said.

Mim shrugged. "Maybe so, but it's the truth." She cast a sideways glance in her grandmother's direction. "They've all got bright red hair. The whole lot of them."

Mammi Vera gasped. "Red hair means one is the devil's own. You know that, don't you, Mim?"

"Of course, Mammi Vera," Mim said, eyes widened in innocence. *I sincerely doubt it, Mammi Vera,* Mim thought.

It had taken two full days last week for Bethany to clean out the second-floor bedroom at the Sisters' House. The sisters' fourteenth cousin twice removed had arrived and settled in, though Bethany had yet to meet him. She brought fresh towels up to the second floor and knocked lightly on the door. "Hello?"

Silence.

The door was locked tight as a drum. She set the towels on a small hallway table and went back downstairs. As she picked up old *Stoney Ridge Times* newspapers from the dining room table, she asked the sisters, "So what is this fourteenth cousin twice removed like?"

Lena sat at the far end of the table, hemming an apron. "Very polite."

"Terribly polite," Ella echoed.

Fannie walked into the room with a pitcher of hot tea. "He has a good appetite."

"Oh, isn't *that* the truth," Ada said.

Bethany stacked the newspapers on a chair. It seemed as if paper multiplied in this house. "Isn't it creepy that he's been here a few days and I haven't laid eyes on him?"

"Why, no, it isn't creepy," Ada said. "He's busy."

"Terribly busy," Ella echoed.

"Where is he now?"

"He's off to the Lancaster Historical Society," Sylvia said, "to do some studying and research on family lineage."

Ada nodded. "He's not a bother at all. We hardly see him."

Fannie's sharp voice added, "Except for meals."

"Yes, that's true," Sylvia said. "He does love Fannie's cooking."

Fannie blushed, pleased to be singled out.

"He gives us the full report of our ancestry during supper," Lena said.

Fannie grabbed a newspaper from the stack to set under the tea on the dining room table. "Feels a little like having someone read you the book of Chronicles. So and so begat so and so, who begat so and so."

Ella wandered away to pick up a newspaper, then sat in a chair to read it.

Why, this was how it happened! Little by little, the sisters undid everything Bethany tried to do. And they were oblivious to the undoing.

Lena threaded a needle and knotted the end. "It turns out that we have an ancestor who came over on the *Charming Nancy*."

Bethany tilted her head. "What's that?"

"The Amish *Mayflower*," Lena said. "One of the first ships to bring the Amish over to America. 1738."

Sipping her tea, Fannie looked up. "1737."

"That's right," Lena said. "He did say that. Well done, Fannie."

"They came over on the *Charming Nancy*," Fannie said. "Enough Amish families to start the first congregation."

At that point the sisters' conversation quickly digressed into the unbearable living conditions of the eighteenth century. Bethany thought they should be more concerned they were living in an unbearable condition in the twenty-first century, but nobody in this room seemed the least bit concerned. She gave up on the living room with all those sisters planted in there talking about the *Charming Nancy* and set off to another room to work for the afternoon.

The next day, Bethany was back at the Sisters' House to work and slipped up to the second-floor guest room. She jiggled the door handle. Locked tight. She sighed, exasperated. That fourteenth cousin twice removed was turning into an irritating mystery.

# 4

Normally, Brooke Snyder thrived on self-discipline. On a typical morning, she would be out of bed at six for yoga and meditation. By eight, she would be in her lab coat in the dark basement of the museum, with the only light coming from infrared lamps so nothing would decay the paintings.

Instead, she spent her mornings strolling around an Amish farm.

Brooke Snyder was a professional art restorer, also called a conservator. She worked for a museum in Philadelphia—researching, cleaning, restoring works of priceless art.

She had been very bright at school; she had been good at everything. Her English teacher encouraged her to pursue a college degree in English Literature. Her P.E. teacher said that with her height—by the age of fourteen she was already nearly six feet tall—she could play volleyball or basketball, or both. But when it came to decision time, Brooke went for art.

She had learned to paint by studying the masters and copying their techniques—something that was part of every artist's training before they refined their own techniques. But Brooke never seemed to get that far. She had such a talent for reproduction that her art professor recommended her for a freelance job at a local gallery that needed help with a fire-damaged painting. One freelance job led to another, then another. She had a reputation for attention to detail, right down to the artist's signature. As soon as she graduated, she was offered a job at a museum.

If anyone asked Brooke about her work, she made art restoration sound like fascinating work, but the truth of it was that it was tedious, painstaking work in a windowless basement, where the average age of her boring colleagues was seventy, and the pay was horrible. Horrible! How could a person survive on such a low salary? She certainly couldn't. How could a young woman ever meet an eligible bachelor? She certainly hadn't.

And that was how she had been tempted to commit a grave error. She'd found herself facing some rather serious credit card debt and complained about it to a co-worker at the museum. It turned out he knew an art dealer who was looking for an artist to commission a painting. After meeting with the art dealer, she agreed to reproduce a Jean-Baptiste-Camille Corot painting for a handsome sum. She would have enough to pay off her credit card debt and some left over to put a down payment on a new car.

She worked extremely hard on that Corot plein air reproduction. She not only duplicated Corot's unique style, but she replicated his painting from every angle: back, front, and sides. She mounted and framed it in an identical way. She even copied the supplier tags. She did a stellar job.

So stellar that the art dealer passed it off as an original and sold it. The art dealer, who was now under investigation for selling several fakes to unsuspecting collectors, had gone missing. The museum curator was furious with her, though she claimed she knew nothing about the art dealer's unscrupulous actions. "Corot, of all artists!" the curator said. "One of the most faked artists of all time."

She knew that. A recent *Time* magazine article said that Corot painted eight hundred paintings in his lifetime, four thousand of which were in the United States.

"But it wasn't an *intentional* fake," she assured him. "My mistake was imitating the original too closely." It pleased her that she had fooled a collector—though, wisely, she kept that thought to herself.

"And adding the artist's signature instead of your own," the curator pointed out. "Intended or not, it is what it is. You created a forgery. A copy." He looked at her with disdain and told her she was fortunate to not be under investigation by the FBI—only because he had vouched for her innocence. And then he fired her.

Copied. There was *nothing* worse in the art world than that word. And yet . . . that's all she really had become, even her aunt Lois—Brooke's most favorite person in the world—had said so. She was a copier.

Brooke thought it might be wise to let things settle down and think out a new path for her future, which, according to the curator, apparently wasn't going to be in the art world. He told her she had committed a cardinal sin, crossed an unforgivable line, which she thought was a little extreme. However, getting out of town for a breather sounded like a good idea, so that's what she did. When her aunt Lois recommended a quiet little inn in Amish country as a place to recalibrate her life, she wiped away her tears, grabbed the idea, and ran with it.

And now Brooke was far, far removed from the art world. She watched the hens in the chicken yard, mesmerized, amused. When had she last stood still and just noticed something as silly and mundane as chickens? She wandered into the large vegetable garden, mostly dormant at this time of year, though she saw the tips of asparagus peeking through straw beds in tidy rows.

In her mind, she re-dressed it into a portrait of summer's full bloom: Glossy basil plants, snowy white impatiens, tomato vines, clay pots overflowing with red geraniums. Bright orange nasturtiums with the delicate blue flowers of a rosemary shrub, silvery sage leaves as a cool backdrop to a cluster of red pepper plants.

She smiled to herself. Maybe she should consider painting garden scenes. Claude Monet? No . . . too obvious. Philippe Fernandez? No . . . too odd. Perhaps Zaira Dzhaubaeva. Yes, she would be the one to study.

*There I go again! Copying.* She hung her head. She couldn't help it. Copying was what she knew to do. Aunt Lois had urged her to drop the copies, skip the restorations, and become an original at something of her own. Anything, she emphasized, choose anything! Become the real thing.

How insulting! Brooke *was* the real thing. She was gifted at what she did—everyone said so. If she studied others long enough, she could fix her mind to think like they thought, act like they would act, speak like they spoke, paint like they painted. Even write like they wrote. Why, she could do anything. "Except be an original!" she could just hear Aunt Lois say.

Two cats came up to Brooke and curled around her legs. She wasn't a cat person, so she untangled her legs and followed a path that led up a hill.

Halfway up the hill, she stopped to absorb the view of the farmhouse from the back. The clapboard white of the house glowed in the sharp morning light. Ivy vines clung to the mortar of the brick chimney, climbing up a drain spout and curling near the green shutters at the windows. The main part of the structure was built in a simple, unadorned rectangle, the typical style of the Amish farmhouse that she'd read about in the tour books. A one-story room bumped haphazardly off the end, probably a later addition. The grandparents' quarters, perhaps?

Down below, she noticed a pretty young woman hanging brightly colored laundry on a clothesline. "Amish dryers" the tourist book had called those clotheslines. Brooke watched the Amish woman move efficiently down the line, with motions as graceful as a ballerina. She was petite, and her clear pale skin made an unusual contrast with her dark hair. She must be Rose Schrock, Brooke realized, the innkeeper. Or maybe she was Bethany, the older sister to Mim? Brooke might have all the women mixed up. Maybe everyone in Stoney Ridge looked the same.

If the woman was Rose the innkeeper, Brooke should head down and introduce herself. One thing she'd already noticed about these Amish—they were always moving on to the next thing. If she didn't catch Rose Schrock now, she'd miss her chance.

One of the cats had followed Brooke up the hill and rubbed against her legs. She scooped down to pick it up, trying not to think of the fleas it might carry, the ticks, the disease. She was doing her best to be fully present and enjoy this farm experience without overanalyzing everything. The sky felt bigger at Eagle Hill. It curved from one horizon line to the other. The fields that had been gray in the early morning had turned to a soft shade of amber brown in the midmorning sun. So beautiful.

It was perfect. Absolutely perfect. Aunt Lois was right. There could be no better place for what she needed right now: a reinvention of herself.

Brooke needed to be here. Every instinct told her this was the place she had to stay, the only place where she could find both the solitude and the inspiration to figure out how to resurrect her career. Her stubborn streak set in.

Right then Brooke made up her mind. She wasn't going to leave this humble Amish inn until she had her new life firmly in its grasp. A simple plan began to take shape in her heart and mind. *I won't leave until I find a fresh wind. A new life direction.*

But . . . what?

On a sunny afternoon, Galen led Silver Queen into the pasture, the foal following closely at her side. Rose closed the pasture gate behind her and walked up to Silver Queen, who bumped her with her nose. Rose scratched her between the ears as Galen put a nylon cord around the foal's neck. It was soft for him to wear for a while as he got used to the feel of something on his neck.

What a wonder a baby was. Rose never failed to appreciate the miracle of a new life, human or animal. So small and sweet, with overlong legs and a dainty little face.

Galen rubbed his legs and back, slow and gentle, until the foal quit fidgeting and stood still for it. "Every day someone needs to be stroking the colt's hooves so that he's used to getting his feet handled."

"He's still a baby."

"No, Rose. He's not a foal any longer. He's a yearling. And he's a promising horse—his conformation is good, his muscle development is right on target. In fact, most yearlings are gelded by now. This colt is far behind in his training from where he should be."

"The boys did a good job for the first few months, but after school started it slipped off to the back burner."

"It's not something that can be ignored and picked up again, on a whim. If you've ever had to shoe a horse that didn't like having his feet handled, you'd know how important this is."

She crossed her arms, annoyed. "I didn't say it wasn't important, Galen. It's just hard to keep up with everything."

Galen reached out and cupped her cheek with his palm, dissolving her annoyance in the time it took to draw a startled breath. "I know. I see."

"Deacon Abraham stopped by yesterday to remind me we're due to host church the first Sunday in May." As if she had forgotten. She thought of all the things that needed to be done to prepare for hosting church: the house would need to be scrubbed, top to bottom. The walls washed down, curtains washed and ironed. Every bureau and cupboard should be cleaned out and organized. The barn needed a serious sweeping out. The front porch was begging for touch-up paint. Windows had to be rubbed until they were squeaky clean. Everything had to be perfect—not for show, but to glorify the Lord God.

Her eyes noticed something new—a broken window on the second floor that looked like it was hit by a stray baseball. She blew out a puff of air. "So much to do."

Galen glanced up and saw the broken window too. "Make a list. I'll help."

"I can't ask that of you."

He took a step closer to her, his eyes smiling in that special way he had, just for her. He raised one hand to her temple and grazed her cheekbone with the tips of his fingers. "Yes, you can. You can ask anything of me." He leaned over to kiss her, gently, brushing his lips against hers.

Their lips had just touched again when they broke apart, startled by the sound of the kitchen door opening as Vera walked out on the porch and settled into the swing. Rose turned away, color rising in her cheeks. How ridiculous! Sometimes, she felt like a schoolgirl around Galen. "You've got your own farm and work to take care of. Spring is the busiest time for you. And you don't have Jimmy Fisher's help anymore."

"I'm surprised to discover how much I've missed his help. I have more work than I can manage." He leaned against the pen with his arms crossed over his chest. "Think there's any chance Edith Fisher would cut him a little slack and let him come back to horses?"

"I don't see how. She needs his help with the chicken and egg business, even more so after her bunion surgery." She bit her lip. "I don't suppose you'd consider taking on Tobe when he's released."

Galen's chin lifted. "Rose, we've been through this before. Tobe doesn't have the temperament for horses. What makes you think he'd even return to Eagle Hill?"

"This is his home. He can't keep running forever. I think he's starting to face up to things—after all, he's the one who pled guilty to withholding evidence. That's a step in the right direction, isn't it?"

"A step, perhaps."

A wave of irritation at Galen came over Rose suddenly. "Couldn't you even give him a chance? For your sister's sake?"

"Naomi?" He looked baffled. "Why would I want Tobe around Naomi?"

"Galen—you must realize there's something brewing between the two of them."

"Not while he's in jail, there's not."

"Definitely while he's in jail. Haven't you noticed the letters they write to each other? She runs to that mailbox every single day. I've seen her! And she walks back slowly, reading that familiar gray envelope."

Galen had a skeptical look in his eyes.

"Before you close your mind to their budding romance, have you even noticed that she hasn't had a single migraine since Tobe returned last fall? Not one."

It wasn't often that Galen King was confounded, but at that moment, he looked at Rose as if she was speaking another language. She turned her attention back to the colt and let Galen resume training Silver Queen. He didn't say another word about the subject of Tobe and Naomi. Neither did Rose. She thought she had said enough.

There was so much Naomi had to thank God for: she hadn't had a migraine since—well, not since Tobe had returned after he'd gone missing for a year. Naomi had suffered from headaches the doctors could neither diagnose nor cure.

It seemed trite, a cliché, but happiness had cured Naomi of the headaches. Happiness and love. For she was in love with Tobe Schrock, and he loved her, and soon he would be released from prison and life could start fresh. Love, she had always thought, could do extraordinary things to people. Now she knew it to be true.

*The Lord works in mysterious ways.* She had always heard that phrase but never knew what it meant until she saw the miracle God was working in Tobe's life, even in jail. Especially in jail. For God was everywhere and all around and couldn't be kept out of any earthly place, not even a federal prison. A prison chaplain led Bible studies in the community area and delivered a Sunday service. Tobe was making strides in his journey of faith. "I feel a weight lift from my shoulders," he had written to her. And another time: "I'm beginning to realize a lot of things don't matter anymore. My chest is much less tight, the awful feeling of running down a long corridor gone." Only God could do this work in Tobe's life. He had been running for over a year and it took God to force him to stop, to take a breath, to catch up with himself. To be still and to know God was God.

And that's exactly what was happening, in a federal prison of all places. The questions Tobe had in his letters, the longings he expressed, the desire to know God, to be a man after God's own heart—why, Naomi fell in love with him all over again. She used to love what he could be, now she loved who he was becoming.

She was grateful for these blessings and many others, but she was also troubled, for when she prayed in her room at night, it was as much from worry as from gratitude. She picked up Tobe's letter that she had received today and re-read it:

*Dearest Naomi,*

*You used to complain that I was too buttoned-up in my letter-writing. Now I wonder if you'll never write to me again after I pour my heart out to you. But here goes, here's the full whoosh of the waterfall.*

*Lately, I've thought of little else but your advice to leave Jake Hertzler in God's hands. The beliefs of the Amish church are easier to talk about in theory than to put into practice. They're counterintuitive to human nature.*

*Is it so wrong to want revenge on Jake Hertzler? So that he doesn't keep hurting others? Because he will, Naomi. Jake is made that way—to steal, to take, to harm, to not care a whit about the consequences. You've said we must forgive him and even to pray for him, but does that mean he doesn't have to face justice? Is that what nonresistance truly means?*

*I just can't do it, Naomi. I can't let him continue to hurt my family. I told the SEC lawyer most of the things Jake had done to Schrock Investments, but not all. A few important pieces—the most important part—I kept to myself, because I want to get out of prison and face Jake myself. It's my responsibility to see it through.*

*Problem is, I have no idea how to go about doing it. I spent a year trying to set a trap for him, but Jake was always a step ahead of me. In fact, he was the one who set the snare for me to step into. That's why I'm here, serving out a prison sentence, while he is off scot-free.*

*I love you, Naomi. And I do give serious consideration to what you have to say on the matter. Pray that I will do the right thing, sweetheart.*

Pray for him? He didn't even need to ask! She prayed for him frequently throughout the days, and often at night. Naomi had been taught since she was small to be grateful in all things and for all things, so despite a feeling of foreboding for this unsettled issue, she gave thanks for it and for what lay ahead.

And then she ate a full roll of Tums.

# 5

Late last night, Mim was informed by her sister Bethany that Danny Riehl had driven Katrina Stoltzfus home from the youth gathering. Bethany felt she should know. "I went back and forth," Bethany had said, "on whether I should tell you or not, and finally decided I would want to know if Jimmy Fisher took another girl home."

Mim only shrugged and gave her a flat look. Why should it matter? Danny had become the permanent substitute teacher at her school. He had to stop inviting her to look through his telescope on starry nights because he felt it wasn't appropriate.

It shouldn't matter.

But it did.

Mim trudged down the driveway on the way to school with her brothers, who felt the need to crush the thin layer of ice that lined every puddle, then howl with approval and sock the air with their fists. She stayed clear of their splatters and wondered why boys always had the urge to break something, even at seven thirty in the morning.

"Yoo hoo!"

Mim spun around to find the new Eagle Hill guest waving to her from the door of the guest flat. She told Sammy and Luke to head off to school and she walked over to see what she wanted.

The guest, a very tall woman with spiky, short blonde hair, thrust her hand out to Mim. In it were dollar bills. "I'm Brooke Snyder." She motioned toward the guest flat. "I'll be staying for a little while. I'd like you to get me a newspaper each day. Preferably the *Times*."

Mim raised her eyebrows. "You want me to bring you the *Stoney Ridge Times*?"

Brooke Snyder blinked. "No. The *New York Times*."

Mim shook her head. "I've never seen that newspaper sold in Stoney Ridge."

She frowned. "Then bring me the closest thing to it. That's not asking too much, is it?"

"I suppose not," Mim said. "But I wouldn't be able to get it to you until late in the day. I have chores in the morning, then I have to go to school. And I have chores in the afternoon."

"That's fine. I'll just save it for the next day's breakfast. Old news is still news."

Mim considered pointing out that the very word *news* meant it was new, thus, old news was an oxymoron. But she didn't think her suggestion would be appreciated. Her family never appreciated her grammatical corrections, so why would a guest whom she'd just met?

"I'm not sure how long I'm going to stay here. Maybe for a while. I want a newspaper for the entire time I'm here, rain or shine. I'll pay you for your trouble." She pushed the dollars into Mim's hand.

"Sure." Mim pushed her glasses back up the bridge of her nose. "Sure," she repeated, nodding vigorously. In fact, it was an ideal opportunity to read her Mrs. Miracle column. Usually, she only saw a copy of the paper if she was at the Sisters' House because her grandmother refused to subscribe. "Rubbish!" her grandmother called the newspaper. Mim spotted the black hats of her brothers as they disappeared over the hill and realized she'd better hurry or she'd be late for school. "Today. I'll bring you a paper later today."

As Mim ran up the hill, she tried to figure out why the guest would bother reading a newspaper like the *Stoney Ridge Times*. It was filled with stories about local people, stories like the one about the mayor who had just been reelected for the sixth time, which might sound impressive until you learned that no one ever ran against him. Then there was the police report, which mostly consisted of parking tickets. Once or twice a month, there were some scandals. Bennie Adams had been fired at the bank because he'd come to work drunk. Junior Jackson's wife had run off with the high school track coach. Those kinds of stories were why Mammi Vera called the *Stoney Ridge Times* the gossip buzz line. The sisters at the Sisters' House had a different point of view. They liked knowing what was going on in town. She wished for the hundredth time that Mammi Vera were more like the sisters—any sister, even Fannie, who was often prickly and her least favorite.

It wasn't that Mim didn't like Mammi Vera. After all, she was her grandmother. She had to like her, or maybe she just had to love her. Maybe it was the liking part she had a choice about. It wasn't Mammi Vera's fault that she wasn't like the old sisters.

That afternoon on her way home from school, Mim stopped at the Bent N' Dent and bought the last copy of the *Stoney Ridge Times*. She spoke to the clerk Katrina, the sister of the incorrigible Jesse Stoltzfus, and asked her to save a copy each afternoon. The sister, she noted, was nice to her despite being irritatingly pretty. Katrina seemed to glide around the store, not walk like a normal person. Of course, *she* didn't wear glasses. *She* would never be called Four Eyes or Owl Eyes by the sixth grade boys.

The Mrs. Miracle column was running twice a week now, and the receptionist had confided in Bethany that there were even rumblings about expanding it to three times a week. Such an opportunity only filled Mim with panic: Someone, somewhere, was going to find out! Bethany was the only one who knew the true identity of Mrs. Miracle. No, that wasn't exactly accurate (and Mim prided herself on accuracy). Ella of the Sisters' House had guessed once, but she had memory woes and had already forgotten. No one else in all of Stoney Ridge suspected that Mrs. Miracle was actually a fourteen-year-old Amish girl.

Mim loved her role as Mrs. Miracle and took it very seriously. When she didn't know the answer to something, she would research it or carefully, cautiously, question the right people. She liked helping others and, not to brag, but she gave excellent advice. Excellent. Mostly, though, she was just reminding people to use common sense. It seemed to be in short supply.

But the Mrs. Miracle column was supposed to be a tiny little side job for her. It brought in only five dollars a week, and it gave her something interesting and challenging to do. No big deal. Just a once-a-week column.

She hadn't expected the readership to explode. She hadn't expected the editor to expand it to twice a week. And now . . . three times a week? Each time she thought of it, she couldn't even swallow. What if she was found out? What if the bishop learned of her secret job? What would her mother say?

She walked as slowly as she could back toward Eagle Hill, reading the newspaper, admiring the Mrs. Miracle column. It was well written, and she tried not to feel proud, but she did. When she had nearly reached the driveway to Eagle Hill, she felt someone over her shoulder.

"My sisters love that column too. They fight over who gets to read it aloud."

Jesse Stoltzfus, of all people! Mim snapped the paper shut and tucked it under her arm. "Mrs. Miracle would say that it's only good manners for a person to let another person know that the person is there."

Jesse was staring at her with his mouth open, as if he didn't hear her properly. He thumped the side of his head with the palm of his hand, like he was shaking water from his ear. "But . . . I did." He tipped his felt hat back on his forehead. "Good thing you're not writing a newspaper column. That was the most confusing sentence a person ever said to another person." He grinned and took off his hat, bowing and sweeping his hat in a big arc. "This person needs to be on his way, if the other person will excuse this person."

Jackanapes! *That* boy always tried to best her. It irked her that Danny—who used to be her special friend before he got so high and mighty and puffed up—he only encouraged Jesse Stoltzfus's gargantuan ego. Just this afternoon, he had read Jesse's composition aloud. "I am sure," Danny told the class, "that all of you were as impressed as I was by Jesse's exciting essay."

Impressed? Mim was dumbfounded. Jesse wrote a heartstopping composition about a time when he was lost in a snowstorm and had to make a snow cave to survive the night. Jesse described the sound of the wind and the bite of the cold so clearly she felt right there with him, in the middle of the blizzard, gasping for breath, trying to push down panic as he dug a snow cave deep down in a world of no light and little air.

How could she be all in a tremble just listening to Danny read about it? It actually hurt to listen—she was *that* jealous of Jesse's writing ability. Mim labored painfully over her writing, every single sentence; Jesse scribbled things down and turned them in before school or during recess. She had seen him! He had forgotten the essay that was due today and dashed it off during lunch.

On the other hand, Danny always caught Mim when her mind was on vacation, though he never suspected Jesse of not paying attention. Danny had one of those tricky voices. It would buzz along for several minutes quite comfortably, then *bang!* he was focused in and asking you a question.

Earlier in the week, Danny had cornered Mim with a question out of the blue, when she was a million miles away. Her mind went completely blank. Throughout the classroom she heard a shuffling of feet and paper, waiting for her to answer him. She could feel everyone's eyes boring into her. Mose Blank was staring at her so intently she thought his crossed eyes might switch sockets. "Parakeets can live nearly twenty years," she blurted out and the class roared with laughter. Turned out Danny had asked her the names of the different kinds of cloud formations in the sky.

Dumb, dumb, dumb.

Then he asked Jesse the names of clouds and of course he knew the answers, including the Latin translations of the words: *cumulus*, heap; *stratus*, layer; *nimbus*, rain; *cirrus*, curl of hair. Wasn't that just like Jesse, to answer more than the teacher had asked for? Danny was delighted. Mim thought Jesse was showing off.

Jesse was one of those boys who sat quietly at his desk doing beautiful schoolwork, never daydreaming or shooting spit wads or chewing gum, and yet he was so full of shenanigans that if Teacher Danny could have once known what was running through that carrot-red-sticky-up-haired head, he would have thrown him out of the schoolhouse in horror.

She sneaked a glance over at Jesse. He was totally absorbed in his geography book, or so it would appear to anyone who didn't know. He must have sensed she was watching him, because he slowly turned his head in her direction. "I've always been fond of parakeets," he whispered, grinning widely.

Did Jesse Stoltzfus ever stop grinning? He grinned when he saw her come in the schoolhouse in the mornings. He'd grinned when she made a fool out of herself by spouting out the lifespan of parakeets (which, incidentally, was a well-known fact). He'd even grinned as he was bringing in wood to stoke the stove and a large spider crawled up his sleeve. *Who* could smile at a spider? She had never known anyone as maddening as Jesse Stoltzfus. Not even Luke, and he sorely tried everyone's patience.

They reached the turnoff to Jesse's driveway and he stopped at the mailbox, opened it, found it empty, then shut it tight. He started up the hill toward his farmhouse.

"Jesse!"

He stopped and turned to face her.

"Did that really happen? That snowstorm?"

He took a few steps toward her, grinning. "Now, why would I make something like that up?" Then he began scissoring up the driveway in great strides and Mim couldn't help but watch. He ran as though it was his nature. It reminded her of the flight of wild ducks in the autumn. Smooth and effortless. The word "glorious" came to mind, but she shook it away and hurried toward Eagle Hill.

The first time that David Stoltzfus delivered a Sunday sermon, a shaft of sunlight broke through the gray skies and came through a crack in the barn roof to touch his face, making him look more saintly than ever. In the short time that David had lived in Stoney Ridge, the people had quickly grown to love him, and in her heart Rose felt a little sorry for the other ministers, who were instantly overshadowed.

It wasn't the other ministers' fault; their sermons were full of good examples and strong admonishments. And yet Rose had to admit that David brought with him some new sense of excitement and inspiration that the other ministers, including the bishop, didn't have.

David fired the church members with an enthusiasm never before known in Stoney Ridge. He was so . . . clear, so vivid. He had a conviction that sermons should be kept to the comprehension level of children, to nourish the spiritual life of young people. He had confidence the adults would still be fed and, of course, he was right.

On this gray morning, he reminded them of how fortunate their congregation was to live in the safety of Lancaster County. He spoke of those, years ago in the Old Country, who had been martyred rather than renounce their faith. He described with vivid detail the horrific persecution their great-great-grandparents had endured. Even Jesse Stoltzfus, whom Mim called abominable, was on the edge of his seat, Rose noticed, listening to his father's sermon with rapt attention.

As they sat in the barn on that Sunday morning, the church of Stoney Ridge was transported miles away to another continent. They felt rich beyond the dreams of kings compared to their ancestors in Switzerland and Germany and France, who had cried out in their dying breath to hold tight to their faith. The barn might have been full of people sneezing and coughing, wet from the trek across miles of roads to get there on a rainy, blustery spring morning, but everyone felt warm and safe and grateful. Their life was a paradise compared to their great-great-grandparents'.

Rose gazed around the barn: at Mim and Bethany, seated behind Vera. At Sammy, at Luke, nodding off; at Galen, who nudged Luke awake with a jab from his elbow—and she gave thanks.

After youth group on Sunday night, Jimmy drove Bethany home. It was a cold night, but the stars were out and the moon was full and the brisk air gave them an excuse to cuddle. Jimmy took the long way home so he could pull up to the shores of Blue Lake Pond. Just to talk, he assured her, but she knew kissing was on his mind. Kissing was always on his mind and he'd been staring at her lips all night. Kissing Jimmy was one of Bethany's favorite things to do, so she didn't object when he stopped the horse and reached out to pull her close to him. But she also had something else to discuss.

"Jimmy," she said, pushing him back slightly. "Kissing is fun and all that, but it's time we started making plans."

Jimmy put an arm around her and wiggled his eyebrows. "I do have plans." He gave her one of his persuasive grins and cupped her jaw to kiss her with a tender consideration. As his lips joined hers, she swayed toward him, her fingertips grazing his chin. When at length he lifted his head, they were both breathing harder as they gazed into each other's eyes.

"Jimmy, don't you want more than that?"

His blue eyes widened in innocence. "Why, Bethany Schrock. I'm shocked!"

"Shootfire!" She snapped forward, cheeks flaming, and smoothed out her apron. "You know what I mean."

He took his arm back and sighed. "Bethany—we've been through this before. I'm trying to get all my ducks in a row." He wiggled his eyebrows again. "And you know how ducks can be."

"Jimmy, be serious, for once in your life. Are you or are you not planning on marrying me?"

"Well, sure. Of course. It's just that I'm not ready yet. I've got a few things I need to do first."

"That's what you told me months ago. It's that horse, isn't it? Lodestar." She crossed her arms against her chest. "You love that horse more than you love me."

"Now, sweetheart, that's not true."

She rolled her eyes. "You're going to keep pining over that horse and using it as an excuse not to get serious."

"I'm not pining for Lodestar. Not much." His smile faded. "I only think about him a few times a day now."

She huffed. "That's a few times more each day than you spend thinking of me."

"I think of you every other minute of every day. Especially how to get you up to the pond for some serious kissing." He leaned toward her to kiss her, but she lunged for the door handle. He reached out to grab her arm before she could slip out of the buggy. "Bethany, hold on a minute. Simmer down."

She closed the door and glared at him. "You just want to kiss so you don't have to talk."

He held his head to one side and smiled at her. "What kind of faith have you in me, that you give me such bad motives?" She ignored him. "Look, I don't want to be a chicken farmer for the rest of my life and I haven't figured a way out of it."

"Can't you get Hank Lapp to propose to your mother?"

"That wouldn't solve anything. Hank Lapp is not a chicken man." He relaxed his grip on her arm. "I wish my brother Paul would return to Stoney Ridge and take over for me."

"Ask Paul to come back."

"I can't. He's settled in at his in-laws, up in Canada. Besides, there were fireworks between my mother and Paul's new wife. I can't ask him to move home just because I prefer horses over poultry."

"But what you really want to do is work with horses."

"I know. But it would take a request from the bishop himself to convince my mother that horses are more important than her chickens." He picked up the reins and gave them a little shake to get the horse moving. "Give me a little time, Bethany." He turned toward her and wiggled his eyebrows in that way that made her smile. "What's the rush, anyway? We've got our whole lives ahead of us." He grasped her hand and wove his fingers through hers.

Later, as Bethany was getting ready for bed, she thought about Jimmy's dilemma and knew he was right, as much as she hated to admit it. He had done a good and noble thing to give up horse training with Galen to help his mother with the chicken and egg business.

But the facts remained: Jimmy loved horses and hated chickens. He had a dream to become a breeder for well-bred, well-trained buggy horses, filling an important need for their church and other districts. Galen had more demand for trained horses than he could fulfill. Last year, as Jimmy apprenticed for Galen, he had developed skills that proved his mettle. It wasn't easy to change Galen King's mind about anything or anybody, but he had grown impressed enough with Jimmy's way with horses that he called him a partner.

David Stoltzfus had just said in Sunday's sermon that God didn't give a desire without planning to fulfill it. Would the Lord give her the desire to marry and have a family if he didn't intend on fulfilling it? Would the Lord give Jimmy a desire to raise horses if he didn't plan to fulfill that?

There were many things about being Amish that frustrated Bethany to no end. What was good for the group was considered good for the individual . . . even if it wasn't. But then, to be fair, there were also many things about being Amish that made life worthwhile.

Have a little faith, Jimmy told her. Where was she putting her faith, anyhow? It had grown leaps and bounds in the last year since she had moved back to Eagle Hill. In many ways, she was a different person than she was a year or two ago.

But her main question wouldn't be silenced, and once again she was asking God: *Would you give us desires if you didn't plan to fulfill them?* She didn't receive an answer, but she didn't feel wrong about asking either. The silence that surrounded her was gentle, not accusing. Perhaps that was enough of an answer. To accept her desires, and Jimmy's, as a mystery.

For now, anyway.

The sun was cresting the hills that framed the back of the farmhouse as Brooke woke. The smoky scent of crisping bacon floated down from the kitchen and in through the open window of the guest flat. Brooke's stomach started to rumble. She threw on a bathrobe when a knock came on the door and there stood Mim, holding a tray that was covered with a red-checkered napkin.

Brooke was relieved whenever she opened the door and found it was someone else besides Vera Schrock, who always looked as if something had displeased her and she was about to issue a complaint. Vera had a tight, drawn look, a near permanent frown, solid and glum-looking. Brooke had expected a similar countenance from the innkeeper, Rose Schrock, and was pleasantly surprised to find Rose to be lovely, warm, and kind, dressed in soft, cheerful colors: turquoise or pink. Vera dressed in drab brown or olive green. No spark, no life. Brooke didn't know how the family abided Vera.

Mim's gaze was fixed on the sky. "The eagles are out." She lifted her chin toward an eagle, soaring above the creek. "They have an aerie in a tree on our property."

Brooke opened the door wide to let Mim cross the threshold. "What's an aerie?"

"It's an eagle's nest. It's huge. Made of sticks and lined with grass and moss. The eagles have been here two years now. Last year, they had one eglet but it died. We're hoping they'll have better luck this year." Mim set the tray on the table in the small living area. "That's why there's yellow tape around that far section of the farm. The Game Commissioner doesn't want bird-watchers bothering the eagles."

"Do they?"

"Yup. Bird-watchers are pretty intense around here. As soon as some eggs are spotted in the aerie, they'll be camped out across the street with their telescopes, day and night."

Brooke smiled. That was the longest speech she had heard come out of Mim Schrock. It pleased her. She was hoping someone, anyone, on this farm would slow down and talk to her a little. She was always noticing them darting around the farm, but rarely still. Especially not those two young boys with the black felt hats—they were in constant motion. Like a blur.

She lifted the large fabric napkin and found a bowl of baked oatmeal, toast with raspberry jam, four strips of thick-sliced bacon, scrambled eggs, orange juice, and a thermos of coffee. "Why, thank you. I thought I smelled bacon frying. It's perfect."

Mim gave a demure nod and darted out the door. Goodness, those Amish were always in a hurry. A cat rubbed against her as she settled at the end of the table. It must have slipped in behind Mim. Brooke thought about banishing it to the great outdoors but decided she didn't mind a little company. Not so much.

Brooke made a grab for the small spiral-bound notebook on the table. Tomorrow, she'd begin to follow the schedule she'd set up for herself:

*Rise at 6:00 Meditation*
*Yoga or brisk walk or hike*

She picked up her pen and added:

*find eagles' aerie*
*Breakfast (but with such a large breakfast, perhaps she should eat, then*
*    exercise)*
*Construct new life plan*
*Lunch*
*Revise new life plan*
*Scheduled time for spontaneity. Sightsee, window-shop, explore, meet*
*    new people*
*Dinner*

*Inspirational reading, journal writing*
*Deep breathing exercises*
*Bedtime 10:00 pm*

Her eyes slipped from the notebook to the *Stoney Ridge Times* newspaper that Mim had left under the breakfast tray. She skimmed the headlines and turned the page as her eyes caught on the Mrs. Miracle column. She nestled into the chair, happily distracted. She'd always loved advice columns.

She leaned closer to the newspaper. Interesting—this column was situated on the upper corner of page three, a perfect spot for the eye to land as the pages opened. She knew enough about newspaper layout from a journalism class in college to know this was no accident; the column must receive high traffic. She skimmed the column and found herself smiling at Mrs. Miracle's no-nonsense advice.

*Dear Mrs. Miracle,*

*My brother is always asking to borrow money from me. He is divorced and never pays his child support. He did, however, recently buy a 48" flat screen TV. He says he needs it so his son will come to his apartment and watch sports with him. What should I tell him the next time he asks me for money?*

*Yours truly,*
*Frustrated*

*Dear Frustrated,*

*It sounds as if your brother believes things, like a television, will solve his problems. Ironically, if he didn't have a television in the first place, perhaps he wouldn't be divorced and living away from his son. I wish more people lived without televisions, as I do. Maybe they would talk to each other instead of letting an electronic machine do all the talking for them. But to answer your question, the next time he asks you for money, tell him no.*

*Sincerely,*
*Mrs. Miracle*

Brooke leaned back in her chair and wondered what Mrs. Miracle might say about her own current dilemma. She could just imagine how she would compose the letter:

*Dear Mrs. Miracle,*

*I need . . . something. I need to reinvent myself. I need to change. A new mantra, a new tagline, a new reason to get up in the morning. Any advice?*

*Most sincerely,*
*Empty of Ideas*

Or maybe . . .

*Dear Mrs. Miracle,*

*My favorite aunt thinks I spend my life sailing on the wind of others' talent. She thinks I am avoiding something by not discovering my own self. I feel there's no point in reinventing the wheel. Why not borrow from the inspiration of others? Look at how the American public imitates celebrities. Is it so wrong to copy others? Any advice?*

*Most sincerely,*
*A Borrower*

Brooke took a sip of coffee. Why not? Why not send a letter to Mrs. Miracle and see if she had an answer for her? She flipped the page of her notebook to a fresh sheet and started to write. When she finished, she found an envelope and a stamp in her purse—she traveled well prepared—addressed it, tucked the letter inside, and set it by the door to put in the mailbox on her brisk walk to find the eagles' aerie.

Why not? Why not see what wise old Mrs. Miracle has to say?

# 6

Mim Schrock liked to collect wildflowers and press them in a book, color intact. Virginia bluebells, coltsfoot, Dutchman's breeches, sweet white violets. After they dried, she would carefully glue them on cards and write their botanical names underneath in her most excellent handwriting. Her mother said she was a real artist.

Bethany stopped by her room one afternoon as Mim was gluing flowers on cards. "Those are pretty."

Bethany never said anything nice just to please you. If she said they were good, then they must be.

"Maybe you could sell them at the Bent N' Dent. Maybe it could turn into a card business for you. That would sure make Mammi Vera happy."

Ever since Mim started eighth grade, Mammi Vera was trying to spur Mim to think ahead about her future, what she would like to do after she finished schooling. "Sie sehnt net weider as die Naas lang is," Mammi Vera would say, with a frown of concentration on her face. *She didn't see further than her nose is long.* Her grandmother assumed Mim didn't have enough on her mind, but the problem was her grandmother had no idea of all that ran through Mim's mind. How could she? She never bothered to ask.

Bethany tossed a manila envelope on Mim's bed. Each week, Bethany dropped off this week's Mrs. Miracle responses and picked up the most recent letters for Mrs. Miracle that were sent to the *Stoney Ridge Times* office. "There's an envelope in there that's supposed to be important. Not sure what's in that, but the receptionist said to make sure Mrs. Miracle saw it pronto."

Bethany waited by the door, arms folded against her chest, as Mim opened and read the letter. It was from the features editor, a man Mim had never met and never wanted to. Bethany said he was quite unappealing, a real curmudgeon. "What's up, Mim? You look as worried as a duck in the desert."

Mim didn't even glance up. "You say that's how I always look."

Bethany lifted an eyebrow. "I've said it before and I'll say it again. I sure hope this Mrs. Miracle gig doesn't blow up in your face. First of all, you're supposed to be eighteen years old to have a column at the newspaper. Secondly, the bishop would not approve of you telling people how to live their life. Thirdly, Rose doesn't know anything about it, so you're being deceitful. Fourthly, Mammi Vera would blow an artery if she knew."

Mim kept her head down. Did Bethany think those concerns hadn't crossed her mind? They did! But Mrs. Miracle had a life of her own.

Bethany waited another long moment, then let out an exasperated snort. "Fine. I've got enough problems of my own." She spun around and walked down the hallway.

As Mim reread the letter, she could hardly breathe. The editor said he had an offer to syndicate the Mrs. Miracle column. Was she interested? Because he was. Call me! he wrote, underlining it twice.

First, she had no idea what syndication meant. Secondly, whatever it was, she didn't want it.

She pulled the dictionary off her desk and looked up the word:

**syndication** | ˌsin-də-ˈkā-shən | *noun* • publish or broadcast (material) simultaneously in a number of newspapers, television stations, etc.: *his reports were syndicated to 200 other papers.*

Oh, boy. Mim threw herself on her bed, headfirst.

Geena Spencer had once been a guest at Eagle Hill and liked Stoney Ridge so much she ended up moving here. She became the housemother to the Group Home for wayward girls, and Bethany couldn't get over the changes there—a person would hardly even recognize it anymore. If a house had a personality, the Group Home used to look sad, neglected, lonely. Now it was smiling, laughing, buzzing with activity.

The very first thing Geena had done as housemother was to get rid of the television. The previous housemother let the television stay on all day and all night. As soon as it had been given away, the wayward girls made noises about being bored and *boom!* That was the moment Geena implemented change number two: each girl would be required to work or volunteer ten hours a week in addition to attending school. But they had so much time, Geena pointed out as they howled and complained about the new rule, why not use it for good? So they did, and it did do good. Mostly . . . for the wayward girls.

On a rainy afternoon in early April, Geena stopped by Eagle Hill and Bethany invited her in for tea and fresh hot scones with a drizzled maple glaze. They had developed a comfortable friendship. By the time the two women came into the kitchen, Luke and Sammy were reaching for second and third helpings of the scones cooling on the countertop. Luke's and Sammy's appetites were a kind of natural calamity. Bethany had watched it with amazement for years and yet it still surprised her how much those boys could eat. Not only did they eat a lot, but they ate it fast. They were appalling.

It was always peaceful when Geena came for a visit; even restless Luke didn't need to be jumping up and moving about. He would hang around just to hear her stories about the wayward girls. They especially loved to hear about a tough cookie named Rusty who had blossomed like a summer rose at the Group Home. An aunt had emerged out of nowhere and asked Rusty to come live with her; things were going well, Geena said. A success story. Of course Luke and Sammy lapped up Geena's stories about her work with the Group Home. The boys hadn't been much of anywhere outside of Stoney Ridge, so it was all romance to them.

"Tell me something you learned at school today," Geena said to Luke as she took a third scone. Mid-bite, her eyes flickered to Bethany, who was staring at her. "Sorry," she said with her mouth full. She pushed the basket toward her. "I had a small breakfast."

Bethany had never seen a woman with an appetite like Geena's. It was impressive for someone who was barely five feet tall and hardly tipped the scales at one hundred pounds, soaking wet. She fit right in with Luke and Sammy.

Luke cut a grin at his brother. "We learned that Sammy thinks the moon was made of real cheese."

"It's a mistake anyone could make," Sammy said, scowling at Luke.

Luke got a devilish look on his face as he turned to Geena. "I just so happened to see you and that SEC lawyer driving through town last weekend."

"His name is Allen Turner," Bethany said, eyes on Geena to see her reaction.

Geena stirred sugar into her tea and held her peace. She never corrected anyone or told anyone he was being childish or immature, but often people seemed to realize it themselves. Not Luke, though. He asked her if she was sweet on Allen Turner, and Geena only sipped her tea, pretending he hadn't asked.

Soon, Bethany had enough of Luke. "You boys go outside so I can visit with Geena."

Sammy was no problem and quickly went his own way. He didn't want to hang around to hear their secrets. Luke needed to be asked twice, as usual.

As soon as the boys were out of hearing, Bethany fixed her gaze on Geena. "Is that true? Did you go on a date with Allen Turner?"

Geena waved that away. "We're old friends. You know that." She added another spoonful of sugar to her tea and stirred it, a little nervously, Bethany observed. "I came by to let you know we're going to set a date to turn the soil for the community garden beds."

Last summer, Bethany and Geena started the community garden as a way to help the down-and-outers in Stoney Ridge. The Group Home worked a plot, and so did other families who were on government aid. The produce from the gardens helped supplement family groceries. It had been hugely successful; this summer there was a waiting list for the plots.

"Oh," Bethany said, but her mind was elsewhere, nowhere near the community gardens.

"You'll help, won't you?" Geena said, between bites of her fourth scone.

Bethany leaned forward. "Geena, I need your advice. What do you do when a person keeps avoiding something because he is overwhelmed by obstacles?"

"Deal with each obstacle, one by one."

One by one. Of course! Why hadn't she thought about that with Jimmy Fisher?

"So, I can count on your help?" Geena said, finishing off her sugary tea.

"Mmm-hmm," Bethany murmured, concocting a plan to knock down Jimmy's biggest obstacle to getting married.

The day suited Mim's mood—wet and cheerless. Earlier today, just after dawn, she was milking Molly only to have the dumb cow shift her big hip and knock Mim right off the milking stool, tipping over the full pail of fresh warm milk. Barn cats, who had been watching the milking from a safe distance, sprang on the spilled milk as if they had conspired with Molly for a free breakfast. When did milking Molly become Mim's job, anyhow?

She plodded along the road to the schoolhouse through the sodden countryside, alone, because her brothers had overslept and she refused to wait for them and risk being late. She made her way carefully around mud and puddles and drowned worms. Even the birds weren't singing this morning.

As Mim approached the schoolhouse, she felt a strange sense that something wasn't right. The schoolhouse was shrouded in mist, cloaked in an oppressive doom. And it was silent. None of the students were outside on the playground, which wasn't at all typical; even rain couldn't keep boys inside when they could be outside.

Something had happened.

Could she have mixed up days again? Was it Saturday? She had done that very thing once, at their old school in York County, and Luke still teased her about it.

But then she saw the backs of a few students huddled together at the open door. She walked up the steps of the schoolhouse and stopped abruptly as she crossed the threshold, expecting something horrific. A dead body, perhaps, or a sinkhole in the center of the schoolhouse that was swallowing it in one bite.

It was nothing like that.

The students' desks and the teacher's desk had been reversed. Everything was in the same spot but facing the opposite direction, a mirror image. Danny stood in the center of the room, a baffled look on his face.

No one had any idea how it had happened.

Early one morning, while Brooke was still in her pajamas, she heard a knock and opened the door to find Mim Schrock with an empty laundry basket in her arms.

"Today's the day we wash sheets."

Mim always had a slightly anxious look, Brooke thought, as she stepped away to let her pass. She enjoyed Mim and tried to detain her with conversation each time she brought breakfast to her. Some might think Mim was dull because she was quiet and watchful, but Brooke could see there was more going on in her mind than she let others know. And it couldn't be a bed of roses living with the gloomy Vera Schrock, who probably hadn't cracked a smile in eons.

Mim headed straight to the bedroom. As she stripped the sheets off the bed, Brooke followed her in and asked, "What would you say, Mim, to a woman who is searching for a new identity? To find herself."

Mim straightened, blinked, pushed her glasses back on the bridge of her nose. "I've actually given this question a great deal of thought lately. What I've decided is that wherever she goes, there she'll be." She pulled the pillowcases off the pillows, one after the other, and bundled the sheets together. "We only have one set of sheets for your bed, so Mom will put them back on later today." She hurried out the door like there was a fire.

Brooke spent the rest of the morning pondering the comment made by fourteen-year-old Mim. "Wherever she goes, there she'll be." There was some truth in those words.

That afternoon, during her "planned spontaneity time," she drove to town to walk around Main Street. She passed the Stoney Ridge Wild Bird Rescue Center and saw a young man inside with a big bird on his gloved arm. Brooke stopped and watched him for a while through the large picture-glass window. If she wasn't mistaken, he was talking to the bird. She had never liked birds, so she moved along. In the air was the scent of bread baking and her tummy rumbled. She couldn't stop thinking about a certain pastry she'd had for breakfast at Eagle Hill yesterday morning. She noticed the Sweet Tooth Bakery and crossed the street.

Inside the bakery, everything looked so delicious in the glass case that Brooke couldn't decide what to pick out. "I'm staying at the Inn at Eagle Hill," she told the clerk, "and the innkeeper made blueberry lemon squares. They were—" Brooke's eyes went to the ceiling—"just amazing! Any chance you have any?"

"No." The clerk seemed greatly annoyed that Brooke would mention anyone else's baking while in her store. She glanced impatiently at the line that was forming behind Brooke.

*What to get, what to get . . .*

"Try the cinnamon roll," a man behind her in line whispered. "They're out of this world."

Brooke took his advice, bought a coffee to go along with the cinnamon roll, and sat down. She took a bite of the cinnamon roll and froze. It was . . . heavenly. Sweet, flaky, just the right amount of cinnamon.

"Was I right?" The customer who made the suggestion stood by her table.

Brooke swallowed down the bite, nodding, trying not to choke. "So right." He was possibly the most handsome man she'd ever seen. His dark blue eyes had the kind of lashes women envy, fair curly hair around his ears, his features had flawless symmetry and beauty. He was dazzling, startlingly attractive. Hard to tell how old he was—but she guessed he was in his late twenties.

He smiled at her, she smiled back, and she pointed to the empty chair. "Please, sit down."

His name was Jon Hoeffner, he said, a scholar, and he was taking a sabbatical from the university to do some research in Lancaster on family ancestry.

"Interesting," Brooke said. "I'd love to hear more." Mostly, she'd love to hear more of anything from this gorgeous creature.

"And what about you?" Jon asked. "Did I happen to hear you tell the bakery clerk that you're staying at the Inn at Eagle Hill?"

Brooke nodded. "Do you know it?"

"I've heard good things about it." He took a sip of his coffee. "So, when you're not vacationing at a quaint Amish inn, what do you do?"

"I am a professional art restorer."

Mid-sip, Jon froze. Then he set the coffee cup down and leaned forward, fascinated. "Tell me more," he said, his smile wide and generous. "Tell me everything."

If it weren't for the fact that they were sitting in a bakery in a tiny Amish town, Brooke would have thought he was flirting, being suggestive. "Ask me whatever you want and I'll answer whatever I want," she said in exactly the same tone, and their eyes met.

# 7

Rose reminded the family of Tobe's mid-April birthday and even organized separate birthday cards from Sammy, Luke, and Mim so that they could each sign them.

This year, Luke was indignant. "Why should I? Tobe never bothers to remember my birthday."

Rose covered Luke's hand with hers, marveling at how big it had become this year. He was inching toward thirteen, an unsettled age. "That was last year. I think Tobe will remember this year. He wants to be part of the family again."

"I'm too old to be sending silly cards to him." Luke snatched back his hand. "It's not like he's my real brother, anyway. He's only my half brother."

Rose felt a flash of anger and gave him a sharp look. "Then why don't you just explain to me what is 'real'? Was it real that winter when Tobe fished you out of the pond you went skating on without checking first to be sure it was frozen over? Was it real when Tobe carried you home from school because you'd broken your arm after falling out of the tree? Tobe *is* your real brother and Bethany *is* your real sister and I won't hear another word out of you on that subject. Is that clear?" She held a pen out to him.

He signed his name on the card and slunk away.

Luke's defiant nature wore her out. She feared there would always be a part of him that was drawn to risk, ignoring obvious dangers and warnings. He, more than the other children, was most like his father. So like Dean.

Today she had received a letter from Teacher Danny about Luke's bold behavior at school—just like the ones she used to receive from Teacher M.K. last year, on a regular basis. She thought he had turned a corner when Will Stoltz moved to town and took him under his wing at the Wild Bird Rescue Center. Luke's fiery temper was less likely to flare up at small things, his passion for birds motivated him to read and study. But Will had less time for Luke after he found his girlfriend, Jackie. Then Jesse Stoltzfus moved in across the street. Two years behind him in school, Luke admired Jesse's brash ways and tried to act and sound like him. He had no patience for Sammy anymore. Too much of a baby, he would tell him, when Sammy tried to follow the boys around.

Luke had slipped backward on his bumpy road to maturity.

Sammy picked up the pen after Luke had dropped it and studied the card before solemnly signing it, using his newly acquired third-grade cursive handwriting. He bit the tip of his tongue as he wrote.

Rose looked at Sammy affectionately. He was still a little boy, full of wonder. Everything fascinated him. A speckled bird's egg. A rainbow sparkling in the sun. He had made a pet out of a raccoon once, and Dean let him keep it for a spell before setting it free.

Sammy was such a funny little thing, quirky and serious but never a moment's trouble to her. Unlike Luke, who was a source of constant mischief and friction. Luke would argue that a blackbird was white.

"I did it!" he exclaimed jubilantly, smiling up at her. He handed the pen to Mim, who had to stop and think carefully what she wanted to say before she signed the card.

Mim was so timid, so unsure of herself. She had inherited her grandmother's pessimism, Rose thought regretfully. She seemed to expect the worst from every situation. Well, perhaps it was better than having expected great things and having got so little, the way Dean had viewed the world.

Mim was losing the baby roundness to her face and turning into a young woman. It was funny how you could look at a person every day and not notice how she was changing until something startled you into seeing her with fresh eyes.

Such a gift God had given Rose when these children were born. The ups and downs, the joys and sorrows—motherhood made her life full and rich, to the point of overflowing.

Rose sealed the envelope and put a stamp on the corner. She hurried to put it in the mailbox before the postman came by. As she closed the lid to the mailbox, she watched a car slow and turn into the driveway. As the car sputtered to a stop, she walked toward it, assuming the driver was lost. Out of the car bounced a young woman, tiny and delicate, with hair the color of spice cake, and a belly bulging with pregnancy. She wore a tight T-shirt with an arrow pointing down toward her abdomen, the words *Under Construction* printed across her chest.

Rose slowed her steps. The young woman looked up at the farmhouse, blue eyes glittering, as cold as a February fog off Blue Lake Pond, before she settled on Rose.

"Do you need directions?" Rose asked.

"Not if this is the Inn at Eagle Hill."

"It is."

Luke's dog, Micky, came charging up to the young woman and she batted him away. "I don't like dogs!"

Rose called Micky back to her side.

"You must be Rose. Tobe's stepmother?"

Rose bristled. She disliked being referred to as a stepmother. She might not have been Tobe's biological mother, but she was a mother to him in every way that mattered. "I'm Rose Schrock."

The young woman smiled sweetly. "I'm Paisley. Tobe's girlfriend. And this," she patted her enormous belly, "is your stepson's soon-to-be-born child."

Rose's eyes swept down to the girl's round stomach. Her mouth opened but nothing came out for a full minute. Maybe longer. She was speechless. Paisley didn't even notice. She just beamed as if she was the happiest person on earth. Rose had no idea what to do or to say. She had never known Tobe to have a girlfriend, not ever, and with a name like Paisley, she was fairly certain she would have remembered.

Paisley waved in the direction of the kitchen. "Let's go inside so I can meet Mammi Vera. She's standing at the window looking at us." Her face lit up even more so, if that was even possible. "Oh! There's the little boys! They're pressing their noses to the window. How charming! I can't wait to meet everyone!" She flounced toward the house, then stopped and spun around. "Rose, be a peach and bring my things." She pointed to the car. "Backseat. The trunk doesn't open."

Rose peered through the car windows. Crumpled bags and empty containers from fast-food restaurants littered the floor. She opened the back door and brought out a battered overnight suitcase and a bulky purse. A feeling of dread filled her, as if a tornado was heading her way but she wasn't sure which direction it came from.

In the kitchen, Rose cleared her throat and introduced Paisley to Vera as Tobe's friend and tried to smile but knew it came out forced and wrong.

Paisley smiled largely at Vera. "Oh, dear Mammi Vera! My sweet Tobe has told me so very much about you! He just adores you." Then she turned to the boys and spoke in a sugary voice to them. "Aren't you two munchkins just the cutest things!"

Mim walked in the kitchen and froze. For a long moment, everyone seemed completely dazed by Paisley's looks and by the way she talked. For a girl with such a small frame, she had the biggest, roundest stomach they had ever seen.

On and on Paisley went, oohing and aahing over what a quaint village Stoney Ridge was and how charming Eagle Hill was. Buttered up by the compliments, Vera's tight face softened. Rose thought Vera would recoil from such overfamiliarity but, to her amazement, she saw her almost preening.

The boys stared at Paisley, their mouths hung open, their eyes opened even wider. Rose put a firm hand on their shoulders and squeezed. "Close your mouths, boys, before a fly lands in them. Time to go feed the livestock."

"Aw, Mom," Luke said, eyes glued on Paisley.

"Go," Rose said, shooing the boys outside. Mim wasn't much better—she was still standing against the doorjamb with a baffled look on her face. "Mim, you help them." Sammy practically stumbled over Mim because he couldn't take his eyes off Paisley. Rose closed the kitchen door and turned to face Paisley. She tried to smile. "Tobe should have told us about you."

"I suppose he's shy like that," Paisley said. "But he'll have to get used to having a wife."

Rose froze. "A wife?"

Paisley laughed at the shocked look on her face. "We haven't tied the knot yet. Soon, though. As soon as he gets out of jail. He needs to make an honest woman out of me."

Vera's eyes went wide and she clutched her chest. Rose wasn't too worried. Vera clutched her chest a lot.

"When did you last see Tobe?" Rose asked.

"Before he went into the slammer." Paisley laughed and patted the bump of her stomach. "Obviously." Her blue eyes darted around the room, taking everything in. "Do you happen to know when he'll be released?"

"Any day now," Vera said firmly, though Rose knew she had no idea.

"Soon, you'll be admiring all this," she said to the unborn baby.

"And how did you say you met Tobe?" Rose said.

"Actually, I didn't say." Paisley peered out the kitchen window. "He was a customer at the restaurant where I worked. It was love at first sight."

"Paisley," Rose said carefully, "do you have any proof?"

"Proof?"

"About Tobe. Try to understand—you seem to know a great deal about us and yet we've never heard a word about you."

Paisley looked at Rose for a long moment, then went to her luggage that Rose had set in the corner of the kitchen. She rummaged around, and then held up a blue shirt.

Rose took the shirt from her. She had made Tobe that shirt three Christmases ago. She remembered every stitch, every seam. Big and square, narrow at the waist. Paisley pulled something else out of her battered suitcase and thrust it at Rose. It was a picture of Tobe with his arm around the shoulders of a then-thin Paisley. "That was taken a year or so ago."

Vera took the photo from Rose and sat down to examine it.

"I can hardly wait to meet the girls and see more of your wonderful house and farm." Paisley peeked into the living room. "It must be wonderful to be so rich!" Her face was flushed and eyes bright, much too bright.

Rich? *Rich!* Rose nearly laughed out loud but didn't dare, with Vera only a few feet away.

Just this morning a neighbor brought over a bushel of cabbage claiming they'd had a bumper crop last fall and needed to start cleaning out the root cellar to get ready for spring. Lately, it seemed, everyone thought of the Schrocks when they needed to share their over-wintered fall vegetables. Eagle Hill had more onions, carrots, turnips, and cabbages than Rose knew what to do with, yet she was grateful for the kindness of their neighbors.

Sammy and Luke felt differently. They would bitterly complain when they faced yet another bowl of stewed cabbage or boiled turnips. She could just predict the scene: one or the other boy would make a face and ask why neighbors never seemed to have an abundance of ice cream or cake. Their ungratefulness would prompt Vera to launch into a long lecture about children in other countries who didn't have enough to eat, then she would wind down by tossing proverbs at them.

Paisley turned to Rose. "Just tell me where to go unpack and I'll take care of myself. I'm very low maintenance."

There was an awkward silence as Rose realized Paisley aimed to stay at Eagle Hill.

Finally Vera broke in. "You can settle into Bethany's room. It has the best view in the house. Second story. It's the room to the right of the stairs. Make yourself at home. Just let Rose know if you need anything."

"Second story? My, how grand!" Paisley flounced up the stairs with her little suitcase.

Rose turned to look at Vera. "You *want* her to stay?"

"Of course I do. If she's carrying Tobe's child, I want her to settle in and make herself at home. Don't you see? She's going to tie him down to the farm. He'll stay here, if he has a wife and child to care for. He'll settle down for good. I always knew it would happen." Vera was fairly glowing with happiness. "Kommt zeit kommt ratt." *When the time comes, there will be a way.*

"Has Tobe ever mentioned her name to you? Because he certainly never said a word to me about a girl named Paisley."

Vera's smile faded. "Love at first sight, she said."

"I find it hard to believe you're not horrified that Tobe might be a father without benefit of matrimony."

Vera patted the hairs at the back of her neck. "Well, sometimes the young get a little ahead of the wedding."

"And what if the child Paisley is carrying isn't Tobe's but some other man's child?"

Vera clutched her chest. "Oh my soul. Why would anyone lie about such a thing?"

"I don't know. But doesn't it seem fishy to you?"

"Maybe you're just being suspicious."

"Vera, I'm just trying to be cautious."

"And I'm trying to be positive. Don't you see? This could be the very thing Tobe needs to join the church."

Rose raised her eyebrows. "And you think a girl like . . . Paisley . . . would want to join the Amish church?"

"Love at first sight, she said." Vera's chin jutted out. "She loves Tobe and a woman will do anything for the man she loves." She sat heavily in a chair, as if exhausted. "Why else would she be here?"

Maybe . . . maybe Vera was right. If Paisley were carrying Tobe's child, maybe he would finally settle down and become the man he was meant to be. Just when Rose thought Vera might be suffering from a little softening of the brain, she up and surprised her with some insightful thing she said. From time to time, Rose felt a surge of affection for Vera, but mainly she felt she brought a lot of unhappiness on herself. Goodness, she went out halfway to invite it.

Rose gazed at Vera, a stout, sad woman in her sixties, a widow, her only son gone. Let her have this hope.

Then another thought crowded in: What about Naomi? What would that hope mean for her?

Naomi felt unsettled, the way air shifted right before a rainstorm was due in. But the sky was delphinium blue and empty of clouds. Restless and at loose ends, she picked up her scissors, grabbed a swatch of pink fabric from her scrap basket, and cut triangles for a new quilt. She needed a new project, something to calm her mind. Her fingers flew without needing a pattern, a skill that irked Bethany. Each triangle was identical to the one before it. When she had finished with the pink fabric, she glanced up and noticed Bethany come up the driveway. She had been working at the Sisters' House today and was on her way home. Naomi thought she might stop by the house, but she beelined into the barn. She set the scissors down and stared out the window, still bothered by something she saw earlier today. Or thought she saw.

Earlier this afternoon, Naomi had dropped off a package at the post office and she spotted a man walking down Main Street. She didn't immediately recognize him until he crossed the street. There was something familiar about the way he walked, arms bent and aggressive. If she didn't know better, she thought the man looked like Jake Hertzler . . . but that was impossible. He was long gone and good riddance to him. She never—not ever ever ever—wanted to set eyes on that horrible man again.

Naomi had only seen Jake Hertzler one time, late at night, though she would never forget it. It would be easy to give in to feelings of hatred for that awful man. But she refused. Instead, she prayed for his soul whenever she thought of him because she knew it was in jeopardy. It was impossible, she knew, to allow hatred to grow in your heart if you prayed for that person. Hatred may visit your heart, but you needn't invite it to stay.

She picked out another scrap of fabric from her basket—another soft shade of pink—and set to work cutting out pieces. She felt a little better, but not much, and she reached into her pocket for a Tums. Something just didn't feel right today.

Bethany went hunting for Galen in his barn and found him, head bowed low, in the tack room, where he was rubbing down an enormous oval collar with a rag of liniment. She watched him work for a moment, breathing in the smell of saddle soap and oil and horses. Galen looked at home in the tack room, but he looked lonely too. "Do you use that for training buggy horses?"

He spun to face her, startling at the sound of her voice. "This collar? No. But Amos Lapp bought a new Belgian for fieldwork and he shies at the collar. He asked me for help, so I thought I'd start with a larger collar so it's not rubbing the horse's neck. I wanted to clean it first."

Clean it? Why, every piece of equipment in this tack room looked like it had been spit and polished that very morning. Meticulous. Fastidious. Galen didn't even use metal nails to drape the leather bridles—only wooden pegs, so nothing would crimp or crack. Curry combs, leather hole punchers, hoof trimmers, shears were hung in designated spots. Rolled leg wraps, bandages, tins of liniment and oil and saddle soap were arranged in a single row above the workbench. Lead ropes were coiled as neatly as lariats. Stacked on a tack trunk was a pile of clean horse blankets.

"Is it always like this?"

He looked around the small room. "Like what?"

"So . . . scrupulously tidy?"

"Yes, except after one of your brothers have been in it." Galen glanced up at the wall wreathed with neatly hung harnesses. "The tack room is one of the most important places in the barn. Everything in its place, and a place for everything."

Why, Bethany should bring the old sisters over to this tack room on a field trip, that's what she should do. They could take a lesson from Galen.

He took the soiled liniment rag, folded it in half, and draped it over a wooden peg as precisely as Rose draped a dish towel over the kitchen sink faucet. "If you're looking for Naomi, she's in the house."

*Oh!* She had become so fascinated with the orderliness of the tack room that she forgot why she had come. "Galen, would you help me find Lodestar?"

He looked up at Bethany in surprise. "You think that horse is around here? I figured he'd be long gone by now."

"Maybe. But maybe not. Jake Hertzler stole Lodestar from Jimmy to make sure everyone knew he had the upper hand, but I don't think he ever cared about the horse other than turning a profit. So wouldn't it make sense that he would try to sell Lodestar again? He's a pretty valuable horse. There are warrants out for Jake's arrest—I doubt he wants to drag a horse around with him while he's on the run."

"I doubt even Jake Hertzler would be bold enough to sell such a distinctive horse at an auction in this county."

"You never met Jake, did you?"

Galen shook his head. "I saw him once in his truck, but it was getting dark. I'm not sure I would know him if I saw him."

"I just have the strangest feeling that he's nearby. I can't explain it."

Galen's dark eyebrows shot up. "Have you seen him?"

"No. Maybe I'm just hanging around Naomi too much. She's always sensing things that aren't visible."

Galen stiffened. He didn't like to hear any implied criticism about his sister. "Naomi has good intuition."

Bethany nodded. "I know, I know. I think that's what I'm starting to pay attention to."

"Maybe you should call that SEC lawyer Allen Turner and tell him what you told me."

"I thought of it, but I haven't actually seen hide nor hair of Jake. It's just a hunch. A feeling. I have no proof."

"The spring auctions are just starting up again. I could ask around about Lodestar."

Satisfied, Bethany turned to go.

"The chance of finding Lodestar again is low, Bethany. But even if I did find him, would you really want him back? I thought Jimmy had made up his mind to give up horse breeding."

Bethany kicked a piece of straw with her shoe. "Haven't you noticed a change in Jimmy? Something's wrong. He's missing his spark. I think he needs that horse back. Maybe once Lodestar is back, everything else will fall into place for him."

"Like . . . proposing?"

*Shootfire!* How did everybody seem to know she had matrimony on her mind? She put her hands on her hips. "I don't know what you're talking about, Galen King."

He grinned. "I'll do what I can. If Lodestar is anywhere in Lancaster County, I'll find him."

Rose made a phone call to the minimum security federal prison where Tobe was being held, saying she had an emergency and needed to get a message to him.

"Just one moment," and there was a shuffling of papers before the voice came back. "Is this a documented emergency?"

"In what way?"

"Is it a matter of life or death for an immediate family member?"

Rose had to admit that no, it wasn't. The operator then suggested she had three choices—she could send a letter to the inmate or have his lawyer call and speak to him or wait for the inmate to use his prepurchased minutes during his free time. Then she hung up without a goodbye.

Rose pressed her forehead against the phone's receiver. Frustrating! Today's mail had come and gone, though maybe Mim could take the scooter into town and deliver it to the post office. Even so, a letter wouldn't reach Tobe for a day or so. Then an answer back might take another few days. It might be four or five days before she heard back from him. Should she try to go visit him? She had offered to visit him but he had discouraged her, telling her he'd prefer letters. To be frank, visiting a prison filled her with panic.

Should she call Allen Turner? He was a go-between for Tobe and his court-appointed attorney. But then she dismissed that thought. She couldn't involve him in a family issue like this.

Back in the house, Rose dashed off a letter to Tobe to find out if he knew a woman named Paisley. She had just arrived at Eagle Hill, with plans to stay. Also, with plans to deliver a baby. His baby.

And did he have *any* idea yet when he might be released from prison?

She had just sent Mim off to town with the letter when she heard Paisley call out to her. "Oh Rose. I've had a little accident. Can you come here? Quickly?"

Rose hurried upstairs to Bethany's room. There in the middle of the quilt Bethany had just finished—the first quilt she had ever made—was a tipped-over bottle of bubble-gum-pink nail polish. The polish had started with a puddle and was now spreading out. Paisley stood in the center of the room, a blank look on her face. "I was polishing my toes and must have knocked the bottle over."

Rose quickly picked up the bottle and lifted the quilt as carefully as she could, so the rivers of polish would remain on that one quilt block and not spread onto others.

"Oh dear, oh dear," Paisley said, fanning her eyes with her hand as if she was trying not to cry. "It's my condition, you see. I have become so clumsy."

Rose's first inclination was to ask her why she would paint her toenails on someone's handmade quilt, but instead she said, "It'll be all right.

Bethany can replace that quilt block and it will be good as new." She was trying to be polite to the girl. It would be a painstaking task to fix this quilt.

"Well," Paisley snuffled like a little child. "If you're sure."

As Rose carried the quilt downstairs to the basement to try to get the stain out, she cringed, thinking of Bethany's reaction. She was going to hit the roof when she saw her spoiled quilt. She had just finished it! Her first quilt.

After Paisley had recovered from her episode of near tears, she found Rose hanging the quilt on the clothesline and said she wanted a tour of the whole farm. Rose showed her the garden, the henhouse, the pastures, Silver Queen and her colt, and the barn. As they walked, Paisley was full of questions like how fast do chickens lay eggs—daily—and how long did it take for a horse to have a colt—about eleven months—and were sheep a good investment—no—and how much money did Rose think the whole place was worth? She asked Paisley what made her so curious about Eagle Hill and she said, "Oh, well. Tobe can't stop raving about the place." She peered into Flash's stall and the old horse peered back at her. "I suppose it's become like home to me."

Rose was just about to ask Paisley where *her* home was, when Sammy came out of the feed room, pushing a wheelbarrow filled with hay. Paisley made a big fuss over him. "You're such a little boy to be pushing that big wheelbarrow!"

Rose cringed. She knew how sensitive Sammy was about his small stature. His cheeks turned red and he got flustered and called her Parsley. She laughed the first time, then she got irritated when he called her Parsley a second time.

"Sammy," Rose said, "I hear Silver Queen neighing for her dinner. Why don't you head out to her."

Sammy grabbed the handles of the wheelbarrow and hurried out the barn door.

As soon as he was gone, Rose turned to Paisley. "Please don't embarrass him. He'll learn your name. It's just a little . . . unusual."

Paisley lifted her eyebrows at Rose and then nodded as if she understood a great secret. "Oh! Tobe didn't tell me that Sammy was developmentally delayed."

"What?" Rose said. "No! Not in the least."

Luke came out of the feed room holding two buckets of oats. He walked through the aisle and out the barn door without a word, his face tight. A moment later, Rose heard a bloodcurdling scream come from the front yard.

"Luke Schrock! What have you done?!"

Oh dear. Bethany must have returned from the Sisters' House and seen the quilt hanging on the clothesline. Rose had tried everything she could think of to remove the nail polish from the quilt, but the stain was permanent. She flew outside and dashed to the clothesline. Tending to the horses in the pastures, the boys dropped the feed and came running toward the clothesline with all their might. Bethany stood by the quilt, examining the stain.

"It wasn't Luke, Bethany," Rose said, trying to stave off an explosion of words aimed at Luke. "It was Tobe's friend, Paisley."

Bethany looked like she was trying not to cry. "What? Who?"

"Her!" Luke pointed to Paisley, walking toward them from the barn, as if she didn't have a care in the world. "And she's staying in your room." He was scowling at Paisley as she approached them.

"That would be me," Paisley said, with an apologetic smile on her face. "I spilled my nail polish while I was doing my toes." She stuck a hand out to Bethany, who was staring at her with a baffled look on her face. "Let's see. You must be Bethany. I'm Paisley. Tobe's Paisley. He's told me all about you."

Off in the distance, Rose noticed something awry. "The goat!" It had gotten into Silver Queen's pasture and pulled hay off the wheelbarrow. The buckets, now empty of oats, lay on their sides, abandoned by Sammy. Silver Queen and her colt were helping themselves to the hay. Rose shooed Luke and Sammy off to finish feeding the rest of the stock.

Rose rubbed her temples. Could this day get any worse?

# 8

Brooke liked Jon Hoeffner. She liked him quite a bit. He was possibly the most charming and easy-to-talk-to man she had ever met. He must be spoken for; a man like him wouldn't be unattached. Could he?

She was taken aback when Jon waved to her at the Sweet Tooth Bakery the very next day when she dropped by.

"Good. I was hoping you'd be here," he said, and her heart skipped a beat.

He seemed to be especially fascinated with her work and asked numerous questions, which was so different from other men who only talked about themselves. "But how," he asked, leaning toward her, resting his forearms on the table, "does restoration differentiate itself from forgery?"

"It's entirely different," Brooke said, trying not to sound a little touchy on the subject. She was still sensitive about the museum curator's accusation that she had been treading in dangerous waters. "Paintings are like fingerprints—they're very unique, and for most forgers, there's simply too much for them to duplicate. People get fooled when they're only familiar with an artist's name and not much else. You need to know what an artist's brushstrokes look like, what his or her favorite subject matters and compositions are, what kinds of mediums, materials, sizes, and formats they usually work in."

Jon didn't seem at all bored, quite the opposite. How refreshing! "I think it's also important to know what the art looks like from the back, how it's usually framed, mounted, or displayed, how and where it's titled or numbered, what gallery it's been in, what labels it's likely to have."

She paused again, aware she was doing all the talking, giving him an option to change the subject if he wanted. But his eyes were glued on hers and he nodded to encourage her to continue. "Then, of course, there's signatures. A lot of forgers make the mistake of not studying an artist's signature. You'd be amazed how many forgers miss something as small as setting the signature where an artist typically locates it."

"Signatures?" Jon said, eyebrows lifting in surprise. "You can duplicate an artist's signature?"

She smiled. "That's one of the easiest things in the world for me to do."

"And you've never gotten caught?"

She bristled. She could practically feel the hair rise on the back of her neck. "I'm a legitimate art restorer. Besides," she tore off a bite of her cinnamon roll, "it's hard to fool someone who knows how to analyze art."

"Show me. Can you copy my signature?" He wrote it out on a piece of paper and slid it toward her.

She picked up the paper and studied his signature, noticing the way he curled his *H*, closed the circles on his *O*. He handed his pen to her and she wrote out his signature, then handed it to him.

"Amazing! It's . . . nearly identical."

She grinned at his response. "It's easy when you know what you're looking for."

"Yes." He smiled back at her. "I can see how that would be true."

Vera marched into the kitchen where Rose was preparing dinner. "Those boys need to keep quiet. For Paisley's sake. She's trying to rest in the living room before supper."

"I just sent them outside to play. They're tossing a ball back and forth."

"They're too loud. They're always loud. They can't do anything quietly."

Rose was cutting an onion to make chicken soup. With a match, she lit the blue ring of fire on the stove top and placed a big soup pot on the burner. She started to sweat the onion with a little olive oil, then added chopped carrots and celery. "Well, they are boys, Vera. They aren't doing anything wrong."

"It's not good for her to be stressed. She says her nerves get easily frazzled."

"Then why did she arrive at a stranger's home toward the end of her pregnancy?" Rose added chicken broth to the pot, shredded chicken, noodles, minced parsley. "What could be more stressful than that? She should be with her own family."

"She doesn't have any family. She told me so." Vera's lips fit into a tight line. She crossed her arms against her chest. "You will try to treat her nice, won't you?"

The soup began to simmer and Rose stirred it with a wooden spoon. "Oh, certainly," she said, feeling more than a little bit aggravated at all the fuss. As Vera went outside to tell the boys to stop playing so loudly, Rose turned her attention back to making dinner, with enough banging and clanging to shake the teeth loose in Paisley's head and frazzle her nerves good.

Finally, Paisley came in from the living room. "Is there any way I can help get dinner ready?"

Rose looked up from stirring dough for biscuits, surprised and pleased. "Would you wash and dry these dishes?" She tilted her chin to motion toward a small mountain of dirty dishes in the sink.

Paisley craned her neck to look behind Rose, frowning. "There's no dishwasher."

"No. We hand wash all the dishes." She set the bowl of biscuit dough to the side and reached for the hot water faucet. Water started to fill the sink as Rose squirted some dish soap into it. She swirled her hand in the water to suds up the soap. "All ready for you."

Paisley took a few steps back. "Oh, bummer. I wish I could help, but I have very sensitive skin."

"Sensitive skin?"

"Yes. Haven't you ever noticed all the skin lotion commercials on TV? The actors are always redheads. Like me." She pulled a ringlet out of her ponytail and twirled it around her finger. "Of course you wouldn't! You don't have a TV!" She held out her hands. "Anyway . . . my hands need special care or I break out in a terrible rash. I wish I could help. I really, truly do." She smiled a weak attempt at an apology and went outside to sit on the porch swing in the sun.

⸺⸰ ◊ ⸰⸻

By the time Bethany had moved a few things out of her room to make space for Paisley, she was calming down from the quilt disaster. A tiny little bit. *Shootfire!* Who was this pregnant Paisley, anyhow? Bethany didn't like her and didn't know why the family was welcoming her with open arms. *Double shootfire!*

She came downstairs to help Rose get supper ready, but the kitchen was empty. There was something good-smelling on the stove top and Bethany peeked inside, hoping Rose had made a broth-based soup and not that awful cream of mushroom that Mammi Vera was so fond of. Whatever it was, it would need to be stretched tonight. She had learned quite a bit about stretching soups from her weekly meal preparation for the down-and-outers at the Second Chance Café. Stretching a cream soup meant dumping in more cream. You ended up with a bowl of hot salty milk. Disgusting.

Bethany had seen Jimmy Fisher earlier in the day, and when she heard he would be dropping by Galen's to talk horses, she invited him for dinner. She peeked out the window, hoping to catch sight of Jimmy, and noticed Paisley walking around on the wooden porch. Then she saw Jimmy come through the hole in the privet.

Before Jimmy reached the porch steps, Bethany saw him stop abruptly, startled, as he realized there was a stranger on the porch. "Hello," he said to Paisley, and Bethany leaned closer to the window, opening it up a crack.

Paisley perked right up and said, in a giggly voice, "Well, hello to you. My, my, my. No one ever told me that I'd be encountering such a handsome man on a dusty old Amish farm."

Jimmy grinned that devilish grin of his, which made Paisley practically swoon. She giggled and held out her hand to him. Paisley's voice dropped to a whisper, but Bethany could tell she was talking up a storm. Jimmy laughed, which made Bethany all the more suspicious of Paisley. If she was so in love with her brother Tobe, then why was she flirting with the first fellow who came along?

Bethany saw Paisley grab the crook of Jimmy's arms and cling tightly. She jumped away from the window and plastered a sweet smile on her face as they entered the kitchen.

"How nice," Bethany said, trying to keep her voice in check. "I see you've met Paisley." She smiled as sweetly as she could. She took a handful of spoons and grabbed some napkins and put them on the table. "Paisley, perhaps you could help set the table for dinner."

Paisley let go of Jimmy as if it took all her strength to pull her hands off him and said she didn't know the first thing about setting tables, but perhaps Jimmy could help? She flashed her dimples at Jimmy and he quickly jumped to her rescue. In fact, Jimmy ended up setting the table as Paisley giggled and told him how clever he was, and Bethany smoldered as she set out butter and jam for the biscuits.

As if stomachs had an alarm clock, the boys and Mim appeared in the kitchen. Rose helped Mammi Vera in from the living room.

"Supper's ready," Bethany said. "Paisley, why don't you sit between Sammy and Luke." She pointed to a chair to sit in, but Paisley had already darted over to be next to Jimmy.

"You can sit there, sister Bethany, and mind those two little rapscallions. I'll keep an eye on this special guy." Paisley offered Bethany her sweetest smile.

Jimmy wiggled his eyebrows at Bethany, which only made her all the more annoyed.

Rose had a belief that many a skirmish could be avoided by the timely appearance of food, but Bethany figured she hadn't shared a meal with someone like Paisley before. All during dinner, sparks flew between Bethany and Paisley like a house cat in a thunderstorm. Jimmy, Bethany noticed with annoyance, had a foolish grin on his face the entire meal, like he was having a wonderful time.

Later that evening, after Rose had cleaned up the kitchen from supper, she heard a knock at the kitchen door and opened it to find Galen smiling down at her, handsome in a black coat and trousers, with Paisley hanging on to his arm. "I just met your newest guest." His voice was happy sounding, but his face was curious and stunned.

As they walked through the door, Galen unhooked Paisley's hand from his and stood near Rose.

Paisley flashed him a saucy smile. "I just can't get over Amish men! Every time I turn around, another dashing fellow appears out of nowhere."

Rose saw the look on Galen's face go from puzzled and amused to wary and cautious. He ignored Paisley's overly effusive comment and turned to Rose. "Would you like to go for a walk?"

"Absolutely." She grabbed a shawl off the wall peg and noticed Paisley's mouth open as if she was going to invite herself along and quickly closed the door behind her. Paisley would have to fend for herself. Something, Rose suspected, she was probably quite good at.

With the barest turn of the head, Galen said, "I've been told you had an eventful day."

"Indeed it was. I'll tell you about it on the way. Who told you?"

"Jimmy filled me in before he headed home tonight."

There was still some fading light left in the sky as they walked behind the house toward the ridge. From somewhere far off came the bellowing of a cow. The chickens had gone to roost in the henhouse, and the chill of evening had begun settling in. Once they had reached the trail that led up the hill, Galen reached out and took Rose's hand.

"I thought you already had a guest using the flat."

"She's not a guest of the inn. She's a guest . . . of the family."

"She's staying in the house?"

"At least for tonight. She says she's a friend of Tobe's."

Galen's eyebrows lifted sharply.

"I sent a letter to Tobe to find out if he does, indeed, know her."

Galen tilted his chin. "Why is she here? She looks like she's about to . . . fresh." Color rose in his cheeks.

"Good grief, Galen. She's not a cow. She's a woman. I'm . . . not exactly sure why she's here. Why now."

Understanding filled Galen's eyes. "So she's carrying Tobe's child?"

Rose yanked her hand out of his and wrapped the shawl tightly around her. "There's no proof that her baby is Tobe's. Only Paisley's word. We've never seen her before in our lives. I tried calling the prison to see if I could get word to him, but it wasn't possible. My letter to him won't even arrive until midweek. Until then, it seems best to be hospitable to the girl."

"Why would she make such a thing up?"

"I have no idea."

"Do you believe her?"

"I . . . can't quite read her. I don't trust her." She walked up the ridge trail ahead of him. "Galen, are you going to tell Naomi what I've told you?"

"Is it a secret?"

"Yes. No. I just . . . would rather wait until I hear something from Tobe."

"But why should it matter to Naomi whose baby it is?"

She stopped and spun around. "You must be joking."

Galen looked at her blankly.

"You must realize Tobe and Naomi have some kind of understanding."

He shook his head, a little too forcefully. "No, they don't. You're mistaken."

"Galen, you think of Naomi as a child. She's a grown woman. She's old enough to make her own choices."

"Tobe might be interested in her, but she has too much sense to—"

"To fall for a Schrock?" That wasn't fair. She regretted saying it as soon as the words spilled out of her mouth.

He looked hurt. "That's not what I was going to say."

"I know you have doubts about Tobe. Naomi knows that too. But you can't predict who you'll fall in love with, can you? No wonder she can't talk to you about their relationship."

"Relationship? He's in jail! They don't have a relationship."

"Once you see Naomi and Tobe together, I believe your doubts will vanish."

"No, I don't think so, Rose." Galen offered a shaky smile. "Why are we talking about such a thing on a beautiful night like tonight?"

They walked up to the ridge in silence, each alone with their own thoughts, a wedge between them. As Rose tried to cope with all the day had brought, she was glad she had come to the top of the ridge to stargaze on this dark night. The clouds kept racing across the moon like smoke from a fire. Drinking in the beauty of a night sky always reminded her of the infinite majesty of God and the finite trivialness of her problems. God was bigger than any problem life could throw at her.

She leaned against him and he put his arm around her.

"Can I do anything? I'd do anything to help."

"I know you would." And Rose did know.

The next afternoon, Naomi walked over to Eagle Hill to see if Bethany wanted to ride with her to the Sisters' Bee over at Edith Fisher's house.

Bethany came out of the door before she reached the porch, an anxious look on her face. "Did Galen tell you?"

"Tell me what?"

Bethany glanced at the house. "Jimmy didn't say anything?"

The pinched look on Bethany's face worried Naomi. "What's wrong?"

"Nothing, really. Well, something is wrong, actually. Someone is terribly wrong, I suppose you could say. And I'd rather you hear it from me first." She sat down on the porch steps and patted a spot next to her for Naomi. "A girl showed up out of the blue yesterday." She pointed to a rusty car that was blocking the driveway.

Micky ran up to Naomi and curled up beside her. "A new guest?" she said, stroking his big head. She loved this silly dog.

"No, not a guest at the inn. She says she's a friend of Tobe's."

Naomi's hand stopped in mid-pat, but Micky looked up at her and she finished the stroke. "Oh."

"A close friend. She says she was his . . . girlfriend. Her name is Paisley. Does that name ring a bell to you? Did Tobe ever mention a Paisley?"

Naomi looked away. "No." She felt a sudden chill.

"I didn't think so." Bethany took in a deep breath. "I have to tell you this before someone else does. This Paisley is pregnant. Very pregnant. Soon to deliver. She says . . ."

Naomi could feel the back of her neck get cold and clammy.

"She says . . . that Tobe is the baby's father." Bethany's fists clenched. "But I don't believe a word she says, Naomi. You shouldn't, either."

In instant response, Naomi's throat tightened with fear and her pulse thrummed fast in her ears. She knew, in a disembodied way, that she would remember this moment forever. She knew the time and the date, and the way she sat on the porch steps with her hand stroking the head of the dog. She knew, with a certainty that she had never felt before about anything, that Paisley was going to bring trouble into her life. Real trouble, threatening everything she had hoped for.

⟶ ☙ ◊ ❧ ⟵

Out the kitchen window, Rose noticed Bethany and Naomi with their heads bent together outside on the porch steps, then she saw Naomi walk back toward her home, shrinking away like an animal that had received a blow. Shoulders slumped, chin down, hands clenched in tight fists. It was a look of Naomi's with which Rose was familiar; it usually was a sign that she was suffering from a headache.

But just ten minutes ago, she had slipped through the privet looking entirely different. Happy, lighthearted, practically glowing.

Rose's heart skipped a beat. *Oh no. Oh no no no.* Bethany must have told her about Paisley.

# 9

⚜

Brooke Snyder set out on her twenty-minute walk eager and happy, her step animated as she strode along the crunching gravel. She walked down the road beside green shoots of new grass that were sleek with dew, glistening in the morning sun, quivering now and then from a breeze. The world was resplendent, quiet and fresh, with sights and sounds of a new day. The creak of a windmill's turning arms, the whinny of a horse in a pasture, the cawing of crows on a sagging telephone line.

Why, the weather alone made her spirits dance. The midmorning sun felt like a golden caress on her back. A few meringue puffs of clouds floated high in the blue sky, a blue so rich it startled the senses.

She passed by an Amish farmer and his son tilling fields, their plows harnessed to six brown, long-eared mules. When the breeze changed direction, she could even smell the good earthiness of the freshly turned dirt. A number of black-and-white cows stood along a wooden fence, rhythmically chewing their cud, regarding her with mild interest as she walked past them. A patchwork cat sat on a fence post, washing its face with an orange paw. A clumsy bumblebee buzzed around her, then dipped into a patch of yellow dandelions. An Amish woman walked briskly past her on the other side of the road, turning her bonneted head at the last moment to give her a shy smile.

The Amish were such ordinary people, but in that very ordinariness Brooke saw goodness and decency. The men were built broad and strong, their thick hands calloused and hard. The women were truly plain by modern standards, with no makeup or hair coloring to camouflage the effects of aging. Clearly, they dressed for comfort rather than style, though she was surprised to see orange crocs on the feet of the woman who just passed by her. They surprised her, these people.

Suddenly inspired, she wished she had brought her sketchpad with her to capture these bucolic scenes. With a start, she realized it was the very first time she'd had such a thought, in which a germ of an idea welled up inside her and she wanted to see it bear fruit, to become something. Her gait slowed as she tried to memorize all she saw on her walk. As soon as she returned to the guest flat, she would get those images down on paper before she forgot them.

But to her surprise, she didn't return back to the guest flat at Eagle Hill for two hours and then she had to hurry. She wanted to find a new outfit in town to wear, one that would bring out the gold flecks in her eyes, hoping she might accidentally-on-purpose bump into Jon Hoeffner later today. The sketches were forgotten.

Later that morning, as soon as Rose saw Brooke Snyder's car drive off, she hurried down to the guest flat to do a quick dusting and change the bed sheets. Brooke Snyder could be a talker, as she had discovered one morning when she brought a breakfast tray to her. She didn't mind chatting a little with the guests, but today she was already behind in her morning work and it was nearly noon.

She was pulling the top sheet off the bed as Paisley walked in and announced, "I'd like some breakfast. Would you mind bringing it to me? I'll be in my room."

Rose's teeth clenched. "Breakfast was hours ago, Paisley. But lunch will be on the table before too long." She yanked the bottom sheet off the bed, a little more firmly than she needed to. "In the kitchen. That's where we eat."

Paisley tilted her head at Rose, then walked around the rooms in the guest flat. "You know, this should do nicely for us. For a while, anyway."

Rose gathered wet towels from the bathroom. "I beg your pardon?"

"I think Tobe and I and the baby will move in down here. Until you can find someplace else to live."

Rose stiffened. "Excuse me? Why would I need to find someplace else to live?"

"Eagle Hill is our home. Tobe's, mine, and the baby." She caressed her high stomach, as if to remind Rose that she was about to deliver a child. There was something about her blue eyes, though, that looked like she was shooting poison darts. She'd never seen blue eyes that were so cold, like arctic ice.

"Paisley, I don't know what Tobe might have led you to believe, but this farm belongs to his grandmother."

"When she dies—and that day doesn't seem too far off, judging from the looks of her—he'll get it all."

Rose bundled the sheets into a ball and tossed them in a wicker laundry basket. "Such news might surprise Vera."

Paisley hesitated. "I'll move down here until it all gets sorted out."

"This guest flat is a business for us. I have reservations for it throughout the summer. Hopefully, even more in the fall. We need the income. I count on it to support my children."

Paisley narrowed her eyes. "I was told that Tobe came from a well-to-do family."

"Tobe might have exaggerated."

"I don't believe you!"

"I'm telling you the truth, Paisley," Rose explained patiently. "There is no money."

Paisley was having none of it. She spun on Rose, lines of stubborn determination forming around her mouth. "Or maybe you're just angling to keep it all for yourself." Her voice grew bitter. "I've read all about your husband in the papers. I know there's money. Somewhere. There's money someplace in this old rat trap of a farm."

Rose struggled to hold on to her temper. "I don't know what you've read or what Tobe has told you, but there is no money."

Darting Rose a last hostile glance, Paisley shot out of the room.

Rose watched her go. She wished she could talk to Tobe. She needed to find out the truth, but at the same time, she didn't want the truth.

As soon as Galen had left for the auction in Mount Joy the next day, Naomi made up a bagged lunch, brushed her teeth, and waited outside for the driver to pick her up. Since she had learned about Paisley yesterday, her anxiety escalated with each passing hour. Today, she was determined to go to the federal prison to talk to Tobe about this Paisley woman. Hiring a driver would cut time off the trip, both ways, faster than the bus. Galen would be gone until late afternoon, and Jimmy Fisher had already agreed to feed the livestock. If things went well, she would be back by suppertime and no one would be the wiser. Except she hoped she would be made wise to the Paisley situation.

As she waited, she felt all those unruly vines of emotion within her start to settle. Of course, of course Tobe would tell her that he had never known a woman named Paisley. Everything would be sorted out as soon as she talked to Tobe. Of course it would.

She reached into her pockets and realized she'd forgotten her Tums, so she hurried back inside to get a new pack, maybe two packs, just as she heard a car turn into the driveway.

She chose this particular driver, Mr. Kurtz, to take her to FCI Schuykill for three reasons: one, he drove fast, and two, he didn't like to talk, and three, he didn't gossip about where he drove his passengers. He never spoke about other people so everyone knew their secrets were safe.

She stared out the window through most of the trip, growing more anxious by the minute. Thoughts of Paisley dogged her, twining together the worry about her and Tobe's future. Would there be a future for them at all? She thought of Bethany's remark that her grandmother was delighted with Paisley's arrival—convinced this young woman was the way to keep Tobe in the fold. Was that what it would take? Could this be God's plan for Tobe? If so, she had completely missed the signals from God and that created another tangling vine of worry. Her stomach tightened into a burning ball, making her regret what she'd eaten for breakfast. *Breathe, Naomi. Deep, deep breaths. Six in, seven out. Or was it seven in, six out?*

She might be worried for nothing. Tobe might tell her that he didn't know a girl named Paisley. That was her best hope. That was what she had come to hear.

Minutes slid by, one into the next. She had chewed through one roll of Tums by the time Mr. Kurtz pulled over in front of the prison. "Want me to come back in a few hours?"

"Do you mind waiting? I don't think I'll be too long. I don't think there will be a wait to get in like there is on weekends."

"I don't mind at all." He gave her a sympathetic nod. "Is it as bad as they say?"

"He says it's not too bad. He's in that adjacent building there, the minimum security prison." She pointed out the window to a nondescript building. "He's not in a jail cell. He says he sleeps in a room with bunks."

"Do you get up here to visit a lot?"

"No. He only gets eight points a month and each weekend visit requires two points. Weekday visits are only one point." That was one of the reasons Tobe didn't encourage his family to visit him—he wanted to save his points for Naomi's visits.

"I've seen on the television that you have to talk to prisoners through a glass partition."

"Not here," Naomi said. "It's a big room with chairs, all in a row."

Mr. Kurtz lit up. "So at least you can hold hands with your fellow."

Naomi felt a blush creeping up her cheeks. "The guards walk around the room, watching everybody."

He opened his palm to reveal a few dollars. "Give them to your young man. I hear money talks in the pokey."

He was such a nice man. She tried to smile, though she knew it came out all wrong. "Thank you, Mr. Kurtz, but money has to go straight to the prison commissary accounts. Tobe says inmates aren't allowed to handle any money." How strange it was that she knew that fact and so many others about prison life.

Naomi was briefly detained while her clearance on the preapproved list was verified at the security gate. Then she was asked to put her house key and the money she'd brought to pay Mr. Kurtz into clear plastic bags before she was led into the visitation room. She sat down on a hard plastic chair to wait for Tobe. Her breathing grew shallow, and she started to feel like she couldn't get enough air. Pins and needles pricked the ends of her fingers, and her whole body began to quake as if she had chills. Over and over she said, "Oh-God-help-me-help-me-help-me please." She kept saying it until she found her muscles start to soften, and then, her symptoms began to relax their grip on her.

Ten minutes later, Tobe was brought in, wearing the prison garb: a khaki button-up shirt and khaki pants, his dark hair shaved close to his skull. Such short hair would have made any other Amish man look like a plucked chicken. But not Tobe. He was so handsome he took her breath away. He saw her and rushed to her. They hugged like long-lost lovers parted unwillingly, which is exactly what they were. Then he kissed her until she felt dizzy and breathless and thoroughly confused.

Some caution seemed to seep back into her and she pulled back, embarrassed by such a public display of affection. He tucked her arm into his and they sat in chairs, facing each other, holding hands.

"I couldn't believe it when I was told I had a visitor today. You were just here, Naomi. Why now?"

"Something has happened."

His smile faded. "Mammi Vera has passed."

"Oh no. No." She shook her head. "Nothing like that."

His smiled returned. "What is it? What brought you all the way to Minersville?"

She looked down at their intertwined hands. "Do you remember a woman named Paisley?"

Tobe stilled. "Yeah. Sure. Why?"

"When did you meet her?"

"Awhile back, while I was scrounging around for that year, living from place to place. She was a waitress. I guess she sort of took a shine to me."

"How well did you know her?"

"She let me crash at her place when I had run out of options. Just for a few nights—then I found a construction job over in Mount Joy and I didn't see her anymore." He tipped his head. "What's all this about?"

She peered at him. "But what I'm asking is, how well did you know her?"

"I told you. Not well."

"Did you know her . . . in the biblical sense?" Naomi's tone was light, her question deadly serious.

Tobe's face went slack. "Why would you ask me a question like that?"

He pulled his hands away and leaned back in the chair. "Why in the world would you ask me such a question?"

"Paisley has come to Eagle Hill. To stay. To deliver a baby she says is yours." Tobe looked at her in disbelief. "Impossible!"

"Is it, Tobe? Is it truly impossible?" She kept her eyes steady on his. She didn't want him to back away from the question. She needed an answer.

In a flash, his face went from fury to guilt to resignation. "No," he said quietly, as the color drained from his face. He looked up, drew a deep sigh, and spoke very gently. "No, it's not *entirely* impossible."

Naomi would remember forever how it felt when Tobe told her that indeed, he had known Paisley, in a biblical way. She felt the shock rush through her, prickling her skin and making her head tingle.

"She's lying. It's all a terrible mistake, Naomi. I would *know* if I had fathered a child with that girl. I would *know* it. I can't imagine why she would do this, out of the blue. But I don't know the kind of person she is."

Naomi squeezed her eyes shut at that last sentence. And yet he knew her well enough to *know* her.

She was very still as she sat and listened to him. Her face changed from time to time, concerned and distressed and compassionate as Tobe explained his tale of loneliness and misery, hastening to put her anxieties at rest: he was just with Paisley a few times and it never meant anything to either of them and he was having such a terrible time when he was in self-exile. She had to force herself to keep from looking stricken, horrified, when he said Paisley must be crazy because he was the last person in the world anyone should choose as a father for their child.

"Could she be lying about the timing? Would you have . . . known her . . . last August? Before you returned to Stoney Ridge?"

Tobe dropped his eyes. "Yes. I was with her one last time, before I returned home. I was a mess, wrestling with coming back home, and I got really drunk. I don't remember much of anything except waking up in the morning at her place again, with people there I didn't even know. I decided right then that I'd go home." He looked up, misery flooding his eyes. "I'm sorry. I'm really sorry."

For a moment, Naomi couldn't breathe. When she took in a full breath, her eyes started to sting. *Oh Lord, don't let me cry. Not here. Not now.*

"Say something, Naomi. Anything." His voice was only a whisper.

She tried to respond but the torrent of words welling up inside her wouldn't budge.

"You're as white as a sheet."

"I'm fine." She wasn't fine. Her muscles and emotions had all turned to jelly.

"Please believe me. I'm begging you. Begging you, Naomi. You're my only sure center. The only thing I need."

"But I'm not, Tobe," she said, strangely calm, though her temples were starting to pound and spots had started to dance before her eyes. "No one can ever be another person's center. That position belongs only to God." She glanced at the clock and said she thought she should leave.

His dismay was enormous. "You can't go now, you've only been here a short time."

"But you've told me everything."

"No, I haven't told you anything really. I've only skimmed the surface."

But she had heard what she came to hear. "I have to go back, Tobe. I would have, anyway, no matter what you told me. I need to get home before my brother returns from the horse auction."

They rose to say goodbye.

"I never, ever intended to hurt you," Tobe said.

Her stomach knotted with worry and she put a hand to her head as if she were coming down with a dreadful headache . . . which she was. "It doesn't matter what you intended. What matters is . . . what is."

What matters is what is.

"Did I do the wrong thing, telling you the truth?" He was a child again, confused and uncertain.

When she first arrived, she had hoped that Tobe would smile his lovely, familiar, heart-turning smile and say, "I've never heard of anyone named Paisley," and they would fall happily into each other's arms. But Tobe didn't say such a thing. It felt like the time when they all thought that Luke had drowned in Blue Lake Pond and it turned out later he'd just gone on home the other way. Well, that's the kind of fear she had now. She knew this kind of fear—it went bone deep.

He reached out to hold her hand. Her throat swelled and tears rushed to her eyes. "I need to go home," she said, backing away from him.

It had begun to rain as Mr. Kurtz drove her home, passing by the fields of green, each surrounded by a hedge of darker green; and Naomi stared hard out of the window willing the tears back into her head. But they came, one after the other, cascading down her cheeks. Her emotions felt like tangled vines, difficult to pull apart, no idea of where they began or ended.

What Naomi had felt as she sat on that porch swing yesterday with Bethany had not been a suspicion, it had been a foresight. She didn't just fear what Paisley's arrival might mean, she knew it.

What matters is what is.

# 10

Mim set her diary down, filled with notes and ideas about how to answer letters to Mrs. Miracle. She was stumped by a recent letter:

*Dear Mrs. Miracle,*

*My father insists that I follow him in the family business. He's worked very hard at establishing a successful business and I admire what he's done. But here's my problem: he's a butcher and I'm a vegetarian.*

*What should I do?*

*Signed,*
*Animal Lover*

"Honor thy father." The words slipped through her mind as she glanced over at her Bible on the corner of her desk. Could you honor your father and still choose a different career path?

She closed her diary, hid it under her mattress, and went next door in search of Naomi, who knew the answer to these kinds of questions.

"Looking for Galen or Naomi?" Jimmy Fisher said as Mim came into the barn over at the Kings', blinking her eyes rapidly as they adjusted to the dim lighting. Three horses stuck their heads over their stall doors, regarding her with interest. Barn swallows swooped from their nests and flew past her toward the open door. Jimmy was brushing a horse held in crossties in the middle of the barn aisle.

"I wanted to talk to Naomi."

"She's away, and so is Galen. I'm helping him out today."

Mim glanced at him with surprise. "Who's minding the chickens?"

He frowned. "I got up extra early and I'll stay up extra late tonight."

Jimmy walked the mare outside to the round training pen and Mim followed behind to watch the training session. He stood in the center, holding on to the long lead line, and made a clucking sound with his tongue to get the horse circling around the pen. He watched the mare's gait with a practiced eye. Now and then, he flicked a whip at her rear hooves to keep her in a gentle canter.

Mim leaned her elbows on the pen's railing. That pinched look Jimmy got on his face when she had asked about his chickens was gone. Come to think of it, that pinched look was on his face rather a lot lately, like his stomach hurt or he'd gotten a popcorn kernel stuck between his teeth. She felt a stab of pity for Jimmy. Here, as he concentrated on the movement of the horse, chirping to her when she slowed from a lope to a jog, praising her when she kept a steady pace, he seemed more like the old Jimmy. Happy, lighthearted, quick to smile.

Bethany was right. Jimmy was in danger of losing his sparkle. Or did she say spark? Either way, it had gone missing.

After the horse had been warmed up, Jimmy unhooked the shank from the mare's halter. He walked over to Mim to set down the whip and pick up a few training tools. "Jimmy, can a son honor his parents but not agree to work in the family business?"

Jimmy's face went blank. "What did Bethany tell you?"

"Tell me about what?"

He looked confused. "About how much I hate chickens."

"She didn't say a word." She didn't have to. Everybody knew that. Everybody!

"Then, why did you ask me such a question?"

"I just . . . was wondering. So what do you think? Can you honor your mother and quit the chicken business?"

Jimmy leaned against the pen railing. "I've been giving this a lot of thought lately."

"Honor thy father. It's in the Bible."

"I know it is." Jimmy looked out at an eagle, drifting high on an updraft, its wings as still as the grasses below, circling and searching for its dinner.

Those words were there. She couldn't deny that. But other bits of verses came to mind. "It also says to walk in truth. And the truth shall make you free."

Jimmy's head snapped around to look at her. "What did you say?"

"Those are someplace in the Bible but I don't know where, exactly. My mom has them written out on index cards and taped to the refrigerator."

Jimmy rubbed his face with his hands.

Mim wasn't sure what she had said that made Jimmy seem bothered.

He picked up a bucket of tools used to condition the horse to unexpected noise. "I'd better get back to work." He walked toward the horse, then spun around. "Thank you, Mim. You've been a big help. You know . . . you give pretty miraculous advice." He winked at her.

What had she said?

After a few casual meetings, Brooke decided to go each day at the same time to the Sweet Tooth Bakery. Jon Hoeffner was always there, in the same seat and table that faced the door—as if he might just be waiting for her. His smile was warm, but it made her nervous. It had been a long time since a man had given her this kind of attention.

And this was the kind of man you could dream about night and day, someone who would occupy all your thoughts. There was a definite undercurrent of romance between them. Jon was strikingly handsome, charming, easy to talk to, and most importantly, he didn't wear a wedding ring. He mentioned very little about his private life, but he spoke well of everyone and badly of no one.

Was Jon toying with her? She couldn't tell. Her intuition read kindness and genuine goodness in him, but she'd been wrong about people in the past.

Brooke was hoping Jon might suggest going out on a date. She thought about asking him—after all, this was the twenty-first century, but some warning voice made her think that she could only keep his attention if she didn't seem to care. It was so silly, all this game playing, yet it appeared to work. "Will you stay in Stoney Ridge long?" she said nonchalantly. It was an act.

He shook his head. "As soon as I wrap a few things up, I'm on my way."

She felt a twinge of disappointment. "Don't you like it here? I do."

"It's a one-horse town and a pretty poor horse at that."

"I don't know about that," she said, stirring her coffee. "There's certainly a lot of drama at the Inn at Eagle Hill."

"Oh?" he said. "What kind of drama could be going on at a quiet Amish farm?"

She told him about the pregnant girl named Paisley who had arrived, out of the blue, claiming to be carrying the oldest son's baby, and how the family was reeling from the news. Come to think of it, she had learned quite a bit about this family just by paying attention. If only more people would learn to listen, they could pick up all kinds of amazing information.

Jon, for example, was a wonderful listener. He leaned close to her as she talked, nodding in all the right places, eyes lighting up as he heard the Schrock family gossip. How many men would find it interesting to hear about an Amish family?

She smiled at Jon. Stoney Ridge was turning into a surprisingly delightful place for her life to find new direction.

She took a sip of coffee and gave a sigh of pure pleasure.

"It's good, that coffee, isn't it?" he said.

As far as Brooke was concerned, it could as well have been turpentine.

Naomi arrived home to find the house was still empty. Relieved, she made up a sandwich for her brother Galen, left it in the refrigerator, and got ready for bed. She could tell that a migraine had begun and was moving from the first phase, which she had felt at the prison—where every sense felt on high alert and almost unmanageable, to the next phase, where a flickering blind spot occurred in the center of her vision, like a spinning black penny. Soon, she knew, the pain would start to throb on one side of her head or the other.

The weather had taken a turn for the worse as the evening wore on. Lightning lit up the room; raindrops splattered the windows. She tried to sleep, then gave up and went down to the basement to the little cot. It was dark in the basement, no sound of crashing thunder, no bright streaks of lightning, no pounding rain.

When Naomi was a child, she used to play the game of "if."

If she got up the stairs before the grandfather clock in the hall stopped striking, then the teacher wouldn't be in a bad mood tomorrow. If the daffodils planted by the front of the house bloomed by April first, she'd get a circle letter from her sisters.

Now she sat in the dark basement with her arms around her knees. If the rain stopped soon, everything would be all right. It wouldn't have happened at all.

But it did. There was no point in pretending it hadn't. The anxiety of what she had learned from Tobe kept coming back—things changing, not being safe anymore.

She dozed off and on, but in the middle of the night, she woke with a start. The panic over Paisley seemed unbearable. She tried to beat back the wild fears that kept shooting through her mind, like violent streaks of colors.

All sorts of horrible possibilities presented themselves in her mind, troubling thoughts that she might be able to dismiss in the daytime but that took hold of her in the dark of night and seemed completely real. As she lay there, she became convinced that Tobe would want to be—and *should* be—with Paisley and her baby, and her breathing quickened and her heart began to beat so hard that it was all she could do not to cry out. She felt so sad, so alone, so lonely. She was ashamed of her own lack of faith, but she conjured just enough to whisper, "I am afraid." She hardly slept the rest of the night.

By noon of the next day, Sadie Smucker came down the basement stairs to check on Naomi. "Galen asked me to come and see if I could help you. He's worried about you." Sadie's voice was sweet and reassuring and Naomi felt thankful she was there.

Sadie placed a cool compress on Naomi's forehead and encouraged her to drink an herbal tea remedy made of Ligusticum. Naomi's body ached, her chest was tight, her head throbbed. She had never felt so sick. "I don't know what's wrong. I've never felt like this before. It must be the flu."

"Can you think of what triggered this migraine? Any food you ate?"

Naomi shook her head. Sadie had helped her create a diet high in magnesium and omega-3 fats to prevent migraines and taught her to avoid other foods that might act as triggers. "Nothing." She put her elbow over her eyes. "I've been so careful, and I haven't had a migraine in months. I thought I was finally getting past them."

Kindly, Sadie said, "I don't think it's the flu. Those migraines have always been your Achilles' heel. Did something happen to upset you?"

Naomi lifted her arm to look at Sadie. She and Sadie had always had a special understanding. Sadie said she used to be very much like Naomi: shy and timid and scared of her own shadow. Naomi couldn't imagine Sadie like that. She might be a quiet person, but she oozed a strong, reassuring presence.

"Naomi, you are sick from despair. This is how the heart speaks to us, through our illnesses." Sadie tipped the cup of tea for Naomi to take another sip. "But you're not alone in this, whatever it is that's troubling you. You're never alone. God hasn't left you. He'll see you through."

Naomi knew that. She knew that God was holding out his hands to her through this situation, asking her to trust him completely. She was trying! She truly believed that God hadn't given her a spirit of fear. This wasn't how he intended her to be. She'd been doing so much better, feeling so much stronger and more sure of herself. Then this situation popped up with Tobe . . . with Paisley . . . and now she was a frightened rabbit again. Afraid of her own shadow.

After finishing the tea, Sadie rested her hand on Naomi's back and began to trace circles with her fingers—across her shoulders and down her spine, back and forth, up and down, again and again. As she did, Naomi's heartbeat slowed and her chest relaxed, and she began to feel calmer.

"Nothing controls and calms the mind like full, deep breathing," Sadie said. "Do you remember what I told you about breathing?" She had taught Naomi how to breathe deeply when the pain was at its worst. When you breathed deeply into the lower lobes of the lungs, she explained, you activated the parasympathetic nervous system, which produced endorphins, which in turn made you feel relaxed and calm and helped you let go of distractions.

Sadie told Naomi to match her breathing to hers, and as she did, in and out, in and out, her fears subsided and she fell asleep.

When she woke again, Sadie was still there, with a small plate of apple slices and cheese. "It would be good if you could eat a little bit."

Naomi sat up slowly. The worst was over, the pain had ebbed. She ate a few bites of apple and was relieved when her stomach didn't reject them. "Sadie, have you ever had second thoughts about Gid?"

Sadie's head lifted in surprise. "What? Where in the world did *that* come from?"

"I just wondered . . . did you ever think you might have made a mistake?"

"I made a promise, Naomi, up in front of the church. You were there. You heard me."

"Yes, you said some words . . ."

"Not just words, Naomi, a promise. A solemn oath. For better or worse, sickness or health. I meant those words." She smiled. "Now, I will admit that I probably expected married life to be all sweetness and light and it's not. Not every day, anyway. Life wasn't meant to be easy. But those are the days I remind myself of that promise I made."

"Yes, but does your marriage make you feel safe?"

Sadie tipped her head to one side and peered at Naomi. "There are more important things in life than being safe."

Naomi stared at Sadie and felt as if she'd just pushed open a window and light flooded into the basement to surround her and lift her, helping her mind shrug off the darkness and take wing. Her heart felt free to beat again and her stubborn streak set in. She was tired of worry and what-ifs. Was she going to let herself be chased away from something precious? No, she certainly wasn't, she decided with sudden conviction.

Right then she made up her mind. She wasn't going to be afraid of this woman named Paisley anymore.

As great with child as she was, Paisley walked with a swish and a certainty. There was nothing demure about her. She was flashy—even Mammi Vera agreed on this. Bethany heard her grandmother tut-tutting about Paisley when she thought no one was listening. Her back hurt terribly, though, she said, and that's why she couldn't help with chores around the farm.

Whenever Bethany would ask when her baby was due and where did she expect to deliver this baby, Paisley would turn the full force of her smile upon her. "There's plenty of time for all that," she would say with a wave of her hand. Bethany would smile back and think to herself, *Paisley is delusional on top of being flashy.* That girl looked full of child, like she was ready to give birth any minute.

But soon, Bethany stopped smiling back. Anytime Paisley was in close proximity to Jimmy Fisher, she found a way to bump against him or touch him.

By week's end, Jimmy wasn't coming around anymore.

One sunny afternoon, Danny asked Mim to stay after school. He waited until the students had all left, then locked up the schoolhouse and walked beside Mim toward Eagle Hill. On the way, he explained that Nancy Blank, mother of Mose, an easygoing ten-year-old boy who was often teased by the others, had come to the schoolhouse earlier in the week. "She's worried about Mose—he's getting pushed around by the big boys on the way home from school each day. She said if she mentions her concern to his father that he tells her to stay out of it. Leroy Blank is the type who thinks being bullied will make a man out of his son."

From the disdainful look on Danny's face, Mim could tell what he thought of that kind of parenting. In an odd flash of maturity, she realized that Danny was probably much like Mose as a young boy—gentle, kind, and a target for bullies.

"I've been watching how the older boys act toward Mose," Danny said. "I haven't actually seen anything to worry about during recesses, but I don't doubt Nancy about the walk home. I wondered if you had any suggestions, other than going to speak to the boys' parents—which might create more problems." He glanced at her. "I thought you might have a solution."

Mim nearly smiled. It was typical of Danny to look for a diplomatic way to solve a problem. "I think he needs to make a friend of Jesse and Luke," she said after some thought.

"Jesse Stoltzfus?" He looked skeptical. Very, very skeptical. "And your brother Luke?"

"He's as smart as a whip, that Jesse. Luke could be too, if he ever set his mind to anything."

"Why not with Sammy? They're closer in age."

"Mose is gentle. He doesn't need another gentle friend like Sammy. He needs an ally."

"How do I encourage Jesse to be a friend to Mose? Or Luke?"

"Maybe put them on a project together. Make them stay after class to help you, so they get to know each other without the other big boys interfering."

Danny pushed his glasses up on the bridge of his nose. "I'll give it some thought. Thanks, Mim. I knew you'd have some good advice."

When Danny thanked her, it almost brought tears to her eyes. It was so easy to solve a little problem for someone else when they asked, and so hard to sort out your own. She gave him a smile, a real smile this time, which she hadn't done in months, and she wondered what Danny would think if he knew she was Mrs. Miracle.

All at once, Danny turned. His face was shadowed, but she could see his eyes—very, very blue eyes—watching her, waiting. "Mim," he started hesitantly, "it won't be long until—"

Who knew what might have happened next? She would never know, because in the next second Jesse and Levi came soaring down the Stoltzfuses' driveway on their scooters, screaming like banshees, and Mim and Danny had to scatter to get out of the way so they wouldn't get plowed over.

The moment was over, it might never come again.

Danny and Mim looked at each other, pretended they hadn't, and went home.

Brooke sat across from Jon Hoeffner at the Sweet Tooth Bakery. A cinnamon roll and a coffee—with two dollops of cream, just the way she liked it—were waiting for her at her place.

Today was the second time Jon had ordered for her and the first time he had paid for her. Things were definitely progressing between them. He was adept at conversation and peppered her with questions about her work, her family, her upbringing, her plans for the future . . . of which she had none.

"Aren't you planning to go back to the museum?"

She stirred her coffee. Could she tell him? Should she? "I was . . . let go."

"Ah . . . the pain of downsizing."

"Not exactly. There was a . . . ," she paused, brushing her hand in the air as if to shoo a fly, ". . . tiny misunderstanding."

Jon's eyes went soft and she melted. There was just something about his eyes. Mesmerizing. "Do you want to talk about it?"

Actually, she would. She wanted to vent to someone safe, someone outside of the art world, and Jon was the ideal person. She didn't have anyone else to talk to about the injustice, the humiliation of getting fired. She told him the whole story, starting with her credit card debt, and the meeting with the art dealer who told her about a client, a man who was a devoted lover of Jean-Baptiste-Camille Corot plein air studies.

Jon interrupted, a quizzical look on his face. "Forgive my ignorance, but who is Jean-Baptiste-Camille Corot?"

Brooke tried to mask the shock she felt. Who didn't know the work of Jean-Baptiste-Camille Corot? "He's an artist from the nineteenth century who was, and is, enormously popular in America. He was an innovator. He bridged the gap between Neoclassical painters and Romantic painters and inspired the Impressionists."

She was afraid she might sound too know-it-all-ish and would scare him off the way she intimidated other men, but Jon seemed fascinated. "Go on," he said encouragingly.

"The Neoclassical painters felt that landscape should have a serious, moralizing purpose. Romantic painters felt the role of nature was to transport the viewer to imaginary places. Corot allowed for both. He responded to nature with his emotions, yet he also was astutely accurate in how he depicted nature—capturing specific weather conditions or the way that light transformed color."

She pulled out her iPhone and googled a few Corot paintings to show Jon. "Do you recognize any of these?" She scrolled through them, but he didn't seem to know the artist. "Corot has a signature brushwork. It starts bold, then matures into a feathery, light touch."

"I don't know much about art, but I'd like to know more. Meeting you makes me all the more determined to learn."

Was he flirting with her? Brooke's heart started to pound. He reached out and took her phone, brushing her fingers with his. He was definitely flirting with her.

"So which of these paintings did you reproduce?"

"None that were well known. When Corot died, it was a surprise to collectors to find over 300 paintings and plein air sketches in his studio. Those sketches became the inspiration for the large, formal works that eventually hung in the Paris salons." She described how she painstakingly practiced Jean-Baptist-Camille Corot's soft brushwork, studied the majority of his paintings, honed his light-drenched palette of colors. She paused. "It hadn't occurred to me before, but I think his landscapes are one of the reasons I feel so intrigued by Lancaster County. The hazy fog we had this morning, the radiance of light—it reminds me of his nature scenes. The topography is light-drenched, luminous . . ." Her voice drifted off. She really needed to start sketching the landscape. It had completely slipped her mind.

"So . . . ," Jon said politely, in a tone to remind her she had veered off topic. "So . . . you reproduced a painting of Corot and sold it to the art dealer."

"That's what was supposed to happen. What actually happened was that the dealer sold it to a collector as an original. When it was discovered, the art dealer had vanished, and even though I wasn't legally implicated, I lost my job."

Jon tilted his head. "There must be a little part of you that feels somewhat pleased you had pulled a fast one on the art world."

Brooke shrugged. It did, indeed.

"And you had absolutely no idea that the art dealer was going to pawn your painting off as the real thing."

"No."

"Come on, Brooke. Really?" Jon leaned forward, eyes twinkling, and gave her a charming rascal smile. "No idea at all?"

She had never admitted such a thing to anyone. Not a living soul. "Well, maybe just a teeny, tiny hunch."

# 11

As Mim swung along the village road after leaving the Sisters' House, good feelings tumbled about inside her. Even if she were soaked in a downpour, nothing could dampen her spirits today. Just moments ago, Ella had greeted her at the door with a big smile. "Welcome back, Mim. I've missed you."

"Isn't Bethany here?"

"Yes, she was here, but she is not you. People are not as replaceable as . . . a pair of boots."

Ella had missed her! Mim smiled inside and out with pleasure.

Sylvia came to the door behind Ella with a message from Bethany to meet her at the Bent N' Dent. Mim needed to hand off her finished Mrs. Miracle letters to Bethany to be dropped off at the *Stoney Ridge Times*. After finding inspiration in her conversation with Jimmy Fisher, she labored long and hard over the right wording in Mrs. Miracle's response to that vegetarian who didn't want to work in his father's butcher shop:

*Dear Animal Lover,*

    *Naturally, I believe in showing respect to parents. It sounds as if you do have respect for your father. Due to these unique circumstances, I think you are going to have to follow your own path.*

            *Sincerely,*

            *Mrs. Miracle*

Mim felt a sudden chill as a car drove past her and her happy feelings slipped away. It might sound certifiably crazy, but she thought she had noticed that car a couple of times now, driving slowly and then zooming past her. She felt she was being watched. But maybe it just reminded her of today's breakfast conversation with her grandmother.

As she was spooning out oatmeal into dishes this morning, Mammi Vera had told Luke and Sammy that the devil was roaming the earth, looking for victims, eyes going to and fro. "Do not succumb to the devil's attempts to lead you into sin," she had warned them as she handed them each a bowl.

Luke said he had never actually seen the devil so he wasn't fearful of him, but he was curious about what he looked like. That comment horrified Mammi Vera; she clutched her chest and went to find her Bible.

Sammy's eyes grew wide and thoughtful as he pondered Mammi Vera's warning about the devil. Mim, less sensitive than Sammy but more sensitive than Luke, tried to dismiss her grandmother's caution, but thoughts of the devil stood hovering in the air over her head.

What had happened to the good feelings that were just tumbling about inside her? They were gone.

Mim cut through a field, near where there was a ditch for water irrigation. A strange eerie sound floated up from inside the ditch—the devil himself, perhaps—so she hurried her steps.

The devil was calling, "Is anyone there? Anyone at all?"

Mim sped up. Then stopped. The devil sounded suspiciously similar to the monstrous Jesse Stoltzfus.

"Are you a demon?" she called.

"Mim, is that you?"

She hesitated. "Maybe."

"Mim, I need your help! The cow fell into the ditch and I can't get her out. Come and help me."

She walked slowly toward the ditch and peered into it. There was Jesse Stoltzfus, with his sticky-up hair, pushing the backside of a cow, who refused to budge.

He looked up at her. "I need your help."

She pushed her glasses up on her nose. "What should I do?"

"Do you think we could use your apron as a kind of rope?"

Her favorite apron! Used as a cow rope. She unpinned her apron and threw it down to him.

"You pull, I'll push."

That would mean she would have to get down near that dirty, smelly ditch water. She frowned and he noticed.

"Mim, there isn't time to be prissy. I need to get this cow out of this ditch and get her to the barn before milking time. Come down here and help me. You don't have to get into the water—just stay on the edge. Or go get my dad. He's at home."

She had just come from home and didn't want to go all the way back again. Besides, Bethany was waiting for her at the Bent N' Dent. She sighed; her happy feelings had thoroughly dissolved. She hid the manila envelope of Mrs. Miracle letters behind a rock, then climbed down carefully into the disgusting ditch. Jesse wrapped the apron around the cow's neck and twisted the ends, then handed it to Mim who was standing on the edge.

"When I count to three, pull with all your might." He steadied his legs behind the cow and prepared to push. "One, two . . ."

Mim started to pull as Jesse pushed and the cow stood her ground, bawling an unhappy cow sound. She thought she might go deaf.

"Are you pulling?" Jesse shouted.

"Yes!"

With that, the cow decided she had enough of getting pushed and pulled and she threw her head, knocking Mim into the water before charging up the side of the ditch. The cow stood on the edge, peering down at Mim and Jesse, batting her big black eyelashes, as if to ask what they were doing in a dirty ditch.

Jesse waded over and offered Mim a hand, which she reluctantly took. She smelled disgusting!

"I'll help you up the side of the ditch."

"No," she growled. "I'll get myself up."

"Suit yourself." He grabbed the abandoned apron-turned-rope, squeezed it out, and scrambled up the ditch. "No one would ever accuse you of being a garrulous girl."

*Garrulous?* What did that mean? It bothered Mim to not know a word. She collected words. She even read the dictionary. Words were her hobby.

Jesse and the cow peered down at her. He looked at Mim as if she had braved a lion in a den. "You have pluck, Mim." He tipped his hat. "Mim is no name for a lass who rescues a lad and his cow in distress. What's your real name?"

"Miriam."

"You have pluck, Miriam." He grinned. "And I will never forget your act of selfless charity during my time of need. Just another charming quality to add to your long list of charmingness. You will make any man proud to call you his wife one day." He bowed, then bobbed up. "And I will be first in line to try to win your hand."

Wife? Win her hand? Was he *crazy*?! "I would never, ever marry you, Jesse Stoltzfus!"

He grinned, saluted her, and turned away, leading the cow with Mim's apron-turned-rope. She tried to scramble up the ditch as fast as Jesse had done, but it took her a couple of tries. By the time she had reached the top, he was halfway across the field.

"I suppose someone will marry you eventually," she shouted. "But it'll have to be someone who is stone-deaf so she doesn't have to listen to your nonsense!"

He waved cheerfully and kept pulling the cow with the rope-apron to keep her moving forward.

She watched him move the cow along until he disappeared beneath a hill. She looked down at her sopping, dripping dress and tried to wring it out. It was very hard to get the last word in with someone as verbose as Jesse. That Jesse Stoltzfus thought he had the world sorted out.

She remembered the manila envelope filled with letters from Mrs. Miracle and ran to the rock where she had hidden it.

It was gone.

Things between Galen and Rose were not as easy as they had been before Paisley arrived. They'd even had sharp words one afternoon, something that had never happened before, when Rose had complained to him that she still hadn't heard back from Tobe, though he must have received her letter by now. She was anxious to know how he would want her to handle this Paisley person. Should she ask her to leave? Could she do that? Because Paisley was surely not telling the truth about Tobe being the father of her baby.

"Maybe there's a reason he hasn't responded quickly," Galen said.

She frowned at him, knowing what he was thinking. "You've made up your mind ahead of the facts."

"The facts are the facts," Galen said bluntly. "Paisley is pregnant and Tobe Schrock is to blame."

Rose was furious! And she was just about to tell him so when she heard someone call her name. It was her new neighbor, David Stoltzfus, walking up the driveway of Eagle Hill with the rope of a milk cow in his hand.

She wanted to finish this conversation with Galen, but what could she do? She went to greet David. With a big grin, he deposited the rope in her arms. "Your boys told me your cow didn't give much milk. Growing boys need milk."

"That's true. But that's because they forgot to milk her for a few days and she started to dry up. So now milking the cow is Mim's job. Thank you, David." Though to be truthful, Rose didn't want another cow. Milk cows were a heap of trouble. She would have been just as happy to have a bit of extra buttermilk now and then.

But she took the rope from David and watched dumbly as Galen shook his hand, turned to her, and said, "I'd better get back." Left, without another word, without a backward glance.

"Do I smell coffee?" David said, looking up at the kitchen.

"Of course. Go inside. I just started a fresh pot. My mother-in-law Vera is in the kitchen. There's some cherry cobbler from last night's dinner."

David grinned. "I'll cross many a hill for a good cobbler."

She smiled. David Stoltzfus was a fine man, even if Mim couldn't abide his son Jesse. Luke, on the other hand, couldn't get enough of Jesse. He was even starting to talk like him. "I'll take the cow in the barn and be right in to join you."

"My youngest named her Fireball."

"What?!"

He laughed. "She just liked the name." He patted the cow on her big head. "She's gentle. Most times."

The cow seemed as docile as could be, but Rose had been fooled before. "Um, well. Fireball it is. Thank you again, David."

Before she went down to the barn, she turned back and saw Galen at the privet hole, his eyes resting on David with a slightly puzzled look.

Paisley asked more questions than Rose had answers for. She was certainly interested in anything that had to do with making money, particularly how much Eagle Hill was worth. Finally, it got so that whenever Paisley would open her mouth to start to ask another question, Rose would cut her off and talk about something completely mundane, like exactly what was her baby's due date and when had she last seen a doctor? Any mention of the impending delivery of Paisley's baby would cause her to frown and soon she would disappear from the room. It seemed as if Paisley was ignoring the fact that she was about to become a mother.

Vera did not like the way Rose interacted with Paisley and told her so, more than once. "Don't you understand why she is asking so many questions about the farm? She is planning for her future with Tobe. And you're making her feel as if it's wrong to ask."

Rose frowned. "Doesn't it seem that a soon-to-be mother should be asking questions about baby care and getting a layette put together? She hasn't given the baby's arrival a second thought."

"She's anxious about it, that's all."

There could be some truth in that. Rose could remember how unsettled she felt before each of her own babies' births. She should keep trying to withhold her opinion about Paisley until she heard something from Tobe—which should be any day now. At least, she hoped so. She couldn't silence Galen's remark that Tobe wasn't responding because he didn't want them to know the truth. She still felt annoyed with Galen, but she couldn't dismiss the notion that he might be right. She loved Tobe, but she knew his tendency to avoid difficulties.

And yet, she told herself, wasn't Tobe serving a prison sentence because he was willing to face a consequence for withholding evidence? Wasn't that a sign of maturity? It was. Why couldn't Galen see that? Why couldn't he be more of . . . a partner, helping her raise children to reach their fullest potential?

It occurred to her that she'd never had a helpmate, a partner. She thought of Fern and Amos Lapp, who worked together on their farm. Or Bishop Elmo and his wife, Dee, who ran a quilt shop together. Two become one. She'd heard it said dozens of times in marriage ceremonies. She and Dean had promised it, but it had never happened.

What if Galen were more like Dean than she had thought? A man who couldn't change his mind or listen to a woman's good sense . . . why, that behavior *was* just like Dean's. Maybe that's what all men were like, deep down. Stubborn and prideful.

One thing she had discovered about Dean, early on—he refused to change. After thirteen years of marriage, they were struggling with the same tangled issues: Dean's pie-in-the-sky dreams, his big promises, and his appallingly poor judgment. He felt she didn't support him, didn't respect him, didn't cheerlead for him. But how could you show support to someone who made terrible decisions, one after the other?

She hated to admit it, even to herself, but Dean's death brought some relief. Sorrow for what might have been, lost hope that things might have improved in time, pressure for all that fell alone on her shoulders now. But a measure of relief. She cringed. Wasn't that a terrible way to think about your dead husband?

She remembered the Christmas when Dean told her that he was going to start his own investment business. No more working for others who took all the profit.

"Why do we need it?" Rose had asked.

"What's need?" He put his arms on her shoulders and looked into her eyes.

"Haven't we enough?" she asked, trying to rephrase the same question.

"It'll be a gold mine. It's made for us." He looked so eager. He said he would love the challenge.

He convinced her that he was right, that the opportunity was made for him and the time was now. But she couldn't ignore the feeling that he was taking on that kind of a career risk just to be a significant man. Just for show. To show some anonymous people who didn't even care.

When Schrock Investments started to flounder, Rose wasn't at all surprised. In fact, she was expecting it. In that way, she had to admit, she wasn't much of a partner to Dean either.

Maybe she was too independent for her own good. Dean had often said so. Maybe she was better off alone.

Certainly, Galen needed someone who could give him babies, not grandbabies. Earlier today, her heart missed a beat when Paisley called her a grandmother-to-be. It hadn't occurred to her that this baby could be her grandchild. Why, she was barely thirty-seven years old!

Rose couldn't get past the disquieting notion that she was missing something important about Paisley. It dangled in front of her, a ripe apple on a tree that she couldn't quite reach.

So many unanswered questions.

She didn't know what to do. She just had no idea what to do.

"Rose, doesn't something seem odd about that Paisley girl?"

Rose looked up from watering the garden to find Bethany, standing with hands on her hips in that defiant way she had. Rose smiled. She didn't know where to begin with all the red flags that had been waving at her since she had met Paisley, but she didn't want to share those worries with Bethany. "What do you mean?"

"She's supposed to be head over heels in love with Tobe, but anytime she's anywhere near Jimmy Fisher, she finds a way to be right next to him, like she's a cat and he's a scratching post."

Rose bit on her lip to hold back a laugh. She turned off the hose. "Tobe will be able to shed light on this topic. Until then, your grandmother is right. We need to be hospitable."

Later that night, as Rose got ready for bed, she took off her apron and stored the pins in the apron belt. She untied the stiff strings of her prayer cap and twisted her head from side to side, stretching the ache of a long day out of her neck. She put the cap on the top of her dresser and her eye caught Allen Turner's SEC business card that she had tucked into the mirror frame. Should she ask him to contact Tobe and find out who Paisley was? But she couldn't even imagine how to frame the request: A girlfriend from Tobe's past has shown up, out of the blue, about to deliver his baby. Would you ask him if he remembers her? She could just imagine the long pause as solemn Allen Turner took in that news, wondering how he got so involved with an Amish family and their trivial woes.

She changed into her nightgown and climbed into bed, its springs squeaking softly as she slipped under the covers. She reached over and opened her Bible, silently reading the words of Psalm 139, lips moving to each word. She needed to be reminded to dwell in the knowledge that God knew all there was to know. Everything.

"O Lord, Thou hast searched me and known me. Thou dost know when I sit down and when I rise up; Thou dost understand my thought from afar . . ."

She read it through twice before turning off the flashlight.

"Dear Lord," she prayed, "please give me answers. Soon. Now. Amen."

Slowly, slowly, she let herself relax into the darkness, closing her eyes, letting the words of Scripture move through her.

The barn was redolent with the familiar musty smell of hay and horses. Mim set her stool at Molly's flank and the pail beneath her speckled udder. Her mother had warned everyone to stay clear of the new cow, to let Galen do the first few milkings. There must be a reason she was named Fireball, she warned Mim. As she started to milk Molly, the plink of the milk in the pail drummed a steady beat. Outside, strutting along the roof of the hen house, Harold the rooster was crowing. She heard horses nickering to each other in the pastures as her brother wheeled hay out to them in the old blue wheelbarrow. How could it be an ordinary day?

Mim pressed her forehead against Molly's warm belly. She wondered idly if cows were ever scared—really scared. She had seen Molly jitter away from Micky the dog, but that was different. A yapping pup at your heels was an immediate threat, but the difference between her and Molly was that when there was no dog in sight, Molly was perfectly content, rhythmically chewing her cud. She wasn't wondering and worrying, while anxiety ate holes through all her stomachs.

Mim closed her eyes and her hands stilled as she wondered how this week had gone so terribly awry. The insufferable Jesse Stoltzfus had stolen her envelope full of Mrs. Miracle letters, and for some reason and without saying so much as a word to her, he had delivered them to the newspaper. They were in yesterday's edition.

Molly shifted her big back hip and Mim snapped to attention. Maybe everything would turn out all right. Maybe Jesse had the decency to deliver them to the *Stoney Ridge Times* newspaper office without opening the envelope. The address was on the front of the envelope and it was sealed. Mim made sure of that because she didn't want Bethany poking through them. Yes. It was entirely possible that she was worrying for naught.

Her father used to say that the perfect state of mind was halfway between Luke and Mim; Luke never saw worries or responsibilities even if he was surrounded by them. But Mim, he would add, always faced a thousand worries long before one appeared on the horizon.

She smiled at her silly fears, at the woolgathering she'd been doing, and lifted her forehead from Molly's warm hide to set to work, making the milk pail ring.

Brooke Snyder hurried to the Sweet Tooth Bakery and was disappointed to see that the store was crowded and that Jon Hoeffner wasn't sitting at their usual table. In fact, he wasn't even in the bakery. Brooke asked the woman who sat at their special table if she was going to be there very long. The woman glanced at the wall clock. "Maybe just a few more minutes and then it's all yours." She motioned to Brooke to go ahead and sit down. "I'm Penny Williams. I work as the receptionist over at the *Stoney Ridge Times*."

"Nice to meet you. I'm Brooke Snyder."

Penny Williams wore pointy glasses and her hair in a tight doughnut bun on the top of her head. "I haven't seen you around. Are you new to Stoney Ridge?"

"I'm staying out at Eagle Hill for an extended vacation. I'm . . . in between jobs." Brooke took a sip of coffee. "I've been reading your newspaper." She leaned across the table. "I would love to have an introduction to Mrs. Miracle."

Penny smiled. "Join the crowd. So would everyone. The features editor, especially. He's been wanting to talk to her for weeks now. But no one knows her true identity."

*Intriguing!*

Penny lowered her voice. "Just between you and me—that column is the reason most people buy this paper. About six months ago, it was on its last legs—it was only getting published a few times a week. But Mrs. Miracle has changed all that. It's back to being a daily newspaper. The editor said he's got an offer to syndicate. That's why he's trying to track her down." She rubbed the tips of her fingers together. "Syndication means big bucks."

Brooke leaned back in her seat. "You're telling me that the paper's livelihood is dependent on someone no one has ever met?"

Offended, Penny stiffened. "I said no such thing. Any paper's livelihood is dependent on advertisers. What I did say was that Mrs. Miracle's column has boosted circulation. Considerably. And that makes advertisers very happy. Which makes the publisher and editors happy too."

"What makes Mrs. Miracle's column so unique?" Brooke added cream to her coffee and stirred. "There are plenty of advice columns."

"Mrs. Miracle sees things in a different way. And she has a knack for pointing people back to the most important things in life. The column used to be once a week, now it's twice a week, and the editor wants it to go to three times a week."

"What *do* you know about Mrs. Miracle?"

Penny shrugged. "Nothing, really. An Amish girl drops off the column and picks up her paycheck and she won't reveal the identity of Mrs. Miracle. I've tried."

Brooke's mouth dropped open. "Are you telling me that Mrs. Miracle is an Amish girl?"

"I said no such thing." Penny's feathers ruffled again. "Absolutely not. Not a chance. Around here, a lot of Amish girls work for the non-Amish— doing errands and housecleaning, that sort of thing. My guess is Mrs. Miracle is a well-to-do woman in her sixties. She's seen it all." She looked at the clock. "I'd better get back to the office. Nice to meet you, Brittany."

"Brooke. Brooke Snyder." But Penny was already out the door and hurrying down the street.

All afternoon, as Brooke strolled through the little Main Street shops, hoping to bump into Jon, she pondered the secret identity of Mrs. Miracle. Could she be Amish? These Plain people kept surprising her. She stopped and picked up a copy of today's newspaper and sat on a sidewalk bench in the sun to read it. Automatically, she turned to the Mrs. Miracle column. As she started to read, she sat up. *There* was her letter to Mrs. Miracle!

So what advice would Mrs. Miracle have for her predicament?

*Dear Borrower,*

*Rather than try to change yourself or copy others, why not try to accept the person you're intended to be? The thing about looking for a new identity is that, when all is said and done, you're still you. Wherever you go, there you'll be.*

*Sincerely,*
*Mrs. Miracle*

Wait. *What?* Brooke had heard that same thing before, but where? Where, where, where? Slowly, awareness dawned on her. Could it be? Could it possibly be?

Fourteen-year-old Mim Schrock *was* Mrs. Miracle.

# 12

Later that afternoon, Rose was down in the barn. She clipped a lead line to the mare and led her out to the pasture, her little foal trotting behind. Her mother-in-law Vera met her out in the yard as she closed the gate. "Rose, what did you say to Paisley to get her all . . . jittery?"

"What do you mean?"

"She's in there pacing around the house like a caged tiger."

Rose rolled her eyes. "An apt description. She seems a little like a tiger."

"You shouldn't be aggravating her so."

Rose stopped in her tracks. "Do you honestly believe her story? You think she's Tobe's girlfriend? Tobe might have sowed some wild oats, but does she seem like the kind of girl he would be interested in?"

"Tobe has been under a great deal of stress. People aren't themselves when they're stressed." Vera bristled. "And he would do the right thing by her."

"Vera, a girl like Paisley could never become Amish. You must see that, don't you? She would only keep him from the church."

"If you would just show a little kindness, she might be interested in joining our people. You're not even giving her a chance."

Rose was astounded. Vera found fault with nearly everyone—all but Dean, her son, and Tobe and Bethany, her favorite grandchildren. And now Paisley was added to the brief list. Paisley, of all people? "That girl came here out of the blue. What do we know about her?"

"She says she's carrying Tobe's baby. What else do we need to know?"

"I won't believe that until I hear it from Tobe."

"You have to be in control of everybody and everything, don't you?"

Rose flinched. Just as she was about to open her mouth to say something she was sure she would regret, Luke and Sammy burst out of the house and ran to meet Rose in the yard. "Paisley said to come quick! She's having her baby! Right now! Right on the kitchen floor!"

Six hours later, a baby girl was born to Paisley at the Lancaster County Hospital. Rose stayed by Paisley's side as she labored. She wiped her forehead with a cool cloth and fed her ice chips, all the while realizing that Paisley was completely, thoroughly unprepared for bringing a newborn into the world. When the contractions rolled over her, overwhelming her, she screamed out in pain and insisted she didn't want to be a mother.

Paisley took in a breath and blew it out slowly. "I'm not qualified."

"Every new mother feels that way. I certainly did."

"Please," Paisley pleaded, clinging to Rose's hand. "Get it out. Whatever you have to do, just get it out."

"You're doing it," Rose said, with a calm she didn't feel. "There's only one way to get through this. You're the only one who can get this baby out . . . and you're doing it."

A long, moaning wail emerged out of Paisley. Her body was finally surrendering; she stopped fighting, and the baby began to move, slowly, down the birth canal and into the doctor's waiting arms.

The room went still. A time that was usually so joyful, buzzing with activity, but no one spoke. The obstetrician and nurses had serious looks on their faces as the pediatrician examined the baby. There was a flurry of whispering, then the baby was briefly shown to Paisley before getting whisked away.

Paisley grabbed Rose's arm. "Something's wrong with it."

Rose looked to the nurse to answer.

The nurse was checking Paisley's blood pressure and kept her eyes fixed on the blood pressure monitor. "The baby's being looked after right now. The doctor will talk to you soon." She unwrapped the blood pressure cuff from Paisley's arms. Then, more kindly, she said, "You must be exhausted.

After we get you cleaned up, you should try to sleep." She nodded in Rose's direction. "You too."

As soon as Paisley drifted to sleep, Rose went back to Eagle Hill to get a few hours' sleep, then returned around noon.

Paisley was curled up in the hospital bed, facing the window, away from the baby in the bassinet next to her.

"How are you feeling?" Rose asked her, before bending to kiss the sleeping baby's forehead.

Paisley didn't want to talk. She wasn't interested in seeing the baby, holding it, nursing it. Rose was appalled; she kept encouraging her to look at the baby, but the nurse assured her that wasn't entirely unusual, under the circumstances.

The nurse motioned to Rose to meet her in the hallway. "The doctor wants to talk to you." She pointed to the pediatrician standing in scrubs by the nurses' station, filling out paperwork.

The doctor sat down with Rose and told her what she already knew after seeing the epicanthic folds around the baby's eyes last night before she was whisked away. She had seen it before. She had known it the moment she saw the baby. This was a special child. One with Down syndrome.

"We ran a number of tests last night and the baby seems to be very healthy," the doctor explained. "Sometimes, these babies have heart defects."

Rose let out a deep sigh. "I assume you've already told this to Paisley?"

He nodded. "She's still in shock. She had no idea the baby would have an issue. Nowadays, an anatomical ultrasound would pick up markers that give indication of chromosomal defects. She said she never had one. I don't see this kind of case very often, where a mother doesn't realize she's going to have a baby with Down's."

"I don't think she had any prenatal care."

He put the pen back in his shirt pocket. "In this day and age, there's a lot of counseling available to help. Most T-21 kids grow up to be loving, caring individuals. As the baby develops, everything will take longer, each new skill will be a huge hurdle, but your granddaughter should have a full and happy life. She'll just need extra time for everything." He patted Rose's arm. "I can't deny it gives me peace of mind to think this child will be raised in an Amish home. I know your people perceive handicapped children differently than the non-Amish."

"Special children," Rose said in a distracted way.

"Pardon?"

"That's what we call them. Not handicapped."

Pleased, he bobbed his head. "That's just what I meant. Exactly that."

His pager went off and he excused himself, so Rose went to sit by Paisley's bed. "Did you notice the baby's ten little fingers and ten toes, Paisley? Perfect."

"She's *not* perfect."

Rose reached out and patted Paisley's bent knee. "Everything will be all right. You'll see." She tried hard to stop her voice from sounding like Paisley's mother or her schoolteacher.

"I've heard that line before." Paisley yanked her knee away and turned her head. "Nothing ever works out the way it should for me."

Rose tried several times to get Paisley interested in the baby, but with no success. Paisley didn't want anything to do with the baby; she just wanted to leave the hospital. The baby had weak muscle tone for sucking, which might make nursing difficult, so the nurse provided a bottle with a specially designed nipple that the baby accepted. Once the baby started to take the bottle consistently, the doctor agreed to let them go home, as long as the baby was brought back for a follow-up physical in two days.

"I think Paisley might adjust to the baby a little better at home than here," he said to Rose as he signed the release papers.

Rose hoped he was right, but knew otherwise.

The last thing Paisley needed to do before she could be released from the hospital was to fill out the birth certificate. She said she didn't care what Rose called the baby so she chose the name Sarah, after a favorite cousin who had Down's. All Paisley cared about was that Tobias Schrock was named as the baby's father on the birth certificate.

"The name you put on that birth certificate has to be legal. Tobe will have to sign the birth certificate to admit to being the father of your child."

Paisley blinked, then scribbled Tobe's name on the line. "And why would he not?"

Well, for one, Rose thought, he might not be the baby's father. She didn't say it aloud, though, because she actually felt a little sorry for Paisley. She couldn't imagine how she would feel if she were in Paisley's shoes right now and so she didn't even try. She thought it would be best to try to support her as she stepped into motherhood. Was it possible for a woman to simply not have a capacity to mother her own child?

With a jolt, she thought of Dean's first wife, Tobe and Bethany's mother, whom she knew little about. Dean rarely mentioned her, nor did Vera. All that Rose knew of Mary Miller Schrock was that she abandoned her young children, divorced Dean, and left someone else to pick up the pieces of a shattered family. Two years later, Rose became that someone.

She cringed, feeling an odd foreboding.

Whoever that fourteenth cousin twice removed thought he was, he still needed to have his sheets changed and wastebasket emptied. The day came when Bethany was fed up waiting for him to show himself. She found a screwdriver and pins and jimmied the lock open to the second-floor guest-room. She turned the knob and cautiously opened the door. She couldn't believe it. She walked slowly into the room. From the unmade bed to the clothes that littered the floor, the room was in complete chaos. Candy wrappers, gum wrappers, old newspapers, soda cans, crumpled dinner napkins, tin foil, cookies, and crackers.

Clothing lay in a soiled heap in the corner. The bed was full of crumbs. The remains of a sandwich lay on the pillow, and an open bag of potato chips had been shoved under the blanket. Nothing had been washed or cleaned since the day the old sisters' fourteenth cousin twice removed had arrived.

Well, she thought, as she stripped the bed, if she had any doubts about his connection to the sisters before today, the condition of this room squelched them. The fourteenth cousin twice removed fit right in with his elderly relatives.

Mim arrived at the schoolhouse early one morning and put her books in her desk. On top of her desk was her "What Pennsylvania Means to Me" essay that she had labored over, graded and returned: B- in big fat red ink.

She slunk into her seat, disappointed and frustrated, angry with Danny Riehl, who thought he was so smart. She opened her desk and was startled to find a red rose—the first of the season, lying on top of her neatly folded and freshly laundered apron-turned-rope that saved the cow in the ditch. There was a card attached:

*A boy met a girl as sweet as caramel,*
*Of all the girls, he thought she was the pinnacle,*
*But she thought he was quite unbearable.*
*To win her hand, he would need help from . . . Mrs. Miracle.*

Mim gasped! Then . . . cringed. Trust Jesse Stoltzfus to make this into a big, big deal. She *knew* he was going to torture her over the identity of Mrs. Miracle. She ripped up the note and scrunched up the rose and stomped to the garbage to throw them away. That Jesse Stoltzfus! He was a loathsome creature. When she turned around, Danny was peering at her with a curious look on his face. "Everything all right, Mim?"

"No! It's not all right. My paper should be an A." She cringed again. Did she really just say that?

He was very Teacher Danny now, sitting at his desk, peering down at her. "I gave you a B- because I believe you can do better."

A few children came into the classroom and put their lunch boxes on the shelf that lined the back wall. Danny glanced at them and lowered his voice. "We can talk about your essay after school, if you like."

She didn't like. She felt just as mad at him as she did at Jesse Stoltzfus. Even madder. Her essay was excellent. Just excellent. He was being intentionally hard on her and she didn't know why.

When Jesse came into the classroom, she purposefully ignored him, though she doubted he noticed. He was too busy crowing to Luke and Mose over the A+ on his stupid essay. When he passed by her desk, he whispered, "B minus?" turned, and wiggled his eyebrows at her. She snapped her head away from his goofy face.

Why couldn't there be another girl in her grade? Or seventh grade. Sixth, even. She was surrounded by horrible, terrible, abominable boys.

On the way home from school that day, she stopped at a horse trough in the field of the nearly-falling-down barn and leaned over to look at her face in the water. "This face," she said, "belongs to someone who can write well enough to have her own advice column in a newspaper, despite what Teacher Danny seems to think. And she has pluck. And this is me, Mim." She stopped. Jesse was right. Mim was no name for someone who could write as well as she could. "Miriam."

What a day. She had been given her first rose, was humiliated by Danny Riehl and mortified by Jesse Stoltzfus. *What* a day.

Rose, Paisley, and the baby returned to Eagle Hill that evening, barely twenty-four hours after the baby had been born. The house was quiet; Vera, Mim, and the boys had gone to bed, Bethany was out with Jimmy Fisher, and Rose was thankful for a quiet entry. There would be time tomorrow for everyone to ooh and aah over the baby.

Paisley went straight upstairs to bed. Rose hadn't heard anyone come into the kitchen but suddenly looked up and found Naomi standing by the doorjamb, looking at the tiny baby sleeping in the Moses basket in the corner. In her arms was a small pink baby quilt she had just completed.

"I had a feeling the baby was a girl," she said, a shy smile on her face.

Somehow, that didn't surprise Rose. Naomi was known for those kinds of presentiments. Rose wasn't sure if she had a unique gift or if she just listened to her intuition better than most. "The baby quilt is her first gift, Naomi." She took the quilt from her and laid it on the table. One-inch squares of pink fabrics in varying shades were perfectly cut, sewn, and quilted with Naomi's precise stitches. "What a treasure you've given her."

But Naomi wasn't even listening. She was transfixed by the baby. That intense look she had on her face—well, for the first time, Rose noticed how she and Galen resembled each other. Naomi's hair was coffee-brown, like his was, her face was angular like his, though their eyes were a different color, and her features were far less classically attractive than her brother's. She wasn't beautiful, but she was. She had the beauty of happiness.

"Can I pick the baby up?" Naomi whispered softly, as if she were standing on hallowed ground.

"Of course," Rose told her. "Her name is Sarah."

She watched as Naomi lifted the tiny baby nervously, almost shyly, and held her to her chest. She said nothing, just walked around the downstairs in a big loop. She mumbled something soft, a prayer or a poem or a tuneless lullaby—Rose couldn't make it out. Naomi's hold on the baby was sure, her love obvious.

After Naomi left, Rose went into Paisley's room with the baby. Seeing that Paisley's eyes were open, Rose started to take the baby to her, but she turned away to face the wall. Rose took the baby to her own room to lie down for a while. She was afraid to trust Sarah with her mother yet.

She dozed lightly, wakened by the baby whimpering, and went downstairs to warm a bottle for her before Sarah started to cry. She sat in the rocker and held the baby against her, reminded of those exhausting days with her own babies: of Mim and of Luke and Sammy. How had she survived them? She remembered feeling too tired to rise.

When the baby had taken all she would from the bottle, Rose wrapped her tightly in a swaddle, the way babies like best, and sat down to rock her to sleep. The moon was full, sending streaming beams of light into the living room.

Little Sarah fell sound asleep, tucked against her breast. She stroked the baby's wispy tuft of dark hair. Was it her imagination or did the baby look more helpless and alone than any other child? As if she knew she was motherless and fatherless from the moment she had come on earth. "You could be worse off," Rose whispered. "Your mother's a fool not to want you, but maybe she was smart to wait until she got to people who would look after you."

But it wasn't really smarts, Rose feared—Paisley just didn't care.

# 13

The full moon flooded Naomi's bedroom with yellow light, as bright as day. She wasn't asleep. She couldn't sleep tonight. She hadn't been able to stop thinking about the baby at Eagle Hill Farm. There was something about her that deeply touched her.

When she held the baby for the first time, she had gazed down into Sarah's little face, and Sarah gazed back at her, her eyes large and shiny. Trusting.

A silent communication had passed between them in that moment, deep and heartfelt.

Naomi had breathed in deeply that sweet newborn smell. Sarah's neck was so small and fragile looking. Her skin was soft and she smelled better than any human being Naomi had ever been near. Unexpected pleasure stole over her. She understood, suddenly, why everything that mothers went through—the long nights, the endless crying, the daily weariness—was worth the sacrifice to them.

Naomi's thoughts drifted to her own mother, long gone, knowing that her mother must have held her in the same way. Her throat swelled and tears rushed to her eyes, but she kept up the gentle motion she had watched Rose use with Sarah to rock her to sleep. Back and forth. Back and forth.

The baby's eyes held innocence and a sort of uncanny wisdom. They continued to look at each other for a long stretch, then Sarah's lids grew heavy and fluttered shut. Rose told Naomi to set the baby in her basket to sleep, but she couldn't bring herself to let her go. She had ended up staying in that rocker for hours.

An owl hooted once, then twice. Naomi should try to sleep. She rolled onto her side to face the wall, away from the bright window. A faint sense that she had forgotten something needled the back of her mind. What was it? Something definitely was missing. Had she left something over at Eagle Hill?

And then it hit her. The thing that had disappeared? Her anxiety. Gone, like a wisp of steam from a teacup. Vanished into thin air.

Her stomach? Settled. Headache? None. Nerves? Steady. Heartbeat? Normal. Breathing? Calm and relaxed.

Astonished, she thought of Sarah, sleeping peacefully in her arms this evening. *She'd* done this, she realized. This tiny gift of a baby had stilled the roiling inside of her. This little person she scarcely knew and already loved.

"I'm going to help you, Sarah," she whispered aloud, as if the baby were still in her arms and could understand her words. "Your mother brought you to us, for whatever reason, and it's the right place for you. I'm going to help you. You're safe here."

Naomi released a deep sigh, and fell asleep.

The next morning, Rose sat on the porch swing, holding the baby in the morning sunlight. The nurse had suggested that the baby get some sun each day to help combat jaundice.

"Hey there."

She looked up to see Galen, a gentle smile lighting his eyes. "Well, hello." She lifted her arms slightly. "Meet our newest houseguest."

He came up on the porch and moved some papers to sit beside her on the swing. He held out a finger for the baby to grab on to. "A special baby."

"Yes. A special child." She smiled at the way Galen was gazing at the baby. He was such a masculine man, all angles, no nonsense—but his face was now soft and tender. To see the baby's little hand grasping his strong finger touched her heart.

He glanced at the papers on the porch swing. "Hospital bills?"

The baby closed her eyes, drifted to sleep. "Yes," Rose said. "Paisley had them all billed to me."

"Well, don't worry about them now," Galen said. "Have a little faith."

Rose wanted to have that kind of faith. She truly believed anything was possible with God. "I think it will take a miracle to get those bills paid."

"We could have a benefit to raise money."

"I can't ask Bishop Elmo for yet another benefit for the Schrock family."

"Sure you can. That's what we do for each other." He nudged her. "You would do it for anyone else."

True, but somehow, it was always easier to give than receive. "Naomi's been a wonderful help. Yesterday she was here all evening, then again this morning."

"She likes babies."

The baby startled awake and Rose transferred her to her shoulder. "Naomi is so remarkably mature." She was like her brother in that way. Mature beyond her years. She glanced at Galen. "I can't imagine what must be running through her mind about Tobe." The moment the words left her mouth, she wished them back.

He flashed her a look of impatience. "You're looking for something that isn't there. Naomi has never even mentioned Tobe. Probably doesn't even think twice about him."

Annoyed, she rose to her feet. "Galen, you're the only one who doesn't think twice about Tobe." She passed the baby to him. "I need to go get a bottle ready. Hold her for a moment, will you?"

"Me?" His voice sounded almost . . . frightened.

She smiled and her irritation with him dissolved. Imagine that. Galen King was intimidated by a little six-pound baby.

Bethany came outside to feed the hens and was startled to see Galen King on the porch swing, holding the baby as if she were made of spun sugar. He looked up when he heard the door open, a shy, embarrassed smile cracking his face, as if he'd been caught.

"I have some news about Lodestar," he said, quickly passing the baby to her.

Bethany couldn't read anything in his demeanor. Galen was such a steady man that good and bad news would probably sound the same, something to be dealt with either way. She sat down on the porch swing to hear what he had to say, awkwardly shifting the baby into her other arm as the baby started making mewling sounds. She wasn't accustomed to newborn babies and had only met this one an hour ago. Where was Rose with that bottle, anyway?

"A farrier knew of a horse that was being used as a mini-backyard breeding factory. The farrier was called out to keep his hooves trimmed on a regular basis. He didn't know the owner and was concerned he might not get paid if no one was around during the shoeing, so he asked to be paid in advance."

"What makes you think it could be Lodestar?"

"He described the horse's unusual looks—that long flaxen mane, the golden coat—from the sound of it, it resembled Lodestar. But I can't be sure."

Bethany sat up in the porch swing. "Let's go find out."

"Now, hold on. There's more to the story. The horse has been kept in a pasture with an electric fence surrounding it. The farrier said the first time he trimmed his hooves, everything was in order. But the second time, the horse looked thinner, dirty and unkempt, like no one was taking care of him. And this last time, the farrier found him in really bad shape. Ribs showing, living in filth, bad water in the rain bucket. Hoof rot too, so he wasn't able to shoe him."

Her heart was beating fast. "Galen, we need to rescue him!"

"It's more complicated than just going and getting him. I'm not even positive it is Lodestar. Besides, the farrier is involved. He said he called Equine Rescue and they're going out this week to check on the horse."

"Could we ask the farrier to take us out to see the horse? Just to see if this horse might be Lodestar?"

"I suppose we could." He took off his hat. "On one condition. I didn't tell the farrier the whole story—about Jimmy Fisher and Jake Hertzler. I just want to take things one step at a time. If it's not Lodestar, we just leave the situation alone and let Equine Rescue handle it. We don't get involved." He looked right at her. "Is that understood?"

"But what if it is Lodestar?" The baby's face scrunched up in distress and Bethany glanced at the kitchen window. Where was Rose?

Galen gave her a warning look. "We'll still take things one step at a time."

"Okay."

He put his hat back on. "You realize we might be walking into trouble, don't you?"

Bethany grinned, even as the baby started to howl. "I do. But to quote Jimmy Fisher, some things are worth a little trouble."

Mim discovered something new about herself: she did not like babies. In fact, she thought babies were revolting and couldn't understand why her mother and Naomi practically stumbled over each other as they went to pick Sarah up and soothe her when she started to howl. Babies might not know how to do much, but they sure knew how to scream. And when the baby wasn't screaming, her mouth was always open and drooling. And those vile diapers! How could anyone so very small need to be changed ten times a day?

Nothing felt normal since Paisley had come to Eagle Hill.

Bethany was preoccupied, her mind seemed a million miles away. Luke was continually in a bad mood and would argue with Sammy at the drop of a hat. Her mother would get upset and send them to their room; she was tired every evening and had no time to talk about school or anything.

Mammi Vera, usually bleak and mournful, was actually acting a tiny bit happy at having a squawling baby in the house. That, too, wasn't normal. She was *never* happy. But Mim noticed that Mammi Vera didn't offer to change Sarah's vile-smelling diapers or wipe the drool off her little pink cheeks.

Mim choked down another bite of oatmeal and wondered if Mammi Vera would notice if she added more sugar. It could be she had already forgotten the first four spoonfuls, but you never knew with Mammi Vera. Some things she forgot right off and others she remembered. Like what someone died from. Old people were always trying to figure out what people died from, or how many sisters and brothers they had and what they died from. That made up half the conversations Mim had to sit through when she helped Bethany at the Sisters' House.

She put down her spoon and stared at her oatmeal, thinking of how huffy her mother became a few minutes ago when Mim shared the suspicions and whispers that were buzzing around the school playground about the fatherless baby at Eagle Hill.

"Suspicions and whispers? That's the most ridiculous thing I've ever heard. What kinds of friends do you think we have?" Her mother's voice shook with anger and Mim was instantly sorry she had brought the subject up. "Three neighbors dropped everything and brought over baby clothes and a crib. Mattie Riehl made a diaper bag and filled it with pacifiers, tiny T-shirts and socks, diapers, bottles, and formula. Galen chopped all that wood for us. Naomi has rocked this baby for hours. Fern Lapp brought supper, and David Stoltzfus offered to do chores as if we'd been friends all our lives."

"I thought you might want to know what other people are thinking," Mim admitted in a quiet voice.

Her mother drew in a deep breath. "Such neighbors wouldn't tell tales and gossip. Love thinks well of others, and the people here have poured out that very kind of godly love and friendship. You worry what they'd think? Down deep in my heart, I know they consider us blessed."

Mim couldn't look her mother in the eye as she stammered, "Those are only some of the neighbors."

"For once your mother is right," Mammi Vera said as she came into the kitchen. "We are blessed by this child."

Mim was shocked. The world was turning upside down. She was astounded that her grandmother wasn't more upset. One of her grandmother's favorite sayings was: Aaegebrenndi Supp riecht welt. *You can smell scorched soup from afar.* Scandals spread like wildfire, she would warn, wagging a finger at them. "I guess I mean, you're supposed to get married and then have babies, right?"

"That's the best way." Mammi Vera peered at the baby, sleeping in a borrowed Moses basket, tucked in a corner by the window where the morning sun streamed through and kept her warm. She tucked a blanket around Sarah's little pink toes. "But things don't always happen in the best way, and once some things have happened, we can't go back and change them to the best way." She looked at Mim. "But it's my belief that every child the Lord sends is a gift, and even when things aren't as they should be, God can make a way out of no way."

"Is that in the Bible?"

"Many times in many stories. Remember how the angel Gabriel told Mary, 'With God nothing shall be impossible'?" Mammi Vera straightened and peered out the window. "Soon, Tobe will be home. You'll see. All will turn out well when Tobe finally comes home."

The farrier drove Galen and Bethany out to look at the horse later in the week. In the corner of a dirty pasture was a muddy, broken-down horse. His head hung low, eyes lifeless, and his ribs stuck out. The saddest discovery of all was that his back feet were buckled together in leather hobbles. "He's in even worse condition than he was a few days ago."

The Equine Rescue truck pulled up at the same time. Two men climbed out and walked to the pasture with grim looks on their face as they saw the condition the horse was in. "There's an electric fence," the farrier pointed out. "I'll turn it off and then we can go in."

Bethany watched him click off a small handle. He tapped the fence with his gloved finger and declared it safe. "The juice is cut off. Go on in."

As they walked in the pasture, through the mud and muck toward the horse, Bethany wasn't at all sure it was Jimmy's Lodestar. This horse was covered in ticks, its eyes had a beaten down look, its ears were flattened back, its mane wasn't flaxen but brown, dirty, and matted. She looked at Galen to see what he was thinking. He was walking around the horse, running a hand down its girth, over the joints in its legs. There was no way this horse could be Lodestar. No chance at all.

Galen looked up at her. "It's him."

"What?! Are you sure? He doesn't look the same."

"It's him." He sounded certain.

The farrier and the men from the Equine Rescue were discussing how to proceed as Bethany tipped over the dirt-filled pan of rainwater and went to go look for fresh water for the horse. Galen had brought a hay bale in the back of the farrier's truck and took it out to Lodestar, who lunged for it. Galen pulled a hoof pick out of one pocket, a bottle of apple cider vinegar and a brush out of the other. With a practiced hand, he unbuckled the hobbles. While Lodestar ate, Galen lifted each foot and cleaned the hoof, then painted vinegar over the frog. An old remedy for hoof rot.

"What happens now?" Bethany asked the men.

"We'll post a warning on the door to the house. If we don't hear from the owner in a few days, we'll return and post another."

She turned to the farrier. "What do you know about the owner?"

"I only met him one time, when he asked me to come shoe the horse every eight weeks. There was something odd about him."

Galen's head snapped up. "What was it that struck you as odd?"

"He only carried a one-hundred-dollar bill. Wanted me to break the change for him, and when I couldn't, he said he would have to pay me next time. I've been on the wrong end of that before, so I told him I only work if I'm paid in advance. It made him mad, but he ended up paying me for two shoeings."

"Do you remember what he looked like?" Bethany said.

"Thirty or so. Nice looking. Clean shaven. Seemed to care about the horse." His lips hardened as he glanced around the paddock. "Nothing like this."

"Was the man pleasant? Charming?" She wanted to know.

"Very. The kind of guy who could charm the spots off a leopard."

It *had* to be Jake Hertzler. It had to be! But Bethany could see the run-down house was empty, deserted. Jake must have left awhile ago, abandoning Lodestar. "What happens if you don't hear back from the owner in a few days? If he never does come back?"

"Then we'll return with law enforcement and confiscate the horse."

Galen's gaze was fixed on Lodestar. "What'll happen to the horse?"

"He'll be taken to a rescue center and rehabilitated. Then he'll be put up for adoption."

"How long could that take?" Bethany said.

"Six months. Maybe a year."

Bethany couldn't bear the thought of this pathetic beast left in this filthy pasture without food and water for another week. And hobbled! One of the men from the Equine Rescue apologized to Galen but told him he would have to put the hobbles back on so they could photograph the condition the horse was in, while the other one wrote up a warning and posted it on the door. Galen looked sadly at the hobbles in his hand and gently replaced them on Lodestar's back legs. The horse turned his head from the hay to stare at Galen, as if betrayed.

As they left the pasture, they reminded the farrier to turn the electric fence back on. "By law, we have to leave everything just the way we found it."

Bethany sidled up to Galen to whisper to him. "We can't leave him hobbled. At the very least . . . not hobbled."

He gave her a slight nod. "Distract them as they walk to their cars," he whispered.

Bethany put herself in front of the men, walking backward, asking them every question she could think of about their work. Behind them, she saw Galen quickly unbuckle the horse's hobbles and hurry across the pasture to join them before they reached the gate and the farrier flipped on the switch to the electric fence.

As they climbed back in the farrier's truck, Bethany said, "Wait! I dropped something by the pasture." She jumped out of the truck and hurried over to the gate. She dropped her handkerchief and leaned over with one hand to pick it up, waving to the farrier and Galen to show them she found it. With the other hand, she flipped the electric fence power switch off. The horse looked at her with sorrowful but mildly curious eyes, munching on the hay. "Okay, Lodestar. I'm giving you a chance. Don't disappoint me."

No one said much on the ride home. They were almost back to Eagle Hill before the farrier broke the silence. "I don't know if that horse will ever be the same."

Bethany looked to Galen for that answer.

"He's young," Galen said reassuringly. "It's amazing how quickly an animal can heal once he's got good food, good shelter, and a little loving care."

With all the excitement of the baby's birth, no one had remembered to check phone messages or pick up the mail. While Naomi was feeding the baby her bottle, Rose walked to the mailbox and pulled out three days' worth of mail. Three days! She shook her head. Then she stopped by the phone shanty and listened to messages.

She hunted for a pen to write down names and numbers as she listened to three different messages from guests who wanted to book reservations in April and May. Her pen fell on the floor, and as she bent to get it, she almost missed the last message. "Rose, this is Tobe. I'm sorry I haven't gotten back to you but there's a reason—I'm getting released this week. I'll be home on Friday. I'll explain about, well, about everything, when I get home."

The first thought that ran through her mind was: Tobe was coming home! Alleluia! And then: Friday? Friday! That's tomorrow! And of course, so like Tobe, he didn't say how he would be returning, or what time. But the important thing—Tobe was finally coming home.

# 14

ethany hurried over to Naomi's. They were planning to go to the
Sisters' Bee at Edith Fisher's and she was running late, as usual. As
she slipped through the privet, something caught her eye. Outside the
far fence, near the road, she noticed a loose horse, unbridled, grazing on
shoots of new spring grass. She looked in the barn for Galen but couldn't
find him, so she grabbed a handful of hay, tucked a rope under her arm,
and walked slowly, slowly toward the horse.

The horse shied but was too weary, too thin, to bolt. "Don't tell me . . .
can it really be . . . is it you?" She held the hay out to the horse and gently
slipped a rope around his neck. She reached out and rested her hand on the
horse's nose. The horse bumped her with his nose, a sign of recognition.
"I know someone who is going to be pretty excited to see you."

Bethany rubbed the horse's long neck, looking him over for injuries.
The horse seemed completely calm. Ears in the upright position.

She ran her hand down each leg, the way she'd seen Galen do, looking
for swelling or bruising or cuts. Then she led the horse into Galen's barn
and into a large box stall, customized with extra latches especially for a
certain horse who liked to escape, but she had a feeling that wouldn't be
a problem any longer.

Jimmy Fisher's Lodestar had come home.

As soon as Bethany arrived at the Fishers' farm for the Sisters' Bee,
she made a beeline to find Jimmy in the pullet barn. It was ten times as
large as the henhouse at Eagle Hill. She had never been in it before and

cringed at the loud sound of the hens, cackling and clucking in their nesting boxes. The air was pungent, fusty and sour, nearly overwhelming her, though it was a well-kept barn with plenty of ventilation. One or two of the hens flapped their wings and pecked at her as she walked down the narrow aisle.

No wonder Jimmy couldn't stand being a chicken boss! These birds were downright ornery.

She found him cutting up apples at a workbench in the center of the barn, tossing the apple slices in a bucket to feed to the hens. When he saw her, he startled. "Bethany, what are you doing here?"

"Jimmy, I found him! Well, Galen helped too."

"Who?"

She paused, unable to hold back a grin. "Lodestar."

He cocked his head and looked at her as if she might be sun touched. "Bethany, are you feeling all right?"

She laughed. "It's really him. Lodestar!"

Jimmy didn't move for a moment, didn't breathe. Then he threw the apple knife down on the workbench so hard it stuck upright, point in the wood. "Where?" His voice made a funny, choking sound. "Where is he?"

"He's not in great shape. He's been mistreated pretty badly. He's lost a lot of muscle mass. But Galen thinks that with good food, good care, love, and kindness, he'll be as good as new." She bit her bottom lip. "Hopefully."

He took a step closer to her, impatience on his face. "Bethany, where is he?"

"In Galen's barn, of course."

Jimmy tossed his worn leather gloves on the ground and blew past her, leaving her alone in the stinky chicken barn.

Micky was getting too old for all the silly games he played like a puppy, but he didn't know it, which was why Rose ignored him when he woke her in the middle of the night with his cold nose on her hand. He hunkered down on the ground and made a whimpering sound, then he ran around and around in a tight circle, jumped up on the bed, jumped off, only to do it all over again. Something was up, so Rose got out of bed. She heard a sound outside and went to the window, just in time to see Paisley's car start up, cough, and sputter down the driveway.

Rose flew into action and bolted down the stairs. "Stop her, stop her! She's leaving! Paisley's leaving!"

Bethany burst out of her bedroom, down the stairs, and ran past Rose to go outside, waving, trying to catch up with the car. At the end of the driveway she gave up and walked back to Rose, furious. "I can't believe she actually left before Tobe got home. I can't believe it!"

All kinds of feelings ping-ponged in Rose's head. Relief that Paisley was gone, that the family would no longer need to walk on a knife-edge of anxiety, that Tobe wasn't home yet to be caught in a quandary about whether to go with her or not.

Then, panic! The baby. The baby was gone! How dare Paisley take that baby away! Rose felt devastated. She was already falling in love with little Sarah.

Suddenly a familiar wail floated down the steps.

Bethany looked at Rose, puzzled. "Paisley didn't take the baby with her?"

The baby's wail grew louder.

"Apparently . . . not," Rose said in a thin, unsteady voice.

In the morning, Rose told Vera that Paisley had vanished. Vera's face suddenly grew gray and wrinkled, as if she had turned a hundred years old.

"The less said about that Parsley woman, the better. The English are very unreliable." Vera's face was in that sharp straight line again. There would be no more said.

When Naomi received Tobe's call that he was coming home, asking her to meet him at the bus stop at three o'clock and to come alone so they could have time to talk, she found herself deliberating over which dress to wear to make her look most appealing—the rose or the teal green—then she pulled herself up sharply and was ashamed to realize how vain she sounded, even to herself. But she wore the teal green one that gave her more color and didn't make her look wishy-washy. She could barely wait to see Tobe. No day had ever seemed longer.

It was nearly time. The bus would be in at three p.m., he said. Only four hours to go. Three. Two. It was time.

Today, fortune was in her favor. Mr. Kurtz was due to arrive at the house at two o'clock during the exact time when Galen happened to have gone to town to buy supplies. No lies were told and none were needed. By three o'clock, Naomi was waiting at the crowded and noisy bus station in Lancaster—so crowded she felt like a hen being crated off to market, so noisy she couldn't hear herself think. She tried to push her way to the front of the crowd as she watched Tobe's bus pull in and stop. She felt a nervous quiver in her belly and unconsciously smoothed her apron again and again.

At the top of the bus steps, his hand clutching the door handle, Tobe paused and his eyes roamed the crowd. The sight of him filled Naomi's eyes with tears. He was so . . . beautiful. Tall, broad, handsome, and he was hers.

She could tell, from the frown on his face, he couldn't find her in the crowd. He stepped down from the bus and started to make his way through the cluster of people. She hurried to catch him and pulled at his sleeve.

"Tobe?" she said, almost hesitatingly.

Tobe spun around.

Their eyes met immediately, but neither of them moved. It was as if words and greetings and reactions had been blown out of them like air after a kick in the stomach. Then words tumbled out.

"I was afraid you weren't coming—"

"How could I not—"

"For hundreds of reasons," he said. Then he gave a quick scan around the bus station to see if he recognized anyone, and satisfied there was no one, he reached out to engulf her in a hug. They left the station with arms linked together and went across the street to a coffee shop to talk. The discreet Mr. Kurtz said he had an errand to run and would return in an hour.

Over coffee, Naomi told Tobe about the baby's arrival, and then about Paisley's midnight disappearance.

He was speechless at the turn of events. Delighted, even. "It proves it, then, doesn't it? I'm not the father. She couldn't face me."

"Maybe. Maybe not. She didn't seem the same after the baby was born.

I'm not exactly sure why. Bethany thinks it's because the baby is a special child. Rose thinks Paisley was under the impression that you came from a well-off family and was not happy to find out that wasn't exactly so—"

"No kidding." He made a scoffing sound. "So why do you think she left?"

"I truly don't know. I hardly traded more than a few words with her while she was at Eagle Hill. After the baby was born, she stayed in bed. She just seemed unhappy and disappointed."

They stopped talking while the waitress brought two mugs, one of coffee, one of tea, and set them on the table.

Tobe poured cream into his coffee and stirred it. "Naomi, I hope you can forgive me." His eyes probed hers as though looking for answers to unasked questions. "Do you?"

She was careful to answer as honestly as possible. "I don't believe that all things that happen are good, but I do believe the Lord can make good come from even the worst things."

He kept his eyes on the brim of his coffee cup. "Even Paisley? Even leaving a baby without a mother? Is there any good in that?"

"A new baby is always a blessing. God wants us to celebrate that."

"I don't know what Paisley told you." She saw his muscles tense as he said the woman's name. "It doesn't matter. No one knows the truth about Paisley. Not even me, but I'll tell you what I do know. Then you'll have to decide who to believe."

She met his gaze. "That decision has already been made."

"Some decisions have to be made over and over." He pulled his eyes away from hers and stared at a bee buzzing against the window of the coffee shop.

Naomi waited for him to elaborate, her hands in her lap, twisting and turning the paper napkin.

"I had met Paisley, years ago. She had worked as a waitress at a restaurant near the office of Schrock Investments. Jake and I used to grab lunch there. During that year when I took off, I stayed at her apartment a few nights while I was trying to find work. Now and then . . . well, we would have too much to drink and get carried away."

Naomi's cheeks reddened, but her grip on the napkin loosened.

With great tenderness he lifted her face up. "Naomi, nine months ago, if I had known what was waiting for me with you . . . I never would've . . .

I never imagined I'd fall in love with an Amish girl who lived next door to my grandmother. I never dreamed of the consequences, that I would be hurting someone I loved." She started to say something, but he put his fingers softly on her lips. "Do you have regrets?"

She didn't hesitate. "Nothing could ever change the way I feel about you, Tobe. Or that we belong together."

Tobe's mouth began quivering and his face crumpled as tears filled his eyes. He brushed the back of his hand across his eyes and drew in a shaky breath before he was able to go on. "Truly? No regrets? Because now is the time to say so." He asked with a kind of stillness in his eyes as if her answer was especially important.

She smiled, feeling light-headed all of a sudden. Feeling lighthearted. "None. Not a one."

Rose kept glancing at the kitchen clock—it was after five—then looked out the window. The table had been laid with more than usual care. All of Tobe's favorite foods had been prepared.

She had wanted to be sure that everything was perfect to welcome Tobe home. Instead, it was chaos. Rain had started and was now pummeling the farm. Baby Sarah seemed particularly fussy this afternoon, Luke was teasing Sammy, something was bothering Mim and she wouldn't say what—she had the energy of a trapped bird. Mammi Vera truculent, Bethany in a mood . . . this would be no way to start a new life. She sighed. If only it would stop raining.

Her thoughts drifted to Paisley's whereabouts. She teetered between relief that the girl was gone and concern that she would come back. What irked her more than anything was that Paisley had left with nothing settled. Nothing!

Rose glanced out the kitchen window again. And suddenly, there was Tobe, walking up the driveway with a satchel in his hand, rain running off the brim of his hat. Her big, handsome, restless son. His smile was tired. Her heart skipped with worry about him, as it so often did. A loud whoop sailed down from the upstairs, then a beat of footsteps clamored down the stairs as Luke and Sammy tried to beat each other out the door to greet their brother. They all rushed out to welcome home the prodigal and soon the farmhouse of Eagle Hill was filled with a happy chaos.

Tobe paid special attention to Mammi Vera, which made her glow with happiness. After supper, which was wonderful and noisy, he admired all the improvements to the farm and said the blueberry cobbler was the best thing he'd eaten in years. But he never held the baby, Rose noticed, nor glanced in the baby's direction when she fussed.

Before turning in, Tobe went to the barn to check on the animals and was gone for quite a while. When he came inside, he had such a pensive look on his face that Vera asked him what he was thinking. "It's so quiet here—I'd forgotten what silence sounds like in the countryside."

"That's why we live here," Mammi Vera said, delighted.

"That's why we live here," Tobe said flatly.

Mim had never felt so at sea. She shifted on the cot to try to get more comfortable. It had seemed to her when she went to bed that she could forget all her worries, that she could sleep and everything was going to be all right, but she awoke in the middle of the night with the horrible realization that two additional people knew she was Mrs. Miracle. Bethany and Ella didn't worry her, they weren't loose cannons. But these two . . . there was no telling what could happen. She tried to push that worry out of her head, but crazy thoughts kept shooting through her mind. Maybe she could go ask Bethany right now. Shake her awake and say, "That lady with the spiky blonde hair in the guest flat found out I'm Mrs. Miracle. Tell me what to do."

Earlier this morning, she had delivered breakfast to the guest flat, like she usually did. Brooke Snyder had a strange look on her face, pinched and pleased. Mim asked if she were feeling well, and she answered her with, "Very well, thank you." She pointed to the newspaper. "So . . . perhaps you'd like to compose a Mrs. Miracle letter while you're here?"

Mim gasped, too surprised to deny she wrote the letters. "You won't tell, will you?"

Brooke turned to Mim, a smile as brittle as toffee fixed to her face. "Why would I tell?"

Mim squeezed her eyes shut and tried to think of something else, or of nothing, but her mind kept circling back to the fact: two people knew she was Mrs. Miracle. She wasn't sure whom she was more worried about: Jesse, whose father was a minister, or Brooke Snyder, who seemed oddly pleased to hold Mim's secret. She got out of bed and looked at her face in the mirror. It was gray-white and there were shadows under her frightened eyes. The room grew gradually lighter, although no warmer. She was doomed.

The disturbing black cloud that came on the horizon for Galen and Rose with the arrival of Paisley was something that they danced around, carefully avoided, and tried to pretend wasn't a problem between them. But when Tobe arrived at Eagle Hill, another storm came and settled on them. This gulf between them was growing huge.

Rose wanted to clear the atmosphere between them. When she discovered the woodpile had been chopped and stacked, she was touched beyond words. She had been so busy lately that she'd hardly had time for Galen. And yet . . . he had chopped a cord of wood for her. And she had forgotten to thank him! She hurried over to catch him when she saw him lead a horse from his barn to the round training pen.

He seemed to be thinking along the same lines of wanting to clear the air. He put the horse in the pen and turned toward her with an eager look on his face.

"I heard Lodestar is back. How's he doing?"

"Well, he's not lacking for attention, I'll tell you that much. Jimmy's in the barn with him now, brushing and preening him like a mother hen fussing over a chick."

"Think Lodestar will make a full recovery?"

"In time. God designed his creatures to heal."

They fell silent then, and a full thirty seconds passed while their gazes held, the only sound was the horse shuffling around in the pen. At last, reaching for her hands, Galen said in a voice so low it was barely audible, "Rose, I want things between us to go back the way they were."

Her face broke into a radiant smile. "I wanted to thank you for chopping all that wood. I . . . can't tell you how . . . I hardly know what to say. It might seem like a small chore to you, but it meant so much to me."

Galen stiffened. In a voice she hardly recognized, he said, "I didn't chop wood for you."

Feeding little Sarah a bottle took nearly an hour, but Naomi didn't mind. The feedings gave her time to study her face, to memorize her row of stubby eyelashes, to watch her temples beating. When the baby's eyes flitted open, she studied the dark gray, looking for signs of the brown or blue or green they would become.

Edith Fisher was, as usual, practical about the baby. "Don't grow too fond of the child," she warned Naomi at the quilting bee the next afternoon. "That unfeeling lout of a mother will be back for her the day it suits her."

What did people mean . . . don't grow too fond of the child? The very first time Naomi had held the baby, a wave of protectiveness almost overwhelmed her. This poor, helpless baby had no one else in the world. How could anyone put a limit to the love she felt for this little girl with the big dark eyes, the head of fuzzy brown hair, the endearing habit of holding her little hands clasped together as if she were praying? It was as if baby Sarah had made her life complete.

Nobody had told Naomi how much she would love this baby because nobody could have known. "I'll do my best for you, little one," she promised to her in a whisper, and she could have sworn Sarah smiled.

The thought that Paisley might have a change of heart and return for her daughter was never far from Rose's mind. It would be awful to have to give Sarah up. She told herself if the mother didn't want her bad enough to come and get her, then she was too foolish to have her.

She knew she had already grown dangerously attached to the baby. She liked to lie in bed with her and watch her try to work her small hands, the tiny, perfect little fists with their miniscule nails. Sarah would peer at her for long stretches, frowning, as if trying to figure life out. But when Rose laughed at her and gave her a finger to hold, she would stop frowning and settle happily.

The morning after Tobe's return, Rose intended to let Tobe sleep in as late as he wanted and was surprised to see him come into the kitchen at dawn as she prepared Sarah's bottle. "What are you doing up?"

He sat on the bench by the kitchen door to get his boots on. "The warden raised poultry. When he found out I was raised Amish, he assumed I know all about chickens, which I didn't. But there was a surfeit of spare time in prison, so I read all I could and the warden let me take care of his chickens." He shrugged. "Better than doing laundry." He pulled out a boot from under the bench. "I heard Harold the rooster crowing, so I thought I'd get up and feed your hens. Mim told me that the old hens were waiting for an opportunity to peck her eyes out." He stuck his foot in one boot. "I used oregano powder in the chicken feed. Made them healthier. Antimicrobial and antibacterial. Mind if I try it?"

Odd, Rose thought, that prison life would be the thing to make a farmer out of Tobe.

"Bethany said you were due to host church soon. I'm sure there's a lot to be done to get ready. I want to help out as long as I'm here."

Her breath caught. Was he already thinking of leaving? He'd only been home one night. "Tobe, I'm going to ask you a question and I want an honest answer." She motioned to Sarah, tucked in her arm. "Is there any chance this baby is yours?"

Tobe dropped his boot and looked up sharply. A long moment passed, then another. "Yes. A small one, a very small chance, but there is."

Rose went cold inside. A hope she had kept burning, sure that he would say he had never known Paisley, extinguished.

"I met Paisley a couple of years ago. She was a waitress at a coffee shop. In fact, Jake introduced us. Then when I was gone that year, working odd jobs, I didn't have a place to stay one night and she let me stay at her place . . . " He hesitated and glanced at Rose.

She lifted her free hand in the air. "I think I can fill in the blanks."

"Rose, Paisley was friendly with a lot of guys. It was never a thing between us."

She glanced down at the sleeping baby. Never a *thing*? "Paisley had a different opinion about that. She said you were planning to marry her as soon as you were released."

"We never, *ever* made plans like that. I haven't even seen her since that . . . those few nights when I stayed at her apartment."

"Why would she claim you're the baby's father if you weren't?"

"I have absolutely no idea. She told a pack of lies and is trying to palm her child off on me."

"She seemed to think you were going to inherit Eagle Hill."

He scratched his chin. "Maybe I said something like that once. Mammi Vera always makes it sound like I will."

"She also seemed upset when she found out that your grandmother wasn't knocking at death's door."

"Is that why she left?" He picked up the boot and jammed his stocking foot into it.

"I don't know. When I told her you were coming home, she became agitated. A few hours later, she vanished. Obviously, she didn't want to see you."

"Well, doesn't that prove to you that I'm not the father of that baby?"

"Sarah. Her name is Sarah. And no—Paisley's disappearance only proved to me that she wasn't a fit mother." She wiped some drops of formula off Sarah's cheek. "The bishop wants to have a talk with you."

Tobe shook his head forcefully. "Oh nooooooo. No, no, no. I'm not baptized. I am *not* about to sit on the sinner's bench over something like this."

"I asked him to come. He's the leader of our church. Stoney Ridge is a small, tight-knit community. A baby has been born who bears your name on her birth certificate—"

Tobe winced.

"—and there needs to be some discussion about what to do with baby Sarah. We need some guidance. All of us." She was trying her best.

Tobe looked down at a spot on the floor for a long moment. Then he lifted his head. "When is he coming?"

"Around eleven this morning, he said. The deacon will be with him."

He slapped his hands on his knees and rose to his feet. "Good. Mim and the boys will be over at Windmill Farm for the afternoon and Bethany will be at the Sisters' House. I want Galen and Naomi to be here. Mammi Vera too." He was sliding away without answering.

"Why?"

"Rose, if you don't mind, I'd rather explain everything when you're all together."

Elmo and Abraham drove up in the deacon's buggy right at eleven o'clock on the dot. Rose was struck by how elderly and frail the bishop appeared as he climbed out of the buggy. He was shaped like an S hook, bending or straightening as he spoke to each person. She knew he played an increasingly smaller part in the events of the church and that most things were done by Abraham, his bustling, energetic deacon.

They all gathered in the living room—Rose, Galen, Tobe, Naomi, Mammi Vera, Bishop Elmo, and Deacon Abraham. Sarah slept in her Moses basket, wedged in between Rose's and Naomi's chairs.

Tobe looked so uneasy that Rose almost felt sorry for him. He had the helpless expression of a man who knew he was looking at disaster but couldn't figure out how to stop it. "This whole situation is very complicated," he said.

"Simplify it so we can understand," Galen said in a sharp tone.

"Galen," Rose said. Her voice sounded a warning note, but he didn't meet her eyes.

Abraham steepled his fingers together. "Tobe, people make mistakes, and once the mistake's been made, you have to move on and figure out what to do next while you try not to make a bigger mistake."

"I don't disagree about making mistakes," Tobe said. "I've made plenty. But I don't believe I'm the father of Paisley's child. I'm going to get a DNA test to prove that and clear up any lingering suspicion."

Elmo was about to say something when Tobe lifted his hand to stop him. "There's something else. Another reason I need to prove to you that I'm not the baby's father because . . ." He glanced at Naomi. She gave him a nervous but encouraging smile. He reached over, took her hand, and breathed a deep breath. "Last fall, Naomi and I were married in a civil ceremony while I was in custody in Philadelphia, right before I was sent to FCI Schuykill."

His words fell like a stone into the room. Everyone went entirely still. The only movement came from Mammi Vera, who started clutching her chest.

"You must be joking," Galen said.

Naomi was looking at her brother calmly, her honest eyes fixed on his.

"It's not a joke, Galen," Tobe said. "It's a fact. It was the best way to ensure that Naomi could have visitation rights at the prison. As my wife, she could be on the preapproved visitor's list and visit as often as she could. If she wasn't a family member, she'd have had to get special permission through the warden. We knew we wanted to marry. Circumstances caused us to speed it up."

Galen went white with the news; he was still white. "Naomi, you visited him at the prison? In Minersville?"

"Yes," she said in a quiet but steady voice. "Often."

"I was only allowed a certain amount of visitor points a month," Tobe said. "Rose, that's why I discouraged you from visiting."

*Ah*. Things were starting to make sense to Rose.

"Why did you never tell me this, Naomi?" Galen's voice was full of emotion.

"What would you have said? What would you have done?"

There was something so bleak and honest in Naomi's tone that Rose could see Galen's fury diminish. Had Galen known, he would have had to inform the church leadership, and most likely, she would have been put under the ban.

Rose wished she could reach out and hold Galen's hand, to let him know that she was there beside him while he absorbed the blow. She knew it was a terrible discovery to him. By contrast, she felt a sweeping relief. She had sensed that Tobe and Naomi had a significant connection and she was actually pleased to think that Naomi stood by him while he was away. She was glad Tobe had someone else in his corner, someone who saw the best in him, someone who cared for him no matter what.

"Well," Galen said and stopped. "This is surprising news," he said, rather stiffly, coldness in his voice.

"We haven't, uh, um, consummated the marriage. We intend to wait until we could have a church wedding." Tobe looked at Naomi, whose cheeks flamed rosy red. "We still intend to wait for that . . . official ceremony."

The bishop let out a deep sigh of relief. "Well, now, this might all work out in the end."

"Not so fast," Galen said. "There's a baby in the middle of this. And a woman who says Tobe is the father of her child."

Tobe nodded. "The DNA test will take care of that."

A trace of stubbornness appeared in Galen's jaw. "And if the baby is yours?"

Irritation crossed Tobe's face. "We'll cross that bridge when we come to it."

The bishop cleared his throat. "Tobe and Naomi, would you give us a few moments to talk?"

Tobe and Naomi left the room and went out to the front porch. Rose heard the faint creak of the porch swing as they sat on it.

Galen glanced at Elmo. "So what do you have to say?"

The bishop and the deacon murmured together for a few moments. Then Elmo leaned back in his chair, a satisfied look covering his face. "What's important is that Tobe and Naomi are going to remain in the Amish church. Naomi has already been baptized. Tobe will need to go through instruction classes to become baptized. We can speed up the classes for him. And then they can be married. Truly married in the eyes of God." His eyes rested on Galen. "And that will be that."

Vera clasped her hands together in delight. "Well, I've always said things have a way of working out."

Galen's face remained stony. "That's your final word?"

Elmo nodded. "It is."

Abraham agreed that it should be done as speedily as possible.

"The important thing," Elmo said, leaning forward, wagging a finger at Galen, "is that they will remain in . . . the . . . church!"

Rose would always remember the way that Elmo's thick round glasses seemed to sparkle as he was telling Galen that. She didn't know if there were tears behind them, or if it was only a trick of the light.

Elmo looked around the room, at each person, then pinned Galen with a stare. "We're all in agreement?"

Rose watched Galen's profile. It was hard and unsmiling. "Yes. Yes, of course." His voice sounded false and Rose knew it.

# 15

While Elmo and Abraham spoke to Tobe and Naomi inside the house, Galen was pacing the front porch like an animal in a cage. As soon as Rose closed the door, he turned around, his lips hardened in a straight line. "The bishop and deacon are only concerned about having Tobe and Naomi remain Amish. You know as well as I do that they'll bend over backwards to keep people in the church."

"God has an interest in this situation too, Galen. We want them to make a meaningful decision for their future. Isn't that what you want for Naomi?"

"Yes. Of course I do. Yes. But not like this."

"Like what, Galen? They fell in love. They wanted to be able to see each other while he was away. They found a solution to that problem. Maybe if . . ." Her voice drizzled off as she wondered if she should say more.

"Maybe if what?"

"Maybe if you hadn't made it so clear that you were against Tobe, that you didn't want him around Naomi . . . maybe they wouldn't have felt the need to keep it a secret."

Galen was still in a temper. "Oh, sure. It's all my doing. It has nothing to do with Tobe's lifelong habit of avoiding difficult things."

"But don't you see? He's not avoiding anything now. Just the opposite. Galen," she said, "a man's past is his past. It's what he contributes to the present that matters. And didn't you hear? He said they were going to be married in the church."

He looked at her as if he couldn't believe she was so naive. "Tobe never said he was going to stay in the Amish church. Yes, he said they were planning to have a wedding in the church. He *never* said an Amish church wedding. There's a very big difference. He's already made his decision to leave." He strode forward a few steps, then spun around. "He's doing the same thing he's always done! He married Naomi secretly, out of nowhere a woman appeared, bore his child, disappeared, and he wants life to carry on, business as usual." He crossed his arms, annoyed. "No consequences."

She felt a raw disappointment in Galen and hoped it didn't show in her face. She tried to keep her voice calm and conciliatory. "Whenever I watch you with your new horses, it seems as if you have a vision of what that horse will be like, once it's trained. Why can't you have that kind of vision with people?"

"Because," he said, searching for the right words, "people are far more complicated than horses."

"But it shouldn't be that way! David Stoltzfus says the word 'worldly' means that you only see what's right before you. We can be worldly when we don't see eternal significance in others."

A confused look swept Galen's face. "David Stoltzfus? The new minister?"

"Yes. He said that very thing."

"That it's worldly to be realistic and objective? To face facts?"

She frowned. "That's not what I meant!" She clenched her fists, a sign she was running out of patience. "Why can't you try and understand Tobe's perspective? Why must you always judge him?"

"Why can't you try to see Tobe clearly?"

"Because . . . with Dean gone, I'm all Tobe has."

"That's not true. He has an entire family to lean on. He has a church, if he wants it." He backed off, rubbing his hands on his thighs self-consciously. After a long pause, he took his hat off and walked closer to her. "Rose, this is starting to divide us."

"*This?*" Rose said, her anger rising. "You mean, the welfare of my son?"

"We have differing views on this subject. Why can't we just set it aside? Agree to disagree."

"Tobe's situation is serious, but there will be other situations with Bethany, Mim, and the boys—we can't always be on opposite sides of the fence about the children."

"That's the problem, right there. Tobe isn't a child anymore. He's a man. By now, he should be. You're going to hobble Tobe from manhood by raising this baby for him." In an uncharacteristic burst of emotion, he nearly shouted, "He will never have to grow up!"

"What do you know about raising children?" Rose flared back.

Galen swallowed. His shoulders stiffened and the wary look returned to his face. His voice came reluctantly, but firmly. "I know enough to see that you try to fix problems that belong to your children, especially Tobe and Luke. Problems that they should find solutions to. Just like you've tried to do with Schrock Investments." He jammed his hat back on his head. "Rose, you keep tethering yourself to the past." He spun on his heels and went down the porch steps.

It was the longest speech that Galen had ever made and it only made her furious. She watched him cross the yard and head to his farm, as if she was watching a stranger.

After the bishop and deacon left, Naomi held and fed the baby so Rose could get some chores taken care of. It took time to get to know a baby—to interpret her cries and figure out how she liked best to be held or cuddled. She had the time to give to Sarah.

"I haven't seen Tobe in the last hour," Rose said as she came into the kitchen, a basket of fresh dry sheets in her arms. "Mim and the boys will be home from school soon. They'll be looking for him."

"He had some thinking to do," Naomi said, "so he took a walk over to Blue Lake Pond."

Rose set the basket on the kitchen table. "Naomi, do you think Tobe will agree to the bishop's plan to join the church?"

Naomi kept her eyes down. "It sounds as if you don't think he will."

"Galen seems to think he won't. I'm not so sure."

Sarah had fallen asleep, so Naomi gently laid her in the Moses basket and covered her with the pink quilt. "Leave Tobe to me."

"And Galen? Think he'll come around?"

"Leave him to me too." But Naomi fingered her pocket to make sure she hadn't forgotten her Tums.

An hour later, Naomi found Tobe at their favorite place—their log at Blue Lake Pond—with his head in his hands. She could see he was troubled. He looked up, startled, when he saw her approach but made room on the big tree log for her to sit down.

"We need to leave Stoney Ridge, Naomi. I'd hoped, I'd thought . . . we were on the same page about this." There was agony and misery mixing in his eyes. "I just wish that your brother—that you—that I—" He gathered her fiercely into a tight embrace, and when he released her, he drew back, holding up a hand to stop her as she was about to say something. "I hope you realize that, by leaving, I'm trying to do the right thing for us."

She was trying to do the right thing too. After all, there was a baby to think of. "And you think that means we need to leave the Amish?"

"I do. You see that too, don't you? You must realize that a lot of your attitudes come from the Amish. You've said yourself that everyone lives in the shadow of the church."

It was true that she had said that, but she meant it in an enveloping, comforting way. Not in the dark, smothering way Tobe interpreted it.

They shifted to sit on the ground, resting their backs against the log, with Tobe's arms wrapped around Naomi, watching the still lake. She listened to everything he had to say, every argument about why they should leave the church. "There's no choices, Naomi. No freedom. You get up in the morning and put on the clothes of your grandparents, you listen to preaching and sing the hymns they once sang, and their faith is your faith and will be the faith of your children's children. Nothing ever changes."

That was exactly what Naomi loved about the Plain life. The slow and steady sureness of time passing, life measured by meaningful customs.

"And where did these old traditions come from? They go so far back no one can even remember why they were important in the first place." He pointed to her blue dress, the one he liked best. "Things like a dress held together by pins and celery at weddings and no screens on the windows. Ridiculous things that make no sense. And people hold on to them as if they were pulled straight out of the Bible."

But this was her life. The sameness, the familiar. Sundays full of old hymns that echoed off the barn rafters, uplifting messages from the preachers, the sharing of the fellowship meal afterward. With weekday mornings full of tossing hay to Galen's horses, afternoons of quilting by the soft light of her favorite window, with keeping house for her brother, with baking bread and gardening vegetables. All the days and nights full of work and prayer and being together. This was the backbone of her life. It was the Plain way and in it she felt safe. She felt loved. *In my heart I am Plain.*

"God gave us a brain and expects us to use it. Instead, everyone just follows the Ordnung like a flock of sheep."

She didn't interrupt Tobe. She let him talk it all out—how few choices they would have, how narrow a life, the way he bristled against conformity, how questions could never be asked, and mostly, the feeling that he would never get free from the clinging disaster of Schrock Investments. She didn't object. She didn't plead. She had always been quick to recognize when something seemed impossible. And a look at Tobe's face told her that this was now the case.

When he was spent of words, she turned to face him. "Tell me again what that year was like for you, after you left home."

"I've told you about it."

"I want to hear more. Where did you work? What friends did you have?"

"I had trouble finding work—I could get some day jobs here and there, working construction or landscaping, but nothing that lasted." He stopped, raising an eyebrow. "I see where you're going. I've thought this out—I'll need to take some classes at a junior college so I can find better work. A real career."

"What about friends?"

He shrugged. "I didn't have many. None, I guess. When Schrock Investments went under, it caused bitter feelings among those I had thought were friends." Then he was silent. "We'll make friends. Eventually. We'll find a church where no one has heard of Schrock Investments."

"And what was missing in that year?"

He looked confused. "I'm not following you."

"After all you've been through, haven't you learned about the most important things?"

He threw up his hands. "How can you say that? I met God in the prison."

"And hasn't that taught you about the most important things?"

He watched her, his expression drawn with concern. "Next to God, you're the most important thing to me, Naomi."

She could see how much he loved her, could see it in the deep softness of his gaze as he looked at her. "Tobe, you must know how important family is to me. Frankly, how important it is to you too. Think of what that year was like without your family."

He looked away.

"I want you to listen to me and not dismiss what I have to say or act like I'm setting out snares to trap you." He opened his mouth to object and she cut him off. "I see it in your eyes, so don't think I don't know what's running through your head. You're underestimating what it would be like for us to live without family. Without our church family too."

She looked down at their hands, twined together. "We would have more to lose than we would have to gain. Being cut off from our family, from our church. We would be sheep without a fold. Look at what the church has done for Rose—they've provided donations to pay back the investors who lost money in Schrock Investments. They've paid off your grandmother's medical bills. They've embraced Sarah without questions or judgments."

"We can find that outside the Amish church too."

She shook her head. "Not easily, Tobe. Our experience would be much like yours—out of work and lonely, cut off from those we love."

He didn't speak for a long while. "Do you think your brother would shun you?"

"Yes." She looked up at him. "And it would break his heart to do it."

A shadow of indecision passed over Tobe's face. "What you're really saying is that you love the Plain life, don't you?"

*What I'm trying to say is, in my heart I am Plain.* "I love my Plain family, and you love yours—maybe more than you know."

"And that's reason enough for you to stay?"

Absolute certainty and conviction welled up inside her and spilled out in one word: "Yes."

Taut silence traveled between them. She could sense him hovering on the edge of decision. In an oddly detached way, she empathized with him. She had hovered on the edge of decision herself after she had learned about Paisley—to remain with Tobe or let him go. It had been a turning-point moment for her, just as this was for him.

He walked toward the edge of the pond, bent down, picked up a rock, and skipped it along the surface of the glassy lake.

She waited, on edge.

Finally, he looked upward, sighed deeply, and turned his full attention to her. "What kind of a husband would I be if I asked you to give up the life you love?"

She walked down the pond's edge toward him. "Are you sure? Absolutely, positively sure? You won't wake up one day and regret this choice?"

"I'd regret hurting you far more."

He leaned forward, holding his hands out to her, and said, "Whatever it would take—I just can't live another moment without you by my side."

She reached out for him and let him pull her toward him, kissing him directly on the lips. She felt his arms tighten around her and they stood locked like this for a time. She pulled back, forehead to forehead, and they looked at each other for a long moment before she spoke. "Tobe, I want you to want it too."

"You've given me everything I've ever wanted."

"I haven't begun to give you anything."

"But you have, believe me. Without you I'd be nothing. You've given me encouragement, and faith, and hope that things will work out, in the end. You've given me the courage to return to Stoney Ridge. And now . . . to stay." He took her hands in his and held them close to his heart. "Now you must give me one more thing . . . you must believe in me. You must believe I'm trying to do the right thing."

"About what?"

"About . . . other things that are still . . . unfinished."

She didn't believe him. Not entirely. It wasn't that she didn't fully trust him, because she did. There was something he wasn't telling her, something he didn't want her to know. And even if he was telling her everything, there was still Sarah to consider. Still, her instinct told her to wait for him—that he would tell her everything when he was ready.

She reached up on her tiptoes to kiss him her answer, feeling a bone-deep happiness she didn't know was possible to feel, this side of heaven, as his arms wrapped around her waist to pull her against his chest. It was a perfect moment.

Soon . . . she would have to face her brother. She reached one hand down to her pocket and patted it. Good. Tums were still there.

By the time Naomi and Tobe arrived back at Eagle Hill, the sun had almost disappeared and the air had thickened with hazy twilight. She said goodbye to him at the hole in the privet, slipped through it, and slowed her walk to a crawl. She was dreading this moment, had been dreading it for months now. She took two Tums and chewed them fast and hard.

In the house, she took her cape and bonnet off, hung them on the wall peg by the back door, and walked into the living room to talk to Galen. He was writing bills at his desk. Naomi noticed his tense jaw and how he was clenching his pen. The guilt she felt about keeping something so important from her brother brought her an instant headache. Where had all her bravery gone?

She tested a please-don't-be-mad-at-me smile that usually worked on Galen, but he didn't look up, didn't acknowledge her presence in any way. "I . . . I wanted to say that I'm sorry."

He radiated a stony silence. This was worse than she thought it would be. Maybe she should just wait until he was ready to talk. As she turned to go to the kitchen, she heard him say, "The worst thing is how deceitful you've been."

She stopped and turned around. "I never lied to you."

"You never told me the truth, either."

Her heart fell. Gone was the warmth and affection that usually flowed between them. She hated that she had done this—brought this kind of hurt to her brother. He had never been anything but kind and caring toward her; she couldn't even remember a time when he'd been angry with her. Glancing down, she noticed that her hands had curled themselves into fists. Finger by finger, she relaxed. "Please, let me explain," she began, hoping he would hear her out.

"There's no need. Tobe Schrock has a strong influence on you."

A protective anger over Tobe buoyed her strength. "What about my influence on him, Galen?" Her chin went up a notch. "Have you considered that?"

He turned back to the bill he was writing.

"We're staying in the church. We're not leaving. It's decided."

Galen's hand stilled. Slowly, he turned to stare at her in wonder. She nearly smiled at his stunned look. Nearly.

"It's true. We just discussed it. Tomorrow we'll go to the bishop and set the date. Tobe has to be baptized first." She walked over to him. "I'm so sorry to have kept this from you. Truly, truly sorry."

Relief and disbelief flooded his face. "I only want what's best for you." His eyes softened and his voice grew shaky. "That's all I've ever wanted."

As he said that, as soon as she heard his voice wobble, tears lodged in her throat. Galen dipped his head. "Rose said . . . she thought I was partly to blame. She said I caused you to feel you had to keep it secret."

"Maybe a little." Naomi smiled, wiping away a tear that was rolling down her cheek. "Maybe a lot. But I don't regret my choice. Getting married the way Tobe and I did—it wasn't meant to hurt you, Galen. It's just that . . . it's just . . ."

When Galen looked up, his eyes were shiny with moisture. "You fell in love."

He said it so softly she wondered if it was more his thought than his voice she'd heard. Maybe she'd only hoped he would say it. "I fell in love. And love does extraordinary things to people."

The next morning, Rose stood by the kitchen window and watched Tobe and Naomi walk together from the buggy after returning from the bishop's home, where they had gone to set a date for a wedding. What a mystery love was: the small figure of this strange strong girl, the tall figure of her own stepson, who seemed even taller since he had fallen in love with Naomi.

They stopped and turned when they saw David Stoltzfus striding up the driveway of Eagle Hill. David dropped by Eagle Hill every other day to check on Molly, he said, though he always accepted the invitation of a cup of coffee in the kitchen with Rose and Vera. On this day, Rose saw Naomi hurry back through the privet and Tobe remain outside with David for a long while.

The two walked together to the porch, then sat on the steps, deep in conversation. Bethany had left the window open to air out the kitchen after burning a pan of granola in the oven. Rose crossed the room to close it and stopped abruptly as she heard Tobe mention the name of Jake Hertzler.

"Why does God allow innocent people to get hurt? My father wasn't a bad man. He was a good man who was trying to help people with their money. God let him die for it. It's like God has no sense of fair play."

Rose held her breath. She wondered how David Stoltzfus might respond to a comment like that. If anyone but Tobe said it, Vera would have called it blasphemous. But David Stoltzfus didn't seem at all shocked or put off. In fact, he asked a few questions to encourage Tobe to keep talking.

Tobe wondered why a loving God could be so unjust to allow Jake Hertzler to have the freedom he seemed to experience. David Stoltzfus had an answer for that. He said it was God's plan to test men's love and goodness for each other. "It's easy to love God," David said. "Nobody has any problem in loving our heavenly Father. The problem is to love people who have sinned against us."

Tobe didn't respond and Rose backed away from the window. Would this ever go away? she wondered. Jake Hertzler's hold on her family went on and on. No one seemed to be able to move forward—not Bethany, not Tobe. Maybe . . . herself too. She had tried so hard to not allow vengeance to take hold of her heart.

A little later, when David came into the kitchen and sat at the table for a cup of coffee, Rose couldn't help but notice how easy it was to talk to him. They had so much in common: their spouses had passed, they were trying to fill the roles of both mother and father to their children. He liked to talk and he was never in a hurry, unlike Galen, who wasn't much of a talker and was always on to the next thing. At first, she felt a little nervous to see David stroll up the driveway of Eagle Hill; she knew he must be busy with the Bent N' Dent and settling his family into the farm. But soon she realized he liked people, he liked visiting, talking. It was nice to be around someone who thought the way she thought, felt the way she felt, understood what she was experiencing. She shouldn't compare David to Galen, but she wondered if she and Galen would ever be able to see eye to eye about children. About Tobe.

During recess one morning, a crowd of children surrounded Jesse Stoltzfus as he sat on the ground and began to unravel one of his socks. Mim sidled a little closer, trying to figure out what he was up to. Whistling through the gap in his front teeth, Jesse wrapped the yarn from his sock around a dried-up old apple. He kept winding and winding, and after a few minutes, he had made a ball.

What was it about boys and balls? If there was snow or a stone or an apple and a sock, there was a ball. And if there was a ball, there was a game. She knew this because of her brothers, Sammy and Luke, who turned any and every thing into a ball. Eggs from the henhouse, pillows from their beds, socks from their sock drawer.

When Jesse had tied a knot to finish off the ball, the children ran to the bases. He looked over at her, standing near the tree where the children carved their initials at the end of each school term, and he waved to her. "Come on and play with us, Mim. Put away your notebook."

She shook her head. She had absolutely no talent for hitting or catching a ball and had given up, humiliated long ago.

He tossed the ball to Luke so the game could get underway, slipped his bare foot into his shoe, and walked toward her.

She ignored him when he stood in front of her. "I have work to do, and you distract me."

"The Mrs. Miracle column?"

"Yes." Mim squinted at Jesse. "And don't you dare say a word."

"Not me." He plopped himself on the ground next to her. "Your secrets are safe with me. Half the time, I don't even listen."

That she believed.

"I don't mean that. Actually, I do. I always mean what I say. I just don't always mean to say it out loud."

"Jesse, why don't you just go play softball with your sock apple ball?"

He didn't budge. "Why don't you ever play softball?"

"I can't hit."

"You're going to have to play in the end-of-year game. Eighth graders versus the sixth and seventh graders. Teacher Danny is playing for them to even out the teams. 'Cuz of me, due to my athletic prowess."

She rolled her eyes. "I can't. I really can't hit."

"We need every player. We have to win." He frowned. "Can you catch?"

"Nope." She shook her head. "But sometimes, I can throw a ball and get it pretty close to where it's supposed to be."

"You mean, pitch?"

She nodded.

"Risky," he said. "I like that in a girl." He looked up at the budding leaves on the tree for a moment. "Miriam, my lovely lass. Have you ever heard of a knuckleball?"

She sensed a trap.

# 16

⟨ornament⟩

Brooke Snyder was naturally nosy and Eagle Hill was turning out to be a place of high drama—always a compelling curiosity to her. Something big had happened the other day but she couldn't tell what and not knowing was driving her crazy. Midday, a buggy had arrived with two very serious and grim-looking Amish men. An hour or so later, Brooke watched from the guest flat window as the two climbed back into their buggy, laughing and smiling and joshing each other.

But all afternoon, she noticed that the Schrock family looked serious and grim. Even those two little boys seemed to sense something was awry when they came home from school. Normally hooting and howling, they went about their chores on the farm subdued, unnaturally quiet.

Brooke would have liked to question Mim Schrock about what earth-shaking news those two Amish men might have delivered, but the girl was studiously avoiding her after she had uncovered Mrs. Miracle's true identity and revealed it to her. Perhaps . . . she should have waited for the big reveal. She hadn't meant to alienate Mim and cut off her information source. She was just so pleased with herself for figuring it out!

And she couldn't stop dwelling on the unfolding drama in that farmhouse. She figured it must have something to do with the boy who returned from jail and the baby. How fascinating! Better than a reality TV show.

This morning, before a cup of coffee—which should have been a waving red flag to Brooke, but she was never good at noticing red flags—she blurted out a question to Vera Schrock as the older woman delivered a breakfast tray to the guest flat. "So, Mrs. Schrock, what do you think the chances are that the missing mother will show up and reclaim the baby?"

Vera froze, set the tray on the kitchen table with a decided bang, and turned to Brooke with an icy stare. "What I think is . . . ," she lifted a hand and pointed a finger directly at her, ". . . that you are a girl who needs more on her mind."

Weather permitting, Jesse organized the eighth graders to stay after school to practice their softball game. On the pitcher's mound, Jesse worked with Mim to show her how to throw a knuckleball.

"It doesn't look very hard to hit," she said. "It looks slow and easy."

"If it works, batters can't hit it."

"And if it doesn't work?"

"If it doesn't, even the pitcher doesn't know where it's going."

That made it sound easier to her. "How does it work?"

"It's a mystery. A small flip of the fingers and wrist, and the ball is thrown with zero spin."

He threw the ball. It seemed to go slowly, and Mose Blank, who was in a younger grade but liked to hang around Jesse, cocked the bat and swung. And missed.

The children, especially the boys, howled with laughter.

Then Mim threw the knuckleball, just the way Jesse had taught her. It went slowly, like his did, and it even got close to the batter, but it didn't have zero spin on it. Mose Blank, who normally struck out, hit the ball over the school fence and into the cornfield next door.

Again, the boys laughed long, unrestrained. From the schoolhouse window, she saw Danny watching. Mim was mortified.

"Well," Jesse said philosophically, "this might require a little more practice than I had anticipated."

On the way home from school, Mim leaned over a horse trough at the farm with the huge falling-down barn and examined her face in the still water. Curly hair surrounding a thin little face with a pointed chin. Gray eyes that were hidden by big, clunky glasses.

Out of nowhere, Jesse Stoltzfus was leaning over her shoulder, peering at her face. His lean face was ruddy from the wind. "Pretty terrific look-ing, I'd say."

She snapped up and scowled at him. *That* boy really thought he was somebody. She could only imagine what her grandmother would have to say to a boy who complimented his own image.

"I was talking about you."

Mim stood perfectly still. "Don't make fun of me."

"But you must know that." Jesse said this as if it was as obvious as the day is from night.

"How would I know? No one ever told me."

"I'm telling you."

"Well," she said, at a loss for words. She felt her face and neck redden at the praise. Mim Schrock hadn't known a compliment from a boy before. She put her hand up to her face so Jesse wouldn't see her flush, but his attention had already moved on to the eagles, circling above the creek that ran along the border of Eagle Hill. They weren't far from the eagles' aerie.

"Luke says there are three eggs this year."

"He would know," Mim said, her voice still shaky from the unexpected compliment.

Jesse's eyes were glued on the eagles as they walked down the road. "I think one of them just caught a fish. Look what's in its talons."

Whenever Mim was nervous, she started to spout off facts. "Did you know that bald eagles can lift about four pounds? And that's one-third of their weight. They have hollow bones and about eight thousand feathers. And they can swim too, unless the water is extremely cold and they get overcome by hypothermia." She knew she should stop, but her mouth just kept going and going. "They have excellent eyesight too. They're at the top of the food chain. The very top." She paused, exhausted of eagle facts.

Jesse was grinning at her.

She eyed him suspiciously. "You already knew those facts about eagles, didn't you?"

"Pretty much, but it gave me a chance for a quick nap." He stroked his chin. "But I think you're slightly off on the eight thousand feathers. There are only seven thousand . . . give or take a few during molting season."

So much for showing off her knowledge.

As they reached their driveways, he turned to her. "About the knuckleball, I have no doubt that you'll come through with waving colors."

"Flying colors."

"I only made a mistake to make you feel superior." He swept his hat off his head and bent over at the waist in an exaggerated bow. "I bid you adieu, my lovely lass." Then he turned and ran up the driveway.

Lovely lass? She felt a smile pull at her mouth but fought it back. She barely made it home and up the stairs on shaking legs as she hurried to her bedroom. There she found Luke and Sammy staring up guiltily from the bed where they had been reading her diary.

"I thought you stayed after school," Luke said, flying immediately to the attack.

"We hadn't gotten to anything really private," Sammy said, far more frightened. "Not yet." He handed her the diary like it was a hot potato.

Miriam Schrock, who was considered a lovely lass, a terrific-looking girl, by one of the most intriguing boys in Stoney Ridge (and there were only two), drew herself up to her full height.

"You can explain all that later," she said. "To Mom and Mammi Vera."

"Don't tell Mammi Vera!" Sammy pleaded. "She'll give us a lecture that will last for a month of Sundays."

"Mom won't like what you've been up to," Luke threatened.

Mim's stomach clenched. In that diary were all the thoughts and questions she had about Mrs. Miracle and Danny Riehl and Jesse Stoltzfus. How far had he read?

When she told her mother what the boys had done, they were grounded for a week. "A person must be allowed to have her private life," her mother told the two sulking boys. "It's a terrible thing to invade someone's privacy."

"But there was nothing in it!" Sammy said.

Mim's mother frowned at him. "To say that is making it worse still."

Mim felt as if she was having trouble breathing. She had no idea how much the boys had read by the time she found them. She wasn't worried about Sammy. He was very young and didn't really understand anything at all.

But Luke . . . he was a continual worry to Mim. Luke was nearly thirteen and thought he knew everything.

If he read the part about Mrs. Miracle and figured it out, that meant that two more people now knew her secret identity. *Two more people!*

It felt like she was falling down a hill. She couldn't stop and she couldn't change direction and she was bound to get hurt.

Bethany looked at Tobe thoughtfully across her coffee. She had made the mistake of politely asking him how the new henhouse was going and he assumed she was actually interested in the answer. He explained in meticulous detail the concerns he had about the timing of the new henhouse coinciding with the annual moulting of the chickens. They might get stressed, he said, and that wasn't good for their health. She was just about to tell him that boring a person to death about chicken feathers could create stress too . . . when suddenly she saw a solution to everything.

Tobe would be the perfect answer.

Later that morning, Bethany gathered Jimmy and Tobe and Naomi to share her idea. A brilliant idea, she thought. "Tobe, you need a job and Jimmy needs a manager for his mother's egg farm."

Tobe tilted his head. "I thought Jimmy was the manager."

"I am," Jimmy said. "But I hate chickens. Despise them. I want to get back to my horse breeding business now that Lodestar has come home." He gave Bethany a wink and a nudge. "Thanks to your sister."

"I don't mind chickens," Tobe said, looking a little embarrassed. "In fact, I sorta like them."

Naomi was almost glowing. "Jimmy, what would your mother think of that arrangement?"

"I don't know for sure," Jimmy said, "but it's worth asking."

"Naomi should be the one to ask her," Bethany said. "She adores Naomi."

Jimmy nodded. "That she does. Still, I can't imagine she'd be agreeable. You know my mother."

"What do you mean?" Tobe said. "I don't know your mother."

"Well," Bethany started, "let's just say that Edith Fisher is considered by all to be a woman whom it might be easy to annoy."

Tobe's eyebrows lifted.

The following day, Edith hammered Tobe with questions about poultry when they stopped by her house. He answered every one correctly, then turned the tables and asked her a few questions. "Have you considered speckled Sussex hens? They're less aggressive than the Old English games you've got. The ones you've got might be good layers, but they're mean birds."

Edith glared at Jimmy.

Jimmy glared back. "How was I supposed to know that? I thought all chickens were mean and evil spirited."

"Sussex are friendly, curious birds. Fine layers too." Tobe folded his arms against his chest. "Though if I were going into the market, I'd go for heirloom hens."

Edith gave him a suspicious look. "What are those?"

"They're heirloom breeds of hens—Ameraucana and Marans. They lay brown and white eggs. Their yolks have a bright color, a rich flavor. Taste better than commercial eggs."

"Do tell." Edith stroked her big cheek. "Like heirloom tomatoes?"

Tobe's dark eyes took on a hint of amusement. "Yeah, I guess. Except that these hens are bred to produce more eggs and eat less chicken feed."

Now he was speaking Edith Fisher's language. Saving money.

"Why not sell chicks to small-flock poultry farmers? And what about expanding to raise and sell meat birds? You've got the space for it and there's a market for local birds. It's called the locovore movement."

That brought a whoop out of Edith. "A movement? We call it the Amish way of life."

Tobe grinned. "English folks want food produced locally and are willing to pay top dollar."

He had Edith in the palm of his hand, but he didn't stop there. "We'll have to make a few adjustments—the best results come from having the brooders in field houses that can be moved from pasture to pasture. The more greens they can eat, the better."

Edith frowned. "We've got hawks here."

"Better netting would solve that," Tobe said.

Edith gave Jimmy a look as if to ask why he had never thought of any of this. She decided that having Tobe manage the chicken and egg business would be an excellent idea. *Fallen straight into their laps* was the way she described it.

"I'll arrive early and stay late," Tobe said.

Edith speared Tobe and Naomi with an unblinking stare. She had always been able to apply pressure with a glance. "Nonsense. After you're *officially* married, you'll live here. You can have Jimmy's room. It's the biggest."

Jimmy's eyebrows shot up. "But . . . what about me?"

"You can move into Paul's old room. Oh, wait. I've turned that into my sewing room." Edith dismissed that worry. "Well, we'll find a place somewhere."

"It's high time for you to move on anyway," Bethany whispered to Jimmy. He looked less certain.

"But . . . what about Galen?" Naomi said. "I can't leave him alone."

Edith waved that concern away with a flick of her wrist. "He's a grown man. It's time he found a wife." She pointed an accusing finger at Naomi. "You're the reason some sweet gal hasn't been able to nab him."

Naomi's eyes went wide. "I just thought he didn't want to be nabbed."

Edith snorted. "Fat chance. He's kept his life on hold for your sake."

A confused look covered Naomi's sweet face. Had that truly never occurred to her? Everyone knew that.

Edith jutted out her big jaw. "That's the only way this will work out. My chickens need twenty-four-hour-a-day care."

Naomi straightened her back. "We'll stay, but we're going to live in the Grossdawdi Haus. We need our own home."

Everyone turned to look at Naomi, shocked by her boldness. Edith Fisher was a bear of a woman. A year ago Naomi wouldn't have raised her glance to her, let alone her voice.

Tobe grinned at Naomi. "If that sounds suitable to you, Edith, then it's a deal. As soon as we marry, we'll move in and I'll take over the chicken business. Jimmy can get back to his horses."

Edith grazed her chicken-hating son with a look. "Fine."

Jimmy Fisher beamed. He positively beamed.

Bethany could have floated away on a cloud of happiness. Everything was finally coming together for her!

But a few days later, Bethany found herself moaning to Geena Spencer about her Jimmy Fisher situation over coffee and gingersnap cookies at Eagle Hill. "Thanks to me, the horse has been returned. And thanks to me again, Jimmy can leave the chicken and egg business and resume horse breeding and training. There's nothing stopping Jimmy from asking me to marry him." She rested her chin on her palms. "Except that he can't seem to get around to it." She sighed. "I think he takes me for granted."

"Most men have no idea what they want," Geena said with the voice of authority. "They are much more simple than women think, but more confused as well."

Bethany looked at her. "What else can I do?"

"You need to tell Jimmy Fisher the truth."

"I have been! I've been telling him that I want to get married."

"Not *that* truth. The truth that you are perfectly happy, that you have no wish to change your life from the way it was. Assure him you are more than satisfied with the way things were. There's nothing that drives men as crazy as that, nothing that makes a woman more attractive to a man than realizing she is content the way she is, not scheming and not conniving to drag him to the altar."

"But that's not exactly true," Bethany said. "I'm not totally content the way I am. I *want* to drag him to the altar."

Geena smiled. "You want Jimmy to think—to *know*—you are a prize he had hardly dared to hope for." She reached over and squeezed Bethany's hand. "Because you are. Don't ever forget there are plenty of young bucks in the woods."

"I wish Jimmy realized that."

"Here's a thought for you: Happiness is an inside job. You can't wait for happiness and contentment to arrive. It's up to you to find it."

Bethany mulled that thought over between bites of a gingersnap cookie. "How'd you get so smart about men?"

Geena swallowed her cookie and shrugged. "It's one of the perks of being a youth pastor. You get to observe hundreds of teenagers who are constantly doing a courting dance."

Bethany jabbed her gently with her elbow. "And what about Allen Turner? From what I hear, he's doing a courting dance of his own."

Geena's cheeks flamed and she hopped up to go. "I'm sure I don't know what you mean."

Mammi Vera marched Luke and Sammy inside, clutching their shirt collars so the boys hung like union suits on a clothesline, a stormy look on her face. Mim wasn't sure what had just happened, but it was bad. Even Luke looked contrite. She ducked into the pantry so she could eavesdrop while her grandmother told her mother what the boys had done.

"The Stoltzfuses have gotten a new refrigerator," Mammi Vera told Rose. "The old one was put by the side of the road with a sign that said 'Free.' As I went to get the mail, I noticed the refrigerator and thought I'd take a look—after all, the one we have is on its last legs. So I opened the refrigerator, and there was *that* one. He fell straight out, stiff as cardboard. I nearly had a heart attack."

Luke, she meant. Mim didn't even need to hear her say it.

"Luke!" her mother said. "You know better than to get inside of a refrigerator. That was so dangerous! You could have suffocated if Mammi Vera hadn't come along when she did."

Luke was strangely silent.

"Oh, he knew exactly what he was doing," Mammi Vera said. "He was waiting for some unsuspecting soul to come along and think there was a dead body in the refrigerator."

"What?" her mother said. "Luke, what were you thinking?"

"It wasn't my idea!" Luke said. "Jesse had it all figured out. He took the back off so there was an air vent."

"But you were playing tricks on people?" Her mother sounded incredulous. "A horrible trick like that?"

In a small and puny voice, Luke confessed. "We didn't figure that Mammi Vera would be the first person to come along. Jesse had it timed for when Mim came out to get the mail."

More silence. Mim wondered what kind of punishment would have an impact on Luke.

"Upstairs," her mother said. "You're not to spend time after school with Jesse Stoltzfus for the rest of the week."

Horrified silence followed. Then Luke and Sammy squealed like pigs stuck under a fence. "Unfair!"

"Go." Her mother sounded hopping mad.

Mim waited a few more minutes after hearing the heavy footfall of the disappointed boys on the stairs, until she could be sure the kitchen was empty and the coast was clear. Her heart sank when she heard the scrape of a kitchen chair along the floor and its creak as her grandmother sat down. "You were right to keep them away from Jesse Stoltzfus. He's the root of the problem. He's the one who starts it all. He has a powerful influence on those boys. Powerful. Luke especially. He admires Jesse far too much. Mim is absolutely right. Jesse Stoltzfus is abominable."

Mim sat down in the corner to wait. It would be a long wait. Once her grandmother settled into a chair, she didn't budge. But Mim didn't mind waiting, not so much. Her grandmother had just given her a near-compliment. First time, ever.

The recent rains softened the soil in the vegetable garden, and Rose planned to spend some time, as soon as Sarah slept, turning the soil around the strawberry plants, then adding straw as mulch to keep the bugs away. Come June and July, these berries would end up in jars of jam, glistening like rubies.

The steady beat of a hammer distracted her for a moment. Tobe had finished building the new henhouse and was now enlarging the yard for the chickens. He said they laid more eggs if they had more room outdoors to peck for insects and have dust baths and generally do what chickens loved best.

Rose turned her attention back to the garden. She was spreading straw down one row, then another, when she looked up and saw Galen, slipping through the privet.

*Now. Tell him now.*

"So you were right, after all," he said, his eyes hidden by the brim of his hat. "About Tobe and Naomi staying in the church."

She took a pitchful of straw out of the wheelbarrow and scattered it around a strawberry plant. "It's wonderful news. Vera is lit up like a child on Christmas Day." She set down the pitchfork. "Naomi said you gave them your blessing."

He looked up and his Adam's apple bobbed once. "Rose, I'm sorry about the other day. About our argument."

"So am I." She set down the pitchfork against the wheelbarrow and walked over to him, taking his hand in hers. *Now. Tell him now.* "We can't do this, Galen. There are too many things between us. We need to cancel our plans to wed." Her voice was gentle, apologetic.

Galen was stunned—for a moment he was unable to speak. Just a few feet from the porch, he leaned his back against the railing very suddenly. "Did I do something?"

"No. It's not that simple. We're just at very different stages of life."

"We're only a few years apart."

Her gaze fell to her lap. She put a pleat in her apron with her fingers, then smoothed it out with her palm. "You're so young. It keeps coming back to me, no matter how much I try to put it from my mind."

"Count the love between us, Rose, the happiness. Not the years."

"I don't mean age in a literal way. I mean . . . the way life has gone for us. The paths we've taken. They've been radically different. For heaven's sake, I'm a grandmother now. We're too vastly different ever to spend a lifetime together."

He was gazing at her intensely but sadly. "No. No, that's not what's troubling you. This is because of Tobe."

She sighed. "I suppose you're right. But I'm right too. It seems as if this situation between Naomi and Tobe has shown us the kind of people we are." The sound of a baby's cry came from the kitchen and Rose pulled off her gloves to head inside, responding without thinking.

He straightened, muscle by muscle, and blew out a shaky breath. "If that's what you want, Rose, then so be it." He looked at her as if he wanted to say more, but he didn't.

A hard, tight knot stuck in her throat. She wanted to tell him that this wasn't what she wanted . . . it wasn't at all what she *wanted* . . . but it was for the best. "I hope we can remain friends. Good friends, like we've been to each other."

Galen looked away so that she wouldn't see his eyes fill up with tears. But she saw all the same.

Jimmy Fisher appeared at Eagle Hill one fine May evening, pleased when Bethany opened the door to his knock. "I came to ask if you'd like to go for a walk."

Bethany said thank you but no. She had plans for the evening.

What? He felt surprisingly put out by this. "Don't tell me you've got plans with someone else?" he asked, only half teasing.

"Goodness no. I'm just helping Naomi work on wedding plans."

Jimmy was at a loss for words. That seemed like something that could be easily rearranged. He waited a moment, assuming Bethany might offer to do just that. But she didn't.

His usual smart joke or casual response deserted him.

Brooke Snyder was getting a little tired of cinnamon rolls. Why didn't Jon Hoeffner invite her out on a real date? Maybe she'd gotten it wrong. Her man radar had always been a little off-kilter, like a crooked weathervane. It was possible that she'd misread him. He might not like her romantically at all.

But then again, he always seemed eager to see her. His face brightened and he was fascinated by what she did with her days—which wasn't all *that* fascinating. She had bought a sketchbook and planned to draw some landscape settings around the area, but she hadn't quite got around to it yet. What had happened to her objective to create a new life while she was staying at Eagle Hill? It seemed to have been pushed aside by her consuming preoccupation with Jon Hoeffner. She spent the morning planning what she would wear when she saw him at the bakery. She spent the afternoons fixing her hair to look just so.

She didn't believe in love at first sight or any such foolishness, but there was something that drew her to Jon. She couldn't say what it was. For all she knew, it was the pull of the moon on the Amish countryside. The only thing she was certain of was that she felt sad when the bakery closed and their coffee and cinnamon roll accidentally-on-purpose dates were over. She counted the hours until she would see him again. Those were the thoughts that spun around in her mind as she sat across from Jon at their special table at the Sweet Tooth Bakery.

"What's going on at Eagle Hill?" he asked.

"Too much, if you ask me. I wanted peace and quiet and, instead, it's been as busy as a weekday at Grand Central Station. The family is going to hold church Sunday soon, so there's a lot of sprucing up going on. Tons of people in and out, painting and hammering and the like. Frankly, the place looks much better." She smiled. "Maybe other churches should do the same thing—threaten to hold church at your home so you'd clean it up now and then. Imagine how many home improvement projects would get finished if you thought you were hosting church for two hundred people."

"I think you mentioned a baby?"

She nodded. "Now that's something interesting. Didn't I tell you? I thought for sure I'd told you all about it. The mother of the baby disappeared. Left the baby and vanished into thin air. I heard her car sputter off in the middle of the night and then the oldest girl—Bethany—yelled for her to come back."

Jon looked shocked. Then he quickly arranged his face in its normal, slightly quizzical, casually interested expression. "Any idea where she might have gone?"

"None."

"Think she'll be back?"

Brooke shrugged. "She wasn't much of a mother type, if you ask me. Seemed very young and immature. Maybe it's for the best, now that the boy is back from jail."

Again, Jon's eyes went wide but just for a split second. "You didn't tell me that, either."

"Didn't I?" *So what?* Why would it matter?

"Sounds more like a soap opera than a quiet Amish farm."

Brooke laughed. "You're right. It does."

And then the subject changed as Jon wanted to know what her plans were for the next week. "Nothing!" she replied, too quickly, too wide-eyed. Then, dropping her head, "Well, nothing that couldn't be rearranged."

He swept a slow glance across the bakery and she studied his profile: those beautiful deep-set eyes, the crisp, straight nose, the dimple in his cheek, that thick, wavy hair. "Maybe it's time to make some plans," he said, offering up that dazzling smile that made her stomach do cartwheels. Their eyes met and she heard her own pulse drumming in her ears.

She was sure, just sure, that he was going to ask her out soon.

# 17

Outdoors it was unmistakably May. Lilacs bloomed, fields were velvet green, purple martins swooped around white birdhouses on tall poles, and Eagle Hill had never looked better. Every member of the family, along with friends and neighbors, had spent days cleaning and sprucing up the farmhouse. The windows had been washed, the floors rewaxed, every cupboard and bureau drawer was swept out and reorganized. Even the barn had been tidied so that you wouldn't recognize it. Not a single spiderweb remained.

"I think the farm was perfectly all right," Vera grumbled as Rose finished preparing the food for tomorrow's fellowship lunch. She looked around her transformed home and saw nothing different.

Tomorrow, church would be held at the farm and Bethany and Tobe would be baptized. Rose wished that Dean could know how well his family was doing. She hoped he did.

The kitchen was a hive of activity and Rose looked on in amazement. Chickens boiled in a huge pot, bacon sizzled in another. Fern Lapp had brought over a large pot of bean soup, Bethany and Naomi had baked loaves of bread and dozens of cookies and brownies, other neighbors would bring additional food.

Bethany put the finishing touches on a tray of brownies and swatted away Luke's hand as he tried to snatch one.

"It isn't fair if we don't get to eat them," he said, a whiny twang to his voice.

"There's bound to be leftovers," Bethany told him.

The next morning, there wasn't a hair out of place, a dirty chin, or a bare foot to be seen. Luke and Sammy looked like little angels, Rose thought. It was always a great surprise to her—the difference a little cleaning and polishing could make.

She had barely rinsed out her coffee mug when she heard the wheels of the first buggy crunching onto Eagle Hill's long driveway. Soon, bearded and bonneted neighbors spilled from their buggies and crossed the yard to gather quietly and shake hands. Children, with freshly polished shoes already coated in dust, darted behind their mothers' skirts and around their fathers' legs. The sheep and goat's pasture had become a temporary holding spot for the many horses that had transported families to church. Galen had brought over a few wheelbarrows filled with hay to act as temporary food troughs.

By 7:45 a.m., a crowd of almost two hundred people milled around the yard. Some of the men leaned against the fences or walls, stiff and stern in their dark Mutza coats, discussing weather and crops. The women gathered together in clumps, their black bonnets nodding as they chatted about canning or gardening or children.

Furniture had been moved out of the downstairs to make room for the long, backless church benches, which arrived by wagon and could be transported from home to home. The benches were placed in every spare inch so that nearly everyone could see the center of the house from his or her seat—the center being where the ministers would preach.

Shortly before eight, as if drawn by a silent bell, the women organized themselves into a loose line and filed into the house. The young single women walked at the front of the line, the older ones at the back.

Rose half listened while Elmo preached a message, her attention focused more on keeping an eye on Luke, seated on the other side of the room from her. Normally she followed every word of the sermon, but this morning she wished the ministers would finish early. She was eager to get to the baptisms of Tobe and Bethany and felt very distracted.

A small plate of graham crackers was making its way around the room for parents who had little ones curled beside them. Rose saw Luke reaching out to grab one and she sent him an arched eyebrow look, straight across the room. Luke's hand hovered over the plate, sensing his mother's message without acknowledging eye contact. His shoulders shrugged in a big sigh and he passed the plate along, untouched. Down the row on the women's side, a little girl was making a handkerchief mouse to amuse her toddler sister. She glanced over at Sarah, sleeping in Naomi's arms.

Mim nudged her with an elbow. "Mom, who is that?"

"Where?"

"Sitting next to the insufferable Jesse Stoltzfus." Who, Mim tried to ignore, was flashing her one of his sweet-rascal smiles.

"It's Jesse's cousin, visiting from Ohio. Why?"

"He can't stop staring at Bethany. And Jimmy Fisher keeps noticing that very thing."

To be sure, Jimmy was scowling at Jesse's cousin, who was staring dreamily in Bethany's direction. She was oblivious, Rose realized, her mind a million miles away.

Mim was glaring at Jesse's cousin, not saying a word, of course, but then, she didn't have to. Rose knew just what her daughter was trying to communicate; it was something Vera would do and she had to stifle a smile. Church, Mim was saying with her pointed stare, was not the place to make eyes at a girl.

The silence lay heavy and warm over the house. Bethany relaxed, they were nearly there. Only a few more moments and the baptism would begin. She breathed in the Sunday smells of laundry starch and shoe blacking and coffee percolating. So familiar, yet on this sunny spring morning, she felt as if she were experiencing church for the first time.

Bethany and Tobe had four crammed sessions with David Stoltzfus studying the Dordrecht Confessions. Usually, a minister spent nine sessions of instruction classes to go through all the Articles, but the bishop was eager to get Tobe baptized. Most likely, Bethany reasoned, he wanted to hurry before Tobe changed his mind.

Bethany expected the instruction classes to be boring, and they mostly were, but her brother made them surprisingly enjoyable. He peppered David Stoltzfus with all kinds of bold and audacious questions that the minister didn't seem to mind at all. In fact, he enjoyed Tobe's inquisitive mind and encouraged questions. It was a pity Jimmy Fisher declined to take part in the classes, Bethany mulled for the umpteenth time, because she knew he would've enjoyed the spirited and lively debates.

Earlier this morning, before church began, Jimmy had sidled close to her and asked if Tobe had smooth talked her into getting baptized with him. It wasn't just smooth talk; Tobe had badgered her into taking the classes with him, but Jimmy didn't need to know that. She gave him a benign smile.

"I just can't understand why you'd want to go ahead with it now. I thought we'd wait and do it . . . you know . . . later."

She tipped an eyebrow his way. "Oh? What's later to you?"

"Well, what's the rush to you?"

"It's hard to explain. But it's a real thing, you know, baptism opening the floodgates of grace."

His mouth formed an O, but the word never made it past his lips. He gave her a strange look, before she moved to the porch where the women were gathering.

When the time came for the baptisms, Bethany looked out at the congregation, all those she knew and loved. Her face grew hot and her voice trembled and she felt herself perspire, but she didn't waiver. Bishop Elmo asked her and Tobe questions: Did they still desire to be baptized? Were they ready to say goodbye to the world and to rebuke the devil? Would they stay in the church until the day they died?

Tobe gulped at that last one, took a long time answering, so long that everyone leaned forward on their benches, straining to hear him. He turned and held Naomi's gaze for a moment. In a loud voice, he said, "Yes. Yes, I will," and there was a sigh of relief among the benches.

Then the bishop turned to the congregation and asked questions of affirmation. He motioned to Tobe and Bethany to kneel for a prayer. A prayer so long that Bethany was sure her knees had sailed past hurting and had gone completely numb. The bishop's wife unpinned Bethany's prayer covering as Elmo took a pitcher of water and poured three trickles of water over Bethany—one for the Father, one for the Son, and one for the Holy Ghost—and she felt the water stream down her face. Then she was up, dripping and wet and cold, and she felt new.

The tables groaned with food. Oval platters offered up sandwiches of peanut butter and marshmallow cream mixed together, slathered on homemade bread. A simple bowl of cut apple wedges sat at each table's end. There were trays of bologna and cheese, dishes of pickles and red beets. Coffee, tea, and containers of unsweetened grape juice—a lively purple from Amos Lapp's own vineyard.

Rose set out a pitcher of hot coffee on the table and noticed Galen standing by the doorjamb. There was something about the set line of his mouth that made Rose decide to go and see what might be wrong. She followed him into the kitchen to find Bethany, Mim, and Vera, standing frozen in a tableau, their faces expressing different degrees of horror.

"Mom, you won't believe it!" Mim said, barely able to speak. She held up a tray of half-moon apple pies with the corners nibbled away. "Every single one!"

"And my brownies!" Bethany gasped, white as a sheet. Teeth marks dented the corners of the brownies. Each one.

"It's the same with the apple snitzes!" Mim's tears were now openly flowing down her cheeks. "Luke. It was Luke. I know it was him."

"No—the one to blame is Jesse Stoltzfus! Ee fauler Appel schteckt der anner aa." *One rotten apple corrupts all those that lie near it.* Vera stood with her shoulders pulled back and her bosom lifted high, her nose wrinkled and her mouth puckered. "And now Jesse Stoltzfus has added sweet Mose Blank into his gang. Mose has been following him like a shadow lately and Nancy Blank is beside herself with worry. She blames Teacher Danny. She said it was his idea to get Mose friendly with that awful Jesse. She didn't want her baby to be bullied and now he's turned into a bully. Leroy Blank is talking of getting Danny turned out as a teacher."

Mim gasped and Rose noticed that she looked both horrified and guilty, all at the same time. Mim fled the room and banged out the door of the house.

Mammi Vera's face was working itself into a terrible anger. "When did that ruffian get into this house?"

"Jesse said he'd help the men with the benches," Bethany said. "I told him I had counted all those brownies before he came in. I saw him eyeing the brownies."

"If only they could have just eaten a few," Rose said.

"It's all ruined," Mammi Vera said. "Entirely ruined. How easily the young can be seduced by the devil." Her voice held that familiar high tinge of hysteria that meant a lecture about the devil was on its way. She got very excited when things were emotional.

Rose had to take action. "Of course it's not all ruined, Vera. Bethany, take the coffee out. Vera, hand me a knife. I'll cut up the brownies and put out a smaller selection."

Galen assembled the criminals together in the kitchen: Jesse, Luke, Mose, and Sammy. "Correct me if I have made an error in identifying you four as the ones who ate bites from the desserts."

The boys looked around the room like rabbits caught in a trap.

"Well?" Galen's voice thundered.

"Sammy wasn't in on it," Luke said.

"I did have a few bites, though," Sammy said, his voice full of regret.

"Do you realize what you did? Bishop Elmo and Deacon Abraham are very interested to hear why you felt you had the right to ruin the desserts that Rose and Bethany and Mim made for today's fellowship lunch. Ruin!" Galen roared the last word.

The boys jumped back in fright.

"But I told them I would handle it," Galen said in his cool, slow way. "I told them you had all volunteered to wash every dish and plate and cup and glass. That it was your contribution. Tomorrow, right after school, you'll put the benches back in the wagon and then return the furniture to the rooms. Then you would come to report to me when it is all completed."

The boys looked at each other in dismay. That would take them all afternoon and evening.

Jimmy Fisher wandered into the kitchen, curious about what was going on.

"What about Jimmy Fisher? Would he like to help—?" Luke began.

"No, Luke, he wouldn't want to," Galen said, "and people like Jimmy Fisher will be delighted to know that you volunteered to put away the benches so they don't have to come back tomorrow to do it."

There was a beat of silence.

"This day will never be forgotten," Galen said. "I want you boys to know that. Every time I see you, this will be at the forefront of my mind."

Sammy's eyes began to fill with tears.

"NOW." Galen glared at the boys. "Get started this minute."

The boys rushed outside to start gathering dirty dishes.

David Stoltzfus stood by the door. "Galen," he said, in a voice of warning. "I think you might have frightened them."

"Good."

"Perhaps you could have just asked me or Anna to handle it. They are our children, after all."

Rose looked at David. "Anna?"

He looked puzzled, then gave his head a shake. "I'm sorry. That was my wife's name. I meant Rose. I meant you should have let Rose and me handle it."

"But you weren't handling it, David," Galen said in a patient voice. "You were outside talking to people, completely oblivious to the mischief that your son had stirred up. I saw what you couldn't—or wouldn't—see."

Rose looked across the room at Galen and their eyes locked. There was a message in those words. David opened his mouth to object and Rose cut him off. "He's right, David. He saw something you didn't see."

The boys hurried into the kitchen, tail between their legs as they walked past Galen, their arms full of dirty dishes.

Rose looked once more at the criminals as they filled the sink with hot water and stirred soap into it. It was probably the first time they had ever washed a dish . . . and they would be washing hundreds today. Because her heart was big and the desserts hadn't been entirely ruined, she gave them half a smile.

As Mim helped Elmo locate his buggy in a long row of buggies standing upright against the barn, the bishop kept exclaiming that it was amazing the way time raced by. It was already midafternoon, he said, astonished by that fact. It was extraordinary how old people thought time raced by. Mim found it went very slowly indeed.

A blue car drove into the driveway. Everyone stopped to watch a portly man get out of the car and look over the crowd, milling about, some moseying over to the pasture thick with horses to hitch them to buggies.

"Where is she?" the man said. "Where's Mrs. Miracle?"

Dread pooled in Mim's stomach.

Bethany sidled closer to Mim. "*That's* the features editor of the *Stoney Ridge Times*." She gave her a look of abject pity. "You are in so much trouble."

And didn't Mim just know it.

The buzz of conversation died down, a silence almost like the respectful hush of church came over the crowd.

Elmo walked up to the editor. "How can I help you?"

"Someone in your church writes the Mrs. Miracle column." He gazed around the yard as Bethany ducked into the house. "Some Amish gal drops off the copy and picks up the paycheck every week. I don't remember who she is, but I know she's here."

Elmo looked thoroughly confused. "I don't understand. What do you want?"

"Mrs. Miracle is ruining me, that's what! Her advice is losing advertisers for the paper. She wrote a letter telling people if they'd just stop buying televisions, they'd end up saving their marriages."

The bishop's spiky gray eyebrows drew together, as if tugged by complicated thoughts. "Well now, there could be some truth to that."

"Not when your biggest advertiser is the Stoney Ridge Electronics." His red face grew redder. "Then she told the butcher's kid to not go into the family business. The Stoney Ridge Butcher Shop just canceled a year's worth of advertising!"

Silence. No one said a word. Bishop Elmo turned and looked around those who remained. "Does anyone know who this man is talking about?"

The editor waved a paper in the air. "I can't make out the sloppy signature, but the name of the person who signed the W-4 form starts with a *B*. Last name starts with an *S*. Now . . . where is she? Who is she?"

*BS* for Bethany Schrock, who had signed the paper because Mim was underage. Mim thought she might faint dead away, right in front of the entire church and her family. Her lungs felt like they were on fire and she knew everyone was looking right at her, boring their eyes into her soul.

"I'm the one you're looking for. I'm Mrs. Miracle."

Heads whipped around to see who had spoken. It was the woman from the guest flat, standing about ten yards from the editor. "I'm Brooke Snyder. Also known as Mrs. Miracle." She smiled widely at him. "I've been meaning to get back to you about syndicating the column. Would you like to come in and talk about it over coffee?"

Mim watched the editor follow Brooke into the guest flat. She was stunned, completely and utterly flabbergasted. There was a burning behind her eyes, a hard place forming in her throat.

Jesse Stoltzfus, who seemed to materialize whenever any drama unfolded, spoke up. "Well, wonders never cease!" he said in a very loud voice. "Mrs. Miracle was right here, under our very noses."

Everyone started talking, and the sound swirled around Mim like the clucking of a flock of chickens. She was wordless. A girl who loved words was thoroughly wordless.

Jesse slipped up behind her, his arms full of dishes. In a voice so low Mim had to strain to hear, he whispered, "Stop shaking and trembling. It may turn out all right. If you're smart, you'll realize you just dodged a bullet."

Mim flashed Jesse a grateful look. But he wasn't looking at her. He was gazing at Rose, standing on the porch, talking to his father.

"You've got a lovely mother," he said. "She's strong but kind."

Mim shrugged. "I suppose."

"I guess people don't ever appreciate their own mothers properly, until it's too late." He kept his gaze on Mim's mother. "She reminds me of my own mother."

She didn't know anything about Jesse's mother, other than she had passed recently. She thought about asking him about her, but he darted away, off to the kitchen with another armful of dirty dishes.

She had always thought Jesse Stoltzfus was nothing but a joker, as happy as a fly in pie. But now she wondered if all his jokes were meant to cover up his sadness.

Vera sat at the kitchen table, rehashing the day, the church service, and the dessert disaster.

"Still, all in all, it was a wonderful day," Rose said, as she brought Vera a cup of tea.

To Rose's surprise, Vera's eyes filled with tears. "If only Dean could have been here. If only he could have seen Bethany and Tobe baptized."

But Dean Schrock was in the Amish graveyard a few miles away.

Rose sat very still. As she gazed steadily at her mother-in-law, she realized dark circles had gathered in the hollows beneath Vera's eyes. And lines had been pressed into her cheeks. When had she gotten so old? And why hadn't she noticed before?

"You should have insisted on an autopsy," Vera said. Every few weeks, she brought up this topic with Rose, probing it like a sore tooth. "You should have had more presence of mind. Even now, two years later, I know people are whispering. I know what they think about us. About Dean. They all think he took his own life. You missed your chance to clear his name once and for all." She wiped her eyes with her sleeve. "And now it's too late."

Vera liked to believe that she knew everything. But Vera was wrong. As hectic as that day of Dean's drowning was, Rose had had enough presence of mind to know she couldn't allow the unthinkable. She told the police no autopsy.

If it had turned out that Dean had done himself in, then he would have been buried outside the walls of the cemetery, where the goats and sheep and cows would walk over the graves of those who had not been allowed to have a Christian burial. Life wasn't yours to take, it was a gift from God and those who threw it back in his face had no place being mourned by the faithful.

Because there was no autopsy to confirm or deny the means of death, Dean was buried with honor and the family could give him a good farewell. It was better, she felt; it gave the family a sort of peace. But she knew, even now, that there was a shadow over how and why Dean had died.

After Vera had gone to bed, Rose fed a bottle to Sarah and rocked her in a chair next to the woodstove. She tried to dwell on the day, on the moment of baptism for Tobe and Bethany, a holy moment. But one thing kept interrupting her thoughts and that was Galen's pointed remark to David Stoltzfus: he had seen something David hadn't seen. He was absolutely right. David was often preoccupied with lofty theology discussions while his son Jesse stirred up all kinds of trouble.

But that wasn't all Galen was insinuating, in his quiet way. She knew that. She and Galen may have their differences, but she could count on him to tell her the truth.

Luke wandered downstairs and came over to look at the baby, then walked around the room. Something was on his mind.

"If Dad's in heaven, he could see us now," Luke said, looking at the ceiling.

Dean seemed to be on everyone's mind tonight. But then, she wasn't surprised. Some days were harder than others, and days of significance, like today, were the hardest days of all. "Of course he's in heaven," Rose said, pushing aside the fear that bubbled up to the surface.

"He wouldn't be in hell, would he?" he asked hesitantly. "Suffering torture for all eternity?"

Rose put down Sarah's bottle and looked at Luke in amazement. "Why would you think that?"

"Mammi Vera said that suicide is a sin that can't be forgiven. She said it's giving up hope." He turned and looked right at her. "Do you know what really happened?"

"Luke," she said softly, "what makes you think that your father took his own life?"

"I remember how upset and angry he was. I remember that he couldn't sleep at night. He was unhappy for a long time."

Now Rose was firm. "It's true, he was under a great deal of stress. But I refuse to believe that your father would have done such a thing."

"But—"

"No buts, Luke," Rose said, with a pain in her chest that she felt would never go away.

Sarah had fallen asleep so she tucked her into the Moses basket and covered her up with a blanket. Then she turned to face Luke. There was something he wanted to say, and she could tell he was trying to put it into words.

"Would it have been terrible . . . drowning? Would it have felt like he was choking?"

Rose gave the matter some thought. "No, I think it would have been very peaceful, you know, like the feeling you get when you're falling asleep and you can't stay awake. You feel as if you're being pulled away. I don't think it would have been very frightening."

"Do you think he thought of us . . . of Sammy and me . . . as he was dying?" Luke's voice was shaking.

"I think he would have been hoping that you'd all be all right, that you'd carry on, that we'd be strong as a family and appreciate days like today, when Bethany and Tobe became baptized."

And then, for the first time in front of her since he was a small boy, Luke let himself go and wept.

# 18

Monday dawned beautiful, warm, and springlike. After Mim and the boys set off to school, Rose fed the baby her bottle on the porch swing. Sarah was already changing—gaining weight, stretching out her spindly arms and legs so she seemed less and less like a tightly coiled newborn. The baby waved a tiny fist in the air and Rose offered her finger for her to grab. Such miniature fingers! So fragile, so perfect. Rose wondered where her mother Paisley was and if she even thought about her. When Tobe crossed the yard from the barn, she stopped him.

He held up a hammer. "I'm finishing up a few things with the henhouse."

A wave of irritation about Tobe came over Rose. Those hens were going to end up with a castle. "Not right now."

His head snapped up, surprised by the tone in her voice. "You sound angry."

"I think it's time you take a look at this child," Rose said. "Really look at her. She might be your daughter, she might not. But she might be the making of you. She might make you into the kind of person you need to be." She walked down the porch steps and handed the baby to him.

"I don't know anything about babies," he said. The baby stared at Tobe with wide eyes, evidently as surprised as he was. "What if I do something wrong with it?"

"Her. Not an it. She's a person. Her name is Sarah. A real live human being."

"She's so very small." Just then the baby began to cry, squirming in his hands. Tobe looked helplessly at Rose, but she made no effort to take the baby. "How can anyone know what a baby wants?"

"The more time you spend with her, the more you start to learn her language. Right now, she's telling you she doesn't like the way you're holding her."

He said he was afraid he might drop the child, who started to twist in his hands like a trapped rabbit. She whimpered, then cried, then yelled so loud she turned red as a beet.

"Put her against your shoulder," Rose said. "You don't have to hold her like that—she isn't a bag of flour."

He dropped the hammer and shifted the baby against his shoulder. "Do you think she might be sick?"

"No, she's fine," Rose said. With that she turned and walked up the porch steps, intending to leave him with the baby, who at once began to cry even harder. But, as abruptly as she had started, the baby stopped crying. She whimpered a time or two, stuck her fist in her mouth, and then quieted. He looked so relieved that he scarcely moved. The baby had wet his shirt with drool, but at least she wasn't crying.

"Talk to her a little," Rose said. She stood at the doorjamb.

"What should I say?"

She made a snort of disgust. "Introduce yourself, if you can't think of anything else," she said. "Or sing her a song. She's sociable. She likes to be talked to."

Tobe looked at her blankly. "I don't know if I'll be able . . . I mean, I'm pretty clumsy."

"All new parents are clumsy," Rose reassured him. "You'll get better at it."

He looked at her sharply. "Why should I have to do this at all? The DNA test will—"

"I don't care about a DNA test. You'll do this because this child needs you. You'll do it because you're a decent man. And if that's not good enough"—she bore down on him—"you'll do it because I'm telling you to."

She felt a little heartless, but she knew he had to learn to do it without her.

Naomi tried not to smile as she listened to Tobe's complaints. Rose had insisted that the family, including Naomi, hand over the bulk of responsibility of the baby to him. They were allowed to give him fifteen-minute breaks now and then, so that he could shower or change clothes, but no help with nighttime feedings or walking the baby back to sleep. She was adamant about that.

After two days of being Sarah's primary caretaker, Tobe was near to weeping with fatigue. There were dark circles under his eyes; he looked as if he hadn't slept in days. He walked the hallways with Sarah in the night, trying to burp her after her third feed of the night. He said he found himself stumbling against furniture, almost incapable of remaining upright.

"How can anyone learn to identify what kind of crying means hunger, discomfort, or pain?" he said. "All crying sounds the same—and it all wakes you up from the deepest sleep. No one ever told me how exhausting it is to be up three, four times every night, night after night. This is awful." He was tired all the time.

It didn't occur to him that Rose and Bethany had been doing that very thing for weeks now, ever since the baby was born. Or that Naomi had cared for the baby during the day.

Then, to his obvious relief, Naomi took the baby from him. "I'm going to grab a nap," he said.

"I'll wake you in fifteen minutes," she said, and his smile faded.

There wasn't much Brooke Snyder wouldn't do for Jon Hoeffner. At times, she wondered if she was falling in love with him. Imagine that! Over cinnamon rolls in a little Amish town. So when he asked her for a small favor, she was elated. "How can I help?"

Jon looked at her squarely, kindly. His lips curved up a little on one side, showing off a dimple in his cheek. He seemed a little sheepish to have to ask her for help, but his boyish embarrassment only melted her. "I have a safety deposit box that I share with my sister. It was something our parents set up before they passed on to glory. My sister and I both have to sign to get into it. I need to get into the safety deposit box because I'm trying to sell my car. I've got to get the title." He blew out a puff of air. "My sister is Old Order Amish and frowns on the life I've chosen—driving a car and using electricity and all that. She refuses to talk to me. It's something called shunning. Kind of like excommunication."

"I've heard of that! I saw a reality TV show about the Amish." Then, after thoughtful consideration, "How awful for you."

Jon nodded. "It's been difficult. I'm left out of every family gathering. It's been . . . well, lonely."

Brooke reached out and covered his hand. "How can I help, Jon?"

"Would you mind posing as my sister at the bank to help me get the pink slip out of the safety deposit box? You'd need to sign in as her, but you could do that, couldn't you? You duplicated my signature perfectly."

A tiny alarm bell pinged inside Brooke's head, but she ignored it. "I suppose the signature part wouldn't be difficult. But what about the ID?"

He smiled. "Not a problem. I've got that covered. My sister doesn't have a photo ID, being Amish, so it's just a matter of getting her Social Security card."

"How would you get it?"

He looked embarrassed. "To be entirely truthful, I saw her Social Security card on the counter awhile ago when I asked her if she'd go with me to the bank. When she refused to go with me, well, I'm not proud of it, but I slipped the card into my pocket. I'll put it back as soon as I get this pink slip taken care of."

She thought about it for a while, stirring her coffee. It didn't feel wrong, but didn't feel quite right, either. *Ping, ping* went the alarm in her head. "You promise you'll return your sister's Social Security card as soon as you get the pink slip?"

"Absolutely! I just couldn't think of any other way . . . not until I thought about how easily you copied my signature. Then I realized, well, you were heaven sent." He squeezed her hands and she melted.

"Okay. When?"

The bakery clerk stood by the door, an irritated look on her face. Brooke suddenly realized it was past five and they were the only customers left in the bakery. They hurried outside so the clerk could lock up.

"I'll let you know when I have the deal completed with the car buyer." He closed the distance between them and pressed a kiss to her cheek. "You're a peach, Brooke. I'm so glad we've met." Jon lifted her chin and kissed her lightly on the lips. He smiled, then walked around the corner and disappeared.

Brooke leaned against the bakery door, feeling like she might explode with happiness. *Ping, ping, ping!* That stupid alarm bell kept going off in her head, so she tried to wipe her mind clean of it and closed her eyes to concentrate on the sweet goodbye kiss Jon had just given her.

Tobe handed baby Sarah to Vera and took the pan of spring peas onto his lap. Rose had to smile. He would rather shell peas than hold a baby, but at least he wasn't shirking his duties with Sarah like she thought he might.

"Where do you suppose that Paisley went off to?" Vera asked him.

"I have no idea," he said. "I called the restaurant where she worked and they haven't seen her in months. They said they fired her because she was helping herself to the cash register."

"Did you try calling the manager of her apartment?"

"I did. They said she was evicted about that same time." He rubbed the underside of his nose with his forearm.

Vera looked up. "But then why was she looking for the key to the apartment?"

Tobe's chin jerked up. "Key? What key?"

"She told me she had lost the key to her apartment and thought you had the only spare. She said it would cost her a fortune to get a locksmith out there, so she really needed to find it."

Tobe's face went white. Slowly, he sat up, his spine poker-straight. The spring pea pan crashed to the floor, and peas bounced all over the kitchen. He didn't even realize what he'd done as he turned to Rose. "Call Allen Turner. Tell him to get out here as fast as he can."

Tobe and Naomi sat on the porch swing, waiting for Allen Turner. Every fifteen minutes, Mim went out to check the phone shanty to see if any messages were waiting from the lawyer. Bethany thought they should take turns waiting at the phone, but Rose said no, that they had plenty to do and staring at a phone didn't make it ring. But no one could get much done.

By the time Allen Turner's car roared up to the house two hours later, Rose breathed a sigh of relief, grateful the boys were still helping Galen feed the horses and weren't in on this. She watched Tobe warily, but color was back in his face.

Allen Turner walked in and sat at the kitchen table, an expectant look on his face. "So. What's the emergency, Tobe?"

"Jake Hertzler is nearby," Tobe said. "I'm sure of it."

Ten seconds of beating silence before Bethany added, "I've had the same thought." Tobe snapped his head to face her. "At least, I know he was here in the last few months."

"Me too," Naomi said.

Mim bit her lip. "Same here."

Allen Turner's head turned from Tobe to Bethany to Naomi to Mim, then back again to Tobe. He seemed thoroughly confused and he was not a man prone to confusion.

Tobe pointed to Bethany. "Is this about the horse?"

She nodded and explained how Galen had found Lodestar, abandoned. She looked at Mim. "What makes you think he's here?"

"There's been a couple of times when a car has driven by me, slowly at first, then it sped up to pass me. The driver was a man, and even though I never saw his face, something about him seemed like Jake."

"That's the same feeling I've had," Naomi said. "I thought I saw someone who looked like him near the post office one day. But it was too dark to tell, for sure."

So far, Allen Turner wasn't impressed by hunches and feelings. He glanced impatiently at his watch and turned to Tobe. Soon, all eyes were on Tobe. He took a deep breath and explained to Allen about Paisley's sudden appearance, about the fact that Paisley had known Jake—quite well, in fact. Much better than he knew her—and then came to the part about the key. "Jake must have sent her here to look for the key."

Allen leaned back in his chair. "Tell me about the key."

"It belongs to a safety deposit box in the York County Savings and Loan. The account is under Dad's and Jake's and Rose's name."

"My name?" Rose said.

Tobe looked at her. "Don't you remember when Dad had you sign some papers to set it up? It was right when Jake started working for Schrock Investments. Jake wanted to put the P&L statements in the box each week. Dad felt it would be wise to have three names on it, so two would always have to go together to sign in."

Rose vaguely remembered when Dean set up the safety deposit box, but she had never used the box. Not once. "Go on," she urged.

"I know Jake and Dad visited the safety deposit box regularly, weekly, but knowing Dad, he would have signed in, spotted someone he knew in the bank, got talking to him, and let Jake go into the vault alone. I found the key in Jake's car on the day—" he glanced at Rose and hesitated— "well, I grabbed it. Along with the ledgers."

"Where is the key?"

"I hid it in a very safe place."

"Where?"

He cut another glance at Rose's direction. "I hid it in my mother's nursing home. In her room."

"What?" Rose said. The word came out as a tiny squeak. "Your mother's . . . *what*? She's . . . *where*?"

Tobe pressed on. "My mother isn't well. She's a paranoid schizophrenic. She lives in a home for mentally ill women."

Vera pinned Tobe with an accusing look. "You're mistaken. Your mother left years ago. She ran away and abandoned the children."

Tobe held her gaze for a moment, then flickered aside. "Bethany knows. She visits our mother once a month."

All eyes turned toward Bethany, but her attention was riveted to a small mark on the tabletop. She was aware that everyone was waiting for an explanation, but she hesitated, taking time to gather her thoughts, before her voice cut into the silence. "That's what my mother wanted everyone to think. She knew that Dad would try to have her come home, and that she wasn't capable of taking care of her children. She checked herself into the facility and had papers drawn up that allowed Dad to divorce her because of abandonment. She planned it all out. She wanted everyone to move on without her."

Rose had often heard of people saying they were rooted to the ground by a shock, and she just realized how apt a description it was. She was not able to move, not able to say a word.

It was almost too huge to grapple with. For years, Rose had felt as if she was picking up the pieces that Dean's first wife had left behind. She was astounded to think Mary Schrock had given her family away to protect them. She felt dizzy, as if she might faint, and she tried to steel herself.

*Vera!* She glanced over to see how her mother-in-law was taking this revelation. Vera remained as colorless as skim milk. Her lips moved silently, but not a sound came out. One hand was touching her heart.

Allen turned to Tobe. "What do you think is in the safety deposit box?"

He lifted a shoulder in a careless shrug. "Money. What else? Enough to get him out of town and set him up somewhere. I think he was siphoning money off the top, right from the start."

Allen Turner released an exhausted sigh. "Why didn't you tell me about the safety deposit box when you were getting interrogated? You could've saved us a lot of trouble."

Tobe looked away. "I wanted to deal with Jake myself. I couldn't figure out how, but that was my intention. My plan." He looked straight at Naomi. "I know better now."

"So you think Jake sent Paisley here to find the key?" Allen Turner said.

"He might've, but it wasn't here," Tobe said. "I hid it at my mother's."

"Wait." Bethany's eyes were round as silver dollars. "Wait a minute. Tobe, what kind of a key? Mammi Vera said Paisley was looking for a key to her apartment."

"She was lying," he said. "It was a small key for a safety deposit box."

Bethany gasped. "I know that key. But it isn't there. During Christmas, I was visiting Mom and she gave me the key. She told me not to lose it. She said it belonged to a little boy and he needed it. I didn't know what she was talking about, Tobe. She doesn't make sense most of the time. I just thought it was a key she had found."

Allen Turner looked like he was about to jump out of his skin. "So *where* is the key?"

"It's up in my room," Bethany said, already at the stairs. "I'll go get it."

"Oh no," Mammi Vera said, touching her chest again. "Oh no."

Rose blew out a puff of air. "Paisley . . . she stayed in Bethany's room."

Bethany came back down the stairs, her face white. "It's gone."

Allen Turner didn't seem at all surprised.

Tobe was practically out of his chair. "What if he's already gotten to the safety deposit box? What if he's emptied it?"

"It's possible. I'll get someone to check on that. But if he hasn't connected with Paisley to get the key, then there's time to set a trap."

"Why wouldn't he have connected with her already? They were working together."

"Calm down, Tobe. My guess is that Paisley is smart enough and shrewd enough to make him have to find her. She's got something he wants, and she knows it. If my hunch is right, then we need to flush him out." Allen Turner bit on his lip, thinking, tapping a pencil on a paper. Then a light came into his eyes. "I'm going to put a notice in the local papers that the York County Savings & Loan Bank is going to drill into all inactive safety deposit boxes and seize the contents."

"Do they do that?" Tobe asked.

"Banks do it frequently," Allen Turner said. "The contents get auctioned off and the money goes to the state."

"Can you do that?" Tobe said.

"Oh yeah." Allen Turner smiled, a first. "If I can force Jake Hertzler to make his move, I'll be waiting for him." Then his smile faded. "But this part is my job. Not yours. Your job is to wait." He looked right at Tobe as he said it. "To wait."

# 19

Mim kept bouncing the baby up and down to stop her from crying, but the decibel level was getting higher. The noise was starting to grate on her. She didn't like babies and they didn't like her.

She had agreed to go with Tobe to the doctor for baby Sarah's one-month checkup, but she didn't realize that meant Sarah would be getting a shot. Mim nearly passed out when the nurse brought in that long needle, but she held the baby snugly in her lap and squeezed her eyes shut and wished she had earplugs.

She also didn't realize that Tobe was getting a paternity test. "It's just a swab of the cheek that gets sent off to the laboratory," he told Mim. "No big deal."

"And if it turns out that you are Sarah's father?" Mim had asked. "That seems like a very big deal." Even though she didn't like babies, she did think Sarah was a nice baby, as babies went. Mostly, she had an uncommonly good smell about her. And sometimes the tip of her tongue peeked through her little pink lips. Mim was amazed at the smallness of it, just as she was at her tiny starfish-like hands.

"I'm not."

"But what if you are, Tobe? What then?"

He frowned at her. "I have to know for sure, Mim."

Afterward, as Tobe was paying the receptionist for the paternity test—cash borrowed from Mim with a promise of a high-interest return—and asking how long the results would take, she tried to calm the baby down.

She jiggled her, she paced the room, she sang to her, she hummed to her, she bounced her. Nothing worked. Sarah flailed and began to cry loud, unstoppable sobs. Little tears rolled down her cheeks, making Mim feel even more terrible, if that was possible. She wanted to cry herself. Tobe kept glancing back at both, a worried look on his face. Finally, he came over and got the bottle of formula out of the baby's diaper bag and sat down to feed Sarah.

As Tobe fed the baby, almost magically, the crying stopped, the baby calmed down, and peace was restored.

"It's like she knows, Tobe."

"Knows what?" The baby looked up at him solemnly, as though committing his face to memory.

Mim bent down to kiss the baby's forehead. "Sarah knows you are the one she can count on. She trusts you."

"Babies are too little to know about trust."

"I'm not so sure about that. Trust is a big part of life. If Sarah already trusts you, you're halfway there."

As usual, just like Sammy and Luke, Tobe wasn't listening to Mim. His eyes were fixed on a distant wall, lost in his private thoughts, as if something was weighing heavily on his mind.

Having Brooke Snyder stay in the guest flat for a steady few weeks certainly helped Rose pay some basic bills, but there were always unexpected expenses. A lamb that had to be treated for colic, Sammy needed to go to the dentist for an aching tooth, Mim needed new glasses, Sarah needed her newborn checkups. Rose still hadn't brought up Paisley's hospital bills to the deacon. Soon, though.

Rose looked over the vegetable garden, now planted for summer's bounty. She felt a deep satisfaction in watching things grow. As a child, she had worked alongside her mother to prepare seedbeds, till the garden, plant and tend crops, and harvest fruit and vegetables at the optimal time. They harvested more fruit than they could haul to market, and nearly everything on her table came from her family's farm: cheese and sausage, bread and eggs and jam, apples and peaches and corn.

She scooped up a handful of dirt. This was how her mother had started.

Year after year, her mother had added to the garden plot, until her father finally gave up on wheat and corn and became a full-time fruit and vegetable farmer. There was always a need for lettuce and carrots and onions and zucchini and pumpkins and strawberries.

She walked past the garden, past the barn, to a neglected section that once housed a pigpen. Perhaps . . . she could do what her mother did. Perhaps . . . *this* might be a potential source of additional income.

If she could turn the pigpen into a garden, she could double the size of her output and start to sell produce at a roadside stand. Or maybe even at the Stoney Ridge Farmers' Market where Bethany used to work.

She should get the pigpen plowed under before spring was too far gone. Tobe could do it, but she wanted him to focus on the baby and not have an excuse to leave her care to others. She thought about asking Galen, but that wouldn't be right. Then she saw David Stoltzfus's buggy drive along the road. "Any time you need any help, just ask," he had told her at church on Sunday. Anytime.

She dropped her handful of dirt and watched it scatter in the wind. Why, now was a time she needed a little extra man's help. She tucked a lock of loose hair back under her prayer cap, straightened her apron, pinched her cheeks, and headed over to David Stoltzfus's.

Jimmy stopped by the Kings' every day to check on Lodestar. When he first saw the horse, the day Bethany had given him the good news, he had been shocked at his weakened appearance. If Jimmy had happened across Jake Hertzler that day, he didn't know what he might have done to him— so severe was Lodestar's neglect. The thought disturbed him, knowing he could harm another man. And yet to see Lodestar's condition was even more disturbing. Another week alone, hobbled, without food or water, and that beautiful animal might have suffered a lonely, painful death.

Galen thought it would be best to keep Lodestar at his barn in a big box stall and Jimmy heartily agreed. Galen's barn was more secure than the small Fisher barn. Though Lodestar didn't seem at all interested in escaping. Just the opposite. He stayed at the back of the stall and only seemed interested in food, not in people. But he was making progress.

His ribs were already starting to fill out, his eyes looked brighter, he held his head up again. The vet said it might take months to fully recover, that stress can have a very negative effect on an animal, but he was cautiously optimistic. "He was rescued in the nick of time," the vet told Jimmy, who told Bethany, who said it was meant to be, and that it proved everything happened for a reason. She had a gleam in her eye when she said it too, which made his throat tighten and his palms sweat.

"First things first," he had told her. "Lodestar needs time and attention to mend properly."

At that, she gave him a probing look, one he couldn't read. It set off that panicky feeling deep within him again.

After Jimmy spent time grooming Lodestar, he led him into an outdoor paddock for a little fresh air and sunshine. He stayed nearby, leaning his back against the paddock, boot heel resting on the lowest rung, so he could observe Galen working in the round training pen. Galen was constantly improvising and trying new things, customizing training to the individual needs of the horses. Jimmy didn't want to miss a trick. He was *that* eager for Tobe and Naomi to hurry up and marry so he could retire as a chicken boss and resume his position as Galen's partner in horse training.

On this breezy May afternoon, Galen was in the pen with a newly pur-chased bay Thoroughbred, a gelding with intelligent eyes. Jimmy walked over to the pen, keeping one eye peeled on Lodestar.

"Want to see my new business card?" He pulled one from his pocket and handed it to Galen.

Galen peered at it. "You're calling yourself a stallion manager?"

"That's what I am. I manage a stallion." He glanced at Lodestar, who was stretching his neck to crop new grass near the paddock gate.

"That title usually indicates a knowledgeable, experienced horseman."

"Exactly."

"Is that so?" Galen handed him back the business card. "So do you have better odds pasture-breeding or with artificial help?"

"Artificial help."

"Wrong." He raised an eyebrow. "A healthy mare can call the shots a lot better than a human can." He flicked the whip to keep the horse loping. "Can you keep stallions together in a pasture?"

Jimmy sneered. "Of course not."

"Wrong again. Horses aren't territorial. As long as there aren't any mares or foals nearby, they don't fight over real estate—only females." He gave Jimmy *the look*—the one that made him feel like he was a dense child. "Maybe you want to hold on to those cards a little longer."

Jimmy tucked the business card into his pocket. "Speaking of being territorial, have you noticed David Stoltzfus hanging around Eagle Hill like a summer cold? Something happen between you and Rose?"

"None of your business."

"He's over there right now, plowing up the old pigpen. Folks say he's got Rose marked off with a red flag."

Galen's whole body drew taut and he eyed Jimmy askance. "I suppose you believe everything you hear?"

Jimmy shrugged. "Pretty much."

Galen had already set his mind on the next task: shaking a plastic milk jug partially filled with gravel at the horse to accustom him to unexpected sounds. Jimmy had always been impressed with Galen's ability to focus. He had never been good at getting his mind to consider two facts at once, much less two big facts. He saw Lodestar mouthing the paddock latch and then unhook it. He ran over to stop him, a big grin on his face. He'd been looking for some sign of bluster from Lodestar, some hint of his uppity nature. His horse was on the way back. Truly back.

Jimmy noticed Bethany across the top of the privet at Eagle Hill, smiled to himself, and reflected that she was a remarkable girl. Against impossible odds, she had found Lodestar. She had thought up a plan to help him get out of the chicken business, which he hated, and back to the horse business, which he loved. He owed a great deal to Bethany.

Yes, she was a truly remarkable girl. She was beautiful, sweet one minute, strong and fiery the next. A fellow would never get bored with a girl like Bethany at his side.

What was he waiting for? He knew she was impatient, eager for him to propose. He decided to bring up the subject soon, maybe the next time he took her for a buggy ride to Blue Lake Pond. He exhaled, a matter decided.

Then he spotted Peter Stoltzfus, cousin to the town menace Jesse Stoltzfus, walk toward the Eagle Hill farmhouse. Bethany met him at the bottom porch step and she laughed at something he said. The sight and sound of it disturbed him, and he was annoyed at himself for being disturbed.

Mim was walking home from the Sisters' House, past the nearly-falling-down barn, when she heard some loud whoops and shouts coming from the barn. She saw three boys climbing on the roof, trying to reach the peak, egging each other on. Boys she recognized. Luke, Mose Blank . . . led by Jesse Stoltzfus.

"First one to the top wins!" Jesse shouted.

One loud crack filled the air, then another sound of creaking timber, and another. Seconds passed. Suddenly the boys disappeared in a blur of motion as the barn roof collapsed. The moment lasted forever. Too scared to move, Mim gave a piercing shriek that rent the afternoon air.

She raced like the wind to get to Eagle Hill, sprinting past the school-house and through Amos Lapp's cornfield and jumping across the creek to reach the shortcut to the farm. The first person she spotted was David Stoltzfus, starting to plow one row of the old pigpen.

"They're dead!" she shouted to him, waving her arms. "Luke and Mose and Jesse! They're all dead!"

David dropped the plow behind the mule and ran to her. "Calm down, Mim, and tell me what happened."

"The nearly-falling-down barn fell down! The boys were trying to climb to the top and it collapsed on them."

Together they ran toward the accident, expecting the worst.

As they arrived at the now-fallen-down barn, Jesse and Luke were climbing out of the debris, dusting off their clothes, grinning and laughing like they were at a Sunday picnic. Mose sat on a rock, holding up his elbow with one hand. His other hand dangled at an odd angle.

It was a fine day for the turning of the sod. Bethany smiled to herself as she saw Amos Lapp and Galen King put their hands together on the shovel and dig into the ground of one of the small garden plots at the Second Chance Gardens behind the Grange Hall. Geena Spencer asked Bishop

Elmo if he wanted to say a few words about the results that came from a caring community.

*Oh, big mistake!* The bishop ended up saying a great many words. He had a habit, when he spoke, of clasping his hands at his spine and rocking back on his heels. When he did, his black shoes would squeak. They squeaked now as he rocked repeatedly, lifting his face to the sky while composing his words.

When Elmo finally wrapped it up, Geena took command, dividing Amish and wayward girls from the Group Home into groups to work together, giving them lists of chores. It was remarkable how much authority a relatively small woman like her could possess, and Bethany admired her tremendously.

All throughout the day, Bethany and Jimmy worked companionably on the garden plots. Toward the end of the day, when normally she might have lingered and ended up going home in Jimmy's buggy—via a stop at Blue Lake Pond—she pondered what to do. Should she stay or leave early? Hard though it was to do, she excused herself and said goodbye.

"You're leaving now?" Jimmy said, surprised and bothered. His disappointment was honey to her soul.

"I have a few things to take care of," she said. And she was gone.

The next day, he was thoroughly put out. "Are you going to keep running away all the time? I was hoping we could plan a picnic."

Big eyes wide, she said that honestly she was sorry . . . she just had a lot of things to do lately. But, of course, she would be delighted to have a meal with him sometime . . .

There was a silence. Jimmy went on to fill it.

"I thought you might arrange it," he said.

In the old days, like every day up to this minute, Bethany would have immediately made plans and offered to prepare a picnic and tell Jimmy what time to pick her up. This time she made no such offer. He reached for her hands, but she pulled them away.

"Oh no, I wouldn't dream of it. If you are asking me to have a picnic, then you must, of course, choose when and where." He was inviting *her*— he must remember that.

Jimmy had, of course, expected Bethany to make the picnic. She realized that the next day as they were sitting on the banks of Blue Lake

Pond, eating peanut butter and sardine sandwiches on day-old bread. She nibbled on the corners of the unappetizing sandwich, smiling, pretending it was delicious.

From far away came a faint sound like old nails being pulled from new wood. Over the treetops flew a wedge of Canada geese, squawking and honking, heading toward the pond. They landed on the surface of the pond with such grace that it moved Bethany to a silent reverence.

Jimmy seemed slightly distracted as he took a bruised apple out of the basket and looked for a spot to bite into. His mind was somewhere else. Eventually he got around to what he wanted to say. "Are you seeing Jesse Stoltzfus's cousin?"

"Who? Oh, Peter?"

"He's been hanging around Eagle Hill."

"He's a very nice fellow."

"Bethany, have I annoyed you lately? In a different way than usual?"

"No, of course not." The warm wind kissed her face, fluttered the ends of her capstrings.

"Are you sure?"

"Nothing I can recall. Why do you think you did?"

"I don't know. You're different. You don't stop by Galen's when I'm over there with Lodestar. You didn't make a picnic today. You don't shoot sparks at me like you usually do. I wondered if you were trying to say something to me . . ."

Her eyes widened innocently. "Like what?"

He looked out at the lake, at two ducks paddling around. "Maybe . . . you're interested in someone else. And I'll admit the thought made me feel like a jellyfish without a backbone."

The face she turned to him wore a polite expression. "You invited me to a picnic and I'm here. And I'm having a lovely time." *Not really.*

He brightened up at once. "A picnic made by my own two hands." He winked at her and threw the sandwich into the lake so the ducks dove for it. "It's just a feeling I've had lately . . ." He took her hands in his. "I wouldn't want to ever lose you, Bethany. In fact, lately I've come to realize how very much you mean to me."

Gone was the lighthearted banter, now he was being serious and caring.

For a moment, Bethany swayed. *This* was the moment she'd been waiting for with him, the moment she had hoped for.

"I value you . . . Bethany . . . and I really do appreciate all you did to get Lodestar back and get Tobe set up to work with the chickens."

There was a beat of silence and she looked at him expectantly, not helping him out.

"I think I'm ready to get engaged."

I *value* you? I *think* I'm ready to get engaged? As if he was doing her a big favor? As if she was a broodmare he was thinking about buying? *Shootfire!* Her heart was pounding, a torrent of words was stuck in her throat, but she forced herself not to reply, not to reveal any hint of emotion. She *wanted* to throw the picnic basket at him, jump on the buggy, and gallop home, leaving the dense oaf to walk home. But she remained composed, cucumber calm.

He squeezed her hands. "Well, say something," he said, anxious to know.

"I don't have any words," she said truthfully. None that were ladylike. None that would be found in *A Young Woman's Guide to Virtue*, Mammi Vera's beloved book.

"Yes would do."

She gave him the sweetest smile she could muster, under the circumstances. "I'll need some time to think it over."

Jimmy blinked. "Why is it so hard to answer now?"

"I'm quite happy with things the way they are," she said, and to her surprise—her complete surprise—she truly was. "Marriage is such an important step—I want to make sure it's the right decision." Maybe Geena was right. Men were simple. And she would need to be equally simple in return. She shrugged. "Besides, what's the rush? We have plenty of time."

Gently, she slipped out of his grasp, rose, and walked toward the lake, tossing the peanut butter and sardine sandwich in bits to the hungry ducks, hoping it wouldn't make them sick and die. She felt lighthearted, almost dreamy. Jimmy, she noticed, when she turned to face him, was sitting where she had left him, his thick, dark brows drawn together in a confused frown.

In a little under two weeks, Naomi King would become Mrs. Tobe Schrock. Her sisters were coming soon to help with wedding preparations, and then the quiet life she and Galen had shared would be over.

Tomorrow, Naomi's sisters, both married with families of their own, would slide into the farmhouse and assume control: suggesting, helping, organizing, giving orders and instructions. Naomi felt a sense of over-powering relief that someone was taking charge. After all the waiting she and Tobe had done over the last eight months, their official wedding day was drawing near. Her heart tripped over itself and her skin flushed with excitement. Did every woman who got married go through this must-pinch-myself-to-believe-it stage? She felt so filled with joy and happiness, she could have burst with it.

And yet she felt a tinge of sadness too, knowing this was the last day she would have with her brother Galen. She worried about him, being alone, being lonely. She wasn't sure exactly what had happened to separate Galen and Rose, but she hoped the frost might thaw between them. She wished Galen would talk to her about Rose, but he was a man who kept his busi-ness to himself, especially business of the heart.

Naomi was sewing the seams of her blue wedding dress and put it aside when she heard Tobe's special rap on the door. In his arms was Sarah, sound asleep. He bent down to graze Naomi lightly on the lips, one kiss, two kisses, a smile, and then he passed the baby into her arms. He looked into her eyes with a combination of serious intensity and warmth. "To-day's the last day."

How sweet! He had realized she was feeling sentimental about her last day she would be living with her brother.

"Today's the last day before the bank is going to drill open the inactive safety deposit boxes."

"Oh . . ." Surprise and deflation colored the single word. "But not really, right?"

"No, but Jake Hertzler doesn't know that." Tobe sat at the table and leaned on his elbows, hands grasped tightly together. "What if he doesn't see the advertisement? He should have shown up by now."

"Maybe he was having trouble locating Paisley and the safety deposit key. She sure did disappear."

"What if he doesn't show up today?"

Naomi sat next to him at the table, shifted Sarah into the crook of her arm, and covered his hands with her free one. "Then we do exactly what we've been doing. We leave Jake Hertzler in God's hands."

When Bethany arrived at the Sisters' House for work on Friday morning, she found the sisters sitting around the dining room table, like they often were, having tea.

"Come in," Sylvia said. "We're all kerfuffled."

"I never liked him," Ella said.

"Who?" Bethany asked, but no one was listening.

"Now, we don't know what the problem was," Lena said.

"Maybe there wasn't a problem," Ada said. "Maybe he finished his work and had to leave."

"Without a goodbye? Without a word to us?" Fannie said, clearly annoyed. "Without a single thank-you for all those weeks of room and board?"

"I never liked him," Ella repeated.

Bethany picked up a pile of newspapers. "Who are you talking about?"

Fannie sighed. "Our fourteenth cousin twice removed. He left this morning."

"Doesn't he go out to do research each day?"

"Not that kind of left. Left, left. He's gone." Ada snapped her fingers. "Just like that."

Bethany stopped and turned. "Why?"

"We don't know. He didn't say a word. Ella heard him packing up before dawn. She went to see what the racket was all about and he just brushed past her, without a word."

Ella nodded. "I never did like him."

"That doesn't make sense," Bethany said. "Are you sure he's really left? Maybe he just had someone he had to see."

"Go see for yourself."

Bethany went up to the second floor. The door to the guest room was wide open. She walked inside and caught a whiff of a familiar scent: Old Spice shaving cream. Unlike the one other time she had been in it, when it was a pigsty, the room was now empty. No garbage in the wastebasket, no clothes on the floor. No sign that anyone had been there. Only the bed was unmade and disheveled. She looked in the closet. Empty. She pulled open the dresser drawers. Empty. She noticed a silver wrapper on the floor and bent down to get it, sniffed it to see how fresh it was: it was unmistakably peppermint gum. Her mind started to race. She could feel her heart start to thump. She spotted something under the bedcovers. She shook out the sheets and a newspaper fell to the ground. She reached down, unfolded the newspaper—the *Stoney Ridge Times*—and felt a shiver run down her spine.

On the front page was the story about the York Savings & Loan, drilling into unclaimed safety deposit boxes and allowing the state to seize the contents. Her hands started to shake as awareness dawned on her. Fighting to control the tremors that shuddered through her, she made her way out of the room on shaky legs, then dropped on the top of the stairs and sat down, holding her head in her hands. Thinking of that man in the same house with those five dear, defenseless sisters, for weeks now, made her feel as if she might throw up.

Jake Hertzler *was* the fourteenth cousin twice removed.

# 20

~~~~~~~~~~~~~~~~~~~~~~~~~~~~~~~

Mim took the broom from her mother and began pushing the dirt toward the corner of the porch.

"Are you feeling all right, Mim?"

Mim leaned on the broom with her cheek. Tears were in her eyes. "Mom, I've done something wrong." The terrible sadness she felt nearly choked off her words.

Her mother took the broom from her and propped it against the wall. "Let's sit down."

They sat on the porch swing and, very simply, Mim began to tell the story about Mrs. Miracle. At no stage did her mother's face look anything except sympathetic. It registered no shock, no disbelief. She seemed to take it all in and to realize the enormity without resorting to panic.

Cold shot through Mim's insides. She put her fingertips against her mouth. "You knew, didn't you?"

Her mother nodded. "Well, I've suspected for a while."

"But . . . how?" She had been so careful, so surreptitious.

"It wasn't hard to figure it out."

"Why didn't you say something?"

"I thought it would fizzle out, just like the letters to the inn fizzled after the bishop had you take down the '*Miracula fieri hic*' phrase on the Inn at Eagle Hill sign. I didn't realize the column was having such an impact until just recently. I've been hearing a lot of murmuring about the advice Mrs. Miracle gave out. Good advice." She smiled at Mim. "To be perfectly honest, I could see that you were gaining confidence in yourself and so I let it be. I put that above the rightness or wrongness of the column. I made a mistake, I think."

Mim had never known an occasion when her mother had been wrong or at a loss for a word. Her father, now, he was different, he had always been scratching his head and saying he hadn't a clue about such things. But Mim felt her mother was born knowing all the answers. "Do I have to tell the bishop?"

Her mother gave that some thought. "Is the column truly out of your hands?"

"I don't have any idea what Brooke Snyder plans to do." She bit her lip. "Should I talk to her?"

Her mother gazed down at the guest flat. "She packed up and left this morning. She said she had gotten what she came for and it was time to leave."

"*What?*" Mim asked, shocked. She had avoided Brooke Snyder all week, unsure of how to handle the betrayal, and now it was too late. Mrs. Miracle was truly gone. For her, anyway.

"Mim, if you are asked about the column by the bishop or the deacon, then you must tell the truth."

"I never actually lied about it. Not to you or anyone else."

Her mother's smile faded. "Mim, there are lies you tell with your lips and lies you don't need your lips for. Once people start telling lies, then they become like spiders who weave their web about themselves. They become stuck—caught by the lies all about them. And then they can't get out of the web, no matter how hard they try." Her mother shook her head in regret over these mendacious unfortunates, and then, as an afterthought, added, "That is a fact, Mim. A well-known fact."

Brooke Snyder hated dogs. She would leap in terror when any dog gave a perfectly normal greeting. She was sorry to leave Eagle Hill today but wouldn't miss that big yellow dog that jumped up on her whenever he saw her. Sorry, but ready to go. This time at the inn had been just what she needed. She felt refreshed, reinvigorated, a teensy bit guilty about making off with the Mrs. Miracle brand, but she assured herself she had done Mim Schrock a favor. A syndicated newspaper column would get too big for a naive Amish girl. It was all for the best.

Brooke had come to Eagle Hill to nurse her wounds and find a new life direction. And she was leaving with a new career as a syndicated newspaper columnist—amazing!—and a boyfriend! Jon Hoeffner might not actually be her boyfriend yet, but things between them were moving in that direction. She had never been happier.

Brooke did have a few misgivings about helping Jon with this safety deposit box signature, but each time she voiced them, he reassured her and she felt better. He was very reassuring, very persuasive. This afternoon, she was to meet him at the York County Savings & Loan so he could get the title. "The fellow who wants to buy my car lives in York County. This way, I'll be able to get the car right to him."

"But how will you get back to Stoney Ridge? Do you need me to drive you back?"

"No. I'm actually leaving Stoney Ridge. I've finished the work I came to do. My cousin said she could drive me. It's all set."

She looked at him blankly. "But where will you be? I mean . . . will I see you again?"

Jon slipped his arms around her waist. "Of course. Absolutely. Just try and keep me away." He kissed her then, a kiss that left her breathless. He made her feel so special.

That was the moment when she decided to leave Eagle Hill. There was no reason to be in Stoney Ridge if Jon wasn't there. And she had taken pains to avoid Mim Schrock this week, though she sensed that Mim was avoiding her too. That cranky grandmother was bringing down the breakfast tray each morning.

When she pulled into the bank's parking lot, she waited in her car for Jon to arrive, feeling another spike of concern. Where was he? It dawned on her that she didn't know what kind of car he drove. Not for the first time, she realized how little she knew about him. He fascinated her—she was determined to discover more. She glanced at her cell phone to check the time, then looked up to see Jon getting out of a car that had pulled up in front of the bank. A woman—his cousin?—would be dropping him off.

Brooke grabbed her purse, and as she got out of her car and walked toward him, she heard the woman shrieking, "You said half. HALF! Don't think I don't know what kind of trick you're capable of pulling."

Jon leaned down to say something through the passenger window. The car peeled away and squealed to a stop in a space across the parking lot. Brooke slowed, hesitating, confused. But Jon didn't seem at all upset. As soon as he saw her, his face broke into that smile that made her knees turn into Jell-O.

"Brooke! There you are." He reached his hands out to her, smiling that charming smile. "You look gorgeous, absolutely gorgeous."

Brooke relaxed. The woman in the car was forgotten.

He took her elbow and steered her into the bank. "Thanks again for helping me with this little problem. Shouldn't take more than a few minutes." He sounded as pleased and grateful as if she had offered to walk his dog while he was at work.

That tiny hitch in Brooke's conscience silenced again. This would only take a moment, he had said. Jon went over to the teller and explained that they needed to open a safety deposit box. He gave the teller his driver's license and signed in the book.

While the teller was distracted with another customer, he slipped a Social Security card into Brooke's hand. "Here you are. Just sign on that line under my name and you're good to go."

Brooke glanced at the Social Security card to study the signature while the teller was away. Rose Schrock. Rose Schrock? She glanced up at Jon. "The innkeeper at Eagle Hill? *She's* your sister?"

"Yes."

"But she doesn't seem like the kind of person who wouldn't help you get the title for your car."

Jon glanced at the teller, who was now occupied on the phone. "Trust me."

Something wasn't adding up to Brooke. She looked into his eyes. "Jon, what's going on here? What's really going on? Who was that out in the car—that woman who said she wanted half? Half of what?"

"I don't know what you're talking about." His relaxed façade stripped away as he stabbed the sign-in book with his finger. "Just sign."

She looked at the signature book and saw Jon had signed his name as Jake Hertzler. Who in the world was Jake Hertzler? She felt a bead of perspiration drip down her spine. "And if I don't?" Her words trailed off.

Jon leaned forward to whisper in her ear as his hand latched onto her forearm. "Then I will have to make a discreet call to the FBI to let them know that Brooke Snyder reproduced a Jean-Baptiste-Camille Corot to be sold as an original on the market." His fingers bit into her arm. "That she admitted as much and I have her confession recorded on my iPhone." He gave her his most charming smile. "There's an app for everything."

She was so stunned, she didn't move a muscle.

He had lied to her! There *was* no title for a car. There was *no* Amish sister. This man was doing something deceitful—something to hurt Eagle Hill innkeeper Rose Schrock. A veil dropped suddenly and she saw the true Jon Hoeffner. She could sense the vindictiveness in those cold, pale eyes, something worse than heartlessness. It was a malevolence with which she simply did not know how to deal.

Jon motioned to her that the teller was approaching and he put a pen in her hands. "Sign."

She could sense his vengefulness growing, and her hand shook as she picked up the pen to write out Rose Schrock's name. The teller glanced at their IDs, compared their signatures, and buzzed them into the vault.

Jon smiled benignly at the teller and turned to Brooke. "Rose, there's no need for you to go in with me. You can leave." He flicked his fingers at her. "Go." He walked into the vault, whistling.

What had she done? What had she just done!? Brooke stared after Jon, realizing only now how weak-kneed she was. She sank onto a bench in the bank, hugging her shaky stomach. *Well, he backed you into a corner, so what are you going to do? Sit quaking like a pup with palsy or get out of here?* She walked, practically ran, to the door and exited the bank, gasping in the fresh air. It was over. *Thank God!*

Brooke searched the parking lot for the car where the woman who had shrieked at Jon was waiting. It was gone.

Then she felt a hand on her elbow and looked into the face of a very serious man in a dark suit. "Ma'am, you'll need to come with me." He took her purse and led her around the side of the bank to a waiting police car. Her eyes were wide in horror and her panic skyrocketed.

"He tricked me! He's still in there. Go after him! Jon. Jake. Whatever his name is. *He's* the one you want. Not me! I'm innocent. I don't even know what he's up to. I thought I was just doing him a small favor."

"Relax, ma'am. We're just waiting for him to finish emptying the box."

Not a moment later, Jon strolled out of the bank, calm as could be, unaware that two undercover police officers were closing in on him. When he spotted them, he dropped his messenger bag and tried to run, but they cornered him against the wall and handcuffed him. "Jake Hertzler," she heard the man in the dark suit say. "I'm with the Securities Exchange Commission. You're under arrest. These officers will read you your rights."

Jon—or Jake? or *whoever* he was—looked angry and defeated as he was led to another police car under the efficient armlock of an officer. Jon was a sham, she thought angrily, he was a fraud. His con man's eyes were as innocent as an altar boy's. How could she have been so naive? So stupid?!

Brooke felt as if she had stepped outside herself and was watching this whole terrible scene without being a part of it. She heard the police officer read Miranda rights to Jon/Jake. He repeated them to her as he told her to put her hands behind her back and slipped handcuffs around her wrists. "You have the right to remain silent . . ." Everything had turned out in the worst possible way. A terrible emptiness took hold of her.

*What have I done?* she thought. *What have I just gotten myself into?*

# 21

Allen Turner called Rose and said he was on his way to Eagle Hill, to expect him around half past eight. He asked if she could gather the entire family together to hear some important news about Jake Hertzler. "I'll pick up Geena and bring her along, if that's all right with you."

Rose assured him that would be fine.

She sent Sammy to bed early, but Luke was invited to be part of the meeting and it pleased him to be singled out. Naomi and Tobe, Bethany, Mim, Rose, Vera, and Luke all sat at the kitchen table, waiting for Allen Turner to arrive.

The clock was ticking and there was a little whir between each tick. Rose had never noticed that before. The clock ticked on with its new whir, and none of them said anything at all.

Allen Turner arrived at 8:30 on the dot with Geena by his side. He sat down in the chair at the kitchen table where he had first interrogated Tobe, months ago. Rose wasn't sure what had happened today at the bank, but she had a feeling that this night, finally, there would be closure. A revealing. *The* revealing.

"We seized the contents of the safety deposit box," Allen Turner said. "There was over one hundred thousand dollars in cash. Jake Hertzler admitted he had been skimming off the top of Schrock Investments during the two years he worked there. Not enough to be noticed, just enough to feather a nest." Allen let out a sigh. "That money will be divided up and returned to investors as part of their claims."

"I'm amazed he confessed to all that," Rose said.

"There's a reason," Tobe said, eyes fixed on Allen Turner. "He wanted to deflect other charges."

"Yes, Tobe's right," Allen said, nodding. "What I wanted to tell you in person was that Jake Hertzler plea-bargained with the state to reduce the charge of homicide to accidental manslaughter."

"Homicide?" Rose was confused. "I don't understand."

"According to Jake's confession, your husband found him fishing at the lake early one morning. Your husband had figured out the whole picture of what Jake had been doing to Schrock Investments—skimming money from the company, keeping a set of cooked books, faking bank statements. Dean Schrock went to confront him.

"They argued, pushed each other, and Dean Schrock slipped off the dock and fell into the lake. Jake said he thought he would come back to the surface, but he didn't."

Tobe leaned forward and jammed a finger on the tabletop. "But what if Jake was lying? What if he pushed Dad in the water? He couldn't swim well. Jake knew that!"

Allen Turner remained utterly calm. "There's a large rock near the dock—a diver confirmed as much this afternoon. Because there was no autopsy, we'll never be able to determine the exact cause of death."

"So Jake just left him?" Bethany said, eyes glistening with tears. "He just left?"

"He pulled him out of the water and onto the dock."

"But," Bethany said, her voice breaking, "how do you know that? How do you know he didn't push Dad in and leave? Are you just taking his word for it? Because he's a liar!"

Allen fixed his gaze on Tobe. "Because there was an eyewitness. Wasn't there, Tobe?"

The entire family snapped their heads in Tobe's direction, staring at him with wide eyes and dropped jaws.

"Tobe, were you there?" Horror sent Rose's heart clubbing at the thought of him watching his father drown.

Tobe gave a solemn nod. "I'm the one who found Dad on the dock. I ran to a cottage and asked them to call 911. I stayed with Dad, I tried to do CPR on him, but he never responded." He rubbed a hand through his hair.

"You did what you could," Rose said softly. She simply could not speak anymore, didn't know how he could. She put her hand on his shoulder.

"And I knew it was hopeless," Tobe continued. "Finally, I ran down the street and called 911 at a phone outside of a convenience store. I waited at the lake until I heard the sirens. But then I slipped away."

"Why were you there that morning? Did Dad take you with him to talk to Jake?"

"I knew about the cooked books Jake had given to the SEC—knew he was trying to pin those on me—and I wanted to find the real books." He swallowed and cleared his throat. "I had a hunch they were in his car trunk and knew Jake liked to fish on summer mornings. I parked down the road from the lake, out of sight, planning to get into his car and get out with the ledgers and key. I didn't realize Dad was with him until I heard them arguing, loudly—you know how sound travels early in the morning on a quiet lake—so I went as close as I could to them without being seen.

"I heard Dad demand the real ledgers—the accurate books—from Jake. He wanted the safety deposit key. Jake denied any wrongdoing and blamed me for the missing money. While they were arguing, I went through Jake's car. I found the ledgers in the trunk and the safety deposit key in the cup holder. I grabbed them and went back to my car. I was going to show them to Dad later . . . but . . . ," he tried to finish but his voice was choked, "there was . . ." He had to clear his throat and start again. "There was no later."

Naomi reached over and put her hand on his forearm, giving him the strength he needed to finish. "During Dad's funeral, I came back to Eagle Hill, hid the ledgers in the basement, kept the key with me, and took off. I knew it wouldn't take Jake long to figure out I'd taken the ledgers and the key. I wanted to try to get back to Eagle Hill but not with Jake on my trail. One day, I realized he was following me. I couldn't think of where else to go, so I ended up at my mother's nursing home. I panicked . . . and hid the safety deposit key in her room."

Bethany clapped her cheeks with her hands. "Tobe, did it ever occur to you that hiding something in the room of a schizophrenic woman who believed people were after her might make her even more paranoid?"

He bit his lip. "I didn't think she had noticed I was hiding something."

Rose felt something in herself uncoil. "Then . . . Dean didn't take his own life."

"No, Mrs. Schrock," Allen Turner said. "He didn't. You can rest assured about that."

"He didn't take his own life. Thank God," Rose whispered. "Thank God." Her vision blurred beneath a wash of unexpected tears and her chest was suddenly choked with feelings—feelings of love and relief and sorrow for Dean. A sob broke from her throat and she covered her face with her hands to gain control. She breathed deeply, wiped tears away from her face, and looked around the table at those she loved so much: Tobe, Bethany, Mim, Luke, resting on Vera. "Did you hear?"

Vera nodded, her eyes shiny with tears. She reached out and grabbed Rose's hands. "I heard. I always knew, deep down." She squeezed her eyes shut. "Was em aagebore is verliert mer net." *What is bred in the bone is never lost.*

"How long?" Tobe whispered in a gruff voice. "How long will Jake be in jail?"

"A long, long time," Allen Turner said. "Brooke Snyder, by the way, was also arrested."

Vera jerked her head up. "The tall lady in the guest flat? How is she involved?"

"She forged a signature at the bank—yours, in fact, Rose." Out of his pocket, Allen Turner pulled Rose's Social Security card and handed it to her. "This Paisley woman was in on it too. She lifted things from Eagle Hill and got them to Jake."

"What's going to happen to Brooke Snyder?" Mim said quietly.

"She said she's willing to testify against Jake, so she'll probably just get her hands slapped. My guess is she'll be put on probation, but her career in art is over."

Naomi cleared her throat. "What about Paisley? Are you going to find her?"

Allen Turner shook his head. "No. We don't need her. She was just a minor player. An opportunist."

"Do you think she'll turn up again?"

He shrugged. "I can't imagine why."

Naomi and Tobe exchanged a glance, then their eyes traveled to the baby, sound asleep in the Moses basket in the corner of the room.

"If you don't have any more questions, that's all I wanted to tell you," Allen Turner said. "It's over. It's finally over."

"There's one more thing," Rose said. "Would you tell Jake something for us? Tell him we forgive him."

The room went still. Even baby Sarah, who had been starting to stir and make noises, grew quiet.

Allen Turner's face went blank. "*What?* You want me to tell him you forgive him? After all that?"

Rose nodded.

"Charges have been filed. That's not going to change." Allen pressed his thumbs against his forehead. "I spent twenty months tracking this guy down. It's not going to stop the due process of the law just because you forgive him."

"I realize that. I'm not asking for him to be released from the consequences of his actions. But as for our family, we are not harboring any ill will toward him." She turned to Tobe, but he wouldn't lift his head to look at her.

Allen Turner tilted his head. "Did you decide that right now? How can you forget what he did? How can you forgive, just like that?" He snapped his fingers to prove his point.

"It wasn't just like that," Rose said. "I decided to forgive Jake Hertzler a very long time ago. Forgiving and forgetting are two completely different things."

"I wish I felt the same way." Allen Turner glanced at Geena, seated next to him. His arms were crossed tightly over his chest.

"Go ahead and tell them, Allen," Geena said gently. "They should know."

Allen shifted uneasily in his chair. "Four years ago, my wife was a professor of accounting at a local college. Jake Hertzler was her student, the most intelligent and capable student she had ever had. Gifted, she called him. Brilliant." He had to stop and compose himself before going on. His voice got even quieter. "And he was the one who broke up my marriage."

Hours later, after Naomi, Geena, and Allen had left and the family had gone to bed, Rose took a hot bath, then read for a while in bed, hoping to fall asleep. An hour passed, then another. Still restless, she went downstairs. So much to sift through! Her mind was reeling with the day's revelations. She lit a kerosene lamp in the living room and sat down to mend a tear in a shirt of Tobe's, grateful for small, simple acts that were like balm to her soul.

Minutes later, she heard a noise and looked up to see Tobe leaning against the doorjamb, Sarah tucked in his arms with a bottle in her mouth. "Can't sleep?"

"No. I could take Sarah if you want to get to bed." No sense in both of them losing sleep.

But he didn't make any move to pass Sarah to him. "Rose, did you mean it when you said you forgave Jake Hertzler?"

"I meant it. I wanted Jake to know, though I doubt he cares. And it certainly doesn't mean it's easy to forget all he did." She knotted the thread and cut it off with her teeth. "I could tell you weren't happy with me for asking Allen Turner to let Jake know we forgive him."

Tobe crossed the room to sit in a chair, unfolded his long legs, and held Sarah up against his shoulder, the way she liked best. "I know you shouldn't pray for something bad to happen to another human, but I have prayed that Jake Hertzler would get a dose of his own medicine."

"Don't be trying to give back pain for pain," Rose said. "You can't get even measures in business like that."

"Don't you see?" He stared down at his hands. "I'm glad he'll be in prison for a long time. I want that for him. I want even worse for him. I even feel a little cheated that I wasn't the one who caught him. I tried. I tried so hard, but he was always two steps ahead of me."

"But you didn't cause it. The evil within Jake caused it all. He can't hurt anyone else. That's what you need to keep in your mind. He can't hurt anyone else." She put the shirt in the basket. "Tobe, you have a new life to live. A wife, a baby to care for. Spending another minute dwelling on the past would be like letting Jake continue to keep hurting you. It's over, Tobe. It's all over. Allen Turner said those very words."

They sat there quietly for a long time, the only sound coming from the hiss of the lamp. Finally, he rose and crossed the room to Rose's chair. He picked up the shirt she had repaired and examined her tiny stitches. "You're good at mending things. Shirts. Families too." He set down the shirt. "I don't say it enough, Rose, but thank you." He went upstairs with the baby asleep, her head tucked under his chin, and soon Rose turned out the light and went to bed.

While she was settling into bed, thoughts ran around and around in her head. All the same, she had a sweet, full feeling inside that warmed her, and soon she too slept, and all was silent in the farmhouse at Eagle Hill.

# 22

Brooke Snyder couldn't even look her aunt Lois in the eye when she arrived at the jail to bail her out. She sat in her aunt's car and stared out the window, sullen, sulky, guilty. Aunt Lois didn't say a word, an anomaly that grew increasingly distressing to Brooke.

"There are two sides to every story," Brooke finally said.

Aunt Lois sighed. "Yes, we know. His and hers. But then there's a third side; the truth. And who is to discover it?" She glanced at her. "Why did you do it?" Her eyes were hard and her voice was cold. "How could you do something so . . . deceitful? So obviously illegal?"

"I didn't mean to do anything wrong."

Her aunt gave her a look of disdain. "Just like you didn't mean to sell a forged painting as an original."

"But I didn't! I just painted a picture. And yesterday, I just signed a signature. I'm the victim here!"

"Brooke Snyder—you are many things, but you are *not* a victim."

Her aunt turned off the freeway and onto the Philadelphia Pike toward Amish country.

Brooke felt a hitch of alarm. "Where are you going?"

"Look in the backseat."

Brooke turned around to see her oil paints, brushes, canvas, and easel. "Where did you get those?"

"From your apartment." Aunt Lois turned off the Pike and onto a back road that led to the rolling hills of Amish farms. "It's time you start seeing yourself through the eyes of God. He didn't give you the gifts you have for copies and forgeries."

Brooke sighed. "I am useless."

"Pish. You're far from useless. You must use the tools God gave you. Find your tools and put them to use. Good use." She pulled the car to the side of the road. "Pick a spot. Any place. You choose your subject. It's high time you become an original."

Brooke looked at her aunt, with her spiky red hair and determined chin, then at her easel and paints, which she hadn't touched since she had reproduced the Corot, then out at the soft, gentle hills, dotted with cows. "Could you head toward Stoney Ridge? There's someone I need to see first."

For the first time all morning, her aunt cracked a smile.

Mim had finished putting fresh sheets on the beds in the guest flat. Two women were coming this afternoon, all the way from Georgia. She thought that might be the farthest distance a guest had traveled to stay at the Inn at Eagle Hill.

She heard a door open and walked into the living room, a pillow tucked under her chin as she struggled to get the case onto it. There, at the door, was Brooke Snyder, the woman who had taken away her newspaper column, merely because she was an ambitious woman.

Mim put the pillow on the small kitchen table. "Is there something you forgot? Or something else you want to take?" She was not rude, but she was very, very cool.

Brooke took a step inside. "I owe you an apology. I stole something from you."

"Yes, you did . . ." Mim stopped and shook her head. No. She didn't, she thought. And once thought, it had to be said. "You didn't steal it. I'm giving it to you." She picked up the pillow to finish stuffing it in the case. "I hope Mrs. Miracle will help you find what you're looking for, just like she did for me."

She turned and went back to the bedroom to fluff the pillow and set it on the bed, ready for the new guests. When she returned to the living room, Brooke Snyder was gone.

The potatoes spattered as they hit the melted butter in the pan and Rose hardly noticed. Her mind was on those new guests who had arrived at the inn this afternoon, stayed ten minutes, and promptly departed. Such an odd pair! They were two cousins, from Georgia, who were going to research their family ancestry.

"Do you have Amish relatives?" Rose asked them.

"No," the taller one said. "Quakers."

Rose looked at them, tilting her head. "You realize, of course, that Quakers came from England, started by George Fox. The Amish came from Europe. Their history is completely separate."

The cousins looked at each other, astounded by that information. "But the Quakers dress like you do."

Rose looked down at her plum-colored dress and black apron. "Not really." Her hand went to her head. "I suppose they do wear bonnets. The Quakers and the Amish share some beliefs, like pacifism, but very little else."

The two cousins were astounded. "Where should we go to learn about the Quakers? Our great-great-great-grandfather was a whaling captain. Ebenezer Folger was his name."

"Then . . . Nantucket Island, I suppose."

And so the two lady cousins left. The guest flat was, once again, empty.

Tomorrow, Rose would need to go talk to the deacon about the pile of unpaid bills that were stacking up on her desk. More bills than money.

She had hoped that she might have that pigpen plowed and extra vegetables already planted to sell at a roadside stand this summer, but David Stoltzfus hadn't gotten back to it after he was interrupted on the day the nearly-falling-down barn had fallen down, and she didn't feel comfortable asking him after their awkward conversation earlier today.

Rose and David happened to be picking up their mail from the mailbox at the same time and he walked across the road. She could tell at once that he had something on his mind to say to her.

"Jesse is going to go stay with my sister, Peter's mother, and her husband for the summer. They need a little extra help on the farm and Jesse, well, he's been . . . missing his mother quite a lot. More than I realized. Seems he needs more than I can give him right now. It's hard, you know . . ." David took his hat off, turning it in his hands. "Rose, we don't know each other well, but I can see that you love God and you love children. It seems like we are both in a similar situation, needing a spouse, needing a parent for our children."

She looked at him, puzzled.

"The problem is, I don't quite know . . . where I stand."

She still couldn't understand what he was trying to say.

"I'm aware, you see, that you are very friendly with Galen King . . . but I don't know how . . ."

*Now* she had a sense of where he was going.

"You see, I don't want to be foolish and hope that you might be interested in me, if there's something . . . so I hoped you might tell me what you think. I've grown very fond of you, Anna, and I hoped you might be growing fond of me too."

"I am." And she was. But her name wasn't Anna.

"Would you consider me?" He looked so hopeful and eager, and almost dreading her reply.

"David," she said gently, "how long ago did your wife pass?"

"It'll be a year on July 9th."

"You must have loved her very much."

"Yes. Yes, I did." He looked at his hat in his hands.

"Do you have any idea how many times you have called me Anna?"

He looked at her, horrified. "I'm so sorry. I . . . didn't realize."

"Don't be. You're still grieving for her. You need time." She looked across Eagle Hill's front yard to see Galen working a new horse in the round training pen near his barn. She was flooded with a vague sense of loss. "Yes," she said softly, "there is something between Galen and me."

David nodded silently, fingering the brim of his hat as if anxious to put it back on. His glance lifted. "Thank you, Rose, for not making me feel like a fool. You're a very special woman." He turned and walked back up the driveway.

That night, Rose tossed and turned, thinking over that conversation with David. She dangled her hand over the edge of the bed to touch the dog's head and stared out the windows at the stars. Suddenly there was a streak across the sky in a flash of light. Seeing a shooting star always made her feel honored, as if God had staged a show just for her. "O the mighty works of the heavens," she whispered. Galen always said that whenever they were outside at night.

Uninvited thoughts of Galen came to Rose at the oddest moments. She'd be pinning up her long hair and would remember him in his barn, running his fingers through a horse's mane to draw out the tangles. She'd be sitting in church, watching the women take turns holding baby Sarah, and she'd remember the tender way he'd held the baby on the porch swing. She'd fill her coffee cup in the morning and remember the way he'd worked so patiently with Luke and Sammy despite how exasperating those two could be.

She sorely missed him.

It had become a schoolhouse tradition, started years ago by Jimmy Fisher. On the last day of school, before the families arrived for the end-of-year program, the eighth graders carved their names in the oak tree that sheltered the schoolhouse with its canopy. The younger students, who would have to return to school after the summer, looked on enviously. The boys had brought pocketknives and were busy digging into the wood of the old tree.

Jesse Stoltzfus had been planning for weeks where he would put his name. Mim wished she could enjoy this moment the way the eighth grade boys did. They acted as if they were being set free from jail. She wasn't sure what it would feel like to not go to school, ever again. She borrowed Luke's knife and scratched out "M. S. was here." She felt there was more to say, but she didn't know what it was.

Danny told the class that he'd accepted the school board's offer to teach another term, so he was no longer the permanent substitute teacher. Instead, he was the permanent teacher. But she wouldn't be there next year. And Jesse was being sent off for the summer. Exiled, he told her, for being a bad influence on younger boys. He said it with that devilish grin of his, not looking at all sorry for his misdeeds, and she thought whoever decided to banish him—probably the deacon—was pretty smart. She wouldn't miss Jesse Stoltzfus and his sticky-up hair and torrent of nonsense. Not one bit. All of Stoney Ridge could breathe a sigh of relief that he would be gone this summer.

She wondered if he'd be back in August or September.

After the barbecue lunch had been eaten, the softball game between the eighth graders and the sixth and seventh graders started off. Jesse didn't want Mim to pitch to the sixth graders because they were too athletic, but he did let her pitch to the seventh graders because they were unusually uncoordinated. Then a boy tripped over his feet on the way to bat and twisted his ankle, so Danny stepped in to take his place at bat.

That was unfortunate, and Jesse Stoltzfus was beside himself at the unfairness of it all, but Mim was ready. She thought of all the crummy B- grades Danny Riehl had given her on her excellent essays this year, just to be mean and spiteful, and how often he treated her like she was just another student. She tried to remember the exact details of how to release the knuckleball. She wound her arm, flicked her wrist, released. The ball flew slow and Danny was ready for it—except it dropped unexpectedly at the last instant, and his bat met nothing but air.

Everyone looked at Mim, stunned. Why, she had thrown a strike at Danny Riehl! She would always be known as the girl who threw a knuckleball! She tried, without success, not to grin with delight.

An hour or so later, everyone packed up to head home. Luke and Sammy had started down the road when Mim remembered she had left her sweater in the schoolhouse and hurried back to get it. As she pulled open the door, she realized, with a heavy heart, this was the last time she would walk into the school.

Starting on Monday, she was going to take over Bethany's two-days-a-week job at the Sisters' House—organizing the rooms—because the deacon kept urging the sisters to prepare to host church one day. She would also be Ella's companion when the sisters had to leave the house on their many errands. Ella had declined enough that the sisters needed someone to shadow her. What the old sisters didn't know was, on Ella's good days, she was dictating the story of her life to Mim. Ella might not remember what she had for breakfast that day, but she did recall every detail of her childhood in Stoney Ridge, nearly a century ago.

It was all Bethany's handiwork—all except the dictation of Ella's life part. That was Mim's brainchild. But the job switch—Bethany said she was tired of trying to keep those sisters organized and she wanted to work someplace where she'd meet more people. She applied for an opening at the Bent N' Dent, available because Jesse wouldn't be working there this summer. Privately—something Mim would never dare voice aloud—she wondered if her sister might have an interest in working at the Bent N' Dent because Peter Stoltzfus worked there. For weeks now, Bethany had been very quick to offer to go on errands to the grocery store, when once she would have avoided it.

Danny was wiping down the chalkboard and turned when he heard the door open. The schoolhouse was empty. She yanked her sweater off the wall hook and started toward the door.

"Mim?"

She stopped and turned toward him. "Miriam. I want everyone to call me Miriam now."

He walked down the aisle of the schoolhouse toward her. "You threw quite a pitch, Miriam. A perfect knuckleball."

"But not the next pitch. You hit a double."

He took a step toward her. "Miriam, the reason I gave you B's instead of A's on your English essays was because I believe you could have done better."

She lowered her glance.

"Anyone who could write such fine prose, posing as Mrs. Miracle, should be writing dynamic essays."

Her jaw dropped open. He *knew* about *Mrs. Miracle*? Did everybody know? Did the whole town? "Jesse told you."

"Jesse? No. It seemed, well, sort of obvious. I guess I recognized your choice of words." His eyes were troubled as he peered at her. "Mim . . . Miriam . . . is there something between you and Jesse Stoltzfus?"

"How do you mean?"

"I don't know." Two red streaks started to crawl up his cheeks. "What about it?"

"What about what?"

"Do you have something going on with Jesse?"

She looked down at her feet. "You took Katrina Stoltzfus home in your buggy."

"She asked me to. She wasn't feeling well and wanted to go home. I was leaving early because . . . well, because it was a clear night and at nine, Venus would be low in the west and Jupiter would be about halfway down to the west and Mars could be seen coming up in the east."

*Oh.* "You act as if you don't even see me. All year, that's how you've acted."

"I've always seen you." His voice went from tenor to soprano in one crack and, visibly nervous, he poked his glasses up on the bridge of his nose. "I wrote your name on the tree."

Her chin jerked up. "You what?"

"I wrote DR + MS, very low down, near a root. I wrote it last year."

"You never did!" She could feel her cheeks grow blotchy pink. Soon, she knew, they would deepen to an all-over heliotrope.

"Let's go and see it," he said. "As proof."

And there it was, just as he had said.

Standing at the base of the tree, Mim and Danny looked at each other and looked away. A lot had been admitted.

Later that night, Mim tossed and turned as she lay in bed. Her sheets felt sticky. She tossed over, once, then twice, flipped her pillow to the cool side and shut her eyes. But she couldn't sleep. And she couldn't stop thinking of Jesse Stoltzfus.

In the middle of the night, Bethany woke to the sound of pebbles hitting her window. Groggily, she pulled herself out of bed and looked down at the yard. Jimmy Fisher was there, sending beams from a flashlight up to her bedroom.

She changed from her nightgown into a dress, wishing she could ignore him and crawl back into bed. "I'm just not sure if I'm in love with Jimmy Fisher anymore," she said aloud, pinning her dress together. Her voice echoed in her head. It was true. She might not love Jimmy. She might, but she might not. It had happened without her knowing, for the love she carried around for him had gone and she hadn't noticed it disappearing.

It was only now that she became aware that it was missing. In fact, she hadn't thought about Jimmy for two full days.

He greeted her with arms stretched out to engulf her, his eyes eager and bright.

Why was he here, in the middle of the night? Bethany wanted to know. "You'd better have a good reason."

"Because I missed you," he said simply. "I wanted to see you again." He slipped his arms around her. "I don't want you to feel I'm rushing you or demanding you give me an answer, but I was hoping by now you would be ready to say yes."

Her heart didn't race anymore, she didn't try to find the right phrase, the best approach. She wasn't eyeing him nervously in case his expression might change. She pressed him away by the arms. "No, Jimmy. I don't have an answer for you. But if you insist on one now, I'd have to say no."

His face went blank. "But . . . but . . . but why? You've been dropping hints to get married for months now. You've talked of nothing else."

She stepped back. "I know, but I think I got tired of waiting and I slipped out of love with you."

A pair of creases appeared between his eyebrows. "It's that Peter Stoltzfus character, isn't it? He's been buzzing around you like a fly around honey."

"What? My feelings for you have nothing to do with Peter Stoltzfus."

He reached out to take her hand and laid it over his palm and ran his other hand over it, as if smoothing a curled page. "Is it possible that you might in time love me again?" He sounded hesitant, unsure. His face was an open book; he looked miserable and hopeful all at once.

Her resolve melted at the desperate look in his eyes. "I suppose anything is possible." Then she turned quickly away from him, feeling unexpectedly sad. She slipped back into the house and was startled to find Rose in the rocking chair, feeding a bottle to Sarah.

"A starlight tryst?" Rose asked with a smile.

"Not really. More like a starlight sayonara. I told Jimmy Fisher things were over between us."

Rose looked up in surprise. "And are they?"

"I think so. He doesn't seem to agree." She sighed. "It seems as if our timing is always off. When he's interested in me, I'm interested in someone else. When I'm finally interested in him, he's distracted with his horse. Now I'm not interested in him anymore and he seems to think he'll perish without me. I'm not sure we'll ever both be on the same page at the same time. I just . . . I want someone who loves me, unreservedly. I don't want to chase someone to the altar." She took off her prayer cap and held the pins in her hands. "Do you think God concerns himself with love?"

"Of course. Of course he does. Look at the love story of Isaac and Rebekah in the Old Testament."

"So . . . if it's meant to be, it will happen?" She let the sentence hang there.

"In God's timing. I'm confident of that." Rose tucked Sarah into the Moses basket and covered her with the pink quilt that Naomi had made for her.

Bethany wished she had those kinds of certainties.

"Don't give up on Jimmy Fisher quite yet. He's making great strides in maturity. Think of where he was a year ago, when his chief delight in life was to set firecrackers off in Amos Lapp's winter wheat to shoo the geese away."

Bethany shrugged. "I hope you're right." She turned to head up the stairs.

"Bethany . . . sometime . . . I'd like to go with you to visit your mother."

Bethany leaned against the doorjamb. "Are you sure, Rose? It's not an easy visit."

Rose nodded. "I'm sure. I'd like to meet the woman who gave life to you and Tobe. I'd like to thank her."

Bethany smiled at her stepmother, and Rose smiled back.

There was a pain in Jimmy Fisher's heart, although hearts were not supposed to hurt. Every day hearts went about their steady beat and no one gave them a second thought, until one day you felt a pain there. Standing next to Lodestar in the middle of the barn, brushing down his coat and mane like he did every afternoon, Jimmy pondered these deep thoughts.

His heart used to sing at the thought of seeing Bethany. She was his Number One. She was his darling. Now, his heart had sunk to his shoes. Peter Stoltzfus was aiming to take his place in Bethany's heart.

Jimmy felt weak, as if his legs didn't want to move. He had never felt weak like this in all his life. He unhooked Lodestar from the ties and led him to his stall. In just a few weeks, the horse was making great gains. His ribs didn't protrude as they had, his eyes were bright and lively, stubbles of hair were starting to grow in the bald spots on his rump. Best of all, he held his head high and pointed his ears forward.

The vet had told Jimmy there was no reason he couldn't be a stud. "You have to remember," Galen reminded Jimmy, "that you have no paperwork, no proof of pedigree, no evidence of Lodestar's lineage, no stud registration."

Jimmy, a born optimist, felt certain that Lodestar's future offspring would test his mettle. "We're back on track, Lodestar," he told the horse as he latched his stall in four places, just in case he did get the notion to escape.

He stopped. Against all possibilities, Lodestar had been found. Against another impossibility, Jimmy was soon to retire from the chicken business. And Bethany had said there was a possibility that she might fall in love with him again. Jimmy *loved* possibilities.

He was going to win Bethany back. Oh yes he was.

# 23

Rose was taking fresh towels down to the guest flat when she noticed Galen and Luke in the empty pigpen, holding the reins to a horse that was pulling a plow to turn the sod. She stopped and watched. Galen was patiently teaching Luke how to plow in a straight line. If the horse veered off, Galen showed Luke how to bring it back into alignment with the other row. Their backs were to her, they didn't see her standing there.

Tears stung her eyes. Despite how busy Galen was preparing his own farm for his sister's wedding, despite how she had hurt him, he hadn't changed. He still made time to help her.

She was struck by how deeply attached she felt to Galen. It was a different love than the heady, exciting feelings she'd had when she fell in love with Dean, and she would have thought younger love was the stronger force. But the feelings she had for Galen were like the deep roots of a sturdy willow tree, whose depth she was only beginning to sense.

She suddenly realized she wanted to grow old with him.

"Talk to him," Naomi said.

"What?" Rose startled in alarm. She hadn't realized that Naomi had come up behind her. Sarah was nestled in her arms.

"You're wondering whether you made a mistake with Galen. Talk to him. It can't do any harm. Talk to him, Rose."

She looked at Naomi, whose clear eyes seemed to see everything and know what was going on in every heart. "Do you always know what people are thinking?"

Naomi laughed. "No. I just try to be a good listener."

"Anyone can be a good listener," Rose said. "That's easy. It's hard to be a wise listener."

After the pigpen had been plowed under and Luke had shown her, proudly, the blisters on his hands that needed tending to, Rose put on a fresh apron and prayer cap and walked through the privet to find Galen. She found him in the barn. He had a gelding's right rear hoof up on his thigh and was scraping caked dirt out of it with a hoof pick. He straightened up as soon as he saw her.

For a moment, she could say nothing at all, only look at him. Her throat tightened, thick with the things she wanted to say to him.

"It's cold today, you'll catch a chill," he said, when he noticed that she was barefoot.

She shrugged, head down, trying to hide the tears that were streaming down her cheeks.

"Why, now, what's the matter?" he asked, concerned.

He put down the hoof pick and walked over to her. He cautiously put his arm around her, as if that might not still be proper—Rose not only accepted it, she moved closer.

"Is something wrong, Rose? Is Vera all right? The baby?"

"Everybody's fine. It's me."

His eyes were filled with worry. "What's the matter with you?"

"Nothing. Everything. I need to ask you something." She stepped back to face him and clasped his hands, tight. "Would you like to marry me?"

There was quiet—complete quiet. And on and on it went, not a word, not a sound. Rose waited, then went on undisturbed, her voice steady. "I'm in love with you, and I can't imagine life without you."

A slow smile, homey and unhurried and sweet, like syrup over hot flapjacks, spread across his face.

"Well, I can imagine it, actually," Rose said, "and it's awful."

That made her grin, and Galen's smile grew bigger, and then he opened his arms and she fell into them. It felt like home to be in his embrace, familiar and safe, but at the same time, exciting and new. They stood there for a long moment. Suddenly the silence was thick and heavy, and he pulled away but held on to her elbows. "Are you sure, Rose? No changing your mind this time? No postponements. We set a date and stick to it. Because I couldn't bear it if—"

She pressed her fingers against his mouth. She leaned into him, melted into the circling of his arms, and lifted her face, a shy invitation. His lips were so soft, so very soft on hers. No kiss had ever been like this. No kiss ever would be.

At Tobe's request, Mim waited by the mailbox every day to intercept the DNA results. She examined every envelope that arrived, but day after day, there was nothing.

"How long can it take to match up bits of tissue?" Tobe complained.

Mim had no idea about laboratories or DNA or bits of tissue, but she had promised to watch the mail for him.

And then, just a few days before Tobe and Naomi's wedding, the letter arrived. Mim had just been in the kitchen with Tobe, who was feeding a bottle of vile-smelling formula to Sarah, when she saw the mailman and ran to the mailbox. She ran back inside, waving the letter. "It's here, Tobe! The DNA results are here!"

In the kitchen, Naomi sat rocking Sarah. Mim froze. Tobe was nowhere in sight.

"The what?" Naomi asked.

Oh, boy. "Um, where is Tobe?"

"He went upstairs to change his clothes because Sarah spit up on his shirt." Naomi put Sarah in the Moses basket. "Did I hear you right, Mim? Did you say that envelope has DNA results?"

Mim didn't know what to say. Tobe walked into the kitchen and saw the envelope in her hand. He and Naomi exchanged a look, telling each other something, the way married people could do without talking, but she didn't know what it was.

Tobe turned to Mim. "Would you mind giving Naomi and me a moment alone?"

Mim put the envelope on the table and backed out of the room. "Sorry," she whispered to her brother as she passed by the doorjamb.

He gave her a gentle squeeze on her shoulder.

It was strange how perfectly normal a day could seem, and yet, Naomi thought, the most important secret of her and Tobe's life was resting in an envelope on the kitchen table. His hand hovered over it, too shaky to pick it up, which suited Naomi just fine. She had never felt so disappointed in anyone. "You weren't going to tell me that you had taken Sarah for a DNA test?"

"When I knew the results, I was going to tell you."

"What difference would the results make, Tobe?"

"It would make everything simpler."

"How so?"

"Sarah is someone else's child. Someone else fathered her, walked away, and got away with it."

"And if that were true?"

"Well . . . then, there's a place for children like her. Somewhere. I'm not sure exactly where, but I could find out. Make sure it's reputable . . ."

His voice drizzled off as the look in her eyes changed from disappointment to fury.

Heart pounding, Naomi tried to keep her voice calm and steady, but she was livid. Had he learned *nothing* in the last year? "And what sort of man would you be if you abandoned her now? What sort of woman would I be? Her mother doesn't want her. Sarah would be taken away to live in foster homes. She's a special child. Her chance of getting adopted is slim. Here, she has so many people who love her and are concerned about her. She's become a part of everyone's life in Stoney Ridge. She's part of our new life together."

Tobe looked surprised. Naomi didn't usually make speeches. He seemed startled at such strong words from her. "Naomi . . . I've been over and over it in my mind. I've thought of little else. But I always come back to this question: How can I bring up another man's child as my own?"

"You're only thinking of yourself. What sort of start in life would Sarah have if you washed your hands of her now? She's a tiny, defenseless baby, who is missing an essential chromosome to have a normal life. Have you thought about her, Tobe? What kind of childhood would she have?"

Tobe jerked his head up, as if surprised by the line of questioning and the bite in her voice.

"Naomi, please listen to me. You asked me what difference it would make if I knew Sarah weren't mine, and I told you the truth. It's just not as simple as you're making it out to be."

"We can be the baby's parents in every way that matters. We loved this child yesterday, we still love her today. We will always love her. It's as simple as that."

After a full minute of silence she said, "Well? Aren't you going to open it?"

But he didn't, only stood rubbing his thumb over the writing, staring at it. Finally, he dropped his arms by his side. In a voice strangled with emotion, he said, "Naomi, what if Sarah happens to be the daughter of Jake Hertzler? I know Paisley and Jake had been . . . together."

"Is that what's been troubling you?" Such a thought had never occurred to her. Not once. She held out her hands to Tobe. He made an uncertain step toward her, taking her hands in his. "If that could be true . . . then it's all the more reason for us to raise her and love her as our own. To bring some good out of this whole sordid situation. You have two very simple roads to go down. To take the baby as she is. Or to walk away from her. Two clear roads."

He didn't move for a long while. He looked at Sarah, asleep in the basket. He looked at Naomi. Then he reached out and tore the letter with the DNA results into tiny pieces. He went over to Sarah and picked her up. "Love," he said quietly, "does extraordinary things to people."

Oh yes, Naomi thought. It does. It has a way of bringing out the very best in people. Her heart was full as she watched Tobe hold the baby close against his chest, tears streaming down his cheeks. In that moment, he had become the man she knew he could be. Little Sarah had done that.

And here Naomi was, getting ready to marry this wonderful man. About to become a mother to a beautiful little girl whom they needed as much as she needed them. The vista of Naomi's life had changed, and she marveled at what lay ahead.

Love did extraordinary things to people. Oh yes, it did.

# Discussion Questions

1. If there's one overriding theme in this novel, it would be this: becoming your best self. Isn't that a hope we all have? For ourselves, for our loved ones. In your opinion, which character—Tobe or Naomi—grew the most and became his or her best self?

2. Some, perhaps most, of the couples in this story seem to be unlikely pairs: Naomi and Tobe, Rose and Galen, Mim and Jesse, Brooke and Jon. Consider Tobe and Naomi. Tobe is impulsive, on a quest to find himself, pulled to the outside world, and is uncertain of what his calling is. Naomi is thoroughly Amish. She leads a very sheltered, quiet life and relies heavily on her intuition and thought life. In many ways, they're complete opposites. Yet why are they drawn to each other?

3. Let's talk about Rose and Galen. Rose is older than Galen in both years and life experience. Galen has a rather narrow view of the world. He loves his sister, he loves his horses. And he loves Rose. Why does their relationship, which has its share of friction, actually work well for each other? They felt differently about important family issues, but in what way were they both right?

4. The novel touches on many themes (love, family, forgiveness, second chances). Which do you think are the most important?

5. Brooke Snyder is a talented but hopelessly insecure young woman. Her aunt Lois said she was always copying because she had never found her "original." Her original self, she meant. How did Brooke's crippling insecurities about herself make her vulnerable to taking

the wrong path? With work? With men? What a message for those of us who struggle with insecurity! And don't we all . . .

6. The importance of family is seen throughout this novel. It's so important to Naomi, for example, that she insists to Tobe that they remain in the Amish church to stay connected to their families. How did family impact Tobe and Naomi, in both positive and negative ways? How has your own family influenced your decisions for good or bad?

7. What do you think Brooke Snyder will end up doing with the Mrs. Miracle column?

8. Paisley is a mess. She's manipulative, selfish, and woefully unprepared to become a mother, especially of a child with special needs. Do you think she did the right thing for the wrong reasons by leaving the baby at Eagle Hill? Or did she do the wrong thing for the right reasons?

9. Galen and Rose experience tension over Tobe's return. Galen is very objective about Tobe and feels Rose has hobbled him with empathy. Naturally, Rose finds herself defending Tobe. "Galen," Rose warned, "a man's past is his past. It's what he contributes to the present that matters." Do you agree or disagree with Rose's remark?

10. Rose and Galen's friction is common among blended families. How does Galen's point of view about Tobe hold merit? Was there any takeaway value in how they both adjusted their expectations of Tobe?

11. Did you guess ahead of time that Jon Hoeffner was Jake Hertzler? If not, what did you think was going to happen with Jon and Brooke Snyder?

12. At the end of the novel, Tobe Schrock tore up the envelope with the results of the paternity test he had taken to determine if he was Sarah's father. He would never know for sure. What did that action mean for Tobe, and why was it such a turning point for him?

13. Another theme in the book is the idea of forgiveness, of second chances. How did you feel when Rose Schrock sent a message to Jake Hertzler to tell him he was forgiven, even though she knew he probably wouldn't even care? Why was it important for her to let her children know that was the intention of their family?

14. What did you think was ultimately the book's lesson?

# Blueberry Lemon Squares
# from the Inn at Eagle Hill

| | |
|---:|:---|
| 2 ¼ cups | all-purpose flour |
| ½ cup | powdered sugar |
| 1 cup (½ lb.) | butter |
| 4 large | eggs |
| 1 cup | sugar |
| 1 teaspoon | grated lemon peel |
| ⅓ cup | lemon juice (use real lemons) |
| ½ teaspoon | baking powder |
| ⅛ teaspoon | salt |
| 1½ cups | blueberries, fresh and rinsed or frozen |

Preheat oven to 350 degrees.

In large bowl, stir flour and ½ cup powdered sugar until blended. Add butter and stir until dough holds together. Press evenly over the bottom of a 9" x 13" pan.

Bake until crust is golden brown, 20 to 25 minutes.

While the crust is baking, beat eggs in a bowl with a mixer on medium speed (or use a whisk). Blend in sugar, lemon peel, lemon juice, baking powder, and salt. After mixing, gently stir in blueberries.

Pour egg mixture into pan over warm crust. Return to oven and bake until filling no longer jiggles when pan is gently shaken, 20 to 25 minutes. Sprinkle lightly with powdered sugar and let cool at least 15 minutes. Cut into 2" squares and lift out with a spatula. Serve warm or cool. If making up to a day ahead, wrap airtight when cool and chill.

Makes 24 squares.

# Acknowledgments

I would like to thank my family for their encouragement and support. In particular, my daughter, Lindsey, for her insights and guiding comments. To my sister, Wendy, too. Both of them read messy first drafts and helped find the good and bad in my work. To A.J. Salch, for answering odd questions about Thoroughbred stallions. To her parents, Kim and Clayton, for providing true stories of childhood mischief that make it so often into my books. Thanks to Mary Ann Kinsinger, who helped me create a baptism scene that rang true.

In terms of print and paper, much gratitude goes to the team at Revell, who transform a bulky Word document into a book. Thank you to Michele Misiak, for marketing brainstorming, to Barb Barnes, for her editorial precision and longsuffering patience. To my remarkable editor, Andrea Doering, for cracking open the world of publication to me and keeping that door open. A special shout-out to my steadfast agent, Joyce Hart of The Hartline Literary Agency, for the dozen roses she sent to celebrate my twelfth contract with Revell. You're all such delightful people to work with.

Hands lifted up high in praise to God for granting me this author gig and giving me a deep love of the written word.

Last of all, but never least of all, my heartfelt gratitude to you readers, near and far, for reading my stories. I love hearing from you—the good, the bad, and the ugly. I can take it. Just don't stop reading!

Fondly,
Suzanne
www.suzannewoodsfisher.com

Coming Fall 2016 from

# SUZANNE
# WOODS FISHER

The Devoted

The Bishop's Family, Book 3

# 1

The bad thing about Ruthie Stoltzfus's job was that it barely paid minimum wage and she had no job security. She was only employed when someone from the Schrock family, who owned the Inn of Eagle Hill, was busy or unavailable, like now.

The good thing about her job was that it was across the road from her home. She liked to think of the now-and-then job as a hotel concierge-in-training, minus the hotel. The Schrocks referred to the position as a filler.

But as for what happened last evening . . . nothing ever—ever!—could have trained her for that. She was still shaky from the shock. The guests who had checked out of the inn yesterday had trashed the little cottage. Completely trashed it! Just as she was locking up after she had worked all day long to clean it up, she saw a man stagger over to her.

"Is this a motel?"

"Not really," Ruthie said. "It's a bed-and-breakfast." And then she noticed the man had a cut on his forehead. "You're bleeding."

He lifted a hand to his head as if startled by the thought. "It's nothing. Look, I need a room for the night."

She looked back at the main house. The lights were out. It was late and they'd gone to bed. But the guest cottage was empty, and she knew Rose would appreciate the income. Still, this man seemed odd. Not in a dangerous way, but he seemed dazed, a little confused. Drunk, maybe? She should send him on his way. But then again, what would he do if she turned him away? He was miles from town. "You'll have to pay cash, up front."

He reached behind him, then patted his pants, his shirt front, alarmed. "I don't seem to have my wallet." He reached into his pockets. "I'm good for the money. If you could just trust me. Just for tonight. In the morning, I'll take care of everything. I promise." His eyes pleaded with her.

In the end, Ruthie ignored her usual overriding caution and let him stay. She walked him over to the guest cottage, showed him how to use the kerosene lights, and left him there. As she closed the cottage door behind her, she felt a hitch in her heart. Had she done the right thing? Or the wrong thing. Birdy, her father's wife, often said that the Bible warned they might entertain angels as strangers in need. Nothing about this man seemed particularly angelic, but he definitely was a stranger in need.

Ruthie crossed the road and turned around, walking backward, as she climbed the steep driveway to her family's home. The light in the little cottage was already snuffed out. The man was probably in bed. She'd made her decision. She had to trust it was the right one, even if the stranger-in-need didn't end up paying for the stay.

She slept fitfully, tossing and turning. In the morning, she woke and dressed in a flash. She left a note for Birdy and her dad on the kitchen table, that she had to get to work early and would miss breakfast. She grabbed her shawl from the wall peg and rushed down the driveway. The cottage still looked as quiet as it did last night, though she wasn't sure what she had expected to find. Burned down? Exploded? Don't be ridiculous, Ruthie, she told herself. You're letting your imagination run away with you.

Rose was already in the kitchen at the main house of Eagle Hill as Ruthie walked right in. She looked up at Ruthie in surprise. "You're here early."

"There's a guest in the cottage," she said. "Late last night, as I was heading home—a man came and asked for a place to stay."

Rose straightened up. She looked out in the driveway. "Where's his car?"

"He didn't have one."

Rose got that look on her face, the one that seemed as if she knew this story wasn't going to end well.

"I might have made a mistake, Rose. He seemed to be in some kind of trouble."

"Did he threaten you?"

"No. Nothing like that. He was very polite." She told Rose the whole story.

Rose went to the window to peer at the cottage. "It's early. Let's wait another hour or so, then I'll take him some coffee."

"Are you mad at me?"

Rose swiveled around. "No. Not at all. Please don't worry, even if the man doesn't pay for the night. You were put in a tough spot and made a decision that felt right to you." She turned back to peer out the window, looking at the cottage, crossing her arms against her chest. "But maybe I'll have Galen take him the coffee."

An hour later, that's just what she did. Galen King, Rose's husband, a no-nonsense kind of man, took a pot of coffee over to the man in the cottage. Not two minutes later, he returned with the untouched coffee tray.

"Is he all right?" Ruthie asked. "Should I call for a doctor?"

Galen set the tray down and slumped into a chair at the kitchen table. "Not a doctor. He definitely doesn't need a doctor." He swallowed. "He needs . . . the county coroner."

And that's why Ruthie couldn't stop shaking. The coroner arrived, and after he saw the cut on the man's forehead, his bleeding knuckles, and discovered there was no identification to be found, he called for Stoney Ridge Police Department. They dispatched their only two cars, sirens blaring, which alerted all kinds of townspeople to come out and see what on earth had happened at the Inn of Eagle Hill. A reporter from the Stoney Ridge Times said this was the biggest story to hit the town in two years, since someone had blown up Amish farmers' mailboxes with cherry bombs.

"Perhaps there's a link," the reporter said, sniffing for any clue he could find to flesh out his story. Hard news, in Stoney Ridge, was as scarce as hens' teeth.

"No link at all," Luke Schrock said with certainty. Rose's son, Luke, was Ruthie's on-again, off-again boyfriend, depending on how much patience she had for him. Lately, it was off-again. Luke seemed almost amused by the activity that was quickly filling up the front yard of his family's property.

Ruthie found Luke's attitude to be callous and would have told him so, but the reporter kept pestering her with questions. When the reporter overheard one policeman tell the other that Ruthie was the only one who had seen and spoken to the man, he cornered her. "What kind of weapon was used to murder him?"

"Murder? Who said anything about a murder?" How awful. What horrible chain of events had Ruthie set into motion last night?

"It's obvious," the reporter said. "The bedroom window was open. The man was found on the floor. It's a cut-and-dry case, elementary crime solving. Someone came in through the open window, killed him, and left through the front door. And now"—the reporter muttered to himself, taking down notes—"we've got ourselves a John Doe, right here in sleepy Stoney Ridge."

The policemen were unrolling yellow crime-scene caution tape over the front door of the guest cottage. Ruthie knew one of the officers, Matt Lehman. He was talking to Rose, so she started toward them, hearing him tell Rose to call tonight's Inn guests to explain that their reservation had to be canceled due to unforeseen circumstances. Then he turned to Ruthie and told her, twice, that she wasn't to talk to anyone about what she'd seen or done until she'd been questioned.

"Right," Ruthie said. "So don't say anything about the blood."

Suddenly the Stoney Ridge Times reporter was by her side again. "What blood?"

"The man's forehead was bloody."

Matt Lehman scowled at the reporter, led Ruthie to the backseat of his police car, and told her to sit there, say nothing, do nothing.

Luke Schrock watched Matt lead Ruthie to the car. "Don't say anything without a lawyer present, Ruthie! You have rights!"

Matt turned to Luke with a sigh. He was well acquainted with Luke. "She's not being arrested."

"Oh," Luke said. He waved a hand in the air. "Well, then, carry on."

Ruthie sat in the police car, arms tightly folded against her chest. Murder. She had let an injured man into the cottage, a criminal, probably, only to have him brutally killed in his sleep.

What did I do? she thought miserably.

A little later, Matt Lehman and the other policeman walked over to the police car to question Ruthie about everything she could remember from last night. It was surprising how many details her mind had taken in and filed away, without realizing it. The stranger was surprised when she pointed out there was blood dripping down his forehead. He had seemed dazed and confused. Even still, he was very polite, very appreciative.

"Why didn't you ask for the man's name?" Matt said. "Why didn't you ask him for any information?"

For that, she had no answer. It was a set of circumstances that had flustered her, made her feel as if she just wanted to get the man settled in so she could go home. The main house was dark, she was alone, the man seemed like he needed to rest. Looking back, she realized how many mistakes she had made. But the stranger hadn't seemed dangerous.

"Who might have broken into the cottage to murder him?" she asked Matt and he looked at her strangely.

"What makes you think he had been killed?"

"The reporter said so. He called it a homicide."

"Aw, no," Matt said, turning to the other officer. "He's gonna get everyone twitchy."

The officer frowned. "They'll all be hearing things go thump in the night."

"But . . . was the man murdered?"

The two police officers exchanged a look. "We aren't sure of anything," Matt said. "Not until we get the coroner's report."

"What about the open window?"

"The innkeeper said there'd been a group in there the other night who trashed the place."

"That was true, but I was the one who cleaned up the cottage yesterday and I didn't notice an open window."

"Ruthie," Matt said. "Are you positive? Absolutely positive?"

"No. I guess not." She wasn't positive of anything anymore.

"Can you think of anything else? Anything at all?"

She squeezed her eyes shut, trying to make herself remember. Her cousin Gabby should have been the one here last night but had moved to Kentucky with her new husband Dane. With Gabby's unique attention for detail, she could've given the policemen a blow-by-blow detailed report.

Her eyes popped open. "He had no wallet." Something else tickled her memory. "When he reached for his wallet, he pulled out a ticket stub. It was to a Lancaster Barnstormer baseball game." She recognized the logo because her brother Jesse often slipped off to go to home games. She was rather pleased with herself. Such recall!

The officers were not as pleased. In fact, they seemed rather disappointed. They closed their notepads and rose to their feet.

Matt handed her a card. "If anything else comes to mind, give me a call." A stain of pink started up the sides of his cheeks. "Or you could have your aunt track me down."

"My aunt?" Her aunts lived in Ohio.

His cheeks went redder still. "The doctor."

Oh! That aunt. "You know Dok? How?"

"I've bumped into her a few times at the hospital." His face was now streaked with red blotches.

Oh. Oh! Matt Lehman was sweet on her aunt! How curious.

As soon as the policemen finished with their questions, Ruthie walked over to the porch of the farmhouse, where Rose King stood waiting for her.

"Are you all right?" Rose asked.

"I suppose so." Ruthie looked at the cottage, at the ribbons of yellow caution tape covering the door. "I'm so sorry. I should never have let that man stay here last night."

Rose put an arm around her shoulders. "You did what you thought was best. Innkeeping is all about dealing with strangers. I'm not sure what I would've done if I'd been in your shoes."

"But look at what it's turned Eagle Hill into. A human zoo."

Rose's gaze swept over the driveway to the cottage. A police car, a handful of horse and buggies, dozens of scooters, clumps of Amish men and women standing together, all curious onlookers. "Well, no doubt it'll all blow over soon."

Ruthie hoped so, but something deep inside her felt this was just the beginning.

**Suzanne Woods Fisher** is the author of the bestselling Lancaster County Secrets and Stoney Ridge Seasons series. *The Search* received a 2012 Carol Award, *The Waiting* was a finalist for the 2011 Christy Award, and *The Choice* was a finalist for the 2011 Carol Award. Suzanne's grandfather was raised in the Old Order German Baptist Brethren Church in Franklin County, Pennsylvania. Her interest in living a simple, faith-filled life began with her Dunkard cousins. Suzanne is also the author of the bestselling *Amish Peace: Simple Wisdom for a Complicated World* and *Amish Proverbs: Words of Wisdom from the Simple Life*, both finalists for the ECPA Book of the Year award, and *Amish Values for Your Family: What We Can Learn from the Simple Life*. She has an app, Amish Wisdom, to deliver a proverb a day to your iPhone, iPad, or Android. Visit her at www.suzanne woodsfisher.com to find out more.

Suzanne lives with her family in the San Francisco Bay Area.

Meet Suzanne
online at

www.SuzanneWoodsFisher.com

Download the

Free Amish Wisdom App